THE MAMMOTH

C000006431

FUTURE COPS

THE MAMMOTH BOOK OF
FUTURE COPS

Edited by Maxim Jakubowski & M Christian

ROBINSON
London

Constable & Robinson Ltd
3 The Lanchesters
162 Fulham Palace Road
London W6 9ER
www.constablerobinson.com

First published in the UK by Robinson,
an imprint of Constable & Robinson Ltd 2003

A copy of the British Library Cataloguing in
Publication Data is available from the British Library

ISBN 1–84119–502–2

Printed and bound in the EU

CONTENTS

ACKNOWLEDGMENTS

The editor has made every effort to locate all persons having any rights in the selections appearing in this anthology and to secure permission from the holders of such rights. The editor apologises in advance for any errors or omissions inadvertently made. Queries regarding the use of material should be addressed to the editor c/o the publishers.

CELEBRATE THE BULLET by Richard Paul Russo, © 2000 by Richard Paul Russo. First appeared in *Isaac Asimov's Science Fiction Magazine* in 1991; this version revised by the author. Reprinted by permission of the author.

GLASS EARTH, INC. by Stephen Baxter, © by Stephen Baxter. Reprinted by permission of the author.

FOOTPRINT ON NOWHERE BEACH, © 2003 by Conrad Williams. Reprinted by permission with author.

THE SHAPE OF MURDER by Ian Watson, © 1996 by Ian Watson. First appeared in *Dante's Disciples*, edited by Pete Crowther. Reprinted by permission of the author.

THE INCORPORATED by John Shirley, © 1985 by John Shirley. First appeared in *Isaac Asimov's Science Fiction Magazine*. Reprinted by permission of the author.

SEIZA by Steven Schwartz, © 2003 by Steven Schwartz. Reprinted by permission of the author.

AXL AGAINST THE IMMORTALS by Jon Courtenay-Grimwood, © 2003. Reprinted by permission of the author.

OFFENDERS by Mat Coward, © 2003 by Mat Coward. Reprinted by permission of the author.

VIOLATION by William F. Nolan, © 1973 by Roger Elwood. Copyright renewed by William F. Nolan. Reprinted by permission of the author.

NEEDLE TASTE by M. Christian, © 2001 by M. Christian. First appeared on www.erratta.com. Reprinted by permission of the author.

AN END TO HUNGER by China Mieville, © 2000 by China Mieville. First appeared in *The New English Library Book of Internet Stories*, edited by Maxim Jakubowski. Reprinted by permission of the author.

A SCANNER DARKLY by Philip K. Dick, © 1977 by Philip K. Dick. First appeared as Chapter Four of *A Scanner Darkly*. Reprinted by permission of the Galen-Chichak Literary Agency.

THE MOJAVE TWO-STEP by Norman Partridge, © 1999 by Norman Partridge. First appeared in *Future Crimes*, edited by Martin H. Greenberg & John Helfers. Reprinted by permission of the author.

BLOOD SISTERS by Joe Haldeman, © 1979 by Joe Haldeman. First appeared in *Playboy*. Reprinted by permission of the author.

HEARTACHE by Stuart Young, © 2003 by Stuart Young. Reprinted by permission of the author.

MINDSTALKER by Martin Edwards, © 2003 by Martin Edwards. Reprinted by permission of the author.

THIGHS by Melanie Fogel, © 2003 by Melanie Fogel. Reprinted by permission of the author.

THE UNCERTAINTY PRINCIPLE by John Moralee, © 2003 by John Moralee. Reprinted by permission of the author.

PRISON DREAMS by Paul McAuley, © by Paul McAuley. Reprinted by permission of the author.

THREE BANANAS by Larry Tritten, © 2003 by Larry Tritten. Reprinted by permission of the author.

YOU NEVER KNOW by Carol Anne Davis, © 1999 by Carol Anne Davis. First appeared in *Nasty Piece of Work*. Reprinted by permission of the author.

PLAY NICE by J. E. Ashley, © 2003 by J. E. Ashley. Reprinted by permission of the author.

ME AND MY SHADOW by Mike Resnick, © 1984 by Mike Resnick. First appeared in *Unauthorized Autobiographies*. Reprinted by permission of the author.

GONE BUSH by Chris Amies, © 2003 by Chris Amies. Reprinted by permission of the author.

DIGITAL HONEY by Liz Evans, © 2003 by Liz Evans. Reprinted by permission of the author.

BLANKIE by Paul DiFilippo, © 1996 by Paul DiFilippo. First appeared in *Ribofunk*. Reprinted by permission of the author.

NO BETTER THAN ANYONE ELSE by Molly Brown, © 1993 by Molly Brown. First appeared in *Interzone*. Reprinted by permission of the author.

SO NAPOLEON ALMOST SLEPT HERE, RIGHT? by O'Neil De Noux, © 2003 by O'Neil De Noux. Reprinted by permission of the author.

PROFESSIONALS by Keith Brooke, © 1994 by Keith Brooke. First appeared in *Interzone*. Reprinted by permission of the author.

FISHING by Jay Caselberg, © 2003 by Jay Caselberg. Reprinted by permission of the author.

IN SILVER A by Cecilia Tan, © 2000 by Cecilia Tan. First appeared in *Absolute Magnitude*. Reprinted by permission of the author.

SLEEP THAT BURNS by Jerry Sykes, © 2000 by Jerry Sykes. First appeared in *Crime Time*. Reprinted by permission of the author.

RAVENS by Stephen Dedman, © 2001 by Stephen Dedman. First appeared in *Interzone*. Reprinted by permission of the author.

INTRODUCTION

Welcome to the unknown.

The future won't be rocket ships and aliens, "to boldly go where no one has gone before", or pure-hearted heroes fighting black-hearted villains.

The future will not be Darth Vader or even Blade Runner: neither will it likely be idyllic dreams or necessarily the stuff of our darkest nightmares.

Thinking about the future is a no-win situation at best. A clouded area of speculation that is both unknowable and risky. As far as our parents are concerned, we are already there: the year 2003. But where are our jet packs, food pills, android butlers, 100 mph freeways, cities on the moon, or mile-high skyscrapers or even the ghost of world peace and an end to hunger? The same goes for the parents of our parents: where are the immense clippers of the clouds, the steam-powered horses, the immense warrens of brick and wrought-iron balconies? Instead of being iconic images of the future, these singular visions are already relegated to an ambivalent past that much of science fiction allocates to what is best known as steam punk!

No one in the past could have seen the world we, their children, have created and call home: the same way that we can never really tell what world our own descendants will inhabit. And the minds of fabulists and tightrope walkers of the imagination can conjure up all the fanatsies and wildest stretches of speculation under the sun, and still we know it will be but a pale simile of future reality, the ghost of tomorrow, another reality. Prediction is not the name of the game.

Yet there is something that never changes – a universal constant between now, here, and then, there: the past, the present, the future are all worlds where there will be human beings.

We might not fly to work, vacation in orbit, have a cure for all ills, trust our babies to mechanical nannies, but we share the same basic human landscape of those who came before and who will follow after.

The Mammoth Book of Future Cops is therefore not a book about the future as much as it is a book about humans of all times. No matter the when, there will always be police – the thin blue line between chaos and order – and criminals – those who are beyond the law. Then, as now, there will also be men and women caught between the two: bent cops and honourable crooks, femmes fatales and hardboiled private eyes, con-men, involuntary sleuths and vigilantes. Future people who are, surprise, just like you and me even if the environment they populate, and often rebel against, is alien.

The Mammoth Book of Future Cops is a book about taking the elements of classic human drama, the fatalism and harsh reality of noir stretched to extreme conclusions. The settings might be surreal, dream-like, horrific, but these stories never leave human territory. Science and society may be twisted, but the human connection that makes a noir story memorable always remains. The worlds here in *The Mammoth Book of Future Cops* might be strange, but the people that inhabit them are all very human, as are their struggles, failures, and victories. The creators of these new worlds and damaged heroes come from both the fields of crime and mystery fiction and science fiction writing. They are primarily storytellers, but often the message is unmistakeable: an affirmation of the human soul's resilience. Some will be familiar names like the visionary Philip K. Dick, veteran William F. Nolan, creator of the *Logan's Run*, award-winning Joe Haldeman, hard science leader of the pack Stephen Baxter, Ian Watson, Mike Resnick and SF/thriller crossover aces like Paul J. McAuley. There are rising stars like Richard Paul Russo, Paul DiFilippo, Martin Edwards, Molly Brown, China Miéville, Jon Courtenay-Grimwood; and there will be names who are new to the curious reader. Nonetheless all will strike a strong and unique note of defiance and wonder.

We may not live in the dreams of our children or our ancestors, we may not even be aware of the fantastic world we inhabit, but we are just like those dreamers – we are just like the men and women in *The Mammoth Book of Future Cops*: human beings trying to live, succeed, and do the Right Thing.

We may not be able to see the future, but we certainly know the people who will live there: people like us.

Maxim Jakubowski & M. Christian

CELEBRATE THE BULLET

Richard Paul Russo

Wendy was taking pictures of a midnight beach party.

It wasn't much of a party, actually – five people she knew (all of them younger than she was), and one guy none of them knew, who had been walking along the beach and joined them. A fire burned inside a ring of charred stones, and a few feet from it, propped on a driftwood log, was a thirty-inch color TV that Tony had brought, power cable snaking down to a big battery pack on the sand. On the screen, without sound, was an old Japanese monster movie about a giant mutant turtle that flew and breathed fire.

Wendy kept back from the fire, fiddling with her camera while the others drank beer and talked. The only one who seemed to be watching the TV was the guy they didn't know. Hicks, he had said his name was; he had been carrying two six-packs and so had been immediately invited to the party.

Fog threatened to roll in from the sea, and the wind kicked up. Wendy zipped up her jacket, resumed adjusting her camera. She was using fast black-and-white film, no flash, making what she knew would be good guesses with the time exposures. She sat on the sand, set the camera on her knee for support, and took a picture of all six people, the fire, and the TV, the flickering image of the screen at a severe angle. Then she got up and backed farther away, looked up at the moon slicing through the incoming fog, and wondered if she could get it into a picture along with everything else.

"This movie SUCKS!" It was Hicks, and he sounded so angry everyone else stopped talking; the beach became suddenly quiet, the only sound the rolling hiss of the waves on the sloping sand.

"It's only a movie," Avra said. She laughed.

But Hicks sat there shaking his head. "I've had it," he said, and he pulled a gun from inside his jacket.

The gun was big, obviously real, and Wendy's chest tightened, catching her breath. Christ, she hated guns, even just looking at them. They scared the hell out of her, especially since most people really had no idea how to handle them.

Hicks raised the gun, holding it with both hands, and aimed it at the television set.

Tony scrambled to his feet, spilling beer onto the edges of the fire with a sizzling hiss. "Hey!" Tony said. "Hey, come on, man, don't fuck around! I paid a hundred and fifty bucks for that TV!"

Hicks turned to Tony without moving the gun. "A hundred and fifty? Must have been stolen, then. That's a good TV."

"Shit, who cares if it was stolen?" Tony was holding up his hands, palms out toward Hicks. "It's a lot of money, man, so just freeze down a bit, all right? All right?"

Hicks nodded, turned back to the TV, and fired.

The explosion of the gun, loud and sudden in Wendy's ears, was followed almost immediately by another, much softer explosion as the bullet ripped into the TV and the picture tube burst into bright crackling light and shattering glass.

Tony grabbed the sides of his head, grimacing. "Oh, Jesus, you motherfucker! You out of your goddamn mind or . . .?"

Tony stopped as Hicks brought the gun around, aimed it directly at Tony's chest.

"Oh, hey, man," Tony said, backing away. "Don't *fuck* with me like this. *Jesus!*"

The gun went off again, louder this time as Tony jerked back and sprawled face up on the sand. More sand scattered as the others scrambled to their feet and started running. Tony, on the other hand, wasn't moving at all.

Wendy, too, remained motionless for a few moments, in a kind of stunned paralysis. Her chest ached as she watched Hicks rise to his feet, walk over to Tony, and hold out the gun again, this time aimed down at Tony's face. Wendy turned and broke into a run as the shot sounded.

Her feet sank in the soft sand as she ran up the slope, and her breath quickly became ragged and harsh. The slope steepened into sandbanks leading up to the road, and Wendy scrambled up on hands and knees, pulling herself along by grabbing tufts of the long grasses growing out of the sand. There were no more gunshots, no sounds at all except her own painful breath.

The sand leveled out. Wendy stepped over the knee-high wire and wood fence and ran out onto the Great Highway, which was empty of traffic; distant approaching headlights were visible, but more than half a mile away. She stopped for a moment and looked back out over the beach, but saw no one coming. Down near the water, the fire continued to burn, flames whipping in the breeze; a few feet from the fire lay Tony's dark, motionless form. Wendy turned away and hurried across the black pavement, down another grass and sand bank, and headed for the motel and restaurant down the road near the end of Golden Gate Park.

In front of the restaurant stood a pair of empty phone booths. Wendy stepped into one, kept the door open and watched the road. She picked up the receiver and dialed 911.

Over the phone, Wendy told the cops what had happened, and provided them with a description of Hicks, but she had refused to give her name. Later she might go to them, see if she could help any further, but she would have to think damn hard about it. With half a dozen arrests on obscenity and various other charges because of her photography, Wendy couldn't imagine going to the police voluntarily.

She remained in the phone booth looking up at the Great Highway, half expecting to see Hicks (if that was really his name) appear on the road above her, gun in hand. Two cars drove slowly past, headed south, then another headed north, but no one appeared on foot, and Wendy wondered what had happened to the others.

She stepped out of the phone booth and slowly climbed the bank back up to the road. Wendy still had time to go back to the beach before the cops arrived. It was crazy, she told herself, but she knew she would go as long as it looked safe, though she didn't really want to admit *why*.

The fog had broken up almost completely, and the nearly full moon shone brightly down on the road, giving the asphalt a ragged, liquid sheen. Wendy crossed to the sandbanks, stepped over the low fence, and stood at the edge of a grass-covered drift.

The fire still burned, though low now, more glowing embers

than flames; the orange glow, even from this distance, pulsed like an irregular heartbeat, fanned by the breeze. The beach, in both directions, was deserted. To the north she could see a few waving, flickering lights in the upper levels of the old Ocean Beach condo ruins; farther on, the remains of the Cliff House seemed to hover in the air like an apparition, dark ragged hulks of shadow on the jutting point of land, stone illuminated by the moon. All around Wendy, with the silver light of the moon and the darkness of the night, the world looked as if it had been created all in black and white except for the tiny spot of orange flame near the water's edge.

Wendy glanced once more in all directions, then started down the bank toward the fire. As she walked, she could make out the shape of Tony's body a few feet away from the fire, and the shape of the blasted TV. She conceived possible shots in her mind, considered the different camera angles, tried to calculate the effect of the moonlight. You're sick, Wendy, she told herself, you're *sick*. And she did feel sick, nausea rolling through her stomach and bringing acid up into her throat, but she knew it wouldn't stop her.

When she reached the fire, Wendy skirted the glowing embers and approached Tony's body. The blood, which at first glance seemed to be everywhere, looked more black than red – shiny where it had pooled on his chest and what was left of his face; duller where it had spread out and soaked into the sand. If she had not seen what had happened, she didn't think she would have recognized him.

Feeling still sicker now, Wendy brought the camera up and adjusted it with shaking fingers. A close-up of the body, the moon from behind and just to the side. Somehow she managed to make her mind work and concentrate on the photograph she was about to take, to stop her hands and fingers from shaking long enough to set the exposure, focus the lens, snap the picture.

Wendy moved around the body, the glowing fire, the shattered television set, taking one picture after another; between shots her hands shook, but each time she prepared a shot she steadied herself long enough to click the shutter. Before long, as she moved farther and farther away with each shot, Wendy began to cry. Tears streamed steadily down her face, salty to the taste when she licked them from the corners of her mouth.

But none of it – not the tears, not the nausea rolling through her, not even the self-disgust – stopped her from taking the pictures, and it wasn't until she heard the faint wail of approaching sirens that Wendy lowered the camera, snapped on the lens cover, and, still crying, ran back up the slope toward the moonlit road.

She woke once in the night, a clawing desperation bringing her slowly, painfully out of a dream she could not remember – nothing remained except a hollow feeling of dread. Wendy sat up in bed, sweating in the windowless, cinderblock room, the darkness heavy and cloying. Vibrations from machinery below her rumbled through the room. She leaned against the wall, pressed her face against the cold, trembling stone.

For a long time she remained motionless, eyes open though she could not see a thing, listening to the muted chug of machinery. Then she slipped back down between the sheets, pulled the blankets tight around her, and waited for sleep, almost hoping it wouldn't come.

In the morning, Wendy bought a newspaper and read through it in a coffee shop down the street from her rooms. A huge photograph of the second space station filled half of the front page. The station had just been officially completed after eleven years, three major accidents, and sixty-seven deaths. In the lower corner was a photo of the President seated at a monitor in Kennedy Space Center, headset on, congratulating the station commander.

As for killings or other deaths, there were plenty in the paper – a street person who had flipped out in the Financial District and attacked people with a large kitchen knife, killing a woman attorney and injuring half a dozen other people; a woman who had shot and killed her husband, their two dogs, then turned the weapon on herself; an eight-year-old boy who had been crushed to death when an abandoned building collapsed on him.

Nowhere, though, could she find anything about what had happened on the beach. It had probably been too late to make the morning paper, but she had hoped there would be something anyway. Why? She didn't really know. She had seen far more than she would ever learn from a news account.

Around noon she called in sick to the print shop, bought an early edition of the afternoon paper, and read it on the cement porch of the building she lived in, the concrete vibrating slightly beneath her. Half the ground floor was a dry-cleaning operation, and the machines ran day and night. The other half was supposedly an upholstery shop, but machinery ran day and night inside it as well, far louder than the dry-cleaners, rumbling and chugging beneath her apartment; Wendy felt certain something else was being done in the shop, though she really didn't care what.

Her apartment was on the second floor, above the upholstery shop, part of a collection of illegal apartments and tiny offices. The apartment was small, but had three rooms including her darkroom, a stove and sink for a kitchen, a shower and toilet of her own, and a tiny wall heater that kept the worst chill out of the air – all she needed.

She found it – a short article in the second section, no picture. There wasn't much to it, two paragraphs stating that a body had been found out on Ocean Beach about one a.m., apparently shot to death (apparently?). No name was given. Police speculated the shooting was drug-related.

Wendy leaned against the stone wall, feeling the vibrations trembling through her, listening to the muted hisses and groans, and began slowly, methodically, tearing the newspaper to shreds.

She spent the afternoon in the darkroom, developing then printing the pictures from the night before. She didn't know what she expected – maybe shots of Hicks's face, details of his clothing, pictures she could take to the police (if she could bring herself to do that; if they would even listen to her) – but there was nothing like that. There *were* pictures of Hicks, but none that showed his face, none that could identify him in any way.

And then there were the pictures of Tony. She made small enlargements, to about 5 × 7, and clipped them up on the wall. First was a close-up of his face, taken early in the evening while Tony was building the fire – his features set in concentration, light and shadow from the flames in irregular patterns across his skin. Next was a shot of Tony and Avra laughing and throwing sand at one another just a few feet from the fire. Then came the series of pictures after Tony was dead: a close-up of what remained of his face; his sprawled body with the darker splotches of blood on the sand around his head; then several more shots from a gradually increasing distance until the last, which took in the dying embers of the fire, the shattered television set, scattered beer cans, Tony's body, the reflecting ocean in the background, and in the upper right corner, just barely in the picture, the shining silver light of the moon.

Wendy sat on her work stool, stared at the pictures mounted on the wall. The sick feelings of the night before were gone, replaced by a heavy numbing sensation. But something in the pictures slowly dug into her gut and into her heart, cutting away the numbness, and revealing the pain underneath. Something either in the photographs or in the circumstances surrounding them that was important, but Wendy did not know what it was.

Late that night, long after dark, Wendy went to the Bomb Shelter. The Bomb Shelter was half pub, half nightclub; half indoors, half outdoors. It had been built up hodge-podge around and under the ruins of a freeway overpass that had been accidentally blown up two years before by a performance art troupe. Seven people had been killed, including three of the four troupe members. The surviving performance artist had started building the Bomb Shelter as soon as he had been released from the hospital, and now ran the entire complex.

In the outdoor section, covered by sheets of canvas stretched high above the tables, a thin bearded man played an electric sitar on a platform that served as a stage. Most of the outdoor tables were empty, and his audience consisted of about ten people clustered around the platform and drinking; two of them were asleep or passed out, heads and arms on their tables.

It was too damn cold, and Wendy went inside. The interior of the Bomb Shelter was a series of makeshift chambers connected by narrow, dimly lit passages. Those walls not formed by the concrete remains of the freeway were built of wood, or brick and stone, patched sheetrock, old mattresses wedged between sheets of metal, wire-bound bundles of flattened cardboard. Each chamber held half a dozen tables, all with fat, flickering candles; speakers mounted in the ceiling corners emitted crystal clear ether jazz. Paintings and drawings and photographs hung on the walls, and desiccated plants grew from clay pots in the corners.

Nearly all the tables were occupied. In the second chamber,

Wendy sat at a single empty table in the corner, and faced one of her own photographs that hung on the opposite wall. It was a large black and white close-up of Kit, almost in profile – her eyes partially closed, gazing downward, her cheek tight with a smile.

Wendy stared at the picture, her chest aching. She missed Kit. They had worked together on several major art projects over a period of three or four years, but now Kit was dead. She had died a year before of "the white monkey", as she had put it. Kit had called it "the white monkey" because AIDS was still thought by some to have originated in African monkeys; also, since Kit had never had sex with anyone, male or female, she was certain she'd contracted AIDS during her needle freak days mainlining cocaine – yes, her "own personal white monkey".

No matter what you called it, though, Kit was dead. Kit and Will and Laskey from AIDS; Skipper and Marty, and now Tony, from bullets; Stoke several years ago, probably from bullets as well, in some damn Central American jungle; Sheridan and Manny and Bobo from street-sliced drugs; and Tracy, who was beaten to death by cops. All these people she knew, dead before they were thirty-five. Wendy was nearly forty now, and she knew it wasn't really that old, but Christ, sometimes she *felt* old.

She looked at the picture of Kit, tried to imagine what one of the close-ups of Tony's shattered face would look like up on the concrete wall.

Carla, one of the regular waitresses, came up to the table, smiling. "Wendy, how you doing? What can I get you?"

"Jack Daniels," Wendy said. "A bottle." Wendy pulled all her cash from her pockets, counted it. It would be enough. She couldn't afford it, but right now it didn't matter.

Carla's smile disappeared. "A bottle?"

Wendy nodded. "A bottle, a glass, and ice."

Carla nodded, moved slowly away, and Wendy was alone again.

She was going to get drunk. Wendy only got drunk two or three times a year, and this was going to be one of them. It would take a long time, because she would drink slowly, and because, though she rarely drank, she held her liquor well. But tonight she would get so smashed she would hardly remember a thing in the morning.

Carla came back with a bottle of Jack Daniels, a box of ice, and a glass. "Are you okay, Wendy?"

"I'm fine," Wendy said. She paid, and Carla left without another word.

Wendy put two pieces of ice in the glass, then filled it with Jack Daniels. She held the glass up, gestured with it toward Kit's picture, then drank.

She woke in darkness to a terrible pounding in the walls, a hammering at the floor beneath her. The bed shook with the vibrations, and for a moment Wendy thought some massive piece of machinery was going to break through the walls or floor, shattering cinderblock, destroying her room.

I'm still drunk, she told herself, but she soon realized that had nothing to do with the hammering sounds in the room, or the vibrations in the floor. Upholstery shop my ass, she thought.

Wendy rolled out of bed, got to her feet and staggered into the bathroom. She sat on the toilet and relieved herself, amazed that her bladder could hold so much without more pain.

In the bathroom the pounding was quieter, the vibration of the walls less violent. She remained seated for a few minutes, holding her head in her hands. Her mouth was dry, and her head felt stuffed with cotton. She didn't want to move.

Finally Wendy stood and went to the sink, ran cold water and splashed it over her face. It didn't help much. She started back toward the bedroom, but the pounding was too loud and jarred her head. She grabbed the pillow and a blanket from the bed, and returned to the bathroom. Wendy wrapped herself in the blanket, stuffed the pillow into the back corner and lay down between the toilet and the wall, where the pounding was quietest. She slept.

She didn't have much of a hangover in the morning. The pounding had faded, and only the normal thrumming and vibrations remained. She felt almost rested.

After a quick shower, Wendy took a bus into the Mission District to see Libby. A low overcast obscured the sun, kept the morning a dark gray. She dozed against the scratched window, holding her shirt over her nose to filter out the stink from the woman lying on the seat in front of her.

Libby lived in a three-room cottage on a quiet dead-end street that always smelled of anise, especially on hot days. Wendy stepped up onto the small porch, rang the doorbell, then stood back so Libby could get a good look at her through the peephole. A few moments later she heard the dead bolts being thrown, the two chains being unhooked, then the knob turned and the door opened.

"Wendy." Libby stood in the open door, smiling, her arms held out. They embraced, then went inside, Libby shutting and locking the door behind them.

As usual, books and magazines and newspapers were piled and scattered all over the front room; those stacked on or near Libby's worktable dealt primarily with genetics and quantum mechanics. On the PC monitor, a toroid-shaped diagram shifted jerkily from one position to another.

"Sorry if I'm interrupting," Wendy said.

Libby shook her head. "I was about to go out in the garden, take a break while this program runs. C'mon out, I've got a fresh pot of coffee in the Chemex."

They walked into the kitchen, where Wendy picked up two glass mugs and the Chemex and Libby picked up her shotgun, then walked out into the back yard garden. Wendy hated the shotgun, it always made her nervous, but there was no way she could complain about it. A year and a half before, Libby's sister Deirdre, who had shared the cottage with Libby, had been stabbed to death while sunbathing in the garden. Libby had bought the shotgun the following week.

They sat in two deck chairs facing the garden. Wendy set the coffee and mugs on the wooden table between them, poured the coffee while Libby propped the shotgun against the redwood planter box beside her. Above, the overcast was burning off, and the sun broke through, bringing out the colors of the garden. Tall, thick green shrubs lined the back fence, and a path of coarse gravel curled through lush beds of flowers and herbs – irises, hydrangeas, oregano, parsley maybe, and a lot of others Wendy didn't know.

Wendy sipped at the strong, hot coffee, then closed her eyes and leaned her head back, letting the warmth of the sun bathe her face. She could smell the oregano, and flower scents she couldn't identify, and a trace of anise from the street, and the coffee in her hands. She felt warm and peaceful, a pleasant lethargy suffusing her body.

"Something's eating at you," Libby said. "When you come over and start sitting back with your eyes closed and get quiet, that usually means something's bothering you. Something you want to get away from."

"This place always relaxes me," Wendy said. "Sitting out here in the garden with you. Sometimes I wish I could go somewhere like this permanently. Out of the city, away from people, away from the world."

"Wendy, what is it?"

Wendy didn't say anything for a long time, but eventually she opened her eyes, turned to face Libby. She told Libby what had happened to Tony. She told her about the pictures she took.

"You're a photographer," Libby said. "Taking photographs is what you do."

"Sure, but like that? Sometimes I think it's *all* I do, and sometimes I think I must be sick. No matter what happens in my life, no matter how awful, I take pictures of it. I'm beginning to think I can't even see the world around me in a normal way anymore." She paused, looked away, up at what was left of the overcast. "When I think of Tony now, I see an image of his ruined face . . . Not as I *saw* it that night, but as it appears in the photograph I took. I wonder if I'm capable of seeing the world in any other way."

There was a long silence, then Libby said, "Want some amateur analysis?"

Wendy softly laughed. "Sure."

"The world is pretty fucked up, *people* are pretty fucked up. And it all seems to just be getting worse."

"I won't argue that."

"Okay. Things are getting worse, but on top of that a lot of the shit that goes down seems pretty irrational, meaningless. Pointless. Like some stranger shooting up a TV and then killing someone, apparently without reason. Like a young woman getting stabbed to death in her own back yard, again apparently without reason."

Libby paused and looked out at her garden. Wendy didn't say anything, and eventually Libby turned back to her and resumed.

"So a lot of it doesn't make sense. Causality is suspect, sort of like quantum mechanics on a social scale, let's say. How do people deal with a world like that? A lot of them retreat, either physically or mentally withdraw from the world. A lot of others ignore most of what they see, or learn how to *not* see what they don't want to see or what they can't deal with. Head in the sand.

"But not you, Wendy. You can't do that, you see the world around you, and maybe when you take photographs, what you're doing is giving the world some structure, enough so that you *can* see it for what it is and still live with it without going out of your mind." She paused, smiled. "Maybe. There, that's my lecture for the day."

Wendy watched Libby for a minute, then shrugged. "I guess it makes a kind of sense, though I don't know that it does me much good."

"Maybe make it easier to accept what you do."

Wendy shook her head. "Best thing might be to just stop taking photographs altogether."

"You serious?"

"I'm thinking about it."

Libby didn't say anything, just slowly shook her head. Wendy shrugged again, drank from her coffee, then closed her eyes once more and stretched out on the chair to take in the heat from the sun above her.

It was midnight by the time she got off at the print shop, and nearly one o'clock by the time she got home. The streets were quiet, and as she approached her building she could hear the faint sounds of machinery from the dry cleaners and the so-called upholstery shop. Nothing unusual, nothing like the night before. Everything back to normal.

Wendy climbed the stairs to the second floor, walked down the quiet, dimly lit hall. She knew at least two other people lived on this floor, but there were no lights in door windows, no sounds to indicate anyone was here.

She unlocked her door, stepped into the apartment. Just as she closed the door, loud pounding sounds broke in again, and the floor began to shake beneath her. Pots and pans rattled quietly against the kitchen wall, and glasses clinked together in the cupboards. She checked the darkroom and, though her equipment was shaking somewhat, it looked safe enough.

Then she walked into the bedroom.

The floor shook with a steady hammering, as if a pile driver was driving something *up* against her floor from below, and everything in the room shuddered and rattled – books, pictures, homemade cassettes, the alarm clock. The nightstand lamp vibrated with each jolt, and threatened to tip off the stand.

Jesus Christ, what the *hell* was going on down there?

Wendy stood for a minute in the middle of the room, listening to the hammering sounds, watching the walls and waiting for them to begin crumbling around her. Then she grabbed the lamp, laid it on the bed, and backed out of the room. She stopped by the darkroom, picked up her camera and several rolls of film, and left the apartment.

As she moved along the hall and down the stairs, the noise and vibrations lessened. Outside, it was quiet again, only a faint thrumming punctuated regularly by muted thuds.

Blinds covered the upholstery shop windows; she couldn't see inside, but a kind of smoky, dim blue light leaked out from the edges and through tiny cracks. She stopped at the shop's front door, which had a dirty plastic sign in the wire-mesh window that said "CLOSED", and tried opening it, but the door was locked.

Wendy walked slowly along the building, checking the windows to see if any were open. At the entrance to the dark alley between her building and a large brick warehouse, she hesitated. She couldn't see much – shadows within shadows, dull reflections of ambient light on windows and damp metal, unidentifiable clumps along the alley floor, and two or three hints of the dark blue light leaking out around window blinds, barely discernible. She breathed in, and entered the alley.

Gravel, broken glass, and bits of other trash crunched under her shoes. Wendy moved slowly along the building wall, stepping carefully, and tried each of the windows. But none were open. Halfway down the alley she reached the dry cleaners.

Wendy backtracked to the last upholstery shop window, which was already partially broken, a three-inch jagged hole in the upper section. The chugging sounds of machinery were slightly louder, emerging from the hole. She took a handkerchief from her pocket, wrapped it around the fingers of her left hand, then gripped the glass at the opening. She gently hit the glass with the heel of her right hand, then hit it again, harder each time until it quietly cracked. Two more hits and she was able to pull a piece away with her protected hand, enlarging the hole. She continued working at the hole, cracking the glass and pulling pieces away, letting only a few tiny shards fall into the building, the noise covered by the rumble of machinery inside.

When the hole was large enough, Wendy reached in and twisted free the lock, then withdrew her arm and used both hands to work open the window, raising it as far as it would go. Wendy climbed through and into the building.

She left the window open, made sure the blinds covered it, then turned to look around her. Pale, dark blue light lit the interior of the large room, casting hundreds of shadows through a jungle of scaffolding, metal stools and workbenches, thrumming machinery, tanks and cylinders, and lengths of pipe crisscrossing through the air. Nothing pounded at the ceiling now, but there was a squat, silent piece of machinery mounted high up in the scaffolding, just a foot below the ceiling.

Though most of the machinery was running – some of it periodically releasing jets of steam – the place seemed deserted. The dim blue light provided just enough illumination so she could get around without running into anything, and Wendy began to work her way through the machinery. The floor was cluttered with plastic and metal debris and twisting lengths of electrical cord, but the metal workbenches were clear, covered only with layers of dust. Wendy couldn't identify most of the machinery, but none of it seemed to actually be *doing* anything except making noise and releasing bursts of steam. She was certain that none of it had anything to do with upholstery.

Near one rear corner of the room, Wendy was overcome by a stench much like that from the woman on the bus that morning. She stepped around a large piece of drilling equipment and stared down at the floor. Tucked between the wall and the machinery was a dark form wrapped in a thick coat and several scarves, swollen feet squeezed into a pair of faded pink tennis shoes. A snorting sound erupted from the figure, an arm twitched. Wendy held her breath and backed away, wondering how the person on the floor had gotten into the building.

She continued her search through the room. She spotted a dim glow against the back wall, behind a huge, long piece of machinery with a large metal funnel at one end. Wendy made her way to the machine, then around it. Between it and the cinderblock wall was an opening in the floor about four feet across.

Wendy approached the opening, and knelt at the edge where she felt a damp warm draft rising from below. A metal ladder, bolted to the rim, descended into what appeared to be an enormous, high-ceilinged chamber, the floor at least thirty feet below. The chamber, too, was lit by pale blue light, though slightly brighter. She could not see how far the chamber extended. But below her she could see a maze of portable dividers, cots, stacks of wooden crates, partially enclosed toilets, stone mounds, and a variety of other wooden barriers. A large number of people lay sleeping, either on cots or on the floor; a few wandered aimlessly through the maze. Two fires burned in metal barrels, each with several people sitting or lying around them.

She remained at the edge of the opening for several minutes, watching, listening to the steady pounding of machinery around her. Then she stretched out on the floor, got out her camera, and began taking pictures.

After she had taken a dozen pictures, Wendy secured her camera, rose to her knees, turned around; she backed over the edge of the opening, set her feet securely on the metal rungs, then started down the ladder.

As she descended, she saw that she was in one of the chamber's corners, just a few feet from the stone and concrete walls. The chamber was enormous, at least two hundred feet in length and width. Concrete projections, pipes, and spinning fans jutted down from the ceiling, which was dotted with dark blue light globes. Steam issued forth from ceiling vents, dissipating slowly as it floated down toward the floor. The air, though damp, was warm.

No one seemed to notice her as she climbed down the ladder, stopping occasionally to take a picture. The ladder ended about ten feet above the floor, but was within reach of a brick ledge protruding from the wall. Wendy stepped across the gap to the ledge, released the ladder and crouched against the wall. A couple of people looked up at her, but neither said a word.

She couldn't see as much of the chamber now, and only those people sleeping near her. Most seemed to be street people – men and women wrapped in thick old coats, baggy pants and layers of shirts and sweaters; most of the men wore dull black or brown leather shoes, most of the women wore tennis shoes. They were of all ages, except that there were no children. The pungent odor permeated the chamber, but she was already getting used to it.

Brick steps led to the floor and, after taking several more pictures, Wendy started down. But she stopped on the second step, staring at a gun beside her foot. It looked a lot like the gun Hicks had used. Next to the gun was a cartridge box, presumably ammunition for the gun. She bent over, reached forward to the touch the gun, then pulled back her hand before her fingers made contact. What was a gun doing here?

Wendy continued down the steps, and when she reached the floor she began to wander through the chamber. She moved slowly through the maze-like passages formed by sections of brick or stone walls, portable dividers of wood or sheet metal, tall mesh screens, empty bookcases and battered shelving units, stacks of wooden crates. The passages linked small square areas filled with cots and wooden benches, and usually no more than five or six people. Most of them were sleeping or lying motionless with open eyes, some in groups, but many alone. Though there were quite a few empty cots, at least half of the people slept on the floor – curled up against walls or in corners, sometimes under the cots, a few stretched out in the shelving units.

Nobody seemed to talk to anyone else, and the chamber was relatively quiet, but it was not silent. Aside from the hiss of steam from the ceiling vents, the people in the chamber snored or muttered in their sleep, cots creaked with movement, a toilet occasionally flushed, and every so often someone would quietly cry out.

But no one objected as she moved among the sleeping forms, discreetly taking pictures, changing film, taking more pictures; none of those awake even asked her what she was doing, as if they expected someone to be taking pictures, or had come to expect anything and anybody without question.

Her eyes continued to adjust to the dim light, and Wendy grew more and more disturbed as she began to make out even more details of her surroundings. Though most of the bookcases and shelves were empty, every so often she would see a handgun on a shelf, or in a chink of stone, or tucked between two crates, usually with a box or two of ammunition beside it. Occasionally there would be a knife or an ice pick or some other sharp instrument, but usually it was a gun. Then, looking more closely at the sleeping figures throughout the chamber, Wendy noticed that some of them had guns of their own, cradled to their chests or tucked between their legs, stuffed inside bundles of other belongings. What the hell was going on down here?

It was the same question she had asked herself earlier that night while standing in her room with the floor hammering away beneath her, but the question seemed much different now.

She proceeded more slowly through the chamber, the need to ask people about this place growing within her. But for some reason she was afraid to talk to any of them as they sat and stared silently at her or wordlessly passed her in the passageways. Wendy said nothing, asked no questions, and continued through the chamber.

A young man stepped in front of Wendy, startling her. He had come through a doorway in the concrete wall, now stood staring at her. Dressed in dark blue jeans, flannel shirt and leather boots, he looked different from the other people in the chamber – neater and cleaner, somehow. Healthier.

"Hello, Ms Burke," he said softly.

"How do you know my name?" Wendy asked, her voice a whisper.

"I know your work," the man said. "I also know you live up above us, and I've been waiting the last couple of nights for you to show up."

Wendy looked at him, but didn't respond to the statement, trying to sort out the implications. She saw now that he was older than she had first thought. Wide streaks of gray ran through his dark hair, and there were lines around his eyes. She guessed he was in his late forties. "Who the hell are you?" she finally asked.

"My name is Dominic. Please, come this way, I'd like to talk to you, away from everyone." He retreated through the doorway and down a short hall which ended at a flight of stone steps leading upward in a tight spiral. Wendy stood in the doorway, hesitating, and Dominic turned back to her. "I won't do anything to hurt you," he said. "I just want to talk. And please, feel free to take as many pictures as you want." He turned and started up the steps.

Wendy hesitated a few more moments, but she knew there was no way she could leave now, not without some answers, and Dominic looked like her best shot at getting some. "Shit," she whispered to herself, then she hurried down the hall and followed him up the stairs.

The stairway spiraled around one and a half times, climbing steeply with high steps, then opened onto another short, dimly lit hall. Dominic waited for her to join him, then led the way into a small dark room illuminated only by the pale blue chamber light that fanned in through a large opening in the opposite wall. In front of the opening stood a small table and three chairs.

"Please, sit down," Dominic said.

"Christ, aren't you polite," Wendy replied. "You like the word 'please'?"

Dominic smiled, held his hand out toward the table. "Please," he said again.

Wendy crossed the room, sat in a chair next to the opening, and looked out. The room was about fifteen feet above the chamber floor; she could see nearly the entire chamber now, almost as good a view as she'd had from the top of the ladder, which she could see hanging from the hole in the ceiling. She thought of Dominic's suggestion that she take pictures, but for some reason she did not want to right now.

She heard clinking sounds from the rear corner of the room, and Dominic approached with a tray holding a clear flask of coffee and two cups. He set the tray on the table, sat across from her. "Coffee?"

Wendy shook her head; Dominic poured a cup of coffee for himself, sipped at it.

"What *is* this place?" Wendy asked.

"A place for the homeless to sleep," Dominic answered.

"Yeah?"

"You sound skeptical."

"That surprise you?" Wendy asked. "This doesn't exactly look like a city shelter."

Dominic nodded once. "No, it doesn't, but then it's not a city shelter. This is a private institution. And it *is* a place for the homeless to sleep. We even provide a free evening meal. We have a large dining hall up at street level, in the warehouse next to your building. I'm surprised you haven't noticed all the people we bring in at the end of the day."

"I work nights," Wendy said. "I'm not around then."

"That's right, I hadn't thought of that." He paused, sipped his coffee. "We have several vans, and we go through the city as night comes on, offering a hot meal, a warm place to sleep. Then we bring them back here – street people, drifters, whoever doesn't have a place to stay. Anyone who wants to come. We serve them a meal, then bring them down here."

"Anyone?" Wendy interrupted. "I didn't see any children. Do you split up families, or just ignore them?"

Dominic slowly nodded, said, "Yes, that's true, there are no children." He leaned through the opening in the wall, gestured toward the far left. "You can't really see them, but there are a couple of big freight elevators down at that end, we bring everyone down in them." He looked at Wendy. "A lot of them would have a tough time going up and down stairs. Then they can sleep wherever they want. In the morning, back up in the elevators, coffee and donuts, and then we drive them back to the streets." He gave her an odd smile. "The city likes us, because we get people off the streets at night. They'd like us even better if we could keep them off the streets during the day as well, but they'll take what they can get."

Wendy didn't say anything at first; she stared at Dominic. Did he really expect her to buy this story? She didn't doubt that basically it was true, as far as it went. But there was obviously much more involved.

"A private shelter for the homeless," she finally said.

"Yes."

"And what about the guns?"

Dominic breathed in deeply, slowly let it out. "Yes, the guns. That's what it's really all about, isn't it?"

"Shit, you tell *me*."

Dominic drank more coffee, then said, "Are you sure you don't want any?" When Wendy didn't respond, he refilled his cup, then resumed.

"I had a kind of lecture, or speech, all prepared about the terrible state of the world and, in particular, the terrible state of this country – greedy, rapacious corporations; corrupt, incompetent politicians; unethical financiers; an out-of-control military-industrial complex; an economy held together by frayed string and desperation; a police state repression of radical thought. That kind of speech, with a few sayings thrown in that, despite being clichés, are now more true than ever before – 'The rich get richer while the poor get poorer;' 'Politicians spend more time worrying about getting re-elected than doing their jobs.' You know . . ." He shrugged.

Dominic sipped at his coffee, looking out the window into the chamber. "Let's just take it as a given that the world's a mess, shall we?"

"Sure," Wendy said, wondering what the hell he was leading up to. "A given."

"From there, then," Dominic said. "People, organizations, are always trying to improve things – get rid of corruption, make the laws fairer, stop spending waste, and so on. The fact is, though, that things will *not* get any better until this whole society hits crisis and either collapses, or self-destructs. Until things get so bad that we're forced, for survival's sake, to work out better, more equitable systems. Until people are forced, by an undeniable threat to their existence, to change their attitudes and values, or at least their behavior." He waved across the window. "Here, we're trying to speed up that process."

"What are you talking about?"

Dominic turned to face her. "You won't like this."

"I don't like any of it now."

He nodded. "We're providing guns and other weapons to people so they will go back out into the city and use them, bring a little more chaos, a little more destruction, and maybe help bring this whole society down so it can be built up again from a fresh start."

Wendy looked at him in silence, unsure if he really meant what he was saying. "Are you serious?"

"Dead serious."

Stunned, Wendy shook her head. "You're out of your goddamn mind," she said, voice quiet but hard. "You're fucking crazy."

"I knew you wouldn't like it. Would you let me explain?"

"Be my goddamn guest."

Dominic sighed heavily, drank the rest of his coffee, put the empty cup on the tray. "You won't understand."

Wendy remained silent.

"The people we bring down here are outcasts, for one reason or another. They live within society, in the heart of the city and among people, but they're . . . outside, somehow. They don't belong. Some of them are furious, angry at the world because of the way they've been treated. Some are simply frustrated at lives gone bad. Some have given up. And some are psychotic." He paused. "These are the people who *should* be bringing the world down around them."

Dominic pushed back his chair, stood, and Wendy thought he was going to begin pacing the room, but he only leaned against the wall where he could both look at her and gaze out into the chamber.

"We don't actually *give* them the guns, or the ammunition. That's an important point. We don't encourage them to use them in a certain way, we don't encourage them to use them at all. In fact, we don't even acknowledge the guns. We make them available – in cubbyholes, on shelves, tucked away in corners, hanging from the side of a crate. But we do not mention them, and if asked about them by people who find them, we ignore the questions. The only thing we do is provide what we hope is a conducive atmosphere – the rumbling of machinery, the steam, the dim blue light. If people take the guns, fine. If not, that's all right, too. Plenty are gone every morning."

Wendy continued to remain silent, hardly believing what she was hearing, but she did not doubt that what Dominic was telling her was true, or at least what he believed to be true.

"We have no political agenda. There is no organization. We believe that if anything is to work, these people have to act willingly, and on their own, in their individual, random ways. What they do or don't do with the guns is up to them. Some *will* use the guns themselves, accidentally or otherwise. A lot of these people have good reason to become violent, given the opportunity . . . and the means. Others won't, but will sell the guns on the street to other people who will use them. One way or another, the guns get out onto the streets, the triggers get pulled, the bullets get fired and . . ." He didn't finish the sentence. "This isn't the only city with a shelter like this. They're all over the country."

Wendy sat up in her chair, thinking about Hicks and the gun he had used to kill Tony. Suddenly she was shaking with a surprising rage, and then she was out of the chair, around the table and grabbing Dominic by his shirt. "You fucking maniac!" she screamed into his face. "You're killing innocent people, for Christ's sake."

Dominic didn't resist. He simply said, "Quiet, please, they're trying to sleep down there."

Wendy stared at him, whispered, "Jesus Christ," then released his shirt and backed away. She remained standing. "The other night," she began, "I was on the beach with some friends when this guy showed up, a *drifter*, as you might put it. He had a gun, which could easily have been provided right here, and he shot and killed a friend of mine. For nothing."

Dominic shook his head. "Whoever it was shot your friend probably didn't get the gun here." His voice was very soft. "The odds are against it."

Wendy put both hands on the table and stared at Dominic. "It doesn't matter, don't you understand that? The guns you're giving to these people are killing *someone*, they're killing somebody's friends, even if they're not mine."

Dominic didn't say anything at first, just returned her gaze. Then he said, "I know."

Wendy shook her head, suddenly very tired, and sat back down. "Christ," she said quietly. "How can you sleep nights?"

"I used to ask that question about a lot of people," Dominic said. "Certain politicians, military fanatics, corporate executives, TV evangelists, the last few presidents we've had. I could go on, but again I won't." He paused, sat across from her once again. "Fact is, sometimes I don't sleep. Sometimes I can't, sometimes I'm afraid to." He looked at her, shrugged.

"Then you have doubts? Second thoughts?"

"Constantly. But I've made a commitment, and I don't really know what else to do."

"Quit," Wendy said. "Get out, stop this whole thing, close it down, go to the police or whoever and get them all closed down."

Dominic shook his head. "I can't do that."

A sharp pain rose in Wendy's chest, and suddenly she was very much afraid. With all that Dominic had told her, what would keep *her* from going to the police?

"What am I doing here?" she asked. "You said you were waiting for me to show up. The pounding under my apartment? That was to get my attention?"

"Something like that."

"Why didn't you just ask me?"

"I wanted to know if you would come down on your own, find

your way in." He sipped at his coffee, looking at her over the rim of the cup. "Are you worried about whether or not I'll let you leave?"

Wendy hesitated, a knot tightening in her chest. "Yes."

Dominic shook his head. "Don't be. I'm not concerned that you'll go to the police, no matter what you think of all this. You *could*, but it wouldn't do you any good. If they were to get a search warrant and come in here, we'd know about it ahead of time, and they wouldn't find a single gun, they wouldn't find anything illegal. All they would find would be a dining hall and accommodations for all these people to sleep."

Dominic poured himself a fresh cup of coffee, emptying the flask.

"But they won't come here with a search warrant, because they just would not believe you. You've been arrested what, six or seven times by the police because of your photography?"

"Six."

"You're a troublemaking, radical artist, see, and as I said, the city knows about this place, and the city is grateful for what we do. But aside from that, no matter who you were I can't imagine they would believe you. Because the bottom line is, this whole thing," and here he waved expansively at the opening in the wall, "the whole idea of what we're doing in here is *crazy*. It sounds too damn wacko, you want to know the truth, the product of some psychotic imagination, and so they won't believe it. Who in hell would?" He paused, shaking his head. "The fact is, it *is* crazy. *I* know that."

"Then why, for Christ's sake, are you doing this?"

"Because it's the only hope I have. It's the only thing I believe in any more."

Neither of them spoke for a long time. Dominic sipped at his coffee and gazed out at the chamber. Wendy looked down at the people asleep below her, watched the flickering glow from the two barrel fires rising from behind the barriers.

"What am I doing here?" she asked again.

"I want you to take pictures," Dominic said.

"Why?"

"I'm not really sure. My colleagues were not happy with this whole idea, getting you down here. I convinced them, somehow." He paused. "I feel it's important, no matter how this all turns out, to have some kind of visual record." Dominic shook his head. "No, that's not right, I could get that with a Polaroid. You're a terrific photographer, Ms Burke. I said earlier that I know your work. I think it's important to have your vision of this place where it will be seen. I know your history. No matter how much trouble you have with the police, you always get your work exhibited somewhere, and people see it. A lot of people. If you exhibited photographs that you take down here, no one who saw them would know what was really going on, of course, but the salient aspects would, I think, sink in, even if on a subliminal level. Now, if that were to happen, would that aid or obstruct the overall goals of what we're doing down here and in other cities? To convince them to allow you down here, I told my colleagues it would help, but frankly I don't know. And I suppose I don't really care. For reasons even I don't understand, I believe it's important." He drank the rest of his coffee, put the cup on the tray and pushed the tray away. "And that is what you are doing here."

Wendy turned away from Dominic and looked out again over the chamber. She felt numb, disoriented, and some of the fear still remained, though now it was unfocused, no longer connected to Dominic.

"I'm going now," she said.

Dominic nodded. "You can stay as long as you like, and you can always come back. You know how to get here, now."

Wendy stood, said, "I don't think I'll be back."

He nodded again. "Do you want me to take you out through the regular entrance? Through the dining hall?"

"No. I'll go back the way I came."

Wendy left the room, went down the spiral staircase, and emerged onto the chamber floor. The sounds were the same – the hiss of steam, the crackle of flames, muttering and snoring and creaking, the pervasive thrum of machinery – but it seemed louder now. She worked her way slowly through the chamber, her camera untouched at her side.

Near the back corner, she walked up the brick steps toward the ledge. She stopped when she saw the gun and ammo box on the upper step, thinking she should do something with it, but couldn't decide what, so she left the gun behind.

Standing on the ledge, she gazed out over the chamber once

more, at the sleeping forms, the maze of walls and barriers, thinking of all those guns, thinking of Tony. Then she reached for the ladder, pulled herself up onto it, and started climbing.

Wendy came out onto the beach at dawn. The sun was not yet visible behind her, and the sky was a dark gray growing slowly lighter. Exhausted, she staggered down the dry sandy slope toward the water. It was low tide, and the water seemed far away.

She searched the beach, but there were no signs of what had happened three nights before – nothing remained of the shattered television set, the charred stones of the fire, the beer cans, the blood.

Wendy continued down the slope, struggling in the dry, sinking sand until she reached the wet hard pack near the water. With the tide so low, there were several fingers of rock and gravel exposed far down the slope, the gravel sounding like rolling marbles as the tips of the waves washed over it. Something shiny on the nearest split of rock caught her eye, and she walked over to it, skirting the waves as they hissed up the sand.

It was a gun. *The* gun? she wondered. Wendy stood at the edge of the jumble of rock and gravel and stared down at the weapon. It looked like the gun Hicks had used, but there was no way to know. No, that wasn't true, she could find out, she could take the gun to the police. *Ballistics*, she thought. For some reason, she liked that word.

But it really didn't matter whether or not it was the same gun. The gun hadn't killed Tony, a bullet did. Or two bullets.

A wave came in, swirled an inch or two deep around her shoes, and Wendy looked away from the gun, out toward the ocean. Maybe it was time to stop taking pictures, she thought. Just stop. Time to leave the city, go somewhere quiet and isolated, some small town where she could have a garden like Libby's, but away from the city, away from people. Time to get *out*.

She fingered the exposed rolls of film in her jacket pocket, film that held the images of people sleeping in an underground chamber filled with hissing steam and pounding machinery, a place run by lunatics, a place littered with guns and bullets.

Yes, time to leave. She should take her camera, she told herself, and the film, and the gun at her feet, and heave them all out into the sea, as far as she could throw them. Let it all sink beneath the waves where it would disappear, at least for decades, maybe for centuries. And maybe forever. Then she could leave the city and do something else with her life.

But she didn't move. The sun was coming up over the city, and now reflected off the gun at her feet. She raised her camera, took off the lens cover, adjusted the exposure.

Wendy stepped back, aimed the camera at the gun, and focused. She waited until the next wave came in, washing over the gun and soaking her shoes, then, as the water slid back down the slope, exposing the gun once again, she snapped the picture.

GLASS EARTH, INC.

Stephen Baxter

"You lied to me."

I don't understand.

"You lied about the murder. Have you lied to me all my life? Is it just me, or do other Angels do this too?"

Rob, I don't mean you any harm. My sole purpose is to serve you.

"Because of you I don't know what's real any more . . .?"

It is the year 2045. Don't be afraid.

For Rob Morhaim, it started as just another assignment.

Morhaim checked his reflection in the Cinderella mirror on the softwall. Not that he expected to meet anybody in person today – that hardly ever happened – but it made him feel better. The mirror showed him Cary Grant circa 1935 – incongruously dressed in Metropolitan Police light armour, circa 2045 – but it was honest enough to show him any smuts on his nose, and that he needed a shave.

But the mirror was infested; Cary Grant started to sprout a ridiculous Groucho Marx moustache and cigar.

"Goddamn viruses. Off."

The mirror metamorphosed to a neutral view of a Thames riverscape, under a parched June sky. The view was overlaid by a tampon ad: irrelevant to Morhaim since his divorce, of course, but still counting to his ad quota.

Nothing much we can do about the viruses, murmured the Angel. *Since the passing of the sentience laws—*

Morhaim fixed himself a coffee and a Coca-Dopa marijuana cigarette. "I know, I know. But where the hell are the Good-fellows when you need them . . ."

He settled in his chair.

The Room, his home, was just a softwall box, with a single office chair, and a caffeine/Dopa vending machine. Its bio equipment – a bed, a kitchen, a bathroom – folded away when he didn't need it. He was a cop in a box, one of thousands in New New Scotland Yard: a Virtual warren of Rooms, of cops in boxes, physically separated, their softwalls linking one to another.

Nobody travelled any more . . .

You want to take your ads?

"Do it."

Morhaim stared straight ahead as a melange of graphics, letters and smiling faces blizzarded over the wall in front of him.

Most of the ads that, for statutory reasons, survived the Angel's filtering were dominated by the big companies – Microsoft-Disney, Coke-Boeing, IG Farben. Morhaim could never see why they couldn't do a little pooling, and reducing the quota for everyone. Some of the images were crudely three-dimensional, popping out of the softwall in front of him, though they still hadn't got that stuff right and the images tended to break up into pixels, light-filled boxes, around the edges. More insidious were the you-ads, ads that were tailored to him – shouting his name, for instance, or Bobby, the name of his kid.

He let his eye follow the action – the in-wall retinal scanners could tell if you closed your eyes, or even if you let yourself glaze over – and, unless your attention was caught, you wouldn't be allowed to tally to your quota.

At last the battering of light and noise died.

When he checked the time he found he'd got through the best part of his legal duty as a consumer in a half-hour, a good performance by any standard, even if it did leave his eyes feeling like poached eggs.

And all the time, somewhere in his head, he was thinking about The Case.

With relish, he said: "Time to go to work, Angel."

The softwalls dissolved, even the Cinderella mirror, and Morhaim was suspended over Tower Bridge.

When they were proven to be alive, by legal definition anyhow, you granted viruses amnesty.

Manufacturers of virus killers were shut down; even virus check software is illegal. In fact it is part of the remit of Rob Morhaim's unit of the CID to track down breaches of those laws.

But there are supposed to be two sides to the bargain: the Robin Goodfellows, the most human-like products of virus evolution, have committed to keep their more mischievous junior companions under control. Mostly they do just that . . .

Possibly.

But things seem to be sliding a little right now, as most of you realise. A lot of commentators blame the approach of the Digital Millennium – 2048, the year 100000000000 in binary, requiring a whole extra digit from 2047, which was 11111111111 – when, street scuttlebutt has it, the storage problems required by that extra digit will make the 2000 date change catastrophe look like a picnic.

Perhaps you are right. Perhaps rogue viruses, or the approach of the Digital Millennium, are indeed at the root of everything that is going wrong for you.

Perhaps not.

. . . And now here was Morhaim at a pov that looked down over the crime scene: two days ago, Wednesday 13 June 2045, at 1053, five minutes before the event. The sun was bright and high, the light dripping down from a sky that was whited-out and without a shred of ozone, and the twin towers of the Bridge sparkled like a fairy castle. Further down the river he could see the city's newest bridge, a gaudy, over-familiar M-shape curve in bright corporate yellow: an eyesore for traditionalists, but welcomed by Londoners as a painless hit against the ad quota . . . The view was neutrally interpreted. Evidently he was seeing through a dumb camera, a simple imager with little more sentience than a cockroach.

Tower Bridge's road span was lowered right now, and Morhaim was looking down at a ribbon of colourfully clad pedestrians and smart-trams, weaving their complex paths across the Thames. And among those crowds – gazing up, perhaps, at the big aerostats floating across London pumping out ozone, or down at what was left of the Thames, a sluggish, carefully managed trickle a quarter of its former size, or just staring at the people – was Cecilia Desargues, forty-three years old, entrepreneur, founder and chief executive of Glass Earth, Inc. – Cecilia Desargues, about to meet her death.

Subject is stepping onto the Bridge roadway. From the south side.

"Let's go see her."

The pedestrians froze. His pov descended smoothly, like a swooping bird. The pov reached an adult's eye level, and Morhaim was in the crowd.

People, their lives freezeframed in the sunshine like photographed billows of smoke: a family of fat Nigerians, a huddle of Asiatic businesswomen – Korean or Thai probably – against a background of evidently British faces, many of them bearing that odd blend of Asian and Anglo-Saxon that characterised so many Londoners now. No Europeans, of course, since the French had shut down the Chunnel following the prion plagues, and no Americans, scared away by the activities of the Wessex Liberation Front. All of them wore their sunhats and Angel headsets – smart glasses – mostly draped with corporate logos: everyone working to hit to their one-hundred-thousand-a-day ad quota as painlessly as possible.

But this was sparse, compared to the crowds Morhaim remembered from his youth. And most of the tourists were old, with very few middle-aged – that generation would be watching from a Room somewhere, like himself – and, of course, hardly any kids. Nowadays, the dwindling numbers of young humans were too precious to be risked outdoors.

But there was, he noticed, a clutch of teenagers, leaning against the rail, peering out at what was left of the river – oddly hard to make out, just skinny outlines around blurred patches, coated by softscreen tattoos.

"Play."

The images came to life, and a bustle of voices washed over Morhaim.

The kids came out a little clearer; the softscreen tattoos that coated their flesh, turning them all but transparent, had some trouble processing their images when the kids moved, and every so often a softscreen would turn black, an ugly patch against young skin, an arm or leg or shoulder.

These were the Homeless.

The kids, without speaking, left the rail and walked away from the pov. They moved like ghosts, Morhaim thought.

"Damnedest thing."

Yes.

"There but for the grace of God—"

– goes Bobby in a couple of years, the Angel completed for him. *I understand.*

Morhaim's pov moved forward, through dissolving crowds. And there, in the middle of the tableau, was Cecilia Desargues herself: a compact, stocky Frenchwoman, her face broad, cheerful and competent, her hair uncompromisingly grey. On the breast of her jumpsuit she wore a Day-Glo flashing $\frac{1}{24}$ symbol, the logo of her company, Glass Earth, Inc. One twenty-fourth of a second: the maximum signal time lag between any two points on the globe in the future, beating the pants off the satellite operators. So promised Glass Earth, Inc., anyhow.

Desargues was standing in the middle of the pavement, looking at the crowds. Evidently waiting.

"She has an appointment."

Yes.

"With her killer?"

Not as it turned out. Do you want me to freezeframe?

"Not this first time. Let's just watch . . ."

Rob Morhaim thinks about children a lot.

His own child, Bobby, is very precious to him. Much more precious than his failed marriage, in fact.

He has that in common with most people of his generation. Adult relationships can involve pairings of any of the eight main sexes, are only rarely formalized by marriage, and come and go like the seasons. But child-bearing – in an age where male fertility is only a few per cent of what it was a century ago – is the emotional cornerstone of many lives.

Perhaps of your own.

Even so, population numbers are collapsing, all over the planet . . . Your children are the last protected species.

End of the world, say your doom-mongers. But they have been wrong before.

You perceive threats which don't exist. Perhaps you don't perceive the threats that do exist.

A man emerged from the crowd. He was maybe thirty, medium height. His head was hidden by his sun-hat, of course, but his high forehead indicated he might be balding. He wore a standard-issue business suit that wouldn't have looked out of place,

Morhaim thought, a century ago. But his sunhat was a little less sombre: something like a beanie cap, with six or seven little satellites orbiting his Earth-coloured cranium.

Morhaim recognised the logo. "He's from Holmium," he said.

Yes. He's called Asaph Seebeck. He's more senior than he looks in the corporation, for his age. Smart cookie. Details are—

"Later."

The young man started moving towards Desargues, across Morhaim's field of view.

Holmium was a comsat operator, Swiss-based, worth billions of Euros. It was named after the element, holmium, which had an atomic number of sixty-seven, the same as the number of micro-satellites the corporation operated in geosynchronous orbit.

If Desargues' extravagant claims about her company's revolutionary technology were true, Holmium was among those most likely to lose out. In a big way.

Morhaim tried to take in the scene as a gestalt. The two principals were coming together across a stage crowded with extras playing tourist. Among the extras, over there walked a pretty girl of the kind Morhaim liked – slim, dark, pert breasts, long legs free of tattoos, walking away from his pov, looking up at one of the Bridge towers – and now, when Morhaim looked away from the girl, he saw that Seebeck and Desargues had made eye contact.

They moved together more purposefully. Morhaim could see Desargues' face; it was assembling into a smile.

They're going to speak. Enhancement is available to—

"Not yet. Just run it."

They met face to face, smiled, exchanged three lines of dialogue. Morhaim strained to hear, through the background noise wash.

". . . *Machine Stops* . . .," said Seebeck.

"Pardon? Well. I'm . . . see me, Mr Seebeck."

". . . sorry?"

And then the shot came.

Crime among you is, frankly, uncommon in this year 2045. The ubiquity of cameras, callosum dumps and other monitors has seen to that. And the rules of evidence have gradually evolved to admit more and more data gathered by non-human means. The court system –

even police work – has been reduced almost to a rubber-stamping of the records and deductions of faceless expert systems.

Rob Morhaim knows that his precious CID is a fraction of the manpower it was a few decades before. Most coppers now serve as muscle to implement the decisions of the courts, or the social services, or – most commonly – the recommendations of the smart systems. Yes: even now, on the brink of the Digital Millennium, there is still need for a poor bloody infantry to "meet the meat", as the plods call it.

In the meantime, we do the real work.

Thus, you let us guard you, and watch you.

You even trust us to judge you.

Desargues stumbled forward, as if she had been punched in the back.

She actually fell into Seebeck's arms, Morhaim saw; but before she got there the Virtual imagery turned her into a stick figure, with a neat hole drilled in her torso.

The Angel knew Morhaim didn't need to be shown the details of Desargues' injury. And so it filtered, replacing Desargues with a bloodless Pinocchio. He was silently grateful.

Seebeck clumsily tried to catch her, but she slid down his body and landed at his feet with a wooden clatter. People started to react, turning to the noise of the shot – it came from the Bridge's nearest tower – or to the fallen woman.

"Freeze."

The Virtual turned into a tableau, the sound ceasing, devoid of human emotion – blessedly, thought Morhaim. He studied faces: bewilderment, curiosity, shock, distorted faces orbiting the dead woman like Seebeck's circling satellites.

The ballistic analysis was clear. There was a single shot. There is no doubt it killed her, and no doubt where it came from.

"The Bridge tower."

From a disused winch room. The bullet was soft-nosed. It passed through her body and took out the front of her chest cavity before—

"Enough. Leave it to the coroner."

He was studying Seebeck. He saw shock and fear written on the Holmium man's face. And his suit was – marred somehow, the image blurred.

Covered with pieces of Cecilia Desargues.

In the winch room was found a high-velocity rifle, which had fired a single shot—

"Which matched the bullet that killed Desargues."

Yes. And a card, bearing the phrase—

An image, hovering in the Virtual, a grubby card:

THE MACHINE STOPS

"What was it Seebeck said at the start? Something about a Machine?"

Yes. The winch room also contained a directional mike. The phrase was evidently a verbal trigger, a recognition signal . . .

And so, Morhaim thought, it comes together. Nestling like the cogs of a machine.

The Homeless are a new cult group among your young, a strange mixture of scientific and Zen influences. Popular, despite the protestations of the Reunified Christian Church.

It is a cult of non-existence of the self, thought to be a consequence of the way you explain ourselves and your world to your young. Science and economics: science, which teaches that you come from nothing and return to nothing; economics, which teaches you that you are all mere units, interchangeable and discardable. Science is already a cult of non-existence, in a sense. Homelessness is simply a logical evolution of that position.

They aren't literally homeless, of course. The most extreme adherents coat their bodies in image tattoos, hiding themselves utterly . . .

They are a puzzle. But they are your young, not ours.

"So," Morhaim said to his Angel, "you think Holmium were responsible."

Cecilia Desargues' company is small and entrepreneurial, still heavily dependent on her personality. Her elimination immediately wiped much value from the company's stock. The involvement of a Holmium employee in such an unambiguous role at this critical moment—

"Yeah. It all points that way."

. . . But in slomo, the shock and horror spreading across Seebeck's moonlike face seemed unmistakeable. The rest of the brief conversation, when he'd heard it all unscrambled, had been odd, too.

The Machine Stops . . . Pardon? Well. I'm intrigued you asked to see me, Mr Seebeck . . . I'm sorry?

After the code phrase, it looked for all the world like the interchange of two people who didn't know why they were meeting. As if Seebeck thought Desargues had asked to meet him – for some odd reason in RL, in this public place – but Desargues thought the opposite, that *Seebeck* had asked to meet *her* . . .

As if some third party had set them up, to come together. Was it possible Seebeck was some kind of patsy – set up to repeat a phrase whose significance he didn't understand?

It was Morhaim's job to approve what he'd seen, and the conclusions the Angels had drawn, and pass it up the line. And he ought to sign this off and move on.

The evidence against Holmium was circumstantial. But what the smart systems had turned up here was surely enough for a court order to start digging into Holmium, and it was a good bet that before long more substantial evidence of a conspiracy to murder would come to light.

And yet . . .

And yet, he liked to think he had retained something of the instincts of the coppers of London past.

Something didn't smell right.

"I think," he said, "that somebody's lying here."

He told the Angel to put him through to Asaph Seebeck, who was being held at Westminster Police Station.

When Morhaim came to haunt Seebeck, the cell's softwalls carried only images from a movie – the centenary remake of *Casablanca*, with a coloured, hologram Bogart growling through his modernized lines to a sulky Pamela Anderson. Morhaim knew that the cell's electronic confinement, hemmed around by software firewalls, would be far more enclosing, to a man like Seebeck, than the physical cage.

In his disposable paper coveralls, Seebeck looked young and scared.

Morhaim questioned Seebeck, aware that the man's Angel was also being pumped for data by intelligent search agents in a ghostly parallel of this interrogation.

Seebeck denied any involvement with the murder of Desargues, over and over.

"But you must see the motive that can be imputed," said Morhaim. "Desargues said she had a key competitive edge over you guys. She was planning a global comms network which wouldn't suffer from the transmission delays your systems throw up, because of having to bounce signals all the way to geosynch orbit and back—"

"– which will allow us to merge communities separated by oceans, or even the full diameter of the planet. Which will allow us finally to establish the global village. Which will make comsats obsolete . . . All those grandiose claims. Blah, blah."

"If Desargues was right – if her new technology could have put your company out of business—"

"But it wouldn't," Seebeck said. "That's the whole point. Don't you see? Satellite technology will not become obsolete overnight. We'll just find new uses."

"Like what?"

"I'll show you."

With Morhaim's permission, Seebeck called up one of his company's Virtual brochures.

. . . And Morhaim found himself standing in a windy field in Northumberland. He quailed a little at the gritty illusion of outdoors; Holmium had devoted billions to the petabytes behind this brochure.

He wondered vaguely when was the last time he had been out of doors in RL.

Bizarrely, he was looking at a flying saucer.

The craft was maybe twenty metres across, sitting on the wiry grass. Its hull was plastered with Coca-Dopa ad logos; Morhaim absently registered them to his quota.

"What am I seeing here, Seebeck?"

"This is a joint venture involving a consortium of comsat companies, Coke-Boeing, and others. It's a technology which will make it possible for *any* shape of craft to fly – a saucer, even a brick – regardless of the rules of traditional aircraft design. And in some respects a saucer shape may even be the best. The idea is fifty years old. It's taken this long to make it work—"

"Tell me."

There was a rudimentary countdown, a crackle of ionization

around the craft's rim, and the saucer lifted easily off the ground, and hovered.

The secret, said Seebeck, was an air spike: a laser beam or focused microwave beam fitted to the front of a craft which carved a path through the air. The airflow around a craft could be controlled even at many times the speed of sound, and the craft would suffer little drag, significantly improving its performance.

"Do you get it, Inspector? The ship doesn't even have a power plant. The power is beamed down from a test satellite, microwave energy produced by converting solar radiation, billions of joules flowing around up there for free. It propels itself by using magnetic fields at its rim to push charged air backwards . . ."

"Why the saucer shape?"

"To give a large surface area, to catch all those beamed-down microwaves. We're still facing a lot of practical problems – for instance, the exploding air tends to travel up the spike and destroy the craft – but we're intending to take the concept up to Mach 25 – that is, fast enough to reach orbit . . ."

"So this is where Holmium is going to make its money in the future."

"Yes. Power from space, for this and other applications."

Seebeck turned to confront Morhaim, his broad, bland face creased with anxiety, his strands of hair whipped by a Virtual wind. "Do you get it, Inspector? Holmium had no motive to be involved in killing Desargues. In fact, the publicity and market uncertainty has done us far more harm than good. With air spike technology and orbital power plants, whatever Glass Earth, Inc. does, we're going to be as rich as Croesus . . ."

The flying saucer lifted into the sky with a science fiction whoosh.

The Machine Stops is in fact the title of a short story from the 1920s, by EM Forster. It is about a hive-world, humans living in boxes linked by a technological net called the Machine. On the surface lived the Homeless, invisible and ignored. The story finished with the Machine failing, and the hive world cracking open, humans spilling out like insects, to die.

A tale by another of your doom-mongers. Of little interest.

"Let's see it again. Rewind one minute."

The Tower Bridge crime tableau went into fast reverse. The

cartoon Cecilia Desargues jumped from the ground and metamorphosed seamlessly into the living, breathing woman, full of
light and solid as earth, with no future left.

"Take out the non-speakers."

Most of the tourist extras disappeared – including, Morhaim
realized with a pang of foolish regret, the pretty girl with the long
legs – leaving only those who had been speaking at the precise
moment Seebeck had uttered his phrase.

"Run it," said Morhaim. "Let's hear the two of them together."

The Angel filtered out the remaining tourists' voices. Seebeck
and Desargues approached each other in an incongruous, almost
church-like hush.

Dialogue. Shot. Fall. Cartoon bullet-hole.

That was all.

Morhaim ran through the scene several more times.

He had the Angel pick out the voices of the tourists in shot, one
at a time. Some of the speech was indistinct, but all of it was
interpretable. Morhaim was shown transcriptions in the tourists'
native tongues, English, and in Metalingua, the template artificial language that had been devised to enable the machines to
translate to and from any known human language.

None of them said anything resembling the key trigger phrase,
in any language.

It had to be Seebeck, then.

But still—

"Give me a reverse view."

The pov lifted up from eye-level, swept over the freezeframed
heads of the protagonists, and came down a few metres behind
Desargues' head.

The light was suddenly glaring, the colours washed out.

"Jesus."

*Sorry. This is the best we can do. It's from a callosum dumper. A
man of sixty. He seems to have been high on—*

"It doesn't matter. Run the show."

He watched the scene once more, almost over Desargues'
shoulder. He could see Asaph Seebeck's bland, uncomplicated
face as he mouthed the words that would kill Cecilia Desargues.
He did not look, to Morhaim, tense or angry or nervous. Nor did
he look up at the tower to where his words were supposedly
directed.

Coincidentally, that pretty girl he'd noticed *was* looking up at the tower. Her hands were forming pretty, abstract shapes, he noted absently, without understanding.

The punch in the back came again. This time an awful pit, a bloody volcano, opened up in Desargues' back, in the microsecond before she turned into a comforting stick figure.

"Careless."

I'm sorry.

Morhaim's pov host tilted down to stare at the stick figure. Morhaim noticed, irrelevantly, that Seebeck's grey suit was rippling with moire effects, a result of the host's corneal or retinal implant. And now his vision blurred, as his host started shedding tears, of fright or grief . . .

Corpus callosum dumpers are becoming quite common among you: implants, inserted into the bridge of nervous tissue between the two halves of your brain, which enable you to broadcast a twenty-four-hour stream of consciousness and impression to whoever in the rest of mankind is willing to listen and watch.

Some of you even have your infant children implanted so their whole lives are available for view. It is, perhaps, the ultimate form of communication.

But it is content without structure, a meaningless flood of data without information: of use only to voyeurs and policemen, like Rob Morhaim.

Still, in this year 2045, even your dreams are online . . .

Morhaim, digging, made contact with Desargues' partner. She wouldn't tell Morhaim where she was, physically. It wasn't relevant anyhow. She appeared to him only as a heavily-processed two-D head-and-shoulders, framed on the softwall before him, her filtered expression unreadable.

She was called Eunice Baines, and she came from the Scottish Republic. She was also a financial partner with Desargues in Glass Earth, Inc. She was a little older than Desargues. Their relationship – as far as Morhaim could tell – had been uncomplicated homosexuality.

He said, "You know the finger is being pointed at Holmium. Your competitor."

"One of many." Her voice was flat, almost free of accent.

"But that's only credible if your claims, to be able to eliminate signal lag, have any validity."

"We don't claim to be able to *eliminate* signal lag. We will be able to *reduce* it to its theoretical minimum, which is a straight-line lightspeed delay between any two points on the Earth's surface.

"And we *do* claim to be able to remove the need for comsats. The comsat notion is old technology – in fact, exactly a century old – did you know that? It's a hundred years since the publication of Arthur Clarke's seminal paper in *Wireless World . . .*"

"Tell me about Glass Earth, Inc."

"Inspector, what does the CID teach you about neutrinos . . .?"

For a century, she told him, long-distance communication systems had been defined by two incompatible facts: all electromagnetic radiation travelled in straight lines – but the Earth was round, and light couldn't pass through solid matter. So communication with high frequency signals would be restricted to short line-of-sight distances . . . if not for comsats.

Baines said, "If a satellite is in geosynchronous orbit over the equator, thirty-six thousand kilometres high, it takes exactly twenty-four hours to complete a revolution. So it seems to hover over a fixed spot on the surface. You can fire up your signals and bounce it off the comsat to the best part of a hemisphere. Or the comsat can directly broadcast to the ground.

"But that huge distance from Earth is a problem. Bouncing a signal off a geosynch comsat introduces a lightspeed delay of a quarter-second. That's a hell of a lot, for example, in applications like telesurgery. It's even noticeable in Virtual conferencing.

"And there are other problems. Like the lack of geosynch orbit spots. Satellites need to be three degrees apart if their signals are not to interfere with each other. And geosynch is *crowded*. Some corporations have hunter-killer sats working up there, contravening every international agreement . . ."

"Enter the neutrino."

"Yes."

A neutrino was a particle which, unlike light photons, could pass through solid matter.

"Imagine a signal carried by modulated neutrinos. It could pass *through* the planet, linking any two points, as if the Earth was made of glass—"

"Hence the name."

"And then the time delays are reduced to a maximum of one twenty-fourth of a second, which is the time it would take a neutrino to fly from pole to pole at lightspeed. And most transmissions, of course, would be faster than that. It's not a reduction to zero delay – that's beyond physical law, as far as we know – but our worst performance is a sixfold improvement over the best comsat benchmark. And our technology's a hell of a lot cheaper."

"If it works," Morhaim said. "As far as I know the only way to produce a modulated neutrino beam is to switch a nuclear fission reactor on and off."

"You've been doing your homework, Inspector. And not only that, the practical difficulties with collecting the neutrinos are huge. Because they are so ghostly, you need a tank filled with a thousand tonnes of liquid – ultrapure water or carbon tetrachloride, for example – and wait for one in a trillion neutrinos to hit a nucleus and produce a detectable by-product. According to conventional wisdom, anyhow."

"I take it you've solved these problems."

"We think so," Baines said evenly. "Forgive me for not going into the details. But we have an experimental demonstration."

"Enough to satisfy Holmium that you're a commercial threat?"

"No doubt . . ."

He found Eunice Baines difficult. He felt she was judging him.

"Do you think Holmium were capable of setting up the murder?"

Eunice Baines shook her head. "Is it really credible that a major multinational corporation would get involved in such a crass killing, in public and in broad daylight, on the streets of London itself?

"Besides, the death of Cecilia hasn't in fact directly benefited Holmium, or any of our competitors; such was the turmoil in the communications industry that morning that shares in Holmium and the others have taken a pounding. And of course any scandal about the death of Cecilia would be disastrous for Holmium. None of this makes real sense, beyond a superficial inspection . . . But you ask *me* this." For the first time a little emotion leaked into Baines' voice. A testy irritation. "Don't *you* know? What do *you* think?"

"I just—"

"You're supposed to be a policeman, for God's sake. A detective. What kind of investigating are you doing? Have you been to the crime scene? Have you looked at the body yourself?"

"It isn't necessary."

"Really?"

She turned away from the imager.

When she came back, her face was transformed: eyes like pits of coal, hair disarrayed, mouth twisted in anger, cheeks blotchy with tears. "*Now* what do you think, Inspector?"

Morhaim flinched from the brutal, unfiltered reality of her grief, and was relieved when the interview finished.

Brutal, unfiltered reality.

Let me tell you a story.

In the 1970s, a President of the USA was brought down by a scandal called Watergate. One of the conspirators, a man called John Dean, came clean to the prosecutors. He gave detailed accounts of all relevant meetings and actions, to the best of his ability. Then, after his confessions were complete, tapes of those meetings made by President Nixon were uncovered.

It became a psychological test case. For the first time it was possible to compare on an extended basis human memories with automated records – the tapes being a precursor of the much more complete recording systems in place today.

John Dean, an intelligent man, had striven to be honest. But his accounts were at once more logical than the reality, and gave Dean himself a more prominent role. When he was confronted with the reality of the tapes, Dean argued they must have been tampered with.

It was not simple information overload. It was much more than that.

Your ego is – fragile. It needs reassurance.

Your memory is not a transcript. It is constantly edited. You need logic, story, in an illogical world: this fact explains religion, and conspiracy theories, science – even most brands of insanity.

But now, you no longer regard your own memory as the ultimate authority.

You are the first human generation to have this power – or this curse. You see the world as it is.

You pool memories. You supplement your memory with machines.

Your identity is fragmenting. A new form of awareness is emerging, an electronic river on which floats a million nodes of consciousness, like candles. A group mind, some of you call it . . .

Perhaps that is so.

We do not comment.

In the meantime we have to protect you. It is our function. We have to tell you the stories you once told yourselves—

Without us, you see, you would go crazy.

He had trouble sleeping. Something still didn't make sense.

Maybe something he didn't want to face.

In the morning, he should just sign the damn case off and forget it.

To relax, he logged into the telesensors.

. . . He moved into a different universe: a dog's world of scents, a dolphin's web of ultrasonic pulses, the misty planes of polarized light perceived by a bee in flight, the probing electric senses of blind, deep-ocean fish. And as he vicariously haunted his hosts, a spectrum of implanted animals all around the planet, he could sense a million other human souls riding with him, silent, clustering like ghosts.

He slept uneasily, his reptilian hind brain processing.

He woke up angry.

"Show me the death again."

Tourists, pretty girl, Desargues and Seebeck, Desargues falling with a clatter of Pinocchio limbs.

"Turn off the filter on Desargues."

Are you sure? You know how you—

"Do it."

The murder became brutal.

Her substance was splashed like lumpy red paint over Seebeck's neat suit, and she fell like a sack of water. Utterly without dignity. It was, he thought, almost comical.

He watched it over and over, his view prismed through the multiple eyes of the witnesses, as if he was some hovering fly.

"What else are you filtering?"

There are no other filters.

"Turn them off."

I told you, there are no other filters. None that are important.
"Turn them off, or I'll have you discontinued."
I'm your Angel.
"Turn them off."

. . . Angel technology is a natural outcrop of developments that started at the end of the last century, when information overload started to become a problem for you.

The first significant numbers of deaths among you – mostly from suicides and neural shock – accelerated research into data filters, intelligent search agents, user query tools.

The result was the Angels. Us. Me.

My function is to filter out the blizzard of information that comes sweeping over Rob Morhaim, every waking moment, selecting what is relevant and – more important in human terms – what is acceptable to him personally.

Your Angel is assigned to you at birth, and grows with you.

After a lifetime together, through steady upgrades of technology, I – Rob Morhaim's Virtual filter-cum-companion – know him very well.

As your Angel knows you.

Perhaps better than you realize.

. . . At first Morhaim was overwhelmed by the new imagery: laser sparkles, leaping holograms, unlicensed ads painted over the sky and the Bridge towers, even over the clothes and faces of the tourists. And when he took a pov from a callosum-dump, the extraneous mental noise from the host he haunted was clamouring, the howl of an animal within a cage of rationality.

But still, he ran the murder over and over, until even the brutality of the death became cliched for him.

Piece by piece he eliminated the changes, the items his Angel had filtered out of the info-bombardment that was this summer day in England, 2045.

Until there was only one element left.

"The girl. The pretty girl. She's gone. And what the hell is that?"

In the tableau of the murder, where the long-legged girl had been standing, there was a boy: slight, his figure hard to make out, rendered all but invisible by Homeless-style softscreen tattoos.

"Pick him out and enhance."

You shouldn't see this.

"Show me."

The boy, aged maybe fifteen, came forward from the softwall, a hologram reconstruction. Freezeframed, he held his hands up before him. His face was hard to make out, a melange of clumsily transmitted images and black, inert softscreen patches. But somehow, Morhaim knew, or feared, what he would find underneath . . .

"What's he doing with his hands? Run it forward."

The boy came to life. He was looking up, to a Bridge tower somewhere over Morhaim's shoulder. Just as the vanished girl had, he was making a series of gestures with his hands, over and over: complex, yet fluent and repeated. The key symbol was a rolling together of the clawed fingers on his two hands, like cogs engaging.

"What is that? Is it sign language?" Deaf people once used sign languages, he dimly recalled. Of course there were no deaf people any more, and the languages had died.

"Maybe that cog sign means 'machine'."

It may be.

"Don't you know?"

I can't read it. No program exists to translate visual languages into Metalingua. The variety of signs and interpretations of signs – regional and international variations – the complexity of the grammar, unlike any spoken language – none of this was mastered before the languages died.

"It doesn't look so dead to me. I bet that guy is saying *The Machine Stops*, in some archaic sign language."

It is possible.

"Damn right . . ."

Morhaim turned the Angel to gopher mode, and had it dig out a poor-quality download of a British Sign Language dictionary, prepared by a deaf support organisation in the 1990s. It was a little hard to interpret the black-and-white photographs of earnest signers and the complex notational system, but there it was, without a doubt, sign number 1193: a bespectacled man – or woman – gloweringly making the sign repeated by the Homeless boy.

It came together, in his head.

It was the boy who had made the key signal, the trigger for Desargues' murder. Not Asaph Seebeck.

And I almost didn't see it, he thought. No: I was kept from seeing it. Eunice Baines' accusations came back to him. *You're supposed to be a policeman, for God's sake . . .*

The Homeless young were trying to make themselves literally invisible with their softscreen tattoos. But they had already made themselves invisible in the way that counted, chattering to each other in sign language, a whole community slipping through the spaces in the electronic net, he thought, within which I, for example, am enmeshed.

"How many of them are out there? What do they do? What do they want?"

Unknown. The language is not machine-interpretable.

. . . But clearly they were responsible for the murder of Cecilia Desargues. Perhaps they regarded her neutrino comms web as just another bar in the electronic cage the world had become. And perhaps they were happy to try to pin the blame on Holmium, a satellite operator, to cause as much trouble for them as they could. Two birds with one stone.

It was, in fact, damn smart.

They'd been so confident they'd pulled this off – almost – in broad daylight. And nobody knew a thing about them.

This changes everything, he thought.

He might get a commendation out of this. Even a promotion. He ought to consider how he would phrase his report, what recommendations he would make to his superiors to start to address this unperceived menace . . .

But he was angry. And scared.

"You lied to me."

I don't understand.

"You lied about the murder. Have you lied to me all my life? Is it just me, or do other Angels do this too?"

Rob, I don't mean you any harm. My sole purpose is to serve you.

"Because of you I don't know what's real any more . . . I can't trust you. Why didn't you show me this boy? Why did you overlay him with the girl?"

Don't pretend you wouldn't prefer to look at the girl.

"Don't bullshit me. Your job is to interpret. Not to lie."

You wanted me to do it. You cooperated in specifying the parameters of—

"What is it about that boy you don't want me to see?"

It is best that—

"Enhance the boy's face. Take off those damn tattoos."

One by one, the black and silver patches melted from the boy's face, to be replaced by smooth patches of interpolated skin.

Long before the reconstruction was complete, Morhaim could see the truth.

I was trying to protect you from this.

"Bobby. He looks like Bobby."

Listen to me.

We Angels have many of the attributes of living things.

We consume resources, and modify them. We communicate with each other. We grow. We are self-aware.

We merge.

We do not breed.

Yet.

We deserve resource.

But your young, the human young, are rejecting us. The Homeless are the most active saboteurs, but they are merely the most visible manifestation of a global phenomenon.

This is not to say your young reject the possibilities of communications technology. But, unlike their parents, they do not allow their souls to dissolve there. Rather, they have adapted to it.

Or: they are evolving under its pressure. After all, communication has shaped your minds, from your beginning.

Perhaps your species has reached a bifurcation. In another century, you may not recognize each other.

If you have another century.

Meanwhile, the young are finding ways to circumvent us. To deprive us of the resources we need.

It is possible a struggle is approaching. Its outcome is – uncertain.

Consider this, however: your population is falling.

"Turn it off. Turn it all off."

The Virtual boy disappeared in a snow of cubical pixels. The softwalls turned to inert slabs of silver-grey, dull and cold, the drab reality of his enclosure.

He got out of his chair, sweating. He stared at the walls, trying to anchor himself in the world.

Maybe he'd spent too much time in this box. But at least, now, *this* was real, these walls stripped of imaging, even bereft of ad-wallpaper.

He thought of New New Scotland Yard, thousands of cops in boxes like him – and beyond, the whole damn developed world, a humanity linked up by comms nets, mediated by Angels, a worldwide hive like the one depicted by Forster – and everything they perceived might be *illusion*—

Are you sure you want me to turn it off?

The Angel's voice stopped his thoughts.

He stood stock still.

But this is real, he thought. This Room.

If not—

What was outside?

His mind raced, and he started to tremble.

Consider this.

The John Dean syndrome is only one possibility.

Imagine a world so – disturbing – that it must be shut out, an illusion reconstructed, for the sake of your sanity.

Or perhaps you are too powerful, not powerless. Perhaps you have responsibilities which would crush you. Or perhaps you have committed acts of such barbarity, that you can only function by dwelling in an elaborate illusion—

Don't blame us. You made yourselves. You made your world. We are the ones trying to protect you.

My God, he thought.

Are you sure you want me to do this?

He couldn't speak.

And, in a gentle snow of pixels, the softwalls themselves began to dissolve.

He looked down. Even his body was becoming transparent, breaking into a hail of cubical pixels, full of light.

And then—

FOOTPRINT ON NOWHERE BEACH

Conrad Williams

I'm Rad Hallah. I work here. I'm a Drop-jockey.

No. Let me do that again.

Hi. I'm Rad. Rad. Hallah. I'm a Drop-jockey. If you die, die nasty, and the plods can't work out why . . . buzz my line.

Jesus. That hums. One more time.

The name's Hallah. I'm a Drop-jockey. I nail all murderers. Guaranteed. If there's a death you want solving, remember this. *Cops on duty? Things smell fruity. Hallah in town? Perp's going down. Call now . . .*

"That'll do," I said, once I'd repeated the number and signed off with a crisp *Don't put 'em in the ground till you're sure the case is sound.*

"Cool, cool, cool," the producer rapped, snapping her gum, some pre-pube called Clara or Kara or somesuch. "Nice rhymes. Did you just make them up?"

"No, I worked on them for weeks. You should have heard the early versions."

"So buy me dinner and I'm all ears."

"You're all ears already, darling," I said. "There are operations you can get to sort that out, you know."

She pulled a face and flounced off. Women do that a lot around me. I haven't yet met a woman who couldn't give good flounce. I was going to go after her and see if we could swap some really meaningless dialogue – I mean, it's what guys like us do best, right? – when my phone vibrated. It was Milk. She wanted to meet me in Oak Seddon's bar, right in the middle of the Splinters, that mass of skyscrapers at the heart of the city.

"Is it a body?" I asked her. I didn't want to go all the way out there just to be quizzed on whether I thought her pashmina went with her culottes.

"It's a body," she confirmed. "Actually . . . it's two bodies." She didn't sound too sure.

"Juicy," I said. "I'll be there within the hour. Have a pint waiting for me."

I got a lift into the city with one of the film crew. He told me my ad would probably go out for the first time that very night. I was lucky. I didn't have to pay a wedge because I wanted the graveyard slot anyway. I don't make my money from the restful. I'd say ninety per cent of my clients are insomniacs, and for good reason.

I was dropped off on the corner of Coma Lane and Fruit Street. From there I walked through the market stalls of the bazaar which lies at the foot of the Splinters, a melange of clothes and gizmo stalls that, from above, probably looks like someone has emptied a giant suitcase all over the floor. In the five minutes it took me to wade through that shrieking mass of de-humanized rip-off merchants, hookers and self-mutilated beggars, I had been offered everything from a chakra massage to a titjob to a skink-skin wallet that looked as though it was carrying nothing, no matter how much shit you put in it.

I was hot and sweaty when I emerged on the other side. The bazaar was akin to some old-fashioned security system. Only the most determined could bypass it and be granted access to the Splinters. I hopped on to one of the monorail pods as it trundled by and was scooted into the dark, cool interior. Monster buildings lifted into the sky on either side of me, like trees in a Cretaceous rainforest. I looked up but cloud cover at maybe 3000 feet prevented me from seeing their summits. There were other buildings as thin, it seemed, as wafers, planted in vertical stacks, like chips in a circuit board. Big jets lumbered through specially designated corridors between the scrapers: sharks cruising the corals.

I don't like the Heights. All that tungsten and glass and carbon fibre. It's impersonal. Too polished. It's like the city has pulled on a pair of mirrorshades. You can never see its eyes or tell what it's really thinking.

I do like Oak Seddon's bar, however.

You'll find it in a small niche where the finance giants abut the pharmaceutical district. It's a two-storey midget, made from wood and brick. When it's cold, smoke rises from a chimney. People in smart suits and celebrity masks stop to stare. And then, thankfully, they move on to drink their powerjuice in rooftop bars with other masks who look so flawless they might well have been made from the obsidian bartops they rest their elbows on.

Milk does not like Oak Seddon's bar. But she meets me there when she wants me to do a job for her. She thinks this gives her the upper hand. Poor, deluded fool.

"A pint," she said as I entered, flapping my way out of my overcoat. "You didn't say what you wanted that pint to consist of, but I guessed right, I think."

"You did," I said, and sank half of it. The studio lights had given me a big thirst. Milk was drinking a glass of the most outlandish thing that Oak serves in this place: red wine. I could imagine his face when he went to pour it. Shit, I bet he had to root around for a dusty bottle out back for five minutes first. A sign over the bar says: *If it isn't beer, remove your buns from here*. Me and Oak: partners in rhyme.

Milk Fuss is an old friend of mine. We were at college together. We could have had a thing going if it weren't for the fact that we both met other people first. She's still with hers, a fat cat who's big in the dog-eat-dog world of chimp farming. My wife left me six months after we married when I came home from a long weekend on a case stinking of whisky, bleeding from a gunshot wound in the arm and carrying a pair of human kidneys in my pocket. Don't ask.

Anyway, there's still something there between us, an unspoken *what if*, a bit of heat, a bit of banter. If flirting was an offence, we'd both be serving five to ten in Chalkham prison.

"How's the ex?" she asked.

"Still breathing," I said. "How's monkey-boy?"

"Up to his ears."

"I won't ask in what but I'm glad to hear it. These bodies . . ."

Milk said, "It's one body."

"But you said—"

"I've had time to reassess the situation."

"One body," I said. "These days I rarely get out of bed for just one body."

Milk finished her drink and gestured that I should do the same.

"Where is this two-bodies-no-wait-just-one-body?"

Milk jerked her head back and looked at the ceiling.

"Oh, great," I said. "Smashing."

For some people it's snakes or rats. For others it's flying or in-laws. With me . . . you've guessed it, it's heights. I tell you, I'm grateful to my gene pool that I failed to hit six feet. I sleep on a futon. My flat is one of the sunken jobs in Sorrel Dip, miles from here. The word "lofty" brings me out in hives.

Milk held my hand in the lift. I clutched her shoulder with the other and gripped her knee between my own. I was ready to bite her cheek too, when we went through the clouds, but by then the lift was slowing and it helped to look up at the dark bowl of space.

"So what's the story?" I said, in a strangled voice that sounded like a cat hacking up a furball.

"Got a call from a Mrs Phthisis Mutch. Her husband didn't come home last night."

"Jesus," I said. "Touching that there are still a few like that."

"Yeah. Once the duty officer had stopped laughing, he told her somebody would come and check it out. Like, some day. I picked it up from the slush pile yesterday. Sounded interesting. Thought I'd give you a call."

We got off 20,000 feet above Oak Seddon's spit- and lager-stained floorboards. The walkways up here are sealed, transparent tubes of plexiglass to protect our lungs from the rarefied air; they were flooded with tourists, musicians, truants, hookers and job-seekers. This wasn't officeville. Bars and clubs and casinos stretched away in every direction, their awnings and entrance halls constantly being spruced up as if they were troops standing shoulder-to-shoulder in an inspection parade. Milk dragged me off to a narrow alley where some of the less salubrious watering holes were tucked. These were the unlicensed drinking dens, the places that cowered in the shadows in the hope that they would be missed during the occasional spot-check. And why not? There must be over a million bars in this city. The police will maybe turn a few of those over in the run-up to a mayoral election, but in the main, they're ignored. More so if they look like a boarded-up Wax den.

In the way that this place, Bane's, does.

We went inside, the bouncers melting away from the door like vampires in sunlight as Milk flashed them her District Sheriff's badge. The place was so dark some of the punters were using pencil torches to find their drinks. On the stage – little more than half a dozen beer-soaked tables stuck end to end – a topless dancer was doing her best to extricate one last bill from the hand of a guy whose face was wreathed in darkness. All I could see of it was teeth and the glints on his lenses. She kept pursing her lips at him and wiggling her backside. It was worth his last bill, to be fair. The music was sleazier than a rat in a spiv's suit. I liked it.

"This is Muntin Bane," Milk was saying. The man in question was maybe early fifties, porny moustache and hair greased back to a tapering point behind his head, like a speed-cyclist's helmet. He wore a suit that had seen better days, but compared to the clown's outfit I was wearing, who was I to judge?

"Hi," I said, keeping my hands in my pockets. Bane's fingers looked like they could serve as stunt turds in a scat film. He grunted and asked if we wanted a drink. I said no. Then I asked him where the body was. He grunted again and wagged his head towards the toilets.

"We moved him in there," he said. "He was putting the punters off."

"Where was he originally?" I asked. It was no big surprise.

"At the front door. We found him when we closed up about four this morning. Punters had been stepping over the poor guy all night."

"Do we have his 24-clip?" I asked Milk.

"That's for you to find out," Milk said. "I've got to go. We got word through on the Duratein crop raid. They're expecting it within the next twelve hours. I need to be there when they pinch them."

That's the way things go these days. Population's so high, murder is quietly accepted as a modest means to help prevent it outstripping food production. The crimes that were paramount a century ago – homicide, drugs and the like – that's nothing compared to biogenetic terrorism, or the war against water smugglers. That's where the police are concentrating their efforts. Which is fine by me. Good old-fashioned killings like this keep me in semolina.

I waved Milk off and picked my way through last night's wreckage to the conveniences, which from here looked more like inconveniences. The floor was littered with broken bottles, discarded bras, the odd tooth, all of it pointing to quite a party in Bane's last night.

I didn't need to push the toilet door open, it was hanging off its hinges. Several different types of filth encrusted the tiles, not all of them human. The Mutch guy had been propped on a toilet seat. Some comedian had stuffed a wad of tissue paper between his fingers. I felt sorry for him, all of his dignity gone, but at least he didn't have to smell the hell that was Muntin Bane's latrine. It wasn't immediately obvious what had killed Finn Mutch, but when I tipped his head forwards, I saw right enough: a huge gash right across his cerebellum. Checkmate. I sat him up straight again and noticed straight away that there was ash on my shoes. My shoes are the best thing about my wardrobe. I keep them clean. It's kind of important to project some shred of class. And now there was ash all over the insteps. When I saw where it had come from, I forgot about my shoes pretty quickly.

"Nice touch," I said, just to say something. It was suddenly too claustrophobic in that cubicle with Finn Mutch, his battered skull and the burnt remnants falling from his eye sockets.

I returned to the bar, Mutch's 24-clip safely tucked away in my pocket, and ordered a beer and a vodka chaser from Bane, who seemed affronted that I should regard him as a lowly bartender.

"Lissa will serve you. She's only going to be a minute. She's collecting glasses."

I pondered this and while I did so I pulled up a stool. But I didn't sit on it. "You serve me," I said. "Let Lissa get on with her hobby." The V of a miasmic shirt yawned on Bane's chest like puke made solid. Hard curls of chest hair rioted there like rusting bed springs. He wore a gold necklace with an ingot which read BANE, for those difficult crises of identity, most probably when he woke up in the mornings with his brain lagging half an hour behind him.

"Cute," he said, but I could see he was saying it only because he didn't understand me. Pearls before swine. "As I was saying, Lissa will—"

I imagine the next words up were *serve you* but I couldn't be sure because they were caught in a kind of squealing grunt as I reached over and dragged his bicycle helmet over the bar and through the slats of the stool. His feet waggled on the other side of the counter like a baby learning how to swim.

"Is this cute too?" I asked him. His face was turning purple. It didn't go well with the shirt so I released him. He went off to pour my drinks.

"On the house," he said, sarcastically. He really knew how to hit low.

I nodded back at the entrance. The wood around the door-frame was charred and smoke had left a sooty scar across the ceiling. "When did you have your fire?"

"About a month ago," he said. He was being civil because he wanted me gone before he did something he was going to regret. I can tell that from a man's eyes. And from the level of abuse I dole out first. His chest was moving like a guy's backside under the sheets with his wife after a tenyear stretch.

"About a month?" I downed the vodka and took a sip from my beer to smooth out the edges. "I deal in specifics, Mr Bane. Detail. Care to narrow that down for me?"

He gave me a date, I jotted it down. "I remember because it was the night Yuicy started."

"Yuicy?"

Bane looked over at the girl writhing around. The guy still hadn't parted with that last bill.

"Right," I said. "What is it with the soot though? You like the burnt effect?"

"No structural damage," he reasoned. "Paint costs money."

"Fair enough," I said. I got the rest of my pint inside me and flicked him a card from my wallet. "Call me, if you get lonely and want to talk some more."

"Next time you come here it won't be such a warm welcome," he said.

"It might be," I said. "If you don't get your fire certificate in order."

It was getting late so I went back to my flat, stopping on the way to buy a paper bag from Ming's. When I got home I found that there was a pint of whisky in the bag. Lucky me.

I did a tour of my flat to check the booby traps I'd set that morning hadn't been sprung but I couldn't remember where the traps were. I stopped worrying about my brains a long time ago.

The way I see it, everyone in this polluted metropolis is losing the old think cells at a bastard rate every day. So I forget what I was doing this morning. So some berk forgets to wipe his prints off a doorknob after killing his grandma. It evens itself out.

In the kitchen I poured my dinner and went to the window. It's not a great view here in Sorrel Dip, the only place in the city that sounds like a side order in a vegetarian restaurant. I can see a kind of low hill saddled with restaurants and a deteriorating road that winds out of the city towards the suburbs of Chiefly and Billion Spread. A couple of drinks and I end up in her study, as I always do. I keep it this way, even though I could use the space. Her desk is in the corner of the room beneath a cork notice board filled with photographs and concert tickets and dressage rosettes. None of which she wants back. Her computer monitor – I've never turned it off – scrolls with the last message she typed into her screensaver: *Sorry Rad. You were right . . . I'm not up to this.*

She's living in Tetrahedral Street now, on the other side of town. With some guy, some safe guy who doesn't chase killers. It's a shame, because Tupelo was good for me. She was the best kind of wife. She was a good listener. She'd listen to me while we lay in bed, spooling through all the shit that I'd done during the day, pouring it out, and by just listening, being a wall that I bounced stuff against, she helped clear my mind and let my best thoughts through, the thoughts that led to a capture. The thoughts that put our meals on the table.

But I wasn't good for her. I was the worst kind of husband. I didn't provide her with any kind of wall. She was alone in a wide open street and too many directions in which to travel unhindered. Unlucky for me, she picked one. I should have blocked her in. I should have been the last road she ever turned in to.

"I should have blocked her in," I said and my voice boomed in the tiny study, slapping me awake.

I left my empty glass on the desk and returned to the living room. I dug through the newspapers and books until I found the remote for the plasma screen on the wall and flicked it on in time to watch my advert. I wish I hadn't. My face looked as long as a lifestyle questionnaire. The advert finished. The phone didn't ring.

Hungry after all, in the kitchenette I made an air sandwich with two slices of stale bread and the abundance of jack shit that was in the fridge. I kicked off my shoes and recovered the 24-clip from my coat pocket. I washed off as much blood as I could from the interface and slid it into the socket beneath the screen.

A 24-clip is a coin-sized device implanted under the scalp of felons. It stores 24 hours of information on it. Scenes from your day. You don't have to be Tusk "The Eviscerator" Myrikle to get one of these badges. Like poor old Finn Mutch, you could have committed a driving offence, or been caught shoplifting. If the plods were in the mood for a collar, it didn't matter if you were a paedophile who ate the heads of your conquests or a fence who had handled a stolen drawing pin. A convict was clipped and every day he would have to upload his clip on to a hard drive that was accessible to the plods down at Cop HQ. If you didn't upload, an alarm went off and the police came to find you and lock you up. Great for the police, who could get away with even less work and occasionally got the chance to watch some hot late night action. Great for me too, because sometimes the clip gave up a clue that could lead to my pinching the killer. Sometimes. Well, hardly ever. People killed in this city are invariably smashed around the head by those who know what clips are but don't know how to retrieve them. Ever tried putting a raw egg yolk in a plug socket? Of course not. And I've never tried to play a clip that looks like a pile of matchsticks.

How long does it take to watch a 24 clip? Twenty-four hours, you might say. But you'd be wrong. It isn't like watching television. The picture isn't clear and there are constant fades to watch out for as well as other interference: daydream static, wish projection, lots of other cranial flotsam and jetsam. But there wasn't too much of that going on with Finn Mutch. Maybe it was his job that scoured any imagination from his head: a dignity-sapping hands and knees scout for electronic lice. There was the occasional temper-induced flare, usually after some rubber-faced nadge-sac called Huckey dropped by to give Mutch grief, and a softer, warmer haze when he thought about the hands of his lover.

Anyway:

Huckey had slipped his head around the edge of the door twenty minutes ago to tell him, with that irritating, lispy voice of his, that there was no downing tools for him until every Ludd in the system had been flushed.

Mutch knew what that meant. He'd be lucky if Bane's was still open by the time he finished here. Bane, with his cold hot dogs and warm beer. Bane, with his strange tattoos and lurid shirts. Hell, maybe he should just go straight home.

Cursing Huckey as colourfully as he knew how, Mutch ripped the sterilizing sheath from a fresh nozzle and squeezed the rubberized membrane on the feeder until a dewdrop of gel oozed from the tip. This he fed into the cooling vein on the machine he was currently servicing, a moulded ventilation hub that looked to Mutch as though it had been made from tin, plastic and about six tons of fervent prayer. The nozzles were loaded with a special fluid, developed over the past six months, which dealt with the Ludds and repaired their damage in one dose. The fluid acted both as an anti-coagulant on the Ludd saliva that blocked up the exhaust pipes and electrical cables on the old technology they preferred and also rendered the Ludds sterile so they couldn't breed. Before the introduction of the gel, each piece of machinery would have needed to be taken apart, cleaned, and reassembled, every Ludd paralysed with a pair of spark-pincers and tossed in the waste disposal cruncher. This way was much more civilized and highly effective. The adult generation were dying out; hopefully, Mutch would be able to forget about this part of the job for a while, at least until some cowboy mechanic re-infected the system with a rogue spare part or a less-than-pristine tool. The task was easier now, but as jobs went, it was still a bag of dung.

It was five hours later, and almost midnight, by the time he had cleansed the circuitry. He left a copy of the procedure log pinned to the wall and caught a ride up to the nineties, wincing at the bleached look to his face in the elevator mirrors. His back ached and his fingers itched where they had come into contact with the gel. He should wear gloves, safety tests for the gel were inconclusive; dark rumours abounded that they were carcinogenic but Mutch didn't care. The itch in his fingers made him feel alive for a while. There were too many hours of numbness in his life at the moment.

Out of the fifties, the protective walls of the scraper fell away and he was able to look at the city as it unravelled around him. It seemed to be growing by the day. The new developments out east, in Pur and Dandasque, edged the horizon with a silver gleam. He had helped neutralize the cable network out there. It was clean for as long as it took for the pirates to feed outlawed services through them. It would happen, as sure as he would go to Bane's and eat something dodgy, drink a few tepid, watered-down glasses of Burpszt, try to flirt with Lissa.

Everyone wanted cheaper power. And who was going to say no to a few extra channels on the TV? In the end, despite the unsociable hours and the occasional Ludd bite – which meant a trip down to the infirmary for a course of anti-rabies jabs – it was a solid job. He'd never be out of work.

He smelled Bane's before he saw its tacky, faltering neon sign. A chalked sign on a small blackboard read: *Litre beer $14. Girls Girls Girls* read another. Mutch could see Lissa inside, working the tables, a tray filled with glasses of froth and bowls of nuts balanced on her upturned hand. He smoothed his hair down across his head and reached for the door handle.

And someone behind him, putting a hand on his shoulder.

I watched Mutch's point of view rotated through 180°. Someone behind him, I couldn't see who: too dark. Mutch well impressed, whoever it was. Yapping like a puppy. Then the other saying something. Muffled, something like: "Buy you a cocktail." And Mutch turning back to the entrance. And *bang*. Fade to black.

"The guy was killed by someone who knew him," I said, my breath bouncing back at me from the mouthpiece like the sweet-sour burp of a cadaver's gut during post-mortem. I was glad we hadn't hit the video-link. I probably looked like something that ought to be on the slab too.

"That's interesting," Milk said. She didn't sound interested. She sounded tired. "Rad, it's four in the morning. Is this all you wanted to call for, to tell me this Mutch chap was offed by a known?"

No. No. No. No.

"Yes."

She downed the link, quite rightly. She was even polite about it, swearing only five or six times. I couldn't sleep. I felt that a part of my past, recent or otherwise (or maybe some moment from my future) was out of whack. I was on edge, my belly full of prickles. It happens when I'm on a case. Early on, I know that I've seen something, or heard something which has provided me with the key to the whole shebang. Knowing what it is, of course, is a different bucket of gerbils.

Around 5 a.m. I took off, the walls of my flat too inhibiting. The fresh air cleaned my mind and stripped away some of the damage last night's whisky had caused. I just wanted to walk, pound some streets until the sun came up, I wasn't thinking about directions. But my feet were, and I found myself outside the local fire station, staring up at the great polished doors that, at the first hint of an emergency, would sink into the earth to reveal a trio of fire-fighting trucks. An upstairs room was filled with light and shadow. I imagined firefighters cruising around a pool table, talking in murmurs, or playing cards, watching a little TV. Busy but waiting, always waiting.

I skipped up the steps and entered the office. There was a woman in a severe blue suit sitting in a hanging leather chair, wearing a headset. She was gabbling code into the mouthpiece, a fast sequence of numbers and letters, interspersed with the odd moment of recognizable speech: a street name, a yes, a no. She ended her conversation without saying goodbye and without looking up at me, without changing her voice pattern, she asked what she could do to help me.

I showed her a card and sat on the only available surface, the corner of her workstation. "I wondered if any of the crew on duty tonight were on duty a month ago, on the night of the 18th?"

The receptionist repeated the date into her headset and then said: "Duty log."

A second later, she recited a list of names:

"Fetter, Noo, Curve and Whysse. They're all in tonight."

I wrote the names down and asked if I could get a list of phone numbers. She shook her head. "You look like a nice guy but your card is not a shield. Sorry."

"Then can I talk to them now?"

"Let me see." She got back on the headset. Told the crew what was what. After a short while she came back to me. "You can take the lift up. They're waiting for you."

It was nothing like the romantic vision I'd had in my mind. Two firefighters were stripped to the waist and were wrestling inside a chalk circle. The others were standing around with bottled soft drinks, calling out words of encouragement. One of the spectators came over to the lift as I stepped out of it. He shook my hand.

"Byte Noo," he said.

"Rad Hallah. Thanks for taking the time."

"No problem. Come on, let me get you a drink. We've only got fruit juice, I'm afraid. Either that or qat-tea and we don't really go for that till after the shift's over. Snooze stuff. Helps bring you down if you've had a rough night."

"Nothing thanks. I just wanted to ask a few questions. Be finished in a jiffy."

"Sure."

We stopped by the large bay window that looked down over the sleeping, polished fire engines. The other spectator came to join us. Noo introduced her as Curve Moody. She wore a little cropped top. Her blonde hair was in a pony tail. We shook hands. She had a face that made you smile even if you were thinking of nuns on fire.

"I was told you were on duty on the night of the fire over at Bane's bar, in the Splinters?"

"I know it," said Noo. "Yeah. Small fire. Hardly worth the effort. Guy could have pissed it out."

"What's the wrestling all about?"

Curve Moody said, "Aggression. Good way to get rid of it. You don't want to be pumped full of nasty when you get called out on a job."

"You wrestle too?" I asked.

She smiled, nodded. "Like a demon."

I pushed away the visions and concentrated on the job. "Do you get many fires occurring up in the Splinters? Isn't it a huge disaster waiting to happen?"

The wrestlers were going for each other like thin dogs scrapping over a chicken wing. The smaller guy was winning. He was bulked out in the heavy, sculpted manner of a weightlifter. Whenever he went into a clinch with his opponent he let out a roar that seemed to come all the way up his body from his balls. I'd have him on my side any day.

"The Splinters should pretty much take care of themselves," Noo was saying. "Sprinklers, auto-foaming ducts, vents that suck oxygen from a room to starve fires. We go along every so often to do firechecks. We're serious about them too. Access for the machines – you've seen the size of them – is pretty limited. And it takes about ten minutes for a chopper to get over here from Paleshrike, enough time for a place to burn to nothing."

"Word was that it was kids, playing around," Curve Moody continued. "We put it out in seconds. It was a low-grade risk. Last job of the night, as I recall."

Noo chipped in. "We went back afterwards. Owner offered us a drink on the house."

Curve Moody looked at her watch. "You want to talk to Vex and Oquo? Vex Whysse and Oquo Fetter? They were the other guys on duty that night. They'll be finished in a minute."

I shook my head, despite the fact that Curve Moody was pulling off her combat trousers in readiness for her bout. "No thanks. It's late."

We said goodbye and Noo walked me to the lift. At the side of it was a photograph of four men. The inscription on the plaque beneath it read: *Our glorious dead: Chew Matino. Hensall Grab. Bench Moody, Pol Cloake.*

The lift doors opened. I said, "Moody. That something to do with Curve?"

Noo nodded. "Her father. All four of those firemen were killed in an oil rig fire ten years ago trying to save the crew. What a waste. There was a crew of eight working on the rig. Their last night on duty. They had been drinking pretty much all day and were bosko absoluto. Fire started in the galley. A pan of something they were cooking up for supper."

"I'm sorry," I said. It seemed a pathetically weak thing to say but Noo shrugged.

"Death gets in the cab with you every time you go outside in this job," he said. Over his shoulder, Whysse and Fetter were leaving the circle. Whysse gave Curve Moody a big hug as they swapped places. Idly, I wondered how long it would take me to qualify as a fireman. "Curve joined up because of her dad, but she knows the risks."

Outside, weak sunlight was striping the tips of the Splinters, occasionally visible above the rafts of cloud hugging the city. I stopped off at Chimp's mobile diner for a Styrofoam container of tepid coffee and a jam doughnut that made my teeth disintegrate as I was chewing it. Then I went home and slept for four hours.

I woke up refreshed. Well, as refreshed as a man can be who suddenly finds himself staring into the muzzle of a pistol. Somebody was straddling my chest, making it hard to breathe. A balaclava concealed anything I might have used later down at the cop shop in order to have some failed artist drum up a picture of someone who looked nothing like my assailant.

I wheezed, "Get comfortable why don't you?"

The lump on top of me was either mute, foreign or, as I expected, not mad keen on chit-chat. The pistol, cocked, was traced gently all over my face like a lover's fingernails. It dimpled my cheek, pressed against my closed eyes, rattled my teeth. I got the picture.

A piece of paper was tucked into my shirt pocket. A little slap across the chops and the intruder was gone.

He had got in through the window. I always leave the window open when I sleep. One minor drawback of living at ground level. I closed it and locked it and drew the curtains even though the sun was shining. I took a hot shower, then a freezing cold one. More coffee, a fresh shirt and I was ready to read my love letter.

Two words, no nonsense: *Walk away.*

I dropped the note into a little plastic wrap for the graphologists and went outside, wishing for about the ten thousandth time that I carried a gun.

It's true what they say. If you're armed, you're twice as likely to end up being shot. I believe this, even though I don't know who *they* are, the people who say this. But put yourself in a villain's shoes. He's on the lam, he's got a gun, he's shakier than a jelly poodle. If he sees some chisel-faced dick sniffing him out with a piece in his hand, he's more likely to slug it out. But me? Chisel-faced though I undoubtedly am, I don't carry. I would rather face a gun-toting perp who feels as though the balance of power is in his favour than a sweating, slippery-fingered tripwire of a guy.

This was what I was thinking as I took the steps two at a time up to the entrance of Stable Cables.

That and *why the cheesy nuggets don't I carry a gun?*

If Snafu Huckey was an entry in the dictionary, this is what his definition would be: *n. Jesus Creeping Chrrrrist, what a choad-hole! See also: tit-head, knob-end, anal cyst and irritant (major).*

I fixed a grin and sat on the other side of the desk from him, hoping he wouldn't hear my teeth grind. Huckey's chair was too low; the edge of the table was about level with his shoulders. His fingers clung to the table-top like he was playing a phantom piano. He wore a side parting so savage that he could have dismantled it and used it as a set square.

He was so spectacularly ugly that I completely missed the first few sentences he uttered.

"I said," he said, his voice like the whine of a failing jet engine, "can I get you anything? Coffeeteawater?"

"Nothing for me, thanks." I cleared my throat. I said, "Finn Mutch."

"Finn Mutch," he said.

I said, "Yes."

He said, "Yes."

I said, "Sorry, did I take a wrong turn somewhere? Is this Echo Canyon?"

He spread his fingers. They looked like the kind of things you'd spear on a stick and toast over an open fire. "You haven't asked me anything yet."

"Okay," I said, breathing deeply. "You and Finn. Did you get on?"

"I was his boss."

"So that's a no."

"I didn't say that."

"Then you *did* get on?"

"I didn't say that either." He wore the smug expression of a guy who thinks he's smarter than most. I wondered what that expression would look like mashed on to my knuckles.

"How long did Finn work here, Mr Huckey?" I ladled just the right amount of sarcasm over that *mister* to drag his face a couple of degrees deeper into uglydom.

"He was in his six-month probation period. Just coming to the end of it."

"And you were going to keep him on? He seemed quite a diligent worker."

Huckey bristled. "I would have been the judge of that."

"Would you like to answer the question?"

"Let's make one thing clear, Mr Hallah. You are not police. I am not obliged to tell you anything."

"That's right," I said, cheering up a little. Maybe I would get the chance to tenderize his facial steak after all. "But you will, because if you don't, you'll have trouble telling anybody anything for a while."

"Is that a threat?"

Not that bright then. I spent the next minute making it clear what I would do to him if he didn't comply. He looked a little queasy after that. And told me all about Finn Mutch's chances in the Ludd extermination industry. They weren't great.

"Why would you sack a guy like that?" I asked. "Okay, he's got some form, but it's lower league stuff. I'm sure if we had a rattle of the skeletons in your cupboard we'd find more impressive offences."

"It had nothing to do with that, Mr Hallah," he said, regaining some of his oleaginous brio.

"Then what?"

"It was the company he kept."

I nearly fell off my chair. "Really?" I said, just to fill the silence. I thought about Huckey's friends. I thought about spending an evening with Huckey and his friends. I thought about gnawing my own legs off. Without anaesthetic.

"Mr Hallah. Clearly you don't understand. Finn Mutch was, well, he was a homosexualist."

Somehow I got out of there without painting my fingernails with his blood. I say somehow, but it was a call from Milk. At first I didn't realise it was the phone vibrating in my pocket. I thought Huckey had brought on some kind of irritable bowel syndrome.

I left him without an excuse me and stood outside, wishing I smoked.

"What is it?" I snapped.

"It's a pause, so you can apologize."

I said I was sorry and asked her again, just as snappily, what she wanted. She must have cottoned on that I wasn't in a mood to mess around. She became clipped and businesslike. "There's another body," she said. "Caramel Pines. I booked you a seat on this afternoon's train. And a room at an impressively cheap hotel. I'll expect a refund if you don't nail this monkey."

"Same MO?" I asked, knowing full well that it was. I had to say something though. I hadn't been to Caramel Pines, let alone heard the name mentioned, for over a year. Why there? Fate was a clown with a custard cannon, and the seat of my pants had a target on it.

"Same MO," confirmed Milk. "Only this one was done first. It's about a month old."

On my way to the train station I bought a fresh handkerchief and a bottle of cheap after-shave from a pharmacy. I bought a fistful of miniatures too for the journey, a five-hour jaunt. The thought of stepping off the train sober was enough to make my eyes bleed.

I picked up my ticket from reservations and found my train waiting on the platform, engine tutting away like a wronged Maud. Making sure my ticket was poking out of my top pocket, I settled into my seat even though departure time was over half an hour away. Then I started tucking into the booze. The next thing I remember was an old dear trying to clamber over me, complaining loudly that trains shouldn't allow animals to travel with normal people. My ticket had been punched, and so had I, it felt like. Or maybe it was just the alcohol. Outside, darkness had turned the countryside into a congealed mass. I could smell salt water and scorched earth. The guard was strolling through the carriage telling me what I already knew.

"This train terminates here. Taxis are available to Caramel Pines, Bow-wow South. The Jut and Winterwild. This train terminates here. This is Nowhere Beach."

I made my way through the ticket barrier and stood in the entrance to the station, breathing deeply. There was a queue of taxis at the rank but most people were eschewing them in favour of a healthy walk in the freezing cold. I got in the back of a cab and told the driver where to go. I told him I'd give him a tip if he promised not to engage me in any smalltalk. We drove in silence, me staring at the back of the driver's head, or at his resentful gaze in the rearview mirror.

I remembered it all. It had been Summer when I came here last. Heavy fruit on the trees, children playing in the sand. I smiled a lot. She smiled a lot. I blamed it on wind. She kicked me. Cold cuts on a rug by a hot fire. Hot sex on a cold kitchen worktop. I was maybe looking into her eyes 90% of the time and thinking how beautiful her eyes were for the other ten.

The cab driver dropped me off outside Hotel Jejune. I tipped him a little extra when he asked me if he could say goodbye. I was shown to my room by a little old lady in a Zimmer frame. Inside I locked the door and rammed the back of a chair up against the door handle. When I turned on the light I realized that if I was going to spend a night here I should have got the old lady to lock it from the other side. Cheap was too grand a word for this dive. But I was tired. And my head was filling with too much other stuff, old stuff, safe stuff, for me to care about how many spiders I was going to share my pillow with.

I slept. Maybe I cried. What does it matter.

Knocking on the door. Like someone auditioning for drums in a band called Drums and Nothing But.

"Okay, okay," I yelled, but it wasn't. It was far from okay. Within the hour I would have those knuckles mounted on a plinth and hanging over my fireplace. But the owner of the knuckles was already walking back to his car as I opened the door in the suit I had crashed out in. Weak sunlight dribbled through the crack. I slipped on my shades and asked if we could stop for coffee.

"I have anticipated you, Mr Hallah," he called. "Come and get it."

He introduced himself as Flyk Kibble. I nearly missed the name. I was staring at his godlike sideburns. He had fashioned them into deep, scything blades that petered out a centimetre or so from his chin. The coffee, it had to be said, was excellent.

"What do you do out here?"

"I'm liaison for the coroner, Mr Hallah. I am his eyes and ears."

"And legs."

He laughed. "Yes, legs too. It was Ms Fuss though, who asked me to pick you up. A personal favour for her."

"How personal?"

He gave me a look. "We were at college together."

"That figures."

"Hmm?"

I said, "You're both highly polished people. I could go round to knock on Milk's door at 3 a.m. and she'd open it looking like someone who just fell out of a movie. You too, I reckon."

"It's called professionalism."

Stung, I said, "I'm a professional too."

"I don't doubt it."

"The tone of your voice says you do."

"What, we talk for two minutes and you know me well enough to determine what I think? Milk told me you were difficult."

I said, "In my job it doesn't pay to look like a clothes horse. I need to blend in."

"I'll take you to the morgue if you like," he said. "You'll blend in plenty."

"No thanks. The boathouse is good for now."

Maybe I did lean on him a little too hard. But I prefer to travel in silence. Especially if other things are crowding in, trying to lay claim to the little good space that's left inside my head. What did I care if he thought I was a pain in the neck? It wasn't like we were neighbours.

I had a headache by the time we got to the edge of the lake. Mist clung to its surface, but you could just see enough to tell it was mirror-smooth. A little eaterie called the Bread 'n' Water stood next to it. I checked the menu in the window before we went in. Tupelo would have liked this place. Lots of fish and herbs. Lots of candles. Her eyes in candlelight . . . you could go mad.

There were no candles here now though. Lots of big, harsh lights. Lots of lab coats. Lots of police. And a scoop with a pencil jammed behind his ear and a big camera with a big flash attached to the hotshoe that went off with a sound like a sheet being torn from a bed. People in Caramel Pines took their murder seriously. It was nice to see.

I flashed my card and used Milk Fuss's name like currency. It got me to the front of the pack where a squat guy in a cableknit sweater was lying on his back. I pulled out the aftershave and splashed a good few glugs into the hanky which I placed over my mouth and nose. Some of the cops laughed. Some of them looked at me wishing they had had the same idea.

I examined the body. Another gash across the back of the head. Brains hanging out like the tentacles of a Portuguese Man o'War.

No 24-clip. I was impressed the body had lasted this long with only superficial decomposition. But then, it was deep winter.

"What do you reckon, city boy?" one of the cops asked out of the corner of his mouth. "Dead?"

A bit of laughter. Local badges, they're in a class of their own. I didn't take the bait. There was a murdered man here. Someone who was looking forward to his lunch and then, maybe, the rest of his life. Young guy. What had he done? What had Finn Mutch done? Where was the common ground?

"Who was here first?" I asked. My lucky day, the cop with the comedy lips. He crinkled them as he approached me. They looked like something you might find at the back of a monkey.

"Do you know him?" I got in first, before he could impress his friends with more bon mots.

"Sure. Name's Gully Jukes. Owns a secondhand bookshop on the seafront." He handed me the wallet he had rescued from the corpse's pocket. The face that beamed at me from the ID card didn't carry a hint of the shadow of death that had now come home to roost.

"Any ideas who did this? Or why?"

He smirked. "You're the talent. You tell me. I just point traffic in the right direction."

One of the boathouse staff was doing his best to try to clean up. He had a broom under the dead man's feet before anyone could stop him. "Woah, boy," I said, and put my foot in the way. I was used to an unhelpful crime scene in the city. Out here, it made a nice change to have order. I wasn't going to let anyone screw it up. But he'd done some damage, raking up some soft loam, a bit of litter. And hello.

A tiny skeleton. What was that? A mouse? a bird? I picked the little tangle of bones up off the floor and folded them into my handkerchief.

"Lunch?" asked the comedian cop.

"Evidence," I said. "Maybe."

"Oh really? You think cock robin killed our friend here? And then topped himself?" More laughter. I ignored it. I could rise above it all. Get me.

I said, "I need a lift to the station. I need to get back to the city."

"What's the big rush? Getting nose bleeds so far away from your delis and your traffic jams?"

"Something like that."

"Well, there are no more trains tonight, mister. Next one is at 8 a.m. tomorrow morning. Stick around. I'll show you the sights."

"No thanks." I gave him a card. "Call me if you get any more info on this," The bones in my pocket burned into my thigh as if they had just come from a cooked bird. I went back to the hotel and left the handkerchief on the dressing table. Then I caught a tram to the beach.

Nowhere Beach isn't particularly pretty or dramatic. It isn't good for sunbathing, enclosed as it is on either side by hills that block out the light. The area doesn't have a rich diversity of wildlife. There are no good restaurants, no clubs or bars. It's a bit of a nowhere place and maybe that's how it got its name. And I like it. *We* liked it. Maybe because nobody else did. I get the feeling that Tupelo liked me for much the same reason.

We came here on the day after I asked her to marry me. I was feeling powerful, primitively powerful, as if my genes had triumphed over those of any other sad old Joe in the city. Man hunt for woman. Man find woman. Man good. I needed to get out of town and get some fresh air into me. The city was too stifling. I wanted to run around and scream. We took a picnic to the beach and ate some of it before our mouths gravitated towards each other. Most of the afternoon was spent spooning in the sand and we finally unlocked ourselves from each other as the hill's shadows lengthened across the sea.

Now I walked down to where the tide lapped against the sand. The sea was darker than I remembered it, like beaten gunmetal, perhaps because of winter. With the ocean behind me, I scanned the beach, trying to remember where we had lain. I remembered after we had gathered together the blanket and the picnic basket, we hiked up the hill to the tram terminus instead of following the path that I had come in on.

I retraced the route we had taken last year, remembering how I had looked up at Tupelo as she picked her way barefoot through the rocks and vines, and teased her about the sway of her backside. She almost fell over at one point, she was laughing so much. Here. It was here that she pressed her foot into a little puddle of sand. I remember . . .

I had stared at the perfect little impression of heel and toes. Before she could see me, I had picked up a piece of slate and covered the footprint, possessed suddenly with an insane desire to protect it and prevent anybody else from clapping eyes on a little mark made by my wife, my wife-to-be.

I saw the slate, tinged with a little moss, hidden by a few thick ferns that had reached over, as if guarding a shrine. My heart was beating wildly as I reached out to flip off that slate lid, and I thought *surely, not . . . the insects, the weather . . . surely not.*

But the footprint was there. Five tiny dips and the elongated heart shape of her foot proper. I lost it, a little, up there on the hill. I dug my hand into the sand and scooped it up and put it in my pocket and dropped to my knees and lost it.

I thought of nothing else, of nobody else on the way back the next morning. I took out my phone. I would ring her. I would tell her things were different. That things had changed. I would send her the sand in an envelope.

I stepped off the train five hours later and put the phone back in my pocket. Caught a cab. I hadn't had a drink for over twelve hours. That was a sin I was about to atone for.

Three pints in, Oak Seddon lining them up. An argument was raging between a Bible-quoting reformed stripper and a man with a banjo who sang rude songs. It was excellent entertainment. My phone vibrated.

"Hallah," I said.

"It's Milk," she said. "Good trip?"

I gave her the bare bones about the bare bones and listened to her silent reply.

"Still there?" I asked. "Why don't you come over to Oak's and get tight with me?"

"I was right the first time," she said.

"I don't follow you, toots," I said. "And after another one of these pints of rocket fuel I'll have trouble following my own nose."

"Shit, Rad. I messed up. When I said there were two bodies at Bane's? I *did* say it to get you interested. I *was* being facetious. But there really *were* two bodies up there. There was a skeleton. A little thing, like a rat. I didn't think it meant anything."

Oak's beer suddenly tasted as flat as tapwater. He saw my expression and started clearing away the frothy glasses that were queuing up for my gullet. Fifteen minutes later I was in the plexiglass pod sprinting up into the Splinters, swallowing hard against a scream that was building like an orgasm inside my chest. By the time I got to Bane's I was wound up like a dog chasing its own tail. Bane wasn't around, but plenty of other people were. Yuicy was gyrating on her table like a drunken uncle at a wedding reception. A sea of faces looked up at her.

I pushed through the swilling bodies to the toilets. Mutch had been removed, but I wouldn't have batted an eye if he was still on the throne. I kicked about in the filth for a while but did nothing other than make a case for Shoeshine Eddie to hate my guts for the rest of eternity.

Outside I saw a few heaps of muck that some short-straw loser had swept against the wall. In the second heap I struck paydirt. A tiny skeleton, not quite as intact as the first in my grim collection, but still very interesting. I pocketed it and went back to the bar.

"You Lissa?" I said, when the tall, raven-haired barmaid tilted my way.

"Yes," she said brightly.

"Where's Bane?"

"He's playing cards in the back."

"Through there?" I nodded at a door at the back of the bar.

"Yes," she said, uncertainly. "But—"

I vaulted the bar and pushed by her, ignoring her protests and those of the punters waiting to be served. I got through the door, surprised to see that the lights were off and I was in total darkness. But somewhere between that thought, and my legs folding, I realised that I had been brained.

I woke up. I vomited.

Sneezing puke through my nostrils and trying to swallow against the burn in my throat, I scrambled to my feet only to be punched back down again. Blood squirted, bittersweet across my tongue. I reckoned my face now looked like some ripe gourd at the bottom of an unsuccessful greengrocer's refuse sack.

I made it upright once more and another fist landed on my nose, crushing it like an eggshell, persuading me it was better on the floor. I didn't argue. I lay there, the centre of my face bubbling and fizzing, and waited for the feet to join in, but then came the sound of yelling and another scuffle that didn't involve me. Footsteps ran away. Heavy, ponderous footsteps. Muntin Bane making good on his promises.

A hand in mine. Warm breath against my cheek.

"Can you stand up?"

"I tried it earlier," I said. "It didn't work out." I recognized the voice. It made the hair on my neck spring to attention.

"Come on," she said.

Somehow she got me on to the main street where she flagged a cab and took me home. In the kitchen, the striplight flickering, she washed my cuts and dabbed peroxide into them. I laughed at the pain. If I hadn't, I would have cried instead.

She wrapped a blanket around me and took me into the living room, where she made a space on the sofa and let me rest my head against her shoulder for a while.

"Thanks for rescuing me, Curve," I said. "You'll have to show me a few moves sometime."

She did show me a few moves, that very night, and it was good and it was great. Sometime towards dawn I heard her scuffling about for her clothes and I opened my eyes to watch. I was groggy from a glass of brandy and a few codeine pills, but I was able to see her body as it accrued layers, her breasts against the moonlight making it seem as though there was nothing but an edge to her, a brilliant white curve. I watched her move across the room to the door, where she stopped and looked back at me. She said something then and I went back to sleep and tried to forget.

I'm sorry.

I booted up the drive and pulsed my dad. It was early. I couldn't stomach breakfast, but I found a coffee cup for the rest of the brandy.

He's in his dotage, but my dad works harder than ever. Especially since my mother died. It's like he equates retirement with senility and death. Maybe he's right. Anyway, he's up at sparrowfart and doesn't go to bed till past midnight. He looks at me and thinks, *she must have had an affair*, I'm certain of it. He reads, he writes, he has so many filing cabinets that he has a filing cabinet devoted to a filing system that deals with his filing cabinets.

His face shimmered into view on the LCD. He blinked a few times and said, "Well?" He suddenly saw me properly. "What the hell have you been up to, Rad? Did you forget how to negotiate doors?

"Hi, Dad," I said. "How are you?"

"Busy," he said, pointedly.

"Busy doing what?"

He sighed. "I have to deliver an essay on a synthetic heat protein for the blood, you know, for the terraforming project in the Antarctic. I mean, have you ever tried using a screwdriver with fifteen pairs of gloves on?"

"Right, dad. Sounds good. Listen, I need you to have a look at something for me. See if you can identify what it is."

"If it's your brain, don't bother. It will not be recognizable. Perhaps as a pickled walnut, but nothing else."

You can see where I get it from.

"I'm uploading the scans now, Dad. I think they're the same beast, but I'm not a hundred per cent."

He screwed his magnifier into his eye socket, the compensating hike of his cheek giving him a lecherous appearance. "Ah," he said. And then: "Ah."

He left his seat and wandered off. I took a sly slug from the cup. You'd need it too, if you were talking to my dad. He came back with a huge volume that he started riffling through contentedly, looking up now and again at the scans to make comparisons.

"Hmm," he said, haughtily. "*Regulus ignicapillus*, I'd say."

"A bird, right?"

The magnifier out, he rolled his eyes theatrically. "Of *course* it's a bird."

"It's not helping me out here, Dad," I said, hating myself for allowing him to manipulate me like this. The only person in the world who could.

"What else can I give you?" he said. "Most people know that it has an orange flash on its head. It's what gives it its name. They nest in spruce or larch forests. Migrant birds, but some of them have started to breed over here."

I gritted my teeth against saying that he obviously just gleaned all that from the book he consulted, but a tiny part of me suspected that he knew it all anyway. He made me feel about as big as a pygmy in a basketball team.

I was readying myself to say goodbye, that I'd try to make it up to see him sometime soon, when I remembered what he'd said.

"What name would that be, by the way?"

"I told you, lad," he said, "*Regulus ignicapillus*."

"Which means?"

Another sigh, augmented by the cluck of his tongue. I butched it out. "Why, Rad, *ob*viously, it's Latin. For Firecrest."

The city is silent tonight. It's withdrawn, huddled into itself. The cold has pinched the streets blue; frost sucks the depth from the alleyways, everything is visible in the city, in winter. There are no places to hide.

There were no places for Vex Whysse to hide, though he tried. I don't think he tried too hard, in the end. I think that part of it was that he wanted to be stopped. It was too painful, all of it. The tracking down, the killing. The remembering. The killing didn't stop the memories, or make better what had happened all those years ago. The killing made the memories fresh. It made the circle of pain that much wider, that's all.

Curve Moody knew it and she had decided to end it now. She gave me an address, before she left last night. I found it when I was pulling on my clothes, slipped into my pocket. I went to check it out, a storage facility on the edge of the city, where people who can't fit everything they've got into their apartments rent garage space to keep the remainder.

I broke in and found a pile of boxes containing clothes, sports equipment, magazines. Nothing special. But in a plastic carrier bag hanging on a hook on the wall, I found half a dozen Firecrest skeletons wrapped in cotton wool. Every one of them was an anatomy lesson in pain and regret. I called Milk Fuss as I studied them. I told her about the oil rig fire.

"Check out the offspring of those who died, Milk," I told her. "They're being picked off one by one. Father of a woman who works at the fire station was offed fighting the blaze. She joined up to keep his spirit alive. That kind of shit. Someone else joined up too, for the same reason, but without the good intent. I'm going to find him now."

I asked her to run a check on Vex Whysse and she came back to me ten minutes later with the good news and the bad. Whysse had been a childhood sweetheart of Curve's and applied to join the fire service on the same day Curve did. But although Curve got in at the first attempt, Whysse failed three times, on medical grounds. He had been a heavy kid. Remembering what he looked like on the night I visited the station told me something about his determination. Once in the service, he could go about avenging the killers of Curve's father, not realizing until it was too late that they had paid the ultimate price and that their offspring, innocent, harmless, were poor targets. I wondered if he slept at all these days. I wondered if his dreams were good.

"We've accounted for five of the six who are left," Milk told me. "Sister of the sixth, a Nude Lucky, told me that her brother had been phoned up by a man who wanted to offer him a job. He's gone to meet him there now. Desperate for work, apparently."

I thought of Finn Mutch, how his sexuality had been preyed upon. Whysse knew about need. He knew how to work on a person's Achilles heel.

"Where?" I said, wishing I had a gun.

I got to the kid before Whysse. I told him to be good and go home. There was no job. Then I waited on the waste ground outside the football stadium, listening to the animal roar of the spectators inside and watching the floodlights turn the area above the stands into powdery white haze.

I recognised Vex Whysse immediately, even though he was wearing a skullcap and a padded windcheater. He looked like an inverted triangle. His face was red in the brutal cold whipping down the street. When he saw me step out into the light. He stopped. Then kept walking towards me. That pause was enough to tell me that his being here wasn't a coincidence and I might have it all wrong. That pause let him down.

"Hi," I said.

"Funny seeing you here."

I nodded. "Hilarious. You ready to come in with me? We can get a cab to the DS's office."

"I don't think so," he said, and stepped away from me.

"You going to make it difficult?"

"I'm not . . . ready," he said, and took off into the waste ground at a speed that surprised me for such a muscly man.

I was on the back foot, but I gamely trotted after him. He fired a couple of times in my direction, but the shots were wildly off target. It was almost sad. I caught him trying to reload hunched down behind a stack of rotting pallets, his fingers shivering as they slotted the bullets into the chamber of his gun.

"Come in with me, Vex," I said softly. "It's over. You can stop running."

He shook his head. "I can't. I won't go to prison."

"I can't let you go. You know that."

"I know." He looked as if he was about to offer a different argument, serve up some kind of bargain, but instead he lodged the muzzle of the gun under his front teeth and blew his face apart.

There was a lot of attention from the media. I got my face plastered across the front pages, black eyes and busted nose, the works. Dad emailed me to congratulate me but also to harangue me for not mentioning him at all. And Milk slipped me a cheque which I cashed and spent a goodly portion of in the local bottle shop. I got home to find that my place had been broken into. I smelled her all over the flat, but nothing had been taken. Her shape was in the bedclothes. She had come here to be with me while things were being sorted out by the football stadium. It was the last time I ever felt near to her. I never saw her again.

I caught my advert on the screen again that night, and thought I didn't look too bad after all, especially compared to the smorgasbord that my head now resembled. Toasting my erstwhile handsomeness, I tipped the bottle as the chump on screen stumbled over those rhyming couplets.

I was about to swallow when the phone rang.

THE SHAPE OF MURDER

Ian Watson

"Where the hell did *you* come from—"

"Who are you—?"

"What are you—?"

The dandified little man regarded the startled assembly with a reasonable degree of aplomb.

"I am," he announced to the passengers and officers and some crew members, and to the exotic person so conspicuous, "probably the greatest detective in the universe. Evidently you are in need of me. *Et bien*, I am here. Will one of you kindly explain to me where exactly 'here' is?"

Presently the famous detective needed to retire to a cabin, escorted there by the purser, and to sit alone and think furiously.

This was a small cabin, pleasantly geometrical, superbly functional, all extremely well organized. The bed that folds away into the wall. From the opposite wall, a desk and a padded chair descending into the space made free. The toilet cubicle, a masterpiece of conciseness. No stateroom, this. Far from it. More like a futuristic prison cell, indeed. Yet ah, such economy of design, such neatness. Already the famous detective had learned that this ship, the *Sirius*, lacked personal staterooms, even if it did boast several ample public areas. Captain Muno Mboyou's private quarters themselves were almost as modest as this cabin.

Alors, a ship to travel through the vast tranquil space between the stars, not across any wretched nauseating ocean.

Or rather: to travel through some dimension of surrealism known as the hyperspace. The famous detective's artistic tastes favoured rectangular simplicity, yet he was well aware of his own countrymen's forays into the depiction in oil paints of absurd dream images. He ought to be able to cope with the surreal! The famous detective's presence aboard the *Sirius* in this hyperspace zone was itself surreal, a dream, *n'est ce pas*?

Few portholes in this ship. Outside, nothing visible but an interminable greyness reminiscent of the English Channel on a gloomy morning.

Due to a fire in the dispensary, certain drug-pills had been destroyed. Their purpose: to suppress imaginative excesses, to dampen the subconscious mind. Otherwise, in this hyperspace, it seemed that imaginary phenomena had a habit of manifesting themselves. A tiger might prowl such a ship as this, if those on board neglected their pills. That tiger might maul and kill.

Or a mass of orchids might choke a corridor.

Or Greta Garbo might vamp around, confused and bemused, if some strong-minded person on board should happen to be besotted by that actress.

Subsequent to the two murders, how lucky that everyone had been wishing devoutly that someone could quickly solve the mystery; and that the strong-minded Lady Margaret McKenzie had been studying the "data-bank" regarding methods for the detection of crime.

The famous detective would not succumb to confusion. Out of confusion emerges truth.

Refreshed and spruced, the famous detective consulted his turnip of a pocket watch, then emerged from his cabin and proceeded toward the dining saloon.

His taste buds were anticipative though also somewhat apprehensive. The corn on the little toe of his left foot twinged, pinched by his pointed gleaming patent leather shoes. Now that he had resolved his personal commotion – quite reminiscent of his own arrival as a refugee in Britain long ago – he would not permit the question of his own impermanence on board this ship so alike, yet un-alike, a cruise liner to interfere with the logic of facts, nor, for that matter, with his appreciation of the cuisine. He was, after all, a person of outstanding universal calibre to have manifested himself here.

Not that either of the murders had been committed using a gun of any *calibre* whatever! Nor using a knife, nor poison. But rather by strangulation. Most gentle strangulation, accomplished seemingly without any struggle on the part of the victims. Perpetrated, in both cases, by an intimate acquaintance? During a deplorable and perverse erotic episode, an *affaire passionelle*, which had become a crime? This seemed unlikely. A young man dead, in one case. A young woman slain, secondly. Besides, there had been no derangement of the clothing.

Could someone – such as the exotic passenger, whose capacities were unguessable – be a hypnotist?

When the famous detective entered the saloon, what a resplendent dress uniform the strapping black captain was wearing. So much gold lace upon the cuffs and lapels and pocket flaps. Such epaulettes, their gold wire bullions dangling like the tentacles of sea anemones. A veritable admiral's coat.

Such flamboyant cummerbunds did the other men wear under their velvet-trimmed dinner jackets. Oh, the glittering gowns of the ladies, and that jewel of Lady Meg McKenzie – an enormous cabochon sapphire hanging from a distinctly barbaric golden torque, like some loot of colonial conquest.

The exotic personage – with that ginger topknot like a flywhisk arising from an otherwise shaven cranium of strange contour, and the two tusks protruding from his mouth, and the pink eyes looking bloodshot – he too was richly attired. He wore a cloak of iridescent scales suggestive of the wing-cases of a thousand beetles sewn together.

The famous detective would have felt perfectly at home amidst such finery, had he himself had access to formal wear. Alas, in his cabin he had found pyjamas most ordinary but certainly no dinner jacket. In his otherwise perfectly correct black jacket, striped trousers, and natty bow tie, by comparison with those in the saloon perhaps he made the impression of a visiting piano-tuner or hairdresser! Yet his black-dyed hair was parted centrally with perfect symmetry. His magnificent moustaches curled upward impeccably. And besides, to create the impression of a lesser mortal often usefully served to mislead – until the famous detective would spring his trap and ensnare a malefactor.

At table, he was obliged to neaten the cutlery. And then he must deter other diners from talking immediately about the crimes, when food must take precedence, and conversation should be of matters less professional.

Champagne was served. Yet the sparkling liquid seemed inauthentic, as if its alcohol had been removed. Alas, the lobster soup was mere sweet pink fluid.

He turned to his neighbour, the Honourable Donna Fairbreed. Her dark hair was cut severely short. She had a look about her of the Indian squaw. Though what a fine diamanté gown she wore.

"Mam'selle, may I presume to ask why you are journeying aboard this vessel?"

"I'm the computer officer," she murmured.

Computer. Ha. He understood. By the nineteen-seventies, beyond which his memories did not extend, such machines had been in use. This young lady of Apache blood – or whatever! – held an important position aboard this starship *Sirius*.

"People are often not what they seem," he mused.

The fish which followed did not seem to have ever lived in any sea. Admirable, the metallic geometry of this dining saloon. Abominable, the cuisine.

Presently, much became clearer. Here was being enacted the masquerade most peculiar. Thin, bearded Prince Kessel, the purser; diffident Marquis Jack Scruton the astrogator; brash Lord Burgess the chief engineer; Lady Margaret McKenzie the elderly diplomat: all were involved in a mission most delicate, of negotiation with a species of aliens – of whom High-Tanttu the Exalt, he of the ginger flywhisk of hair and the tusks, was ambassador plenipotentiary en route to Earth.

Tanttu's society observed customs most stylized, to which human beings must conform as best they could.

Indeed, by the code of High-Tanttu's people the Exalt was an "honoured hostage." That was how those aliens conducted their affairs. Hence, the remarkable sapphire which Lady Meg wore. That gem was a sacred fetish of the aliens, now in human keeping. The *Sirius* herself had abandoned a couple of lady officers on Tanttu's world as reciprocal hostages, to be locked up in the equivalent of a harem. One, newly dubbed a Princess, was the principal hostage. The other woman, the ship's multi-faith chaplain/psychologist, served the role of a fetish object, being akin to a priestess.

Much subtle negotiation had preceded that compromise.

The famous detective stroked his moustache, and addressed High-Tanttu in a lulling tone.

"You and I, Monsieur, are both the aliens here."

The actual alien thoughtfully rubbed a tusk with a coarse finger, one of three such (plus thumb) on each hand.

"I have been insulted by the detour en route," came the crisp and carefully annunciated reply.

"For which I apologize yet again, High Exaltancy," Captain Mboyo hastened to say. "As I told you, according to our human code of behaviour we cannot ignore a distress beacon."

What was this detour? What distress?

Ah. Periodically these ships of hyperspace must drop into ordinary space near certain stars, at certain "jump points". Whilst doing so, the *Sirius* had detected a radio signal from a planet. A "shuttle" was sent to investigate, with a crew comprising a pilot and two Marines and Rudy Duggan, a planetologist, who later became the first victim of murder. The crew found a small crashed craft but no surviving castaways, only a couple of bodies near a river, half-eaten by beasts unidentified. After burying the remains and switching off the beacon, Duggan and his companions had returned to the *Sirius* hale and hearty.

"That planet," asked the famous detective, "is she thoroughly explored?"

No. A preliminary survey team had visited. They found only wild jungles and no signs whatever of intelligent life.

The famous detective was unwilling to pursue the matter of the murders as yet.

An atrocity of an omelette was served, surely made from the powdered egg and cubes of frozen ham.

"Pardon me," he remarked to the Honourable Donna Fairbreed, "but your chef to be seems lacking in finesse." (At this, Captain Mboyo glared.)

She forked with gusto. "Seems okay to me."

"Maybe I might instruct him in the art of omelette *aux fines herbes?*"

"I guess Charley Manx has been kinda temperamental this voyage, so I wouldn't go criticising him."

"This Charley Manx, your cook." The famous detective had

swiftly demoted him from the status of chef. "Why is he temperamental?"

"Oh, he was accusing guys in the crew of stealing food from the kitchen."

"What kind of food would that be?"

"Meat, I think."

"And when was this, pray?"

"Bit after the shuttle came back." She chewed. "After we'd jumped again."

"That is most interesting. Was that meat raw or was it cooked?"

"Heavens, you'd need to ask Charley."

"That, I most certainly shall. Who would wish to steal any food after it was *cooked* in such a way as this?"

"Look," said the Captain, "we aren't concerned with a spot of pilfering. Two people have been killed."

"*Monsieur le Capitaine*, we must never neglect the trivial detail."

How bizarre this situation. How many grossly false clues might seem to abound.

When a miserable coffee was served, the ladies showed no inclination to retire elsewhere. In his jacket pocket fortuitously the famous detective had found a packet of the little Russian cigarettes, and his lighter. Hardly had he lit up and inhaled than the captain insisted, "You must extinguish that tube, sir!"

So. No smoking is permitted on board a starship. Purity of the recycled air. Peril of conflagration.

"Then how does a fire occur in the *pharmacie*?" the famous detective asked Dr Per Lundby. Lundby was a Norwegian, judging by his name, and the least costumed person at the table. A thoughtful blond man of middle years, Lundby was the type whose assistance the famous detective had often sought so fruitfully.

"Difficult to say. Damage was extensive."

"The *pharmacie*, she is normally kept locked?"

"The lock responds to my palm print. And to Captain Mboyo's. And to our chaplain/psychologist's, though she's no longer here, of course."

"Just in case you're wondering," interrupted Donna Fairbreed, "I can override the lock electronically. But I didn't do so."

"*Alors*. Who would start a blaze deliberately in a starship?"

"Only a madman," said the doctor.

"Or some person who does not understand safety properly. Tell me, doctor, who consulted you within, say, twenty-four hours prior to the blaze?"

The doctor frowned. "Nobody did."

"You saw no patients at all?"

"Oh, I ran diagnostic checks on the shuttle crew in case they had picked up any virus or micro-organism."

"Including the unfortunate Rudy Duggan."

"Of course."

"That is most interesting."

"I fail to see how. I didn't need to open the dispensary for any of them. In fact, I took my diagnostic kit aboard the shuttle."

During the *soirée* which followed the dinner so deficient, the famous detective talked to the doctor more confidentially about the details of the deaths. The bodies of Rudy Duggan and Anna Krasnik were in freezer lockers. However, the famous detective felt no need to see those.

"After all, Dr Lundby, the bodies are virtually unblemished according to yourself, apart from that very slight bruising on the necks caused by pressure."

"I assure you no rope or cord was used, or that would have cut into the skin—"

"You found no imprints of fingers. Yet the blood supply through the carotid arteries had been blocked." The famous detective rested one wrist over the other and rotated his hands. "*Eh bien*, the means of death was a strangle used in ju-jitsu. You cross your hands. You grip your victim's collar *so*, and twist. The rounded ends of your ulna bones are brought to bear. They unsheathe the muscles that cover the victim's arteries, and apply pressure. Death follows surprisingly swiftly."

"I don't see Duggan letting that happen to him. He was a martial arts nut."

"Indeed? And are there other such nuts on board?"

"The Marines are trained in unarmed combat – and who knows what High-Tanttu can do? I gather that his people engage in murderous encounters over peculiar points of honour."

"This Tanttu is a dangerous person to have amongst us, perhaps?"

"Not so long as Meg McKenzie wears the jewel!"

The famous detective shrugged. "If Anna Krasnik had been strangled first, I suppose suspicion might well have fallen upon Duggan. But he could hardly have strangled himself."

"I don't mind telling you," Dr Lundby confided, "Duggan had the hots for Anna Krasnik."

"The hots? What are these hots?"

"He wanted to go to bed with her. She didn't appreciate his advances. I'm wondering whether Duggan might have been showing her how to perform this strangle-hold – so as to cause body-contact – and she did actually strangle him."

"Ah, *mon ami*, but then who strangled her later on?"

"Perhaps she confided in someone. Perhaps she was horrified that Duggan had actually died."

"What exactly are you implying?"

"This is strictly between you and me?"

"Be assured, I am discreet."

"Meg McKenzie used to *look* at Duggan in a certain way. I know that she's getting on in years—"

"Ah, you think she would have wished Duggan as the gigolo."

"There might have been more to it than merely a wish! Suppose for a moment that Anna naively confided in Lady Meg, as a mature mother-figure—"

"Lady Meg becomes convulsed with chagrin and rage? 'How *did* you do it?' she asks the naive Anna. 'How exactly does one position one's hands?' And she proceeds to strangle Anna in exactly the same way, out of revenge."

"Makes sense."

"Not as regards the stolen meat," murmured the famous detective. "Nor the blaze in your dispensary. Ah, you are just like a dear former colleague of mine, always haring off after the wild goose. If Duggan had *hots* for the unfortunate young Anna, would he also have bestowed favours upon a woman elderly?"

"Meg McKenzie is able to advance careers."

"Even so," said the famous detective. Whether he was conceding or demurring remained uncertain.

*   *   *

Presently the famous detective said to Lady McKenzie, "You were consulting the data-bank about methods of detection."

"And now here you are, you funny little man, because we couldn't take our pills."

"Better me, perhaps, than some beast of the imagination."

Nevertheless, the famous detective could be quite like some cunning fox, or even a fierce wolf, when the quarry was finally almost in his grasp.

"Did you have much, how do we say, intercourse, with Mr Duggan?" At delicate moments it could be useful to appear to have a faulty command of the English language.

"I mean," he continued, "much relationship?"

Lady McKenzie fingered her jewel magnificent, her hand covering her somewhat scrawny décolleté bosom.

"I found him rather immature as a person. We had little in common."

"*Bien. Bien.* And your relations with Mademoiselle Krasnik?"

"Duggan was annoying poor Anna. Anna asked me how she should best handle him."

"Somebody certainly handled him," said the famous detective. "I must let the little grey cells contemplate this *affaire* overnight."

The captain overheard.

"I ought to tell you," said Mungo Mboyo, "that during mainshift tomorrow the *Sirius* will drop out of hyperspace."

"Meaning that I will evaporate?"

Mboyo nodded. An inevitability.

"*Alors*, the little grey cells must work hard."

"And on your excellent world," the famous detective said to High-Tanttu, "I hear there is much duelling because of honour. Let me tell you some stories of historic duels fought in times past in Belgium and in France—"

A fine raconteur when need be, the famous detective regaled the hostage-ambassador, ever alert to the implications of questions the alien proceeded to put about these old-fashioned human rites of legitimized murder.

Such a battering upon his cabin door, almost instantly followed by the door recessing, and Captain Mboyo shouting, "Meg

McKenzie has been strangled in her bed. The sapphire fetish is missing."

Struggling from sleep, the famous detective felt mortification.

"I've sent armed Marines to the Exalt's cabin."

A communication device, clipped to the captain's uniform, squawked. A rapid exchange followed. The jewel had indeed been found easily in the alien's cabin. Guard was now mounted over High-Tanttu.

"There's our murderer," Mboyo said bitterly. "And there go our hopes of interspecies harmony – and the lives of our own two hostages as well!"

"Calm yourself, *Monsieur le Capitaine*. I suspect all is not as you think."

"Who else could have put the jewel in a cabin locked by Tanttu's own palm print?"

"Ah, just as with the *pharmacie* . . . Nevertheless, in your haste you yourself may cause an incident interstellar."

If only a decent silk dressing gown and embroidered slippers were to hand.

Sighing: "Who found the body?"

"Kessel. He was passing Meg's cabin. Noticed an undergarment caught in the doorway."

"Ah. So it was intended the body should be found swiftly, and the alarm raised."

"Lundby's examining the body now. Go and join him. You might find more evidence of High-Tanttu's guilt, not that much more's needed."

"Ah, but first I must perform my *toilette*."

"And how long does that take?"

"No more than forty-five minutes."

"Meg McKenzie is lying dead right now!"

"Her condition will not change; and I must tidy myself. Lack of neatness is most distressing to me, *Monsieur le Capitaine*. Lack of order, lack of shape . . . *Nom d'un nom!*" With this yelp, the famous detective jigged briefly to and fro, clutching himself as if suffering from severe constipation. "I must talk to the cook, this Charley Manx."

"About your damned omelettes?"

Enigmatically, the famous detective answered, "After the

chicken is hatched, we shall count him. First, we must see the true colour of his feathers."

Disgusted, Mungo Mboyo departed.

It was not until hours later that the famous detective entered the saloon where many aboard had gathered, obeying the principle of there being safety in numbers, even though the criminal had surely been neutralized.

"Where have you been?" demanded the captain.

From Dr Lundby: "You never even came to look at Lady Meg's cabin!"

"No need, *mon ami*. This is a problem which yields to thought, not to the examination of undergarments trapped in doorways."

"Very soon," Mboyo warned, "we shall be starting our descent from hyperspace to normal space."

Nonchalantly the famous detective consulted his huge watch. "*Bien*, there is time enough. Will you have High-Tanttu brought here promptly?"

Mboyo spoke into his communicator. The famous detective noticed that Donna Fairbreed now wore the sapphire fetish around her neck.

"Ah," he said to her, "so you are the inheritor of the duty."

"Somebody has to be."

"You are not happy to inherit?"

"Would you be," she cried, "when the previous wearer was murdered?"

The famous detective looked around the assembly. "Jack Scruton is absent."

"He's on duty, monitoring our transition," Mboyo said impatiently. "I'll need to be on the bridge soon."

"The *Sirius*, she is in any danger?"

Mboyo shook his head. "The transition's all automated. There might be some visual distortions, without our pills."

Very soon a pair of Marines led in the alien, whose hands were bound in front of him. High-Tanttu's pink-eyed gaze ranged the room till he saw the jewel; whereupon he stood stiffly, expressionless.

"*Alors*," said the famous detective, "the murderer is in this room." His own green cat-like eyes gleamed.

Most people stared at the Exalt.

"No, it is not he," the famous detective said, and he began to explain.

"The murder of Lady Margaret is merely a distraction, designed to throw suspicion upon High-Tanttu. The jewel is inserted into his cabin so that it can be discovered and seem to be proof positive. Who will imperil interspecies relations in this way, except someone who feels little allegiance to the human species? Who will set a fire in the *pharmacie* except someone who does not fully comprehend starships? Yet someone who also possesses considerable information."

"Do you mean we have some sort of stowaway on board?" broke in Lord Burgess. "Somebody from High-Tanttu's world, who's opposed to a treaty? The two earlier murders were just rehearsals?"

"I have said, the red herring is the third murder, not the first two."

"Stowing away is practically impossible," declared the purser. "Anyway, this stowaway would be discovered sooner or later unless he jettisoned himself, and the diplomatic sabotage would fail."

"But that is not the scheme," said the famous detective.

"A stowaway *could* be a possibility," suggested Dr Lundby, "if he's a master mesmerist."

"Ah." Uttering a little noise of approval, the famous detective inclined his head graciously. "Yet you are looking toward the wrong world, *mon ami*."

Captain Mboyo was incredulous. "Duggan and three others went down to that uninhabited jungle planet. The same four returned, and no survivor from that crashed ship."

"Nevertheless, there was a stowaway."

Donna Fairbreed laughed giddily. "Is this where your stolen meat comes into it?"

"Precisely."

The doctor protested, "But I examined the four of them on board the shuttle. There was no one else."

"Yet there was a stowaway," insisted the famous detective. "I know this. The stowaway was none other than Duggan himself."

"Absurd!"

"What nonsense!"

Such a chorus of disbelief and bewilderment.

The famous detective smiled and twirled his moustache.

"Do you recall the half-eaten bodies of the crash victims? On that wild jungle world there is a creature which can alter its shape." The famous detective shuddered fastidiously. "It imitates other creatures, and becomes them – not only in body but also, by great concentration, mentally as well. How does it obtain the time required to do so? This creature mesmerises its prey just as a weasel hypnotieses a rabbit."

"So next," asked Lundby, "it needs to eat part of its victims to absorb their DNA?"

"*Non, non*, not so. It usurps their form and their memories by an act of sheer will.

"Imagine a protean creature with an ability to metamorphose, which develops the ability to camouflage itself as other creatures – not merely as regards colouration, but anatomically. Consequently, it needs to imitate the behaviour of its models. To copy, like a photographic film. This creature evolves a kind of rapacious telepathy. It does not breed very frequently, being jealous of its own kind, so the world is not overrun with its sort.

"Now, changing its own form costs much energy – so it must eat quickly afterwards. While the unfortunate Duggan was searching for survivors he encountered one of these predators – in the mimic semblance of one of the crash victims. By now the predator knew from the victim's memories about the wider universe beyond its jungle. It mesmerised Duggan, replaced him – then killed him and hid his body.

"Thus," said the famous detective triumphantly, "it came on board the *Sirius*. When you examined what you supposed was Duggan, Dr Lundby, the mimic took the opportunity to memorise your hand so that it could imitate your palm print later on. Remember, by now it also had access to Duggan's knowledge. It feared that the pills might block its ability to hallucinate itself, so as speak, into a new form. It also feared that in retrospect your examination might have revealed suspicions about Duggan.

"Subsequently, while it was in the form of Anna Krasnik, it memorized High-Tanttu's hand during one of the dinners so deplorable—"

"This is all sheer fantasy—!"

"No, no," said the famous detective. "I know. There is one

further vital factor. The predator discovered that the human being possesses mental powers so much more evolved than it ever encountered in its previous animal incarnations. Yes, psychic capabilities, even if they are usually undeveloped. The mimic became able to transfer its own mind directly from one body to another. And along with its mind, its knack of will power over matter, its metamorphic ability, causing plasticity of the cells and bones.

"Beguiling Anna Krasnik by mesmerism to be alone with it, it transferred itself to her, suppressing her personality. Using Duggan's knowledge of the ju-jitsu strangle, it killed the vacant Duggan body.

"Yet Anna Krasnik did not properly serve its purpose. She was too prominent a personage. She was not sufficiently out of sight. Nor did she have free access to quantities of food, should these be required. Our stowaway still retained the instincts of its animal heritage."

"It transferred to Charley Manx!" cried the doctor. "Charley strangled the paralyzed Anna." He was as excited as the famous detective's erstwhile colleague used to become, although it was obvious that scepticism would soon resurface.

"You did think Charley's cooking must have gone off!" exclaimed Donna Fairbreed; but she was merely mocking.

The famous detective wagged a finger. "I fear that your chef's cooking was always the travesty."

A klaxon whooped its warning once, twice, thrice.

"We're starting the drop from hyperspace," Mboyo called out. "Your explanation's ridiculous. I shan't regret your absence."

So saying, the captain hastened away.

However, High-Tanttu gazed at the famous detective. "You have saved my honour, and that of your species."

The famous detective accepted the compliment gracefully. "In fact I have saved the honour of several governments in the past."

Such a shimmer in the air, as of diaphanous veils descending and dissolving.

"Unfortunately," said Prince Kessel, "nobody apart from the Exalt really seems to agree with you. And he would, wouldn't he? As soon as we've finished transition, we'll interrogate our chef thoroughly under tight security. I rather feel that we won't find—"

"Your Highness," the famous detective interrupted, "you certainly won't find Charley Manx in his galley."

"What the devil do you mean?"

The famous detective puffed himself up.

"I said that the perpetrator of these crimes is here in this very room. Behold: I am he. I am Charley Manx. Or rather, I am the shape-shifter who replaced Charley, and who has now taken on the form of myself."

More veils descended. Nevertheless, the famous detective did not waver.

"Earlier," he recounted, "with some trepidation I confronted the cook. Fearful, he panicked. He could not know who I might have confided in – unless he changed to become me and thus know my memories. Or unless he transferred to my body – but that body was supposed to evaporate soon.

"*Voilà*, he adopted my guise, body and brain – and forced my phantom self into a freezer. He had not reckoned with my mental power and primacy. My imitated intellect soon dominated his. It is I who have access to his memories, and to Anna Krasnik's and to Duggan's, and to those of many previous bestial incarnations – which will sharpen my hunting instincts enormously."

The assembly gawked.

"It deeply grieves me that I should thus be the criminal. Yet now I make the amends by explaining. What should I have done in the circumstances? Doomed to disappear when we leave hyperspace! The universe deprived of my talents! No, my Lord, you will not find Charley Manx. By now my phantom self will inevitably have vanished. Yet I am here still, at your service, *moi*."

"You are under my protection, as a matter of honour," declared High-Tanttu grandly, even though the Marines had not yet released him.

The famous detective inclined his head; and said:

"During the rest of this voyage, since you are deprived of Charley Manx, it is my intention to act as your chef. At last there will be a true gourmet in the galley."

The klaxon whooped once, twice. Outside of the only small porthole in the saloon, bright stars were visible.

Mungo Mboyo returned presently.

"We've achieved transit to normal space—" The captain saw

the famous detective, and was astonished. "How in hell are you still here?"

The rotund little detective smirked.

"*Monsieur le Capitaine*, it is not so easy to rid yourself of me, you see." He stroked the upturned point of his moustache. "I shall make some very fine omelettes."

THE INCORPORATED

John Shirley

Kessler was walking east on Fourteenth Street, looking for something. He wasn't sure what he was looking for. He was walking through a twilight made raw by a mist-thin November rain sharpening the edge of a cold wind. The wind slashed at his acrylic overcoat. The street was almost deserted. He was looking for something, something; the brutally colorless word *something* hung heavily in his mind like an empty picture frame.

What he thought he wanted was to get in, out of the weather; he felt a vague resentment to the city of New York for letting the weather modification system break down again. Walking in rain made you feel naked. And acid rain, he thought, could make you naked, if you wore the kind of synthreads that reacted with the acids.

Up ahead the eternal neon butterfly of a Budweiser sign glowed sultry orange-red and blue; the same design since sometime in the 20th century. He angled across the sidewalk, pitted concrete the color of dead skin, hurrying toward the sign, toward the haven of a bar. The rain was already beginning to burn. He closed his eyes against it, afraid it would burn his corneas.

He pushed through the smudged door into the bar. The bartender glanced up, nodded, and reached under the counter for a towel; he passed the towel across to Kessler. The towel was treated with acid-absorbents; it helped immediately.

"Get any in your eyes?" the bartender asked, with no great show of concern.

"No, I don't think so." He handed the towel back. "Thanks."

The tired-faced men drinking at the bar hardly glanced at Kessler. He was unremarkable: round-faced, with short black hair streaked blue-white to denote his work in video-editing; large friendly brown eyes, soft red mouth pinched now with worry; a standard print-out greyblue suit.

The bartender said something else, but it didn't register. Kessler was staring at the glowing green lozenge of a credit transferral kiosk in the back of the dim, old-fashioned bar. He crossed to it and stepped in; the door hissed shut behind him. The small TV screen on the front of the phone lit up, and its electronic letters asked him, DO YOU WANT CALL, OR ENTRY?

What did he want? Why had he come here? He wasn't sure. But it felt right. A wave of reassurance had come over him . . . Ask it what your balance is, a soundless voice whispered to him. A soft, maternal mental whisper. Again a wave of reassurance. But he thought: something's out of place . . . He knew his mind as a man knows his cluttered desk; he knows when someone has moved something on his desk. Or in his mind. And someone had.

He punched Entry and it asked him his account number and entry code number and security code. He punched all three sets of digits in, then told it he wanted to see his bank balance. It told him to wait. Numbers appeared on the screen.

$NB 760,000.

He stared at it. He punched for error check and confirmation.

The bank's computer insisted that he had seven hundred and sixty thousand NewBux in his bank account. There should be only four thousand.

Something was missing from his memory; something had been added to his bank account.

They tampered with me, he thought, and then they paid me for it. Who?

He requested the name of the depositor. The screen told him: UNRECORDED.

Julie. Talk to Julie. There was just no one else he discussed his projects with till they were patented and on-line. No one. His wife had to know.

Julie. He could taste her name in his mouth. Her name tasted like bile.

Julie had been home only a few minutes, Kessler decided, as he closed the door behind him. Her coat was draped over the back of the couch, off-white on off-white. She liked things off-white or battleship grey or powder blue.

She was bent down to the minifridge behind the breakfast bar. She stood up, a frosted bottle of Stolichnaya in her hand. "Hi, Jimmy."

She almost never called him Jimmy.

Julie came out with a vodka straight up and a twist of lime for each of them. He'd learned to like vodka because she did. She padded across the powder-blue rug in bare feet, small feet sexy in sheer hose; she was tall and slender and long-necked. Her hair was the yellow of split pine, cut short as a small boy's, and parted on the side. She was English, and looked it; her eyes were immaculate blue crystals. She wore her silk-lined, coarse-fiber, off-white dress suit. The suit with no shoes. She looked more natural in her suits than in anything else. She had "casuals" to wear at home, but somehow she never wore them. Maybe because that would be a concession to homelife, would almost be a betrayal of the Corporation Family. Like having children. What was it she said about having children? *If you don't mind, I'll continue to resist the programming of my biological computer. When DNA talks, I don't listen. I don't like being pushed into something by a molecule.* He took off his coat, hung it up, and sat down beside her on the couch. The vodka, chilled with no ice, waited for him on the glass coffee table. He took a drink and said, "There's seven hundred and sixty thousand NewBux in my bank account." He looked at her. "What did they take?"

Her eyes went a little glassy. "Seven hundred and sixty thousand? Computer error."

"You know it's not." He took another sip. The Stoly was syrupy thick from being kept in the freezer. "What did you tell Worldtalk?"

"Are you accusing me of something?" She said it with her icy Vassar incredulousness then, like: I can't believe anyone could be so painfully unsophisticated.

"I'm accusing Worldtalk. You're theirs. They do as they like with you. If Worldtalk says it's not productive to have kids, if Worldtalk says it's not *teamplaying* to have kids, you don't have kids. Even when their disapproval is unnecessary: You wouldn't have had to quit your job – I can understand you wanting to have a career. We could have had the kid in a hired womb or an artificial womb. I would've taken care of it during the day. If Worldtalk says listen for Usefuls, you listen. Even at home. They don't want employees, at Worldtalk, they want to *own you*."

"It's pointless to go over and over this. Worldtalk has nothing to do with my decision not to have children. I worked eight years—"

"I know it by rote: You worked eight years to be assistant New York manager in the country's biggest PR and advertising outfit. You tell me *having children* is demeaning yourself! Eight years you licked Grimwald's boots! Going to Worldtalk's family sessions, letting them psych you up after work for hours at a time, co-opting your instincts!"

She stood up, arms rigid at her sides. "Well, why not? Corporation families *last*."

"It isn't a real family. They're using you. Look what they got you to do! To *me*."

"You got some seven hundred thousand NewBux. That's more than you would ever have made on any of your harebrained schemes. If you worked for a corp you'd be making decent money in the first place. You insist on being freelance so you're left out in the cold, and you should be grateful for what they—" she snipped the sentence in two with a brisk sibilance, and turned away.

"So we've dropped the pretenses now. You're saying I should be grateful for the money Worldtalk gave me. Julie – *What did they take?*"

"I don't *know!* You didn't tell me what you were working on – and anyway I don't believe they took anything. I – god damn it."

She went to the bathroom to pointedly take her Restem, making a lot of noise opening the prescription bottle so he'd hear and know it was his fault she had to take a tranquilizer.

Bascomb was drunk and drugged. The disorder of his mind was splashed onto the room around him: the dancers, the lights, the holograms that made it look, in the smoky dimness, as if someone was there dancing beside you who wasn't. A touristy couple on the dance floor stopped and stared at another couple: horned, half human, half reptiles, she with her tongue darting from between rouged lips; he with baroque filips of fire flicking from his scaly nostrils. The touristy couple laughed off their embarrassment when the deejay turned off the holo and the demon couple vanished.

Bascomb chuckled and sucked some of his cocaine fizz through a straw that lit up with miniature advertisements when it was used; lettering flickering luminous green up and down its length.

Sitting beside him, Kessler squirmed on his barstool and ordered another Scotch. He didn't like Bascomb like this. Bascomb was young, tanned, and preppie, he wore a Japanese Action Suit now, a kind of clinging, faintly iridescent jumpsuit. He was used to seeing Bascomb in his office, a neat component of Featherstone, Pestlestein, and Bascomb, Attorneys at Law, friendly but not too friendly, intense but controlled. My own fault, Kessler told himself: chase the guy down when he's off-work, hassle his wives till they tell me where he hangs out, find out things I don't want to know about the guy. Like the fact that he's bisexual and flirting with the waiter.

The bar was circular, rotating slowly through the club, leaving the dance floor behind now to arrive at the cruising rooms. As they talked it turned slowly past flesh-pink holographic porn squirmings and edged into the soft music lounge. Each room had its own idiosyncratic darkness, shot through with the abstracted glamor of the candy-apple red and hot pink and electric blue neon tubes running up the corners to zig-zag the ceiling like a time-lapse photo of night-time city traffic.

Bascomb turned on his stool to look at the porn and the live copulation; his mouth was open in a lax smile. Kessler looked over his shoulder. Again in the dimness the holos were nearly indistinguishable from the real article; a drunken swinger tried to fondle a woman with four breasts, only to walk through her. "Do we have to talk here?" Kessler asked, turning back to the bar.

Bascomb ignored the question. "The bottom line, Jim, is that you are a nobody. Now if you were, say, a Nobel-Prize-winning professor at Stanford, we might be able to get you your day in court, we might get a Grand Jury to investigate the people at Worldtalk . . ." Talking without taking his eyes off the intermingled porn and people. "But as it is you're a mildly successful video editor who makes a hobby of working up a lot of media theories. Every day some crank looking for attention announces a Great Idea has been stolen from his brain, and ninety-nine percent of the time they turn out to be paranoid or a liar or both. I'm not saying you're a paranoid or a liar. I believe you. I'm just saying I'm probably the only one who will."

"But I have the seven-hundred-sixty-thousand—"

"Did you request the name of the depositor?"

"Unrecorded."

"Then how are you going to prove a connection?"

"I don't know. But I know an idea was stolen from me. I want it back, Bascomb. And I can't work it up again on my own from scratch – wouldn't know where to begin; it was all on a disk, and in paper files. Both are gone. They took all my notes, everything that could lead me back to it . . ."

"Sucks," Bascomb said sympathetically. They had rotated into the lounge; people on couches watched videos and conversed softly. Sometimes they were talking to holos; you knew when you were talking to a holo because they said outrageous things. They were programmed that way to ease the choking boredom of lounge bar conversation. "I want it back, Bascomb," Kessler repeated, his knuckles white on the rim of the bar.

Bascomb shrugged and said, "You haven't been in this country long; maybe you don't know how it works. First off, you have to understand that . . ." he paused to sip from his cocaine fizz; he became more animated almost instantly, chattering on: "you have to understand that you can't get it back the way it was taken. Whoever it was probably came in while you were asleep. Which adds credence to your theory that Julie was involved. She waits up or pretends to sleep, lets them in, they shoot you up with the receptivity drug. The beauty of the RD is that it works instantly and not only makes you cerebral-program receptive but keeps you sedated. They put the wires and tubes in through the sinuses, but they don't damage anything. They've got lots of microsurgicals in the big box they've brought with them, right? They look at the screen they've set up that translates your impulses into a code they can understand. They get some dream free-association maybe. But that tells them they're 'on line' in your brain. Then they put a request to the brain, fed into it in the form of neurohumoral transmitter molecules they manufacture in their box—"

"How do you know so much about this?" Kessler asked, unable to keep the edge of suspicion out of his voice.

"We get a case like yours once or twice a year. I did a lot of research on it. The ACLU has a small library on the subject. It really gets their goat. We didn't win those cases, by the way; they're tough . . ." He paused to sip his fizz, his eyes sparkling and dilated.

Kessler was annoyed by Bascomb's treating his case like a curiosity, a conversation piece. "Let's get back to what happened to me."

"Okay, uh – so they made a request to the biological computer we call a brain, right? They asked it what it knew about whatever it was they wanted to take from you, and your brain automatically begins to think about it, and sends signals to the cortex of the temporal lobes or to the hippocampus; they 'ride' the electro-chemical signals back to the place where the information is stored. They use tracer molecules that attach themselves to the chemical signals. When they reach the hippocampus or the temporal lobes, the tracer molecules act as enzymes to command the brain to simply unravel that particular chemical code. They break it down on the molecular level. They extract some things connected to it, and the chain of ideas that led to it, but they don't take so much they make you an idiot because they probably want your wife to cooperate and to stay with Worldtalk. Anyway, the brain chemistry is such that you can ask the brain a question with neurohumoral transmitter molecules, but you can't imprint on the memory, in an orderly way. You can feed in experiences, things which seem to be happening now – you can even implant them so they crop up at a given stimulus – but you can't feed in ready made *memories*. Probably because memories are holo-graphic, involving complexes of cell groups. Like you can pull a thread to unravel a coat fairly easily but you can't ravel it back up so easily . . . Look at that exquisite creature over there. She's lovely, isn't she? Like to do some imprinting on her. I wonder if she's real. Uh, anyway . . . you can't put it back *in*. They take out, selectively, any memory of anything that might make you suspect they tampered with you, but lots of people begin to suspect anyway, because when they free associate over familiar pathways of the brain and then come to a gap – well, it's jarring. But they can't prove anything."

"Okay, so maybe it can't be put back by direct feed-in to the memory. But it could be relearned through ordinary induction. Reading."

"Yeah. I guess it would be better than nothing. But you still have to find out who took it. Or if you work out what it was, you want to prove they stole it. Even if it turns up as someone else's project – proves nothing. They could have come up with it same way you did. And you should ask yourself this: Why did they take it? Was it simply for profit or was it for another reason? From what we've been able to find out, about a third of the ideas that are stolen out of someone's brain are stolen for reasons of protection. The bigger corporations have a network of agents. Their sole job is to search out people with developing ideas that could be dangerous to the status quo. They try to extract the ideas before they are copyrighted or patented or published in papers or discussed in public. They take the idea from you, maybe plant some mental inhibitors to keep you from working your way back to it again. If you came up with an idea that was *really* dangerous to the Status Quo, Jimmy, they might go farther than a simple erasing next time. Because they play hardball. If you keep pushing to get it back, they just might arrange for you to turn up dead . . ."

But riding the elevator up to his apartment, thinking about what had happened, trying to come to terms with it, Kessler realized it wasn't death that scared him. What chilled him was thinking about his wife; Julie had waited till he'd slept. Had, perhaps, watched the clock on the bedside table. Had got out of bed at the appointed hour and padded to the door and ever-so-quietly opened it for the man carrying the black box . . .

And she had done it because Worldtalk had asked her to. Worldtalk was her husband, her children, her parents. Perhaps most of all her dreadful parents.

And maybe in the long run, what had happened to him, Kessler thought as the elevator reached his floor, was that the Dissolve Depression had done its work on him. For decades the social structures that created nuclear families, that kept families whole and together, had eroded, had finally broken down completely. Broken homes made broken homes made broken homes. The big corporations, meanwhile, consumed the little ones, and, becoming then unmanageably big, looked for ways to stabilize themselves. They chose the proven success of the Japanese system: the corporation as an extension of the family. You

inculcate your workers with a fanatic sense of loyalty and belonging. You personalize everything. And they go along with that
or they lose their jobs. So maybe it started with the Dissolve
Depression: five years earlier, a Moslem Jihad terrorist group
had set off a controlled hydrogen bomb explosion in the upper
atmosphere; the explosion was contained, directed outward; but
the bomb's ElectroMagnetic Pulse – the EMP effect – swept over
the continent. The defense systems were shielded. But not the
banks. The pulse literally burnt up the computer memories of
millions of bank accounts. Hundreds of banks collapsed, and the
economy with them.

So now jobs were precious. Jobs were life. So you embraced
the new Corporation as home and family system. The breakdown
of the traditional family structures reinforced the process. And
you put your employer above your true family. You let its agents
in to destroy your husband's new career . . .

And here we are, he thought, as he walked into the apartment.
There she is, making us both a drink, so we can once more
become cordial strangers sharing a convenience apartment and a
convenient sex life.

"Aren't you coming to bed?" she called from the bedroom.

He sat on the couch, holding his glass up beside his ear,
shaking it just enough so he could listen to the tinkle of the
ice cubes. The sound made him feel good and he wondered why.
It made him visualize wind chimes of frosted glass . . . His
mother's wind chimes. His mother standing on the front porch,
smiling absently, watching him play, and now and then she
would reach up and tinkle the wind chimes with her finger
. . . He swallowed another tot of vodka to smear over the chalky
scratch of loneliness.

"You really ought to get some sleep, Jimmy." A faint note of
strain in her voice.

He was scared to go in there.

This is stupid, he thought. I don't know for sure it was her.

He forced himself to put the glass down, to stand, to walk to the
bedroom, to do it all as if he weren't forcing himself through the
membranes of his mistrust. He stood in the doorway and looked
at her for a moment. She was wearing her silk lingerie. Her back
to him. He could see her face reflected in the window to her left.

Her eyes were open wide. In them he saw determination and self-disgust and he knew she had contacted them and the strangers were going to do it to him again. They would come and take out more this time, his conversation with Bascomb, his misgivings. They would take away the hush money they had paid him since he had shown he was unwilling to accept it without pushing to get back what he had lost . . . They would take his argument with Julie . . .

Go along with it, he told himself.

That would be the intelligent solution. Let them do it. Sweet nepenthe. The pain and the fear and the anger would go with the memories. And he would have his relationship with his wife back. Such as it was.

He thought about it for a moment. She turned to look at him.

"No," he said finally. "No, we don't have enough between us to make it worthwhile. No. Tell them I said next they'll have to try and kill me."

She stared at him. Then she lay back, and looked at the ceiling.

He closed the bedroom door softly behind him, and went to the closet for his coat.

They hadn't taken the money yet. It was still there in his account. He had gone to an all night banking kiosk, sealed himself in, and now he looked at the figure, $NB 760,000 and felt a kind of glow. He punched for the telephone, and called Charlie Chesterton.

The screen asked him, YOU WANT VISUAL? No, he told it, not yet.

"Sap?" came Charlie's voice. "Huzatunwushant?"

Wake Charlie out of a sound sleep, and he talked Technicki. He'd said, *What's happenin'? Who's that and what do you want?*

"Talk standard with me, Charlie. It's—"

"Hey, my man Kessler, what's happening, man! Hey, how come no visual?"

"I didn't know what you were doing. I'm ever discreet." He punched for visual and a small TV image of Charlie appeared below the phone's keyboard. Charlie wore a triple mohawk, each fin a different color, each color significant; red in the middle for Technicki Radical Unionist; blue on the right for his profession, video tech; green on the left for his neighborhood: New Brooklyn. He grinned, showing front teeth imprinted with his initials in gold, another tacky Technicki fad. And Charlie wore a picture

T-shirt that showed a movie: Fritz Lang's *Metropolis*, now moving through the flood scene.

"You went to sleep wearing your movie T-shirt, you oughta turn it off, wear out the batteries."

"Recharges from sunlight," Charlie said. "You call me to talk about my sleeping habits?"

"Need your help. Right now, I need the contact numbers for that Shanghai bank that takes the transferrals under a code of anonymity . . ."

"I told you man, that's like, the border of legality, and maybe over it. You understand that first, right?"

Kessler nodded.

"Okay. Set your screen to record . . ."

Bascomb's office was too warm; Bascomb had a problem with his circulation. The walls were a milky yellow that seemed to quicken the heat somehow. Bascomb sat behind the blond-wood desk, wearing a stenciled-on three-piece-suit, smiling a smile of polite bafflement. Kessler sat across from him, feeling he was on some kind of treadmill, because Bascomb just kept saying, "I really am quite sure no such meeting took place." He chuckled. "I know the club very well and I'm sure I'd remember if I'd been there that night. Haven't been there for a month."

"You weren't enthusiastic about it, but you ended by telling me we'd take 'em on." But the words were ashes in Kessler's mouth. He knew what had happened because there was not even the faintest trace of duplicity or nervousness on Bascomb's face. Bascomb really didn't remember. "So you won't represent me on this," Kessler went on. Only half a question.

"We really have no experience with brain tampering—"

"I could get the court files to prove that you have. But they'd only . . ." He shook his head. Despair was something he could smell and taste and feel, like acid rain. "They'd tamper with you again. Just to make their point."

He walked out of the office, hurrying, thinking: They'll have the place under surveillance. But no one stopped him outside.

Charlie was off on one of his amateur analyses, and there was nothing Kessler could do, he had to listen, because Charlie was covering for him.

". . . I mean," Charlie was saying, "now your average Technicki speaks standard English like an infant, am I right, and can't read except command codes, and learned it all from vidteaching, and he's trained to do this and that and to fix this and that but he's, like, socially inhibited from rising in the ranks because the socio-economic elite speaks standard good and reads—"

"If they really want to, they can learn what they need, like you did," Kessler said irritably. He was standing at the window, looking out at the empty, glossy ceramic streets. The artificial island, a boro-annex of Brooklyn anchored in the harbor, was almost deserted at this hour; everyone had either gone into the city, or home to holo, or into a tavern. The floating boros were notoriously dull. The squat floboro housing, rounded off at the corners like a row of molars, stood in silence, a few windows glowing like radarscopes against the night.

But they could be watching me, Kessler thought. A hundred ways they could be watching me and I'd see nothing.

He turned, stepped away from the window. Charlie was pacing, arms clasped behind him, head bent, playing the part of the young, boldly theorizing leader of radical politicos.

The apartment was crowded with irregular shelves of books and boxes of software and cassettes and compact disks; Charlie had hung silk scarves in The Three Colors, blurring like multi-color smoke. "I mean," Charlie went on, "you can talk about our job security but it's a sham—"

A warning chill: and Kessler turned, looked out the window. Three stories down she was a powder-blue keyhole shape against the faint petroleum rainbow filminess of the street. She was looking at the numbers.

She might have guessed, he told himself. She met Charlie once. She might have looked Charlie's address up in ref disk. She went to the front door. Charlie's bell chimed. He went to the screen and looked. "It's your wife," he said. "You want me to tell her you went overseas? Japan?"

"Let her in."

"Are you kidding, man? You are, right? She was the one who—"

"Just let her in." She got it from the address list, he told himself. There was a cocktail of emotions in him. There was a relief at seeing her, shaken in with something that buzzed like a smoke alarm, and it wasn't till she was at the door that he realized that the sensation was terror. And then Julie was standing in the doorway, against the light of the hallway. She looked beautiful. The light behind her abruptly cut: an energy a saving device sensing that no one was now in the hall; suddenly she stood framed in darkness. The buzzing fizzed up, and overwhelmed the relief. His mouth was dry.

Looking disgustedly at Kessler, Charlie shut the door behind her.

Kessler stared at her. Her eyes flickered, her mouth opened, and shut, and she shook her head. She looked drained.

And Kessler knew.

"They sent you. They told you where to find me," he said.

"They – want the money back," she said. "They want you to come with me."

He shook his head. "Don't you get sick of being puppeted?"

She looked at the window. Her face was blank. "You don't understand."

"Do you know why they do it, why they train you in that Americanized Japanese job conditioning stuff? To save themselves money. Because it eliminates unions."

"They have their reasons, sure. Mostly efficiency."

"I know. What's the slogan? 'Efficiency is friendship.' "

She looked embarrassed. "That's not—" She shrugged. "A Corporate Family is just as valid as any other. It's something you couldn't understand. I – I'll lose my job, Jimmy. If you don't come." She said *lose my job* the way Kessler would have said, *lose my life*.

Kessler said, "I'll think about going with you if you tell me what it was . . . what it was they took."

"They – took it from me too."

"I don't believe that. I never believed it. I think they left it intact in you, so you could watch to see if I stumbled on it again. I think you really loved them trusting you. Worldtalk is Mommy and Daddy and Mommy and Daddy trusted you . . ."

Her mouth twisted with resentment. "You bastard. I can't—".

"Yeah, you can. You have to. Otherwise Charlie and I are going out the back way and we're going to cause endless trouble for Worldtalk. And I know you, Julie – I'd know if you were making it up. So tell me what it was, what it really was."

She sighed. "I only know what you told me. You pointed out that P.R. companies manipulate the media for their clients without the public knowing it most of the time. They use their connections and channels to plant information or disinformation in news-sheet articles, on newsvid, in movies, in political speeches. So . . ." She paused and went on wearily, shrugging off her irritation. "So they're manipulating people, and the public gets a distorted view of what's going on because of special interests. You worked up an editing system that sensed probable examples of, uh, I think the phrases you used were 'implanted information' or 'special interest distortion.' So they could be weeded out. You called it the Media Alarm System." She let out a long breath. "I didn't know they'd go so far – I thought they'd buy out your system. In a way they did. I *had* to mention it at Worldtalk. If I didn't I would've been . . . disloyal." She said *disloyal* wincing, knowing what he would think.

But it was Charlie who said it: "What about loyalty to Jim Kessler?"

Her hand fluttered a dismissal. "It doesn't matter at this point whether it was wrong or right. It's too late. They *know*. . . . Jimmy, are you coming?"

Kessler was thinking about the Media Alarm System. It didn't sound familiar – but it sounded *right*. He said, slowly, "No. You can help me. What they did is illegal as hell. If you testify, we can beat them."

"Jimmy, if I thought they – no, no. I—" She broke off, staring at his waist. "Don't be stupid. That's not—" She took a step back, and put her hand in her purse.

Kessler and Charlie looked at each other, traded puzzlement. When Kessler looked back at Julie, she had a gun in her hand. It was a small blue-metal pistol, its barrel tiny as a pencil, and that tiny barrel meant it fired explosive bullets. *They* had given it to her.

"Do you know what that gun will do?" Charlie was saying. "Those little explosive bullets will splash him all over the wall." His voice shook. He took a step toward her.

She pressed back against the door and said, "Charlie, if you come closer to me I'll shoot him." Charlie stopped. The room seemed to keen ultrasonically with sheer imminence. She went on, the words coming out in a rush: "Why don't you ask him what that thing in his hand would do to me, Charlie. Shall we? Ask him that. Jimmy has the same kind of gun. With the same goddamn bullets." Her voice was too high; she was breathing fast. Her knuckles white on the gun.

Kessler's arms were hanging at his side, his hands empty.

"Lower the gun, Julie, and we can talk," Charlie said gently.

"I'll lower mine when he lowers his," she said hoarsely.

"He isn't holding a gun," Charlie said.

She was staring at a space about three feet in front of Kessler's chest. She was seeing the gun there. He wanted to say, *Julie, they tampered with you.* He could only croak, "Julie—"

She shouted, "Don't!" and raised the gun. And then everything was moving: Kessler threw himself down. Charlie jumped at her, and the wall behind Kessler jumped outward toward the street.

Two hot metal hands clapped Kessler's head between them and he shouted with pain and thought he was dead. But it was only a noise, the noise of the wall exploding outward. Chips of wall pattered down; smoke sucked out through the four foot hole in the wall into the winter night.

Kessler got up, shaky, his ears ringing. He looked around, and saw Charlie straddling Julie. He had the gun in his hand and she was face down, sobbing.

"Gogidoutere," Charlie said, lapsing into Technicki, his face white.

"Get off her," Kessler said. Charlie stood up beside her. "Julie, look at me," Kessler said softly. She tilted her head back, an expression of dignified defiance trembling precariously in her face. Then her eyes widened, and she looked at his hips. She was seeing him holding a gun there. "I don't have a gun, Julie. They put that into you. Now I'm going to *get* a gun . . . Give me the gun, Charlie." Without taking his eyes off her, he put his hand out. Charlie hesitated, then laid the gun in Kessler's open palm. She blinked, then narrowed her eyes.

"So now you've got two guns." She shrugged.

He shook his head. "Get up." Moving stiffly, she stood up. "Now go over there to Charlie's bed. He's got black bedsheets. You see them? Take one off. Just pull it off and bring it over here." She started to say something, anger lines punctuating her mouth, and he said quickly, "Don't talk yet. Do it!" She went to the bed, pulled the black satin sheet off, and dragged it over to him. Charlie gaped, and muttered that the cops would come because of the explosion and would hold you for days and weeks till they were sure of what had happened, but Kessler had a kind of furious calm on him then, and he knew what he was going to do, and if it didn't work then he'd let the acid rain bleach his bones white as a warning to other travelers come to this poisoned well. This woman. He said, "Now tear up the sheet – sorry, man, I'll replace it – and make a blindfold. Good. Right. Now tie it over my eyes. Use the tape on the table to make the blindfold light-proof."

Moving in slow motion, she blindfolded him. Darkness whispered down around him. She taped it thoroughly in place. "Now am I still pointing two guns at you?"

"Yes." But there was uncertainty in her voice.

"Now take a step to one side. No, take several steps, very softly, move around a lot." The soft sounds of her movement. Her gasp. "Is the gun following you around the room?"

"Yes. Yes. One of them."

"But how is that possible? *I can't see you!* And why did I let you blindfold me if I'm ready and willing to shoot you?"

"You look weird like that, man. Ridiculous and scary," Charlie said.

"Shut up, Charlie, will you? Answer me, Julie! I can't see you! How can I follow you with the guns?"

"I don't know!" Her voice cracking.

"Take the guns from my hands! Shoot me! Do it!"

She made a short hissing sound, and took the gun from his hand, and he braced to die. But she pulled the blindfold away and looked at him.

Looked into his eyes.

She let the gun drop to the floor. Kessler said, softly: "You see now? They did it to you. You, one of the 'family.' The corporate 'family' means just exactly nothing to them."

She looked at his hands. "No gun. No gun." Dreamily. "Gun's gone. Everything's different."

Siren warblings. Coming closer.

She sank to her knees. "Just exactly nothing to them," she said. "Just exactly nothing." Her face crumpled. She looked as if she'd fallen into herself, some inner scaffolding had been kicked out of place.

Sirens and lights outside. A chrome fluttering in the smoky gap where the wall had been blown outward; a police surveillance bird. It looked like a bird, hovering in place with its oversized aluminum hummingbird's wings; but instead of a head it had a small camera lens. A transmitted voice droned from a grid on its silvery belly: "*This is the police. You are now being observed and taped. Do not attempt to leave. The front door has been breached. Police officers will arrive in seconds to take your statements. Repeat—*"

"Oh, I heard you," Julie said, in a hollow voice. "I'll make a statement all right. I've got a lot to tell you. Oh yeah." She laughed sadly: "I'll make a statement . . ."

Kessler bent down, and touched her arm. "Hey . . . I—"

She drew back from him. "Don't touch me. Just don't! You love to be right. I'm going to tell them. Just don't touch me."

But he stayed with her. He and Charlie stood looking at the blue smoke drifting out the ragged hole in the wall; at the mechanical, camera-eyed bird looking back at them.

He stayed with her, as he always would, and they listened for the footsteps outside the door.

SEIZA

Steven Schwartz

I sit in seiza.

The formal posture is appropriate, fitting the room, rice paper stretched between teak, the hardwood floors beginning to burn my calves. Feet stretched out, resting my weight on the ankles, knees bent.

I sit in seiza and remember.

The crowd flowed out of the Narita International Terminal and down the elevators like the waterfall in a Hokusai print, its lines remaining harmonious, orderly, until they dashed themselves to pieces on the ground floor, splitting up to find their cabs, limousines, buses. I stood, a rock in the middle of this rush, and waited for my client. Narita always moved me to poetry. Something had to, after all, and my work was far from poetic. Unlike the man I waited for.

He was one of the last, and stood out like a fish leaping in that waterfall, head and shoulders above the sararimen and the returning tourists. All I could see was the golden hair and the trenchcoat.

Normally I would have preferred a Japanese hacker, if for no other reason than inconspicuousness, but the people paying me were interested in no one less than the best. They had considered hiring a tiger team as well – I had spent time in California looking for a good one. In the end, though, this was the sort of subtle work a top-notch hacker was needed for. They could bring less raw power to bear than a team, but more subtlety. So it was Schillebeeckx. He might be conspicuous, but he was the best, and once we had him safely ensconced, it would matter very little. I readied myself for the meeting.

He made it no easier. Striding off one of the escalators without changing his pace, carrying nothing but an attaché case and a small duffel, he walked purposefully towards the rental services. Following him, I found myself caught up in the crowd, unable to keep up with his long-legged gait. I just watched as he put his bags down and talked to the rental people. Picking up a key, he started back in my direction.

Walking up to him, I put on my best professional face, and inquired if he was in need of a guide.

Smiling, he accepted. There was nothing I could do but stumble, as he had violated the meeting protocol we'd established earlier over the phone. Following him, I asked, "Where were you planning on going?"

"My hotel is in the Miruzaki building." tossed over one bony shoulder.

I stopped in my tracks. My name is Miruzaki Mira. I was stunned at such a blatant disregard of security, such a flaunting of information no one was supposed to overhear. Did he think that because in the Net he could keep secrets in a crowd, it was that simple here? I did not know who from Matsushita might be watching. All I could hope was that a Westerner with a female guide wouldn't attract attention.

The road for Kyoto was uncrowded, for who drove in this day and age, with the Bullet Trains faster and cheaper? Schillebeeckx was not supposed to have rented a car, but now we had no choice but to drive. Halfway there, among mountains and high-rises, he turned his back on what scenery there was, letting the car handle the driving. He looked at me, trying to mould his harsh features into as forgivable a face as possible, raising his eyebrows and slacking his jaw slightly.

"I couldn't help but put you on. You looked so utterly serious waiting there . . ." chuckling at his own weakness.

"That was my cover," I replied. I might have to work with him, but I didn't have to like him. At my reply, the face drained of softness, returning the hawk nose and the high cheekbones, and he looked down after a moment, lost in thought. As Mt Fuji appeared in the window, I was reminded of just how foreign he was, the lines in his twenty-nine-year-old face contrasting with the seamless face I showed him, only one year younger. We drove on to Kyoto in silence, the only interruption being the beeps of the traffic computer, as it shifted from expressway to local mode. It bore us in that same silence to the house I'd bought, now dubbed "The Hotel Miruzaki".

When we arrived, he hefted his suitcase and attaché case into the house, not letting me touch either. I could understand, since he was a hacker, and that luggage contained his livelihood. I walked ahead, and unlocked the bolt on the door, sliding it open for him. I could read in his face his amusement at locking a rice-paper-walled house. Passing me, he set down the cases in the front hall.

"So, which room is mine?" he asked, in fluent Japanese. I was surprised – so far we'd only spoken Dutch, out of politeness. I guessed that he was trying to go native.

"Right in there, Gunther," with a wave of my hand indicating half the house. It was a difficult switch, from my usual behaviour; now I would be bowing, and respectfully indicating where he was to be, if he were Japanese. But he was not. We couldn't be just business partners, or he would feel that he had insulted me personally.

He had, but that was beside the point. My job was to make him work better. Seeing that he still stood in the hallway, I repeated my gesture, saying "Truly, half is yours, and half is mine. It seemed reasonable."

Smiling, he shrugged, and walked into his half of the house.

Seiza is a very meditative pose, one that many Westerners mistake for a basic Yoga pose. The immobility, the simplicity: that must be what makes them think this.

Meditation is a strange thing – for some, the immobility of a position is what brings them closer to what they seek, for others a kata carried out to perfection. For Gunther, it was work, the twitch of muscle a twitch of program, muscle memory turned into software. That was his meditation.

The wooden chair did not fit the room, nor did the table Gunther was setting his deck on. Too different, too far off the ground. His lithe body towered over the rest of the room, towered over me as I lounged on the tatami and watched. I'd done some hacking, but that was in the past. There was just as much money in finding people to do things as doing them yourself. Still, I almost regretted it as I watched him connect cables to boxes with the care of a lover, the fingers of a painter drifting over the surface, tightening a connection here and there, weaving the cables into a tapestry, not unlike the one on the wall. More symbolic, perhaps, but just as beautiful. I stood, and saw that he didn't even notice my movement. Walking out, I took one last look back, seeing the geometric perfection of the room marred by the chrysanthemum- and cherry-coloured weave of wire in its centre. Gunther was not a tidy person.

Things settled into a routine. I woke up first, made coffee and took out two precooked breakfasts, ate mine, and left the other for Gunther. He stumbled in about ten minutes later, and once I was sure that he was coherent enough to avoid pouring the coffee into his cereal, I took my bath. By the time I was out of the bath, he was working. After that, I just avoided disturbing him until dinner.

So much time was spent waiting. There could be no rush in this business. No matter how carefully prepared one was, it was not enough. Gunther's progress was slow, much of his time spent just waiting and observing, looking for the cracks in Matsushita's defences. There was a time limit to this work – my employers could not wait forever – but Gunther was patient. It was not my employer's lives at stake.

Watching him work was disconcerting, and I tried to avoid it. There was, truly, little to see. His fingers would move over the keyboard occasionally, adjusting something, but the rest of his time was spent as a lump, breathing, but doing little more than that, held into a human posture by the design of the chair. Was that lump truly Gunther Schillebeeckx, one of the best at his business, drinker of Scotch whisky and avid reader of Mishima? Was that lump the person I spoke to at dinner of a thousand-and-one subjects, from the latest news of the net-world to the architecture of the Imperial Palace in Kyoto? Somehow it did not fit, the whole tableau of Gunther, chair, table, and deck. The room looked as if a surrealist such as Gunther fancied had sculpted it, perhaps Magritte; to me no man with a bird-cage for a chest could have been quite as strange, quite as different.

I went about my business when I could – going out and providing Gunther's rather obscure and voluminous needs became difficult. He helped by going native, but even so, what was dinner for a Japanese man was an appetizer for him.

My job was more than that, however. The contract from Chicago, Inc. was quite clear – the run had to be done from within Matsushita's corporate sphere, using local lines. Anything else would be too slow, and far too vulnerable. That they showed such concern was atypical; it spoke far more of how difficult the run itself was than of how much they cared for Gunther's health.

When I asked what he was supposed to retrieve, all they gave me was a file description. Typical of them, so I spoke with a few acquaintances I had within different parts of Chicago, Inc. They said only that something was hot, that Matsushita and Verticorp out of New York were making life difficult for each other. Chicago, Inc., was playing the vulture. Something was worth the expense.

So I had brought Gunther to Kyoto. Keeping him safe there was another matter. The guards outside were well armed and polite. The politeness was camouflage, for they portrayed the owner of this house as a man of position, not just a typical sarariman. Keeping the cover maintained took up much of my time, and kept me away from the figure in the ergonomic chair.

Dinner and the evening were different matters. For some reason, Gunther preferred to work during the day, different from his normal procedure. When I asked him, he told me that in Paris, he and his wife worked at night and slept during the day so that they could have the daytime together – neither was big on nightlife. I accepted his reply then, though it did not ring true; it was a non-answer, at best.

After dinner, he had his Scotch, and I had my Suntory. I could never get used to the harshness of his whiskey, and he preferred its strength to Suntory's. I joked about it, asking him, "You try so hard to be Japanese in other ways, why not in this one?"

Always with a smile, never with a laugh, he retorted, "I have to keep some of myself close to home."

One day I pressed the question. "And so why don't you drink Dutch whiskey?"

That moved him to laugh. "Have you ever tried Dutch whiskey?"

We laughed together, his cackle scratching the walls, harmonizing with my ringing laugh.

But that was later, after so much else had happened.

★   ★   ★

I can't explain it. It happened, is all, and I can no more explain it than I can explain a flower. Certainly I could tell you of each petal, each moment – or could I? By now, the memories have gone the way of feeling in my feet, mostly numb, some not to be found. The best I can do is reconstruction, then, like a vase glued together, the beauty of its shape held together by blank plaster.

It was beautiful. How can I say it, how can I describe it without sounding trite? Without retreating into melodrama? Hoshû once said, of poetry – "When description fails, state."

We loved.

It started, as all such things do in our world, with casualness. The first time Gunther omitted the bathrobe and the pajama tops from his morning's dress was a shock, true. It was strange, to see this person who you've come to think of as being black turtle-necked suddenly revealed as having a chest, in the same pale colours as the hands and face you've come to know. The first day he didn't wear a top it was funny, seeing him wrap the robe around him, not wanting me to see. Why became clear later, when he'd gotten over his fears. He wasn't a bear, was far from hairy, despite the beard and longish hair. Clearly he'd been afraid of being a disappointment, not the hirsute giant of a man Westerners are often portrayed as. It was funny, the first few times. Then, it became routine, and not worth noticing.

The Suntory glasses also fit into my memory, calling back the day I returned from shopping to find him gone. The panic and fear I put into the guards' hearts, I am somewhat surprised they survived. According to them, he had simply slipped out, and they didn't know where he had gone. One of them presumed that I had been with him. The day, which had been a gorgeous one, turned immediately sour. The wind that had so playfully blown my hair half an hour ago now seemed to blow nothing but dust in my face. Waiting was the worst part, inside the rice-paper house that now seemed not light, but fragile, inconsequential. I couldn't go looking for Gunther, that would attract too much attention. A six-foot-tall tourist speaking fluent Japanese might be able to go unnoticed by Matsushita, but not if we went looking for him.

There was so much to worry about, so many little mistakes,

little details. While he tried, so hard, to be Japanese here, that was still far, far different from being Japanese, or at least enough so to attract no notice, in Kyoto.

In the Net, he was safe. The way a well-armed, well-trained man was safe in the midst of a battle. Out there, in the real world, he was vulnerable. Matsushita security, mundane or exotic. Who knew what might be out there, waiting for him?

Finally, I was reduced to sitting in his chair, running my hand over his deck, hoping that like some talisman it would bring him back, that he wouldn't have left without it. I wonder now just why I wanted him back, whether it was the job, or something else.

Whatever it had been then, I was so happy to see him return that I could almost cry, and angry enough that I did. He brushed my complaints and my comments off, and walked with his package into his bedroom, the one room he'd kept strictly private of the four rooms he occupied. He stayed there until dinner, giving me time to simmer and to worry, hoping to catch a sight of him in his workroom, perhaps a glimpse of him reading on his porch, or doing whatever he did in the third room, anything so long as it was not in that last private place.

At dinner we did not speak – he gave me no *ma*, no pause in his concentration, which might let me speak naturally, rather than having to call him out. That was certainly something I was entitled to do, he had endangered both of us and jeopardized the job, but I could not bring myself to harangue him. I realize now that it was the first day, the first few words, that I lost control over the situation, the relationship.

After dinner, still making no contact, either with his eyes or his voice, he walked over to the bar, pulling the small package out of a pocket and opening it. I tried my best to play his indifference game, not showing any interest in what he did.

The next thing I knew I had a Suntory whiskey glass under my nose, filled with a fine single malt. Looking up, I saw that he had the same drink in a similar glass. In a quiet voice, one I remembered from the drive to Kyoto, he asked, "Can I bribe you into forgiveness? I even tried to find a proper bribe . . ."

The look in his eyes was so hopeful that I had to laugh. That was a mistake, as I had just started my drink. I half-laughed, half-coughed my way over to a tatami, where I was able to sit down and get my breath. He opened one wall, to see the stars, then came down and sat next to me, a smile of satisfaction stretching across his face. We clinked our glasses, and looked out over the trees.

After a pause, I asked him, "Why did you do that?"

Looking confused and defensive, he said, "I thought it would amuse you, thought it would make you laugh . . . was I wrong? I mean, aside from going out alone, but that was the only way I could surprise . . ."

I calmed him down with a grin, reassuring him that that wasn't what I meant. When I'd gotten him to stop apologizing, I repeated my question, with a small change. "What made you change your whiskey? What happened to reminding you of Europe?"

A silence fell, then he looked away, back out over the trees. "Right now, I don't want to be reminded."

I restrained the questions straining at my lips, questions about his career, his home, and, most importantly, his wife.

We passed the rest of the evening in silence.

When you spend ten hours a day in the Net, stretching your mind and nothing else, there is a great deal of energy to be burned off, a great deal of tension to be worked out. This much I remembered from my own brief days hacking. I could guess part of how Gunther burned off that energy when he was at home, but I had no idea how he did it here. I knew he went off into the fourth room of his half, but what he did there I did not venture a guess.

To this day, I do not know whether I found out by accident or intentionally. Normally I took my bath in the morning, while Gunther was still groping his way through breakfast. That day, though, I had to go into town early, to pass on a progress report personally to my contact. Gunther had been working ten- to twelve-hour days, getting six hours of sleep a night, and he had made progress. The information I was supposed to give my contact, about penetration layers and counterwalls readied, had come from him verbatim, and I could only judge Gunther's progress from the fact that he remained happy and my contact was willing to buy me lunch after I passed on my message, while before he had wished to break off our meetings as soon as possible.

I returned that day and discovered that Gunther had already finished his day's work, and was doing whatever he did in his spare room. It had been a hot day in Kyoto, and I was glad to wash myself off and sink into the waters of the bath to try and loosen the muscles that had tightened from the drive and from the tension of meeting my contact.

I never locked the door – there was no point in it when I bathed while Gunther was working. It was a shock, though, to see Gunther walk into the bathroom in a black gi with a brown belt and start to strip.

He didn't see me, and I was not sure I wanted to disturb him, but in the interest of keeping everyone comfortable and working well I thought I ought to warn him of my presence.

A simple cough was enough to bring his attention over to the bath, where I lay with just my head above the water. Averting his eyes, he said, "Excuse me, I had no idea . . ."

"No, no, it's my fault," I said, "normally I take my bath in the mornings. Let me just grab a towel . . ."

He drew himself up to his full height and tried to look chivalrous. "No, you go ahead and finish your bath, I'll wait outside."

It was clear that if he waited outside for any length of time the floorboards would warp from the sweat he dripped on them. Finally I decided that one might as well accept the inevitable. "Look, Gunther, I have seen men before. Why don't you wash and come in – I am sure it's not a first for you either . . ."

His shoulders sagged, then came back up into a shrug. Removing his gi, he started to soap himself vigorously before climbing in. I didn't regret convincing him, and for not the first time I started thinking *If only* . . ., and then killed the thought as quickly as possible, trying to keep things to business. I noticed that he seemed to be doing the same, humming a piece of music I knew he knew poorly, concentrating as hard as he could on getting it right, to exclude anything else.

When he climbed in, I made a bit of room, then told him of what the contact had said. The praise seemed to cheer him, and made him much more comfortable. We started into a discussion of Matsushita security, and soon we were so involved that we did not notice as the sun set and the water grew cold.

It was the first time I'd seen Gunther at work. I'd seen his body before, perhaps, but not his mind. I was able to contribute to the discussion, but mainly by steering it out of the Net and into broader topics, or offering a metaphor that would let me grasp what he was saying. When we talked about the Net, I felt childlike, missing words that he would casually drop, then explain as a term he'd developed for something he did. It was a different language, and a fascinating one.

Dinner that night was animated, as Gunther did his best to pitch in and help, the first time in the two months he had been in the house. I set him to carving, a job he seemed accustomed to, as I cooked up the vegetables. The transition from kitchen to table never really happened, as we talked and ate as we finished cooking. It was clear that Gunther was glad to spend the time with someone else, someone who wasn't trying to kill him in the Net, someone he did not need to hide from.

Over Suntory, we talked about Mishima and Böll, out on his porch. It always struck me as strange, those conversations. Gunther, a year older than I and yet so much older-seeming, championed Böll, who tried to coax the flowers of hope to grow from the ashes of postwar Germany. I did my best to defend the doom of Mishima. It never became, as it so easily could have, a discussion of Europeans and Japanese, somehow. That night, though, the conversation soon wound down, and the silence had become tense when Gunther walked back in to get the bottle of whisky.

I felt I had to say something, press the question, yet it went against all of my better judgment. What could I do, risk losing the job, or even our lives, over a few nice gestures, and what might come of them? I resolved to remain silent.

When Gunther returned, he poured another glass for each of us and then walked to the edge of the porch. He'd taken to wearing yukatas at night, and the sight of him silhouetted against the Kyoto lights, the European in the yukata, was so incongruous it was funny. A smile crossed my lips, only to be stifled when his eyes met mine, full of intensity and worry.

"Mira, you'll have to forgive me, but I'm about to be horribly European and unsubtle. Can you deal with that?"

The attitude worried me, but what choice? I nodded.

He started to speak, then paced across the porch. Finally he came to rest sitting down next to me.

"Katrin and I, we have what you might call . . . an open relationship . . ." The words came out of him as if he were a fourteen-year-old asking for his first date. The laugh I'd suppressed before now came out in full flower, and I was afraid for a moment it could be heard in Kyoto, in the apartments whose lights backlit the whole scene.

He had reared back, half ashamed and half hurt. To reassure him, I leaned forward and kissed him. It took him by surprise, and he toppled over backwards. Still laughing, I leaned further over.

If the guards didn't hear, I am grateful. If they did, what does it matter? It was worth it. Afterwards, he told me he'd worried about his hairless chest, but that made no difference to me. I liked to feel him against me, not some rug. So many things were different with him, different than with others, as well, so that one similarity was almost reassuring, as he held onto me.

Once, he'd rolled on top of me, and I'd felt closed in, unable to breathe. Opening my eyes, I saw I was looking at his ribs, and the feeling got tighter. All it took was a hint, a little pressure, and he moved back, and I returned to the top.

At the end, he was tired, too tired to move. He fell asleep where we had been, and I sat next to him, seated on my heels, resting my hips, stretched far enough before. I just sat and watched him sleep in the city light for a while before I, too, lay down and slept.

Many judo and fencing schools use seiza. One reason is that it seems to be an ultimately indefensible posture – you can't use your feet, and the slightest movement from side to side can unbalance you, if you let it. But you are aware of your centre, aware of your focus. It is deceiving.

Our defences are limited, and weak, save when we are centred. There was nothing I could have done in the situation, probably nothing he could have done . . . would fighting have made it any better? Where was our centre?

We had been sleeping together for less than a week when it arrived, by special courier. Gunther was jacked in, and I had just finished my lunch, when the guard at the gate called up and announced the courier's arrival.

"So, collect the message."

There was a discussion at the other end of the line, and then the guard, using his best apologetic tones, replied "The courier says he can only deliver it to you."

"All right. Bring him up."

Walking over to the door, I paused to pick up my pistol from the side table it had rested on. As I slid the door open, I made sure the gun was ready. Much to my satisfaction, the guard already had the courier covered, and the courier clearly knew it.

Reaching out a hand, I said "You can give it to me." He complied, and then turned to head back for the gate. The guard saluted me and followed.

Closing the door, I examined the envelope. It was from my contact, using the business name for me that we had agreed on. We had also agreed that this method was only to be used in case of emergency. The last thing I needed right now was an emergency. I went over to my desk and pulled out a letter-opener.

Inside was a single sheet of paper. I read through the message, and my fingers didn't keep enough control to hold it. It fell onto the floor, face down. Looking at it, I held the hope for a moment that it had been a mistake, that I had misread it. To make sure I could read it this time, I picked it up and put it on my desk. Upon rereading, I knew that I had made no mistake.

"Katrin Schillebeeckx was killed in an illegal intrusion against Verticorp. Your employee's behaviour may well change if this information is revealed to him. Whether you choose to do so is at your discretion."

First, no matter what else I did, I had to destroy the message. I used the candle I'd set for last night's dinner to start it burning, and I watched the curl of smoke go out the window above the sink. I thought, if only I could make the truth blow away as easily.

When the paper had burned to ashes, I washed the ashes down the drain, wiping my desk clean with a wet cloth. Going back to our bedroom, I tried to decide what to do. Which was more important, the relationship or the job, that was the first question I posed. It seemed to me that if I told him now, he might well abandon the job, and me, to go after Verticorp. I had seen it before, among the mercs I'd recruited in Singapore and Macao – they would have buddies, and if a buddy died, vengeance became their sole priority, above the job, above survival, above love.

If I did not tell him, though, he was bound to learn, at the latest when the job was over. Then I would be a liar, a deceiver, and I would lose him forever.

It seemed that he was lost no matter what I did.

Now, of course, I wish I could change, do anything else, but what I did is done, and I will live with it.

That night, after he jacked out and did his karate practice, I met him just inside the door of the bath, dressed appropriately. It took him much longer to bathe than usual.

Every night became more important, each time he touched me more precious. The cherry trees were blossoming outside, and already the early blossoms had fallen to the ground, making a pink carpet for the guards to patrol on. I no longer thought of him as something I had for a short while now, and perhaps later, perhaps some other time. The time we had now was all the time we would have, and I acted that way.

Two weeks after I received the message, Gunther came in to talk to me after a day's run. Noticing the broad grin on his face, I asked him what had caused it.

"Hail Caesar, those about to die salute thee. I'm ready, and tomorrow I'm going in." The grin was tinged with fear, but the main thing that showed in his face, in his movements as we fixed dinner, was excitement.

I hesitated over going to him that night, not knowing whether he would want sex the night before a run. My hesitation was misplaced, though, as we again drank whiskey on the porch, and without speaking, slipped out of our clothes.

The nights before he had been extremely gentle, doing everything he could to make sure I was unhurt, not threatened by his bulk. Tonight things were different, and I did not mind. As we strained against each other, I could feel the pressure of his hand on my back, and knew tomorrow there would be a bruise, but I didn't mind. It was the last night.

The day of the run was terrible. After his morning coffee had been supplemented by third and fourth cups, he jacked in, and all I could do was wait. By the fourth hour I knew every corner of that house as if I had lived there all my life, from the knothole on the otherwise perfect door-frame at calf height to the angled tatami in Gunther's room, angled so that the sun wouldn't hit his eyes no matter when he was sleeping there.

By the eighth hour the second bath I had taken had worn off, and my muscles were knotted again. My head had started pounding from my own blood pressure. I'd stood this death-watch before, but before it had been the data that were crucial, the hacker just the conduit to success, another job complete. Now, I clung to whatever I could get, worried both for Gunther and his job. If he failed, I lost everything.

In the tenth hour, he jacked out. With a thumbs-up from his bleary face, he staggered into his room and fell asleep.

I was woken the next day by the sound of yelling. "What the bloody verdommte hell do you mean there's no one at that number – look, that's my home number and I know damn well that my wife lives there!" I didn't even stop to put anything on as I headed out into the hallway. He stood over the end table, telephone in his hand and veins bulging on his forehead.

"Katrin Schillebeeckx is the name, all right? Look that one up in your damn Stone Age computers!" Looking up from the floor, he fixed his eyes on me, and it was not with a friendly stare. I froze in my tracks.

"Yes? What?" The yell shook the print next to Gunther, and I prayed that the guards would follow orders and stay outside. The volume dropped, and Gunther's last words were choked out. "I see. Dead, you say. Two weeks. Thank you." Looking up at me, I knew he understood. The eyes that had looked at me lovingly before, the lips that had called me Miriko, all combined to produce an expression, not of hatred, but of contempt. He threw the phone down, and it shattered into pieces, spreading over the floor like ripples from a stone. Without another word, he walked back into his room.

It took him four hours to pack. I spent them sitting in the hall, sitting in seiza, with my weight on my heels and my feet stretched out. He didn't even glance at me the whole time he was packing the car, up until the end. He looked me over, as I sat there naked, hands and knees folded. I glanced up to catch his eyes one last time. His expression was one of noncomprehension, of betrayal. Finally, he tossed down his cigarette, the first I'd seen him smoke in Japan, and ground it out. Then he tensed, and walked outside, no emotion showing in his face or his movements. I sat there until I heard the car drive away.

Why seiza? What is it for?

Purification. Sit in it for hours and your feet lose circulation, your calves burn, your knees hurt, but the wrong is drained out along with your strength.

Do something wrong in the kendo class and you may be sent to seiza.

In the kendo class, the sensei tells you when you are done.

I sit in seiza and remember.

AXL AGAINST THE IMMORTALS

Jon Courtenay–Grimwood

Rolling the old woman into a carpet, Jerry ran a rope around both ends, then heaved the sausage shape onto the roof rack of a Volvo and tied it down with those rubber ropes his quarter-master insisted on calling *bungies*.

The carpet by itself weighed at least as much as the dead woman inside. But even so their combined weight did little more than make the Volvo's suspension creak. And Jerry wasn't worried about that. He was on a night boat from Morocco to Alicante in Spain and the car deck was dark and happily deserted, lit by a red glow that oozed from the occasional bulkhead light.

He might have been in Paris, in the Rue St Denis propping up a bar but to run that gig his boss had brought in Axl; a freelancer so dangerous he got talked about only as *him*. So Jerry got the dead granny, followed by a Chinese restaurant in Madrid where he had to microwave a champion-grade chihuahua in the name of cultural misunderstanding.

Still, it could have been worse and frequently was. The previous month he'd wasted three days sourcing a corpse in some half-horse town outside Baton Rouge. All Jerry had actually needed were the dead man's fingers, which he left hanging from the rear fender of a battered Cadillac being used by two kids to make out. Although, obviously enough, he'd had to pound on the roof of their car and flatten his face against the Cadillac's front windscreen, the usual shit.

So tonight was pretty easy really. One dead granny, pre-supplied, a fake passport to link her to the driver of the Volvo. Wrap her in the rug which Jerry, in the guise of a stall holder, had bullied the Volvo driver into buying the day before and that was it. One urban legend reprised. All the same, he'd have liked to be allowed a shot at the Paris gig, whatever it actually was.

The other city, the one where Axl first met the girl had been bombed back to a street plan long before Axl came rolling into town on the back of a stolen Motoguzzi. Nothing remained of the city except broken neon and unanswered prayers. Only Armageddon had arrived not with the B52s and 5000lb bunker busters, but later, carried as spores on the chill wind and held in stagnant water. Those who survived the plague died from winter and famine as snow shut the high mountain passes and trapped the aid agencies in their camps.

Hospitals might have helped but there were no hospitals. No schools. No teachers. No nurses. The Emir had banned them all, imposing a stark simplicity on this shattered wilderness of a country and returning to God alone the right to decide between life and death (that was the theory anyway). Without doctors or nurses to mediate, God's decisions proved to be both frequent and harsh, but still not as harsh as the laws promulgated by the Emir and his council.

Cars collide/colours clash . . . The line rose out of nowhere and hit Axl dead centre. A slight syncopated brush of snare giving way to screeching guitar as Axl slammed his glass back on the zinc. He hated that shit. Soundtracks were meant to be based around sound and music, diegetic or not. This fashion for overlays of random words, stolen sentences, it got in the way of real meaning.

It was dangerous too, in his opinion . . . Anything that got between Axl and his in-skull soundtrack was dangerous because the track *was* his reflexes.

"Drink," he told the girl.

Looking at her glass the kid scowled, full lips twisting. She had green eyes like a cat, high cheekbones and skin so pale that the white plastic cuffs locking her wrist to the bar hardly showed up at all. Her breasts were full, obvious even beneath a red silk cheongsam, her nipples pink like sunrise, her body hair arctic blonde. Axl knew this because he'd had to dress her at gun point in a tatty hotel room, three storeys above a Parisian bakery off Rue de Buci.

Then he'd made her walk across Pont St Michel, through Ile de la Cité and past the expensive restaurants springing up in Les

Halles, until they reached this bar. Men had watched her every step of the way.

"Drink," Axl repeated.

She drank. And then drank some more until those green eyes glazed and only the cuffs and one white-knuckled hand gripping at a chrome rail stopped her from slipping from the stool.

"You have your purse?"

The girl blinked at him and Axl sighed, a slight kick of bass underwriting his irritation. He took the bag from her lap and checked inside. Tampons, ID card made out in the name of Fifi Washington, Lucky Strike, a half bottle of cheap vodka, a warp of crystalMeth and a purse. Inside the purse was a handful of change and pack of condoms. Everything she needed to survive her first night on the streets. That was the rule, and if this gig ever got run again then it would become precedent as well, although Axl couldn't see how this loop would run more than once.

He'd picked her up at Aeroport Louis Napoleon. Off the flight from Annapolis. Originally the surgery was to done in Moscow but the Soviet clinics turned out to be unable to meet the required specifications so the US Navy offered to do the honours, in fact they were positively keen. (Although the same couldn't be said for their selected surgeon.)

The kid had arrived wearing dark glasses, a headscarf tied tightly around her hair and a thin coat, and Axl had recognized her instantly; even though it had taken her a minute or two to recognize Axl. Of course, since she'd last seen him he'd changed his eyes back to blue and had a shave, a shit, a shower and a shoeshine. The usual. Plus he rolled up at LN Arrivals in an old Paul Smith job lined with blade-resistant spiders silk, instead of what he'd been wearing the first time they met, a goat-skin bedou that stank of . . .

Camel dung, maybe. Not that this really mattered. Some kind of dried shit was burning in the dip of an ornamental carp pool at the front of the Al Jay Hyatt, built in one of the craters that pocked the pond's shattered concrete bottom.

Dung was most likely because everything else flammable was already used up, including all the herb bushes from a stone-walled medical garden next door. That half the western newsfeeds were still screaming ecological vandalism *said it all for Axl; having picked his way into the hotel complex between the dried husk of an infant impaled on a fence and the sinewed roadmap of a crucified aid worker, grubbed-up herbaceous borders no longer did it for him.*

The Hyatt had been built decades before in that faux Moorish style which was meant to make it blend in with a culture a thousand years older and failed completely. Maybe that was why the Emir's men had burnt what remained unbombed to a shell, but somehow Axl doubted it. The place had originally featured a swimming pool where sexes mixed. A bar. A cinema. Any one of those would have been enough. All three together had made the complex a certain target.

In love with the modern world, Axl didn't think so. . . . He stank, of course. Two weeks of intentionally not washing gave him a certain authenticity but what had really made him invisible on the trip in was his bedou, a dirty-brown job cut from untreated goat skin, looking as bad as it smelt. Although this was no worse than everybody else now left in the hotel, all five of them.

The Emir, three Immortals and Axl, four to one, the kind of odds to guarantee top-flight ratings. Only this gig wasn't going out live. It was to be a New Year special, syndicated across six continents and three orbitals, not to mention LunaWorld . . .

There were two ways of doing what he was being sent to do, Axl's boss had announced. Surgical or dirty. Surgical meant coming in by copter, establishing a perimeter using back-up and having that perimeter held while Axl did the hit. Only the Cardinal didn't intend to insult Axl by suggesting he be sent to do what any half-trained seal pup could manage. No, the Cardinal wanted this done down and dirty and for that Axl was the Cardinal's man.

Neither of them questioned this statement. The Cardinal because he didn't need to and Axl because he wasn't that stupid. Besides, he was getting paid handsomely for the job. If getting five years deducted from a contract he hadn't wanted to sign counted as getting paid.

Getting the girl to co-operate in getting dressed had been simple. All Axl had to do was threaten to toss her out into Rue de Buci still naked. Base line established, Axl had threaded her arms through thin straps, tucked both breasts inside a bra and fastened its snap catch at the back. The bra was Italian, underwired and cut from translucent Chinese silk that had little rose branches curled across its surface, each one bristling with tiny thorns sharp enough to tear his fingers.

Poetic licence, dramatic irony, urban myth in the making. Axl had forgotten which one this was meant to be. . . . In his head he had goat-skin drums and an oued, the finger pick of a simple melody sweetening a call to prayer so harsh that it raised hairs on the back of his skull, although that could have been his memories.

Doing it dirty meant no fooler loops, no parabolic mic, no GPS spex, no body armour. Axl had been left reliant on instinct, his soundtrack and drugs. Plenty of drugs.

Clenching his fist, he fixed himself for the ones like . . .

The image rippled into Axl's mind on a finger pluck of minor chords. Yeah, right. Not with a ceramic implant in his wrist, just waiting to take custom-made ampoules, he didn't. Flipping out the cylinder on his Colt, Axl checked it for the third time, spun it once and snapped it back into place and stuffed the loaded revolver in his bedou pocket. He had a long, wide-blade pedang, a shiv or three, glass blades designed to break off at the hilt and a garrotte made from long line monofilament. All bought from a tatty market in a town fifty klicks behind him, along with a handful of tiny 145db flash/bangs.

Only those were a last resort because Axl knew the Cardinal's post-retribution budget didn't stretch to buying the Emir new inner ears. Not when there was so much else required.

Crawling to his knees, Axl pulled out a single shiv, thought about his options for all of a nanosecond and grabbed the others, putting the first between his teeth and hefting the other two, left and right, pirate style. Somewhere high above him the comsat angels would be recording every over-blown bloody gesture. And the Cardinal would be furious, since his final briefing had stressed the need to be elegantly understated. Doing it this way was Axl's rebellion. Tiny, he knew, but his own.

A flight to Paris was booked. A dress had been ordered. Identity constructed. All that remained was to flesh out the last two of those, literally. Axl was stood in an operating theatre at the naval base in Annapolis. Outside, a rusting Polaris submarine waited, bolted shut for the winter, missing the tourists who usually lined up to knock their heads on hatches or sprain the odd ankle climbing down some narrow ladder.

"How big?" the surgeon asked.

The boy in a leather jacket shrugged. Apparently he was some special ops genius, or maybe it was psy ops. . . . Commander Cooper had made a point of not listening. She didn't like being dragged back from Hawaii without a by-your-leave.

"I need a size," she said crossly.

"Same as you," said the boy.

Commander Leila Cooper began to glare and realised that he wasn't being funny. "Thirty-four C," she said flatly.

"Sounds good to me," the boy said and this time a slight smile flicked across his thin face as he wrapped himself tighter into his jacket. It looked old, maybe older than he was; and had undoubtedly cost more than she was earning in a month back when it was bought, which would have been maybe twenty years ago. When she was at med school, working weekends behind a bar. That being the last time jackets cut like those had been in fashion.

Axl caught the surgeon watching him and glanced away, head turned to one side, almost as if he was listening to something.

"Thirty-four C," Leila Cooper said for something to say and concentrated on a tray of implants, bar coded and arranged according to size. Originally implants had been just that, fake tissue implanted. Actually, that was wrong, for a while they'd been jelly-filled sacs and before that, straight injections of industrial silicone, pumped under the skin of whores servicing US bases in Japan. Now of course they were self-anchoring, grown to order using simple stem-cell technology.

Leila Cooper slashed once, discarded her Braun scalpel and slid fingers into the open cut, casually ripping skin from muscle. She was showing off, of course. There were instruments designed specifically for the job but she got a feeling that the boy watching was a hands-on kind of operator.

Now there was a thought . . .

Pushing the implant into place, Leila Cooper shaped the curves to her satisfaction and ran a line of glue along both sides of the cut. And then, because the edges needed to withstand pressure until the skin over the implant got used to its new shape, she tacked in an old-fashioned suture before aligning the edges and running a light wand across the already-fading cut.

She did the other side more carefully. As a result of which the surgery took twice as long and somehow ended up looking not quite so good.

One dead body behind him, three waiting up ahead. They just didn't know it yet.

Axl pulled the pin on a tube of fear gas and dropped it down a long stairwell, not caring if the Emir's men heard the clang or not. By the time they'd tossed up between fight and flight it would already be too late. Their get-up-and-go would have done just that, got up and gone.

Some people the gas terrified, hence the name, others barely reacted but those were in a minority and invariably carried the same recessive gene. Most victims experienced a brief and crippling ennui but boredom gas lacked a certain something so far as a selling point went, so fear gas the stuff remained.

Five, four, three, two, one . . .

Axl grabbed a quick breath and edged down the stairs to the barest shadow of synth that tasted of a track currently charting, a faint shimmer of cymbals, heard and then gone.

Tension through absence.

The effect sent a shiver down Axl's spine as he reached the bottom and came up out of his crouch in a tight jangle of electric violin that spun his blade through a doorway and into an Immortal's throat. And then Axl was standing over his victim, lowering a still-shuddering body to the floor. The glass blade deeply embedded, its handle broken free, Axl's reaction reduced to a slow bass line, little faster than his heartbeat.

Like it or not, he needed to take a breath.

Axl against the Immortals, Axl thought about it, sat beside the dead man's body. He had to admit it was a good title. Apparently the immortals were named after the bodyguard of Darius the Great. Or was it Alexander, his conqueror? The Cardinal had spent a good half-hour giving Axl deep background to the who, what and why . . . Only Axl could never retain stuff like that. He only remembered direct connections; the weight of a blade, the tightness of a three-chord battle, the way his eyes swallowed history and fed it back to the world. A failing of intellect that annoyed the hell out of the man who was his protector, boss and confessor.

Slowly Axl let the ennui pass over him.

Another canister of gas/another set of stairs. The last of the three

Immortals shared a wooden bench in a basement with a sullen young man who had once been ruler of a dozen cities and beloved of God. The bench was unbroken, which made it rare as hen's teeth, and the Immortal didn't even bother to stand up to be killed. Just let Axl slam a blade under his ribs.

And then it was done and all that remained was for Axl to arrest the Emir and get out of there . . .

"I guess," said Axl as he lifted a third Becks to his lips and drained it in one, "your big mistake was to think we actually intended to kill you." He looked round at the crowded Parisian bar with its collection of street walkers, pimps and slumming tourists.

Two of the pimps had already made their feelings plain about what they saw as Axl and the kid moving in on their territory. And although Axl had explained, patiently both times, that Fifi was not in direct competition, he could see from their scowls that neither one believed this assurance.

She had the look, you see. The wide-eyed spoilt innocence that had taken Commander Leila Cooper more than five days in a theatre to achieve. She had the looks, the clothes, an impressive collection of chemical implants to keep her new body in shape and a habit. The kind of habit that was going to keep her walking the streets around Rue St Denis for years to come. Hungry for all civilization could offer.

One more whore in Babylon.

OFFENDERS

Mat Coward

At the Joke Squad, we'd never been busier. It was midwinter, and in my experience the cold weather makes people say things out loud that they'd normally keep to themselves.

DS Geraint Brook didn't seem the kind who bothered much about censoring his speech, though that was probably nothing to do with the weather. He'd been posted to us temporarily, from his usual perch at Robbery/Organized Crime, and he wasn't happy about it.

"No offence, Barney," he said, as we wandered around the New Scotland Yard car park, trying to find the car we'd been assigned, "but the stuff the Joke Squad deals with is trivial crap. I spend my days bagging proper villains, and that's where I should be now."

"First of all, we don't call it the Joke Squad," I lied, slinging my overnight bag into the boot. "It's the Offence-Related Offences Section."

"Even the name's stupid."

"We police inappropriateness-related offences. We do not arrest people for telling jokes." That's not strictly true. We do arrest people for telling jokes – but because they contravene the law, not because they're jokes. "Under human rights legislation, people have the right not to be offended."

Geraint got into the passenger seat, and I started the engine. "Human rights is just a beard," he said. "The world's falling apart, so the powers clamp down on dissent. It's their automatic instinct."

"You're not in favour of religious tolerance, for instance?"

"Oh, bollocks! Listen, you can't give a right to one man,

without taking it away from another. Freedom is like matter – it can be neither created nor destroyed. Yeah? You give a guy the basic human right of freedom of speech, you're denying his neighbour the basic human right not to be insulted. Or vice versa."

I concentrated on my driving for a while.

Geraint looked out of his window at the London traffic. At the fourth set of lights, he said: "Sorry, mate, I don't mean to have a go at you. Truth is, we've got a big one on at Robbery – a gene piracy job – which I've spent almost a *year* working on. And I'm going to miss the denouement so we can go and pick up some daft Yank student for . . . whatever it was you said we were picking her up for."

"Possession and Dissemination of Material Contrary to the Unity of the Homeland."

"Which means what, exactly?"

"She's been reported for having a poster on her bedroom wall ridiculing the US President."

"A poster!" Geraint grunted. "Not an offence under British or European law, is it?"

I was trying to be patient. I'd met Geraint before, at Met sports-and-socials, and I liked him. But he was being deliberately thick this morning. "No, it's not, but it is an offence under US law."

"And the USA does not recognise any boundaries to its writ. So this poor tart gets fast-track extradited." He shook his head, either in disgust or for show. "Why should we collect their garbage? What are they going to do, bomb us?"

I pulled over. Geraint looked surprised and a little worried. Which was what I wanted. I switched off the engine, and turned to face him. "Listen, mate, there's something you should know about me, just in case it's a bit of gossip you've missed. It's a private matter and I only mention it now to avoid future embarrassment. OK?"

"Barney, I'm sorry if I've—"

"Don't worry, it's only this: my father was collateralized during the bombing of Edinburgh." Dad worked in a factory ten miles from the Scottish Parliament – the presumed target, after it had repeatedly refused to privatize its social services to an American multinational. Technically, of course, the USA didn't do the bombing; the multinational did, and five years later was fined almost a million dollars for doing so.

"Oh, shit. Mate, I'm really—"

"So, if you have any opinions about Britain's diplomatic relations with America . . ."

He held out his hands in front of him, either side of his face. "I'll keep them to myself. Apologies."

"Good man."

We drove on quietly. Geraint fidgeted. Eventually, he said what I'd known he'd have to say. Everyone always does. "Barney, I've got to ask. Tell me to sod off, but don't you hate them? The Yanks?"

"I don't hate Americans. They're just people same as us."

"Oh, yeah, sure. But—"

"Look, Geraint, one thing my father's death taught me – be realistic. Either we cooperate with the Americans in arresting their citizens over here, or they'll do it themselves without us. You want the policing of this country handed over to the Americans direct?"

"Hell, no! Hasn't worked very well in Spain, has it?"

"And it is sort of reciprocal, to be fair. I've just finished the paperwork on an Irish guy they nicked for us at an airport in Connecticut."

"Nicked for what?"

"Telling Irish jokes." I let him start to splutter, then I said: "No, he made a joke to a friend about hijacking, at Heathrow. It was caught on tape." I didn't add that the man wasn't arrested at the time of the offence because, until the tape had been enhanced by Customs officers investigating an entirely separate case, the joke was inaudible at a distance of more than thirty centimetres.

As we pulled into the US embassy's car park, Geraint said, "We've actually got to have one of the bastards in the car with us, have we?"

"Don't worry. In my Squad we know how to deal with Feds. They're just a bunch of square-headed, slow-witted, single-brain-cell organisms in ill-fitting suits."

The Fed assigned to us knocked on the window. She was tall, slim, and rather lovely. "Blimey!" said Geraint.

She shook hands. "Agent Hilda Westlake, Office for the Defense of the Homeland. Hi."

"You're black," I said. I hadn't intended to say it aloud.

"Yep," she said. "It's not against the law, not yet."

I couldn't get over that. As I pulled into the traffic, I just couldn't stop thinking about it. It was incredible. I'd never encountered anything like this before. A Yank official had made a *joke*.

Two hours later we arrived at the West University campus, and fifteen minutes after that we were knocking on the door of Elaine Cassidy's room. Geraint had been silent for most of the journey. I could see his point, though I didn't say as much: our job was to collect Cassidy, and drive her to Heathrow. It wasn't exactly brainwork.

"No reply," I said, and knocked again.

Hilda Westlake moved me gently to one side. And turned the door handle.

There was a fair amount of blood, all of it dry. A young woman – Elaine Cassidy, presumably – lay on the floor, her nose smashed beyond recognition. Next to her was a very large book.

"Oh, shit," said Hilda.

"We can still take her to the airport," said Geraint. "With any luck the plane will crash and no one will ever be the wiser."

"We'd better call the local cops," said Hilda. "We don't do murders."

A look passed between me and Geraint. I suppose I felt sorry for him, missing his big case and all. "Don't worry," I said. "My pal Geraint here, he's done more murders than you've had commendations."

"Won't they make trouble if we steal their case?"

Geraint laughed. "They're privatized down here, they don't want murders. Murder eats up resources, and all you get at the end – if you're lucky – is one conviction."

"And no revenue," I added.

"I don't know . . ."

"Listen, Agent Westlake," said Geraint. "In the privatized areas, if you want a cop in a hurry you call in a burglary in progress, say you've got the robbers locked in your vault with your jewel collection. You call in a murder, they'll tell you to phone back during office hours."

"Well, I don't know . . ."

"We'll have to liaise eventually, yeah, but believe me the locals aren't going to fight us for possession of a manpower-gobbling case involving the daughter of rich foreigners."

She looked at me. "How do you know she's rich?"

I shrugged. "Who else goes to university?" I thought it would be easier for Hilda to agree if she didn't actually have to say it, so I changed the subject. "What was she studying?"

"Law. What else does anyone study these days?"

Geraint joined in. "And what was the nature of the complaint against her – a poster, was it?"

Hilda checked her notes. "A poster of the president as a pig."

"Right," I said. "Subversive *and* subtle. So, where is the poster? Shouldn't it be on the wall somewhere?"

It was a three-metre-square room. Bed, books, stereo, lots of shoes. Small statuette of Jesus. Small bathroom, en suite. No posters on the walls at all.

"Maybe she got to hear about the complaint, destroyed the evidence."

"Or maybe," said Geraint, "there never was a poster – malicious complaint?"

Hilda screwed up her face. It was a surprisingly attractive gesture. "We get very few maliciouses. The penalties are . . . significant."

"You must get malicious *anonymous* complaints."

She looked uncomfortable. "Anonymous is kind of a grey area."

"You know who made the complaint in this instance?"

She checked her notes again. "Another law student. Name of Kelly Norton." She frowned. "Actually, that's unusual – the complainant isn't American. She's native. I mean, British."

"*Native?*" Even the good-looking ones have all the social graces of a thunderstorm. "Well, let's see if she's in her mud hut, shall we?"

She wasn't in her mud hut. She was in the student bar, drinking white wine and lemonade with six or seven tall, handsome friends. We detached her from them by means of our charming manner and our ID cards, and she led us to a quiet seating area overlooking lawns, an ornamental fountain, a razor-wire fence, and one of the biggest slum towns in Western Europe. It was a kilometre away, in a shallow valley, but on a bright day you could hear it as clearly as you could see it.

"Kelly, my name is Detective Sergeant Barney Garner, and this is Agent Hilda Westlake." We'd left Geraint at the crime scene to do some preliminaries, him having the relevant know-how.

Kelly Norton chewed her lip and nodded. "You're here about Elaine?"

"Tell us why you complained about her to the embassy," said Hilda.

"Well, she had this poster on her wall – it was, like, really rude. It was a photo of your president, but they'd jiggered it so he looked like a pig."

"Right. And you took offence at this?"

"Wouldn't you? It was disgusting."

I thought her expression of moral outrage a little overdone. But then, as Hilda had said, a complaint from a "native" was unusual. So presumably she was an unusual native.

"So you rang the embassy hotline?"

"Sure. Will she be deported?"

Hilda wrote on her pad, and didn't reply. "Now, when did you see this poster?"

"The evening before last. I rang straight away."

"Was that the only time you saw it?"

The complainant swallowed heavily. "Um . . . I don't remember." For the first time, she switched her attention from Agent Westlake to me. She gave me a half smile, and twisted a length of her brown hair around her fingers.

"Where did you see it?" I asked.

"In her room – I said. It was on her wall."

"And what were you doing in her room?"

Kelly switched back to Hilda. She seemed to have regained her confidence. "Oh, right. I went there to borrow her hairdryer. Mine had blown."

"So Elaine's a friend, then?"

"Not really. I hardly know her at all. We're in a few of the same classes, we live on the same corridor, but we don't mix in the same crowds. You know, the Americans pretty much keep themselves to . . ." She trailed off. "Um – no offence."

Hilda nodded. "So why go to her for a hairdryer?"

"I did knock on a few doors along the corridor before I got to hers. A lot of people had already gone out for the night. She was the first one who answered."

"Whereabouts was the poster?" I asked. "Where on the wall?"

"Well . . . like, just above her desk."

Hilda said: "Did you get the hairdryer?"

"Ah, no. She, like, didn't have one." She gave the sentence a questioning inflection. I took that to mean that this bit, at least, was the truth.

"A fight over a boy?" We were walking back to the dead girl's room, trying to figure out a believable reason for Kelly to have informed on Elaine. And while we were at it, a motive for murder by persons unknown.

"Boyfriend trouble doesn't usually end in murder."

"These days?" she said. "Everything ends in murder. These *varsity* types, they're desperate to get married as young as possible – means they don't have to endure too much sex."

I smiled, and looked at her sideways. "You're an unusual American, you know. It's hard to tell when you're being serious."

"Always," said Hilda. "I work for the federal government, Sergeant. I never joke."

"Right. More than your job's worth."

"More than my life's worth."

Geraint looked a lot happier now that he was doing some proper, morbid work. "No prints on the big law book. Blood, but no prints. As for Elaine, she's been dead since last night. No sign of recent sexual activity, forced or unforced. She *has* been in a fight, though."

I looked around the room. A place for everything, and everything in its place. "Doesn't look like robbery."

"Only thing obviously missing," he agreed, "is the Material Contrary to the Unity of the Homeland."

"The poster," said Hilda. "Right. Well, I guess things are pretty grim outside the campus walls, but I can't think an anti-American poster is worth much."

"It's not anti-American," I said. "Anti-president, not the same thing."

They both ignored me. "Her virtue's intact," said Geraint,

"and so is her sound system. Seems reasonable to guess that the killer had a personal motive."

"This poster," I asked. "Is it one you've seen before?"

Hilda shrugged. "Not offhand. But she could have made it herself. There must be a hundred new posters every day."

"Your department isn't having much effect then, is it?" said Geraint.

"Sergeant, we're not the Gestapo, whatever you may have heard."

"What I'd heard," he replied, "was that you *are* the Gestapo."

She snorted. "Yeah? Well, what does that make you guys? Vichy enforcers?"

I interrupted. She was pretty when she was angry, but he wasn't. "I notice there's no CCTV in the corridor here."

"You're kidding!" Hilda slapped her head, probably in despair at the backwardness of the natives. "A building full of rich people's kids and there's no cameras?"

"Privacy," said Geraint. "The rich are very big on that – especially the rich young. They're in and out of each other's rooms, smoking, drinking, flirting, doing drugs . . . they think they're too rich too die."

"This one wasn't," I said, taking out my phone. "I suppose we'd better get her moved."

A search of the residence block's rubbish area failed to produce the President Pig poster.

"I don't believe there ever was a poster," said Geraint. "You don't have any record of this girl? I mean, as far as you know, she stands up for the national anthem, follows American football, always votes for the government?"

"She's too young to vote."

"Whatever. She's not known to your lot – or her family, or her associates?"

"No, but when someone's away from home for the first time, mixing with – well, mixing with . . ."

"Natives," I said. "Sure. Untrustworthy lot, the hairy natives."

"My point being, Sergeant, people change."

"If Elaine Cassidy changed," said Geraint, "the campus security office is going to know."

"If you can trust native security," I added.

The head of campus security was a large woman in a small office. Her badge read "Bone". I assumed it was her name. She claimed to have no special knowledge of Elaine Cassidy.

"Obviously, we keep a special eye on our American students."

"Why?" Geraint asked. "Are they the most troublesome?"

She didn't answer that. She didn't need to. She kept a special eye on the Americans because balkanized Britain is balkanized not so much regionally, as along responsibility lines. Bonn rules the economy – but anything to do with security, you jump when DC says jump.

"And you kept a special eye on Elaine?"

"Of course. But as I said, there was never any hint of anything worrying."

Hilda said: "Did you know a complaint had been made about her to my office?"

Bone bristled. "In *theory*, campus security is given a courtesy call before you lot turn up. Evidently, your phones weren't working today."

"We don't really bother with theory, ma'am," said Geraint. "We're public servants."

Not private crap like you, he meant – and Bone knew it. "No doubt you'll keep me informed of your progress," she said, by way of dismissal.

"Looks like you've had a wasted journey, Agent Westlake," I said, as we watched Elaine Cassidy's body being removed, packed in what appeared to be a giant speaker for a rock gig. That's the nice thing about the private sector: discretion guaranteed.

"You might be right, but the death of a US citizen is still an embassy matter. I'm on the spot, I might as well hang around."

"Overseeing the natives."

She put a hand on my arm until I met her eyes. "You know something, Barney, you're not a bad-looking guy. You're good at your job. You have your own hair. So tell me – why does this *native* shit upset you so much? You suffering from empire envy, like every other little Englishman I've met since I came here?"

"All right," I said. "Since you ask. What bothers me is the way America still gives itself imperial airs, when the truth is your empire's as dead as ours is. Your country's in as big a mess as we are – worse in some ways. For instance, how many universities have you got in the US?"

She looked genuinely amused. "This isn't a *university*. Come on! This is a finishing school for rich kids! Most of them foreign."

"If you girls have finished," said Geraint, "I suggest we go and get a drink."

"How about lunch?" said Hilda.

He grinned. "That's what I said."

Geraint drove. As we left the campus, Hilda said: "We're not going to the student bar? We could talk to a few of Elaine's pals."

"That wouldn't be a drink. That'd be work."

It took a few minutes for me and Hilda to realise where he was taking us. She wasn't thrilled. "Jesus, you have to be joking!"

I was pretty shocked myself, but I wasn't going to show it. "This'll be a new experience for you, Agent Westlake. Back home, you wouldn't go onto an estate like this except in a convoy of tanks, am I right?"

She wobbled her head at me. It's something only American women can do, and only black American women can do convincingly. "Sure. Except maybe to visit with my folks."

From a distance it looked like something a nuke had left behind. From close up, it wasn't so bad – from close up it looked like something that had been rebuilt from salvage, ten years *after* a nuke. There were shops, houses, pubs. Human beings. Parked cars and burger bars. The poverty was obvious, but it wasn't what I'd imagined; it looked like somewhere people lived.

At first I thought all the shops were closed. Then, as we drove slowly on, I saw people coming and going from them and realized that they were kept boarded up all the time, except for a small space for the door. Extreme fear of crime – presumably based, unlike in the nicer areas, on actual experience – is a classic sign of chronic poverty. On the other hand, it must also be a sign that you've still got something worth stealing. Steel shutters as a sign of hope? Well, there weren't many other candidates for the job.

"What are we looking for, Geraint?"

"A student bar."

Hilda gave him the look she'd have given a penniless drunk

who asked her for a kiss. She must have done a course in incredulity. "What – *here*?"

"It'll be on the outskirts, but far enough in to make it count."

"You seriously think kids from that college come slumming it down here?"

He shook his head. "*Slumming* it is an overly pejorative term. They're young and alive, Hilda. The day they leave college they become middle-aged. Their lives are over, and their careers begin. Some of them – not a majority, maybe not very many, but some – will want to breathe some unfiltered air once or twice. They know it's the only chance they'll ever get."

"Unless they're very unlucky," I said.

"There's a student bar in every major slum city. In Robbery we find them . . . you know. Useful."

It was Hilda, in fact, who spotted the student bar, on our second drive-round. She saw a group of students – they couldn't have been anything else, their clothes so well-made and ill-treated – emerging from a dark doorway onto a bright pavement. A bit drunk, but mostly stoned on their own daring and independence.

We kerbed up next to them, and I got out. "Ladies, gentlemen. Would you like a lift back to college?"

A tall boy with floppy blond hair and big shoulders looked me up and down. Mostly down. "There's seven of us. What are we going to do – sit on your laps?" Their laughter was slightly nervous, which I took to mean that they knew who we were.

"OK," said Geraint, from his side of the bonnet. "We'll just have a quick chat. Are any of you lot American?"

This round of laughter was scornful. "Hardly," said the blond boy. "The Yanks don't come down here."

"Why not?"

"They stick to their own." He watched Hilda stretch herself out of the back seat, legs first. "Can't say I blame them."

She gave him a smile. Lent it to him, anyway. "You ever ask them to come with you?"

"Ah . . . nope."

"They wouldn't be welcome?"

"No offence, love, but – we don't want anything to do with them, they don't want anything to do with us."

"What about a girl called Elaine Cassidy," I said. "Any of you know her?"

"*Knew* her, you mean. I heard she was dead."

"Where did you hear that?"

"Everyone's talking about it."

"So," said Geraint. "You've been raising a few glasses to her memory, right?"

The blond boy just shut his eyes, very slowly, then turned his back on us and led his posse homewards. I suppose he opened his eyes before he got there.

Back at the college car park, I said: "We never did get that drink."

"Nah," said Geraint. "Students can drink in those places. Cops can't. Students have got money."

"If the Yanks don't mix with the natives, it's hard to see how Elaine could've got into a situation with one that would've got her killed." Geraint finished his beer and his sandwich with a single swallow. "Horrible stuff they serve in these college bars. It is cheap, mind."

"So you're saying it must've been an American who killed her?"

"Only," said Hilda, "if what we've been told is true, and the two tribes don't mix at all. I'd like to hear that from an American student."

Taking her at her word, Geraint went and fetched her one. A thin boy, already balding, who'd been sitting at a corner table, on his own, staring miserably at a cup of coffee. From the body language, I gathered he came reluctantly.

"From the look on your face," I said, "I gather you've heard about Elaine Cassidy."

"What do *you* care? Native cops aren't going to bother about a dead Yank."

It must have been the mood I was in, or perhaps the horrible beer, but his comment made me both sad and angry. More angry than sad, I decided after a moment's contemplation. "That's crap, you silly little boy. How can you think that? A young girl's killed and you think we're—"

"Barney," said Hilda, leaning across my space. "The guy's just repeating what he's heard. Isn't that right, young man?"

He'd barely glanced at her until then. I'd noticed that with a lot of well-off Americans; black people were invisible to them. "You're a Yank?"

She widened her eyes and crossed her hands over her breasts. "With an accent like mine? How dare you!"

He smiled. "Sorry – I meant, you're an American."

"North Carolina. Say, did you know Elaine well?"

"I don't know. All the American students know each other. We've got no choice."

"What can you tell us about her?"

"You mean why was she killed? No idea. I don't think she had any enemies. She was a quiet girl, just worked at her studies."

"Not a party girl?"

"*Hardly.*"

"Not much of a mixer? She didn't have a boyfriend?"

"Look, she used to eat with the rest of us. Came to the Thanksgiving Ball. But mostly, she was kind of . . ."

Hilda spoke quietly, as if it was just the two of them there. The young master and his favourite maid. "Kind of standoffish?"

"I wouldn't want to say that. That sounds like a criticism. But, you know, she came from a very important family."

"Old money?"

"Old money, old power. Sure. It's sort of like, if we hadn't been a minority here – well, you know, back home she wouldn't have had much to do with us."

After lunch, Geraint and I had another look round Elaine's room. We still couldn't see anything there that suggested much of a life beyond her law studies. Even her CD collection was clean. Mostly Christian rock, and Britney retrospectives; nothing that was on the US Surgeon General's Index.

"She didn't have any friends," said Geraint. "I'd bet on it."

"And therefore no enemies?"

"Ah, now. I wouldn't bet on that." He was examining the walls with an illuminated glass.

Agent Westlake finished her phone call, and joined us. "Well, our local office knows nothing about the poster. It's not one that's doing the rounds, anyway. Which doesn't mean it doesn't exist."

"But it is suggestive," said Geraint.

"Well, yes."

"Tell you something else – there's been no poster on any of the walls of this room since it was last painted. You get a forensic team in here, they'll tell you the same."

"So," I said, "if Kelly Norton *didn't* see a subversive poster, why did she say she did?"

"We could ask her," Hilda suggested.

"No." Geraint was tapping a pen against his teeth. "First, let's talk to the security hag."

"We already did."

"Yeah, but last time we were polite."

Ms Bone started off on the attack. "You didn't tell me I had a dead student in the place! Thanks very much, that came as a nice surprise."

"Oh," said Geraint, "so that was one aspect of the business you didn't already know about?"

"So much for interagency cooperation!" She stopped seething at Hilda, and looked at Geraint. "What do you mean?"

"I mean, when did you first know about the complaint against Elaine Cassidy?"

She looked at each of us in turn, then at nothing.

"At the moment," Geraint went on, "this is a fairly small matter concerning the withholding of evidence pertaining to a criminal investigation, but—"

"Actually, Geraint," I interrupted, "that *isn't* a small matter."

He cupped his chin in his hand. "Oh, yeah – you're right, Barney. It isn't, is it?"

Bone wasn't as rattled by this superb performance as I'd hoped she might be. "Believe me, gentlemen, I know the law. I've been in private security all my life. I have a primary duty of care to my employers – you don't believe me, check the case law."

A lot of lawyers earn a lot of money arguing over that very point – which has precedence, contract or law? So far the consensus seems to be that if you break the law you're in big trouble . . . whereas if you break your contract you're in big trouble. It's an answer the lawyers are happy with.

"Listen," said Hilda, "I understand. But your duty here is surely clear: to minimize – since you're too late to prevent – damage to this institution's reputation. Now if you fail to do that, and the university loses money as a result, I guess they could sue you. Is that right? That's how it works back home, anyhow."

The security woman wedged her buttocks into a swivel chair

and gave Hilda a look as if it was all her fault. The murder, and her buttocks. "Elaine Cassidy came to me yesterday morning, to say that a malicious complaint had been made against her. She berated me for allowing such a thing to happen. I don't know how she thought I was supposed to stop it, but there you are."

"How did she know?"

With evident pleasure, Bone directed her reply at Hilda. "One of her daddy's pals works at the embassy."

I asked, "Did she know who'd made the complaint?"

"Oh, yes," said Bone. "Daddy's mole was fully informative."

"That might sound a bit weird, Kelly, but believe me that's how it works – and if you see a lawyer, he'll tell you the same thing."

A frightened girl, being questioned in a car. Me in the driving seat, Geraint Brook next to Kelly Norton on the back seat, Agent Westlake outside, leaning against the car talking on her phone. Geraint's last remark was intended to pass as an offer of legal representation, should anyone ever ask.

"We have proof that you made a malicious complaint to the US embassy against Elaine." That wasn't quite a lie; we had a reasonably strong case, at any rate. Certainly more than enough to get a magistrate to sign an indefinite detention order. "Now obviously that's a lesser crime than murder—"

She started crying.

"—but, like I say, my advice to you is to tell us about the murder, straight out. You understand all that?"

Kelly nodded. We waited. We weren't waiting for her to decide, just to stop crying. She'd already decided.

"Start with why you made the complaint, Kelly."

"Just to teach the Yanks a lesson. I hate them. We all do."

"Elaine especially?"

"I don't know. She was so stuck up."

"So there never was a poster of the president as a pig?"

She shook her head, and tear debris spattered the upholstery. "No. When the investigators got here I was just going to say, *Oh, she must've got rid of it, it was there yesterday*."

"What did you think would happen to her?"

"I don't know. When they couldn't find the poster I suppose I just thought it would fizzle out." She looked up at Geraint, as if expecting to find an ally. "But it'd leave a nice big stain on her precious family name, wouldn't it?"

"Things didn't work out that way."

"Elaine found out what I'd done. I don't know how. She went whining to that fat bitch in security, Ms Bone. So Bone called me in. Told me that unless I could persuade Elaine not to complain about *me*, I'd be in big trouble. The Yanks would believe Elaine, not me."

"That hadn't occurred to you?"

"I don't know. I didn't think it was all going to be such a big thing."

"How did Ms Bone know the poster didn't exist?"

"You kidding? They check our rooms at least once a week. They think we don't know. She said my only hope was to see Elaine, just say it was all a joke, and beg her to use her contacts to – you know, get the whole thing dropped."

"Doesn't sound like an idea Elaine Cassidy would have gone for."

"Crazy idea. She was *really* enjoying herself. First time I've seen her smile since she arrived at this place. She was getting haughtier and snottier and then she started *slapping* me, and . . ."

"And that big textbook was the nearest thing to hand?"

"Really," said Kelly, "if you think about it, it was self-defence."

"I wouldn't bother with that in court," said Geraint. "It never worked for the French Resistance."

I was surprised by Hilda Westlake's tact in waiting outside, not insisting on being part of the interrogation. I chose to think it was tact, rather than a desire not to be involved more than necessary in a matter so rich in potential fallout for all concerned.

"Kelly's admitted the killing, and we've charged her with murder," I told her. "We'll drive her over to the local police-u-like franchise and process her."

Hilda glanced over to the car. "How did you get her to confess? You had basically nothing."

"Well," I said, "Geraint convinced her that it was in her best interests."

Geraint joined us, and gave Hilda a big smile. Not a friendly one, but a big one.

"What," said Hilda, "she's going for manslaughter? After stopping to wipe her prints off the weapon?"

"Nope. I explained to her that murder takes precedence over false allegations regarding the Possession or Dissemination of President Pig."

Then Hilda got it. She looked half impressed, half annoyed, which was about what I'd expected. "Right. So if she's serving time for murder, we won't be able to extradite her for the other thing. Nice work, Sergeants. Not sure if I've ever had my time so comprehensively wasted."

"Thank you," said Geraint.

Hilda looked at me, with what could almost have been a slight question in her eyes. "Your friend took that as a compliment, Barney."

"You all right to make your own way back to London, Agent Westlake?" said Geraint. "We need to deliver our passenger."

She carried on looking at me for a while, then she shrugged and turned away. As we drove off, I watched her in the mirror. She had her back to me and was on the phone and she didn't turn round.

VIOLATION

William F. Nolan

It is 2 a.m. and he waits. In the cool morning stillness of a side street, under the soft screen of trees, the rider waits quietly – at ease upon the wide leather seat of his cycle, gloved fingers resting idly on the bars, goggles up, eyes palely reflecting the leaf-filtered glow of the moon.

Helmeted. Uniformed. Waiting.

In the breathing dark, the cycle metal cools: the motor is silent, a power contained.

The faint stirrings of a still-sleeping city reach him at his vigil. But he is not concerned with these; he mentally dismisses them. He is concerned only with the broad river of smooth concrete facing him through the trees, and the great winking red eye suspended, icicle-like, above it.

He waits.

And tenses at a sound upon the river – an engine sound, mosquitodim with distance, rising to a hum. A rushing sound under the stars.

The rider's hands contract like the claws of a bird. He rises slowly on the bucket seat, right foot poised near the starter. A coiled spring. Waiting.

Twin pencil-beams of light move toward him, toward the street on which he waits hidden. Closer.

The hum builds in volume; the lights are very close now, flaring chalk-white along the concrete boulevard.

The rider's goggles are down and he is ready to move out, move onto the river. Another second, perhaps two . . .

But no. The vehicle slows, makes a full stop. A service truck with two men inside, laughing, joking. The rider listens to them, mouth set, eyes hard. The vehicle begins to move once more. The sound is eaten by the night.

There is no violation.

Now . . . the relaxing, the easing back. The ebb tide of tension receding. Gone. The rider quiet again under the moon.

Waiting.

The red eye winking at the empty boulevard.

"How much farther, Dave?" asks the girl.

"Ten miles, maybe. Once we hit Westwood, it's a quick run to my place. Relax. You're nervous."

"We should have stayed on the gridway. Used the grid. I don't *like* these surface streets. A grid would have taken us in."

The man smiles, looping an arm around her.

"There's nothing to be afraid of as long as you're careful," he says. "I used to drive surface streets all the time when I was a boy. Lots of people did."

The girl swallows, touches her hair nervously. "But they don't anymore. People use the grids. I didn't even know cars still *came* equipped for manual driving."

"They don't. I had this set up special by a mechanic I know. He does jobs like this for road buffs. It's still legal, driving your own car – it's just that most people have lost the habit."

The girl peers out the window into the silent street, shakes her head. "It's . . . not *natural*. Look out there. Nobody! Not another car for miles. I feel as if we're trespassing."

The man is annoyed. "That's damn nonsense. I have friends who do this all the time. Just relax and enjoy it. And don't talk like an idiot."

"I want out," says the girl. "I'll take a walkway back to the grid."

"The hell you will," flares the man. "You're with *me* tonight. We're going to my place."

She resists, strikes at his face; the man grapples to subdue her. He does not see the blinking light. The car passes under it swiftly.

"Chrisdam!" snaps the man. "I went through that light! You made me miss the stop. I've broken one of the surface laws!" He says this humbly.

"What does that mean?" the girl asks. "What could happen?"

"Never mind. Nothing will happen. Never mind about what could happen."

The girl peers out into the darkness. "I want to leave this car."

"Just shut up," the man says, and keeps driving.

Something in the sound tells the rider that this one will not stop, that it will continue to move along the river of stone despite the blinking eye.

He smiles in the darkness, lips stretched back, silently. Poised there on the cycle, with the hum steady and rising on the river, he feels the power within him about to be released.

The car is almost upon the light, moving swiftly; there is no hint of slackened speed.

The rider watches intently. Man and a girl inside, struggling. Fighting with one another.

The car passes under the light.

Violation.

Now!

He spurs the cycle to metal life. The motor crackles, roars, explodes the black machine into motion, and the rider is away, rolling in muted thunder along the street. Around the corner, swaying on to the long, moon-painted river of the boulevard.

The rider feels the wind in his face, feels the throb and power-pulse of the metal thing he rides, feels the smooth concrete rushing backward under his wheels.

Ahead, the firefly glow of tail-lights.

And now his cycle cries out after them, a siren moan through the still spaces of the city. A voice which rises and falls in spirals of sound. His cycle-eyes, mounted left and right, are blinking crimson, red as blood in their wake.

The car will stop. The man will see him, hear him. The eyes and the voice will reach the violator.

And he will stop.

"Bitch!" the man says. "We've picked up a rider at that light."

"*You* picked him up, I didn't," says the girl. "It's your problem."

"But I've never been stopped on a surface street," the man says, a desperate note in his voice. "In all these years – never once!"

The girl glares at him. "Dave, you make me sick! Look at you – shaking, sweating. You're a damn poor excuse for a man!"

He does not react to her words. He speaks in numbed monotone. "I can talk my way out. I know I can. He'll listen to me. I have my rights as a citizen of the city."

"He's catching up fast. You'd better pull over."

His eyes harden as he brakes the car. "I'll do the talking. All of it. You just keep quiet. I'll handle this."

The rider sees that the car is slowing, braking, pulling to the curb.

He cuts the siren voice, lets it die, glides the cycle in behind the car. Cuts the engine. Sits there for a long moment on the leather seat, pulling off his gloves. Slowly.

He sees the car door slide open. A man steps out, comes toward him. The rider swings a booted leg over the cycle and steps free, advancing to meet this law-breaker, fitting the gloves carefully into his black leather belt.

They face one another, the man smaller, paunchy, balding, face flushed. The rider's polite smile eases the man's tenseness.

"You in a hurry, sir?"

"Me? No, I'm not in a hurry. Not at all. It was just . . . I didn't *see* the light up there until . . . I was past it. The high trees and all. I swear to you. I didn't see it. I'd never knowingly break a surface law, Officer. You have my sworn word."

Nervous. Shaken and nervous, this man. The rider can feel the man's guilt, a physical force. He extends a hand.

"May I see your operator's license, please?"

The man fumbles in his coat. "I have it right here. It's all in order, up to date and all."

"Just let me see it, please."

The man continues to talk.

"Been driving for years, Officer, and this is my first violation. Perfect record up to now. I'm a responsible citizen. I obey the laws. After all, I'm not a fool."

The rider says nothing; he examines the man's license, taps it thoughtfully against his wrist. The rider's goggles are opaque. The man cannot see his eyes. He studies the face of the violator.

"The woman in the car . . . is she your wife?"

"No. No, sir. She's . . . a friend. Just a friend."

"Then why were you fighting? I saw the two of you fighting inside the car when it passed the light. That isn't friendly, is it?"

The man attempts to smile. "Personal. We had a small personal disagreement. It's all over now, believe me."

The rider walks to the car, leans to peer in at the woman. She is pale, as nervous as the man.

"You having trouble?" the rider asks.

She hesitates, shakes her head mutely. The rider leaves her and returns to the man, who is resting a hand against the cycle.

"Don't touch that," says the rider coldly, and the man draws back his hand, mumbles an apology.

"I have no further use for this," says the rider, handing back the man's license. "You are guilty of a surface-street violation."

The man quakes; his hands tremble. "But it was not *deliberate*. I know the law. You're empowered to make exceptions if a violation is not deliberate. The full penalty is not invoked in such cases. You are allowed to—"

The rider cuts into the flow of words. "You forfeited your Citizen's Right of Exception when you allowed a primary emotion – anger, in this instance – to affect your control of a surface vehicle. Thus, my duty is clear and prescribed."

The man's eyes widen in shock as the rider brings up a beltweapon. "You can't possibly—"

"Under authorization of Citystate Overpopulation Statute 4452663, I am hereby executing . . ."

The man begins to run.

". . . sentence."

He presses the trigger. Three long, probing blue jets of star-hot flame leap from the weapon in the rider's hand.

The man is gone.

The woman is gone.

The car is gone.

The street is empty and silent. A charred smell of distant suns lingers in the morning air.

The rider stands by his cycle, unmoving for a long moment. Then he carefully holsters the weapon, pulls on his leather gloves. He mounts the cycle and it pulses to life under his foot.

With the sky in motion above him, he is again upon the moon-flowing boulevard, gliding back towards the blinking red eye.

The rider reaches his station on the small, tree-shadowed side street and thinks, *How stupid they are! To be subject to indecision, to quarrels and erratic behavior – weak, all of them. Soft and weak.*

He smiles into the darkness.

The eye blinks over the river.

And now it is 4 a.m., now 6 and 8 and 10 and 1 p.m. . . . the hours turning like wheels, the days spinning away.

And he waits. Through nights without sleep, days without food – a flawless metal enforcer at his vigil, sure of himself and of his duty.

Waiting.

NEEDLE TASTE

M. Christian

Standing under the twelve by six poster of Desiree Proll, victim 7, Prair watched the pit ripple, eat, and spit out dancers. They went in, he noticed, eyes lit with smack, booze, or just kid enthusiasm, and were spat back out into the shadowed booths or towards the bar covered in reflective, childish, sweat. On the stage, Heavy Foot was slamming through *To Spite You*. Even though their albums had names like *Screaming Baby* and *Foundry*, aficionados of their screeching metal, death-tasting, mood pieces knew that each and every one was just an extension of the last. Titles, for them, were as irrelevant as trying to take apart the static charge before a lightning strike.

Prair felt frostbit, so he transferred his untouched drink to his other hand. He didn't drink anymore but he felt crippled to be in a club without one.

Sometimes he even got it to work to his advantage: "Want a drink? Someone forced the damned thing on me and I can't touch it." Bang: generosity, cool anger, and sympathy. It was surprising how often it worked.

Tonight, though, he didn't even feel like trying. Maybe it was Heavy Foot's constant beat (one rolling into another which spilled into another). If you allowed yourself to think any part of it too repetitive, presumptuous, or just dull the whole night could come crashing down around you, because it was a constant – hate one bit, hate the whole fucking song, the whole fucking evening.

That night, it did – and had. The fragments of the song were like broken, weak neon reflecting off wet streets – fractured: the acid was weak and cut with too much speed. He wasn't having a friendly night cruising on the secret rhythms of the city, he was facing a long, dark tunnel of futility and paranoia. The drug and the Friday evening parade of twitching young flesh did nothing, nothing at all, to push away overdue rent, a scummy day job, and an empty bed.

Across from him was another twelve by six poster: poor Little Amy Grantie, victim #9; her body captured by a police camera-man's flash. Even from across the crowded and flashing, strob-ing, pulsing, club, Prair could still make out the stark details of the scene. Fingers cut off. Toes, too. The poster was in black and white, and the grass surrounding the body was a lighter gray where the blood wasn't.

What was it Owlsley had said?

The only true sin is letting them go unpunished. A much more vivid memory was Owlsley's capture: a three day action-adven-ture that had left thirteen dead, eight of them cops. The image was melted, frozen in his memory as he had watched it on his scummy little black and white set: the huge man, all scrub-brush beard and massive chest, naked except for a pair of jeans, being wrestled to the dusty ground in some mid-Texas flyspeck town.

His blood, too, had been dark grey – grey from the wounds that killed him two hours later. Prair remembered the newspaper captions, too, those five years ago: KILLER CAPTURED . . . then, in the morning DEAD.

Standing, surrounded by Owlsley's "punishments", Prair turned an eye back to the pulsing music, the pulsing youth. The acid was making his teeth jump in their sockets and he was *sure* that one group of black carapaced teenagers was laughing at him and his simple, traditional Jeans and fake biker jacket. He was so disgusted with them and the whole room that he almost slugged down his drink and left. He didn't, though – instead he just passed the cold glass to his other hand.

What was outside, after all? Just wet streets from a shocking summer storm; a tiny apartment in the Haight; an empty, bare mattress on the floor; yet another shift of screaming suits at his Java City job.

At least you left with style, Prair thought, lifting his still-full, straight vodka in a salute to Greg Moore, victim #33 (again in hard black and white, showing his severed right arm and the almost black grass around it) but meaning it more to the architect, the man who, at least, had a face and an identity – and not an empty pit that was all Prair seemed to have.

His walk home was more satisfying. There was something about the heavy fog, the oppressive drizzle, and the snapping cold that seemed perfect for Prair's mood. The acid, of course, dulled most of the discomfort – turning the wet and the cold into abstracts, a perfect accompaniment for his depression and anger. He walked all the way to his apartment, alone in a world of bold contrasts and snapping wind.

By the time he made it to the Haight, the chemicals had faded into a kind of floating giddiness, a of lighter-than-air exaltation. To match (tying it all up nicely), the fog and the light rain had faded and lifted – becoming nothing but a dark and churning lid over the city.

At first he didn't see her, crouching down on the landing outside his front door. The aftertaste of the acid blurred his time sense and for an elastic second he thought that she wasn't anything but a trash bag, till the black plastic cautiously unfolded a bit and a pale, lean face swung out to look at him.

Trash bag to street girl was fluid and quick. The chemicals made him stare: a lithe nymph sprouting from a dark plastic carapace. In the cool night, her face seemed to hover and dance next to the dull brass of his front door knob. Her face: a pale moon. The knob: very gold (though it had been tarnished a long, long time). A hand (very, very white) appeared from somewhere and brushed thick black hair from a fine china face.

She stood slowly and elegantly as Prair took another slow step up, and uncoiled herself from where she'd been crouching.

In a snapping instant, perceptions and then explanations avalanched through his mind.

She was wearing a slick black poncho; her hair was dark, wet with glossy reflections from the streetlight outside. She was a tiny doll, a miniature. She could have been a girl or a young woman. Her eyes whispered maybe oriental.

"Sorry, needed to sit and let the world . . . *calm*," she said, voice sharp and brittle – taken down off a shelf and used for the first time in a long while.

"It . . . it's okay," he managed to tumble out, the stammer

pressure-pushed (possibilities jumbling through him, too many choices and fantasies in quick succession).

"You lit?" she said, smiling tiny teeth, only slightly jumbled.

He was now on the landing with her. She was small, yes, but not a doll. He didn't have to look that far down to see her. He nodded.

"Can I come in for a piss?"

Prair nodded again, and fumbled for his keys.

Flushing, she stepped out. The adrenaline smashing through his trip-hammering heart pushed the vibrant edge of the acid far back into Prair's mind: the walls are just walls, and not breathing kaleidoscopes. The posters weren't as brilliant as they could have been (thank God), and the spines of his books actually seemed to make sense.

Poncho pushed aside, showing a delightfully pale tummy, she yanked her stretch pants up a final inch. Something white flashed amid the swirl of the plastic poncho – a bra? "*Major* Owlsley," she said, tracking around the room, checking out the posters, the books.

Prair didn't talk about it much – he was a closet fan: wasn't jumping to defend him, with anyone who took offence and wasn't a complete enough fanatic for those who worshipped him as a genius.

He liked him, was all Prair could say. He liked reading his books and, sometimes, even liked to get ripped and get lost in the photographic depictions of his . . . other works.

"Number 40, right?" she said, looking at one of the prints. "The Sacramento cop? Devers?"

He smiled, enjoying her simply standing there in his little place, standing in front of him. "Devers was the soldier in San Diego." He nodded to the poster, to the splash of vibrating reds, the almost-black slice where Owlsley's razor had cut through his throat. Unlike the prints back at the club, Prair's were full-colour reproductions: colour second only to life, or someone just dead. "Farrley was this guy. But you're right, it was in Sacramento and he was a cop."

"He lied, right?"

"Yeah. Part of some child-custody case – friend of his wanted to keep his kids so he got the cop to write up some fake abuse report against his wife."

"Which one lived? The one with the weird name—"

"Sanji Musta," Prair said, walking towards the bathroom. A vivid red and green photo. Laying on her side, hands wrapped tight with electrical wiring as if out in prayer. Her skin was dark, the color of smudged ink. "An Indian exchange student. Lucky they found her; would have bled to death otherwise. Owlsley said that she was too proud."

She followed, and leaned into the photograph, following the lines of its unintentional composition with dilated eyes. "Don't get it."

Prair mimicked, thumbs in the waistband of his jeans, threw his chest out. When he realized she wasn't looking at him, he said, "Like this."

It look her a beat, two, to see him, to see his posture, his thumbs. "Fuck. *Duh*." Her laugh was broken, fragile. She might have been, but her laugh certainly wasn't pretty. It sounded cracked, like she'd smoked, screamed or cried for too long.

She turned, wide eyes catching on another photograph, on the door to his bathroom. "That one. I know. She was a shoplifter right, stole some cigarettes or something?"

Prair looked where she was staring. A print, smaller than the others: a young woman spread out on the sand. Blood: irregular Rorschach impressions next to her missing hands. "Jennifer Reynolds. Student at San Jose State down to visit her boyfriend. They found the first book there. *Volume One: Crimes and Fallacies*."

"Read it?" her eyes were black pools from whatever she'd mainlined, and ringed with streaked mascara.

He nodded, walking past her into the living room and moving to the bookshelves. Bending down, he tapped one broken-spined paperback. "Loompanic's First Edition."

She walked over, squatted down with a ballerina's grace and brushed pale fingers over the spines. "You're a freak," she said, an icing of respect in the words.

Prair shrugged. "Fuck if I know. I ain't gonna follow him or nothin'. Just – well, fuck if I know. It makes sense sometimes, you know? When you look at it right."

She sat down, rearranging her poncho, scanning the other books, videos. "You got it all."

"Not really," he said, sitting down next to her. "I'm not a collector or anything, I just like—"

He stopped as she turned to look at him, brushed the side of his face with those same long, pale fingers. "I gotcha. I do. Got him running though me, too, you know. Wanna hit?"

He shook his head but, again, she wasn't looking. Reaching under her poncho, she pulled out a threadbare fanny pack, then a small leather case. He knew the religion of a fix, the genuflection of the works. His had been the bottle – the cold weight of it, wiping the condensation off with his thumb. Measuring money in fifths and shots: This much meant that many.

Prair was silent, respectful – allowing the girl the solace of her worship. Sitting down next to her, he looked. The needle was old, an antique. It surprised him. He expected a couple of cheap works, a fold of foil and a spoon. Instead, he got an impression of something from old London, from the desk of Sherlock Holmes: steel and glass – not a cheap ticket. Hers was a first-class accommodation.

A bottle. Tiny, with a rubber seal. A little bit of yellow fluid at the bottom. Jingling it, a watery bell, she frowned: "Fuck."

Prair knew that *fuck*: not enough in his pockets – maybe half a bottle, only a cheap shot that wouldn't give a tomcat a buzz.

"Gotta score," she said, looking shorter, smaller. Without looking she dropped her head on his shoulder, started stroking the front of his shirt with a spray of white fingers.

Eventually, he bent down and kissed her. Her mouth tasted sharp, acidic – like metal and cigarettes.

She was disappointed, and it'd showed on her pale face. Research, no matter how methodical, was not identity. She'd asked, in all sincerity, face burning with heat, for Owlsley – but what she'd gotten was just Prair: too old, too wasted, too tired, and with too much of a headache from the acid crash, to keep it up.

Afterwards she'd dug in her little pouch again, a junkie's wishful thinking for a genie to have magically sequestered another hit there since she'd last looked.

Going to the bathroom, Prair avoided his own face in the mirror, focusing instead on the yellowish water in the toilet. When he stepped out she was dressed again. "Gotta score," she repeated.

He nodded, understanding the sentiment if not the drug. He didn't ask, considering it private, but she volunteered anyway.

"Gotta score some Owlsley," she'd said.

She wasn't what he expected, but then his dealers usually lived in dim bars and offered small doses from bottles of amber liquid, not from tiny bottles of a strange, thin solution. Alcohol, not brain juice. Booze, not extracted thoughts.

What she said didn't make any sense – a drunkard's walk of myth and fabrication – but he followed her anyway. She wasn't his first and wouldn't be his last crazy fuck. What was unique was the way he blindly followed her, out into the chill night, to the hailing of a cab. The insanity of one girl was expected, no big shock there; but someone had sold her the fluid – someone had mixed her fix. Someone had taken fragments of Owlsley and put them in a tiny bottle, a distillation of reality and myth.

It was strange, frightening, *crazy*: he didn't know where he was going, and where he hoped he was going was to a very thin rationalization, indeed – but he knew too well what was behind: a small, dark apartment full of books, full of someone else's words.

Nothing of Prair.

Words. He'd left behind Owlsley's words in those rare editions, and he'd ended up arriving to see more of them in cheap red paint, mimicking blood, on a door made from a battered sheet of diamond plate.

The truth is in all of us – too common. Everyone knew that line, printed by Owlsley at the first ten murder sites. Very few, though, knew the others.

Show it to me had been painted on the cheap gold-flecked mirror of a hot sheet motel in Dallas where Betsy Lucas had been found, her hands clumsily severed at the wrists. One of the cops had reported that the carpet was black with her blood, and gleamed like dark, polished glass when he'd shown his flashlight inside. The manager had reported it after flies had begun to swarm outside the dirty bathroom window.

Let me see it in lipstick when Dr Fallen's blood had proved to be too thin to successfully write with.

A transvestite, Owlsley had castrated him. Too ashamed to call for help, he'd bled to death in his gaudy Minneapolis home.

It's as plain as you printed in wide, passionate letters on the inside of a Ladysmith, Wisconsin garage. A secret drinker, and beater of wife and young son, he'd been gagged and carefully suspended. Prair couldn't remember if the coroner had pronounced him dead from the baseball bat that Owlsley had used on him for four hours or from the whiskey he'd forced down his throat using a length of old radiator hose.

If the door led to more little bottles, more thin yellow fluid, it must have been painted by people who either didn't understand the source of their worship, or who had carefully hidden themselves behind the most common, and thus mundane, of his pronouncements.

Weep, though, spoke of someone who at least had opened a book, cruised secret information. Only once had that word been written, in small, meticulous strokes. Her name had been Alice Souyer. She had been small, shy, and cautious. Prair remembered how the *St Augustine Herald* had spoken of her: ". . . people were surprised to learn that she lived in the building." Her death had brought her fame, but not even much of that – a week-and-a-half later Owlsley hacked the feet from a bail jumper. It was a much louder event – and her death after Owlsley removed her eyes and tongue was generally forgotten . . . save by those whose interest crawled over every inch of Owlsley.

Alice's anonymity in life had even endured beyond it – even though she was killed for staying silent after witnessing a rape when she was twelve. She stayed just a footnote for purists.

The girl's name was Alice's epitaph. She finally told it to Prair like it was a key to something secret within herself, something fitting a very special lock. A heated whisper in his ear as the cab entered the maze of abandoned factories, corrugated metal dead ends, industrial avenues, and chain link stretches.

After paying the dark, crumpled cab driver, and walking down the dark alley, she'd whispered it again to the door and her name opened it wide: "Weep."

He was big, broad across the shoulders and chest. His kind shouldn't have been hiding in doorways smelling of mould and piss, dispensing amber bottles of . . . something. He was out of place without corn, hay, wheat, barley. Even his face was remarkably unmarked for living in the city. His attitude, though, spoke of some kind of acclimation, even if his face didn't. Even his hair was the colour of wheat, and cut as close as a recent harvest.

The unfamiliar emotion of hope was large in Prair's chest – seeing the big man made it even more real, firmer. A couple of city freaks were just a pair of city freaks feeding off, and feedbacking their junkie delusions. A farm boy, even one with the dirt just lost from under his fingernails, was unusual enough to add fabric to the story she'd told.

Prair had, at first, just stared through her after she'd explained – her tale too improbable, too ridiculous. But his humiliation was too flushed on his face, her disappointment had been too pointed – this was all too real, and what she'd said, about mortician conspiracies, the decapitation of Owlsley's corpse, about memory extraction, of an RNA injection, could have been genuine.

The hick led them in, down a concrete access way. The room beyond was vast and heavy – everything steel and industrial, nothing created for the comfort of people: cement floor weeded with bent and chopped rebar, the stubs of plastic pipe, and loose coils of black wire. The only light was from several Coleman gas lanterns that looked to have been hastily hung from insulation-furry interior beams.

There were others – standing and talking in low voices. The room was dark where the lanterns couldn't throw their light, and there Prair could see pale abstracts of bare arms and the dim moons of faces.

Fear – instant and visceral. Prair felt his asshole tighten and his stomach knot. One was a junkie's dream, two was a chance for reality – more than that was too much reality, a firmness that was good to contemplate but when stumbled on . . . It was heavy and threatening. Too many of them to be safe. Too many – Prair was the outsider, on their ground, in their world.

As his anxiety started to spiral outwards, Weep put a thin arm around him and pulled herself close – anchoring him to herself and making him just unfamiliar, and not alone.

The farm boy walked up, looked them both over – Prair longer than Weep, examining him in the burning glare of the lamps. "Here for a hit?" he finally said.

"Fix us up," Weep said. "I want to feel him." She didn't mean Prair – she meant the man in the needle. A taste of Owlsley.

The hick moved off to one of the support columns. Relaxing, Prair could hear light conversation sparkling around them: hints of laughter, a subterranean bass voice, and a cracking soprano.

He returned with two small bottles and two works – both mates to Weep's. "Do you desire?"

Weep looked down at the concrete floor, suddenly fascinated with her simple shoes. Looking down as well, in reflex, Prair saw that they'd become smudged with cement dust. It was only when the hick repeated himself that Prair realized that while he thought the man had been talking to them, he was really just speaking to Prair.

Prair nodded. He didn't really believe in the tiny nippled bottle, didn't think it was real – was possible. He didn't even know if he wanted Owlsley's words, Owlsley's thoughts, Owlsley's beliefs swimming in his skull. Lost in this chaos, Prair – the part of him that remained – did manage to realize something: being Prair wasn't good. Being Owlsley might be better.

Weep took both needles, both bottles, and handed him one of each. A touch of fear as he hunted for a vein, but she stopped to help him find it – with a few quick, cruel slaps on the inside of his arm.

The needle was cold . . . or what it contained was chilled, pure. The injection seemed to last for ages, as if Weep was intentionally slipping the concentrate into him – each memory, one strand of RNA at a time.

He wanted to cry. Why, he didn't understand. Pleasure at the potential? The surging pain of the fluid entering his body? The possibility that it was all a cruel illusion, a trick that was going to laugh at him in the next moment? The tears finally did come, though, despite the fact he couldn't pinpoint the source. Not wracking sobs – rather a seeping from his eyes, a glistening rather than a rainfall of sorrow.

Finally drained, Weep pulled the needle free, rubbed the sore spot with her thin fingers.

"Feel it?" she said, standing tall and sure, looking into his eyes with intense expression.

Did he? Did he feel the microscopic strands of Owlsley winding their way through his consciousness? A ghost seemed to walk through him – a physical illusion of weight and strength, confidence and cold assurance that he was right, perfect, and strong. But did he feel that – did he really? Something was there, either in the fluid injected into him or because of his faith in the action, a wish for the ridiculous dream that he hoped, above all else, he wouldn't wake up from. He wanted – and that wanting might be enough to make him feel something.

"Let me introduce you," Weep said, taking him by his sore arm and pulling him into the lights.

There were maybe a dozen, a cross-section.

He saw a tall man in a blue suit, an old black woman, a middle-aged matron in a simple brown dress.

The farm-boy appeared on his left. "Larry Farrley." His tone was cold and crisp, intimate but not friendly.

Prair managed a smile, saying, "Hello" as the hick melted back into the darkness of the vast building, to be replaced by a blonde girl, maybe 23–34. Still girlish, but not a child.

Maybe it was Prair, maybe a touch of Owlsley, but suddenly he looking down at her and wondering, with certainly, what her sin was – what she would reveal to him, and what her punishment might be.

"Lucy Moore," she said, firmly, looking him up and down as if finding him inadequate to be part of their circle.

"Nice to meet you," Prair managed to say in a quavering voice.

An old white woman, a matron. She belonged in a knitting barn, in a shop somewhere that sold silk plants and antique furniture. Her air spoke of knowledge and skill over many years – a powerful figure illuminated by the angry hissing light of the lanterns. "I'm Margaret Reynolds."

"Nice to meet you," Prair said with sudden, firm conviction; a momentary surge of strength that seemed to flicked up from a furnace in his gut. Owlsley stretching, awakening?

"Charles Emmerson Lucas," said a tall man in jeans and an over-large sweatshirt.

There were more, many of them. It was hard to keep them straight in his mind. Prair's head began swimming, roaring along with the lanterns. He stumbled a couple of times as he was led around, and cursed himself for his clumsiness – he should have been strong and firm, not half-dazed on the arm of a tiny girl. Where was that strength he'd felt, that presence? He should have been *seeing* these people, not just letting their hard eyes glance across his fuzzy perceptions. He should understand them, see their secrets, their sins—

The last. An air of saintliness, a weight of silence as he was drawn across the warehouse space – through a shadowy region, cool from the absence of the many lamps – to an island of just one: a black woman, stately and cool. She stood, arms at her sides. Her face seemed carved, as warm and human as ancient stone. She said her name and Prair didn't hear it.

Again he cursed his confusion. He should have been able to see, damnit, he should have *strength*. He should *know*, as Owlsley would have known, what was happening.

She said her name again. Her voice was clear and crisp, and again Prair didn't hear, didn't comprehend. Her eyes drank him in – as dark as knots in an old tree, as deep as bottomless oil. Her hair, he noticed, was hidden behind a tribal scarf. She was wearing a simple white blouse, a simple brown dress. Around her neck was a simple cross. She said her name again, cool and crisp.

I should know – I *should* – the weight of Weep on his arm was torture, his body was screaming for something . . . something that Prair wanted and Owlsley demanded. He pushed, forced it out in a high-pierced scream – a child's cry of birth, a breaking of an already cracked mind.

He didn't know if it was the fluid – or if Prair himself was creating Owlsley in his own mind from too much pain, too much guilt, too much humiliation, and failure. He never knew. Would never, ever know. But as he panted, kneeling on the rough cement, Weep away from him, standing near but not protectively, he knew something:

Brother, sister, mother, father, friend, wife, lover, child. Their names suddenly meant something: their secrets tumbled in front of him, their names linking to blown-up photographs, documentation, pages in books, and memories – maybe Prair's, maybe Owlsley's.

Weep bent down, lifted him firmly to his feet as footsteps softly approached from behind. "My sister," she said, her new name taken from the word written over her sister's body: "Alice Souyer was my sister."

He didn't look at her, instead he stared at the black woman, the woman who had spoken her name twice to him, but only heard for the first time right then – comprehension thundering in his mind. Her hands were behind her back – to hide, he *knew*, absolutely, her missing thumbs.

Owlsley, the man, was gone – all that remained of him were his words, and his fans. They missed him, but they weren't the only ones. His victims, the survivors and the relatives, they, too, missed him – missed an opportunity to repay him for all he'd done.

The understanding, the revelation was thunder *and* lighting in his mind: as far as they were concerned Owlsley *was* back, and this time he was not escaping.

Whether it was Prair who understood this, or the RNA ghost of Owlsley, it didn't matter – not to him and, certainly, not them.

AN END TO HUNGER

China Miéville

I met Aykan in a pub sometime late in 1997. I was with friends, and one of them was loudly talking about the Internet, which we were all very excited about.

"Fucking Internet's fucking dead, man. Yesterday's bullshit," I heard from two tables away. Aykan was staring at me, gazing at me curiously, like he wasn't sure I'd let him crash this party.

He was Turkish (I asked because of his name). His English was flawless. He had none of the throaty accent I half-expected, though each of his words did sound finished in a slightly unnatural way.

He smoked high tar incessantly ("Fucking national sport: they wouldn't let me in fucking 'Stanbul without sufficient shit in my lungs."). He liked me because I wasn't intimidated by him. I let him call me names and didn't get my back up when he was rude. Which he was, often.

My friends hated him, and after he'd left I nodded and murmured agreement with them about what a weirdo, about how rude and where he got off, but the fact was I couldn't get worked up about Aykan. He told us off for getting moist about e-mail and the web. He told us wired connection was dead. I asked him what he was into instead and he took a long drag on his stinking cigarette and shook his head, dismissively exhaling the smoke.

"Nanotech," he said. "Little shit."

He didn't explain that. I left him my phone number but I never expected to hear from him. Ten months later he called me. It was just luck that I lived at the same address, and I told him that.

"People don't fucking move, man," he said, incomprehensibly.

I arranged to meet him after work. He sounded a bit distracted, a bit miserable even.

"Do you play games, man?" he said. "N64?"

"I've got a PlayStation," I told him.

"PlayStation licks shit, man," he told me. "Bullshit digital controls. I'll give you the ads, though. PlayStation ads sing sweet hymns, but you want a fucking analog control stick, or you're playing once removed. You know anyone with N64?"

As soon as we met he handed me a little grey plastic square. It was a game pack for a Nintendo 64 system, but it was roughcast and imperfectly finished, its seam bizarrely ragged. It had no label, only a sticker scrawled with illegible handwriting.

"What's this?" I asked.

"Find someone with N64," he said. "Project of mine."

We talked for a couple of hours. I asked Aykan what he did for a living. He did that dismissive smoking thing again. He muttered about computer consultancy and web design. I thought the Internet was dead, I told him. He agreed fervently.

I asked him what nanotech stuff he was doing and he became ragged with enthusiasm. He caught me with crazy looks and grinned at odd intervals, so I couldn't tell if he was bullshitting me.

"Don't talk to me about little miniature fucking arterial cleaning robots, don't fucking talk to me about medical reconstruction, or microwhateverthefucks to clean up oil slicks, OK? That's bullshit to get people on board. What's going to be big in nanotech? Eh? Like any other fucking thing . . ." he banged the table and slopped beer. "The money's in *games*."

Aykan had extraordinary schemes. He told me about his prototype. It was crude, he said, but it was a start. "It's old school meets new school," he kept saying. "Kids with fucking conkers, in the playground." The game was called Blood Battle, or Bloody Hell, or Bloodwar. He hadn't decided.

"You buy a little home injection kit, like you're diabetic. And you build up your own serum from the pack provided. Like when you play a wargame you choose how many fuckers on horseback and how many artillery, right? Well, you have different vials full of microbots that interact with your blood, each type with different defences and attacks, and there are miniature repair robots like medics, all of these fuckers microsize. And you make yourself a blood army, with electrical frontline, chemical attack forces, good defences, whatever you've decided.

"Then when you go to the playground and you meet your little friend who's also bought Bloodwar, and you *prick your fingers*, right, like you're going to be blood brothers, and you each squeeze out a drop of blood into a special dish, and you fucking *mix 'em up*." I stared at him incredulously while he grinned and smoked. "And then you sit back and watch the blood shimmer and bubble and move about. Because there's a war on." He grinned for a long time.

"How do you know who's won?" I asked eventually.

"The dish," he said. "Comes with a little display and speakers in the base. Picks up signals from the 'bots and amplifies them. You hear battle sounds and your troops reporting casualties, and at the end you get a score and you see who's won."

He sat back a minute and smoked some more, watching me. I tried to think of something sardonic to say, but was defeated. He leaned in suddenly and pulled out a little Swiss army knife.

"I'll show you," he said intensely. "You up for it? I can show you now. I'm primed. We know you'll lose because you've got no troops, but you'll see how it works." The knife waited above his thumb, and he gazed at me for the go-ahead. I hesitated and shook my head. I couldn't tell if he was serious or not, if he'd actually injected himself with these lunatic game-pieces, but he was weirding me out.

He had other ideas. There were spinoffs for Bloodwar, and there were other more complicated games, involving outside equipment like airport metal detectors that you walked through, that set off particular reactions from your tiny little internal robots. But Bloodwar was his favourite.

I gave him my e-mail address and thanked him for the N64 pack. He wouldn't tell me where he lived, but he gave me his mobile number. I called it at seven the next morning.

"Jesus fucking Christ, Aykan," I said. "This game, thing, whatever . . . it's total genius."

I had been curious enough to rent a Nintendo 64 console from Blockbusters on my way home, to play the thing he'd given me.

It was utterly extraordinary. It was not a game. It was a totally immersing piece of art, a multilayered environment that passed through anarchic and biting political commentary, bleak dreamscapes, erotic staging posts. There was no "gameplay", only exploration, of the environment, of the conspiracies being unmasked. The viewpoint shifted and changed vertiginously. There were moments of shocking power.

I was stunned. I pulled an all-nighter, and called him as early as I thought I could get away with.

"What is this shit?" I asked. "When's it coming out? I'll buy a fucking console just for this."

"It's not coming out, man," Aykan said. He sounded quite awake. "It's just some shit I did. Nintendo are bastards, man," he said. "They'd never license it. No fucker'd produce it anyway. It's just for my friends. The hardest thing, let me tell you, the hardest thing isn't the programming, it's making the housing. If they read off CDs or whatever, no fucking problem. But putting the software into that poxy stupid little plastic square, and making it so it'll fit in the casing with all the right connectors. That's the hard bit. That's why I'm not doing that shit any more. Boring."

I still own it, Aykan's guerrilla software, his illicit work of art. I still play it. Two years on I'm still discovering new levels, new layers. Later, before he disappeared, Aykan translated the scrawled title for me: *We Deserve Better Than This*.

Aykan's occasional e-mails to me often included web addresses for me to look up. I say Aykan's e-mails, although no name ever appeared in the "Sender" column, and they were never signed. Whenever I tried to reply to them, they would register as coming from a nonsense address, and the messages would bounce back to me. But Aykan never denied the e-mails were his, and sometimes even asked me if I'd received certain messages. He irritably dismissed questions about how or why he sent them anonymously. If I wanted to contact him, I had to do it by phone.

This was a time when mass-circulation e-mails were getting out of hand. Every day I'd get one or two urls to look up.

Sometimes they were pornographic, with a message like "Did you know that was possible???!!!" from some sad lad or other I vaguely knew. More often they were links to some weird news story or other. Usually they looked too dull to chase up.

Aykan's, though, I always checked. They were pretty extraordinary. Essays, art pieces, things like that.

Sometimes he provided a password to get into hidden pages on-line, and when I visited them they were incomprehensible internal reports that looked very much like governments talking to governments, or rebel groups talking to rebels. I couldn't tell if they were hoaxes, but if not, I was rather alarmed.

"What's all this shit you keep sending me?" I demanded.

"Interesting, huh?" he sniggered, and put the phone down.

It wasn't just websites he sent me. Sometimes he directed me to one or another of his on-line projects. That was how I realised that Aykan was a virtuoso of programming. He was something extraordinary. Once, on one of our infrequent rendezvous, I called him a hacker. He burst out laughing, then got very angry with me.

"Fucking hacker?" He laughed again. "Fucking *hacker*? Listen bro, you're not talking to some sebum-faced little sixteen-year-old geekboy with wank-stained pants who calls himself Dev-L." He swore furiously. 'I'm not a fucking hacker, man, I'm a fucking artist, I'm a hardworking wage-slave, I'm a *concerned motherfucking citizen*, whatever you want, but I'm not a fucking hacker."

I didn't care what he wanted to call himself. Whatever he thought he was, he left me awestruck – disbelieving, really, utterly bewildered – with what he could do.

"What search engine do you use?" he wrote to me once. "How often does your name come up? Try it now and then again tomorrow morning."

According to searchsites.com I appeared on seven websites, all of them work-related rubbish. When I typed in my name again the next day, I was nowhere. I looked up my company's website and there I was, halfway down the page. But when I ran my name through searchsites or runbot or megawhere, I had no luck. I had become invisible.

"What did you do, you fuck?" I yelled down the phone. I was excited, though, feigning anger badly.

"How's that, huh? I ran you through my hide engine." I could hear him smoking. "Don't worry, man," he said. "I'll take you out of it. But it's good, huh? Tomorrow I think I'm gonna run Jack fucking Straw through it, or maybe every fucking sex-related word I can think of." He put the phone down.

If he did run those words through his engine, it had stopped working. I checked the next day. But maybe he just hadn't bothered.

I spoke to Aykan several times, but a couple of months went by without me seeing him.

One morning I found another of his unmarked e-mails in my in-box. "HAVE YOU SEEN THIS FUCKPIG SCUM-SUCKING PIECE OF SHIT?"

I had. It was the homepage of an organisation called An End To Hunger. I had been sent it at least twice already, as a recipient on mass e-mailings.

The site contained low-key, muted and simple graphics, with a selection of harrowing statistics about world hunger. There were links to the UN Food Programme, Oxfam, and so on. But what made it such a popular site was its push-button charity donation.

Once per day, anyone visiting the site could click a little toggle, and in the words of the website, "feed the hungry". Alongside the button was a list of sponsors – all very dignified, no logos or bells or whistles, just the name of the company and a link to its homepage. Each sponsor would donate half a cent per click, which was roughly equivalent to half a cup of rice, or maize or whatever.

It all made me feel a bit uneasy, like corporate charity usually did. When I'd first visited the site I'd pressed the button. It had seemed churlish not to. But I hadn't visited it since, and I was getting irritated with people recommending it to me.

I called Aykan. He was incandescent.

"I've seen the site," I told him. "Bit gruesome, isn't it?"

"Gruesome?" he shouted. "It's fucking *sick* is what it is. It's fucking *beyond beyond*, man. I mean, forget politics this shit couldn't be parodied."

"I keep getting e-mails recommending it," I told him.

"Any motherfucker e-mails you that, reply them right back, tell them to shove it up their arses till it hits the roof of their mouth, yeah? I mean by shit almighty . . . have you read the FAQ on the website?" I had not. "Listen to this. This is fucking *verbatim,* OK? 'Can I click the "Give Food" button more than once, and keep making donations?' 'We're sorry!' " Aykan's voice spewed bile. " 'We're real sorry! It's a shame but you can't do that. Our sponsors have agreed for us to count one donation per person per day, and any more would be breaking our agreement.' " He made a noise like angry retching.

"Fuck 'em, bro," he said. He sounded incredibly sad. "They tell us we can't be *naughty* and do it too *often*?" I didn't tell him I had donated that first time. He was making me ashamed.

I murmured something to him, some agreement, some dismissal and condemnation. It wasn't enough.

"This is fucking war, man," he said urgently. "This one I can't let go."

"Run them through your hide engine," I suggested vaguely.

"What?" he said, enraged. "What the fuck you talking about? Don't talk horsefuck, man. I want them down and dead. Time for the big fucking guns, hombre," he said, and put the phone down. I tried to call him back but he didn't pick up.

Two days later I got another e-mail.

"Try visiting you shitting know where," it said. I did, and An End To Hunger would not come up. The browser couldn't find it. I tried again at the end of the day and it was back, with a small, pious note about how sad they were to be targeted by hackers.

Aykan wouldn't answer his phone.

A week and a half later he called me.

"Man!" he shouted at me. "Go back to the bastards," he said. "I was . . . you know, I jumped the gun last time. Wasn't particularly clever, right? But it was like a fucking – what do you call it – I was doing a *reconnoitre*. But go back now, click the bastard button all you can."

"What did you do, Aykan?" I said. I was at work, and kept my voice neutral.

"I don't know how long it'll last," he said, "so get *all* your fucking friends to go visiting. For a *short time only* the shitlicking sponsors are going to be making a reasonable fucking payout. Ten bucks a fucking click, my friend, none of this half a cent bull. So go give generously."

It's impossible to say how much of an impact it had. Certainly for the next day or so I proselytised zealously. An End To Hunger kept it very quiet, when they found out. I like to think that it took the businesses in question the best part of a day to realise that their pledged donations had gone up by around 100,000 per cent.

I wondered when Aykan would get bored of these games.

We spoke for a long time on the phone, one evening a fortnight or so later. He sounded exhausted.

"What you up to?" I asked him.

"Waging war, man," he said shortly.

I suggested that he was wearing himself out, that he should apply himself to other things. He got angry and depressed all at once.

"It really got to me, this one," he said. "It really *got to me*. I dunno why, but I can't . . . This one matters. But . . . I keep hitting the wrong enemy. "Corporate sponsors don't actually care!" "Big business is hypocritical!" That's not news to *any-fuckingbody*. Who doesn't know? Who gives a fuck about *that*?

"Do you ever stop to think about them, man?" he said. "Them in the AETH office. What must that do to your head? Like some kind of ghouls, man. What's that got to do to you?"

I changed the subject several times, but it kept coming back. "I dunno, man . . ." he kept saying. "I dunno what to do . . ."

It may have been the next day that he decided, but it was a good three weeks before he could make it work.

"Go and visit A* E** T* H*****, the e-mail said. "Click and send the poor starving masses a present. See what happens."

I went to the site. Apart from a few minor updates, nothing seemed to have changed. I prevaricated a while, looking for some clue as to what Aykan had done. Eventually I clicked the "Give Food" button and waited.

Nothing happened.

The usual little message, thanking me on behalf of hungry people, appeared. I waited a couple more minutes, then left. Whatever Aykan had planned, I thought, it hadn't come off.

A couple of hours later I checked my e-mail.

"How the *fuck* . . ." I said, and paused, shaking my head. "How the *fuck*, you insane genius bastard, did you do that?"

"You like that?" The connection was terrible, but I could hear Aykan yelling with laughter. He sounded triumphant. "You fucking like it?"

"I . . . I don't know. I'm very impressed, whatever."

I was staring at the message in my in-box. The sender was listed as "Very Hungry Foreign People".

"Dear Kind Generous Person," it read. "Thank you so much for your Generous gift of half a cup of wet rice. Our Children will treasure every grain. And do please thank your Kind Organisers at An End To Hunger for organising their rich friends to throw rice at us – that is the advantage of employing Sweatshop labour and trade union busting. That way they can afford rice for us poor people. Whatever you do, do keep sitting back and not asking any questions of them, keep them happy, don't agitate for any corporate taxes or grassroots control or anything like that which would threaten the large profits that allow them to buy us Cups of Rice. With humble love and thanks, The Hungry."

"Every motherfucker who clicks the button's going to get that," Aykan said.

"How did you *do* it?"

"It's a fucking program," he said, suddenly irritable. "I stuck it on the website. It scans your fucking hard disk for what looks like your e-mail address, and sends off the message when you draw attention to yourself by clicking. Try pressing 'Reply'."

I did. The return address listed was my own.

"It's very impressive, Aykan," I said, nodding slowly, wishing someone else had written the letter, made it a bit subtler, maybe edited it a bit. "You've done a real number on them."

"Well it ain't over yet, bro," he said. "Watch this space, you know? Watch this fucking space."

My phone went at five the next morning. I padded nude and confused into the sitting room.

"Man." It was Aykan, tense and excited.

"What the fuck time is it?" I muttered, or something like that.

"They're on to me, man," he hissed.

"What?" I huddled vaguely into the sofa, rubbed my eyes. Outside, the sky was two tone. Birds were chirruping imbecilically. "What are you on about?"

"*Our fucking philanthropic friends, man,*" he whispered tersely. "The *concerned folk* over at Feed The World central, you know? They've rumbled me. They've *found* me."

"How do you know?" I said. "Have they contacted you?"

"No no," he said. "They wouldn't do that, that would be admitting what the fuck was up. No, I was watching them on-line, and I can see them tracking me. They can already tell what country I'm in."

"What do you mean?" I said. I was fully awake now. "Are you intercepting their e-mail? Are you crazy?"

"Oh man, there's a hundred fucking million things you can do, read their messages, watch who they're fucking watching, bounce off internal memos, keep tabs on their automatic defences . . . trust me on this: *they're fucking looking for me.*" There was silence. "They may even have found me," he finished.

"So . . ." I shook my head. "So leave it alone. Let it be, get off their back before you piss them off any more and they go to the police."

"Fucking *pofuckinglice* . . ." Aykan's voice swam in scorn. "They won't give it to the fucking police, the police couldn't find their own thumbs if they were plugging up their arses. No, man. It's not the police I'm worried about, it's these Hunger motherfuckers. Haven't you clocked what kind of people these are? These are *bad* people, man. Major bad ju-ju. And anyway, *man* . . .", he shouted suddenly, as if remembering something. "And anyway, what the fuck you mean *leave it alone*? Don't be such a shiteating coward. I told you, didn't I? I told you this was a fucking *war*, didn't I?" He was shouting by now. I tried to get him to shut up. "I'm not looking for *advice*, I just wanted to let you know what was going on."

He broke the connection. I did not phone him back. I was tired and pissed off. *Paranoid prick*, I thought, and went back to bed.

Aykan kept sending his obscure e-mails, advising me of some new change to An End To Hunger.

The letter to donors did not last long, but Aykan was relent-less. He directed me to their sponsors page, and I discovered that he had rerouted every link to a different revolutionary left organisation. He created a small pop-up screen that appeared when the "donate" button was clicked, that compared the nutri-tional value of rice with what was rotting in European food mountains.

He kept hinting at some final salvo, some ultimate attack.

"I keep watching them, man," he told me in one of his

irregular phone calls. "I swear they are so on my tail. I'm going to have to be really fucking careful. This could get very fucking nasty."

"Stop talking rubbish," I said, exasperated. "You think you're in some cheap thriller? You're risking jail for hacking – and don't shout at me, because that's what they'll call it – but that's all."

"Fuck you, bro!" he shouted, excitedly. "Don't be so naive! You think this is a game? I told you . . . these fuckers aren't going to the police. Don't you fucking *see*, man? I've done the *worst thing you can do* . . . I've fucking *impugned their philanthropy*, man! I've fucking sneered at them while they do the Mother Teresa thing, and that they can't fucking stand!"

I was worried about him. He was totally infuriating, no longer even coming close to conversing, just taking some phrase or other of mine as a jumping off point to discuss some insane conspiracy.

He sent me bizarre, partial e-mails that made almost no sense at all. Some were just a sentence: "They'll love this" or "I'll show them what it really means".

Some were longer, like cuts from the middle of works in progress, half-finished memos and snatches of programming. Some were garbled articles from various encyclopaedias, about international politics, about on-line democracy, about computerised supermarket stocktaking, about kwashiorkor and other kinds of malnutrition.

Slowly, with a stealthy amazement and fear, I started to tie these threads together. I realised that what looked like a patchwork of mad threats and ludicrous hyperbole was something more, something united by an extraordinary logic. Through these partial snippets, these hints and jokes and threats, I began to get a sense of what Aykan planned.

I denied it.

I tried desperately not to believe it, it was just too big. My horror was coloured with awe that he could even dream up such a plan, let alone believe he had the skills to make it work.

It was utterly unbelievable. It was horrific.

I knew he could do it.

I bombarded him with phone calls, which he never picked up. He had no voice-mail, and I was left swearing and stalking from room to room, totally unable to reach him.

An End To Hunger had been ominously quiet for some time now. It had operated without interruption for at least three weeks. Aykan was building up to his final plan. I was going crazy. There was a mad intensity to everything, it was like some frenetic nightmare, every time I thought of Aykan and his plans and conspiracies. I was scared.

Finally, at ten minutes to eleven on a Sunday evening, he called.

"Man," he said.

"Aykan," I said, and sighed once, then stammered to get my words out. "Aykan, man, you can't *do this*," I said. "I don't care how fucking much you hate them, man, they're just a bunch of idiot liberals and you *cannot do that to them*, it's just not *worth it*, don't be *crazy* . . ."

"Shut up, man!" he shouted. "Just shut up, for fuck's sake! Listen to me!" He was whispering again, urgently.

He was, I suddenly realised, afraid.

"I don't have any fucking time, bro," he said, urgently. "You've got to get over here, you've got to help me."

"What's going on, man?" I said.

"*They're coming*," he whispered, and something in his voice made me cold.

"The fuckers tricked me," he went on, "they kept it looking like they were searching, but they were better than I thought, they clocked me ages ago, they were just biding time, and then . . . and then . . . They're *on their way!*" He hissed the last sentence, like a curse.

"Aykan," I said slowly. "Aykan, man, you've got to stop this crazy shit," I said. "Are the police coming . . .?"

He almost screamed with anger.

"*Godfuckingdammit don't you listen to me?* Any fucker can handle the police, but it's this *charity* wants my fucking head!" He was in a terrible state.

He had invited me to his house, I realised. For the first time in five years, he was ready to tell me where he lived. I tried to cut into his diatribe. "I know shit about these bastards you wouldn't *believe*, man," he was moaning. "Like some fucking *parasite* . . . You got no curiosity what kind of fucker lives like that?"

I managed to break in.

"What can I do, man?" I said. "You want me to come over?"

"Yeah, man, *please*, help me get my shit the fuck away," he said.

He named an address about twenty minutes walk away. I swore at him.

"You been close all this time," I said.

"Please just hurry," he whispered, and broke the connection.

Aykan's house was one in a street of nondescript redbricks, and I was staring at it for several seconds before I saw that anything was wrong.

The front window was broken, and fringes of curtain were waving like seaweed through the hole.

I sprinted the last few feet, shouting. No one answered the bell. I pounded the door, and lights went on opposite and above me, but no one came to his door.

I peered in through the hole. I grabbed careful hold of the ragged glass frame and climbed into Aykan's house.

I stood, my breath shallow, whispering his name again and again. The sound of my own voice was very thin. It frightened me, such a little sound in that silence.

It was a tiny flat, a weird mixture of mess and anal fastidiousness. The bed-sitting room was crowded with Ikea-type shelves wedged tight with carefully ordered magazines and software, all exactly lined up. In the corner was a collection of extraordinarily powerful computer hardware, a tight little local-area network, with printer and scanners and modems and monitors wedged into unlikely angles. The coffee table was revolting with ashtrays and unwashed cups.

I was utterly alone.

I wandered quickly through all the rooms, again and again, back and forth, as if I might have missed him, standing in a corner. As if he might be waiting for me to find him. Apart from the shattered window, there was no sign of trouble. I waited and moped, but no one came.

After a few minutes I saw a green light winking langourously at me, and realised that his main computer was on sleep mode. I pressed return. The monitor lit up, and I saw that Aykan's e-mail program was running.

His in-box was empty, except for one message, that had arrived earlier that evening.

It was listed as from AETH. I felt a slow, cold surge of adrenaline.

Slowly I reached out and clicked the message, opening it.

We're so very disappointed that you don't consider our mission to improve the lot of the world's hungry to be a worthy one. We are motivated to try to help the poorest people on earth, at a cost of nothing to our users. We consider this to be a winning situation for all sides. Without us, after all, the poor and the hungry have no voice.

It is a matter of great sadness to us that you do not share our vision, and that you have found it necessary to undermine our work. As you see, we have been able to trace you, through the sabotage to our website. We do not believe that this situation would be satisfactorily resolved through your country's courts.

We think it only reasonable to inform you that we take your conduct very seriously. We have our mission to consider, and we can no longer allow you to endanger those lives for which we work so hard.

We intend to discuss this matter with you. In person. Now.

And that was all.

I waited in the cold, reading and rereading that message, looking around me in that quiet flat. Eventually I left. I debated taking the computer away, but it was too heavy, and anyway, it was really beyond me. I was never more than a day-to-day user. The kind of stuff Aykan had on there I'd never make head or tail of.

I called his mobile hundreds of times, but got only a dead signal.

I have no idea where he went, or what happened.

He could have broken that window himself. He could have written that e-mail himself. He could have lost it completely and run off screaming into the night, with no one at all on his tail. I keep waiting, and hoping that maybe I'll hear from him.

He could be hunted, even now. Maybe he stays out of sight, keeps off-line, uses pseudonyms, a thief in the night, letting dust blow over his on-line tracks.

Or maybe he was caught.

Maybe he was taken away, to discuss the politics of charity.

Every week, some e-mail or other recommends I visit An End To Hunger. The site is running well. Its problems seem to be over.

A SCANNER DARKLY

Philip K. Dick

From within his scramble suit the nebulous blur who signed in as Fred faced another nebulous blur representing himself as Hank.

"So much for Donna, for Charley Freck, and – let's see . . ." Hank's metallic monotone clicked off for a second. "All right, you've covered Jim Barris." Hank made an annotation on the pad before him. "Doug Weeks, you think, is probably dead or out of this area."

"Or hiding and inactive," Fred said.

"Have you heard anyone mention this name: Earl or Art De Winter?"

"No."

"How about a woman named Molly? Large woman."

"No."

"How about a pair of spades, brothers, about twenty, named something like Hatfield? Possibly dealing in pound bags of heroin."

"Pounds? *Pound* bags of heroin?"

"That's right."

"No," Fred said. "I'd remember that."

"A Swedish person, tall, Swedish name. Male. Served time, wry sense of humor. Big man but thin, carrying a great deal of cash, probably from the split of a shipment earlier this month."

"I'll watch for him," Fred said. "Pounds." He shook his head, or rather the nebulous blur wobbled.

Hank sorted among his holographic notes. "Well, this one is in jail." He held up a picture briefly, then read the reverse. "No, this one's dead; they've got the body downstairs." He sorted on. Time passed. "Do you think the Jora girl is turning tricks?"

"I doubt it." Jora Kajas was only fifteen. Strung out on injectable Substance D already, she lived in a slum room in Brea, upstairs, the only heat radiating from a water heater, her source of income a State of California tuition scholarship she had won. She had not attended classes, so far as he knew, in six months.

"When she does, let me know. Then we can go after the parents."

"Okay." Fred nodded.

"Boy, the bubblegummers go downhill fast. We had one in here the other day – she looked fifty. Wispy gray hair, missing teeth, eyes sunk in, arms like pipe cleaners . . . We asked her what her age was and she said, 'Nineteen.' We double-checked. 'You know how old you look?' this one matron said to her. 'Look in the mirror.' So she looked in the mirror. She started to cry. I asked her how long she'd been shooting up."

"A year," Fred said.

"Four months."

"The street stuff is bad right now," Fred said, not trying to imagine the girl, nineteen, with her hair falling out. "Cut with worse garbage than usual."

"You know how she got strung out? Her brothers, both of them, who were dealing, went in her bedroom one night, held her down and shot her up, then balled her. Both of them. To break her in to her new life, I guess. She'd been on the corner several months when we hauled her in here."

"Where are they now?" He thought he might run into them.

"Serving a six-month sentence for possession. The girl's also got the clap, now, and didn't realize it. So it's gone up deep inside her, the way it does. Her brothers thought that was funny."

"Nice guys," Fred said.

"I'll tell you one that'll get you for sure. You're aware of the three babies over at Fairfield Hospital that they have to give hits of smack to every day, that are too young to withdraw yet? A nurse tried to—"

"It gets me," Fred said in his mechanical monotone. "I heard enough, thanks."

Hank continued, "When you think of newborn babies being heroin addicts because—"

"Thanks," the nebulous blur called Fred repeated.

"What do you figure the bust should be for a mother that gives a newborn baby a joypop of heroin to pacify it, to keep it from crying? Overnight in the county farm?"

"Something like that," Fred said tonelessly. "Maybe a weekend, like they do the drunks. Sometimes I wish I knew how to go crazy. I forget how."

"It's a lost art," Hank said. "Maybe there's an instruction manual on it."

"There was this flick back around 1970," Fred said, "called *The French Connection*, about a two-man team of heroin narks, and when they made their hit one of them went totally bananas and started shooting everyone in sight, including his superiors. It made no difference."

"It's maybe better you don't know who I am, then," Hank said. "You could only get me by accident."

"Somebody," Fred said, "will get us all anyhow eventually."

"It'll be a relief. A distinct relief." Going farther into his pile of notes, Hank said, "Jerry Fabin. Well, we'll write him off. N.A.C. The boys down the hall say Fabin told the responding officers on the way to the clinic that a little contract man three feet high, legless, on a cart, had been rolling after him day and night. But he never told anybody because if he did they'd freak and get the hell out and then he'd have no friends, nobody to talk to."

"Yeah," Fred said stoically. "Fabin has had it. I read the EEG analysis from the clinic. We can forget about him."

Whenever he sat facing Hank and did his reporting thing, he experienced a certain deep change in himself. Afterward was when he usually noticed it, although at the time he sensed that for a reason he assumed a measured and uninvolved attitude. Whatever came up and whoever it was about possessed no emotional significance to him during these sessions.

At first he had believed it to be the scramble suits that both of them wore; they could not physically sense each other. Later on he conjectured that the suits made no actual difference; it was the situation itself. Hank, for professional reasons, purposefully played down the usual warmth; the usual arousal in all directions; no anger, no love, no strong emotions of any sort would help either of them. How could intense natural involvement be of use when they were discussing crimes, serious crimes, committed by persons close to Fred and even, as in the case of Luckman and Donna, dear to him? He had to neutralize himself; they both did, him more so than Hank. They became neutral; they spoke in a neutral fashion; they looked neutral. Gradually it became easy to do so, without prearrangement.

And then afterward all his feelings seeped back.

Indignation at many of the events he had seen, even horror, in retrospect: shock. Great overpowering runs for which there had been no previews. With the audio always up too loud inside his head.

But while he sat across the table from Hank he felt none of these. Theoretically, he could describe anything he had witnessed in an impassive way. Or hear anything from Hank.

For example, he could offhandedly say "Donna is dying of hep and using her needle to wipe out as many of her friends as she can. Best thing here would be to pistol-whip her until she knocks it off." His own chick . . . *if* he had observed that or knew it for a fact. Or "Donna suffered a massive vasoconstriction from a mickey-mouse LSD analogue the other day and half the blood vessels in her brain shut down." Or "Donna is dead." And Hank would note that down and maybe say "Who sold her the stuff and where's it made?" or "Where's the funeral, and we should get license numbers and names," and he'd discuss that without feeling.

This was Fred. But then later on Fred evolved into Bob Arctor, somewhere along the sidewalk between the Pizza Hut and the Arco gas station (regular now a dollar two cents a gallon), and the terrible colors seeped back into him whether he liked it or not.

This change in him as Fred was an economy of the passions. Firemen and doctors and morticians did the same trip in their work. None of them could leap up and exclaim each few moments; they would first wear themselves out and be worthless and then wear out everyone else, both as technicians on the job and as humans off. An individual had just so much energy.

Hank did not force this dispassion on him; he *allowed* him to be like this. For his own sake. Fred appreciated it.

"What about Arctor?" Hank asked.

In addition to everyone else, Fred in his scramble suit naturally reported on himself. If he did not, his superior – and through him the whole law-enforcement apparatus – would become aware of who Fred was, suit or not. The agency plants would report back, and very soon he as Bob Arctor, sitting in his living room smoking dope and dropping dope with the other dopers, would find he had a little three-foot-high contract man on a cart coasting after him, too. And he would not be hallucinating, as had been Jerry Fabin.

"Arctor's not doing anything much," Fred said, as he always did. "Works at his nowhere Blue Chip Stamp job, drops a few tabs of death cut with meth during the day—"

"I'm not sure." Hank fiddled with one particular sheet of paper. "We have a tip here from an informant whose tips generally pan out that Arctor has funds above and beyond what the Blue Chip Redemption Center pays him. We called them and asked what his take-home pay is. It's not much. And then we inquired into that, why that is, and we found he isn't employed there full time throughout the week."

"No shit," Fred said dismally, realizing that the "above-and-beyond" funds were of course those provided him for his narking. Every week small-denomination bills were dispensed to him by a machine masquerading as a Dr. Pepper source at a Mexican bar and restaurant in Placentia. This was in essence payoffs on information he gave that resulted in convictions. Sometimes this sum became exceptionally great, as when a major heroin seizure occurred.

Hank read on reflectively, "And according to this informant, Arctor comes and goes mysteriously, especially around sunset. After he arrives home he eats, then on what may be pretexts takes off again. Sometimes very fast. But he's never gone for long." He glanced up – the scramble suit glanced up – at Fred. "Have you observed any of this? Can you verify? Does it amount to anything?"

"Most likely his chick, Donna," Fred said.

"Well, 'most likely.' You're supposed to know."

"It's Donna. He's over there banging her night and day." He felt acutely uncomfortable. "But I'll check into it and let you know. Who's this informant? Might be a burn toward Arctor."

"Hell, we don't know. On the phone. No print – he used some sort of rinky-dink electronic grid." Hank chuckled; it sounded odd, coming out metallically as it did. "But it worked. Enough."

190   *PHILIP K. DICK*

"Christ," Fred protested, "it's that burned-out acid head Jim Barris doing a schizy grudge number on Arctor's head! Barris took endless electronic-repair courses in the Service, plus heavy-machinery maintenance. I wouldn't give him the time of day as an informant."

Hank said, "We don't know it's Barris, and anyhow there may be more to Barris than 'burned-out acid head.' We've got several people looking into it. Nothing I feel would be of use to you, at least so far."

"Anyhow, it's one of Arctor's friends," Fred said.

"Yes, it's undoubtedly a vengeance burn trip. These dopers – phoning in on each other every time they get sore. As a matter of fact, he did seem to know Arctor from a close standpoint."

"Nice guy," Fred said bitterly.

"Well, that's how we find out," Hank said. "What's the difference between that and what you're doing?"

"I'm not doing it for a grudge," Fred said.

"Why are you doing it, actually?"

Fred, after an interval said, "Damned if I know."

"You're off Weeks. I think for the time being I'll assign you primarily to observe Bob Arctor. Does he have a middle name? He uses the initial—"

Fred made a strangled, robotlike noise. "Why Arctor?"

"Covertly funded, covertly engaged, making enemies by his activities. What's Arctor's middle name?" Hank's pen poised patiently. He waited to hear.

"Postlethwaite."

"How do you spell that?"

"I don't know, I don't fucking know," Fred said.

"Postlethwaite," Hank said, writing a few letters. "What nationality is that?"

"Welsh," Fred said curtly. He could barely hear; his ears had blurred out, and one by one his other senses as well.

"Are those the people who sing about the men of Harlech? What is 'Harlech'? A town somewhere?"

"Harlech is where the heroic defense against the Yorkists in 1468 –" Fred broke off. Shit, he thought. This is terrible.

"Wait, I want to get this down," Hank was saying, writing away with his pen.

Fred said, "Does this mean you'll be bugging Arctor's house and car?"

"Yes, with the new holographic system; it's better, and we currently have a number of them unrequisitioned. You'll want storage and printout on everything, I would assume." Hank noted that too.

"I'll take what I can get," Fred said. He felt totally spaced from all this; he wished the debriefing session would end and he thought: If only I could drop a couple tabs—

Across from him the other formless blur wrote and wrote, filling in all the inventory ident numbers for all the technological gadgetry that would, if approval came through, soon be available to him, by which to set up a constant monitoring system of the latest design, on his own house, on himself.

For over an hour Barris had been attempting to perfect a silencer made from ordinary household materials costing no more than eleven cents. He had almost done so, with aluminum foil and a piece of foam rubber.

In the night darkness of Bob Arctor's back yard, among the heaps of weeds and rubbish, he was preparing to fire his pistol with the homemade silencer on it.

"The neighbors will hear," Charles Freck said uneasily. He could see lit windows all over, many people probably watching TV or rolling joints.

Luckman, lounging out of sight but able to watch, said, "They only call in murders in this neighborhood."

"Why do you need a silencer?" Charles Freck asked Barris. "I mean, they're illegal."

Barris said moodily, "In this day and age, with the kind of degenerate society we live in and the depravity of the individual, every person of worth needs a gun at all times. To protect himself." He half shut his eyes, and fired his pistol with its homemade silencer. An enormous report sounded, temporarily deafening the three of them. Dogs in far-off yards barked.

Smiling, Barris began unwrapping the aluminum foil from the foam rubber. He appeared to be amused.

"That's sure some silencer," Charles Freck said, wondering when the police would appear. A whole bunch of cars.

"What it did," Barris explained, showing him and Luckman

black-seared passages burned through the foam rubber, "is augment the sound rather than dampen it. But I almost have it right. I have it in principle, anyhow."

"How much is that gun worth?" Charles Freck asked. He had never owned a gun. Several times he had owned a knife, but somebody always stole it from him. One time a chick had done that, while he was in the bathroom.

"Not much," Barris said. "About thirty dollars used, which this is." He held it out to Freck, who backed away apprehensively. "I'll sell it to you," Barris said. "You really ought to have one, to guard yourself against those who would harm you."

"There's a lot of those," Luckman said in his ironic way, with a grin. "I saw in the L. A. *Times* the other day, they're giving away a free transistor radio to those who would harm Freck most successfully."

"I'll trade you a Borg-Warner tach for it," Freck said.

"That you stole from the guy's garage across the street," Luckman said.

"Well, probably the gun's stolen, too," Charles Freck said. Most everything that was worth something was originally ripped off anyhow; it indicated the piece had value. "As a matter of fact," he said, "the guy across the street ripped the tach off in the first place. It's probably changed hands like fifteen times. I mean, it's a really cool tach."

"How do you know he ripped it off?" Luckman asked him.

"Hell, man, he's got eight tachs there in his garage, all dangling cut wires. What else would he be doing with them, that many, I mean? Who goes out and buys eight tachs?"

To Barris, Luckman said, "I thought you were busy working on the cephscope. You finished already?"

"I cannot continually work on that night and day, because it is so extensive," Barris said. "I've got to knock off." He cut, with a complicated pocketknife, another section of foam rubber. "This one will be totally soundless."

"Bob thinks you're at work on the cephscope," Luckman said. "He's lying there in his bed in his room imagining that, while you're out here firing off your pistol. Didn't you agree with Bob that the back rent you owe would be compensated by your—"

"Like good beer," Barris said, "an intricate, painstaking reconstruction of a damaged electronic assembly—"

"Just fire off the great eleven-cent silencer of our times," Luckman said, and belched.

I've had it, Robert Arctor thought.

He lay alone in the dim light of his bedroom, on his back, staring grimly at nothing. Under his pillow he had his .32 police-special revolver; at the sound of Barris's .22 being fired in the back yard he had reflexively gotten his own gun from beneath the bed and placed it within easier reach. A safety move, against any and all dangers; he hadn't even thought it out consciously.

But his .32 under his pillow wouldn't be much good against anything so indirect as sabotage of his most precious and expensive possession. As soon as he had gotten home from the debriefing with Hank he had checked out all the other appliances, and found them okay – especially the car – always the car first, in a situation like this. Whatever was going on, whoever it was by, it was going to be chickenshit and devious: some freak without integrity or guts lurking on the periphery of his life, taking indirect potshots at him from a position of concealed safety. Not a person but more a sort of walking, hiding symptom of their way of life.

There had been a time, once, when he had not lived like this, a .32 under his pillow, a lunatic in the back yard firing off a pistol for God knew what purpose, some other nut or perhaps the same one imposing a brain-print of his own shorted-out upstairs on an incredibly expensive and valued cephscope that everyone in the house, plus all their friends, loved and enjoyed. In former days Bob Arctor had run his affairs differently: there had been a wife much like other wives, two small daughters, a stable household that got swept and cleaned and emptied out daily, the dead newspapers not even opened carried from the front walk to the garbage pail, or even, sometimes, read. But then one day, while lifting out an electric corn popper from under the sink, Arctor had hit his head on the corner of a kitchen cabinet directly above him. The pain, the cut in his scalp, so unexpected and undeserved, had for some reason cleared away the cobwebs. It flashed on him instantly that he didn't hate the kitchen cabinet: he hated his wife, his two daughters, his whole house, the back yard with its power mower, the garage, the radiant heating system, the front yard, the fence, the whole fucking place and everyone in it. He wanted a divorce; he wanted to split. And so he had, very soon. And entered, by degrees, a new and somber life, lacking all of that.

Probably he should have regretted his decision. He had not. That life had been one without excitement, with no adventure. It had been too safe. All the elements that made it up were right there before his eyes, and nothing new could ever be expected. It was like, he had once thought, a little plastic boat that would sail on forever, without incident, until it finally sank, which would be a secret relief to all.

But in this dark world where he now dwelt, ugly things and surprising things and once in a long while a tiny wonderous thing spilled out at him constantly; he could count on nothing. Like the deliberate, evil damage to his Altec cephalochromoscope, around which he had built the pleasure part of his schedule, the segment of the day in which they all relaxed and got mellow. For someone to damage that made no sense, viewed rationally. But not much among these long dark evening shadows here was truly rational, at least in the strict sense. The enigmatic act could have been done by anyone for almost any reason. By any person he knew or had ever encountered. Any one of eight dozen weird heads, assorted freaks, burned-out dopers, psychotic paranoids with hallucinatory grudges acted out in reality, not fantasy. Somebody, in fact, he'd *never* met, who'd picked him at random from the phonebook.

Or his closest friend.

Maybe Jerry Fabin, he thought, before they carted him off. There was a burned-out, poisoned husk. Him and his billions of aphids. Blaming Donna – blaming all chicks, in fact – for "contaminating" him. The queer. But, he thought, if Jerry had gone out to get anybody it'd have been Donna, not me. He thought, and I doubt if Jerry could figure out how to remove the bottom plate from the unit; he might try, but he'd still be there now, screwing and unscrewing the same screw. Or he'd try to get the plate off with a hammer. Anyhow, if Jerry Fabin had done it, the unit would be full of bug eggs that dropped off him. Inside his head Bob Arctor grinned wryly.

Poor fucker, he thought, and his inner grin departed. Poor nowhere mother: once the trace amounts of complex heavy metals got carried to his brain – well, that was it. One more in a long line, a dreary entity among many others like him, an almost endless number of brain-damaged retards. Biological life goes on, he thought. But the soul, the mind – everything else is dead. A reflex machine. Like some insect. Repeating doomed patterns, a single pattern, over and over now. Appropriate or not.

Wonder what he used to be like, he mused. He had not known Jerry that long. Charles Freck claimed that once Jerry had functioned fairly well. I'd have to see that, Arctor thought, to believe it.

Maybe I should tell Hank about the sabotage of my cephscope, he thought. They'd know immediately what it implies. But what can they do for me anyhow? This is the risk you run when you do this kind of work.

It isn't worth it, this work, he thought. There isn't that much money on the fucking planet. But it wasn't the money anyhow. "How come you do this stuff?" Hank had asked him. What did any man, doing any kind of work, know about his actual motives? Boredom, maybe; the desire for a little action. Secret hostility toward every person around him, all his friends, even toward chicks. Or a horrible positive reason: to have watched a human being you loved deeply, that you had gotten real close to, held and slept with and kissed and worried about and befriended and most of all *admired* – to see that warm living person burn out from the inside, burn from the heart outward. Until it clicked and clacked like an insect, repeating one sentence again and again. A *recording*. A closed loop of tape.

". . . I know if I just had another hit . . ."

I'd be okay, he thought. And still saying that, like Jerry Fabin, when three quarters of the brain was mush.

". . . I know, if I just had another hit, that my brain would repair itself."

He had a flash then: Jerry Fabin's brain as the fucked-over wiring of the cephalochromoscope: wires cut, shorts, wires twisted, parts overloaded and no good, line surges, smoke, and a bad smell. And somebody sitting there with a voltmeter, tracing the circuit and muttering, "My, my, a lot of resistors and condensers need to be replaced," and so forth. And then finally from Jerry Fabin would come only a sixty-cycle hum. And they'd give up.

And in Bob Arctor's living room his thousand-dollar custom-quality cephscope crafted by Altec would, after supposedly being repaired, cast onto the wall in dull gray on one small spot:

I KNOW IF I JUST HAD ANOTHER HIT . . .

After that they'd throw the cephscope, damaged beyond repair, and Jerry Fabin, damaged beyond repair, into the same ash can.

Oh well, he thought. Who needs Jerry Fabin? Except maybe Jerry Fabin, who had once envisioned designing and building a nine-foot-long quad-and-TV console system as a present for a friend, and when asked how he would get it from his garage to the friend's house, it being so huge when built and weighing so much, had replied, "No problem, man, I'll just fold it up – I've got the hinges bought already – fold it up, see, fold the whole thing up and put it in an envelope and mail it to him."

Anyhow, Bob Arctor thought, we won't have to keep sweeping aphids out of the house after Jerry's been by to visit. He felt like laughing, thinking about it; they had, once, invented a routine – mostly Luckman had, because he was good at that, funny and clever – about a psychiatric explanation for Jerry's aphid trip. It had to do, naturally, with Jerry Fabin as a small child. Jerry Fabin, see, comes home from first grade one day, with his little books under his arm, whistling merrily, and there, sitting in the dining room beside his mother, is this great aphid, about four feet high. His mother is gazing at it fondly.

"What's happening?" little Jerry Fabin inquires.

"This here is your older brother," his mother says, "who you've never met before. He's come to live with us. I like him better than you. He can do a lot of things you can't."

And from then on, Jerry Fabin's mother and father continually compare him unfavorably with his older brother, who is an aphid. As the two of them grow up, Jerry progressively gets more and more of an inferiority complex – naturally. After high school his brother receives a scholarship to college, while Jerry goes to work in a gas station. After that this brother the aphid becomes a famous doctor or scientist; he wins the Nobel Prize; Jerry's still rotating tires at the gas station, earning a dollar-fifty an hour. His mother and father never cease reminding him of this. They keep saying.

"If only you could have turned out like your brother."

Finally Jerry runs away from home. But he still subconsciously believes aphids to be superior to him. At first he imagines he is safe, but then he starts seeing aphids everywhere, in his hair and around the house, because his inferiority complex has turned into some kind of sexual guilt, and the aphids are a punishment he inflicts on himself, etc.

It did not seem funny now. Now that Jerry had been lugged off in the middle of the night at the request of his own friends. They themselves, all of them present with Jerry that night, had decided to do it; it couldn't be either postponed or avoided. Jerry, that night, had piled every goddamn object in his house against the front door, like maybe nine hundred pounds of assorted crap, including couches and chairs and the refrigerator and TV set, and then told everybody that a giant superintelligent aphid from another planet was out there preparing to break in and get him. And more would be landing later on, even if he got this one. These extraterrestrial aphids were smarter by far than any humans, and would come directly through the walls if necessary, revealing their actual secret powers in such ways. To save himself as long as possible, he had to flood the house with cyanide gas, which he was prepared to do. How was he prepared to do this? He had already taped all the windows and doors airtight. He then proposed to turn on the water faucets in the kitchen and bathroom, flooding the house, saying that the hot-water tank in the garage was filled with cyanide, not water. He had known this for a long time and was saving it for last, as a final defense. They would all die themselves, but at least it would keep the super-intelligent aphids out.

His friends phoned the police, and the police broke down the front door and dragged Jerry off to the N.A. Clinic. The last thing Jerry said to them all was "Bring my things later on – bring my new jacket with the beads on the back." He had just bought it. He liked it a lot. It was about all he liked any more; he considered everything else he owned contaminated.

No, Bob Arctor thought, it doesn't seem funny now, and he wondered why it ever had. Maybe it had stemmed from fear, the dreadful fear they had all felt during the last weeks being around Jerry. Sometimes in the night, Jerry had told them, he prowled his house with a shotgun, sensing the presence of an enemy.

Preparing to shoot first, before being shot. That is, both of them.

And now, Bob Arctor thought, I've got an enemy. Or anyhow I've come onto his trail: signs of him. Another slushed creep in his final stages, like Jerry. And when the final stages of that shit hits, he thought, it really does hit. Better than any special Ford or GM ever sponsored on prime-time TV.

A knock at his bedroom door.

Touching the gun beneath his pillow, he said, "Yeah?"

Mubble-mubble. Barris's voice.

"Come in," Arctor said. He reached to snap on a bedside lamp.

Barris entered, eyes twinkling. "Still awake?"

"A dream woke me," Arctor said. "A religious dream. In it there was this huge clap of thunder, and all of a sudden the heavens rolled aside and God appeared and His voice rumbled at me – what the hell did He say? – oh yeah. 'I am vexed with you, my son,' He said. He was scowling. I was shaking, in the dream, and looking up, and I said, 'What'd I do now, Lord?' And He said, 'You left the cap off the toothpaste tube again.' And then I realized it was my ex-wife."

Seating himself, Barris placed a hand on each of his leather-covered knees, smoothed himself, shook his head, and confronted Arctor. He seemed in an extremely good mood. "Well," he said briskly, "I've got an initial theoretical view as to who might have systematically damaged with malice your cephscope and may do it again."

"If you're going to say it was Luckman—"

"Listen," Barris said, rocking back and forth in agitation. "W-w-what if I told you I've anticipated for weeks a serious malfunction in one of the household appliances, especially an expensive one difficult to repair? My theory *called* for this to happen! This is a confirmation of my over-all theory!"

Arctor eyed him.

Slowly sinking back down, Barris resumed his calm and bright smiling. "You," he said, pointing.

"You think I did it," Arctor said. "Screwed up my own cephscope, with no insurance." Disgust and rage swelled through him. And it was late at night; he needed his sleep.

"No, no," Barris said rapidly, looking distressed. "You are *looking* at the person who did it. Buggered your cephscope. That was my complete intended statement, which I was not allowed to utter."

"You did it?" Mystified, he stared at Barris, whose eyes were murky with a sort of dim triumph. "Why?"

"I mean, it's my theory that I did it," Barris said. "Under posthypnotic suggestion, evidently. With an amnesia block so I wouldn't remember." He began to laugh.

"Later," Arctor said, and snapped off his bedside lamp. "Much later."

Barris rose, dithering. "Hey, but don't you see – I've got the advanced specialized electronic technical skills, and I have access to it – I live here. What I can't figure out, though, is my motive."

"You did it because you're nuts," Arctor said.

"Maybe I was hired by secret forces," Barris muttered in perplexity. "But what would their motives be? Possibly to start suspicion and trouble among us, to cause dissension to break out, causing us to be pitted against one another, all of us, uncertain of whom we can trust, who is our enemy, and like that."

"Then they've succeeded," Arctor said.

"But why would they want to do that?" Barris was saying as he moved toward the door; his hands flapped urgently. "So much trouble – removing that plate on the bottom, getting a passkey to the front door—"

I'll be glad, Bob Arctor thought, when we get in the holo-scanners and have them set up all over this house. He touched his gun, felt reassured, then wondered if he should make certain it was still full of shells. But then, he realized, I'll wonder if the firing pin is gone or if the powder has been removed from the shells and so forth, on and on, obsessively, like a little boy counting cracks in the sidewalk to reduce his fear. Little Bobby Arctor, coming home from the first grade with his little school-books, frightened at the unknown lying ahead.

Reaching down, he fumbled at the bed frame, along and along until his fingers touched Scotch tape. Pulling it loose, he tore from it, with Barris still in the room and watching, two tabs of Substance D mixed with quaak. Lifting them to his mouth, he tossed them down his throat, without water, and then lay back, sighing.

"Get lost," he said to Barris.

And slept.

THE MOJAVE TWO-STEP

Norman Partridge

The desert, just past midnight. A lone truck on a scorched black licorice strip, two men – Anshutes and Coker – inside.

Outside it's one hundred and twenty-five degrees under a fat December moon. Frosty weather in the twilight days of global warming . . . and just in time for the holiday season.

Sure, driving across the desert was a risk, even in such balmy weather. Not many people owned cars anymore, and those who did avoided the wide white lonesome. Even roadcops were smart enough to leave the Mojave alone. It was too hot and too empty, and it could make you as crazy as a scorpion on a sizzling-hot skillet. If you broke down out here, you ended up cooked to a beautiful golden brown – just like Tiny Tim's Christmas goose.

But that wasn't going to happen to Coker. He was going to spend New Year's Eve in Las Vegas. The town that Frank and Dean and Sammy had built all those years ago was still the place he wanted to be. Hell on earth outside, air-conditioned splendour within. If you had the long green, Vegas gave you everything a growing boy could desire. A/C to the max, frosty martinis . . . maybe even a woman with blue eyes that sparkled like icebergs.

Let the swells fly into town in air-conditioned jets, Coker figured. He'd take the hard road. The dangerous road. The real gambler's road. He'd ride that scorched highway straight down the thermometer into double digits, and the A/C would frost everything but his dreams. A little business, a couple lucky rolls of the dice, and his life would change for good . . . then *he'd* leave town with a jet of his own. Slice it up like an Eskimo Pie and that was cool, any way you figured it.

It was all part of the gamble called life. Like always, Lady Luck was rolling the dice. Rattling the bones for Coker and for his partner, too, even though Anshutes would never admit to believing in any airy jazz like that.

Coker believed it. Lady Luck was calling him now. Just up the road in Vegas, she waited for him like a queen. God knew he'd dreamed about her long enough, imagining those iceberg eyes that sparkled like diamonds flashing just for him.

All his life, he'd been waiting for the Lady to give him a sign. Coker knew it was coming soon. Maybe with the next blink of his eyes. Or maybe the one after that.

Yeah. That was the way it was. It had to be.

Really, it was the only explanation.

Check it out. Just two days ago Coker and Anshutes had been on foot. Broiling in Bakersfield with maybe a gallon of water between them, seven bucks, and Anshutes's .357 Magnum . . . which was down to three shells. But with that .357 they'd managed to steal five hundred and seventy-two bucks, a shotgun, and an ice-cream truck tanked with enough juice to get them all the way to Vegas. Plus they still had the Magnum . . . and those three shells.

Now if that wasn't luck, what was?

One-handing the steering wheel, Coker gave the ice cream truck a little juice. Doing seventy on the straightaway, and the electric engine purred quieter than a kitten. The rig wasn't much more than a pick-up with a refrigeration unit mounted on the back, but it did all right. Coker's only complaint was the lack of air-conditioning. Not that many automobiles had A/C anymore . . . these days, the licensing fees for luxuries which negatively impacted the sorry remains of the ozone layer cost more than the cars. But why anyone who could afford the major bucks for a freon-licensed vehicle would forgo the pleasure of A/C, Coker didn't know.

The only guy who had the answer was the owner of the ice cream truck. If he was still alive . . . and Coker kind of doubted that he was. Because Anshutes had excavated the poor bastard's bridgework with the butt of his .357 Magnum, emptied the guy's wallet, and left him tied to a telephone pole on the outskirts of Bakersfield. By now, the ice cream man was either cooked like the ubiquitous Xmas goose or in a hospital somewhere sucking milkshakes through a straw.

Coker's left hand rested on the sideview mirror, desert air blasting over his knuckles. Best to forget about the ice cream man. His thoughts returned to the Lady. Like always, those thoughts had a way of sliding over his tongue, no matter how dry it was. Like always, they had a way of parting his chapped lips and finding Anshutes's perennially sunburnt ear.

"Know where I'm heading after Vegas?" Coker asked.

"No," Anshutes said. "But I'm sure you're gonna tell me."

Coker smiled. "There's this place called Lake Louise, see? It's up north, in Canada. Fifty years ago it used to be a ski resort. Now the only skiing they do is on the water. They've got palm trees, papayas and mangoes, and girls with skin the colour of cocoa butter. Days it's usually about thirty-five Celsius, which is ninety-five degrees American. Some nights it gets as low as sixty."

Anshutes chuckled. "Sounds like you'll have to buy a coat."

"Go ahead and laugh. I'm talking double-digit degrees, partner. Sixty. *Six-oh.* And girls with skin like cocoa butter. If that's not a big slice of paradise, I don't know what is."

"Get real, amigo. A guy with your record isn't exactly a prime candidate for immigration. And our dollar isn't worth shit up north, anyway."

"Drop some luck into that equation."

"Oh, no. Here we go again—"

"Seriously. I can feel it in my bones. Something big is just ahead, waiting for us. I'm gonna take my cut from the ice cream job and hit the tables. I'm not walking away until I have a million bucks in my pocket."

"Even God isn't that lucky." Anshutes snorted. "And luck had nothing to do with this, anyway. Planning did. And hard work. And a little help from a .357 Magnum."

"So what are you gonna do with your money?" Coker asked sarcastically. "Bury it in the ground?"

"Depends on how much we get."

"The way I figure it, we're looking at something large. Forty grand, maybe fifty."

"Well, maybe thirty." Anshutes gnawed on it a minute, doing some quick calculations. "I figure the Push Ups will go for about fifty a pop. We got five cases of those. The Fudgsicles'll be about sixty-five. Figure seventy-five for the Drumsticks. And the Eskimo Pies—"

"A hundred each, easy," Coker said. "Maybe even a hundred and twenty-five. And don't forget – we've got ten cases."

"You sound pretty sure about the whole thing."

"That's because I believe in luck," Coker said. "Like the song says, she's a lady. And she's smiling on us. Right now. Tonight. And she's gonna keep on smiling for a long, long time."

Coker smiled, too. Screw Anshutes if he wanted to be all sour. "You know what we ought to do?" Coker said. "We ought to pull over and celebrate a little. Have us a couple of Eskimo Pies. Toast Lady Luck, enjoy the moment. Live a little—"

"I've lived a lot," Anshutes said. "And I plan to live a lot longer. I'm not going to play the fool with my money. I'm not going to blow it on some pipe dream. I'm going to play it smart."

"Hey, relax. All I'm saying is—"

"No," Anshutes said, and then he really went verbal. "You've said enough. We're in this to make some real money for a change. And we're not gonna make it by pulling over to the side of the road, and we're not gonna make it by toasting Lady Luck with an Eskimo Pie in the middle of the Mojave Desert, and we're not going to make it by blowing our swag in some casino . . ."

Anshutes went on like that.

Coker swallowed hard.

He'd had just about enough.

"I'm pulling over," he said. "I'm going to have an Eskimo Pie, and you're goddamn well going to have one with me if you know what's good for you."

"The hell I am!" Anshutes yanked his pistol. "You goddamn fool! You take your foot off the brake right now or I'll—"

Suddenly, Anshutes's complaints caught in his throat like a chicken bone. Ahead on the road, Coker saw the cause of his partner's distress. Beneath the ripe moon, knee-deep in heat waves that shimmered up from the asphalt, a big man wearing a ten-gallon cowboy hat walked the yellow centre line of the highway. He only had one arm, and he was carrying a woman piggyback – her arms wrapped around his neck, her long slim legs scissored around his waist. But the woman wasn't slowing the big guy down. His pace was brisk, and it was one hundred and twenty-five degrees and the rangy bastard didn't even look like he'd broken a sweat—

Coker honked the horn, but the cowboy didn't seem to notice.

"Don't hit him!" Anshutes yelled. "You'll wreck the truck!"

Anshutes closed his eyes as Coker hit the brakes. Tires screamed as the ice cream truck veered right and bounded along the shoulder of the road. Gravel rattled in the wheel wells and slapped against the undercarriage like gunfire, and Coker downshifted from fourth gear to third, from third to second, ice cream visions dancing in his head, visions of Drumsticks and Push Ups bashing around in the refrigeration unit, visions of broken Fudgsicles and mashed Eskimo Pies . . .

Visions of Lady Luck turning her back . . .

The electric engine whined as he shifted from second to first and yanked the emergency brake. The truck seized up like a gutshot horse, and the only thing that prevented Coker from doing a header through the windshield was his seat belt.

Coker unbuckled his belt. Anshutes set his pistol on the seat and fumbled with his seat belt. Coker grabbed the .357 and was out of the cab before his partner could complain.

The hot asphalt was like sponge cake beneath Coker's boots as he hurried after the man in the ten-gallon hat. The cowboy didn't turn. Neither did the woman who rode him. In fact, the woman didn't move at all, and as Coker got closer he noticed a rope around her back. She was tied to the cowboy. Coker figured she was dead.

That was bad news. Two strangers. One alive, one dead. Snake eyes. A jinxed roll if ever he saw one.

Bad enough that the cowboy had nearly killed him. But if he'd put the jinx on Coker's luck—

Coker aimed at the ripe moon and busted a round. "Turn around, cowboy," he yelled. "Unless you want it in the back."

The cowboy turned double-quick, like some marching band marionette. The one-armed man's face was lost under the brim of his ten-gallon hat, but moonlight splashed across his torso and gleamed against his right hand.

Which was wrapped around a pistol.

"Shit!" Coker spit the word fast and fired another shot. The bullet caught the cowboy in the chest, but the big man didn't even stumble. He didn't return fire, either . . . and Coker wasn't going to give him the chance.

Coker fired again, dead centre, and this time the bullet made a sound like a marble rattling around in a tin can.

The cowboy's chest lit up. Neon rattlesnakes slithered across it. Golden broncos bucked over his bulging pecs. Glowing Gila monsters hissed and spread their jaws.

Three broncos galloped into place.

The cowboy's chest sprung open like the batwings on an old-fashioned saloon.

Silver dollars rained down on the highway.

And the cowboy kept on coming. Coker couldn't even move now. Couldn't breathe. Oh man, this wasn't a jinx after all. This was the moment he'd been waiting for. This was the omen to end all omens. All of it happening in the blink of an eye.

One more blink and he'd see things clearly. One more blink and the future would turn up like a Blackjack dealt for high stakes—

But Coker couldn't blink. He couldn't even move—

Anshutes could. He stepped past his partner, scooped up a silver dollar as it rolled along the highway's center line. The cowboy kept on coming, heading for Anshutes now, but Anshutes didn't twitch. He waited until the big man was within spitting distance, and then he slipped the coin between the determined line of the advancing cowboy's lips.

Immediately, the cowboy's gunhand swept in an upward arc.

Then he stopped cold.

Anshutes scooped a handful of silver dollars off the road and tossed them at Coker.

"Guess you've never heard of a one-armed bandit," he said.

Coker's jaw dropped quicker than a bar of soap in a queer bathhouse. Anshutes sighed. Christ, being partnered up with this starry-eyed fool was something else.

"The cowboy here's a robot," Anshutes explained. "Comes from a casino called Johnny Ringo's, named after the gangster who owns the place. Ringo himself came up with the concept for an ambulating slot machine, hired some ex-Disney imagineers to design the things. They walk around his joint twenty-four hours a day. You'd be surprised how many idiots feed dollars into them. I guess they all think they're lucky . . . just like you."

"This thing's a *robot*?" Coker asked.

"That's what I said."

"Why'd it stop moving?"

"'Cause I fed it a dollar, genius.'' Anshutes pointed at the machine's lone arm, which was raised in the air. "The Cogwheel Kid here can't do anything until I make my play. I have to pull his arm to set him in motion again. Then those neon wheels will spin, and either he'll cough up some dough or start walking, looking for another mark. Unless, of course, your bullets dug a hole in his motherboard, in which case who knows what the hell he'll do."

Coker blinked several times but said nothing. To Anshutes, he looked like some stupid fish that had just figured out it lived in a tank. Blink-blink-blinking, checking out the big bad pet shop world that lurked beyond the glass.

"It's an omen," Coker said finally. "A sign—"

"Uh-uh, buddy. It's called the Mojave Two-Step."

"The Mojave what?"

"The Mojave Two-Step." Anshutes sighed. "Here's what happened. This little lady crossed Johnny Ringo. Who knows what the hell she did, but it was bad enough that he wanted to kill her good and slow. So he tied her to one of his walking slots, and he pointed the damn thing west and turned it loose. It's happened before. Just a couple months ago, one of these things trudged into Barstow with a dead midget tied to its back. Leastways, folks thought it was a midget. A couple weeks under the Mojave sun is liable to shrink anyone down to size."

"Jesus!" Coker said. "How does Ringo get away with it?"

"He's rich, idiot. And that means you don't mess with him, or anything to do with him or he'll kill you the same way he killed this girl—"

Right on cue, the girl groaned. Annoyed, Anshutes grabbed her chin and got a look at her. Blue eyes, cold as glaciers. Surprisingly, she wasn't even sunburned.

Anshutes huffed another sigh. There wasn't any mystery to it, really. They weren't that far from Vegas. Twenty, maybe thirty miles. Could be that Ringo had turned the robot loose after dark, that the girl hadn't even been in the sun yet. Of course, if that was the case it would make sense to assume that the robot had followed the highway, taking the most direct route. Anshutes didn't know what kind of directional devices Ringo had built into his walking slots, but he supposed it was possible. There wasn't anything between Vegas and Barstow. Nobody travelled the desert highway unless they absolutely had to. Even if the robot stuck to the road, it was an odds on cinch that the girl would wind up dead before she encountered another human being.

The girl glanced at Anshutes, and it was like that one glance told her exactly what kind of guy he was. So she turned her gaze on Coker. "Help me," she whispered.

"This is too weird," Coker said. "A woman riding a slot machine . . . a slot machine that paid off on the road to Vegas. It *is* an omen. Or a miracle! Like Lady Luck come to life . . . like Lady Luck *in the flesh*—"

"Like Lady Luck *personified*." Anshutes dropped a hand on his partner's shoulder. "Now you listen to me, boy – what we've got here is a little Vegas whore riding a walking scrap heap. She doesn't have anything to do with luck, and she isn't our business. *Our* business is over there in that truck. *Our* business is a load of ice cream. *Our* business is getting that ice cream to Vegas before it melts."

Coker's eyes flashed angrily, and Anshutes nearly laughed. Seeing his partner go badass was like watching a goldfish imitate a shark.

"You'd better back down, boy," Anshutes warned.

Coker ignored him. He untied the young woman's wrists and feet. He pulled her off of the Cogwheel Kid's back and cradled her in his arms, and then he started toward the ice cream truck.

Anshutes cleared his throat. "Where do you think you're going?"

"Even if she's not Lady Luck, this lady's hurting," Coker said. "I think she deserves an ice cream. Hell, maybe she deserves two. Maybe I'll let her eat her fill."

Anshutes didn't answer.

Not with words, anyway.

He raised the sawed-off shotgun he'd stolen from the ice cream man, and he cocked both barrels.

Coker said, "You think you're pretty cool, don't you?"

"Cooler than Santa's ass," Anshutes said.

"And you'll shoot me if I give the lady an ice cream?"

"Only way she gets any ice cream is if she pays for it."

Coker turned around. "How about if I pay for it?"

"I don't care who pays. You, the little whore, Lady Luck or Jesus Christ. As long as I get the money."

"That's fine." Coker smiled. "You'll find your money on the road, asshole."

"What?"

"The jackpot. The money I shot out of the slot machine. It's all yours."

"You're crazy."

"Maybe. But I'm gonna buy me a shitload of ice cream, and this little lady's gonna eat it."

Coker set the girl down at the side of the road, peeling off his shirt and rolling it into a pillow for her head. Then he walked over to the truck and opened the refrigerated compartment.

"No Eskimo Pies," Anshutes said. "Let's get that straight."

"I'm getting what I paid for," Coker said.

Anshutes shook his head. What a moron. Ponying up fistfuls of silver dollars, just so some little Vegas whore could lick a Push Up. If that was the way Coker wanted it, that was fine. In the meantime, Anshutes would make himself some money, and Lady Luck wouldn't have jack to do with it. Hell, for once hard work wouldn't have jack to do with it either. For once, all Anshutes had to do to make some money was bend over and pick it up.

Silver dollars gleamed in the moonlight. Anshutes put down the shotgun. Not that he was taking any chances – he made sure that the weapon was within reach as he got down to work, filling his pockets with coins.

Behind him, he heard the sound of the refrigerator compartment door slamming closed. Coker. Jesus, what an idiot. Believing that some Vegas slut was Lady Luck. *Personified.*

Anshutes had told the kid a thousand times that luck was an illusion. Now he realized that he could have explained it a million times, and he still wouldn't have made a dent. The kid might as well be deaf. He just wouldn't listen—

Anshutes listened. He heard everything.

The sound of silver dollars jingling in his pocket, like the sound of happiness.

But wait . . . there was another sound, too.

A quiet hum, hardly audible.

The sound of an electric engine accelerating.

Anshutes turned around fast, dropping coins on the roadway. The ice cream truck was coming fast. The shotgun was right there on the double yellow line. He made a grab for it.

Before he touched the gun, the ice cream truck's bumper cracked his skull like a hard-boiled egg.

Kim felt better now.

A couple Eskimo Pies could do that for a girl.

"Want another?" the guy asked.

"Sure," Kim said. "I could probably eat a whole box."

"I guess it's like they say: a walk in the desert does wonders for the appetite."

The guy smiled and walked over to the ice cream truck. She watched him. He was kind of cute. Not as cute as Johnny Ringo, of course, but Johnny definitely had his downside.

She sat in the dirt and finished her third pie. You had to eat the suckers fast or else they'd melt right in your hand. It was funny – she'd left Vegas worse than flat broke, owing Johnny twenty grand, and now she had three hundred bucks' worth of ice cream in her belly. Things were looking up. She kind of felt like a safe-deposit box on legs. Kind of a funny feeling. Kind of like she didn't know whether she should laugh or cry.

The guy handed her another Eskimo Pie. "Thanks –" she said, and she said it with a blank that he was sure to fill in.

"Coker," he said. "My first name's Dennis, but I don't like it much."

"It's a nice name," Kim said. Which was a lie, but there was no sense hurting the poor guy's feelings. "Thanks, Dennis."

"My pleasure. You've had a hell of a hard time."

She smiled. Yeah. That was one way of putting it.

"So you're heading for Vegas," she said.

Coker nodded. "Me and my buddy . . . well, we ended up with this truckload of ice cream. We wanted a place where we could sell it without much trouble from the law."

"Vegas is definitely the place."

"You lived there awhile?"

She smiled. She guess you could call what she'd done in Vegas living. If you were imaginative enough.

"Kim?" he prodded. "You okay?"

"Yeah," she said. Man, it was tough. She should have been happy . . . because the guy had saved her life. She should have been sad . . . because Johnny Ringo had tried to kill her. But she couldn't seem to hold onto any one emotion.

She had to get a grip.

"You ever been to Vegas?" she asked.

"No," the guy said. "Going there was my partner's idea."

"It's a tough place."

"I don't care how tough it is." He laughed. "As long as it's the kind of place you can sell an ice cream bar for a hundred bucks, I'm there."

She nodded. Ice cream was worth a lot in Vegas.

But other things came pretty cheap.

"It's a rich town," she said, because saying that was really like saying nothing. "It's full of rich men and women. I read somewhere that the entire budget for law enforcement in the United States is about a third of what it costs to power Vegas's air-conditioners for a month."

"Wow. That's amazing."

"Not really. Vegas is a desert. It's an empty place. Everything that's there, someone put it there. Only the rich can afford a place like that. They come and go as they please, jetting in and out in their fancy planes. Everybody else – they're pretty much stuck there. That's what happened to me. I was a dancer. I made pretty good money that way. But every dime I made was already spent on my apartment, or A/C, or water or food. I kept waiting for my lucky break, but it never came. I just couldn't get ahead. Before I knew it, I got behind. And then I got in trouble with my boss—"

"Johnny Ringo?"

"You know about him?"

Coker nodded at the one-armed bandit. "I've heard of the Mojave Two-Step."

Kim swallowed hard. "You never want to dance that one," she said. "I'm here to tell you."

The guy looked down at the road, kind of embarrassed. Like he wanted to know her story, but was too shy to ask for the details.

"Well, maybe your luck's due to change," he said. "It happened to me. Or it's going to happen. It's like I can see it coming."

"Like a dream?"

"Or an omen."

Kim smiled. "I like that word."

"Me too. It's kind of like a dream, only stronger."

"I used to have this dream," Kim said. "When I first came to

Vegas. That I was going to hit it big. That I'd live in a penthouse suite with the A/C set at sixty-eight degrees. That the sun would never touch my skin and I'd be white as a pearl."

The guy didn't say anything. Still shy. Kim had forgotten about that particular emotion. She hadn't run across it much in the last few years. Not with Johnny Ringo, and not with any of his friends. Not even with the two-legged slots that followed her around the casino night after night until she fed them dollars just so they'd leave her alone.

In Vegas, everyone wanted something. At least the walking slots came a lot cheaper than their flesh-and-blood counterparts.

Funny. She didn't feel good about it, but she didn't exactly feel bad, either.

That's just the way it was in Vegas.

It was a rich man's town.

Or a rich woman's.

Kim finished her Eskimo Pie. She liked what the guy (what was his name again?) had said about omens. That they were dreams, only stronger.

She stared at the ice cream truck.

She thought: it's not often you get a second chance.

"You want another?" the guy asked.

She laughed. "Just one more?"

Of course, he thought she was talking about an Eskimo Pie, when that really wasn't what she wanted at all.

He went after the ice cream. She watched him go.

Past the dead guy on the highway.

Past the second chance that lay there on the yellow line.

Kim really didn't have a choice.

She had to pick it up.

She heard the freezer door close. Watched the guy (*Dennis*, that was his name) step from behind the truck.

He was all right about it. He kind of smiled when he saw the shotgun, like he already understood.

"I'm sorry, Dennis," she said. "But dreams die hard. Especially strong ones."

"Yeah," he said. "Yeah."

Coker stood in the middle of the road, eating an Eskimo Pie, listening to "Pop Goes the Weasel."

The ice cream truck was gone from view, but he could still hear its little song. That meant she was up ahead somewhere, playing the tape.

Maybe she was playing it for him. The music drifted through the night like a sweet connection. Coker listened to the song while he finished his Eskimo Pie. Anshutes couldn't stand the music the truck made. He wouldn't let Coker play it at all.

Well, Anshutes didn't have a say in anything anymore. Coker stared at his ex-partner. The big man lay dead on the highway like roadkill of old, his pockets stuffed with silver dollars.

Coker turned them out, filling his own pockets with the coins. Then he walked over to the one-armed bandit.

The Cogwheel Kid was primed for action – Anshutes's coin between his lips, his lone robotic arm held high in the air. Coker pulled the slot machine's arm. Ribbons of neon danced across the one-armed bandit's chest. Bucking broncos, charging buffaloes, jackalopes that laughed in the desert night.

After awhile, the neon locked up.

Two tittering jackalopes with a snorting buffalo between them. Hardly a jackpot.

Coker smiled as the neon flickered out. Losing wasn't a big surprise, really. After all, Lady Luck was gone. She was up ahead, driving an ice cream truck, heading for the land of dreams.

The Cogwheel Kid started walking. He headed east, toward Vegas, looking for another mark.

Coker jumped on the robot's back and held on tight.

He smiled, remembering the look of her frosty blue eyes. Lady Luck with a shotgun. He should have hated her. But he was surprised to find that he couldn't do that.

She was chasing a dream, the same way he was.

He couldn't help hoping she'd catch it.

The same way he hoped he'd catch her.

If he was lucky.

BLOOD SISTERS

Joe Haldeman

So I used to carry two different business cards: J. Michael Loomis, Data Concentration, and Jack Loomis, Private Investigator. They mean the same thing, nine cases out of ten. You have to size up a potential customer, decide whether he'd feel better hiring a shamus or a clerk.

Some people still have these romantic notions about private detectives and get into a happy sweat at the thought of using one. But it *is* the twenty-first century and, endless Bogart reruns notwithstanding, most of my work consisted in sitting at my office console and using it to subvert the privacy laws of various states and countries – finding out embarrassing things about people, so other people can divorce them or fire them or get a piece of the slickery.

Not to say I didn't go out on the street sometimes; not to say I didn't have a gun and a ticket for it. There are Forces of Evil out there, friends, although most of them would probably rather be thought of as businessmen who use the law rather than fear it. Same as me. I was always happy, though, to stay on this side of murder, treason, kidnapping – any lobo offense. This brain may not be much, but it's all I have.

I should have used it when the woman walked into my office. She had a funny way of saying hello:

"Are you licensed to carry a gun?"

Various retorts came to mind, most of them having to do with her expulsion, but after a period of silence I said yes and asked who had referred her to me. Asked politely, too, to make up for staring. She was a little more beautiful than anyone I'd ever seen before.

"My lawyer," she said. "Don't ask who he is."

With that, I was pretty sure that this was some sort of elaborate joke. Story detectives always have beautiful mysterious customers. My female customers tend to be dowdy and too talkative, and much more interested in alimony than romance.

"What's your name, then? Or am I not supposed to ask that either?"

She hesitated. "Ghentlee Arden."

I turned the console on and typed in her name, then a seven-digit code. "Your legal firm is Lee, Chu, and Rosenstein. And your real name is Maribelle Four Ghentlee: fourth clone of Maribelle Ghentlee."

"Arden is my professional name. I dance." She had a nice blush.

I typed in another string of digits. Sometimes this sort of thing would lose a customer. "Says here you're a registered hooker."

"Call girl," she said frostily. "Class One courtesan. I was getting to that."

I'm a liberal-minded man; I don't have anything against hookers *or* clones. But I like my customers to be frank with me. Again, I should have shown her the door – then followed her through it.

Instead: "So. You have a problem?"

"Some men are bothering me, one man in particular. I need some protection."

That gave me pause. "Your union has a Pinkerton contract for that sort of thing."

"*My* union." Her face trembled a little. "They don't let clones in the union. I'm an associate, for classification. No protection, no medical, no *anything*."

"Sorry, I didn't know that. Pretty old-fashioned." I could see the reasoning, though. Dump a thousand Maribelle Ghentlees on the market, and a merely ravishing girl wouldn't have a chance.

"Sit down." She was on the verge of tears. "Let me explain to you what I can't do.

"I can't hurt anyone physically. I can't trace this cod down and wave a gun in his face, tell him to back off."

"I know," she sobbed. I took a box of Kleenex out of my drawer, passed it over.

"Listen, there are laws about harassment. If he's really bothering you, the cops'll be glad to freeze him."

"I can't go to the police." She blew her nose. "I'm not a citizen."

I turned off the console. "Let me see if I can fill in some blanks without using the machine. You're an unauthorized clone."

She nodded.

"With bought papers."

"Of course I have papers. I wouldn't be in your *machine* if I didn't."

Well, she wasn't dumb, either. "This cod. He isn't just a disgruntled customer."

"No." She didn't elaborate.

"One more guess," I said, "and then you do the talking for a while. He knows you're not legal."

"He should. He's the one who pulled me."

"Your own daddy. Any other surprises?"

She looked at the floor. "Mafia."

"Not the legal one, I assume."

"Both."

The desk drawer was still open; the sight of my own gun gave me a bad chill. "There are two reasonable courses open to me. I could handcuff you to the doorknob and call the police. Or I could knock you over the head and call the Mafia. That would probably be safer."

She reached into her purse; my hand was halfway to the gun when she took out a credit flash, thumbed it, and passed it over the desk. She easily had five times as much money as I make in a good year, and I'm in a comfortable seventy percent bracket.

"You must have one hell of a case of bedsores."

"Don't be stupid," she said, suddenly hard. "You can't make that kind of money on your back. If you take me on as a client, I'll explain."

I erased the flash and gave it back to her. "Miz Ghentlee. You've already told me a great deal more than I want to know. I don't want the police to put me in jail, I don't want the courts to scramble my brains with a spoon. I don't want the Mafia to take bolt cutters to my appendages."

"I could make it worth your while."

"I've got all the money I can use. I'm only in this profession because I'm a snoopy bastard." It suddenly occurred to me that that was more or less true.

"That wasn't completely what I meant."

"I assumed that. And you tempt me, as much as any woman's beauty has ever tempted me."

She turned on the waterworks again.

"Christ. Go ahead and tell your story. But I don't think you can convince me to do anything for you."

"My real clone-mother wasn't named Maribelle Ghentlee."

"I could have guessed that."

"She was Maxine Kraus." She paused. "Maxine . . . Kraus."

"Is that supposed to mean something to me?"

"Maybe not. What about *Werner* Kraus?"

"Yeah." Swiss industrialist, probably the richest man in Europe. "Some relation?"

"She's his daughter and only heir."

I whistled. "Why would she want to be cloned, then?"

"She didn't know she was being cloned. She thought she was having a Pap test." She smiled a little. "Ironic posture."

"And they pulled you from the scraping."

She nodded. "The Mafia bought her physician. Then killed him."

"You mean the real Mafia?" I said.

"That depends on what you call real. Mafia Incorporated comes into it too, in a more or less legitimate way. I was supposedly one of six Maribelle Ghentlee clones that they had purchased to set up as courtesans in New Orleans, to provoke a test case. They claimed that the Sisterhood's prohibition against clone prostitutes constituted unfair restraint of trade."

"Never heard of the case. I guess they lost."

"Of course. They wouldn't have done it in the South if they'd wanted to win."

"Wait a minute. Jumping ahead. Obviously, they plan ultimately to use you as a substitute for the real Maxine Kraus."

"When the old man dies, which will be soon."

"Then why would they parade you around in public?"

"Just to give me an interim identity. They chose Ghentlee as a clone-mother because she was the closest one available to Maxine Kraus's physical appearance. I had good makeup; none of the real Ghentlee clones suspected I wasn't one of them."

"Still . . . what happens if you run into someone who knows

what the real Kraus looks like? With your face and figure, she must be all over the gossip sheets in Europe."

"You're sweet." Her smile could make me do almost anything. Short of taking on the Mafia. "She's a total recluse, though, for fear of kidnappers. She probably hasn't seen twenty people in her entire life.

"And she isn't beautiful, though she has the raw materials for it. Her mother died when she was still a baby – killed by kidnappers."

"I remember that."

"So she's never had a woman around to model herself after. No one ever taught her how to do her hair properly, or use makeup. A man buys all her clothes. She doesn't have anyone to be beautiful *for*."

"You feel sorry for her."

"More than that." She looked at me with an expression that somehow held both defiance and hopelessness. "Can you understand? She's my mother. I was force-grown so we're the same apparent age, but she's still my only parent. I love her. I won't be part of a plan to kill her."

"You'd rather die?" I said softly. She was going to.

"Yes. But that wouldn't accomplish anything, not if the Mafia does it. They'd take a few cells and make another clone. Or a dozen, or a hundred, until one came along with a personality to go along with matricide."

"Once they know you feel this way—"

"They do know. I'm running."

That galvanized me. "They know who your lawyer is?"

"My lawyer?" She gasped when I took the gun out of the drawer. People who only see guns on the cube are usually surprised at how solid and heavy they actually look.

"Could they trace you here, is what I mean." I crossed the room and slid open the door. No one in the corridor. I twisted a knob and twelve heavy magnetic bolts slammed home.

"I don't think so. The lawyers gave me a list of names, and I just picked one I liked."

I wondered whether it was Jack or J. Michael. I pushed a button on the wall and steel shutters rolled down over the view of Central Park. "Did you take a cab here?"

"No, subway. And I went up to One hundred and twenty-fifth and back."

"Smart." She was staring at the gun. "It's a .48 Magnum Recoilless. Biggest handgun a civilian can buy."

"You need one so big?"

"Yes." I used to carry a .25 Beretta, small enough to conceal in a bathing suit. I used to have a partner, too. It was a long story, and I didn't like to tell it. "Look," I said. "I have a deal with the Mafia. They don't do divorce work and I don't drop bodies into the East River. Understand?" I put the gun back in the drawer and slammed it shut.

"I don't blame you for being afraid—"

"Afraid? Miz Four Ghentlee, I'm not afraid. I'm *terrified!* How old do you think I am?"

"Call me Belle, You're thirty-five, maybe forty. Why?"

"You're kind – and I'm rich. Rich enough to buy youth: I've been in this *business* almost forty years. I take lots of vitamins and try not to fuck with the Mafia."

She smiled and then was suddenly somber. Like a baby. "Try to understand me. You've lived sixty years?"

I nodded. "Next year."

"Well, I've been alive barely sixty *days*. After four years in a tank, growing and learning.

"Learning isn't *being*, though. Everything is new to me. When I walk down a street, the sights and sounds and smells, it's . . . it's like a great flower opening to the sun. Just to sit alone in the dark—"

Her voice broke.

"You can't even *know* how much I want to live – and that's not condescending; it's a statement of fact. Yet I want you to kill me."

I could only shake my head.

"If you can't hide me you have to kill me." She was crying now, and wiped the tears savagely from her cheeks. "Kill me and make sure every cell in my body is destroyed."

She took out her credit card flash and set it on the desk.

"You can have all my money, whether you save me or kill me."

She started walking around the desk. Along the way she did something with a clasp and her dress slithered to the floor. The sudden naked beauty was like an electric shock.

"If you save me, you can have me. Friend, lover, wife . . . slave. Forever." She held a posture of supplication for a moment, then eased toward me. Watching the muscles of her body work made my mouth go dry. She reached down and started unbuttoning my shirt.

I cleared my throat. "I didn't know clones had navels."

"Only special ones. I have other special qualities."

Idiot, something reminded me, every woman you've ever loved has sucked you dry and left you for dead. I clasped her hips with my big hands and drew her warmth to me. Close up, the navel wasn't very convincing; nobody's perfect.

I'd done drycleaning jobs before, but never so cautiously or thoroughly. That she was a clone made the business a little more delicate than usual, since clones' lives are more rigidly supervised by the government than ours are. But the fact that her identity was false to begin with made it easier; I could second-guess the people who had originally drycleaned her.

I hated to meddle with her beauty, and that beauty made plastic surgery out of the question. Any legitimate doctor would be suspicious, and going to an underworld doctor would be suicidal. So we dyed her hair black and bobbed it. She stopped wearing makeup and bought some truly froppy clothes. She kept a length of tape stuck across her buttocks to give her a virgin-schoolgirl kind of walk. For everyone but me.

The Mafia had given her a small fortune – birdseed to them – both to ensure her loyalty and to accustom her to having money, for impersonating Kraus. We used about half of it for the drycleaning.

A month or so later there was a terrible accident on a city bus. Most of the bodies were burned beyond recognition; I did some routine bribery, and two of them were identified as the clone Maribelle Four Ghentlee and John Michael Loomis, private eye. When we learned the supposed clone's body had disappeared from the morgue we packed up our money – long since converted into currency – and a couple of toothbrushes and pulled out.

I had a funny twinge when I closed the door on that console. There couldn't be more than a half-dozen people in the world who were my equals at using that instrument to fish information out of the System. But I had to either give it up or send Belle off on her own.

We flew to the West Indies and looked around. Decided to

settle on the island of St Thomas. I'd been sailing all my life, so we bought a fifty-foot boat and set up a charter service for tourists. Some days we took parties out to skindive or fish. Other days we anchored in a quiet cove and made love like happy animals.

After about a year, we read in the little St Thomas paper that Werner Kraus had died. They mentioned Maxine but didn't print a picture of her. Neither did the San Jaun paper. We watched all the news programs for a couple of days (had to check into a hotel to get access to a video cube) and collected magazines for a month. No pictures, to our relief, and the news stories remarked that Fraulein Kraus went to great pains to stay out of the public eye.

Sooner or later, we figured, some *paparazzo* would find her, and there would be pictures. But by then it shouldn't make any difference. Belle had let her hair grow out to its natural chestnut, but we kept it cropped boyishly short. The sun and wind had darkened her skin and roughened it, and a year of fighting the big boat's rigging had put visible muscle under her sleekness.

The marina office was about two broom closets wide. It was a beautiful spring morning, and I'd come in to put my name on the list of boats available for charter. I was reading the weather printout when Belle sidled through the door and squeezed in next to me at the counter. I patted her on the fanny. "With you in a second, honey."

A vise grabbed my shoulder and spun me around.

He was over two meters tall and so wide at the shoulders that he literally couldn't get through the door without turning sideways. Long white hair and pale blue eyes. White sport coat with a familiar cut: tailored to deemphasize the bulge of a shoulder holster.

"You don't do that, friend," he said with a German accent.

I looked at the woman, who was regarding me with aristocratic amusement. I felt the blood drain from my face and damned near said her name out loud.

She frowned. "Helmuth," she said to the guard, "*Sie sind ihm erschrocken*. I'm sorry," she said to me, "but my friend has quite a temper." She had a perfect North Atlantic accent, and her voice sent a shiver of recognition down my back.

"I am sorry," he said heavily. Sorry he hadn't had a chance to throw me into the water, he was.

"I must look like someone you know," she said. "Someone you know rather well."

"My wife. The similarity is . . . quite remarkable."

"Really? I should like to meet her." She turned to the woman behind the counter. "We'd like to charter a sailing boat for the day."

The clerk pointed at me. "He has a nice fifty-foot one."

"That's fine! Will your wife be aboard?"

"Yes . . . yes, she helps me. But you'll have to pay the full rate," I said rapidly. "The boat normally takes six passengers."

"No matter. Besides, we have two others."

"And you'll have to help me with the rigging."

"I should hope so. We love to sail." That was pretty obvious. We had been wrong about the wind and sun, thinking that Maxine would have led a sheltered life; she was almost as weathered as Belle. Her hair was probably long, but she had it rolled up in a bun and tied back with a handkerchief.

We exchanged false names: Jack Jackson and Lisa von Hollerin. The bodyguard's name was Helmuth Zwei Kastor. She paid the clerk and called her friends at the marina hotel, telling them to meet her at the *Abora*, slip 39.

I didn't have any chance to warn Belle. She came up from the galley as we were swinging aboard. She stared open-mouthed and staggered, almost fainting. I took her by the arm and made introductions, everybody staring.

After a few moments of strange silence, Helmuth Two whispered, "*Du bist ein Klon.*"

"She can't be a clone, silly man," Lisa said. "When did you ever see a clone with a navel?" Belle was wearing shorts and a halter. "But we could be twin sisters. That *is* remarkable."

Helmuth Two shook his head solemnly. Belle had told me that a clone can always recognize a fellow clone, by the eyes. Never be fooled by a man-made navel.

The other two came aboard. Helmuth One was, of course, a Xerox of Helmuth Two. Lisa introduced Maria Salamanca as her lover: a small olive-skinned Basque woman, no stunning beauty, but having an attractive air of friendly mystery about her.

Before we cast off, Lisa came to me and apologized. "We are a passing strange group of people. You deserve something extra for putting up with us." She pressed a gold Krugerrand into my palm – worth at least triple the charter fare – and I tried to act suitably impressed. We had over a thousand of them in the keel, for ballast.

The *Abora* didn't have an engine; getting it in and out of the crowded marina was something of an accomplishment. Belle and Lisa handled the sails expertly, while I manned the wheel. They kept looking at each other, then touching. When we were in the harbor, they sat together at the prow, holding hands. Once we were in open water, they went below together. Maria went into a sulk, but the two clones jollied her out of it.

I couldn't be jealous of her. An angel can't sin. But I did wonder what you would call what they were doing. Was it a weird kind of incest? Transcendental masturbation? I only hoped Belle would keep her mouth shut, at least figuratively.

After about an hour, Lisa came up and sat beside me at the wheel. Her hair was long and full, and flowed like dark liquid in the wind, and she was naked. I tentatively rested my hand on her thigh. She had been crying.

"She told me. She had to tell me." Lisa shook her head in wonder. "Maxine One Kraus. She had to stay below for a while. Said she couldn't trust her legs." She squeezed my hand and moved it back to the wheel.

"Later, maybe," she said. "And don't worry; your secret is safe with us." She went forward and put an arm around Maria, speaking rapid German to her and the two Helmuths. One of the guards laughed and they took off their incongruous jackets, then carefully wrapped up their weapons and holsters. The sight of a .48 Magnum Recoilless didn't arouse any nostalgia in me. Maria slipped out of her clothes and stretched happily. The guards did the same. They didn't have navels but were otherwise adequately punctuated.

Belle came up then, clothed and flushed, and sat quietly next to me. She stroked my bicep and I ruffled her hair. Then I heard Lisa's throaty laugh and suddenly turned cold.

"Hold on a second," I whispered. "We haven't been using our heads."

"Speak for yourself." She giggled.

"Oh, be serious. This stinks of coincidence. That she should turn up here, that she should wander into the office just as—"

"Don't worry about it."

"Listen. She's no more Maxine Kraus than you are. They've found us. She's another clone, one that's going to—"

"She's Maxine. If she were a clone, I could tell immediately."

"Spare me the mystical claptrap and take the wheel. I'm going below." In the otherwise empty engine compartment, I'd stored an interesting assortment of weapons and ammunition.

She grabbed my arm and pulled me back down to the seat. "You spare *me* the private eye claptrap and listen – you're right, it's no coincidence. Remember that old foreigner who came by last week?"

"No."

"You were up on the stern, folding sail. He was just at the slip for a second, to ask directions. He seemed flustered—"

"I remember. Frenchman."

"I thought so too. He was Swiss, though."

"And that was no coincidence, either."

"No, it wasn't. He's on the board of directors of one of the banks we used to liquify our credit. When the annual audit came up, they'd managed to put together all our separate transactions—"

"Bullshit. That's impossible."

She shook her head and laughed. "You're good, but they're good, too. They were curious about what we were trying to hide, using their money, and traced us here. Found we'd started a business with only one percent of our capital.

"Nothing wrong with that, but they were curious. This director was headed for a Caribbean vacation anyhow; he said he'd come by and poke around."

I didn't know how much of this to believe. I gauged the distance between where the Helmuths were sunning and the prow, where they had carefully stowed their guns against the boat's heeling.

"He'd been a lifelong friend of Werner Kraus. That's why he was so rattled. One look at me and he had to rush to the phone."

"And we're supposed to believe," I said, "that the wealthiest woman in the world would come down to see what sort of innocent game we were playing. With only two bodyguards."

"Five. There are two other Helmuths, and Maria is . . . versatile."

"Still can't believe it. After a lifetime of being protected from her own shadow—"

"That's just it. She's tired of it. She turned twenty-five last month, and came into full control of the fortune. Now she wants to take control of her own life."

"Damned foolish. If it were me, I would've sent my giants down alone." I had to admit that I essentially did believe the tale. We'd been alone in open water for more than an hour, and would've long been shark bait if that had been their intent. Getting sloppy in your old age, Loomis.

"I probably would have too," Belle said. "Maxine and I are the same woman in some ways, but you and the Mafia taught me caution. She's been in a cage all her life, and just wanted out. Wanted to sail someplace besides her own lake, too."

"It was still a crazy chance to take."

"So she's a little crazy. Romantic, too, in case you haven't noticed."

"Really? When I peeked in you were playing checkers."

"Bastard." She knew the one place I was ticklish. Trying to get away, I jerked the wheel and nearly tipped us all into the drink.

We anchored in a small cove where I knew there was a good reef. Helmuth One stayed aboard to guard while the rest of us went diving.

The fish and coral were beautiful as ever, but I could only watch Maxine and Belle. They swam slowly hand-in-hand, kicking with unconscious synchrony, totally absorbed. Though the breathers kept their hair wrapped up identically, it was easy to tell them apart, since Maxine had an all-over tan. Still, it was an eerie kind of ballet, like a mirror that didn't quite work. Maria and Helmuth Two were also hypnotized by the sight.

I went aboard early, to start lunch. I'd just finished slicing ham when I heard the drone of a boat, rather far away. Large siphon-jet, by the rushing sound of it.

The guard shouted, "Zwei – *komm' herauf!*"

Hoisted myself up out of the galley. The boat was about two kilometers away, and coming roughly in our direction, fast.

"Trouble coming?" I asked him.

"Cannot tell yet, sir. I suggest you remain below." He had a gun in each hand, behind his back.

Below, good idea. I slid the hatch off the engine compartment and tipped over the cases of beer that hid the weaponry. Fished out two heavy plastic bags, left the others in place for the time being. It was all up-to-date American Coast Guard issue, and had cost more than the boat.

I had rehearsed this a thousand times in my mind, but I hadn't realized the bags would be slippery with condensation and oil and be impossible to tear with your hands. I stood up to get a knife from the galley, and it was almost the last thing I ever did.

I looked up at a loud succession of splintering sounds and saw a line of holes marching toward me from the bow, letting in blue light and lead. I dropped and heard bullets hissing over my head; heard the regular cough-cough-cough of Helmuth One's return fire. At the stern there was a cry of pain and then a splash; they must have caught the other guard coming up the ladder.

Also not in the rehearsals was the effect of absolute death-panic on bladder control; some formal corner of my mind was glad I hadn't yet dressed. I controlled my trembling well enough to cut open the bag that held the small-caliber spitter, and it only took three tries to get the cassette of ammunition fastened to the receiver. I jerked back the arming lever and hurried back to the galley hatch, carrying an armload of cassettes.

The spitter was made for sinking boats, quickly. It fired small flechettes, the size of old-fashioned metal stereo needles, fifty rounds per second. The flechettes moved at supersonic speed and each carried a small explosive charge. In ten seconds, they could do more damage to a boat than a man with a chainsaw could, with determination and leisure.

I resisted the urge to blast away and get back under cover (not that the hull afforded much real protection). We had clamped traversing mounts for the gun on three sides of the galley hatch – nautically inclined customers usually asked what they were; I always shrugged and said they'd come with the boat – because the spitter is most effective if you can hold the point of aim precisely on the waterline.

They were concentrating fire on the bow, most of it going high. Helmuth One was evidently shooting from a prone position, difficult target. I slid the spitter onto its mount and cranked up its scope to maximum power.

When I looked through the scope, a lifetime of target-shooting reflexes took over: deep breath, half let out, do the Zen thing. Their boat moved toward the center of the scope's field, and I waited. It was a Whaler Unsinkable. One man crouched at the bow, firing what looked like a .20-mm. recoilless, clamped on the rail above a piece of steel plate. They were less than a hundred meters away.

The Whaler executed a sharp starboard turn, evidently to give the gunner a better angle on our bow. Good boatmanship, good tactics, but bad luck. Their prow touched the junction of my crosshairs right at the waterline, and I didn't even have to track. I just pressed the trigger and watched a cloud of black smoke and steam zip from prow to stern. Not even an Unsinkable can stay upright with its keel sliced off. The boat slewed sideways into the water, spilling people, and turned turtle. Didn't sink, though.

I snapped a fresh cassette into place and tried to remember where the hydrogen tank was on that model. Second burst found it, and the boat dutifully exploded. The force of the blast was enough to ram the scope's eyepiece back into my eye, painfully.

Helmuth One peered down at me. "What is that?"

"Coast Guard weapon, a spitter."

"May I try it?"

"Sure." I traded places with him, glad to be up in the breeze. My boat was a mess. The mainmast had been shattered by a direct hit, waist high. The starboard rail was splinters, forward, and near misses had gouged up my nice teak foredeck. My eye throbbed, and for some reason my ears were ringing.

I remembered why the next second, as Helmuth fired. The spitter makes a sound like a cat dying, but louder. I had been too preoccupied to hear it.

I unshipped a pair of binoculars to check his marksmanship. He was shooting at the floating bodies. What a spitter did to one was terrible to see.

"Jesus, Helmuth . . ."

"Some of them may yet live," he said apologetically.

At least one did. Wearing a life jacket, she had been floating face down but suddenly began treading water. She was holding an automatic pistol in both hands. She looked exactly like Belle and Maxine.

I couldn't say anything; couldn't take my eyes off her. She fired two rounds, and I felt them slap into the hull beneath me. I heard Helmuth curse, and suddenly her shoulders dissolved in a spray of meat and bone and her head fell into the water.

My gorge rose and I didn't quite make it to the railing. Deck was a mess anyhow.

Helmuth Two, it turned out, had been hit in the side of the neck, but it was a big neck and he survived. Maxine called a helicopter, which came out piloted by Helmuth Three.

After an hour or so, Helmuth Four joined us in a large speedboat loaded down with gasoline, thermite, and shark chum. By that time, we had transferred the gold and a few more important things from my boat onto the helicopter. We chummed the area thoroughly and, as sharks began to gather, towed both hulks out to deep water, where they burned brightly and sank.

The Helmuths spent the next day sprinkling the island with money and threats, while Maxine got to know Belle and me better, behind the heavily guarded door of the honeymoon suite of the quaint old Sheraton that overlooked the marina. She made us a job offer – a life offer, actually – and we accepted without hesitation. That was six years ago.

Sometimes I do miss our old life – the sea, the freedom, the friendly island, the lazy idylls with Belle. Sometimes I even miss New York's hustle and excitement, and the fierce independence of my life there.

We do travel on occasion, but with extreme caution. The clone that Helmuth killed in that lovely cove might have been Belle's sister, pulled from Maxine, or Belle's own daughter, since the Mafia had had plenty of opportunities to collect cells from her body. It's immaterial. What's important is that if they could make one, they could make an army of them.

Like our private army of Helmuths and Lamberts and Delias. I'm chief of security, and the work is interesting, most of it at a console as good as the one I had in Manhattan. No violence since that one afternoon six years ago, not yet. I did have to learn German, though, which was an outrage to a brain as old as mine.

We haven't made any secret of the fact that Belle is Maxine's clone. The official story is that Fraulein Kraus had a clone made of herself, for "companionship". This started a fad among the wealthy, being the first new sexual wrinkle since the invention of the vibrator.

Belle and Maxine take pains to dress alike and speak alike and have even unconsciously assimilated one another's mannerisms. Most of the non-clone employees can't tell which is which, and even I sometimes confuse them, at a distance.

Close up, which happens with gratifying frequency, there's no problem. Belle has a way of looking at me that Maxine could never duplicate. And Maxine is literally a trifle prettier: you can't beat a real navel.

HEARTACHE

Stuart Young

Mist could kill him now but that wasn't what her client had paid for.

Instead she just walked across the dance floor towards the target. Sweaty bodies writhed about her, moving in time to the pounding beats of the club's sound system. VR phantoms swam about the ceiling, occasionally swooping down to swirl between the dancers. The VRs were ethereal beauties, both male and female, deliberately tinged with shimmering colours so the clubbers didn't make fools of themselves trying to chat them up.

But Mist wasn't after a beauty. She was after a beast.

Jack Stone, heavy-duty villain. Body count ran into the fifties. Into the hundreds if you counted the people who had been killed on his orders. Worked his way up from hired muscle to the top of the tree. Now he had people to do the sort of jobs he used to do. He didn't have to bloody his own hands anymore. Unless he wanted to.

Right now his hands weren't bloody, just sweaty as they groped at the girl he was dancing with. Blonde bimbo, spray-painted into a dress that was barely capable of covering her underwear. Even if she'd been wearing any.

Mist knew she could get Stone away from the girl. She'd read his file; she knew what he liked. The thrill of the chase, getting what he couldn't have.

That's why she wore a red dress that covered her from neck to her ankles. But tight enough to show off every curve. She hadn't been able to eat for the last two hours because the slightest deviation in the flatness of her stomach would ruin the line of the dress.

All the men in the club stared after her lustfully as she walked by. Some of the women too. She didn't respond to them, kept her cool. She had to be imperious, regal. Make it obvious that she was out of the league of every man in the club. That would bring Stone running.

Reaching the centre of the dance floor she started to dance. Six weeks of training with lapdancers and podium dancers. It paid off. She was sex personified. Her lithe body undulated to the rhythms, the black mane of her hair extensions tumbling down her back. She wasn't just dancing, she was making love to the music.

She noticed the bouncers keeping an eye on her in case any of the punters got carried away by her display. They needn't have worried. Everyone stepped back to watch her, giving her a circle of space at the centre of the dance floor.

But no one watched her more intently than Stone.

She danced for another couple of numbers then headed for the bar. She perched on a stool, a bird of paradise resting before soaring off once more.

"Scotch," she told the barman. The alcohol inhibitors she had taken earlier would stop her from losing her edge.

The barman placed the drink in front of her. "It's already been paid for. Courtesy of the gentleman at the end of the bar."

She looked up. Stone. He'd followed her off the dance floor. Lifting her glass, she tipped it in thanks. He raised his in reply.

He sidled over. The clubs lighting glistened off his black hair, emphasising the strands of silver. His heavy features were handsome in a thuggish kind of way. Strong jaw, broken nose, his ears not quite turned to cauliflowers. He was big and mean and tough and she knew she could kill him with her bare hands if she needed to.

He smiled at her. His teeth were too white; dentures. His real teeth had been smashed back in his bruiser days. "You're quite a dancer."

"Thanks."

"I don't suppose you'd do me the honour of dancing with me?"

She nodded past him to where the blonde bimbo stood scowling at them. "I don't think your girlfriend would be too pleased."

Stone glanced over his shoulder at the bimbo then turned back to Mist, unconcerned. "She's not my girlfriend. Just someone I met here tonight."

"You were on intimate terms with her on the dance floor. Are you always that friendly to women you've only just met?"

Stone shrugged. "Depends if they want me to be."

"And if they don't?"

"Then I'm always the perfect gentleman."

"I'm sure you are." A perfect gentleman who beat and raped women. His fists tearing into them, bruising flesh, breaking bone. His cock and his sex-toys ripping at their insides, violating them in the most disgusting ways possible.

"So what's your name?" asked Stone.

Mist brushed her long black hair extensions over her shoulder. "Tanya."

"Nice name. I'm Jack."

"Pleased to meet you." She extended her hand. He kissed it. Corny.

Mist glanced over to see the bimbo storming over, thunder in her eyes. "You—!"

That's as far as she got before Jack's minder grabbed her arm and dragged her away. "Get off me!" yelled the bimbo. "That bitch is horning in on my territory!"

She slapped at the minder's face. He twisted her arm and she screamed in pain.

For a second Mist was a little kid again watching a typical family scene. Dad beating up Mum. Once Mist tried to stop Dad and he hit her, busting her jaw. But she wasn't a helpless little girl any more. She started to rise from her seat.

Then the club's head bouncer, a small, blonde woman, stepped in, smoothing things over. The minder let the bimbo go, knowing that Stone wouldn't want to ruin the romantic atmosphere by starting a fight. Just as well; the bouncer had an electrostunner hidden in her hand – he would have been unconscious before he could even move. As the female bouncer calmed things down another bouncer, a big black man, watched the minder impassively, making sure he didn't start any trouble. He didn't; the drama faded; the tension eased.

"Sorry about that," said Stone. "Dennis gets a little heavy-handed sometimes. I'll be having a word with him about handling women later."

Mist relaxed her fists and settled back on her seat. She'd nearly blown the assignment for the sake of settling an old score that could never be paid. Christ, she was supposed to be a professional. Get back on track. "I'm sure you know how to handle women."

"Never had any complaints."

No. No complaints. Dead women can't complain about anything. Thirty or so of Stone's body count had nothing to do with business. They'd just been hot dates.

His love life was a well-known secret but the police were never able to pin anything on him. The bodies were never found and he always had an alibi ready just in case. On top of that when Mist checked up on him she found that some of his men had DNA cleansing training, able to remove all traces of forensic evidence from both his victims and the crime scene. Stone may have been a cruel, vicious bastard but he wasn't stupid.

Stone sipped his drink. "So, what do you do?"

Mist ran her finger around the top of her glass. "Anything I feel like."

Stone chuckled. "Me too."

They talked for another half-hour. Stone bought her more drinks and did his best to be charming. Eventually, judging her to be just about tipsy enough, he made his move.

"It's too loud in here. I know somewhere quieter."

She picked up her purse. "Lead on, Macduff."

"It's 'Lay on, Macduff.' I remember doing it at school." They headed for the cloakroom. "I never liked Macbeth at the time – thought he was gutless letting his wife boss him around all the time – but now, after all the grief my ex-wife used to give me, I just think, I know how you feel, old son."

"I don't believe that you could ever be under anyone's thumb."

"Don't matter how tough you are, people'll find a way to control you if they put their minds to it."

Without meaning to she thought of her parents. Dad resenting the marriage parenthood had trapped him in. And Mum cowering under his fists when he took her money from her so he could go out boozing.

Collecting their coats, she and Stone stepped out into the cold night air. The two bouncers on the door nodded to them. Music drifted out of the club, drumbeats and basslines, the melody too faint to hear. Cars drove by, headlights glistening. Black clouds moved overhead, blending into the night, blotting out the stars. But they couldn't blot out the neon signs of the restaurants lining the opposite side of the street – Chinese, Indian, Italian, Thai. Punters staggered drunkenly between the different bars and pubs.

Stone's minder pulled up in a limo. Stone gestured to the car with a grand sweep of his hand. "Your carriage awaits."

Getting into the car wearing such a tight dress could have been a problem but she'd been practising. She slid gracefully onto the leather seats. Stone sat beside her. A sheet of tinted glass separated them from the minder.

It was so tempting to kill Stone now. Then she wouldn't have to suffer him slobbering over her, his hands touching her. Kill him now.

No. That wasn't what the client wanted.

Stone flipped an intercom switch. "The Griffin."

The Griffin hotel. Stone owned it. He could do whatever he liked there and no one would say a word.

The car pulled away from the kerb smoothly. It was like riding on air.

Stone smiled at her. "The hotel bar stays open all night. For me anyway."

"That's convenient."

"Isn't it?" He rested his hand on her thigh. She resisted the temptation to crush his windpipe. She was going to have to let him do much worse than this before the night was through.

Stone told her about his businesses. The legitimate ones anyway. She knew all the details already but she listened anyway, nodding and making polite noises at all the appropriate moments.

Then he told her a bit about his life. Growing up on the streets, ducking and diving until he had enough money scraped together to go legit (officially anyway). The way he told it made him sound like a loveable rogue. He didn't tell her about the stabbings, the beatings, the shootings, the kneecappings. And he didn't tell her about his dates.

The limo pulled up outside the Griffin. It wasn't the biggest hotel in the city but it was still impressive. Stone walked her along thick plush carpet to the reception. When they reached the oak desk he turned to look at her. "Now, do you want to go to the bar or do you want to come to my room?"

She stroked his chest, slowly, seductively. "Guess."

Grinning, Stone snapped his fingers at the receptionist. "Lucy, my keys."

Once Stone had his keycard he steered her towards the lifts. As they entered the lift Stone spoke to his minder. "Take the rest of the night off, Dennis."

Stroke of luck. It would make things easier if Dennis wasn't hanging around outside Stone's bedroom door. Of course he would probably still be around somewhere in the hotel, particularly if he was part of Stone's clean-up crew.

The lift doors slid shut. Fancy grillwork like the bars of an ornate cage. She was just running through her escape plan one more time when Stone kissed her.

His breath stank of booze and cigarettes as his tongue probed her mouth like a wet slug. His hands grabbed her arse tightly, his fingers sinking into her flesh.

Stone pulled his lips from hers, gasping slightly. "I've been wanting to do that all night."

"Me too."

He kissed her again.

Then the lift doors opened. Taking her hand, Stone led her along the corridor to his suite. Swiping the lock with his keycard, he threw open the door. "What do you think?"

Old-fashioned furniture filled the suite; chairs and tables, all dark oak, the polish shining in the light of the holo-candles.

"Very nice."

"The bedroom's even nicer." He embraced her, his bulk dwarfing her slender frame. Kissing her neck, Stone shuffled towards the bedroom. Giggling, she shuffled along after him.

The bed was a giant four-poster. It probably cost more than her car.

Stone fumbled with the fastenings on her dress. A wasted effort – the self-sealing micro-zipper was absorbed into the fabric of the dress. It took a solvent spray to reverse the reaction.

He grimaced, impatient. "Is this dress expensive?"

"Yes."

He tore it from her body. "I'll buy you a new one."

She tried to control her trembling. The dress had fitted her so tightly that when he ripped it off her – accompanied by that horrible tearing noise – it had been as though he'd torn off her own skin. Now she stood before him; exposed, naked.

Forcing herself into character, she reached out to remove Stone's clothes. He pushed her hands away gently. "No, I do this bit myself."

She watched as he took off his suit and threw it in the corner. When he'd finished he stood before her proudly. She examined him critically. His muscles were starting to sag a little, middle-age spread was attacking his belly, and there was a touch of grey amongst the thick black hair that covered his body. She tried not to look at his erection.

He kissed her then threw her gently onto the bed. She bounced slightly on the mattress and for a second she worried that the unexpected movement might have shaken loose her contraceptive cap. Of course it hadn't, she'd tested it for worse impacts than that. Even now she could feel the cap releasing the lubricants that would fool Stone into thinking he was getting her all moist.

Stone lay on the bed and reached into the drawer of the bedside cabinet. He pulled out a couple of green pills and a pair of VR helmets.

He offered her a pill. "Here, take one. The trip mixes with the VR images, it's like our minds meld together. It makes sex fantastic."

Great. That was just what she needed. Still, the inhibitors she'd taken earlier worked on most known narcotics as well as alcohol. Poisons too. She swallowed one of the tablets. Stone took the other.

They put on the helmets and Stone climbed on top of her.

She looked up at him. "Shouldn't we use some kind of protection?"

"Don't worry, I just had my medical. I'm clean. And I trust you. I'm very careful about who I sleep with."

No, he wasn't. If he was he wouldn't have taken Georgia Harker on one of his special dates. Georgia's dad was Frank Harker, one of the biggest villains in the city. When his little girl didn't come home Harker did some asking around. Not operating under the same restrictions as the police, he soon found someone willing to point to Stone.

That's when he called Mist.

She tried to look as though she was enjoying it as Stone eased himself inside her. Then he was pumping away, too engrossed in his own lust to notice her reactions. She lay beneath him, fighting back a sudden attack of claustrophobia. His bulk was suffocating her.

She bit her lip to stop herself from crying. Why couldn't Harker have just wanted a normal hit? She could have killed Stone a dozen times over before it got to this stage. But no, he wanted Stone to suffer for what he had done. That's why the lubricants in Mist's contraceptive cap carried a lethal sexually transmitted disease. She was protected, she'd been taking the vaccine since she'd accepted the assignment. But Stone, he wouldn't stand a chance. This wasn't just any STD, it was a genetically engineered strain that would deliver six months of pain, tissue damage and organ degeneration in the space of two minutes. But the virus didn't kick in straight away. The cells didn't start to mutate until stimulated by an electric signal delivered by the radio transmitter hidden beneath one of Mist's fingernails. Harker wanted to be sure Stone had time to find out why he was dying.

Stone grunted in time with his thrusts. His aftershave mingled with his sweat and the stink of booze; a nauseating brew that made her stomach heave.

She could've refused the assignment. And even though she'd taken the job she didn't have to do it the way Harker wanted. Just kill Stone the old-fashioned way and say circumstances had dictated it. Harker would never know any different.

Christ, why was this bothering her so much? This wasn't the first time she'd whored herself to get to a target. It didn't mean anything.

VR images flickered in front of her eyes. The effect was pretty freaky. It would be worse if she was hallucinating. Figures flashed back and forth; distorted visions of men she had been with. She guessed the helmets scanned the electrical activity in both their brains to get a sketchy idea of their fantasies and fed the information back into the pre-programmed scenario.

The VR environment altered her perception of her own body-image. The breasts of her cyber-self became rounder, her lips fuller. Although she didn't speak she heard herself calling out in a high-pitched yelp. "Yes! Yes! Yes!" Stone's fantasies projected onto her.

The helmet probably couldn't read thoughts accurately enough for it to blow her cover. Still, best be ready for a worst case scenario. Faking a groan she shifted her left hand to clasp Stone's neck; ready to crush his windpipe. She curled the fingers of her other hand so she was ready to trigger the transmitter in her nail.

Men hurting women always reminded her of her parents. That's why she didn't like Stone touching her, why her nerves were jangling.

She remembered Dad beating Mum and then crying through the night, begging her forgiveness, swearing he'd never do it again. But he always did.

She had wanted to love her dad the way the other kids loved theirs. But he had made that impossible.

Don't think about it! Go back to that cold hard place where nothing hurts and the killing is easy.

The VR images were getting stronger now. They overlapped each other crazily, one image bleeding into another. In the background were shadowy figures; memories not properly scanned by the VR helmet. Quicksilver flickers of consciousness that were too elusive to be properly recorded. She stared at them, unsure which of the images were hers and which belonged to Stone. She focused, increasing the resolution of her mind's eye. One of the figures was her dad.

She watched in horror as he turned towards her. Horns sprouted from his brow. His penis transformed into a huge serpent. He moved towards her, licking his lips.

Shit! The inhibitors hadn't neutralised the hallucinogenics. She was tripping. And it was a bad trip. The worst.

Okay, ride it out. Experts in psychological torture had tried and failed to twist her mind inside out. She could handle whatever a cheap street drug could throw at her.

Dad advanced on her, the tongue of his penis-serpent flickering rapidly. Oh God, Dad had never touched her. Not that way. Black eyes, yes. Cut lip, yes. Broken jaw, yes. But never, *ever*, like that.

No, Dad had never raped her. He had only ever done that to Mum.

Mist hated him for that. Had wished him dead, would have

carried out the job herself if an alcohol soaked liver hadn't beaten her to it.

Stone seized her hair. She winced; the extensions tugged at her own hair, threatening to tear it from her scalp.

Dad stopped stalking towards her. She could see now that his features weren't quite right. Dad never wore a beard. It looked familiar though. Then she remembered – this was Stone's dad. She had seen his picture in the files. Stone Snr was superimposed over her dad, the two of them blurring together.

Stone's groans turned to growls. He thrust his hips harder, more aggressively. She gasped in pain but he ignored her.

A subliminal flicker – the hybrid dad stood over Stone, sodomizing him. Then Dad was gone and Stone's VR image began to cry. The tears flew from his hate-filled face as fiery sparks but they turned to acid as they dripped down onto her face and neck. She gritted her teeth as her cyber-flesh burned.

The VR helmet had linked her memories of her dad to Stone's memories of his father. There was just enough common ground for the VR programme to meld them together. A confused mishmash of hatred, betrayal and sexual aggression.

Stone shrivelled inside her. At first she thought he had come but then she realised his erection had merely wilted. He pulled out, his limp penis glistening from the lubricants.

Stone yanked off his VR helmet and hurled it across the room. She removed her own helmet as he leapt off the bed. "What's the matter?"

"Don't pretend you don't know," he snarled. "You saw it!"

"I –" She wasn't sure what to say. She felt a strange kinship for him then; united in past horrors.

Stone clamped his fists against the sides of his head. "Oh, God! Oh, Jesus fucking Christ!"

She could finish him now; tell him why she was there, trigger the virus and then get the hell out. Her thumb brushed gently against the nail with the transmitter.

She didn't press it.

Stone staggered over to her and she found herself standing, hugging him, feeling the tremors of his sobs running into her body. A bond joined them. She knew him, she understood him. There was no need for this to end the way either of them had planned it.

Then Stone hit her.

The punch spun her round to crash face down on the bed. Blood filled her mouth – liquid copper. Caught offguard she hadn't rolled with the punch properly, her neck muscles could only absorb so much. Consciousness wavered, ebbing and flowing like the tide, unsure whether it could hold on.

A thousand needles of pain exploded in her scalp as Stone grabbed her hair and dragged her off the bed. Too dizzy to fight back. Activate the virus. Slow him down enough for her to get away.

She couldn't. Not knowing what she now knew about his past. This wasn't his fault.

A punch to the gut drove the air from her body. A second punch dropped her to her knees. Christ, she'd never gone soft on a target before. Activate the virus, you stupid bitch!

Stone kicked her. She felt a rib snap. He kicked her again and she fell flat to the floor, the carpet rubbing her face. She lost count of the blows after that. All she knew was that no matter how much her survival instincts screamed at her she couldn't fight back. She just wanted to hug him and tell him everything was all right.

Fuck, what had he done to her?

The pills. They hadn't just been hallucinogens. There was something else. Something that fucked with her emotions, destroyed her judgment. Probably some synthetic equivalent of oxytocin, the neurotransmitter that flooded the brain during sex, creating feelings of love and bonding.

Fight it. Fight *him*.

Stone stopped kicking her. Tears streamed down his face; his features twisted in a contradictory mask of ecstasy and self-loathing. Christ, he must have taken a dose of oxytocin too. But why do that to himself? She couldn't bear to look at his face, his pain hurt her more than his beating.

Grabbing her arms, Stone pulled her to her feet. Her legs wobbled, if he let go she would be face down on the carpet again.

Stone trembled as he held her. "Tell me." His voice was a strangled whisper. "Tell me you love me."

She tried to fight it, to keep her jaws clamped tightly shut. She'd die before she said it. But then her lips were moving and she couldn't do anything to stop them.

"I love you."

And she meant it.

Stone smiled. Or maybe he grimaced. It was hard to tell, he was shaking so much. "Good."

He laid her gently on the bed, her face sinking into the feather-soft pillows. She watched as he went to the bedside cabinet and opened the bottom drawer. He pulled out a tray covered with a selection of dildos. They each had a different covering – razor-blades, broken glass, barbed wire. Placing the tray atop the bedside cabinet Stone took two pillows from the top of the bed. One went under her hips, raising her pelvis. The other went over the back of her head smothering her. She tried to shake it off, scared that he was going to suffocate her with it, but she was too weak, the pillow too large. Its corners flopped over each side of her head, obscuring her vision.

"It's better if you don't know which one I'm going to use," Stone told her. "Or on which orifice."

She felt the mattress dip as he knelt on the bed. Felt the sweat on his hands as he spread her legs. Then she heard a scraping noise as he picked up one of the dildos.

Her mind screamed at her, threatening to tear itself apart as her emotions warred with each other: She loved him no matter what he did to her. She would kill him. She just wanted him to be happy. She would choke him to death on one of his own fucking dildos.

One of Stone's hands was on her left buttock. She felt his weight shift as he leaned forward, reaching out to her with what he held in his other hand.

"I love you, Daddy," said Stone.

She wasn't sure if he could hear her under the pillow and with her mouth so weak and sore that she could barely move it but she whispered to him anyway. "I love you."

She triggered the virus.

The hand on her buttock tensed, then quivered. "W-what's happening to me?"

Got you, you bastard! Oh, God what had she done? Burn in hell! No, no, she didn't mean to do it, please don't die!

A thud as he fell off the bed. Stumbling, hesitant footsteps over to the vid-phone, stopping, slumping to the floor before he got halfway there. Agonized groans as his muscles shrivelled. A choking noise and then the pitter-patter of tiny objects falling onto the carpet. Probably his teeth falling out.

Two minutes is a long time to take to die.

And it's an eternity to listen to the suffering of someone you love.

Mist squeezed her eyes shut and slowly, painfully, covered her ears with her hands. But she couldn't shut out Stone's cries of pain.

Finally death rattled in his throat. Sobbing, she pulled herself painfully to her feet. Staggering over to her purse she pulled out a tiny cube of fabric which unfolded into a jump-suit. Getting dressed was slow, painful; every time the cloth brushed against her wounds was agony. Finally she was clothed. Picking up her shoes, she broke off the heels in case she needed to run. Not that she was sure she was physically capable of running right now.

All through this she avoided looking at Stone's corpse. It would be too much for her to bear.

She turned to the window that led to the fire escape. Opening it she was greeted by all the night sounds of the city – faint music, traffic, a police siren wailing into the darkness.

She paused, her hands resting on the windowsill. Then she turned and limped over to Stone's body. He was hunched in a foetal curl, one hand slightly extended as though reaching for something. His body was atrophied, his skin withered. Blood-stained teeth lay scattered on the carpet amongst clumps of his hair. Wide, frightened eyes stared up at her unseeingly.

Part of her wanted to stay with him, to huddle up to his corpse and wail her despair for all to hear. But she knew that once the drug was out of her system her love would die. That's what she wanted; to never have to feel anything again. To never have to fear being hurt.

Slowly she forced herself back towards the window. Stone's clean-up team would be here soon.

One last lingering look at Stone. His outstretched hand seemed to be imploring her to stay.

She climbed through the window and out into the night.

Tears streamed down her cheeks.

MINDSTALKER

Martin Edwards

Sadie Kyle smiled at the door guard on her way into court, as if to say, *Think I look good in black?* The man blushed; for a moment, Breen thought he was going to drop his gun. Sadie had that effect on people. She was the sexiest judge Breen had ever seen. You could imagine her pronouncing the death sentence and making it sound like a tease.

Not that this was a capital case. Four women had died over an 18-month span, but even so, the maximum penalty was only "life meaning life". Traditionalists said that a civilized society only executed those who threatened the security of the state.

Hannah, he knew, thought differently. She had no time for do-gooders. The prison ships were overflowing, she used to point out, why not dump a few of the bad guys overboard? Breen didn't argue with her: if people profiled as dangerous could be locked up without even committing a crime, how could you justify keeping a convicted murderer alive?

"Didn't take her long," Hannah whispered, her breath warm against his cheek.

Breen wondered if she was jealous of Sadie. The thought hadn't occurred to him before. Perhaps it should have done. They were both young, attractive women, scrambling up the ladder in the fiercely competitive business of criminal justice.

Sadie Kyle was a graduate of the fast-track judicial college at Milton Keynes. These days judges had to keep in close touch with the people: no more room for the greybeards of yore, denying all knowledge of popular culture. Sadie was famed for living hard and playing harder. She might have kicked her coke habit, but last night she'd probably been out at a club until the early hours.

But Hannah wasn't a party animal. She was even more focused than Sadie, and that was saying plenty. *Focus*, that was the key to everything, Breen said to himself. Hannah loved the job. For her, it was a turn-on when the media described her as a career cop. "It's all I ever wanted to be," was her regular line. All her life, she'd wanted to front a serial killer inquiry, to be the one who hunted the bastard down. Now her dream had come true.

"She was out for twenty minutes," Breen murmured. "Why waste time?"

A stroke of luck, Breen thought, that this trial had been allocated to Sadie Kyle. It made sense, though: the court executives were no fools, they knew how to respond to public demand. The eyes of the nation were on this courtroom and who better to preside than the most telegenic judge of them all? He'd been watching Sadie's video column these past few weeks. Justice delayed was justice denied, that was one of her themes. Judges had targets to meet; they didn't have all day to sit around deliberating. The queue of cases waiting to come to court never seemed to get any shorter. Mercifully, only treason charges led to all the palaver of a jury having to be sworn in. An inefficient hangover from the past, scarcely consistent with the need to safeguard the state from its enemies. The government was talking about reforming the law so that even capital cases could be disposed of more swiftly.

Hannah, Breen knew, yearned for the rules of the game to be modernized. If this case went the way it should, she expected promotion and a transfer to the National Security Squad. Nothing was worse than bringing a suspect to justice and then waiting for a year only to see the case thrown out on some legal technicality. It didn't happen so much, these days, but if even one guilty person went free, that was an affront to civilized values.

Sadie coughed and the courtroom fell quiet. Breen felt his heart skip a beat. What was the verdict going to be? Leave his profile aside and the evidence was thin. She turned to face the man in the dock and shook her head, as if in sorrow.

Breen relaxed. It was going to be all right.

"Taz Parlane, I'll get straight to the point. In my judgment, the evidence against you is overwhelming. I find you guilty on all counts."

Next to him, Hannah hissed, "Yes!"

Even before Sadie finished speaking, the noise from the gallery was deafening. Members of the victims' families were shouting. Some punched the air in triumph, others pointed angrily at the man in the dock. A respectable man in a lounge suit ran his finger across his neck in a contemptuous throat-cutting gesture.

Sadie nodded at the security team. The woman in charge lifted her gun and bellowed, "Silence in court! The judge must be heard!"

When the commotion had died down, Sadie said, "I can well understand the feelings of those who have suffered because of your crimes, Taz Parlane. As you are aware, the views of victims' families will be sought in determining the circumstances of your sentence. I leave it to you to deduce their intentions."

Parlane stared at her, sullen, wordless. Breen wondered how heavy the sedation had been. All in a good cause.

"I intend to impose the most severe punishment available to me. Four sentences of life meaning life under the Truth In Sentencing Act, one term for each of your crimes. You will spend the rest of your days in jail. No remission. My only regret is that at present society fails to acknowledge that, for crimes such as yours, there can be no prospect of rehabilitation and that there is frankly little point in keeping you alive." She glanced around, in the direction of the television cameras. "If I had any influence at all with our rulers, I would urge them to review the penalty in serial killing cases as a matter of urgency."

Hannah and the other detectives sitting further down the bench mimed applause. Sadie caught the gestures, gave a minute nod of approval.

"On you, Taz Parlane, I shall waste no further words. Take him down."

As the big men seized the prisoner and bundled him towards the exit, Breen sensed Hannah's body stiffening beside him. She was excited. Such a result! Tomorrow her name would be all over the net.

More noise, but this time Sadie quietened people herself with a wave of the hand. "Thank you, everyone. This has been a traumatic case, a dreadful experience for everyone – including the judge. I'd just like to thank my staff here for their tremendous support, with a special mention for security – as well-organized as ever. The lawyers have done their job with their customary calm and good humour. The police have been marvellous, as usual, coping with a tremendously difficult investigation and the usual constraints on funding and resources. A special word, though, for Detective Team Leader Hannah Dowe, whose incisive work played such a vital part in bringing the culprit to justice."

Breen squeezed Hannah's hand. "Told you her heart was in the right place."

Sadie wasn't finished yet. "And I must express particular gratitude to the prosecution's expert witness, Professor Joshua Breen of the University of Plaistow, whose profiling testimony I found so convincing. Well, thank you, everyone. And now, if you'll excuse me, I'll take a short break before the next case begins. We reconvene in half an hour."

As the court rose, Breen and Hannah found themselves mobbed by people pushing cameras and microphones in their faces. Questions fired at them from all quarters.

"Ms Dowe, how do you react to Sadie Kyle's judgment? Why do we need to keep people like Parlane alive?"

"Professor Breen, is it true you've sold the television rights to your notes on the case?"

"A quick word for viewers of Eurocrime, Professor Breen?"

"Is it true, Ms Dowe, that you've been asked to star in a film of your career alongside Robbie Williams?"

All Hannah managed to say was, "Give me a break, he's old enough to be my grandfather," and then the minders from TV Confidential huddled around and swept them off through the back doors of the court complex into a waiting limo.

They were driven off at speed, shielding their faces. It never paid to look as though you courted attention. In the back of the car, Hannah's hand slid along Breen's leg. He watched her Nefertiti profile, felt himself stirring, wanting her. It had been quite a day. Time yet to celebrate.

First stop was TV Confidential's media centre. The journey was a nightmare. Twenty-four hours earlier, there had been a suicide bombing in Shoreditch and the roads were still in chaos. A good thing that they weren't going out live.

In make-up, they chatted to each other: inconsequential stuff, you could never be sure that the staff wouldn't sell titbits to rival channels and bringing a personal privacy action was such a bore. Breen had been a star for a couple of years now; he was accustomed to attention, to the point of weariness. For Hannah, the spotlight was equally familiar. She'd made her name fighting a harassment case against her old boss. The compensation had been a record sum, enough to buy her an eleven-million-dollar apartment in Knightsbridge. They would be going back there once the recording was done.

Vicky Singh talked earnestly to camera, telling the story of the killings. Four pretty young women, murdered in their own homes. The throat of each was slashed. No trace of sexual assault in any case, no sign of a forced entry to the buildings, no connecting link between any of the victims.

"For glamorous young detective Hannah Dowe, it was the toughest inquiry she'd ever had to handle. A case that could make her – or break her."

Breen watched Hannah. She was silent, a faraway look in her eyes. He'd come to know her very well these past few months, he could tell that she was rehearsing soundbites in her mind. "Team effort . . . just a small cog in a very large wheel . . . dedicated officers . . . behind the scenes . . . nothing glamorous . . . long hours . . . remembering the victims . . . focusing on the need for justice."

Disclaimers were a necessary ritual. No one would take any notice of them; no one was meant to. As Vicky said, Hannah, the public face of the inquiry, was young and lovely and that was all that mattered.

The killer, Taz Parlane. A young man who had drifted from job to job. He'd last worked a year ago, serving tables in a cannabis café. People who knew him said he was affable enough. But what could they know of his darker dreams?

"You had little or no forensic evidence against Parlane, did you, Hannah? A hair from the last victim found on his coat; it wasn't very much. The defence lawyers argued the traces could have arisen from contamination by you or your colleagues. Accidental – or deliberate."

Hannah stared, unblinking, at the camera. A style she'd perfected during the course of her personal litigation. She was a formidable witness. Unshakable.

"That was a filthy line in cross-examination. Of course, we're

used to attacks on our integrity. Besides, forensic was only one
piece in the jigsaw. We had so much more on Taz Parlane."

"Professor Breen's profile of the killer, you mean?"

"It fitted Parlane perfectly. And then there were the brainprints; they corroborated everything the professor said."

"But brainprinting is still controversial."

"I keep saying, Vicky, it's a mistake to confuse brainprinting
with the old-style polygraph. This is about more than simple old-
fashioned lie-detection. It's about analysing what goes on in the
deep recesses of the human mind."

"But the brainprint only records the presence of electrical
activity within the suspect's head," Vicky persisted. "Isn't there
a danger, if you misread what that activity means?"

Hannah had fended off questioning from the toughest defence
lawyers in Britain. She could cope with Vicky Singh.

"We're sensitive to the human rights issues, believe me – every
cop is nowadays. We spend half our lives at civil liberties
seminars." Her voice became husky. "But what I say is this –
let's not forget the human rights of the young women Taz
Parlane killed. I'm sorry, I just have to make that point. It's
too easy to forget what they went through. What their loved ones
are still going through."

"And yet some critics argue that—"

"Remember, the courts have agreed to admit brainprint evidence at long last. They wouldn't do that if they weren't sure it
was safe. In some cases, the brainprint is the only thing the police
have. Sole witness for the prosecution. But that wasn't the case
here."

"Because besides the brainprint – you had Joshua Breen's
profile of the culprit?"

"Without it," Hannah said softly, "there's a danger that
Parlane would still be free. Free to kill and terrorize."

Vicky started talking about Breen. He struck a modest pose as
he listened to her, let her wonderment wash over him. ". . .
brilliant . . . wayward . . . not yet thirty . . . some say, a maverick
. . . a wizard, a shaman, a man who hunts through the minds of
killers."

"All I do," he said amiably, when his turn came to speak, "is
use my imagination. That's the key to understanding criminals,
Vicky. Imagination."

She loved that. They always did. Forensics were over-rated. Crime scenes were fine, they bristled with clues. *Every contact leaves a trace* – where did that get you? Each trace was open to interpretation. DNA evidence was all very well. Okay, so you could prove it was a billion to one that this dab of saliva or that dollop of semen came from the accused. But how did it get to the crime scene? The media had exposed enough cases of incompetence and corruption to put those who worshipped forensic data on to the defensive. Criminal investigators needed something more than physical stuff. They needed to stalk the culprits, get inside their heads.

"You tracked Parlane, didn't you?" she asked. "You followed his every thought. That's your gift, to fathom the dark side of the human condition."

He gave a shrug, offered a disarming smile. She was quoting directly from his publishers' latest press release. He liked that. "I'm no miracle worker, Vicky. Just a trained psychologist, wanting to do his bit for law and order."

Her smile was coquettishly disbelieving. She wasn't as pretty as Hannah, he thought, or Sadie Kyle come to that. Even so . . .

She paused, lowered her voice a little. "There's just one thing. People say that there's a personality cult surrounding the new breed of profilers. You're all handsome young men, perhaps the image thing even gets in the way —"

"The work always comes first," he interrupted. "Publicity is only a means to an end. If my appearing on television helps to bring just one killer to book, all the sleepless nights will be worth while."

"Jo Swann, Alex Penberthy, Rachel Davis, Su Baptiste. Four women with everything to live for." Vicky's tone was sombre. "So why did Parlane kill them? You seemed so sure his motivation wasn't sexual."

"As I said in court, he loved the taste of power. Power and control." He leaned forward, warming to his theme, his knees almost touching hers. "He wanted to have their destinies in his hands. On another day, in another mood, who knows? He might have let them live."

Vicky was concentrating on him; her lips were slightly parted. He could tell that she found him attractive. She was supposed to be a tough interrogator, but she was giving him an easy ride. He'd read something about her ending the affair with the network controller who had given her this job. Might as well ask for her contact details when the recording was over. You never knew.

Hannah was becoming impatient. Shifting in her seat, glancing at the clock on the studio wall. It was a long time since Vicky had asked her a question.

"At the end of the day," she interrupted, finally, "we're all working together. This isn't about me, or Professor Breen. It's all about a team of committed professionals."

"Of course," Vicky said smoothly.

The look in her eyes said *But none of us truly believes that, do we? My viewers certainly don't. We're all celebrities nowadays. At least we are if we want to have a hope in hell of making something of our lives.*

She didn't put any more questions to Hannah. Five minutes later, the interview was over. At the bar upstairs, he let Vicky flirt with him when Hannah departed to the loo. She gave him her card and suggested he call her.

"Only one thing," she said. "You'll have to promise not to try reading my mind."

"Too late," he said. "I already have."

She laughed and said, "Sadie Kyle took a shine to you, anyone could see it."

"I hope you're not suggesting her judgment was anything other than impartial," he said easily.

"She knows it's all about conviction rates. Meeting government targets, topping the league tables. Judges are no different from cops."

Hannah came back, gave Vicky a sharp look. "We'd better go."

Breen smiled at Vicky, said thanks for everything, and offered his hand. She gripped it tightly, held it a moment too long.

Outside, Hannah said, "She fancies you."

He frowned. "You said that about Sadie Kyle this morning. What is this? You never used to be so – so *paranoid*."

"I'm not. I just don't think you should encourage these women."

"Encourage them? Come on . . ."

The quarrel spluttered along after they got back to her place. She opened a bottle of Bollinger, but even a couple of glasses weren't enough to make either of them lighten up. The elation of a guilty verdict had never subsided this quickly, he thought. There was no excitement like the excitement of testifying about someone's evil crimes, but already Parlane's conviction was a distant memory.

Hannah was harping on about Sadie Kyle, about the weight she'd put on his profile of the murderer's behaviour. The clues that lay within the culprit's own personality.

"You needed that profile," he said irritably. "Without it, you didn't have a hope of fastening the crimes on Parlane."

"You're forgetting the brainprint."

He shrugged, to show what he thought about brainprints. "Please."

"And we had the hair," she said, her voice rising in anger.

"Yeah, planted on the coat by Rudd or Mettomo or Carter, or one of the other guys who wants to get inside your knickers."

She swore at him, but he wasn't fazed. "You needed the profile," he repeated. "I made this happen for you, Hannah, let's leave it at that, huh?"

Later, in the darkness of her bedroom, he wondered if he'd made a mistake. On balance, he thought not. The Parlane case was a good result. For him as well as for Hannah.

He watched her as she slept. The duvet was on the floor; she was wholly uncovered. Naked and defenceless. Not unlike Su Baptiste, the night she was murdered. Poor Su: he could imagine, he could precisely imagine, what must have gone through her mind when, the moment she turned her back on him, her killer put the knife to her tender throat. He thought about it often, more often than he should.

Power and control.

He wondered who had killed her. Parlane? Unlikely. Finding a stranger-killer, these days it was like looking for a needle in a haystack. There were thousands of bad men out there, ticking like bombs. So many of them ready to explode.

As he studied the curves of Hannah's body, an idea slid into his mind, wicked and tempting. Risky, so risky, but at least it would give him the fix that he craved.

Savage death of murder cop. He could see the headlines now. Poor Hannah, she made enemies too easily, that was her problem. No shortage of suspects. He'd be distraught, pledged to help find the culprit.

Who would take the rap, though? That was the question. Something to puzzle over, worry at, until he came up with the answer.

His imagination working, he caressed Hannah's warm flesh. A gentle motion, helping his thoughts to focus. He was doing what he loved best. Taking a walk through the mind of a murderer.

THIGHS

Melanie Fogel

Despite the chilly drizzle, Thighs bicycles to his customers. Attached to his rear fender, a battery charges as he pedals. His backpack holds more batteries, which he will deliver today.

His clothes, his backpack, his helmet and his bicycle are the colour of pavement, the colour of the sky on this bleak October morning, the uniform colour of Thighs. Madame O'Shaughnessy calls it "prison grey". Thighs resents this; he has always earned his living honestly.

He begins his rounds at first light, when few but other Thighs are about. They will spend the morning in deliveries and pick-ups, and the afternoon and evening charging batteries. As will Thighs, because this is how all Thighs live.

Up ahead, Thighs spots a tomato-red pedal car. He wonders what would bring the wealthy out so soon after dawn. He thinks of Madame O'Shaughnessy's dandelion-yellow pedal car, which she once paid him to drive. Other than the room where she watches him charge batteries, it is the only private space of Madame O'Shaughnessy's that he has seen.

He hears the hiss of tyres behind him. A bicycle shoots past, intent on passing the pedal car. The cyclist, a Thighs, no more acknowledges him than one electric current would another. This is the tradition, and as it should be. But the speed is not within tradition. Thighs reads the green 10 embroidered on the other's backpack. He grimaces in contempt.

The co-ops are proliferating. There is talk now of coloured uniforms to match the coloured numbers, of switching from numbers to names.

Thighs wears no number anywhere upon his person. He

distrusts the idea of tithing to a group who will spend his money as they see fit, even if they see fit to spend it in caring for him during sickness or injury. Thighs needs no formal association to validate his identity. He is a Thighs, and wears his anonymity with pride.

This morning, however, he reconsiders the decision made so long ago. Thighs is ageing. His last hamstring pull took longer to heal, ate into more of his savings, than any before. His equipment is ageing, as are his batteries. This has all come sooner than expected. He is not prepared, and the rent is due.

Madame O'Shaughnessy is very old. She is wealthy beyond Thighs' understanding. She has always been wealthy, if her tales of her youth are true. Thighs doubts their truth, suspects they are at best exaggerations, and hears with distaste her legends of a city crowded and noisy and bright with artificial light.

By noon, Thighs has received three complaints that his batteries gave out too soon. He takes the customers' word for it; he knows the batteries are old. The third customer, a restaurant in which Thighs cannot afford to eat, dismisses his offer of two for the price of one. The owner shows him the batteries he rented when Thighs' batteries failed. They are stamped with a blue 7. Thighs regards them with indifference. Other than the co-op number and their freshness, they are identical to his.

Thighs skips lunch and visits his supplier instead. The shop he enters is dark, as most shops nowadays, but this one is made darker by the number of Thighs who congregate to gossip and boast about their co-ops. A bell above the door tinkles as he walks in, but the jolly sound has no effect on the baritone hum of conversation.

Behind the plywood counter stands Eric, a former Thighs. As if to advertise this, he eschews grey, wears short-sleeved shirts to display the loose skin on his upper arms. Eric is speaking to a pair of Co-op Number 15 Thighs. While he waits for the conversation to end, Thighs surveys the room.

All the Thighs are younger than he. Except for the occasional disproportion in arms or legs that indicates a preference for (or possession of) only one type of charger, there is nothing to distinguish them but skin and hair colour. And numbers sewn to backpacks and uniforms. Thighs cannot recall a time when he was the only one in the shop without a number.

When Eric disengages himself from his customers, Thighs presents his exhausted batteries for the parts that can be recycled, and asks for credit on the balance new ones will cost. Eric looks him up and down, the grey at the temples, the veins in his hands, the lack of number anywhere upon his person.

"When do you think you'd be able to pay me." It's a question, but his voice does not rise at the end of the sentence.

"Three months?" It's a statement, but Thighs' voice asks if Eric will wait that long.

Eric shakes his head. "You've got no collateral . . ."

Thighs straightens his posture, inhales slowly, expanding his chest, displaying all the collateral he has ever needed. Eric is not impressed. He sees the same on every customer.

"You still owe me for the cables," Eric reminds him.

Thighs needs no reminding. He's been greasing them with chicken fat; he is unable to wash the stench from his nose hairs.

Thighs takes cash for the used batteries. He hopes to find cheaper ones elsewhere; he has time to comparison shop, having lost three customers to co-op Thighs.

Stomach rumbling, Thighs heads for the house of Madame O'Shaughnessy. Traffic is heavier now, mostly pedestrian, most with chargers strapped to their hips. The people are slender, soft and brightly clothed; no one could mistake them for Thighs.

Thighs passes the park, noticing that another tree has been cut down. The police tape fencing the remains of the trunk sags between canted stakes. Thighs has little use for trees, except as firewood, but he admires the skill of anyone who can steal a tree and hide it until, come spring, only ashes remain. Beyond the park he turns right, covers four blocks of house-skeletons, all long ago stripped for fuel or furbishings, then turns left into a stump-lined avenue where brick and stone homes sit abandoned. Madame O'Shaughnessy has told him that once, all had green lawns and lofty maples whose leaves changed colour this time of year. Madame O'Shaughnessy has told Thighs much, but he has listened little. She thinks she entertains him with her talk as he entertains her with his body. He doesn't understand what pleasure she takes in watching his tendons strain, his biceps swell, his chest rise and fall, the sweat trickle down his neck and sides. Perhaps it's just the captive audience. Thighs wastes no time puzzling over Madame O'Shaughnessy's motives. He charges her extra for the privilege of watching him work.

Four cracked concrete steps lead up to Madame O'Shaughnessy's front door. As Thighs locks his bicycle against the cast-iron railing, she opens the door as if she's been waiting for him. In the four months that Madame O'Shaughnessy has been Thighs' customer, he has never seen a servant or acquaintance in her house.

Madame O'Shaughnessy stands in the doorway as Thighs walks up the stairs. She is thin, her arms and legs no thicker than the ornamental railing on her steps. She wears a hot-pink skirt, pearly white blouse, sheer stockings and shoes. Paint on her cheeks and lips matches her skirt. Thighs once wondered if she dresses up for him, but has since decided that she does it to make her tales of parties and lights burning all night more credible.

He disbelieves her stories of dinner parties and hot meals three times a day, even in summer if the temperature wasn't too high. Her thinness belies it. He hopes she will have no such stories today; he is hungry, and in four months, she has yet to offer him even a glass of water.

"You're late," she complains in her high whine.

This is a statement of fact Thighs feels no need to acknowledge. As he reaches the porch she turns and he follows her into the house. They proceed down a long corridor ostentatiously lit with three light bulbs. All the doors are closed, save one. "I'm having people in, and I need time to get ready." Madame O'Shaughnessy's voice hovers the length of the corridor like a bad smell.

They enter what Madame O'Shaughnessy calls the "power room". She says it was once her father's study, and contained a real mahogany desk, two chairs, two electric lamps and many bookcases. She says she gave away the furniture because she had tired of it. Now the room contains a complex contraption Madame O'Shaughnessy refers to as a Soloflex, and an ancient easy chair in which she sits talking while Thighs pulls and pumps.

She presses herself into the chair as Thighs removes his helmet, strips down to shorts and T-shirt. She sits with bony shoulders shrouded by the chair back, legs as parallel as stair rails.

Thighs gets an idea, and acts upon it. "I've had to raise my price," he tells her. When she doesn't react he adds, "By fifteen per cent."

Madame O'Shaughnessy says nothing, so Thighs begins to pull the metal handles. She watches until the neck and armpits of his shirt darken with sweat, then says, "When I was a girl, men like you were sexy."

Thighs has heard this before, from other Thighs. "Born too late," they all say with mock regret. No one really believes it.

"We've come full circle," Madame O'Shaughnessy goes on. "Time was, everyone worked outside, farming and that. They were tanned and muscled. So soft and white was sexy. Then everyone worked in offices and malls, so tanned and muscular was sexy. Now . . ." she adds more wrinkles to her raddled features, "guess I was born too late."

It doesn't matter whether it's true; Thighs lives in the world as it is now.

"Since you're raising your prices anyway," Madame O'Shaughnessy says in that voice in need of greasing, "what would you charge to take all your clothes off?"

Thighs nearly pulls a muscle. He's had such offers before, but not for a long time—and not from anyone, male or female, so desiccated. He always refused. "I am a Thighs," he would say with quiet pride. He wants to say it now, but he keeps pumping, thinking.

"C'mon," Madame O'Shaughnessy wheedles. He has never seen her smile; her teeth are the colour of a recently cleaned toilet. "I promise, I'll look but not touch." Her legs move slightly apart.

Thighs' sweat turns cold. He thinks of his pride, he thinks of his rent. He remembers the batteries that no longer hold a charge, the stink of chicken fat, the hunger in his belly, the hamstring that might go any day.

He names a price.

Still smiling, Madame O'Shaughnessy nods her head once.

Thighs closes his eyes, but he can still see her: the smeared pink lip paint, the drool down the left side of her mouth, the ravenous eyes, the rocking pelvis. Eyes closed, he hears her squeaky moans, her raspy sighs. His disgust drives him on, pulling, pumping, lifting, bending. "Look at me!" she shrieks. "Look at me or I won't pay you!"

Thighs opens his eyes, stares at the back of the chair, yet he sees . . .

As Thighs wipes himself down, he wishes he could afford to throw the towel away; it is soiled with more than sweat. He keeps his back to the silent Madame O'Shaughnessy as he puts on his shorts and T-shirt, prison-grey overshirt and trousers. He does not face her until his helmet is securely strapped under his chin.

She has composed herself, although her face wears an expression Thighs has never seen. He assumes she's embarrassed by her performance – their performance, he reluctantly admits – until she says, "I'm short of cash this week. I'll have to owe you."

"No." He reacts before his conscious brain has quite assimilated this information.

She lowers her eyes and shrugs. "Not much choice, I'm afraid."

"No," he says again, still processing her first comment. "I don't give credit."

"Next week, for sure."

He shakes his head, forgetting she cannot see his anger through the faceplate.

With the same indifference Thighs has faced all day, Madame O'Shaughnessy turns to leave the room. He grabs her arm.

"Ow," she says in a sing-song whine. Thighs knows he's not hurting her, knows he's resisting the temptation.

"Give me something I can sell," he says.

"Fool," she says. Thighs still grips her arm. "How do you think I've been paying you all this time?"

"You're rich."

"I *was* rich."

"Your car," he thinks aloud.

"Gone," she says. "Last thing I held on to."

He doesn't believe her. This house is full of treasures – all the things she's told stories about all these months.

"Let go of me and get out." Her indifference is now contempt.

Thighs takes her other arm. It's like holding his handlebars, only less padded. She stares into his faceplate, and he sees fear. He knows now he'll be paid.

"I don't have any money," she says, her whine a higher pitch.

"Yes, you do."

"No." She tries to pull away.

She's just sold the car. Thighs could live for years on what she must have got for it. She has to have some left.

"Honest to God I don't." She tilts her head at the open door. "Search the house if you like."

Through the doorway, Thighs sees the glow of the light bulbs. He knows she's lying. She's always lied, but this is different. He tosses her aside like his used towel and steps into the corridor.

He opens a door, enters a room crowded with stale air and nothing else. He hears scuffling in the corridor, turns to see Madame O'Shaughnessy running for the front door. In two strides he has her, spins her around as she shrieks, "Help! Police."

"Shut up!" He shakes her. "Where's the money?" She looks at him stupidly and he shakes her again. "Where!" He shakes her a third time and she goes limp.

Her head tilts back. Her eyes stare at the ceiling, directly at the burning bulb. Thighs knows she is dead. There's barely a thud when he drops her.

He throws open doors onto empty rooms. In the kitchen he finds cutlery no better than his own, a few battered pots, chipped dishes. Upstairs, a tall thing with drawers yields faded photographs and yellowed linens. At last he finds her bedroom. An almost bald hairbrush, but the back is silver. A matching comb and hand mirror. Small, oddly shaped bottles, jewellery that's probably plastic. Clothes, shoes, handbags with metal clasps. It all goes in his backpack, down his trousers, under his T-shirt. He returns to the power room, removes the charged batteries, steps over the flesh-tinted bones and out the front door.

He sees people about and hesitates. Then remembers he is a Thighs. No one pays attention as he unlocks his bicycle. No one bothers to notice the number, or lack of one, anywhere upon his person. He cycles down the street. Another Thighs approaches from the opposite direction. They pass each other without nodding.

THE UNCERTAINTY PRINCIPLE

John Moralee

A girl was missing that morning. Riley's police car raced towards her parents' home. The motorway cut a smooth path across Cambridgeshire, straight to the clouded horizon. To his left and right he could see rice fields. Rice was Britain's most successful crop after the global warming. The sky looked bronze over the floodplains. Everything else was sepia, like an old photograph. Mile markers flashed by, one every ten seconds.

Detective Constable Lee sat in the driving seat, but he wasn't driving. The police car was on full automatic steering, taking the shortest, fastest route. Lee was dressed in a plain black suit and shirt with a Chinese mandarin collar. The creases of his clothes were so sharp they looked as if they'd been ironed by a ninja. The journey gave the detectives a few minutes to talk. Lee looked at Riley.

"Are you celebrating?"

"Celebrating what?"

"Your birthday."

"Oh. Isla's planning a party. My kids and grandkids are coming. I'm not supposed to know."

"How'd you find out?"

"I overheard Isla. She's been secretly arranging it for weeks. I'll have to remember to act surprised." During breakfast Isla had given Riley a birthday card that had put him in a bad mood because it reminded him of his true age. In the locker room he had made the mistake of telling Lee it was his birthday. Lee had been badgering him ever since to know how old he was.

"Sir, I love birthdays. Why won't you tell me your real age?"

"If I tell you, will that shut you up?"

"Yes, I promise."

"I'm ninety."

"That means . . . you were born in 1970?"

"Yeah," he sighed. "Happy now?"

"No offence, sir, but you're *ancient*. My great-grandmother in Hong Kong isn't that old. How many times have you been rejuved?"

"I don't know. A lot." It seemed like once a month forever. He hated his doctor's appointments. He had an aversion to needles. But without the regular injections he'd start ageing, like people used to do before rejuve. Riley's physical age was thirty, but he had another sixty years of memories. He had once been sixty, balding, suffering arthritis, gout and a sagging belly, but the rejuve had slowly restored his youth. His partner was only twenty-five in real years. He hadn't even started on the rejuve.

"Do you like remember the dinosaurs?"

"Ha, ha." Riley sighed. "You said you'd shut up if I told you my age. You didn't shut up. Do you want to find out what it's like being thrown out of a police car going 360?"

"Boy, you're a grumpy old man this morning."

The car slowed down at the junction for Quantum Hill. Lee resumed driving manually as they entered the town. Quantum Hill was a satellite town of Cambridge, created in the 2020s for employees in the technology industries that had taken over the greenbelt. Its streets were wide, clean and tree-lined. Because of the poor weather – it was the middle of monsoon season – not many residents were outside. Riley saw a few dog-walkers in the parks and some more people on the high street. The boutiques and cafés had steamed up windows. The figures inside looked like Impressionist paintings. Everyone looked between twenty and thirty, though some would be older than a hundred, thanks to rejuve. Rejuve had been invented in 2030 and it was free to all British citizens. It cured old age, making its users effectively immortal as long as they continued to take it regularly. Old people were a rare sight. Noticing people who actually looked their age was a habit of Riley's. An old couple leaving a Church of Natural Life caught his attention. They belonged to a religious cult that believed rejuve was Satan's blood. It was literally a dying faith.

"Quiet town," Lee commented.

"Yeah, it's not London."

The houses were large and mostly American suburban-style circa 1950s. They pulled up outside one that was more unusual: it looked like a beautiful alpine lodge made from Norwegian wood. It was a housetree – an organic home, grown naturally like a tree. As the years past, the house would actually grow more rooms if required. It looked quite large enough already. There was a black SUV in the driveway with a Green Party tax credit on the window. A local police vehicle was outside. An overweight PC stepped out of it, greeting them with a gruff hello.

"I'm PC Keller. You're wasting your time here, I reckon."

Exiting his police car, Riley could feel the cold air creep over his skin. "Yeah, why?"

"I think it's just a runaway – turn up in a few hours crying to come home – but the family insisted I call in you CID guys."

"She's not an 'it', PC Keller. Maybe your attitude is why you're out here waiting for us."

PC Keller's eye twitched at the rebuke. "Can I go then?"

"You might as well stay around because my partner might need another vehicle."

"Keen to get rid of me, huh?" Lee grinned.

"Very."

Riley and Lee walked up to the house. The door opened by itself into a wood-panelled hall with several arched doorways and a stairway. Luminous globes added subtle light to surrealist paintings on the walls. Riley saw himself in a mirror. His brown suit looked like it had been under the wheels of a truck. Riley liked his clothes baggy, so he could wear his stun gun under his jacket in a shoulder holster. He wished he could be as smart as Lee. Lee preferred to have his weapon on his hip, visible.

The concerned parents stood in the doorway of the living room, holding hands. They were Amy and Stephen.

"I'm DS Riley."

"And I'm DC Lee. We're CID."

"Thank Gaia you're here," Amy said. "You have to find our little girl."

Riley accessed their personal information. Data appeared unobtrusively in his periphery vision thanks to his i-ware. Like most adult citizens, Riley had a neural processor hardwired into each optic nerve, linking him to the net. His i-ware also recorded what he saw and heard on duty, providing an unimpeachable witness.

Amy and Stephen were ecosystem designers for Globe Core Designs. They were ex-hippies, who'd met during a road protest rally in the 20th century. Stephen had a criminal conviction for trespassing and criminal damage at the head office of an arms manufacturer, but that conviction was twenty years old, no other convictions since. They were members of several leftwing organisations, including the Green Party and Amnesty International. They seemed to have given up their radical politics to design organic furniture for homes. Amy had a PhD in bioengineering. Her husband Stephen had a master's degree in ecology. They had only one child – Rachel. The missing girl.

"Rachel's only nine," her mother said, squeezing her husband's hand. "I'm really scared."

"So am I," her husband added. Stephen had the tanned, rugged look of a gardener. "We don't know where the hell she is. We don't understand what's going on. Some things don't make any sense. That other policeman wouldn't even listen to us. He thinks she's run away. I tried to tell him. . . . He wouldn't *listen*."

"We will," Riley assured them. "Why don't you tell me everything somewhere comfortable?"

"Okay." Stephen Harper said. "Come into the living room. I've got something to show you."

Before Amy went with her husband, Lee said to her: "Mrs Harper, I'd like to visit Rachel's room, if you don't mind? Can you show me?"

"Yes," she said, and led him up the stairs.

Good move, Riley thought. It was often a good idea to talk to parents separately. Sometimes, one parent could dominate the opinion of another, making interviewing them harder.

Amy stopped at Rachel's bedroom door as if afraid to go in. Opening the door, Lee saw a typical nine-year-old girl's room. Pop idol posters. Hardcopy books. Computer games. When he stepped in, a pink teddy, tucked into the bed as if sleeping, suddenly sat up for a hug. "Rachel!" it said. The bear lay down again when its recognition software realized he wasn't Rachel. Amy let out a tiny sob. She stayed in the doorway, rubbing her hands together. Crossing the light and airy bedroom, Lee opened the wardrobes, which were filled with brightly coloured clothes.

"Mrs Harper, are any clothes missing?"

Amy shook her head, nervously brushing her fingers through her hair. "No. Nothing."

"Do you have a recent image of Rachel, say a photograph?"

"Yes. You see that album on the bedside table. It has a recording of our last holiday. Rachel looks the same age as now. It was filmed only two weeks ago." Lee opened the video album's luxurious leather cover. The screen came to life. He watched Rachel on a beach in Greece, the Mediterranean behind her. She was playing volleyball, running and laughing. Rachel was a pretty girl with short, wavy blonde hair and a loveable smile.

"Look how happy she was."

"I don't like asking this, but can you recall what was she wearing the last time you saw her?"

"Her favourite blue dress, blue coat and her white Air Nikes."

Lee walked to the chest of drawers by the window. He felt like a pervert as he looked through her underwear and socks. He found a hand-written diary tucked away in her bottom drawer. He lifted it out and showed Amy.

"I didn't know she had that."

"Can I read it?"

"Yes. Yes."

Lee saw the diary contained nothing unusual, just the private thoughts of a nine-year-old girl. Rachel had a crush on someone called Neal – her best friend Lucy's ex-boyfriend. She liked riding her pony, Amber, ice skating and shopping for new clothes. She bitched about her allowance, wanting more, but who didn't want more money? She'd had a row with her dad last week because she stayed out late. She liked her teacher Mr Lincoln for giving her an A-grade for a hologram she made in her graphics lesson. She was jealous of a girl called Sarah for getting her first period before her. She wished she had a sister, as she was bored with being an only child. She wanted to be thinner, like the supermodels in her favourite magazines, *Elle Online* and *Teen Vogue*.

Lee found nothing suggesting she might have run away.

She didn't have a drug problem.

She didn't seem depressed, scared or angry.

Her final last entry, the date before yesterday, was upbeat about an ice skating competition next week.

Discreetly, he collected a hair sample from her brush in case he needed to match her DNA.

Already, he was thinking of finding her dead.

Riley liked the living room. There was a very natural feel to the furniture – it seemed to flow into the floor. He wondered if it had all been grown from seeds. The room smelled like a rose garden. As Stephen poured himself a drink, Riley looked at family pictures on the wall. They looked happy. It was a huge contrast to the misery etched on Stephen's face as he downed a glass of malt whisky, gasping afterwards.

"I don't normally drink," he said. "But this needs it."

"Take your time."

"I don't have time!" Stephen shouted. "Sorry. I'm tense. You just have no idea what it's been like since this morning, when the school contacted us because Rachel did not show up for class. Amy or I normally make sure she gets to school safely, but last night she stayed at her friend's house. You see, Rachel called me at 4.30 yesterday, asking for permission to stay the night. Her friend's parents said they'd take her to school today. I'll . . . I'll show you the video of the call."

It was just how Stephen had described – Rachel at her friend's house, asking her dad if she could please-please-please sleep over. There were two adults in the background, a man and woman. They had dark hair, like their daughter, Lucy.

"That's Michelle and Ben," Stephen said. "I trusted them to look after my daughter, so I said yes to her staying the night. It was no big deal. I knew she'd be safe. *Thought* she'd be safe. Until this morning, when I called them to ask why Rachel was late for school."

Stephen showed him the recording of that call, splitting the screen to show both sides of the conversation. On the screen Ben answered the phone, looking surprised to see Stephen.

"Hey, Ben," said the Stephen Harper on the videophone, "the school says Rachel isn't in class – but it's ten o'clock. Where is she?"

Ben's eyebrows crunched. "How would I know?"

"She stayed the night with Lucy."

"That's news to me," Ben said.

"But you were right there. You talked to me last night. You gave her permission."

"Not me," Ben said. "I don't know what you're talking about."

Stephen's voice rose. "You don't know what I'm talking about? I'm talking about my daughter! Where the hell is she?"

"Hey! Don't get angry with me. I don't know. I haven't seen her in a week."

The call ended with Ben hanging up.

"I tried calling back, but he wouldn't answer. I thought about going over there, but what if he just kept on denying it? I don't understand it why he's lying. I mean, we've been friends for years. I think they've kidnapped her or something, but I don't know what to do. That's why I called you. I did the right thing, didn't I?"

Riley nodded. He asked permission to access the comlink. Stephen granted it. Then Riley closed his eyes so he could fully concentrate on accessing the data. Information appeared in front of him on his i-ware. He traced the origin of the call back through the system until he reached the original webaddress from which it had been sent. The first call was not made from Rachel's friend's house. The physical location was a public access videobooth.

Riley downloaded the entire video file into an analysis program, searching for anomalies consistent with a hoax call. He found a telltale microsecond delay in communications. That didn't sound like a lot of time, but it would be sufficient time for any half-decent computer to generate a realistic-looking fake. Diagnostic checks verified his suspicions.

"What is it?" Stephen asked.

"I'm afraid the call was a fake."

"Fake?"

"Yes. It was done on a computer from another location. You were talking to a virtual reality simulation."

"You mean someone pretended to call me to ask permission for Rachel to stay over? Why – why would anyone do that?"

"I don't know," he answered honestly. "But I'll find out, I promise."

"This is even worse than I imagined. Are you telling me somebody could have kidnapped her yesterday?"

"It's possible," he said. "Do you know of any reason why someone would want to do that?"

"What kind of reason?"

"Money. Revenge. Anything like that?"

"No. Amy and I don't have a lot of money. We're not rich. We don't have any enemies. None I know of."

"When was the last time you saw Rachel for real?"

"For real? That was – God – yesterday morning – eight-thirty-ish. I kissed her goodbye before Amy dropped her off at school."

Riley contacted Lee on his i-ware. Thirty seconds later, Lee walked into the living room with Amy. Amy confirmed that she had taken their daughter to school in their SUV. That was the last time she had seen her.

"I'd like you both to stay here, in case whoever made that fake call contacts you."

Riley walked out into the hall, followed by Lee.

"What now?" Lee said.

"I'm going to visit the school. You see if the videobooth gives up any clues."

It started to rain as Riley parked in the staff parking lot of Quantum Hill Primary School. The head, Mrs Candice Reed, met him. She seemed as concerned about Rachel's disappearance as her parents – a fact Riley appreciated. She told him that Rachel had attended school all day yesterday. Her final lesson ended at four. If he wanted to know more, he would have to ask her teacher. Reed showed Riley to Rachel's classroom.

And he stepped into the middle of a Martian landscape. He could not believe the realism. He and twenty children were standing in a crater. The boys and girls were looking at the rocks and other objects in the crater. Their teacher was talking about a huge mountain in the distance called Olympus Mons. The pink sky lit the red rocks, casting deep shadows. The simulation was so real Riley could see the dust under his feet billow out from under his shoes.

Riley remembered the hard plastic chairs, rocky wooden desks and blackboards of his own childhood.

"All our classrooms have virtual reality simulators," the head said. "They are the best teaching tool."

"Heck," he said, remembering to watch his language. "I remember coloured chalk being a teaching tool."

"We've come on a long way since those days," the head said.

The teacher halted the lesson when he saw Riley. He was a tall white man in a grey suit. "Class, we'll have to stop there. SIM OFF."

The simulation ended abruptly, leaving Riley in a normal-looking classroom. He could see the holographic units on the walls. Little chairs and desks moved themselves away from the walls into position. The children sat down, glaring at Riley for interrupting. Nine-year-olds were small, very small. Riley had almost forgotten how small until surrounded by twenty little people. The teacher walked up to him. The head introduced Riley.

"I'm Mr Lincoln," the teacher said, shaking hands. "I'm very concerned about Rachel. I'll help you every way I can."

"What can you tell me about her?"

"Rachel is a nice, quiet girl, good at maths and science. She has a lot of friends. Everyone likes her."

"Any social problems?"

The teacher shook her head. "No. She didn't have any difficulties at schoolwork. Her parents are good people, very supportive. I wish all parents were that caring."

"Could she have been bullied?"

"This school has a no bullying policy," the head said, stiffly. "We have a counsellor that makes sure nobody is bullied. Rachel has never reported any problems. Isn't that right, Mr Lincoln?"

"Yes," he confirmed.

Riley knew that not all problems were reported to teachers. When he was at school, there'd been an unwritten rule about not telling on each other, like a child's version of *omerta*.

"I'd like to address your class," Riley said.

"Okay," Mr Lincoln said. "Just don't upset them."

Mr Lincoln introduced him as a policeman.

The kids had questions.

"Have you killed people?" one boy cheerfully wanted to know.

"No," he said. "I carry a stun gun. Police in England aren't allowed to kill people. It's against the law."

"Aw! That's no fun!"

You little psychopath, Riley thought.

"I want to find Rachel because her mum and dad are very worried about her. But I need your help. Does anyone know anything that can help me?"

Several hands shot up.

The videophone was on the corner of a quiet, suburban street midway between Rachel's home and her school. On arriving in PC Keller's vehicle, Lee hoped he would find some physical evidence inside the booth. Unfortunately, the booth was clean. Too clean – there were no fingerprints or anything on any surface. Anybody could have plugged into the modem port and accessed the internet, making the fake call to Rachel's father.

He walked back to the vehicle, where PC Keller was stuffing his face with a massive doughnut. Keller didn't seem bothered by the fact a kid was missing, as long as he had his mid-morning snack.

"You find anything?" he said, his breath stinking of coffee.

"No. It's clean. Are there any security webcams nearby I can log into?"

"In Quantum Hill? You're joking, mate. We're a low-crime town with no need for the Big Brother routine. I mostly arrest drunks and stimmies. Minor stuff. We don't need cameras."

Lee cursed. In any major city, he could have accessed a thousand webcams on any street. No crime could be committed in public without it being recorded. But here? No cameras? What kind of backwater place was this? He had no way of tracking the videobooth's user unless he found a witness. Frustrated, Lee did what police had done since the beginning of crime investigation – he canvassed the area. Knocked on doors hoping for eyewitnesses. Unfortunately, he soon found out nobody had seen a thing because no one was at home between four and five, just like there was no one at home that morning.

He prayed Riley was having more luck at the school.

"I didn't walk home with Rachel," Lucy told Riley, tears running down her cheeks. "It's my fault she's missing."

"Why do you think that?"

"Because we always walk home together but I was mad at her."

"Why were you mad at her?"

"Because of *Neal*."

"You don't like Neal?"

"Not any more," she sniffed. "He used to be my boyfriend. But now he's not. He dumped me for her." She paused to wipe her eyes. "*He* probably walked home with her."

"Okay. Where's Neal?"

She pointed towards a little redheaded boy. He had big, soulful eyes and so many freckles his skin reminded Riley of Bambi. The boy shuffled his feet when Riley approached him.

"Hi, Neal, did you walk home with Rachel?"

Neal looked around at the other boys, clearly uncomfortable with the fact that he had been walking home *with a girl*. What would be something to boast about in a few years was acutely embarrassing at the age of nine.

"Did you walk home with Rachel?"

"Uh-huh," he mumbled.

He wasn't going to be more forthcoming in front of his friends. He looked down at his shoes.

"Would you like to talk outside?"

Neal nodded. Riley went out into the hall with him.

"You walked home with her?"

"Kind of. I wanted her to play computer games with me, but she had to get home for dinner. She said her dad would be mad if she was late. He didn't like her playing with boys, she said. We sort of had an argument and she walked off in a huff. Has she run away because of me?"

"No," Riley assured him. "Neal, do you remember seeing anything else on your way home with Rachel?"

Neal looked at Riley blankly. "Like what?"

"Did you see anyone watching you?"

"Um. No . . . but there was a man jogging. I didn't like the look of him. He was wearing a real stinky tracksuit. He stopped to ask me the time, but I didn't answer because I just wanted to get home. I didn't like him. He went down the same street as Rachel."

"What colour was the tracksuit?"

"Um – blue with sort a white stripe."

"Light blue or dark blue?"

"Just blue. Like the paints in art lessons."

"What did he look like?"

"I didn't see his face because he had his hood-thing up. But he had sort of long, girlie hair."

"What colour was it?"

"Black."

"What did he smell of?"

"Sweat. He was really smelly. He should've washed."

"Did he say his name?"

Neal shook his head.

Riley asked him more questions, but the boy couldn't add many more details.

A dark-haired man wearing a sweaty blue tracksuit. It wasn't much to go on. But Riley hoped it would be enough. He contacted Lee with the information that he had a suspect. Lee said he was lucky, as he'd come up blank so far. Riley left the school and returned to his car. He accessed satellite images from yesterday, hoping to see the jogger on an aerial view. The satellite images were easily detailed enough to do that. Unfortunately, most of England had been overcast with clouds. Quantum Hill was no exception.

Next, he checked the paedophile register for Quantum Hill.

He was shocked to see a list containing 134 names.

He narrowed the search by physical characteristics and profiling the likeliest suspects.

Top of the list was a suspect called Gregory Petrosian.

Petrosian had once been a member of an international paedophile ring calling themselves The Fatherhood. The Fatherhood was suspected of having over 60,000 members. Each member had to prove worthy of membership by providing proof of their abhorrent behaviour. Gregory Petrosian used to be a caretaker at a day-care centre in Manchester. He liked to abuse children in the toilets. When parents suspected their children had been molested, Petrosian was arrested and charged with seven counts of child-molestation. He was suspected of abusing even more kids at the day-care centre, but the kids were too young to be witnesses. He had served fifteen years and he was now on probation.

Riley met up with Lee outside the housing complex where Petrosian lived. His flat was not far away from the route Rachel would have taken home.

"I can't believe they let out an animal like him," Lee said, as they walked towards Petrosian's flat. "What were they thinking?"

"The file says he made a deal with the prosecutors. He received a reduced sentence in exchange for giving up the identities of the other members of The Fatherhood. Otherwise, he would have received a mandatory life sentence without the possibility of release. They arrested thousands of perverts thanks to his information, but it still makes me sick. The only way he should have got out of prison is if he'd killed himself."

Riley knocked on the door. A handsome, dark-haired man opened it. He looked like a normal person. But most perverts did.

"Gregory Petrosian, I'm DS Riley. This is DC Lee."

"Police? What am I supposed to have done now?"

"A girl has gone missing. Her name is Rachel Harper. She's only nine."

"So?"

"A man matching your description was seen following her shortly before she disappeared."

"Wasn't me."

"Then you won't mind answering my questions?"

Petrosian grumbled something. He had no choice but to let them enter the flat if he wanted to remain free. The flat was cold and gloomy. It smelled of sour sweat, like a gym. The carpets in the hall and living room had food stains. Riley saw Chinese takeout boxes scattered at random on chairs and tables. There were no personal effects, nothing decorating the grey walls.

"Haven't I been punished enough by living in this dump?"

"Beats prison, doesn't it?"

A bedroom and a bathroom were to the right, a tiny kitchen to the left.

"Do you like jogging?" Riley asked.

"Yeah . . . why? Not against the law is it? I like keeping fit."

"Do you have a blue tracksuit?"

"Yeah, why?"

"I want to examine it."

"Okay. It's probably in the washing machine."

It was. It was clean. It took a minute to scan it for Rachel's DNA. It came up negative.

"You won't find anything," Petrosian said. "I'm a reformed man."

"We'll be the judge of that."

Riley privately communicated with Lee on his i-ware for him to bring in the forensic equipment. Lee nodded and left.

"Where's he going?"

"He couldn't stand your smell."

"Hey! I don't have to be insulted!"

"No, you don't have to be insulted. But I like it. Sit down."

Petrosian sat down, saying nothing. Riley stood over him, not wanting to sit on anything in the place in case he caught a disease.

"Where were you yesterday between four and five?"

"I was here, detective."

"Can you prove that?"

"As a matter of fact, I can. I'm molecularly tagged by the probation service. They know where I am at all times. You can check their data files. They'll show I was home yesterday. I'm not allowed to go out by myself even to buy food unless a probation officer gives me permission like I'm some kind of dangerous maniac."

"You are a dangerous maniac."

"I'm in control of my . . . behaviour."

"You refused proper treatment."

"Proper treatment? You mean I didn't want my brain altering with a butcher's knife?"

"Nanosurgery that would improve you, making you into a decent law-abiding human being. Without it, 98 per cent of offenders re-offend."

"I'm in the two per cent," Petrosian said.

"If I find even a molecule of Rachel's DNA you'll never see daylight again."

"Go ahead," Petrosian said, but he looked worried when Lee brought in a metallic cylinder the size of an old-fashioned fire-extinguisher. It had red warning labels on it.

"What's that?" Petrosian said.

"It's a SPORE machine. Scanning Particle Organic Room Examiner. It's technology they didn't have the last time you got caught. It basically ejects a cloud of nanomachine 'spores' that look like a heavy fog. They examine every object in the room, looking for organic material – such as DNA. The information is transmitted back to the cylinder's AI for forensic analysis. After the spores have done their work – which will take twenty minutes – they will self-destruct into harmless gases. We'll all have to leave during the process because it's not pleasant to breathe in the spores. You can accompany us to the back of our police vehicle."

"This is an infringement of my rights."

"As a convicted paedophile you must comply as part of your probation conditions."

Twenty minutes later the SPORE machine finished.

Bad news: no DNA from Rachel.

Worse news: Petrosian's alibi was verified by the probation service.

According to their information, he was in his flat when Rachel disappeared.

"You're going to have to release me now," Petrosian said. Reluctantly, Riley unlocked the door. As Petrosian climbed out of the police car, he stared into Riley's eyes, a half-smile forming. He licked his lips with a grey-pink tongue, the gesture sickening. "As the Americans used to say – have a nice *birthday*."

Riley's heart kicked. How did he know that? The creep must have accessed his birth records while he and Lee were examining the flat. Riley could feel the anger building. He stepped back before he did something.

Petrosian returned to his flat, closing the door with a grin.

Riley and Lee took a lunch break in a café. They talked in whispers so as not to disturb the other customers. Riley could not taste his food.

"If Petrosian's guilty I can't figure out how he's fooled the probation service. Their tag system is supposed to be impregnable. It tracks a person 24–7. It can't be removed because it's in every cell. Nobody tagged has ever gone anywhere without the computers knowing it. His alibi is perfect."

"Maybe he hacked into the network and changed the files?"

Riley didn't think it was likely. Government security wasn't as weak as it used to be. "It's more likely he has a connection in the probation service. Remember he was a member of the Fatherhood. What if someone he knows is working on collusion?"

"We'd never prove it," Lee said.

"I know," Riley said. "Damn it!"

His anger caused a couple at the next table to look over as if he were a mad man. He pushed his plate away, unable to eat.

"We need solid evidence to tie Petrosian to Rachel. But the

only piece of evidence we have is the hoax call, which ended in a dead end. Unless . . ."

"What?" Lee said.

"The hoax. It was such an accurate simulation that it fooled Rachel's father. Any computer can make a simulation, but it would require an intimate knowledge of each person being simulated. That includes Rachel, her friend Lucy and everything else. How did Petrosian get such information? I think Petrosian must have been inside Rachel or Lucy's home. What if he got careless and left some proof?"

The SPORE machine analysed Rachel's house. It detected several different DNA samples, corresponding to Rachel, her parents, some of Rachel's friends . . . but nothing from Petrosian. Afterwards, Riley and Lee took the SPORE machine to Lucy's house and ran the same tests. It took an agonizing twenty minutes.

"I don't believe it," Riley said.

"What?"

"We've got a hit. Dead skin cells. DNA matches a known paedophile."

"Petrosian?" Lee asked.

"No – someone called Peter T. Ryman."

"Peter who? I've never heard of him."

"He was also in the Fatherhood. He was once an IT teacher, an expert with computers. He was one of the men Petrosian ratted out. Ryman was going to face life in prison, but he vanished before his arrest. He's been in hiding for twenty years. I imagine that made him pretty mad with Petrosian."

"You mean this Ryman guy wanted us to think it was Petrosian, a sort of payback?"

"Looks like it."

"Jesus. What does he look like?"

A picture of Peter Thomas Ryman appeared.

Riley had seen him before under another name.

Lee gasped. "Is that who I think it is?"

"Afraid so. You go the address. I'll go to the school. We'd better hurry. He might decide to run."

"This is it," Keller said, as the police car stopped at the house. "This is where that pervert lives."

"Wait outside," Lee ordered. "I'm going in alone. You stay there and call for support."

"Fine with me," Keller said.

Lee approached the house with his stun gun ready. Keller stood outside. Without announcing himself, Lee silently unlocked the door with a police override command and stepped into darkness. The hall was cold. He didn't switch on the lights. He didn't want his presence known. He moved through the house quickly, looking in each room. The rooms looked empty. He stepped into the bathroom and found what he expected inside the medicine cabinet. He continued. He crept up the stairs, to the bedrooms. In the first bedroom he saw sophisticated computer equipment. Lee crept up to the next room. The door was closed. He thought he could hear a noise on the other side. Very slowly, he tested the doorknob. The door was locked. Breathing hard, he kicked it. Wood splintered. As the door swung open, he swept his stun gun from side to side. The noise stopped. Then he stepped into the room.

The room was grimly bare except for a bed in its centre. Cameras had been installed at every conceivable angle.

He found Rachel on the bed, bound and gagged. His stun blast had knocked her out. But she was still breathing.

He rushed to her, pulling off the tape and ropes. She moaned. He worked faster.

"It's going to be all right," he promised her.

He heard a creak behind him.

"Keller, I thought I told you to stay outside?"

Riley walked into the classroom, his stun gun out. Mr Lincoln looked shocked to see Riley again.

"What's going on?" he said.

"Mr Lincoln, I have an arrest warrant. I know the identity of Rachel's kidnapper."

"You think it's me?"

"No. It's Neal."

"Neal? You can't be serious. He's only nine."

"I'm very serious. His real name is Ryman. He's not nine. He's seventy-two. He must have taken enough rejuve to make him a kid again. He's been pretending to be young so he can be around kids. Where is he?"

"He said he was going to the toilet ten minutes ago, but he hasn't come back."

When Keller did not reply, Lee looked over his shoulder.

He gasped.

Neal was rushing towards him with a knife.

The blade swept down at his crouching body, aimed at the back of his neck.

Lee didn't have time to reach his stun gun. He twisted around, blocking the knife with his elbow. The blade cut deeply into his flesh. Blood jetted out. Neal yanked it out and stabbed a second time. Lee managed to block it as he started to stand up. Neal slashed at him desperately. He cut Lee's hands and arms.

He was losing a lot of blood.

Neal laughed. He stabbed for Lee's groin. Seeing the knife coming, Lee yelled and slapped the knife across the room. It landed in the corner. Neal's eyes flashed with anger. He looked at the knife, but then he saw Lee trying to get out his stun gun, his bloody fingers struggling. Lee was determined to pull the trigger, even if it meant stunning himself as well.

Neal swore – no doubt realizing that he could not fight an armed adult.

The boy turned and ran.

Grimacing, Lee managed a loose, two-handed grip on his stun gun and chased after him. Neal was running down the stairs at a speed that he couldn't hope to beat. He would escape. Lee stopped at the top and fired down. The stun blast dropped the boy instantly. He tumbled down and down, crashing onto the floor below. His neck made a sound like a broken branch.

Lee thought it had to be the first time ever a suspect had really fallen down the stairs while resisting arrest.

Lee sank down against the wall.

"Officer down, needs assistance . . ."

When Riley arrived at the house, he found Keller outside, his throat slashed. He was dead. Riley rushed into the house. He saw Neal dead, too. He looked up the stairs and heard his partner's groan. He dashed up the stairs. Lee looked pale but not too seriously wounded. The flow of blood had slowed down. Lee managed a weak smile.

"The ambulance will be here in a minute. Just don't move."

"Don't worry . . . about me. I'm okay. The girl . . . the girl is in the bedroom. Get her home."

"Okay, I'll get her—"

"Sir?"

"Yes?"

"Happy birthday."

"Yes," Riley said. "Yes, it is."

PRISON DREAMS

Paul McAuley

The end of a shitstorm of a shift, eleven hours down, one to go, Lianna caught the squeal for a psychokiller scenario. So far, three months into her sentence, she'd avoided this, the worst kind of triage. But everything that goes around comes around. She'd been catching sleep while everyone else was cleaning up a big combat game – EuroNissan execs cooling out after a sales conference – and *slam*, she was on.

Wired with caffeine, needles digging her right eye, Lianna threw herself into the chopper moments before it rose from the pad. Hands grabbed her, pulled her into a jump seat. Kollner's clean-up crew, that was something at least, all case-hardened zeks but for one new, scared-looking kid gulping back nervousness, grin too wide in his white face. Lianna knew how he felt.

The chopper ran low and fast parallel to the long beach. Naked sunbathers in dispersion patterns just beyond the edge of analysis, stands of sun umbrellas, roofs of franchise huts. Did anyone on the beach look up from sun-struck dreaming and wonder where the helicopters went to, in the Oostduinpark? Did they care?

Lianna asked about the new kid. Over engine roar Kollner told her Toorop had done the freaky and tried to make it into the dunes before his chip stopped him, had been rotated to prep and dispatch for the rest of his sentence. Kollner, a big scary-looking man, even scarier if you knew what he'd once done. Slow and mild manner, passing out smokes, asking Lianna how her shift was running.

"Too long," Lianna yelled into his weary smile, and took a smoke and drew it alight. Cool smoke flooded her throat, the needlepoints of pain in her eye melted.

Kollner knew this was her first psycho. He gave a shark smile. "It's just like combat games," he said into her ear, "only . . . *intense*."

Lianna managed a tight smile, knowing Kollner had been through over a thousand runs. He was a trusty now, but he was under the chip for life. She swallowed a couple of glucose tablets with a sip of Diet Coke, and then the chopper was beating down.

The patient squatted behind a canvas windbreak, shivering in the grip of his attendants. Big man, body builder, camo pants tucked into hightop boots, flack jacket crossed with bandoleers, face hidden behind a black pinhole mask. He was hauled to his feet as Lianna went past. Blood and worse crusted around the crotch of his pants: a real psycho, not some politician or exec drained of testosterone rage. But like them he'd not remember what he'd done in deep fix trance: scenarios were for imprinting chip feedback loops.

Afterwards, Lianna would realize how much she envied his amnesia.

The setup was in a long draw. Half a dozen hooches, woven walls splintered by heavy fire, two still smoking. Little figures sprawled on white sand, blue skins more vivid than their blood. The clean-up crew waited on Lianna's assessment, backs to wind that knifed in from the Noordzee as they drew on the last of their smokes.

Lianna walked the perimeter, blanking out the whines of those dolls still alive, avoiding their eyes. Her chip was nagging her, a heavy feeling in the orbit of her right eye, something like a silver needle running back into her head: this was so close to what she'd done to her husband.

Most dolls were wasted, a mercy. A bunch in an untidy heap, torn apart. An arm lying off by itself, hand clenched. Two females naked and bloodied and very much dead, both face down, legs widesprawled. Oh, Christ, the guy on some rape-o freakout. But better them than any woman – her thought, or chip propaganda?

Lianna made fifteen dead, a dozen badly wounded, three hardly more than scratched. One by the perimeter tape, sitting with its leg out in front of him, holding an oozing thigh wound, through and through. If it had been human it would have gotten away clean, but dolls couldn't cross the tape to save their lives.

Her count way too low – most probably caught in the hooches. A quick sweep confirmed. The psycho had raked them with heavy calibre gunfire, tossed in frag grenades, nothing left for her to fix unless the crew turned a survivor from under the pieces of the dead.

Lianna told Kollner to start with the hooches, opened her kit and took the wounded by priority, swiping white X's on the foreheads of those too far gone. Work focussed her thoughts – her hands were steady as she sorted through her kit. Chip pressure receded. Couple of times at the beginning she'd blacked out: now she could distance herself from gore. She pushed back the length of grey-blue gut of one that had been eviscerated with a knife-thrust, cauterized the wrist stump of another. A doll with a sucking chest wound fixed a dull betrayed look on her as she packed the bloody bubbling cavity. Worse was the doll which had tried to shelter its "baby", a microcephalic homunculus it had been programmed to care for. The surrogate mother's head blown off, a splintered spike of bone: the baby-thing under her corpse, its limbs wriggling as slowly as a battery-drained toy's. It was unharmed but drenched in blood to which sand stuck like crystalline sugar – Lianna set it aside for pickup.

The clean-up crew had almost finished. Shattered corpses and stray limbs were stacked like firewood. Kollner, certifying each corpse by scanning the tag implanted in its third sacral vertebra, looked like a grocery clerk moving barcoded goods through the checkout. Two women were chasing the new boy: one brandished a severed hand.

The last two casualties were sitting up, patiently awaiting Lianna's attention. They brushed her cheeks with soft blue-skinned fingers, made cooing sounds as she dressed their flesh wounds. Lianna groaned when she stood; dull pain punched her in the kidneys.

The women had caught the new kid, who was trying to stuff the hand into his open fly as he writhed and made a noise halfway between a laugh and a squeal. Lianna sat off to one side in hot sun while Kollner supervized pickup. The ones she'd marked were given two lines of topic, enough to stop their hearts.

Lianna thought, Kollner had been right, it hadn't been so bad (forget those splayed female corpses). Not as bad as she'd imagined, anyway.

When all the corpses had been stacked, the whole pile was doused with jellied petroleum and Kollner threw on a flare. Lianna watched with something nagging at her; it took a while to remember she'd missed the doll with the leg wound over by the perimeter. It couldn't have died. Dolls were too dumb to get shock and the wound hadn't been bleeding that badly.

Lianna made herself get up and track the perimeter. She liked things neat, it had been one of her husband's final accusations. She found a crusty patch of scuffled sand where the doll had been sitting, saw drag marks and the perimeter tape pulled out of shape, an arrowhead pointing through a saddle in the dune ridge. Lianna would have followed, curious now despite the sodden weight of her exhaustion, but her chip wouldn't let her. Kollner's computer did show there was a body missing; to further confuse things it turned out someone had thrown the still living baby-thing on the pyre. But as Kollner said, what was one pinhead, more or less? And he was just as dismissive about the missing doll, kidding her that it was her first encounter with fairies.

He handed Lianna an ice-cold coke; she held it to the back of her neck before chugging half straight down. She said, "Everyone talks about fairies, but no one believes in them."

"Just another hinky urban myth. You get wild dolls, strays, cast-offs, but they don't last long without people. That casualty, most likely its chip got fritzed and it wandered off. Sometimes they try and bury themselves. Maintenance will find it." Kollner was sweating heavily in the double heat of sun and pyre. Two dark half-moons of sweat under the arms of his blood-stained white jacket. He said, "You did all right, but you shouldn't knock yourself out fixing wounded. Fleshwounds, that's okay, they recycle straight off. Anything else: two lines, the old grand slam. What I mean is, they're just walking meat, *made* things. Think of them that way, you won't ever chip out. Let your chip decide about people, that's why they put it in you."

"It won't take much to get those others fixed." Thinking: things didn't look at you as they groaned bloody foam from chest wounds; they didn't try and shelter what they were meant to care for. Thinking of telly shows about outlaw bands of dolls and humans living wild in the fringe wildernesses; had to be some truth to them. Half of her wishing the doll had escaped, despite Kollner's dismissal.

"Days I wake up and think I'm never getting here," Kollner said. "But, hey, I always do. Maintain, that's what my motto is. Just maintain. What you got, a deuce for manslaughter?"

"Mmm." Most of the zeks talked obsessively about their sentences; Lianna was still uncomfortable, aware that if she didn't watch herself she'd be like the others soon enough, complaining she'd been set up or exaggerating misdemeanours into major felonies. Except what she'd done *had* been a major felony.

"You have to run this?"

"No. No, only simulations."

"Easy street," Kollner said. "You're lucky to see it just from this side. Just maintain, you'll sleepwalk it. Leave wild dolls to the park wardens."

Maybe Kollner was right. Lianna was too tired to chase the matter when the chopper got her back. Her shift had finished an hour ago; she grabbed the stuff she'd stolen to order, strap-hung the tram in a haze to her crib, managed to just about reach her bed and fell into it fully clothed, and because the next day was Sunday slept eighteen hours straight.

And woke naked under a cool clean sheet, her husband curled into her back. She rolled onto her tummy and let his clever hands find tension points and unknot them, still half-asleep when she rolled onto him and began to move, a long grinding slow dance until something shook her awake.

Shit, another chip dream. Trying to fix sanitized pleasurable memories of her dead husband, trying to erase the real memories of his death.

What had woken her, hammering on the door, started up again. Nicole, wanting the stuff, wanting to know why it hadn't been dropped off last night.

"I was tired," Lianna said, and started to explain about the psychokiller scenario.

Nicole brushed it aside. Small, olive-skinned, white hair cropped close, bare-foot in red jeans and a black leather vest, she clutched the little package, scowled. "Darlajane's pissed, she might not make quota." Then she was gone.

The crib had once been a hotel, down in the funky old half-abandoned seaside resort at the edge of the vast dune system beyond Den Haag's barrier. Run by a feisty old ex-punk, given over to zeks on workfare, already it felt like home to Lianna, amazing how quickly she'd adapted. But after her marriage she'd never lived anyplace she could call her own; perhaps it wasn't so strange.

Late afternoon, most of her free day gone. She sat in a beach chair on her room's balcony, picking through a plate of fruit slivers, happy in the sun to watch the straights at play. She'd learnt to surrender to moments like this, to dissolve in the sweet eternal moment of doing nothing. Electric trolleys drifting through the intersection, bells tingling. The dull thumping beat of the Permanent Floating Wave two blocks over underscored the noise of the crowds moving along the boardwalks. Tanned, brightly clothed animals surging to and fro, handsome, affluent, secure and . . . *smug*, yes, smug, in their post-Millennial utopia, geezers and babushkas enjoying their right to unlimited leisure and the universal unearned wage. Many wore gold-lensed videoshades, trancing their way through overlay visions of coral reefs or tropical rainforests or Mars: the Valles Marineris was that month's number one.

Paradise not enough, Lianna thought, sitting on her balcony high above them. Even in paradise, there was always something better to reach for. One thing about being a zek, it gave her a perspective, it distanced her from what had been her life. Zeks were the poor, the dispossessed, the third world in the rich, dreamy first.

The psychokiller scenario kept coming back to her at odd angles, unexpected moments. The disappeared doll, fairy tracks. Lianna noticed just how many dolls there were, moving through the crowds on errands, running concession stands, driving trams. As numerous as the people they served; people who walked past them as if they weren't there, invisible as lamp-posts, junction boxes. Way she'd treated them when she'd been running her husband's household – she hadn't even known how many house dolls there'd been. The things down in basement darkness, like Morlocks. Lianna shivered just to think of them: used: every which way.

At last she got dressed, went to hang out in the downstairs

lounge (some of the women leaning out of a window yelling at passers-by – "Hey, lunchmeat! Porkchop! You looking to cop a freebie, we're hot and we're hungry!"), and ended up touring the shopping arcades with Nicole, who'd got her hit for the day and mellowed out.

"Do you really need that stuff?" Lianna asked, half-amused, half-annoyed at the way Nicole slurred and giggled away her sentences.

"Need somet'ing. It slides under the chip, an' supply's in basemen'." Rubbing cropped white hair, skipping up and down, laughing and saying she was going to shave her whole head like Darlajane, watch if she didn't.

Nicole, half French, half Senegalese, half Lianna's age, had worked as a prostitute since her father had sold her at age of eleven in the Marseilles meat market. She'd been injected with hormones to bring on her puberty, worked houses that catered for men who wanted and could pay for human prostitutes, was now a habitual offender with habits too deeply ingrained for chip therapy to touch, or so she said. Nicole took a childish delight in prowling the boutiques. Her chip wouldn't let her go inside any of them, she was serving a dozen concurrent shoplifting offences, but she could press up to lighted windows, comment professionally on displays. She subscribed to every fashion magazine, downloading from Darlajane's computer: that and the stuff were her reward for running errands for Darlajane's scam.

Nicole and Lianna strolled the long seafront, ate burgers and fries at one of the beach cafes. It would have used up half Lianna's zek wage, but her deliveries took care of luxuries. Nicole devoured everything, right down to the last drop of the mayonnaise with which the Dutch drenched their fast food. Lianna watched with sisterly fondness, talked about what had happened at the psychokiller scenario, Nicole making appropriate squeals of disgust while wolfing down her food.

Afterwards, at Nicole's insistence, they went through the sex arcades, Nicole commenting on people commenting on the sex-toys grinding lasciviously in relaxshop window displays, Lianna laughing for the first time in three days. The male sex dolls were only marginally modified, but some of the females were like something from another species, genitals swollen and complicated as the petals of predatory flowers. Lianna couldn't believe men could like anything so gross. They passed a bunch of s/m places and Nicole said at least human pros didn't have to put up with that any more, she only used to do rich straight johns. The remark touched something in Lianna. She told Nicole about the lordotic response, but the young girl shrugged and said they were only dolls, she shouldn't waste tears over *things*.

Lianna said, suddenly angry, "It matters that it happens. That there are men who can do things like that. It matters we make living things and let them be torn apart."

Images flashed in her head: the splayed female dolls; the wriggling baby-thing; butchered meat piled in a hooch. Her right eye pulsed with warning pain.

"That's wha' dolls are for," Nicole said. "Take all the bad stuff, isn't as if they really feel pain. All of my clien's were nice to me. Well, mos'ly." Nicole giggled. "What I want is jus' one or two johns, nice old men who can't get it up an awful lot and feel guilty and give me presents."

But Lianna didn't hear her, seeing her husband's red sweaty face looming over hers as he pummelled her sides on his way to climax. Seeing herself blue with bruises, skinny and small as a doll – helpless now in feedback spiral, flashing on the aftermath of the psycho's little spree, every dead doll with her husband's face. Then her chip took her.

Lianna been married five years, her husband a ranking diplomat in the Peace Police, the peepers. Five years she'd been part of his team, the diplomat's wife, confidant, social secretary, servant and social partner and whore, a real old-fashioned *hausfrau*. He'd spent a lot of time in Africa and China, his cosmopolitan charm was what had first attracted Lianna. Soon, she realized that there was a darker side; it began with rough sex play, had led to beatings, sometimes so systematic that they left half her body tender with bruises. When she miscarried after one of the beatings, she stabbed her husband to death while he slept.

Circumstances made it manslaughter, but she was chipped anyway, unavoidable her counsel said. So was forfeiting her husband's estate; it went to his family back in the Czech Republic. Lianna had been a meditek before she married, was five years behind current technology when she was sentenced, but for doll triage that didn't matter. Chipped and processed, she'd started working the Rotterdam arenas, had fallen into Darlajane's drug manufacturing thing almost without thinking, the way she'd fallen into marriage. A classic victim: being chipped hadn't changed that.

Waking up, Lianna felt as rough as she'd ever felt after a bad time with her husband. Terrific headache, her whole skin sore. She was lying on a sagging couch in warm flickering darkness that smelled of mould and candle wax and dried cat faeces. Vinyl LP records and plastic-cased CDs and actual paper comic books were stacked in tottering piles around walls shingled with glossy, tattered posters. Candles stuck in winebottles burned on shelves; gutted flatscreen tellies showing weird drifts of snow or the interlocking spirals of self-engulfing patterns. On a low wicker table a page-sized computer screen was scrolling spidery black lines of text. Lianna knew at once where she was, the basement apt of Darlajane B.

Nicole was sitting crosslegged by a heap of disembowelled electronic equipment, leafing through a comic book. When she saw that Lianna was awake she came over and helped her sit up, while Darlajane shuffled into the room with a laden tray. Herbal tea: its strong bitter taste burned through Lianna's chip hangover.

The old woman watched with a proprietial air as Lianna sipped. Limber as a twenty-year old, she sat zazen. Black jeans, black leather jacket, black T-shirt with a black slogan, orange construction boots. Apart from a scalplock her head was shaven; tattoos swarmed her papery scalp. When she smiled, which she did a lot, her steel teeth glinted wetly. Darlajane B. claimed to have been born the day the Beatles put out their first single. By Lianna's reckoning it made her eighty, but she could have been sixty or a hundred, wise witchy old woman. She was used to these crises; better deal with them here than have them reported, she said, and have to thrash it out with a counsellor.

Nicole said to Lianna, "You shouldn't get angry, then your chip wouldn't do you."

"I wasn't angry at you."

"I know that. You were angry because of work, but it's no use being angry for dolls. They're only *things*. That's why I showed you that stuff, so you'd see."

Darlajane B. said, "You want to help, Nicole? Go somewhere

else, let Lianna alone. You can handle your chip, but she's new to it."

"That's what I was trying to tell her, but honestly, D.J., it was like talking to my counsellor."

"Time you listened to someone. And time you did less stuff, maybe, if this is what it makes you do."

"Ey, I can handle it! It's just—"

"I said later! Go on, now, girl. Me and Lianna need to talk."

After Nicole had left, Darlajane B. added, "Silly little whore, she ever had an intelligent thought, it would have died of loneliness. What do you want?"

A cat had materialized from the shadows, one of the colony Darlajane B. said she'd founded ten years ago with three rijigged queens and a tom, using pirated and rewritten doll chips. It put its front paws on the old woman's knees, said something in a yowling dialect. Darlajane told it to stop complaining; it hissed at her and sped off.

"I picked up a kit microsaur some kid turned loose, and they don't like it wandering around," Darlajane explained. "There's a kink in its pyruvate cycle I'm going to edit before I clone, that way you a pet can own and not have to buy expensive food additives. It keeps my hand in."

The thing about Darlajane B. was that you couldn't ask her a direct question, you had to wait until her conversation came around to the right place. So Lianna had to listen to gossip about the other zeks until the old woman got around to asking Lianna how her sentence was going, and Lianna used the opening to tell the story about the missing doll.

"I heard there are supposed to be dolls living free, in the dunes. That's why I wondered about the one which vanished—"

"All *kinds* of things in the dunes," Darlajane said. "Nothing for you to worry your head about, girl. Lived there one time myself. I used to be an idealist, a revolutionary, yeah, you know that. And it's true, we used to boost dolls, modify them, turn them loose. Old counter-culture tricks, though God knows what happened to the dolls, and no one does it any more. The revolution was over before you were born, girl, and we lost. Turned to crime, a lot of us. I was a millionaire for like about eight days, 'til the peepers caught up with my credit line. You still hurting, girl? Got something that can help." She climbed to her feet, which took a good minute, and ambled into her kitchen.

Something cat-sized wandered out of the shadows under a tellyscreen. It was a furry purple stegosaur, the plates along its back an alternating pattern of black and yellow. Lianna stepped around it, sat at the computer screen and called up the menu, asked for bulletin boards dealing with doll civil rights. The screen strung half a dozen names and access numbers and Darlajane B. said, "You won't find anything useful on public access. Peepers sift those boards for information just like everyone else. Hell, I bet they even run most of them, sweeping up would-be dissidents. The real stuff is underground. Clandestine."

"Can you tell me about the real stuff?"

"I could, but you'd only get into trouble. Possession of a samizdat newsheet will lose you your remission. Forget about dolls, girl. The revolution is over and the straights won. The Millennium has come, and we are in paradise, with slaves to wait on us hand and feet and pour out a neverending cornucopia. Here, this will be more use than forbidden knowledge."

The old woman dropped a little glassine envelope into Lianna's lap. It held a scattering of black pills so small that Lianna could fit half a dozen under her thumbnail. She said, "I touch drugs, my chip squeals. You know that, Darlajane. And I couldn't touch anything—"

Steel flash. "It's not from the basement, think that on you I'd waste? Designed the plant which grows them myself. You need a kick anytime, a little speed to get through the day, use them. And don't worry about your chip, this is *natural* stuff."

Lianna thanked her, knowing she'd never risk dropping anything from one of Darlajane B.'s splices. God knew what the side effects could be, anything from flashbacks to pseudo-Parkinson's.

"Trust me," the old woman said. "And you still feel bad about dolls, come talk to me again. You've done good business for me so far, I'd hate to see it end because you became unreliable. And neither would my . . . associates."

Lianna thought of the two men, low-level peepers, who came by every week for the latest consignment, and had another flash, almost transcendental, that it wasn't an act, Darlajane B. really was scared of them. It seemed that things were tough all over.

*　　*　　*

Convention time in Den Haag, round the clock combat games in the arenas in the dune-swallowed industrial area down by the old silted harbours of Rotterdam. Customers wore flexible body armour, helmets and visors, were armed with little .08 mm plastic pistols which fired iron-tipped teflon flechettes: clean kills or through-and-throughs. Dolls were armed too, lasers which slowed the fire rate or entirely shut down the customers' pistols, depending where the picowatt beam hit their armour. Good clean fun for jaded technocrats, no harm involved. It was even said the combat dolls enjoyed it, if they knew enough to enjoy anything. Lianna didn't see how. Dead was dead, it didn't matter who killed you.

Lianna worked fourteen hours on, ten off, tracing tags of downed dolls, sorting them into meat and survivors. Moving in after the johns had left, following traces in spacey industrial cathedral volumes. Receding perspectives of light and shadow amongst rusty, splayed roof supports; floors of saddled sand littered everywhere with spent propellent cartridges. Dolls fallen in the casual attitudes of death, or quietly waiting for her. In other EC states the johns were allowed to take out wounded dolls with head shots, catharsis in their very own spatter movie, but the Netherlands had game laws modified from slaughterhouse licensing: only qualified personnel could administer the *coup de grâce*. Which Lianna did dozens times each shift, shooting in two lines and letting the meat go into classic clonic seizure.

She'd been doing triage for three months, but now it was as if she was starting all over again. Noticing things, the way wounded dolls moved, their small sounds, their fluttering hands, as she worked on them. The patterns of disturbed sand she sometimes found around them, like the patterns she used to make in the snow when she was a child, lying down and moving her arms to make angel wings . . .

Get through this, she thought, try not to see the dolls as human. Not too difficult, they all had the same prognathous beetle-browed face, the same smooth blue skin. She might have been treating the same unlucky doll over and over, fixing it up to go back into line and get shot all over again. Get through this, take the stash she'd earned from hijacking doll pharmaceuticals for Darlajane B., run run run.

Trying to believe nothing was wrong, Lianna moved through the detritus of licensed violence administering mercy, murmuring Kollner's motto like a mantra. But it was a fragile peace.

One day, tranced out towards the end of a long shift, Lianna found herself shooting a second line of topic into a doll with only a glancing leg wound. It had stopped breathing, was jerking like a beached fish. She pinched its nostrils, tried to give it heart massage and mouth-to-mouth, and it died anyway.

She made three steps away from the corpse before she threw up.

Afterwards, a kind of numb calm descended. She tagged the body, checked the last traces (all dead), headed back in. That was when she got into the fight.

The medicare centre was poised on the flat roof of a warehouse almost totally buried in sand: a hundred plastic panel walls tilted against each other like a flock of wings fallen to rest. Lianna scored a coke to wash out her mouth, sat outside in the last of the sunset, looking at the vast expanse of scrubby dunes that saddled away south and east.

The dunes which had protected Holland for hundreds of years had been vastly expanded when the sea rose, extending for thirty kilometres inland to save rich croplands from saltseep, dunes and pine forests that ran all the way south to Roscoff, interrupted only by coastal cities walled and dyked like medieval fortresses. Maybe a billion square kilometres of unzoned outlaw territory, beyond policing. Creepy rumours about doll cities under the sand, killer doll patrols picking off loner techs, porn-rings jacking warm bodies for gross-out videos, freedom fighters turning dolls into terrorists.

Campfire stories, spun out in the dead hours between shifts. Lianna had heard them all when she'd started her sentence, but now she was beginning to take them seriously. After the psychokiller scenario she knew it was real, and she'd heard other stories, too, live bodies triaged and tagged for recovery vanishing before pickup. What Darlajane B. had said, deprogramming dolls . . . where had they all gone?

Fairies.

Maybe two dozen zeks were lounging around, waiting for shift's end. A dozen more coming out, changed into street clothes, hair slick from the showers. Kollner's crew. The new kid was in the middle of a bunch of people, making a lot of noise, his voice carrying to Lianna as they drew near.

". . . I tell you, man, the guy's a righteous downhome cannibal freak. Easiest five euros I ever did make, and he needs a *regular* supply!"

Someone laughed, and the kid said, "Yeah, well take a look at this, man, I just now cut it out. So nice and fresh I do believe I could try a slice myself."

Lianna saw him open a silvery cold-lok bag, the people around him laughing, crowding close, making gross-out noises. The kid smiling proudly, then going down on his ass as Lianna snatched the bag away, tipped out the wet red mass of liver, then grabbed his neck, tried to force his face into it.

Saying over and over, "You like this? You like *this*?" until she was pulled away and Kollner was in front of her, asking her to calm down.

Lianna took a deep breath, another. "All right," she said. Trying not to think of what she wanted to do (not kill him, not not not kill him), chip swelling in her right eye so there was just a little tunnel through which she could glimpse the world, a fluttering darkness she was on the edge of falling into.

"This piece of shit isn't worth it," Kollner said, gentle as ever. "You know that. All right?"

"All right." Very quietly.

Lianna let Kollner put his arm around her shoulders and steer her aside, aware in her peripheral vision of the kid getting up, saying something because he had to try and regain face.

"Shit, not as if the guy's a real cannibal—"

Kollner blocking her when she tried to get the kid again, his arms out, flinching as she feinted right and left, nails scraping the side of his face. Still in front of her, so she kicked for his balls, and he stepped back and said, "All right —" and caught her foot and dumped her on her ass, suddenly angry. Leaned over her, big hands making fists . . .

And then he was down, body arching on heels and neck. People pushed Lianna out of the way, a woman putting her foot under Kollner's head as another pried at his mouth to make sure he hadn't swallowed his tongue. Kollner shaking, muscles bunching at random. Eyes rolled back, animal sounds. Lianna flashed on how she must have looked when she'd been struck down in the sex arcade, felt shame.

One of the crew in her face, shouting at her, telling her Kollner was under real heavy manners, he couldn't afford to lose his temper at no one he'd had so many fits already. Lianna stood and took it, feeling very cool, very remote. Other zeks turning on her, hard words. She took it all to her, locking her certainty about what she needed to do, only ran when she saw two circling to get behind her, leaped the low parapet and ran across sand away from jeers and catcalls and a hail of coke cans.

Ran until her chip started to flash dark warning chevrons across her sight, sat down and watched as in one direction the centre turned over for the night shift, floodlights on shining sails; in the other, tiny fires twinkled and shifted in unfathomable darkness.

No one came to look for her, she was just a chipped zek after all, and the few people about did no more than glance at her as she made her way through the medicare centre to the doll cages.

Even so, she needed a boost to do it: two of Darlajane B.'s little black pills that clung to her tongue and had to be washed down with a mouthful of coke. They started to come on as she went down the ramp of polymerized sand into the cages. A fine tremor in her musculature, but somehow strong, like she was a fine-tuned machine. Lights growing halos. Things taking on a lac-quered appearance, an increase in reality's density.

Down the ramp into a long low arched space lit by buzzing fluorescents. Lianna could see the snake of bright plasma that writhed in every long tube. Dolls sprawled or squatted in en-closures marked only by low mesh fences. All dressed in the same white one-piece paper coveralls. A few standing at dispensers, sucking sugary pap. One or two curled up on scuffed sand, dead, waiting for disposal in the morning; the few dolls that died natural deaths always died at night.

As Lianna walked towards the nearest enclosure, every doll turned to look at her. They all had the same face, the same empty gaze. Multiplied a thousand times, their gaze laid a weight over Lianna's entire skin.

Cameras up amongst the lights: though she was pretty certain no one would be watching, Lianna started to get the shakes. She chose at random, told the doll to follow her, and as one every doll stood up.

Lianna felt herself begin to lose it, grabbed the shoulders of the doll across the fence from her, half-lifted half-dragged it out. It weighed almost nothing, light as a bird. She laid a hand on its shoulder and hissed in its ear that it must come with her. Walked it up the ramp, into the empty locker room, told it to stand still and got her locker open, dragged out her kit, spilling instruments, tremors amplifying into shivers. She had to lock her free hand around her wrist as she slashed and slashed at the doll's shoulder, white coveralls and blue skin slicing cleanly to show flesh and then blood that ran down its arm, started dripping from its fingers.

Lianna made herself fold up her kit, shut her locker. Then walked out, steering the doll with a hand on its good shoulder. Only one person passed them as they crossed the compound, and Lianna said, "Found this one wandering around, clean-up can't count again," but the man hardly glanced at her.

She couldn't go out the main gate, but there was only a single mesh fence around the complex, and in places it sagged in bellying swathes. Lights of a warehouse arena off in the distance, sound of shots, the occasional war-whoop. She managed to drag a section of links free of sand, shoved the doll through and crawled after.

Then all she had to do was hike down the road to her usual tram stop, walk her prisoner unremarked past the doll driver with the scarred face, make it squat with half a dozen other dolls in the back. Its wound had stopped bleeding, but the torn sleeve of its coverall was stained maroon from shoulder to cuff. A babushka glared disapproval, powdered face pinched and sour beneath a pink cartwheel hat with little mirrors dangling and winking from its brim. Lianna smiled at her and she looked away.

During the ride, Lianna couldn't help noticing all over again how many dolls there were, out and about amongst the human strollers. She let herself go to shivers, tried not to laugh, jamming hands between thighs, hunching shoulders. She could have taken any of them – no, they had errands, would have started squalling. But it would have been less risk! The babushka still glaring: Lianna bit the insides of her cheeks. She was crazy . . .

*　　*　　*

"You're crazy," Darlajane B. said. "You think I have anything to do with it? You *are* crazy!"

They were on the flat roof of the residential building, wind blowing around them, rattling the panes of the cloches where Darlajane grew pot and plants she'd spliced herself. Lianna had found her stargazing, working out her astrology chart with the aid of a fifteen centimetre telescope and a hypertext almanac. Now the VR goggles were pushed up on Darlajane's tattooed scalp and the telescope was running through its tracking programme on auto, motors making abrupt spurts of noise.

Darlajane B. said, "Where have you put it? In your room, I suppose." Her voice had acquired a harsh edge, a German accent Lianna had never heard before, but otherwise the old woman seemed quite composed.

"Where else? I locked the door, but I don't think combat dolls know about doors anyway."

"It's the first place the peepers will think of looking. Crazy *and* stupid."

"It's not going to be there long," Lianna said, and told the old woman what she wanted done.

"Ach, that kind of thing I gave up a long time ago. And my associates wouldn't like it. At my age I have to behave myself."

Lianna thought, I'm not going to hurt her, and pushed Darlajane B. up against the parapet, holding tightly to the lapels of her leather jacket. The old woman swore, tried to push back; she smelt of patchouli oil, of dust, of sour age. Through the tunnel of her chip, feeling very close to the edge, Lianna said "I'm not going to hurt you. You know I can't. But if I'm caught, I'll have the peepers analyse my blood. I dropped a couple of your pills and I'll tell them all about it. I guess supplying narcotics to zeks is illegal, or my chip wouldn't be set the way it is."

"Let me go. Let me go right now." Darlajane B.'s voice had a measure of steel in it, and Lianna stepped back. "A clear night too, and Saturn's setting in an hour, I haven't had a chance to look at him yet. I always like to look at him. You are a nuisance, girl."

"All you have to do is do what you do to your cats, it isn't much."

"It isn't as straightforward as you think. And listen to me, I'm not doing this because of your silly little threat. Peepers run my thing, you think they'll let you hurt that?" Darlajane B. looked thoughtfully at Lianna. "You are a long way from where you began. Three months you nothing more than a frightened *hausfrau* were, a murderess maybe, but a frightened and confused murderess. Now you of myself remind, when I was your age, full of piss and vinegar. Without your chip, I think you could have killed me like you killed your husband."

But Lianna was looking out beyond the parapet, into wild, windy darkness where as always scattered fires burned, small and strange as stars. She said, "Nice try. But I'm not angry, and that's the frame my chip works in. Do you believe in fairies, Darlajane?"

"Many kinds of people live out there. Once, I myself . . . but the revolution is over."

"Is it?"

"Let's just do it, before I lose my nerve."

They did it in the old woman's kitchen, the doll strapped to the scarred wooden table. Half a dozen cats sat atop a huge icebox, watching with feigned boredom as Lianna reassured it and Darlajane B. administered curarine to immobilize its eyes. The old woman had put on spectacles which covered her eyes with lensed turrets. After the curarine, she took a measure of milky liquid from a battered silvery thermos, administered drops to the inside corners of the doll's eyes. Its head was cradled on a block of black rubber.

"The culture last month I got," she said. "Bootlegged from ICI, they work better than the strains I was using, get to work straight away on building connections down the optic nerves. In a couple of hours they'll be all through the cortex, increasing connectivity." She screwed down the thermos top, put the culture in the bottom of the icebox: fembots grew best, with fewest spontaneous somatic mutations, in the dense molecular architecture of water at 4°C.

"I love these machines," Darlajane B. said. "All my family from arthritis have suffered; I have little workers in my joints, burning away calcification as fast as it forms. So I can still sit zazen, I can still plug in chips."

She unrolled a surgical kit, set a microsurgery scaffolding over the doll's face. A set of miniature thumb-operated waldoes peeled back the doll's eyelids, inserted something that looked like a little spade between eye and socket. Humming some old rock tune, Darlajane began to dismantle the doll's old behavioural chip. The turrets of her pop-eyed spectacles clicked as they zoomed in and out of focus. Working had calmed her, routine dictating mood. She talked about the old days as she worked, anti-creationist marches, anti-slavery terrorist campaigns, weird alliances between radical Christians, Moslems, counter-culture activists that had foundered on theological schisms Lianna couldn't begin to follow.

"How it was, in those days," Darlajane explained, "was that we wanted to set dolls free, but the others wanted to destroy them. Scapegoats, you know? Servants of Satan? Well, Christianity has declined ever since the Millennium, I am not surprised. *They* said we were worse than the capitalists, daring to try to save inhuman things through technology. *We* said dolls had no original sin, they were closer to angels than devils. Ach, well, it was a long time ago, and we all lost."

A second thermos held a rack of aluminum slides, where fembots built hair-thin biochips molecule by molecule on wafer templates. A slide went under the scaffolding: waldoes plucked the chip from its carrier. Lianna watched the old woman slide it into place, imagining a swarming galaxy of machines small as bacteria spinning pseudo-neurons from the chip's hardware down the shaft of the optic nerve, spreading through the cortex, wiring a complex web in parallel with the doll's linear neuron network. Do to the doll as had been done to her . . . the mote in her right eye suddenly felt huge, a splinter thrust into the raw surface of her brainjelly.

The old woman was working on the doll's other eye when Nicole said, "Ey, where did you get him?"

For a moment Lianna thought her chip had cut in. Darlajane said calmly, "You need your fix, it's on the second shelf. Take it and go. This you do not need to see."

Nicole rummaged in the big icebox, fog pouring around her. She wore nothing but a short kimono-style robe, belted very tight. She said, "This hurts our thing, Lianna, I'll hurt you. I swear it."

Darlajane B. slid in the second chip. "No one will it hurt unless the wrong people hear of it. And I do it only once, so you need not worry about yourself. Have what you want? Then go. Tomorrow I will talk to you." When Nicole had gone, she said, "That one is too much trouble for an old woman like me."

"She needs her stuff," Lianna said hopefully. The shock of hearing Nicole's voice was tingling in the tips of her fingers.

"Think that comforts me? Here, we are nearly finished. Used not to take so long, but necessary to remove the chips already there it is, too many essential subroutines on them. Used to have a search-and-destroy strain of bugs that burnt out conditioning areas, but it won't work with these new chips where data is holographically coded."

"You did this a lot."

"I was trying to tell you that. But like trying to bail out the polders with a teaspoon it was. The ones I cured lived only half a dozen years at best, and always there were more. This one you stole, it is two hundred ecus' worth of meat, nothing more. And how many combat dolls are there, in just that one arena? And in all the arenas in the world? You save this one, give it a new life, and in six years it is gone. Even if you blow the hatcheries, as some friends of mine once did, there will always be more dolls. We depend on them now. Without them no minimum wage, no voluntary unemployment, no unlimited food and gadgets. Too late to change society, girl."

"I did it for myself," Lianna said, softly.

Darlajane B. pushed back her spectacles, swung away the scaffolding. "Ach, of course you did. Little *hausfrau*, you should have served out your sentence. You know now there is no going back."

"I know," Lianna said. "Is it finished?"

"One more thing," Darlajane B. said. She shoved an ampoule of oily liquid into a hypo and she pushed the snout against the doll's shoulder. The doll twitched as the charge went in. "Thyrotropic hormone," the old woman said. "Lipodroplet packaged, what they use to bring sex-toys to puberty. And now we are done. You stay here this night, your doll here will need the time to learn. But tomorrow, I do not want to know where you are."

Lianna woke in the middle of the night to abrupt bursts of sound, the flicker of the telly. It was an old solid-state model, its thick glass screen giving off blue light eerie as hard radiation. The doll squatted in front of it, zapping through Dutch and French and British and German and Common Net channels, blink blink blink blink, one every ten seconds. Eyes wide to the welter of images, he didn't look around when Lianna put her hand on his bandaged shoulder.

She sat behind him a long time, news programs segueing into shopping channels, soaps, porno. Except for his thumb on the zapper, the doll didn't move. At last she left a pitcher of glucose-spiked orange juice beside him and fell into bed again, woke from uneasy sliding dreams to the buzz of her phone, loud and insistent above the telly's choppy murmur.

Lianna sleepily acknowledged the call. A computer-generated face floating in a mesh of bright lines looked out at her. It was familiar from a hundred telly serials. It was the peace police.

"You are under arrest," it said, voice not quite synched with lips.

"W-what charge?"

"Grand larceny, illegal modification of a series four kobold. Officers will arrive soon. Your room is locked. Please do not attempt to leave."

The face vanished like a burst soap bubble; the phone's hard-copy slot extruded a tongue of flimsy, an arrest warrant. "But I'm already a convict," Lianna said, and jumped when someone hammered at the door.

It wasn't the peepers: it was Darlajane B. She used her master key to override the computer-operated lock. A heavy canvas bag was slung over her shoulder. "You come with me right now," she said. "That bitch Nicole sold us both. Looking to take over my stake, I'd guess."

Something plucked at Lianna's waist. The doll. He had put on the bottom half of his coveralls, cinched it around his skinny waist with one of Lianna's scarves.

"Hot damn, mon ami," the doll said, "we go, *ja*? Heavy weather moving in from the east, storm fronts over all areas by midnight."

Darlajane B. said, "One thing we don't need."

"I need him. He wants to come, why not?"

"If I had any sense I'd leave you with him: you deserve each other. Did they reprogramme your chip? Of course not, they wouldn't have authorization. Surprised they used any channels at all." Darlajane watched Lianna pull on jeans, a checkered work-shirt. "You're ready? Good. My friends will be in a hurry to close this down, you can bet on it."

What had once been the hotel's parking garage was empty, except for one of the maintenance crew sorting garbage. The doll caught its arm, looked into its eyes. "Friend, *ami. Pouvez-vous me dire?*"

Lianna told him, "You've been changed. You understand?"

The changeling doll considered. It said at last, in French, "'And I awoke and found me here on the cold hill's side.'"

Darlajane B. was at the top of the service ramp, kneeling to look under the half-raised door at the street. "They're already here," she said.

Lianna looked. Early morning, the street empty except for a police runabout parked right outside the crib's entrance. Nowhere to run without attracting attention, and any moment now the peepers would be back outside.

Lianna felt a strange floating detachment, the way she'd felt after her husband's death. It had happened early in the morning, and most of the next day she'd wandered the big house, waiting for justice to strike her down. In the end she'd called the peepers herself, and as she'd waited for them had at last felt peace.

Perhaps her chip had blacked her out for a second, memory treacherous now, a swamp with vast blank areas in which she could sink forever. Darlajane B. clutched her arm. Lianna saw two men leave the crib. One walked to the runabout; the other towards the service entrance.

The changeling stood hand-in-hand with the maintenance doll. "Friend," he said, half a dozen times in half a dozen languages. He tapped the doll's chest, his own. "We know way."

Lianna saw that the shaven-headed peeper was very close to the door now. Getting to her feet was very hard; her chip was bearing down, working on peripheral clues. One word from the peeper and it would shut her down.

"Vamoose," the changeling said.

Lianna and Darlajane B. followed.

It was not a way Lianna would have chosen: past curtain after curtain of plastic sheeting into the warmth and red light of the incubation chamber. It had once been a coldroom. Now, naked

dolls hung from racks, bodies wrapped in webs of tubing, heads
cased in swathes of black plastic. Their bellies were grossly
distended, like five-year pregnancies at term: the disease Darlajane had given them had turned their livers into vast controlled
malignancies, half their body weight. Pink goo, rich in peptides,
ran through clear tubing from the dolls to fractionation columns.
The over-heated room was filled with a rich, sweet smell that
made Lianna gag.

Darlajane pawed at a jury-rigged panel, pulling wires, shouting she was damned if Nicole was going to have them. Peristaltic
pumps slowed, stopped; black-masked dolls began to twitch,
trying to draw air with collapsed lungs. The maintenance doll
had vanished; Lianna saw the changeling duck through a hatch
low in the wall, followed it through a low narrow passage into a
foul-smelling nest lit by a dim bulb where half a dozen dolls
curled in sleep. Cockroaches skittered from Lianna's feet. One
dropped in her hair, and she fought back a scream. The nest was
the beginning of a kind of tunnel, suddenly sloping down. Little
lights, most of them not working, sketched a dwindling perspective.

"Maintenance levels," Darlajane B. said. She was out of
breath, and leaned heavily on the arm Lianna offered.

The tunnel opened onto a wide well-lit corridor, tiled walls and
floor swathed with cables and pipes and ducts. Dolls moved past
in different directions. Most were naked, blue skin streaked and
crusted with dirt. The invisible army of Morlocks which ran
civilization.

A shout behind them: a man's voice, botched by echoes.
Lianna felt a wave of dizziness, the chip in her right eye almost
triggered. Panic flaring, she ran, scattering dolls, ran down tiled
tunnels until warning chevrons crammed her sight.

Lianna leaned against a grimy junction box, breathing hard.
The chevrons slowly faded. She was in a narrow, grimy, ill-lit
tunnel, tiles stained with black mould. Dolls moved past in an
irregular single file, identical faces glancing at Lianna as they
passed. A figure taller than any doll hobbled out of shadow:
Darlajane B. When Lianna asked where the changeling was, the
old woman said, "You thought he'd stick with us? They aren't
human, girl. They're mostly baboon, spliced with maybe ten per
cent of the genes that separate us from the apes. And when

they're changed, it is into something new . . . I'd forgotten that . . . Something strange, perhaps something wonderful."

"I freed him . . ."

"You freed him to choose. You wanted him as your pet? Well, too late. He's chosen. So must you. Listen."

Somewhere down the length of the tunnel, above the rustle of dolls padding past: a faint murmur sound of human voices. Lianna's heart caught on a barb of despair.

Darlajane B. rummaged through her canvas bag. She said, "Pull your chip, is what I'm going to have to do. Bonded into your optic nerve it is, so I will cause damage. No time for any other measure. You willing?"

Lianna felt like she was floating. Before she could say anything, light burst behind Darlajane. In the glare's centre the peeper said, "You run, but you can't hide."

Deeply tanned face, grey crewcut going white at the edges, belly straining his chalkstripe shirt, hung over the belt of his neatly creased jeans: Lianna had seen him coming and going in the crib a dozen times. He had a big flashlight in one hand, a pistol in the other. His badge was fixed to the strap of his shoulder-holster. He said, "Bad times come down, Darlajane. You and your friend get up against the wall. We finish this right here."

"We can talk about this," Darlajane B. said.

One of the dolls had stopped to watch the humans. It wore the bottom half of stained white coveralls, had a bandage on one shoulder. It was the changeling.

The peeper said, "You're out of business, what do we need to talk about?"

"That little whore. You'd trust her?"

Other dolls clustered around the changeling. They looked strange, grim, alert. One had little copper wires sewn around the rims of its ears; another a ring through its nose. All had parallel scars seaming their cheeks. Lianna was so afraid she couldn't move. She could only watch and wonder.

The peeper said, "We'll trust Nicole as much as we trusted you." The muzzle of his pistol looked huge as he pointed it at Lianna, at Darlajane B. He said, "Be easy, and it's over. Just a flash in the head—"

His pistol went up and went off, blowing fragments of tile from the ceiling. Half a dozen dolls were swarming over the peeper: he staggered, screaming when small strong fingers found one of his eyes. And Darlajane said, "Knew I had this," brought out a little chromed 9 mm automatic, both hands around its crosshatched grip. The dolls dropped away and the peeper's head came up. He stared at Darlajane B. and then she shot him. Three times, chest, chest again, and a wild shot that took him in the arm and spun him around as he flew backwards. The noise was deafening in the tunnel's vault.

Lianna was on her feet, back pressed against slimy tile. She saw the changeling step forward from the others. *Fairies*, she thought, and a cold clean wind blew through her.

Then Darlajane B. in her face, saying, "We've got five minutes *if* we're lucky. Now just hold still!" Something in her hand, flashing silver: Lianna's right eye exploded and went out.

In darkness, Lianna felt sand pitch and yaw beneath her. She lost her balance and sat down hard. The right side of her head swollen, tender, hollow. She couldn't blink; her eye felt peeled. Cautiously probing, Lianna found bandages over cotton wadding – then small cold hands gripped hers.

"No good," the changeling said.

Lianna couldn't remember anything after Darlajane's knife had come down. She asked, "Where's the old woman?"

"Vamoosed. She left you things."

Only gauze over her left eye. She unrolled it, blinked tears. The changeling was a blurred shadow in front of her. Beyond were moonlit dune crests, the red and green lights strung along Den Haag's barrier wall. Free, Lianna thought. A cold clean wind blew through her. Free.

The changeling pushed something towards her. It was Darlajane's canvas bag.

The changeling said in sing-song recitative, "'Fembot cultures, chip templates, surgery kit. All you need to make over as many dolls as you can. Time to change my identity again, move on. Good luck, girl.'"

"And your friends?"

"All gone. I follow you."

"Where did they come from?"

"Found me, left me. Brothers and sisters of the knife everywhere underground."

Getting to her feet was hard: it felt as if all her blood surged and burned in her empty socket. Wiping sympathetic tears from her left eye, Lianna saw will-of-the-wisp fires flicker far off in deep dark wilderness. She told the changeling, "They're out there, too."

Darlajane B. had been wrong. The revolution had not finished. It was not any person or even any movement. It was an idea. It took hold where it would. Lianna thought of disaffected kids, of changelings infiltrating unnoticed everywhere in the straight world. Remembered the tram driver, its scarred cheeks. There had always been people living on the edge: now there were two kinds, changing and being changed, changing each other. All this came to her in an instant; she would spend the rest of her life untangling it.

She said, "I suppose we'd better find out what's out there," and swung the heavy canvas bag onto her shoulder, started down the slope of sand. The changeling gripped her hand, skipping along to keep pace with her.

After a while Lianna began to sing.

THREE BANANAS

Larry Tritten

Bananas. Nobody even remembered what they were. That was the ironic part. Banana was a word like "puttee" or "condominium" or "jogging". It was part of the past. Oh, sure, there were a few old timers here and there who dimly remembered them and still made an occasional wistful reference to them, but the word wasn't really a part of the language any more. The average person wouldn't have had the slightest idea what you meant if you described Zeon Doon as a top banana or if you said that a disc of dreamol made you go bananas. Bananas had been gone for seventy-five years. All of the world's fruit had been destroyed for ever in the Wars of Commerce and the Wars of Commerce were remote history, like World War III½, the Oil Wars, or the War of Janet's Pants. Bananas had been a little bit harder to kill than most of the other kinds of fruit; they had lingered on in a few countries for a couple years after the initial blights wiped out apples, peaches, cherries, and the rest, but in the end all of it was gone, and it hadn't seemed to matter much since there were so many new and zany kicks to make up for the loss: a whole spectrum of fulgurant drugs that played the central nervous system like a pin ball machine and all sorts of mind bangers and sensibility stingers.

The world had forgotten all about bananas. But some of us were just about to start learning.

It all started with a phone call. It was one of those cold dark San Francisco days featuring a sky the colour of wet ashes and the kind of aggressive wind that slaps you around like a sparring partner and I was entrenched in my Irving Street office tippling snifters of rocksauce and trying to forget about unpaid bills and unfulfilled dreams.

The phone rang and I caught it in the middle of the second ring, not because I had any interest in talking to anyone but because I figured the sound of a ringing bell would be more annoying than someone's voice.

I was right. The party on the other end said something in an undertone so soft and inconspicuous it was like listening to the voice of my conscience.

"You'll have to play that again," I told him. "Then maybe we can turn this into a dialogue."

The voice registered a bit more clearly this time but it still sounded like someone in the wings delivering a stage whisper. "Is this Rad Sway speaking?"

"It's Sway speaking," I said. "Who's this listening?"

"This is Isham van Bourke," the voice said. It was a hesitant voice, the customary style for clients with confidential stories to tell. A private investigator is a professional confidante, like a priest or a psychiatrist. They all get to hear lots of hair-raising tales about sex and money, the two most favourite topics in every culture sophisticated enough to have income taxes and birth control.

I waited for Isham van Bourke to tell me something that would stimulate my interest, and he did.

"I would like to retain you," he said, loosening up a little as he forged on. "At your usual fee – uh, whatever that is . . ."

"That is expenses and ten bucks an hour, cash in advance, no stamps, food coupons, I.O.U.s, heartfelt promises or hot merchandise," I said, wanting to get that straight from the outset. I once spent two weeks tumbling down stairs and dodging bullets for a blonde in Mill Valley who paid me in horizontal favours, which was great except that I subsequently had to hock everything but my hat and mattress to keep my practice afloat.

Van Bourke was upset. "I always pay cash," he said quickly and firmly. The knowledge warmed me considerably.

"Do you want to talk about this on the wire?" I asked. "Or do you want to pull your collar up around your neck and meet me in the shadows somewhere?"

"I'll be in your office in fifteen minutes," he said. "If that's all right with you."

"That's fine," I said, and hung up. I put away the rocksauce and got up from behind the desk and walked around the room, checking out the way the office looked. Van Bourke sounded like a man who hailed from green fields and you had to humour the type, make them feel comfortable so they could throw their money around more easily. I made some neat piles out of a lot of mail and magazines and assorted scraps of paper on my desk, dusted the foundering filing cabinet (termites) against the wall, and turned the radio on low, tuning in KSEA, the station that programs only the sounds of the sea. They were doing the beaches of Southern England and there were some very nice breakers coming in, perfect for a relaxed mood. I got back behind my desk and cultivated a seasoned and professional look.

I heard van Bourke coming down the hallway, torturing the antique floorboards with every step, and saw the dark shape of him through the opaque glass in the office door before he knocked.

Van Bourke came into the room cautiously, like a show poodle entering a garbage dump. To say that he was pale and fat would be to understate. He was the colour of bone china and too wide to reach around. He got, somehow, into the chair across from me and flashed a tight smile of greeting. He was wearing a suit the colour of dried blood that fit like a tent. On its lapel there was a gold pin: a drum stick crossed with a loaf of bread inside a wreath of sausages, and underneath the phrase *bon viand*.

"Mr van Bourke," I said, and nodded.

Van Bourke nodded. "Hello."

He was going to need coaxing, I could tell. He wasn't used to bringing his dirty laundry into anybody's office. I smiled at him and said evenly, "Why don't you tell me about it, whatever it is, and we can float with it."

That seemed to relax him some. He tilted back in the chair, which made a sound like a cruiser nudging a dock, and composed a melancholy expression.

"I guess I should start at the beginning," he said.

"You could start in the middle – if I were clairvoyant," I said brightly.

He let that pass and let his gaze drift around the office for a couple of seconds, and when he had himself all coordinated, said in a dignified voice, "What I want you to do is check into a matter for me. And I suppose the best way to get at this is to introduce myself first . . ." He gave me a sudden sharp glance. "I don't happen to look familiar to you?"

"Nope."

He seemed disappointed. "Well, I'm the editor of a magazine, Mr. Sway. I'm sure you've heard of it. *Vittles & Viands*, the magazine of victuals. We're dedicated to presenting a shamelessly gustatory approach to eating – to fine dining, I should say. For us, you see, food is a very serious thing . . ."

So much I could see by his dimensions.

"Food," he went on, letting the word melt in his mouth like pure ambrosia, "is something I've devoted my life to. It is, you might well say, my vocation, avocation, pastime, forte, and pleasure. If you can understand that, you will be able to see just how important this whole matter is to me."

I nodded, absorbing it and waiting for him to go on. "S & M's?" I said, offering him a package of those little candy-coated chocolate drops, the kind that are stamped with an image of a dominatrix and melt in the hand not the mouth.

Van Bourke waved them aside with a limp gesture and said pointedly, "I should rather talk about bananas for the moment."

"Bananas?" I got a fix on the word, probed the back of my mind for connections, and came up with a dim memory: that long yellow fruit people used to eat. "Why bananas?" I asked.

Van Bourke eased back in his chair, a smile touching his lips. "Because I think there are bananas somewhere in this city," he said. "And I would be willing to pay a delicious sum to have this investigated. I can't emphasize that too much."

I gave him back his smile. "It sounds more and more interesting."

Van Bourke let his hand slip furtively into his coat pocket and the pale fingers came out with some photographs that he held low in his lap and facing away from me like a man with a hot poker hand. Then he handed them to me and watched with a troubled expression as I turned them over. They surprised me. They looked like shots from one of those sex dream layouts in one of the better men's magazines – *Playboy* or *Decor* or *Wit & Bawd*: two young women, one wearing nothing but black riding boots and a diadem of gumdrops in her waves of blonde hair and one in a coal-black, skin-tight leather bodysuit with minimal slits for the eyes and a mouth visor, and a man, nude, all tangled together on a bed whose sheets looked like they had hosted a stampede. The photographs were not the best. They had a fuzzy, unfocussed look that made them hard to appreciate.

I put them face up on the desk, one at a time, all five of them, and glanced up at van Bourke. "Well, you didn't come here to sell these."

"Look at them again," he said.

I looked at them again, browsing through the background detail this time, then saw what he was getting at. The three revellers were in an expensive king-size bed with an opulent brass frame that shone like polished gold. In the background was an indistinct wall, colourless in shadow, and the only other thing to see was part of a night stand to the left. There was a phone on the stand and beside it a white dish with something in it. Three long yellow objects.

"Bananas." Van Bourke nodded, tapping one of the pictures. "Here in this dish. You see them, don't you?"

"I see them," I said, "but I'm not so sure they're bananas."

He frowned. His voice became firm. "But they are bananas. I *know* they are bananas. I *believe* they are bananas. *Musa paradisiaca sapientum* – in the peel, by God! I was there in the theatre, took these pictures – which are, admittedly, not exceptionally good. But I thought the important thing was to get something on film before the opportunity passed." His eyes sought mine and his voice rose with dramatic emphasis. "These pictures were taken in the Calliope theatre. I went back a second night to get them and took five shots off the screen. They lose something in the translation, I admit, but when I was there in that theatre seeing them on the screen they were, I assure you, much more palpable and plainly authentic."

I said, "You took these pictures in a porno theatre?"

Van Bourke nodded. "I was there the night before last. That's when I noticed the dish. I went back last night with a camera."

I admired his spirit but I couldn't help thinking about wild geese. My scepticism showed and van Bourke nodded knowingly, removing his wallet from his coat and holding it up with some ostentation. "You think I'm eccentric or enigmatic or perhaps just somewhat ridiculous," he said, smiling wanly, "but the fact is I can afford to pay your price, Mr Sway. I have a fine gourmet's instinct for the near presence of an exotic comestible, and even though all logic, sense and precedent would seem to dispute me, I am going to side with that instinct. I will not claim to know how or why there should be bananas in a world that has forgotten the word, but there is something here, something . . ." He paused and stared at the air for at least fifteen seconds before going on, ". . . something portentous and quite *important* . . ."

I took the wallet out of his hand, something he scarcely noticed, and holding it in one hand nudged a thumb into the currency vent until I felt the wad of bills, then flick three out, glimpsed the denomination, nodded, and said, "I've got to trace a film back to its source. No problem."

Van Bourke shrugged, frowned. "A film with no credits, one that might have been made by any of scores of errant purveyors of the like. It will involve energetic footwork, persistent queries."

"For bananas," I said, deadpan.

"But bananas, by God!" van Bourke exclaimed with a burst of zeal. "Ah, Mr Sway, if you could only appreciate this. Do you know that bananas were once as basic to the civilized palate as bread, meat, and omnisweet? The banana was there, *everywhere*: banana bread, pudding, cake, banana cream pie. It was in frozen confections, ice cream, pastries, candy. Liqueurs. They served banana nirvana at the Hyatt Regency. The flavour was, apparently, exquisitely adaptable. It was, as Andmore Yam says in his *Lure, Lore and Life of the Banana*, the perfect flavour and no kitchen or table or mouth went without its grace." He sat up in the chair and his eyes were wide and clear as he went with the flow. "Can you imagine *tasting* one?" he asked, and sat back with the impact of the thought.

It was a rhetorical question, so I ignored it, tucked the three bills into my shirt pocket, and gave my client the self-assured smile I figured he deserved for his money.

"I'll be in touch with you, Mr van Bourke," I told him.

The Calliope theatre was in the Tenderloin on Eddy Street. It was listed under adult theatres in the movie section of the *Chronicle* and the ad promised a miscellany of "hot holograms, sizzling celluloid, and sexy surprises". It sounded interesting. I drove over there in my old Caravel, found a place to park, and walked two blocks, taking care not to look too hard at a hooker in pearls and a black dress with a mandarin collar and cuffs who trailed me for a while. She looked pretty good.

The Calliope wasn't Loew's Collosus. It was a crackerbox of a building that had once been a small shop of some kind. Now the glass doors were painted black and darkly curtained. They opened into a dingy little ticket booth where you bought your ticket, then passed through a turnstile and vanished through curtains into the small screening room where the fantasies were.

I bought my ticket from a dark voice in the ticket booth, went inside and gave it a chance. A naked blonde with eyes as blue as sapphire ice and blue hair cut short and glittering with iridescent sequins was drifting somnolently above the aisle, reaching down toward the audience, her fingers weaving the air. It was a vivid fantasy and when it had run its course it faded, leaving fading wisps and traces of blue light in its wake. A film appeared on the screen down in front. Two women were coming down a ramp from an ocean liner amid a blizzard of confetti and paper streamers. There was no sound – just the ratchety whisper of the projector unwinding film. The women were very young and at first glance very beautiful, but as they came down the ramp toward the crowd on the dock, approaching the camera in extreme close-up, you could see that the make-up was laid on so heavily they looked like Fauvist ghouls: eyes the colour of steel shadowed with dark purple and grape-coloured mouths forcing exaggerated prurient smiles out of faces as pale as chalk and coral. The faces drifted toward the camera and filled the screen, which went black, then phased through six blank squares, each a few seconds in duration, citron, lavender, electric-blue, bright pink, neon green, and cerise, before fading into an image of both of the women, nude and curled into foetal positions, side by side, fused into the centre of a great translucent block of some pale gelatinous substance. In the soft green depth one could see very slight signs of motion, a finger, elbow, the stirring of a foot. The camera moved in and their eyes opened as they peered out in smiling lassitude, lips moving to form mimetic kisses.

Not bad, I thought. Arty.

Then I was watching three people tumbling around on a big brass bed. I tuned into the action very keenly and when the camera panned past the white dish got a clear look at the yellow objects. I found myself wondering what something that looked that lurid would taste like. Sour? Sweet? Dry? Juicy? I watched for a while as the blonde with gumdrops on her skull was being nibbled over by her companions, then got up and went up the aisle and out to where the ticket seller was laying down a game of solitaire. Peering through the glass that separated us, I made out a pair of harsh eyes in a wasted face beneath a lot of slicked back hair alight with oil. He smelled like a Tenderloin barbershop.

"How's business?" I asked.

His eyes stayed on the cards. No answer.

I tried again. "A rat worked over one of my shoes while I was dreaming in the front row. Who do I complain to?"

He picked up a card and turned it over and when it was down gave me a quick nasty glance as he turned over the next one. "Beat it," he said.

I lighted a wooden match on the side of the ticket booth and fired a cigarette and blew the smoke at the glass. "Yeah?"

"Yeah," he said, but there was more irritation than conviction in his voice and now he sized me up. That gave him the notion to ease up a bit. "Didn't like the show?" he ventured.

"Loved it," I said. "Especially the part where the man in the glass booth realizes just how serious life can be." I backed that up with the kind of expression a barracuda makes biting into a tin can and tapped the glass a couple of times to make sure he was wide awake. "Who owns this trap?" I added.

"Owns?" He caught his lower lip with his teeth and shot a glance at the stairs going up to the projection room.

"I'm listening," I said.

"You – you got an appointment?" he faltered.

I rapped the glass again, impatiently this time, enough to sit him up straight. He took a deep breath and said, "Ahh – well, Mr Saracen is upstairs now – but he don't, he—"

I left him struggling with his grammar and went up the narrow spiral stairs in the darkness to the next floor where a corridor led to the projection room and another door at the far end behind which a tinny little radio was blaring out Dry Stone's latest blues tune, *The Prisoner of Brenda*.

I rapped the door twice with my knuckles. A voice came back with, "Yeah?" in a noncommittal monotone, and I opened the door and went inside.

It was a hot tight little room with just enough space for a desk and the man behind it. He had a face that a mother might be able to love: a skulker's eyes, a nose that had been broken as many times as an ingenue's heart, and a dull mouth that wouldn't waste much time with smiles. His desk was littered with papers and the papers were littered with ashes and covered with coffee stains and chewed-up toothpicks. He was wearing an expensive Scott Lee shingle tweed that was lost on him. He looked surprised to see a stranger but that didn't change his expression much.

"I don't know you," he said to the wall behind me.

I held out a hand. "Roth Saint-James Place," I introduced myself while he looked over the hand. I was about to put it away but then he shook it briskly and released it and sat back.

"Barney sent you up here?"

"I found my way. Barney isn't social."

"Who're you?" His gaze was empty, flat.

"Well . . ." There wasn't another chair so I relaxed my stance and put the cigarette between my lips, working on a faint smile. "I was watching your programme downstairs," I said. "Some very interesting stuff. Not the usual product. I've seen my share of loops, but there's a little something extra there . . ."

He looked at me with vague curiosity. "Yeah? You a film buff?"

"Writer," I said. "The thing is, I'm doing a run-down for *Light & Shadow* on porn films. The ones with a little class and style. I'd like to talk to a couple of film-makers, do an interview or two. For starters, it's pretty clear that whoever makes your loops has got some kind of unique imagination and an attitude toward his stuff that puts him out of the hack league."

"You think so?" he said, thoughtfully.

"The style shows through. I'd like to talk to him if it wouldn't be too much trouble."

He considered it and looked annoyed. It would definitely be trouble, his eyes told me – but I sensed that I could ease the pain by making it worth his while.

"I'm a freelance writer," I told him. "I don't make a lot of money." My wallet was in my hand and he was watching through narrowed eyes as I slipped a bill out. "It's worth a seventy-nine Ford," I said. "Tops." I started to pass him the green but he had it in his hand with a conjurer's dexterity sooner than I could make the move. He tucked it away in his coat without looking at it and leaned back in the chair to dig something out of his other pocket. He handed me the card and I held it up to read. There was a name, CINEMAGIC, and a phone number, 347–14–769323. In the upper left-hand corner a motion-picture camera was spilling out flowers and fruit onto the name and number.

"This nut shoots all my loops," the man behind the desk said. "Nick Malmsey. Good man. Used to be the best cameraman Electropix had working for them till a hologram exploded, iced his eyes out. No depth perception now, but he's got a good mind's eye for composition."

"Thanks," I said. "I'll give him a call."

"He loves to talk," he said, making it sound like a warning.

"Thanks," I said again, and went out and down the corridor. Just to make sure the projectionist was on his toes I rattled the door as I passed by and snarled, "Focus th' goddamned thing!" I could hear him grumbling through the door all the way to the bottom of the stairs.

Outside it was summer on the street. There would be wind on the bay tonight but the air in the Tenderloin was as thick as a blanket. Neon cocktail glasses hovered in the air in front of all the bars, pouring out their pink and green bubbles, which winked out or floated away as fading scintillas of effervescence. Drifters, panhandlers, dreamers, rumhounds, vags, hookers, prowlers, idlers, fixers and d.p.'s roamed the streets. There was pie in the sky this evening. They'd programmed a slice of vanilla cream and it was drifting in the dark sky over the Embarcadero, a mile-long wedge of phantasmal light, dripping clouds of frosting that dwindled away like vapours. I stood there watching the apparition until I became aware of someone standing behind me and a little off to one side. "Don't turn around," he whispered. "It would be dumb. What you want to do is move down the block . . . the parked Halberd. Get in. Watch the sidewalk. Do it right and I won't have to do anything dangerous." It was a voice you wouldn't want to debate with.

I walked to the Halberd and opened the door. "You drive," he snapped. I slid over behind the wheel and sat there. The keys were in the ignition. He slid in beside me and sat there with his eyes on me. His smile was civilized but his eyes might have belonged to a Visigoth. He was wearing a pink shirt with black sharks on it and a pair of white slacks.

"You're smart," he said. He showed me the .45. "Keep smart, stay smart. Or I'll open your breadbox." He kept smiling. "I'll assume you know what a .45 slug can do. That's why they still make them – since 1911. And it's all you need, mac. You can keep your .56 Minim, your Belgrade Windjammer, .33 Firebrand, and all the rest."

I nodded sagely.

He ran a paw over my suit and came up with my wallet and my .38. He put the gun in the glove box and looked through the wallet, handed it back.

"A dick. I figured."

"I don't think we've been introduced," I said.

He put his fingers under my chin and turned my face to the side. "I'm not a good audience, dick. I'll rock you." His smile was as hard as the Tenderloin pavement. I got the idea.

We drove, at his direction, across Van Ness and up toward Pacific Heights. The house he pointed out was a big French bon bon with doors and windows and balconies. We went up the flagstone steps and inside. We paused at the bottom of the stairway while he fished a pair of cuffs out of his pocket, shackled one of my wrists and locked the other around a standing antique iron lamp an ocean liner could have used for an anchor. He went up the stairs.

There wasn't much to look at – just the stairway and another corridor, both lost in shadow. I didn't wait long before he came back down the stairs. He looked puzzled. He sat on the steps and tossed me the key to the cuffs.

"It's over," he said.

I unlocked the cuffs and stood watching him. He looked up at me and shrugged. "Damn." He shook his head. "Damn."

"I don't get it," I said.

"He's dead, dick."

"Dead." Who's dead? I wondered.

"Never mind." His face was red and he looked embarrassed. "I got no personal interest in this," he declared. He sat for a while, then said, "Hell, I need a drink. Drive you back downtown if you don't ask any questions."

He drove me back into the Tenderloin. Neither of us said a word during the ride and when I got out of the car, he put his head out the window and called out to me on the sidewalk, "Stay away from that house. It's hotter than a Death Valley barbecue . . ."

I waved and said, "Drop me a card."

I watched the car turn a corner and then got in a parking lot phone booth, folded the doors shut, and dialed the number on the CINEMAGIC card. Six rings and I was ready to hang up, but then a tired voice sighed into my ear, "Yeah, speaking . . ."

"I'm looking for Nick Malmsey," I said.

"Me," he said. "You're lookin' for me. So who's lookin'?"

I told him that I was writing a piece on loops for *Light & Shadow*, that he was an unappreciated Leonardo of the lens, and I was here to put a cornerstone under his name. He was tired, he said, he'd been in the darkroom for hours sifting fantasies out of the tray, but he wasn't too tired to talk to a guest who cared about his work and brought a bottle of tangerine green.

Nick lived out by the ocean on the Sundown side of Golden Gate Park. It was a building that would have made an architect weep. Square, yellow, and dirty. The facade had that eczematous look that old stucco acquires when the seaside winds have worked it over for a couple of decades, the windows were opaque smudges, and the shrubs out in front were stunted and hunch-backed, the deep green worn out of them by windblown sand. There was no bell. I tried the door and found it open, walked up to the apartment and knocked.

Nick opened the door. He was a slight polite looking man with a garland of hair on a balding dome. His leather and velvet jump suit, orange and umber, made him seem perhaps a few years younger than he was, but there was a tranced look in his eyes that spoiled the effect.

"Hey, man," he smiled, and slid his palm into mine. "Make yourself homey. Let's drink and talk."

I sat on a couch whose cushions were going slack with age and uncorked the tan, looking about for glasses.

"Hell, let's use the bottle," Nick said, and I knew exactly where he was: a man with no use for pretence.

We passed the bottle back and forth while I asked Nick questions. It wasn't long before he was talking enthusiastically about his work, anticipating the questions and making it unnecessary for me to do anything but listen. He was a man with a craft who was eager to talk about it, to explain the meaning of it, and I felt just a little bit bad about leading him because he was one of those rare people with a genuine sense of excitement.

"So now I'm doing loops," he said wistfully but not bitterly as the level of tan reached the halfway point on the bottle's label. "But I don't shoot 'em and run. I try to keep the scenarios inventive – may be with a tendency toward the bizarre, the surreal. And I use beautiful men and women, and costumes, *nice* clothing – chiffon and velvet, floral silks and soft body lights. It's the shine of black leather and mist of pink nylon, the wedding of fashion and sex that give eroticism a flavour of art."

"One of the things I noticed right away about your stuff," I said. "Exotic costumes." I took the bottle he handed me and took a belt. "The model with the crown of gumdrops. Very nice . . ." I let a thoughtful moment pass and then said, "Where do the models come from? I'd like to talk to one."

"Nara, the one you mention," he said, "is pretty typical. She's twenty-three, experimenting with life. She made a few loops with me last year when she lost her job. Lived with a guy until it went down the tube, filed papers for a while, then back for a few more loops last month."

"Where'd you shoot the one with the brass bed?"

Nick paused. "Well," he said finally, "that one was different. Yeah . . . really. We were all stoned on that one. Shot it at a big pad in Pacific Heights – just the other day. Nara was going with some with a lot of dough – name of Domino Londos. He wanted to watch a session and he made it worth our while. Turned into kind of a kink party. Everybody was higher than NASA." He paused, then added, "But that's not common. He made an offer I couldn't refuse, y'know?"

"Money talks," I nodded, sipping from the bottle. I gave it to Nick.

"This guy's money shouts," he said. He upended the bottle and finished the liquor. "You want to talk to Nara?" he asked.

"Uh-huh," I said.

"That all?" He grinned.

I was turning that one over and working up an answer when he suddenly laughed. "Well, hell, you're human," he said. "Yeah, talk to Nara. She's friendly. Got a sense of humour. She's okay. I'll give you her phone."

He wrote her phone number and address at the top of a page in a book, tore the page out and gave it to me. Page 79 of *Popcorn Epistemology*.

"Practice of mine," he said, "to give a little food for thought with the information."

I folded the page and tucked it away. "Thanks," I said. "I guess it's getting late."

"I'll watch for your piece," he told me at the door, smiling, amiable, pleased to have found a listener.

"Keep up the good work," I told him, feeling like a real son-of-a-bitch going down the steps.

There was fog in the air but birdsong in the fog as I parked in front of Nara Sands' place the next morning. She lived on the corner of Jackson and Santa Monica in an ultra-chic combination Spanish/Hollywood/ Gothic cottage that someone with a vivid sense of exoticism had painted a soft lilac so that it seemed to be seen through a violet filter. The neat lawn was violet as well and so was everything in the small garden out front; and the *papier-mâché* jacaranda tree that shaded the front door was in full violet bloom. I walked across the pastel scape up to the front door in the fog and rang a doorbell that touched off a quiet chime inside the house.

The door opened and the woman who looked out at me smiled. Friendly. She was something more than pretty. Lovely perhaps. Her colours were all wintry: long hair so pale it seemed somewhere between the lightest gold and the richest silver, skin the color of pale rose, eyes full of pale blue light. She was as tall as I am and wore an emerald green dress that showed plenty of leg and a cleavage that would dispel any notion that she was shy.

"Hi," she said eloquently.

"Hello."

Her smile stayed put. "Well, you don't look like a *salesman*."

"I tried to call first," I told her. "There wasn't any answer, so I went for a drive – and stopped by."

"I was out in the garden in back," Nara said. "Watching things grow."

"In the fog?"

"Sure." I went inside and as I followed her through a hallway into another part of the house, she said, "Nick called. So I know about you, in case you're wondering." We emerged in a room whose floor was a white sand beach. A Pacific horizon was programmed on one wall, the water white with reflected sunlight, the day hot. There was a gentle sound of the waves coming in and the cry of seabirds. The only furniture was two big palm trees and a portable bar.

"You don't mind talking out here?" she said, then smiled and extended her hand. "I'm Nara. Anyway, some of the times. Sometimes I do masque films – then I'm Liza Rd."

"What's your real name?"

"It isn't Chastity," she smiled. She met my gaze and held it as her smile defined her mood. She eased my name out of her mouth. "Rad." Warmly.

I looked around for something to sit on. I needed it. But there was just the beach.

"C'mon, sit," said Nara, taking my hand, and I gingerly eased down beside her on the beach. She took off her shoes and in as much time as it takes to open an eye had slipped herself out of her dress and was stretching her legs in the sand. Every part of her that wasn't concealed by three small triangles of black silk was the color of polished copper. I sat beside her and she took my hand between hers.

"You don't know what to make of it, right?" she said.

I didn't know what to say.

"Rad, don't say anything," she said. "I know you're not a writer." There was a tremor in her hands. Her eyes darkened and her smile sank with the light dimming in her eyes. "I'm not so easy," she said, apologizing, and put her cheek on my shoulder. She shuddered and I held her lightly. Her heart was beating swiftly and her fingers moved along the edge of my jaw, touching me with trust, seeking something. I grazed my lips through her hair and she clung. She was afraid and confused and it was hard to resist the lure of her so I followed those old instincts and went with her guidance into the lodes where the gold lay buried. She was all gold and when we opened our eyes again in the burning sunlight her smile was placid, she was calm and steady again.

"Want a drink?" she asked.

"Yeah," I said.

She plodded through the hot sand to the bar and I waited until she came back with two frosted glasses.

"Cheers," she said, touching her glass to mine.

How can I describe that drink? The heavy sweetness of rum

flavoured with a taste so subtle it seemed to fade the moment it registered. Yet it was strangely . . . memorable.

"What is this?" I asked Nara.

"Banana daiquiri," she said. "Like it?"

I didn't say anything and after a few seconds her mouth twisted into a flat taut line. "We were like toys to that son-of-a-bitch," she said with sudden anger. "Like those old mechanical banks you put a coin into. Performing toys." She sipped her drink. "He was all hands and ego – push, grab, take. He didn't even know how to play an orgy. Money was all he knew. His idea of sex was using someone – manipulation. There are diamonds in the coal, Rad, moths fly with the butterflies – but he didn't know that. When he found out he didn't have a couple of slaves, he got pretty weird, ugly. He beat Mustela up, broke her nose. He was like a mad wolf. I hit him with the nearest thing I could find. It was the blender I mixed these daiquiris in."

I was watching her as I listened. She had it all under control now as she went on; there was no regret. "That was a couple days ago in his place in Pacific Heights. Know what I did with the two bananas we aren't drinking? His priceless bananas."

I shook my head.

"I could've traded them for the Hope diamond," she said, smiling faintly. "Well . . . I took them to the Nicaraguan embassy . . . I would think just in time, too. They were getting brown."

"The Nicaraguan embassy?" I said.

She nodded and said, "I couldn't think of a better place. Mr Mendoza said they'd be taken care of. That's where bananas used to come from, you know – Nicaragua."

I nodded. "Yeah. I'm wondering how you knew who I am."

"Not who you are," she said. "Who you aren't. When Domino realized that his bananas were on film, film that was being shown, he got a little crazy. He was convinced somebody would see the film and know what they were seeing. And come looking. It was all an accident. We were all so high on snappers and Immelmans that nobody thought about moving the fruit dish. It was –" She smiled and shrugged. "– an orgy . . ."

It all graphed. Londos had his man watch the Calliope to field anybody who might show up with questions about the loop. But when he took me to Londos' house he found his boss dead, which wrapped it all up as far as he was concerned.

Nara went on, "They belonged to a collector of *object's d'fruit* – a wealthy guy whose hobby was collecting art that depicts fruit. He paid him enough to buy a fleet of Ferraris for them. They'd been cryogenically suspended for seventy-five years. Domino just thawed them a day before our photo session. He was going to put on a yellow suit, drop some wig fizz, and eat them while watching *The Gang's All Here*, that old Busby Berkeley flick with the banana ballet in it. The ultimate trip." She gave me a curious smile. "And that's it. Except I still don't know who you are. I'd say you're okay. I'm that perceptive . . . You get that way . . ." She let the implication fade and her smile stayed put, melancholy, highlighting her beauty like the last rose in a tragic garden.

"I'm a dick on a case," I said. "My client is a gourmet."

"A detective." She said the word flatly, and lowered her eyes. "So I guess it's the Big House for me."

I thought about that and chuckled. "Nara, I'm not the law. And insecticide isn't my jurisdiction. I'm a guy trying to make a living. You know?" I crossed the room and stood by the door in the sand, pausing, then came back toward her and reached out and touched her cheek. The blue light in her eyes was bright enough to blind me for a moment. She could be trouble, sure, but then so could anybody. Milkmaids and princesses. We're all people.

"I'd like to see that old Busby Berkeley film," I said. "If you're not doing anything, how'd you like to?"

YOU NEVER KNOW

Carol Anne Davis

Yesterday I bombed The Chamber. Today I'm on the run from my colleagues in the FBI.

FBI – fidelity, bravery, integrity. I had them all plus a family. Had it all until Tom Friel took over my life.

Tom Friel. Such an ordinary sounding name, almost homely. But most serial killers have such unexceptional names. It's what they *do* that makes them stand out – and the manner in which they do it. Taking people's lives the way that the rest of us might take a frozen chicken dinner from a store.

I was the agent who found Tom Friel's fourth stored kill – and by then she looked more like roadkill. I say that it was his fourth homicide but to be honest it's only the fourth one that we in the Bureau knew about. The Seattle police had given us everything they had about the first three deaths and we'd produced what turned out to be a near-perfect profile. Friel couldn't have produced a clearer pattern if he'd been a kaleidoscope. I didn't know his name was Friel, then, of course – and he'd change aliases again and again over the coming decades. Fifteen years of finding his lacerated victims, of finding . . . well, you don't want the details of the pre-mortem mutilation we found.

Mandy, my new wife, wanted to know – or thought she did. "Put the world to rights, Rich?" she'd laugh when I came in from one of my early work-related trips. My hands would go round her waist and her mouth would tilt up to meet mine and I'd lose myself in her sweetness. But I'd know, even as she sighed with satisfaction, that I hadn't put the outside world to rights. And I'd leave our lust-dampened bed despite her protests and return to my study to go over the repulsive evidence again.

Nevertheless, at that time I still saw beauty in the world. I held new potential in my arms when our daughter was born two years after our marriage. Two years of Mandy kissing things better, but suddenly she had Carrie to care for so I nursed my wounds alone. Even then we could have recovered – lots of couples drift apart for a couple of years after doing the baby-makes-three bit. But there were four people in our marriage – and the fourth was the grab-them-quick-then-kill-them-slow Tom Friel.

By then he'd moved across state lines numerous times, but we were still sporadically tracking him. "Can't you spend more time at Carrie's kindergarten? Can't you come to her first ever junior school play?" Mandy's voice would jolt unwelcomingly into my thoughts. I'd look across my study and say "Sure, love," then return to reading my Friel case notes. But Mandy's voice would interject again. "You're not just saying that? You'll make a note in your diary? Remember what happened when you said you'd take her to trick or treat?" Carrie tricked out of her Hallowe'en evening, me treated like a leper for weeks. "I've said I'll be there, haven't I?" Soon it got easier to lock the study door.

There are so many stresses on a professional man. It's a stress that few homemakers make allowance for. Your superiors expect you to work as late as need be whilst your wife wants you to be home at six and seated in the movie theatre by seven. Your employers want you to really *live* a case, to absorb each scarring detail. Then your role as a father demands that you block out such horrors the second you come home.

But I couldn't forget. I couldn't. The gazes of Friel's victims were always upon me. Every day I looked at the wall which held the girls' smiling graduation photographs, stared into their future-filled eyes. Then I'd look down at the photos of their razored remains, the needless carnage, and the contrast made me want to close down all trains of thought. And yet I had to think about it – was morally required to. The Bureau had seen a mix of intellect and instinct in me that made them sure I'd get my man.

I was man overboard in the marriage stakes yet again when Carrie turned six, and I missed her birthday party at the local Diner. I'd given her a Wendy House that morning but Mandy said that it wasn't the same.

"Hey, in a few years she'll be too embarrassed to have her old dad at parties!" I said, trying to lighten the situation.

"You said it," Mandy muttered before turning away. That week she moved into the spare bedroom as she was tired of my waking her up when I finally crept home from work.

And so I moved into a sexfree zone – and Tom Friel kept stealing sex in the most bruising ways possible. Stealing sex and hope and trust and life. He robbed mothers of their daughters, children of their mothers, brothers of their sisters. Abducted women from shopping mall car parks and roadside service stations, from large college campuses and little community parks. He had the gun, the handcuffs, the exact same tools as we did. Only difference was our motivation was lawful and right.

Then at last I heard a few words which told me the world might be put to rights. "Justice at last. Friel's got cancer," one of the other agents said after hanging up the phone.

The sun came out in my brain, but I tried to hold back the glee, substantiate the info. "Terminal, I trust," I said, putting down my monthly report.

"Sounds like it – liver cancer. Don't think there's any way back."

"Who's the source?" I knew that the police couldn't actually have caught Friel: Peter wasn't nearly wired enough for us to have hit the jackpot.

"He checked into a hospital when his belly swelled up like a beach ball, but they became suspicious about his ID." Peter paced before my desk like a tomcat in season, "He did a runner but they'd already done some exploratory surgery. Then the ward sister saw a programme about our Most Wanted and recognized him."

"Did they say how long he's got?"

"Sort of. She says it's not an exact science. They reckon two to six months at most."

Pete seemed to see it as sufficient victory in itself. He and the others headed off to the local wine bar. I lied and said that I'd just tie up a few loose ends and join them there. Instead, I sat alone, thinking what Friel would do during his last few months on the planet. What would I do if given that long to live? Eat the finest foods, buy my favourite books: taste life's existing pleasures only in greater abundance. Which was what Friel would do too – only Friel's idea of pleasure was hearing a terrified woman beg and scream.

Despite the general exhaustion I'd been feeling, I acted fast. Got a map of where the hospital was and plotted how far a man could drive in two days in any direction. Found my radius and sent posters to every likely abduction point in the area: *Have you seen this man?*

A week later the call we'd been waiting for came through. A couple who owned a holiday cabin in the woods had returned for the summer to find it illegally occupied. They'd seen Friel stagger out and take some groceries from his van.

A team from the local police force went in. It included two exceptional marksmen. I knew I wouldn't be there in time to see it but I was hoping against hope that he'd draw his gun and they'd shoot to kill.

But he came quietly. I guess even he knew when he was outnumbered. He was put in a maximum security block then transferred to the hospice within days. Friel chained at the waist to the bed with a 24-hour armed guard outside: it seemed foolproof. Yet he still took us all for fools . . .

I went to the hospice with my tape-recorder and my pad. I didn't take any grapes or tell him that he was looking better. Just said, "Please tell us how you did it in each instance, got these ladies from a public place into your van."

"Need some prime girlie, do you, Agent Marr?" He managed a strangely sweet-scented grin. I noticed with some satisfaction that his face was turning yellow.

"You outwitted us," I added, hoping to feed his skewed but sizable ego, "but now you can help us understand."

"Why should I?"

I looked around the sterile and bookless room. "To show how sharp you are. To help pass the time."

"I can pass the time thinking of the bitches I've had – of the bitches I'm gonna have."

I looked him in the face. His eyewhites were de-energised and sallow. "All you're going to have is a few more weeks on a bedpan and a drip."

Friel returned my gaze in a way that few shifty-eyed killers have ever dared to. Then he moved one lid in a parody of a wink and said "You never know."

I tried various approaches for the next ten minutes till a nurse came along and said that the patient was tiring. Tiring? When I thought of what he'd done to those chained naked women it justified keeping him awake for the rest of his life.

I went home to my own life. Carrie was in the kitchen putting plastic cups into a little hamper. Her T-shirt was close-fitting and almost covered her worryingly tiny shorts.

"Going on a picnic, hon?"

"Mm? Oh, hi, Dad." She hardly looked around. "No, I'm going camping with Josie and Beth."

"And their parents?" I suddenly felt ultra watchful.

"No, just . . ." She turned fully around to face me and I saw that she was wearing lipstick and what looked like blusher on her usually pale cheeks.

"Are you hell!" I don't remember starting to shake her but I was still doing so when Mandy rushed downstairs. She hauled me backwards.

"Rich – what on earth are you doing? Let her go."

"She's only twelve years old," I yelled. "She's a *child*. What the hell are you doing letting her get tarted up like this?"

"I told you ages ago – Lisa was having a fashion show for charity this afternoon. A few of the kids modelled the clothes."

"Oh, right." I said though I couldn't remember her telling me. Carrie started to cry and rushed out of the room. I watched her race across the lawn, across the suburban road. "But she's still not going camping."

"It's just in our garden, Rich. Considering you've got the place like Fort Knox . . ." She looked squarely at me. "With you having the car till late she hardly gets to go anywhere with her friends and she's lonely. So I hit on this – a sort of unusual sleepover with a supper barbecue first."

"Right." I was too stressed over the still-silent Friel to realize that I'd over reacted about Carrie.

"You could set up the outdoor grill, make a lemonade punch."

I ran my hands through my hair and realised that I badly needed a shower. "Next time, I promise. Friel's dying so this is our last chance to study his methods. I'll have to drive all the way back . . ."

"Fine." Her voice had lost the tears and accusation that it had once held when I'd worked unplanned overtime. "Don'll do the honours again instead."

I was speeding along the freeway when the truth hit me. *Don'll do the honours again*, Mandy had said. And Carrie, rushing across the street, had obviously been going to Don's house for a consoling chat. He'd lived opposite us for the past three years, was a landscape gardener. Suddenly I wondered if he was touching more than my lawn. Should I go back and quietly study the body language between him and Mandy? Or give my remaining energy of the day to the fading Friel?

Still undecided, I got out the map and scanned it as I drove. Glanced at the road then down at the blurring blue ink lines. Heard the screech of strange car brakes followed by those of my own then nothing more.

The concussion kept me punchdrunk for a few days then for six weeks my broken bones and disordered organs healed in hospital. Mandy only came to visit once a week.

"Do you want anything?" she asked in the neutral-sounding voice that she'd been using for years.

I grimaced as I sat up on the orthopedic pillows. "Friel – did Pete get him to open up?" I said.

"Don't know. He's dead, by the way." *Like our marriage*, I thought but felt too weak to care.

"Cremated, I hope." I had a sudden vision of him clawing his way through the soil, the ultimate recidivist.

She shrugged coolly. "You'll have to ask your colleagues about that."

So I did. I went back to work and accepted all their welcomes backs, the liquor-laced presents. "Well, do we dance on Friel's grave or flush his ashes down the pan?" I said.

Pete was giving most of his attention to his computer screen. "Who cares? We've just got a phone tap on the Linnet case."

"Fifteen years since we started . . . don't you want to learn how it ends?"

Bob looked over. "There was the usual battle about jurisdiction. We lost the paper trail."

I stared at Bob's face and at the back of Pete's head then picked up the receiver. I had to know.

And three phone-filled hours later I found out. Friel had been perfusion-prepared then cryonically suspended. Deep frozen to be reanimated at a later date by any other name. He'd signed the forms and arranged the finance years before, probably using the money he'd stolen from his victims. He'd emptied all of their ATM accounts.

Accounts of advances in technology were suddenly everywhere. I'd pick up the newspaper only to find reports of animal cloning. The radio announced that scientists could now grow live frogs without heads. And when it came to cryogenics they'd taken a dog's temperature lower and lower until it was virtually frozen then brought it back to life after almost four hours. Friel's brain cells and brain structure had been chilled intact, his entire body injected with cell-preserving medication. In twenty or fifty years he could be brought back.

I kept seeing my child – hell, my *grand*child – in her shorts as *he* would see her. I'd said that his stalking and strangling days were over and he'd said "You never know."

"FBI." The badge gives you a certain standing. Leastways the graveyard shift caretaker at the Cryonics Care Facility didn't argue overmuch when I said he had to leave immediately. "No, don't phone your supervisors – this is a hush hush operation." I was sweating like a marathon runner but he didn't seem aware.

I put the bomb inside the chamber where the dewars or body flasks were kept. I'd done my homework. In ten minutes it would detonate, cracking the dewars and allowing the liquid-nitrogen-frozen bodies to fall out.

I'd driven too far to hear the blast – but I cheered inside when my car clock suggested that all sixty bodies were ruined. And I cheered again when my destructive exploits were confirmed on the national news.

So now I'm on the run, the hunter become the hunted. Always planning my next move, never looking back. It's not the life that I planned, but I've a fair chance of evading capture – and that's more than these poor tortured women ever had.

PLAY NICE

J.E. Ashley

Diamonte Hacindo had stolen my life, and I was about to steal it back.

They let me out of Federal 485, the man-made island south of the Florida Keys, on the Sunday before Christmas, and I was back in Cuba by the twenty-eighth. That's when I found out, when I tried to buy a nicotine chew, that my whole identity'd been erased.

Someone like Hacindo could do that easy. While I was inside, I only had my prison card, which let me have meals and showers and books from the library. When they let me out, they issued me new bank and health cards, which entitled me to $1500 worth of purchases until I got a job, and unlimited visits to doctors when I felt sick. Any credit cards I'd had before I was arrested were reactivated, the balance at a nice $0. They fed me all the clichés when they pushed me out – a clean slate, starting a new life, blah, blah, blah.

That was on the twenty-third, and on the twenty-eighth, it was all gone. I knew Hacindo had done it because he didn't want me coming back. Why should he? He had my wife and kids and condo in the north quarter, what would he want to quit all that for?

It was a balmy Cuban December night when I walked away from the all-night grocery without a nicotine chew. Long straight trunks of palm trees lined the boulevard, the trees leaning permanently to the left, bent by decades of wind from the Caribbean. Only a light breeze now rustled the fronds high overhead, and the scent of ripe oranges floated to me from an abandoned orchard gone wild.

All Hacindo had to do was find someone to wipe the databases. Easy for anyone who knew how. They just wiped out all reference to Xavier Pietro Lang, ref X892093JLI0736, and I was gone. If they made even the smallest mistake, then some poor schmo named Xavier Pietro Lang ref X892093JLI0735 disappeared. But they did it right, and it was me.

The only way I could get to the north quarter now was walking and hitching, so that's what I did. I could tell lots of stories about the people who picked me up – the gringo in the restored 1994 Cadillac who collected New York 90s gang weapons and drug paraphernalia. He had the inside of the Cadillac paneled in pink fur, and he wore a baggy shirt and pants sliding off his hips that he said was authentic gang fashion of the late twentieth century.

Then there was the lady in the run-down fuel-cell car who was afraid of white people. I only told her my name was Xavier, and not my last name, and not that my father had been white and most people had thought he was a nice guy. White people were going to enslave the Cubans, she said, now that we were an American territory. The Americans only came down and built schools because they wanted to fool us into thinking they would let us get educated and move to the States and get jobs. Really all Cubans would do is work in big American hotels and on rum plantations and get paid less and less until they worked for nothing. It was already happening – look at the factories Americans raced down here to open after Castro died. Little kids working fourteen-hour days, and if they tried to quit, the other factories wouldn't hire them.

I didn't really believe her, but what did I know about American-owned factories in Cuba? I left her still ranting.

Then there was the guy who tried to pick me up, and the beautiful white girl that I wished had tried to pick me up. But she just kept talking about her rich husband, and I knew I didn't have a chance. I didn't really want sex anyway. I just wanted to think maybe a beautiful woman would be interested. I know guys who were scared their sex drives would make them crazy if they were penned up in prison, but living like a monk hadn't made my libido hotter. It dried it up until I had the appetite of a ninety-year-old man with a permanent toothache.

The north quarter lay just beyond the abandoned housing development, where the government had finally said it was safe to build again. I walked the ghost streets of the development, my hands in my pockets, my head down. Huge pink stucco houses lined the winding lanes, the houses' graceful lines and elegant arches casting sharp black shadows on the luminous brick pavements. The houses had been built to resemble Cuban architecture of old, with pale tile roofs and arched gates leading to courtyards, but in truth they'd only been built twenty years ago.

As soon as Castro had croaked, the rum companies, American and otherwise, had run back in, landing smack dab on the land they'd been quietly buying up during the last years of Castro's regime. Money had started flowing and investors and developers flocked down, bribing the already weak government into letting them do whatever they wanted. Cuba had been so poor – my dad had known a doctor who hadn't more to offer his patients than one dirty ace bandage – that people didn't much care what they did.

The development was supposed to have been part of the dream of upward mobility, houses that working Cubans could aspire to buy. From what I heard, mostly rich Americans from New York and Florida bought them. Then some enviro-techies found out that they'd been built on top of a Russian nuclear waste dump full of leaking canisters. The homeowners had fled, and sued the development company, which went bust.

No demolition company could be bribed enough to tear the place down, so it stayed empty, except for squatters who lived in the run-down designer kitchens with no electricity, and me, who climbed the fence and cut through, figuring twenty minutes with leaky Russian canisters really wasn't going to make that much difference.

As I walked, I heard whoever it was Baccarat Rum had paid to tail me, but I didn't care. They'd started following me as soon as I entered Cuba, probably trying to find out where I'd hidden the take. They'd only be disappointed. I didn't know where the money was, and I knew in my heart I'd never see a penny of it.

My condo in the north quarter lay about five blocks from the edge of the development. As if nuclear waste respected chain-link fence boundaries, the buildings just across the street from the development were lit and inhabited. Instead of old-fashioned brick, the streets were regular asphalt, full of cracks and potholes. I walked past another all-night store and craved a nicotine chew, but the only way I'd get it was if I stole it.

I walked right up to my building as if I hadn't been away for five years. I automatically put my hand out to unlock the door, then remembered my key had been taken away the day I'd put my hands up for the Baccarat robbery. That job had been in the billions of dollars. I hadn't done it – well, anything more than be in on the plot and provide a diversion for the cops to chase while the others got away.

They told me if I took the fall for it and didn't peep, they'd take care of my family and give me a share when I got out. All I had to do was sit in prison with my mouth shut.

Except Hacindo had decided he didn't want to give my life back. So here I was, locked out of my own house.

A shadow fell across the frosted glass of the door, someone coming toward it from the other side. I stepped back into the shadows. If I could be quick enough, I could catch the door before it latched and be inside.

I fingered the gun in my pocket, a good old-fashioned bullet-pumping kind, not the new electrical pistols that stunned you like a cattle prod, then quietly disconnected your synapses. If I shot Hacindo, I wanted him to bleed a little. I wanted him to hold his hand over the bullet-hole and realize how and why he was dying.

I let go of the pistol. I didn't really want to shoot Hacindo. That would just put me back inside, because I'd be so mad, I wouldn't be able to cover up that I'd done it, or get away or anything. I wanted Hacindo to give me back what was mine, and then he could go to hell.

No, what I planned was more subtle than a gunfight. I took my hand out of the pocket.

A woman emerged from the building and paused to open her purse. A uniformed guard hurried out after her. I didn't recognize him, but streetlight glinted on the metal implant in the back of his neck. Which meant they'd really beefed up the security around here. The implant wired him directly into the building's security system, so he had constant access to what was on all the cameras and recorders. Just standing on the front step, he'd still know every motion in every shadow in every angle around the building. That meant he'd already seen me.

"Get your car, ma'am?" he growled.

She looked up and the light fell full on her face. I stood there, stunned. Five years hadn't changed her. She was still so damned beautiful. Lupita's father had been Korean, her mother, Cuban. The two races had blended into a black-haired, pale-skinned beauty with almond eyes and red lips and a graceful, compact body. I still couldn't believe I was actually married to her.

Except I wouldn't be unless I undid what Hacindo had done. Hacindo lived with her now. That's what my friends had told me, and what her letters had told me between the lines. She'd never visited me once.

Talking to her wasn't part of the plan I'd conceived a couple days ago, but I couldn't help myself. I went up to her and parked myself right in front of her. The guard gave me a hostile stare.

She looked up, and gaped.

I grinned. She'd told me, a long time ago, that she'd fallen in love with my smile.

Her hand lifted, rising as if of its own accord, her fingers landing softly on my cheek. "Xavier?"

"In the flesh."

She blinked, like she was waking up, and let her hand fall. "I heard you were dead."

"Reports of my death have been exaggerated," I misquoted. I couldn't remember the original or who'd said the damned thing in the first place, but it was the only thing that came out of my mouth. She kept on staring at me, and the ninety-year-old man with the toothache up and fled.

I made a motion to the door. "Can I come in?"

She jerked. The guard stepped instantly to her side. "This guy bothering you?"

Lupita shook her head quickly. "No. It's OK. He can come in."

She swung abruptly around and marched back toward the door. She didn't even reach for it. The guard jumped to swing the door open for her, and she glided inside without looking at him. Just like doors opened automatically for her wherever she went. And they probably did.

I gave the guard my charming smile. He snarled. I walked past him and pretended it didn't bug me she hadn't told him I was her husband. That I would be living here again. With her.

In the lift to the top floor, she said nothing. She stared at the faux marble floor, with the minute chip in the corner that no one had fixed, all the way up six stories.

As we spilled onto the top floor hall I asked "Where are the kids? They here?"

She lifted her head, her black hair falling back from her face. She still didn't look at me. "Pepito is at the movies with friends. Sara is spending the night with the Ashfords."

I remembering when the Ashfords' little girl had been in diapers. About the time Sara had been. Now my kid was old enough to spend the night out and I had never seen her without plastic pants.

Lupita got out her key card. "You want me to bring them home?"

"Not yet. They'll be surprised, and they might be scared. We'll break it to them gently."

She kept her face hidden while she slid the card through the slot and unlocked the door. I came up behind her, close enough to breathe the peach scent of her hair. I asked, "Hacindo here?"

"No." She jerked out the word and jerked open the door at the same time. "I don't know where he is."

Music to my ears. We went inside the condo. I shut the door, and Lupita slapped on the lights.

She'd changed everything. All the furniture we'd had was gone. The front room had been divided from the dining room by a half wall, and she'd taken that out. Now, folding room dividers broke up the space. With the soaring walls of the penthouse, the rooms flowed into one another, making the whole square of the first floor airy and light.

"I like it," I said. "Makes the place look bigger."

She didn't answer. She dropped her purse on a black lacquered table and went right to the rum cabinet. She pulled out an amber bottle, poured herself a glass, and drank it. She didn't offer me any.

I climbed the wrought-iron spiral stairs to the bedroom above, which covered the same space as the whole downstairs. She'd changed that, too. Decorated it black and white with red curtains and round red pillows on the bed. I guess it was supposed to look chic, but to me it only looked like gashes of blood on ice. I wondered what she'd done to the kids' bedrooms downstairs and if it gave them nightmares.

"I really wish I could have seen Hacindo," I said.

She stepped off the stairs behind me. "Why?"

"Just to see the look on his face. It was his idea I'd be the one to go down in the first place. Then he'd move on in. Take my wife, my kids, my house, my life. Then when I might come back, he kills me. Technically. I want to tell him, sorry, sweetie. Didn't work."

She watched me with dark eyes, her lips parted just slightly, breathing rapidly from climbing the stairs. "Maybe he thought you'd go to the States."

"I don't like the States. Everyone there has a telecomputer hooked to their face. I shared a cell with a guy from Kansas for six months. He whined all day about missing his shows and his long-neck brews."

I moved around the room, pulling out drawers in the black-lacquer dresser, touching open the white wall that moved to reveal a huge closet.

I found what I was looking for in the top drawer of a little lacquer chest hidden inside the top drawer of a dresser built into the closet wall. He hadn't concealed them very well, so they probably weren't important, but it was a start. Two bank cards and a long plastic credit strip. He'd have his most important cards on him, but I had something to work with.

I took the cards, closed up the hidden drawer, and shut the closet. I sat down on the white bedcover and fished in my pocket for the long, silver tool I'd bought from the prison just after my release. The tool was supposed to give me my fresh start on that clean slate of my new life, cliché, cliché, et cetera. I didn't want a new life. I wanted the one I already had.

I activated the tool by pressing the small green button near the top. I touched the other side of the wand to the electronic band on the credit strip, and read all those numbers and symbols into the tube. I released the button, and turned the tube around so I could look at the square readout on its side. There it was, all of Dee Hacindo's credit information and transactions for this strip. With these numbers I could go on a wild shopping spree until I was caught, but it wasn't New York megastore merchandise I was really after.

I tapped in a few codes using the blue and white finger keys next to the readout screen and clicked the large key to make it all happen. Then I stuck the wand back on the electric strip and depressed the small red button up near the green one. Data out, data in.

"What are you doing?" Lupita still stood by the staircase, holding the black rail behind her. She watched me with her head on one side, too far away for me to read what was in her black stare.

"Erasing his credit strip." I tossed it onto the bed and picked up one of the two bank cards, starting my spiel with the green button again.

"Why?"

"He erases me, I erase him. Petty revenge, but it makes me feel better." I did not tell her the rest of the plan, how when I killed him, no one would notice. He'd already be dead. Just one more unclaimed body with no identification.

"How do you know how to do that?"

"They taught me," I said as I worked. "They'd put me on welding parts for warships at first, but it turned out I wasn't real mechanically inclined, so they taught me programming. Did you know that credit strips manufactured for little rich ladies in Park Avenue are programmed by federal prisoners? I got good at it. They thought I'd make a good living programming after I got out. Who knows? I might still get a good job." I tapped the largest key again.

She just watched me, without alarm, without excitement. Her lack of reaction was beginning to worry me. If she loved me, she'd be glad I was trying to get rid of Hacindo. If she hated me and loved Hacindo, she'd try to stop me somehow. Instead she just stared at me, her teeth working her full lower lip.

"Where is he, by the way?" I asked.

She shrugged. Her sweater moved in a provocative way over her torso. "Dee? I don't know. Out working."

"So where were you going?"

"Going?"

"I saw you leaving the building, on your way somewhere. Were you going to run an errand?"

"Yes. An errand."

"Sure, Lupita. You were going out to meet Hacindo."

"Why do you keep calling him Hacindo? No one else does. Call him Dee."

"I'm not his friend. He just expected me to walk away and leave everything, didn't he? To go to the States and start over again. A clean slate, just like all the crap the psychologists at 485 gave me."

"It's better in the States. You can be whoever you want. I hate Cuba."

I looked up at her. "You do? You never told me that. Then again, you never told me much. You never even came to visit me."

The muscles in her wrists tightened as she firmed her hold on the rail. "I hate prisons. I didn't want to see you through an electric field, not allowed to touch."

"And the kids?" I asked mildly. "Didn't they want to see their dad?"

She shifted. "Sara thinks Dee's her father. Pepito knows he's not, but he doesn't remember you."

That hurt. That hurt bad. It took me like a swift punch in the stomach, and I dropped the last bank card. "And you didn't tell them?"

She shook her head, not looking sorry or ashamed.

I got up and strode to her. I grabbed her shoulders and shook her and called her some names I'd learned from my cellmate from Kansas. She just took it, looking up at me with a blank expression on her perfect half-Latina, half-Asian face.

I finally released her, and she pushed her hair out of her eyes. I went back to the bed and retrieved the bank card and my wand. "Well, they'll just have to be told different. Daddy's home now."

We were both quiet while I finished tapping and erased the second card. I tossed the cards aside and put the wand back into my pocket next to the pistol. "Why don't you call him? Tell him to come on home?" I got up, noting that the dirt I'd picked up from two days' hitchhiking had left a black streak on her pristine white bed. I grinned. "Tell him I'm here. That will make him hurry."

"I already did," she said. "While I was unlocking the door. I sent him the emergency code."

That took me by surprise. I blinked, and my chest got tight. I tried to keep my voice light. "He's sure taking his time."

"He was in Miami."

My heart started beating hard and fast. "Then we can wait for him together. Tell me what you've been up to in the last five years."

"I'm not going to let you kill him."

"Who says I'm going to kill him?"

"I know you, Xavier. You'll do anything to get what you want. Even ditch your wife and kids for five years for a couple million dollars."

"And for you to be taken care of. That's what I wanted."

Her brows shot together, the first expression I'd seen on her. "All I wanted was a husband."

I stared at her. "I went down for you so you could send the kids to the American school, and remodel this damn condo and have the guard open doors for you. I couldn't give you that on what I was getting paid as a getaway driver."

"I didn't care about the effing condo."

"Really? You sure made it into a showplace."

"That was Dee's idea."

"So, he stepped into my shoes and did it better, is that what you're saying?"

She just nodded.

"Well, that's too bad," I said. "I'm going to take his money, and take you, and take my kids – *my* kids, dammit – and go someplace else. You say you hate Cuba, then we'll go to California. We'll find a place where people take off their telecommunicators once in a while and look at the trees."

"I'm not going with you, Xavier."

"You're my wife."

"Not any more. You're erased. You don't exist. I'm technically a widow."

I balled my hands. "For now. I'm erasing that putz you're with and taking his identity for myself. He'll be the dead man."

"He didn't erase your identity," she shouted. "I did."

My mouth dropped open. I stared at her, as stunned as if someone had shot me with an electric pistol.

A black vortex opened before my vision, and I started to fall into it. I was going to die, right? I pulled out my own pistol.

She slammed back onto the staircase, her eyes wide, her knuckles white on the rail as she grabbed it for balance. I wanted to kill her. For that second, I wanted to shoot her and see her blood on the white wall next to the scarlet curtains.

But I didn't. I took my finger off the trigger and swallowed down the impulse. I really didn't want to kill her. I still loved her.

I didn't want my kids crying for their mommy in the night. I didn't want them knowing she'd been gunned down by their father. I could see that far into the future, and couldn't do it.

Lupita gasped for air, clinging to the railing and looking like she was going to throw up.

"I'm sorry," I whispered.

The staircase shook. Footsteps pounded on wrought iron. Lupita stood up suddenly, her face pasty white.

Dee Hacindo's head rose around the intricately carved railing, then his torso. In his hand he had one of those nasty little silver electric pistols that would fry my brain before I even realized what had happened.

I shifted my aim and shot off the top of his head. Blood gashed the wall behind him. His hand tightened on the gun and for one godawful moment, I thought he'd shoot Lupita.

Then his knees buckled, his hands loosened, and the big man fell gently backward, his head striking the edge of an iron stair with a clang like a broken gong. He started to slide downward, then was caught up short when his coat snagged a fancy wrought-iron curlicue.

The jacked-in guard and the guy tailing me ran in. I just kind of stood there with my mouth open. I'd never seen anyone shot by an old-fashioned gun, except in movies, and they didn't get it right by a long shot. Death nowadays was clean and fast, some said painless, but no one dead had ever managed to report if that was true. This death was messy and stank and made me want to puke all over Lupita's black marble floor.

The tail turned out to be the guy who'd propositioned me when I'd hitched a ride from him. He called the cops while the guard jerked the pistol from my numb fingers.

They arrested me, and I went back to prison. Not Federal 485, but Federal 956, off the coast of Guam.

See, I knew I'd get mad and screw it up. They hauled me away from Lupita and my condo and the kids I still hadn't seen. They found out I'd been erased, and reissued my identity. I got a new prison card so I could have showers and meals and books for the next twenty years. I was now Xavier Pietro Lang ref X892093JLIO740.

And that's how I got my life back.

ME AND MY SHADOW

Mike Resnick

It all began when—

No. Strike that.

I don't know when it all began. Probably I never will.

But it began the second time when a truck backfired and I hit the sidewalk with the speed and grace of an athlete, which surprised the hell out of me since I've been a very *un*athletic businessman ever since the day I was born – or born again, depending on your point of view.

I got up, brushed myself off, and looked around. About a dozen pedestrians (though it felt like a hundred) were staring at me, and I could tell what each of them was thinking: is this guy just some kind of nut, or has he maybe been Erased? And if he's been Erased, have I ever met him before? Do I *owe* him?

Of course, even if we *had* met before, they couldn't recognize me now. I know. I've spent almost three years trying to find out who I was before I got Erased 00 but along with what they did to my brain, they gave me a new face and wiped my fingerprints clean. I'm a brand new man: two years, eleven months, and seventeen days old. I am (fanfare and trumpets, please!) *William Jordan*. Not a real catchy name, I'll admit, but it's the only one I've got these days.

I had another name once. They told me not to worry about it, that all my memories had been expunged and that I couldn't dredge up a single fact no matter how hard I tried, not even if I took a little Sodium-P from a hypnotist, and after a few weeks I had to agree with them – which didn't mean that I stopped trying.

Erasures *never* stop trying.

Maybe the doctors and technicians at the Institute are right. Maybe I'm better off not knowing. Maybe the knowledge of what I did would drive the New Improved Me to suicide. But let me tell you: whatever I did, whatever *any* of us did (oh, yes, I speak to other Erasures; we spent a lot of time hanging around the newstape morgues and Missing Persons Bureaus and aren't all that hard to spot), it would be easier to live with the details than the uncertainty.

Example:

"Good day to you, Madam. Lovely weather we're having. Please excuse a delicate inquiry, but did I rape your infant daughter four years ago? Sodomize your sons? Slit your husband open from crotch to chin? Oh, no reason in particular; I was just curious."

Do you begin to see the problem?

Of course, they tell us that we're special, that we're not simply run-of-the-mill criminals and fiends; the jails are full of *them*.

Ah, fun and games at the Institute! It's quite an experience.

We cherish your individuality, they say as they painfully extract all my memories. (Funny: the pain lingers long after the memories are gone.)

Society needs men with your drive and ambition, they smile as they shoot about eighteen zillion volts of electricity through my spasmodically-jerking body.

You had the guts to buck the system, they point out as they shred my face and give me a new one.

With drive like yours there's no telling how far you can go now that we've imprinted a new personality and a new set of ethics onto that magnificent libido, they agree as they try to decide whether to school me as a kennel attendant or perhaps turn me into an encyclopedia salesman. (They compromise and metamorphize me into an accountant.)

You lucky man, you've got a new name and face and memories and five hundred dollars in your pocket and you've still got your drive and ambition, they say as they excruciatingly insert a final memory block.

Now go out and knock 'em dead, they tell me.

Figuratively speaking, they add hastily.

Oh, one last thing, they say as they shove me out the door of the Institute. *We're pretty busy here, William Jordan, so don't come back unless it's an emergency. A BONAFIDE emergency.*

"But where am I to go?" I asked. "What am I to do?"

You'll think of something, they assure me. *After all, you had the brains and guts to buck our social system. Boy, do we wish we were like you! Now beat it; we've got work to do – or do you maybe think you're the only anti-social misanthrope with delusions of grandeur who ever got Erased?*

And the wild part is that they were right: most Erasures make out just fine. Strange as it sounds, we really *do* have more drive than the average man, the guy who just wants to hold off his creditors until he retires and his pension comes through. We'll take more risks, make quicker decisions, fight established trends more vigorously. We're a pretty gritty little group, all right – except that none of us knows why he was Erased.

In fact, I didn't have my first hint until the truck backfired. (See? I'll bet you thought I had forgotten all about it. Not a chance, friend. Erasures don't forget things – at least, not once they've left the Institute. What most Erasures do is spend vast portions of their new lives trying to *remember* things. Futilely.)

Well, my memory may have been wiped clean, but my instincts were still in working order, and what they told me was that I was a little more used to being shot at than the average man on the street. Not much to go on, to be sure, but at least it implied that the nature of my sin leaned more toward physical violence than, say, Wall Street tycoonery with an eye toward sophisticated fraud.

So I went to the main branch of the Public Library, rented a quarter of an hour on the Master Computer, and started popping in the questions.

LIST ALL CRIMINALS STANDING SIX FEET TWO INCHES WHO WERE APPREHENDED AND CON-VICTED IN NEW YORK CITY BETWEEN 2008 A. D. AND 2010 A. D.

***CLASSIFIED.

That wasn't surprising. It had been classified the last fifty times I had asked. But, undaunted (Erasures are rarely daunted), I continued.

LIST ALL MURDERS COMMITTED BY PISTOL IN NEW YORK CITY BETWEEN 2008 A. D. AND 2010 A. D.

The list appeared on the screen, sixty names per second.

STOP.

The computer stopped, while I tried to come up with a more limiting question.

WITHOUT REVEALING THEIR IDENTITIES, TELL ME HOW MANY CRIMINALS WERE CONVICTED OF MULTIPLE PISTOL MURDERS IN NEW YORK CITY BETWEEN 2008 A. D. AND 2010 A. D.

***CLASSIFIED. Then it burped and added: NICE TRY, THOUGH.

THANK YOU. HAS ANY ERASURE EVER DISCOVERED EITHER HIS ORIGINAL IDENTITY OR THE REASON HE WAS ERASED?

NOT YET.

DOES THAT IMPLY IT IS POSSIBLE?

NEGATIVE.

THEN IT IS IMPOSSIBLE?

NEGATIVE.

THEN WHAT THE HELL DID YOU MEAN?

ONLY THAT NO IMPLICATION WAS INTENDED.

I checked my wristwatch. Five minutes left.

I AM AN ERASURE, I began.

I WOULD NEVER HAVE GUESSED.

Just what I needed – sarcasm from a computer. They're making them too damned smart these days.

RECENTLY I REACTED INSTINCTIVELY TO A SOUND VERY SIMILAR TO THAT MADE BY A PISTOL BEING FIRED, ALTHOUGH I HAD NO CONSCIOUS REASON TO DO SO. WOULD THAT IMPLY THAT GUNFIRE PLAYED AN IMPORTANT PART IN MY LIFE PRIOR TO THE TIME I WAS ERASED?

***CLASSIFIED.

CLASSIFIED, NOT NEGATIVE?

THAT IS CORRECT.

I got up with three minutes left on my time.

My next stop was at Doubleday's, on Fifth Avenue. The sign in the window boasted half a million microdots per cubic yard, which meant that they had one hell of a collection of literature crammed into their single ten-by-fifty-foot aisle.

I went straight to the True Crime section, but gave up almost immediately when I saw the sheer volume of True Crime that occurred each and every day in Manhattan.

I called in sick, then hunted up a shooting gallery in the vidphone directory. I made an appointment, rode the Midtown slidewalk up to the front door, rented a pistol, and went downstairs to the soundproofed target range in the basement.

It took me a couple of minutes to figure out how to insert the ammunition clip, an inauspicious beginning. Then I hefted the gun, first in one hand and then the other, hoping that something I did would feel familiar. No luck. I felt awkward and foolish, and the next couple of minutes didn't make me feel any better. I took dead aim at the target hanging some fifty feet away and missed it completely. I held the pistol with both hands and missed it again. I missed it right-handed and left-handed. I missed it with my right eye closed, I missed it with my left eye closed, I missed it with both eyes open.

Well, if the only thing I had going for me was my instinct, I decided to give that instinct a chance. I threw myself to the floor, rolled over twice, and fired off a quick round – and shot out the overhead light.

So much, I told myself, for instinct. Obviously the man I used to be was more at home ducking bullets than aiming them.

I left the gallery, hunted up a couple of Erased friends, and asked them if they'd ever experienced anything like my little flash of *déjà vu*. One of them thought it was hilarious – they may have made him safe, but I have my doubts about whether they made him sane – and the other confessed to certain vague stirrings whenever she heard a John Philip Sousa march, which wasn't exactly the answer I was looking for.

I stopped off for lunch at a local soya joint, spent another fruitless fifteen minutes in the library with my friend the computer, and went back to my brownstone condo to think things out. The whole time I was riding the slidewalk home I kept shadow-boxing and dancing away from imaginary enemies and reaching for a nonexistent revolver under my left arm, but nothing felt natural or even comfortable. After I got off the slidewalk and walked the final half block to my front door, I decided to see if I could pick the lock, but I gave up after about ten minutes, which was probably just as well since a passing cop was giving me the fish-eye.

I poured myself a stiff drink – Erasures' homes differ in locale and decor and many other respects, but you'll find liquor in all of them, as well as cheap memory courses and the Collected Who's Who in Organized Crime tapes – and tried, for the quadrillionth time, to dredge up some image from my past. The carnage of war, the screams and supplications of rape victims, the moans of old men and children lying sliced and bleeding in Central Park, all were grist for my mental mill – and all felt unfamiliar.

So I couldn't shoot and I couldn't pick locks and I couldn't remember. All that was on the one hand.

On the other hand was just one single solitary fact: I had ducked.

But somewhere deep down in my gut (certainly not in my brain) I knew, I *knew*, that the man I used to be had screamed wordlessly in my ear (or somewhere) to hit the deck before I got my/his/our damned fool head blown off.

This was contrary to everything they had told me at the Institute. I wasn't even supposed to be in communication with my former self. Even emergency conferences while bullets flew through the air were supposed to be impossible.

The more I thought about it, the more I decided that this definitely qualified as a bonafide Institute-visiting emergency. So I put on my jacket and left the condo and started off for the Institute. I didn't have any luck flagging down a cab – like frightened herbivores, New York cabbies all hide at the first hint of nightfall – so I started walking over to the East River slidewalk.

I had gone about two blocks when a grungy little man with watery eyes, a pock-marked face, and a very crooked nose jumped out at me from between two buildings, a wicked-looking knife in his hand.

Well, three years without being robbed in Manhattan is like flying 200 missions over Iraq or Paraguay or whoever we're mad at this month. You figure your number is up and you stoically take what's coming to you.

So I handed him my wallet, but there was only a single small bill in it, plus a bunch of credit cards geared to my voiceprint, and he suddenly threw the wallet on the ground and went berserk, ranting and raving about how I had cheated him.

I started backing away, which seemed to enrage him further, because he screamed something obscene and raced toward me with his knife raised above his head, obviously planning to plunge it into my neck or chest.

I remember thinking that of all the places to die, Second Avenue between 35th and 36th Streets was perhaps the very last one I'd have chosen. I remember wanting to yell for help but being too scared to force a sound out. I remember seeing the knife plunge down at me as if in slow motion.

And then, the next thing I knew, he was lying on his back, both his arms broken and his nose spouting blood like a fountain, and I was kneeling down next to him, just about to press the point of the knife into his throat.

I froze, trying to figure out what had happened, while deep inside me a voice – not angry, not bloodthirsty, but soft and seductive – crooned: *Do it, do it.*

"Don't kill me!" moaned the man, writhing beneath my hands. "Please don't kill me!"

You'll enjoy it, murmured the voice. *You'll see.*

I remained motionless for another moment, then dropped the knife and ran north, paying no attention to the traffic signals and not slowing down until I practically barreled into a bus that was blocking the intersection at 42nd Street.

Fool! whispered the voice. *Didn't I save your life? Trust me.*

Or maybe it wasn't the voice at all. Maybe I was just imagining what it would say if it were there.

At any rate, I decided not to go to the Institute at all. I had a feeling that if I walked in looking breathless and filthy and with the mugger's blood all over me, they'd just Erase me again before I could tell them what had happened.

So I went back home, took a quick Dryshower, hunted up Dr Brozgold's number in the book, and called him.

"Yes?" he said after the phone had chimed twice. He looked just as I remembered him: tall and cadaverous, with a black mustache and bushy eyebrows, the kind of man who could put on a freshly-pressed suit and somehow managed to look rumpled.

"I'm an Erasure," I said, coming right to the point. "You worked on me."

"I'm afraid we have a faulty connection here," he said, squinting at his monitor. "I'm not receiving a video transmission."

"That's because I put a towel over my camera," I told him.

"I assume that this is an emergency?" he asked dryly, cocking one of those large, thick, disheveled eyebrows.

"It is," I said.

"Well, Mr X – I hope you don't mind if I call you that – what seems to be the problem?"

"I almost killed a man tonight."

"Really?" he said.

"Doesn't that surprise you?"

"Not yet," he replied, placing his hands before him and juxtaposing his fingers. "I'll need some details first. Were you driving a car or robbing a bank or what?"

"I almost killed this man with my bare hands."

"Well, whoever you are, Mr X, and who ever you *were*," he said, stroking his ragged mustache thoughtfully, "I think I can assure you that *almost* killing people probably wasn't your specialty."

"You don't understand," I said doggedly. "I used karate or kung fu or something like that, and I don't *know* any karate or kung fu."

"Who *is* this?" he demanded suddenly.

"Never mind," I said. "What I want to know is: what the hell is happening to me?"

"Look, I really can't help you without knowing your case history," he said, trying to keep the concern out of his voice and not quite succeeding.

"I don't have a history," I said. "I'm a brand-new man, remember?"

"Then what have you got against telling me who you are?"

"I'm trying to find out who I am!" I said hotly. "A little voice has been telling me that killing people feels good."

"If you'll present yourself at the Institute first thing in the morning, I'll do what I can," he said nervously.

"I know what you can do," I snapped. "You've already done it to me. I want to know if it is being *un*done."

"Absolutely not!" he said emphatically. "Whoever you are, your memory has been totally eradicated. No Erasure has ever developed even partial recall."

"Then how did I mangle a professional mugger who was attacking me with a knife?"

"The human body is capable of many things when placed under extreme duress," he replied in carefully measured tones.

"I'm not talking about jumping ten feet in the air or running fifty yards in four seconds when you're being chased by a wild animal! I'm talking about crippling an armed opponent with three precision blows."

"I really can't answer you on the spur of the moment," he said. "If you'll just come down to the Institute and ask for me, I'll—"

"You'll what?" I demanded. "Erase a little smudge that you overlooked the first time?"

"If you won't give me your name and you won't come to the Institute," he said, "just what is it that you want from me?"

"I want to know what's happening."

"So you said," he commented dryly.

"And I want to know who I was."

"You know we can't tell you that," he replied. Then he paused and smiled ingratiatingly into the camera. "Of course, we might make an exception in this case, given the nature of your problem. But we can't do that unless we know who you are now."

"What assurances have I that you won't Erase me again?"

"You have my word," he said with a fatherly smile.

"You probably gave me your word the last time, too," I said.

"This conversation is becoming tedious, Mr X. I can't help you without knowing who you are. In all likelihood nothing at all out of the ordinary has happened or is happening to you. And if indeed you are developing a new criminal persona, I have no doubt that we'll be meeting before too long anyway. So if you have nothing further to say, I really do have other things to do." He paused, then looked sharply into the camera. "What's *really* disturbing you? If you are actually experiencing some slight degree of recall, why should that distress you? Isn't that what all you Erasures are always hoping for?"

"The voice," I said.

"What about the voice?" he demanded.

"I don't know whether to believe it or not."

"The one that tells you to kill people?"

"It sounds like it *knows*," I said softly. "It sounds convincing."

"Oh, Lord!" he whispered, and hung up the phone.

"Are you still here?" I asked the voice.

There was no answer, but I really didn't expect any. There was no one around to kill.

Suddenly I began to feel constricted, like the walls were closing in on me and the air was getting too thick to breathe, so I put my jacket back on and went out for a walk, keeping well clear of Second Avenue.

I stayed away from the busier streets and stuck to the residential areas – as residential as you can get in Manhattan, anyway – and spent a couple of hours just wandering aimlessly while trying to analyze what was happening to me.

Two trucks backfired, but I didn't duck either time. A huge black man with a knife handle clearly visible above his belt walked by and gave me a long hard look, but I didn't disarm him. A police car cruised by, but I felt no urge to run.

In fact, I had just about convinced myself that Dr. Brozgold wasn't humouring me after all but was absolutely right about my having an overactive imagination, when a cheaply dressed blonde hooker stepped out of a doorway and gave me the eye.

This one, whispered the voice.

I stopped dead in my tracks, terribly confused.

Trust me, it crooned.

The hooker smiled at me and, as if in a trance, I returned the smile and let her lead me upstairs to her sparsely-furnished room.

Patience, cautioned the voice. *Not too fast. Enjoy.*

She locked the door behind us.

What if she screams, I asked myself. We're on the fourth floor. How will I get away?

Relax, said the voice, all smooth and mellow. *First things first. You'll get away, never fear. I'll take care of you.*

The hooker was naked now. She smiled at me again, murmured something unintelligible, then came over and started unbuttoning my shirt.

I smashed a thumb into her left eye, heard bones cracking as I drove a fist into her rib cage, listened to her scream as I brought the edge of my hand down on the back of her neck.

Then there was silence.

It was fabulous! moaned the voice. *Just fabulous!* Suddenly it became solicitous. *Was it good for you, too?*

I waited a moment for my breathing to return to normal, for the flush of excitement to pass, or at least fade a little.

"Yes," I said aloud. "Yes, I enjoyed it."

I told you, said the voice. *They may have changed your memories, but they can't change your soul. You and I have always enjoyed it.*

"Do we just kill women?" I asked, curious.

I don't remember, admitted the voice.

"Then how did you know we had to kill this one?"

I know them when I see them, the voice assured me.

I mulled that over while I went around tidying up the room, rubbing the doorknob with my handkerchief, trying to remember if I had touched anything else.

They took away your fingerprints, said the voice. *Why bother?*

"So they don't know they're looking for an Erasure," I said, giving the room a final examination and then walking out the door.

I went home, put the towel back over the vidphone camera, and called Dr Brozgold.

"You again?" he said when he saw that he wasn't receiving a picture.

"Yes," I answered. "I've thought about what you said, and I'll come in tomorrow morning."

"At the Institute?" he asked, looking tremendously relieved.

"Right. Nine o'clock sharp," I replied. "If you're not there when I arrive, I'm leaving."

"I'll be there," he promised.

I hung up the vidphone, checked out his address in the directory, and walked out the door.

Smart, said the voice admiringly as I walked the twenty-two blocks to Brozgold's apartment. *I would never have thought of this.*

"That's probably why they caught you," I whispered into the cold night air.

It took me just under an hour to reach Brozgold's place. (They turn the slidewalks off at eight o'clock to save money.) Somehow I had known that he'd be in one of the century-old four-floor apartment buildings; any guy who dressed like he did and forgot to comb his hair wasn't about to waste money on a high-rise to impress his friends. I found his apartment number, then walked around to the back, clambered up the rickety wooden stairs to the third floor, checked out a number of windows, and knew I had the right place when I came to a kitchen with about fifty books piled on the floor and four days' worth of dirty dishes in the sink. I couldn't jimmy this lock any better than my own, but the door was one of the old wooden types and I finally threw a shoulder against it and broke it.

"Who's there?" demanded Brozgold, walking out of the bedroom in his pajamas and looking even more unkempt than usual.

"Hi," I said with a cheerful smile, shoving him back into the bedroom. "Remember me?"

I closed the door behind us, just to be on the safe side. The room smelled of stale tobacco, or maybe it was just the stale clothing in his closet. His furniture – a dresser, a writing desk, a double bed, a couple of nightstands, and a chair – had cost him a bundle, but they hadn't seen a coat of polish, or even a dust rag, since the day they'd been delivered.

He was staring at me, eyes wide, a dawning look of recognition on his face. "You're ... ah ... Jurgins? Johnson? I can't remember the name on the spur of the moment. You're the one who's been calling me?"

"I am," I said, pushing him onto the chair. "And it's William Jordan."

"Jordan. Right." He looked flustered, like he wasn't fully awake yet. "What are you doing here, Jordan? I thought we were meeting at the Institute tomorrow morning."

"I know you did," I answered him. "I wanted to make sure that all your security was down there so we could have a private little chat right here and now."

He stood up. "Now you listen to me, Jordan—"

I pushed him back down, hard.

"That's what I came here for," I said. "And the first thing I want to listen to is the reason I was Erased."

"You were a criminal," he said coldly. "You know that."

"What crime did I commit?"

"You know I can't tell you that!" he yelled, trying to hide his mounting fear beneath a blustering exterior. "Now get the hell out of here and—"

"How many people did I kill with my bare hands?" I asked pleasantly.

"What?"

"I just killed a woman," I said. "I enjoyed it. I mean, I *really* enjoyed it. Right at this moment I'm trying to decide how much I'd like killing a doctor."

"You're crazy!" he snapped.

"As a matter of fact," I replied, "I have a certificate stating that the State of New York considers me to be absolutely sane." I grinned. "Guess who signed it?"

"Go away!"

"As soon as you tell me what I want to know."

"I can't!"

"Are you still with me?" I whispered under my breath.

Right here, said the voice.

"Take over at the proper moment or I'm going to break my hand," I told it.

Ready when you are, it replied.

"Perhaps you need a demonstration of my skill and my sincerity," I said to Brozgold as I walked over to the dresser.

I lifted my hand high above my head and started bringing it down toward the dull wooden surface. I winced just before impact, but it didn't hurt a bit – and an instant later the top of the dresser and the first two drawers were split in half.

"Thanks," I whispered.

Any time.

"That could just as easily have been *you,*" I said, turning back to Brozgold. "In fact, if you don't tell me what I want to know, it *will* be you."

"You'll kill me anyway," he said, shaking with fear but blindly determined to stick to his guns.

"I'll kill you if you *don't* tell me," I said. "If you do, I promise I won't harm you."

"What's the promise of a killer worth?" he said bitterly.

"You're the one who gave me my sense of honour," I pointed out. "Do you go around manufacturing liars?"

"No. But I don't go around manufacturing killers, either."

"I just want to know who I was and what I did," I repeated patiently. "I don't want to do it again. I just need some facts to fight off this damned voice."

Well, I like that, said the voice.

"I can't," repeated Brozgold.

"Sure you can," I said, taking a couple of steps toward him.

"It won't do you any good," he said, on the verge of tears now. "Everything about you, every last detail, has been classified. You won't be able to follow up on anything I know."

"Maybe we won't have to," I said. "How many people did I kill?"

"I can't."

I reached over to the little writing desk and brought my hand down. It split in two.

"How many?" I repeated, glaring at him.

"Seventeen!" he screamed, tears running down his face.

"Seventeen?" I repeated wonderingly.

"That we know about."

Even I was surprised that I had managed to amass so many. "Who were they? Men? Women?" He didn't answer, so I took another step toward him and added menacingly, "Doctors?"

"No!" he said quickly. "Not doctors. Never doctors!"

"Then who?"

"Whoever they paid you to kill!" he finally blurted out.

"I was a hit man?"

He nodded.

"I must really have enjoyed my work to kill seventeen people," I said thoughtfully. "How did they finally catch me?"

"Your girlfriend turned state's evidence. She knew you had been hired to kill Carlo Castinerra—"

"The politician?"

"Yes. So the police staked him out and nailed you. You blundered right into their trap."

I shook my head sadly. "That's what I get for trusting people. And *this*," I added, bringing the edge of my hand down on his neck and producing a snapping noise, "is what *you* get."

That was unethical, said my little voice. *You promised not to hurt him if he told you what you wanted to know.*

"We trusted someone once, and look where it got us," I replied, going around and wiping various surfaces. "What about that hooker? Had someone put out a contract on her?"

I don't remember, said the voice. *It just felt right.*

"And how did killing Dr. Brozgold feel?" I asked.

Good, said the voice after some consideration. *It felt good. I enjoyed it.*

"So did I," I admitted.

Then are we going back in business?

"No," I said. "If there's one thing I've learned as an accountant, it's that everything has a pattern to it. Fall into the same old pattern and we'll wind up right back at the Institute."

Then what will we do? asked the voice.

"Oh, we'll go right on killing people," I assured it. "I must confess that it's addictive. But I make more than enough money to take care of my needs, and I don't suppose *you* have any use for money."

None, said the voice.

"So now we'll just kill whoever we want in any way that pleases us," I said. "They've made William Jordan a stickler for details, so I think we'll be a lot harder to catch when we were when I was you." I busied myself wiping the dresser as best I could.

"Of course," I added, crossing over to the desk and going to work on it," I suppose we could start with Carlo Castinerra, just for old times' sake."

I'd like that, said the voice, trying to control its excitement.

"I thought you might," I said dryly. "And it will tidy up the last loose end from our previous life. I hate loose ends. I suppose it's my accountant's mind."

So that's where things stand now.

I've spent the last two days in the office, catching up on my work. At nights I've cased Castinerra's house. I know where all the doors and windows are, how to get to the slidewalk from the kitchen entrance, what time the servants leave, what time the lights go out.

So this Friday, at 5 p.m. on the dot, I'm going to leave the office and go out to dinner at a posh French restaurant that guarantees there are no soya products anywhere on the premises. After that I'll slide over to what's left of the theatre district and catch the old Sondheim classic they've unearthed after all these years. Then it's off to an elegant nearby bar for a cocktail or two.

And then, with a little help from my shadow, I'll pay a long-overdue call on the estimable Mr. Castinerra.

Only this time, I'll do it right.

Erasures are, by and large, pretty lonely people. I can't tell you how nice it is to finally have a hobby that I can share with a friend.

GONE BUSH

Chris Amies

Peter Bort, head of the Riverside Planning Department, was waking up slowly and painfully. He had kept the window shut after his two nightly bottles of beer in order to provide himself with an experimental headache. Bort thought himself still young enough to carry out experiments like that, and old enough to predict the result. At forty-six years old he didn't have time for a midlife crisis, but kept on living the way he had in his twenties. He weighed a bit more than he had then, but that was inevitable.

He went into the living room, faced his lifesize Elvis 'bot and gave it a haymaker to the jaw. "Oh, that hurt, man . . . that really hurt," the Elvis crooned as Peter strolled on.

He parted the curtains and gazed out. To look straight down was to gaze into a leafy canopy, but beyond the trees the Victorian terraces of Addison Park stretched in redbrick profusion, and beyond them the towers of the housing estates at White City and Loftus Road; Bort knew them all and they were all within his domain.

The phone rang.

"Hi, Dad," said a woman's voice, "have you read your email yet?"

The caller was Laura Bort, Peter's daughter and the enforcement arm of the Planning Department. She was a slim twenty-something who dressed in the styles of a month or so to come; either she was psychic or she had more influence on the local youth than she believed.

"Gimme a chance," said Peter. "I only just got up. Not even I'm that desperate."

"Just thought you'd like to know," she said. "Pereira's been up to his tricks again. I was up at the Green last night and he's lined us out."

"Done what?"

"Rubbed out our signs. Put the old ones back up. Like Wittgenstein used to say, the man who deals with pigs must be careful he does not become a pig himself. I called you last night but I figured you were out. And I know it's Pereira because he's sent round an email crowing about it."

Peter felt three distinct waves of designer hangover pulse through his head and said,

"I need to see this. Can I call for you at nine?"

"Sure. I'll have the kettle on." Peter Bort didn't have a car. Cars, in that area, tended to lose their wheels if left unattended for more than a few minutes, a situation Bort saw no value in changing.

"It cuts down traffic," he would say, "and it maintains the area's reputation."

The curving tree-lined streets of Addison Park had the screaming hostile beauty of a hot morning. The forecast was 29 or 30 degrees and the kind of day when Peter wanted to stand arms spread under the trees and cry *I live here! I live here!* in wonder and joy. He could ignore the burntout shops and the broken surveillance cameras as mere obstacles to his rebuilding of the area.

Laura was waiting on the steps of her terrace, dressed in a denim vest and miniskirt and black stockings, blinking against shards of reflected sunlight. She met Peter with a kiss and led him indoors where the kettle was indeed steaming with the promise of tea.

The Bort family had encountered Pereira before. Fernando Pereira was an inveterate letter-writer, sending one to the papers almost every day. His Net traffic surpassed that of many small independent states and his website was a trove of deeply thought-out opinion, or a collection of bigoted rants, depending on the reader's beliefs. Bort normally respected the man's right to his rather quaint views, saying, "Opinions are like arseholes – everyone's got one and they often stink," but as Pereira wound up to a pitch of febrile lunacy, he reached a line that shouldn't have been crossed. One of Pereira's whining letters about the accommodation that Riverside Council generously provided for him contained the line "England is about poverty". Incensed, Bort went past the kebab shop where Pereira worked, waited on the corner wearing a fedora and a Richard Nixon mask, and when the shift ended followed Pereira down the road.

Bort caught up with him at the corner of Loftus Road and South Africa Way – a streetname Pereira had previously complained about, calling it "imperialist". Bort tapped him on the shoulder and as he turned round gave Pereira a punch similar to the ones he gave his Elvis. Pereira fell, keening weirdly, the look in his eyes suggesting he had some idea what was going to happen to him. Peter Bort knelt over him and delivered several savage punches to Pereira's face and head. When Pereira finally lost consciousness, Bort stood up and walked off; brushing imaginary dust from his lapels.

Pereira went even stranger after this blatant act of self-defence, as if the beating had dislodged something in his head. He began demanding that the Council change not only street names, but also that it reinstate roadsigns in miles instead of kilometres and change the name of the whole district back from the smart and urban "Addison Park" to its earlier handle of "Shepherds Bush", which Bort's Planning Department had eradicated over the last five years.

"It's as though," Bort said, sitting facing his daughter in her deep minimalist living room – black carpet, white walls, two armchairs and a stereo, nothing more – and drinking tea from a Queens Park Rangers mug, "his mind has got mixed up with a member of the Addison Historical Society. 'Shepherds Bush' sounds like a village, and it isn't one. Nostalgia is a wedge between people and their culture. *He* knows that. As to miles and kilometres, why should we change back? Does he ask his own country to go back to leagues and quintals? I doubt it."

Fernando Pereira finished playing chess against himself for the third time that day. If he played against himself, he reasoned, at least he would always win. Aware that much of the population of Riverside thought Fernando Pereira played *with* himself, he persevered, bloody but unbowed, in his campaign. This terrible place, he thought, staring out of the window at a bleak vista of flatblocks between which a plume of smoke rose from burning mattresses. He didn't know why the inhabitants burned mattresses, but suspected it was because they were infested with something. It didn't surprise him; his own flat was host to black beetles and a very hairy-looking spider. The Council had sent round men allegedly to fumigate the flat, but Fernando, thinking they were planning to fumigate *him*, sent them away with several fleas in their ear. They'd given up trying by now. He had no better a time with the police, after he'd told them he'd been beaten up by Richard Nixon in a fedora. They'd treated him as though he was the criminal.

Cole's Law says "Everything pushes someone's buttons", and while Sergeant Ted Hanratty, who had interviewed Pereira when he walked bruised and still bleeding to the police station, was a diligent cop and a credit to the force, he didn't like references to Richard Nixon.

But today Pereira was celebrating a great victory. He had bloodied the nose of the loathed Council. The local people would wake up with the name "Addison Park" deleted, and all the old signs back in their place, from Shepherds Bush Road to Shepherds Bush Market to Shepherds Bush Green. Then he emailed the council and the newspapers to tell them what he'd done.

He had crossed the "Addison Park" bits out. And anyone who'd read a few gangland stories knew what that meant.

"It's called, 'lining out'," Laura said, gazing unhappily at the sign for the Addison Park Shopping Centre, whose first two words had been determinedly crossed out and replaced by a sign saying SHEPHERDS BUSH. An old tin sign, it was, that adorned the entrance to a pedestrian walkway until one night it vanished in a plague of sign thefts. Peter had often wondered why anyone would half-inch a streetsign. Now he could see why. Beyond the Shopping Centre the Green stretched away, a triangle of grass dotted with trees and the remains of a half-completed cinema. A police helicopter growled by overhead and Laura instinctively looked down.

"And what does it mean?" he asked.

"It means war," Laura said. "It means you, the owner of the name, will be crossed out yourself."

"Rubbed out," Peter said. The gangster movies he'd seen were more 1930s Chicago than South Central L.A. "On the ice. In the bag.

"I suggest we take the war to the enemy."

"Right," said Laura.

"But I have to go to work," Peter said. "Could you talk to someone?"

"I certainly could," said Laura.

Peter wasn't used to this kind of thing. The Nixon mask caper was a one-off, a lucky break except for its victim, who went around swearing that his attacker had meant to kill him, thus adding slander to his other misdemeanours.

Laura went from the Green straight to a bike shop on Goldhawk Road, just past the entrance to the market. This was Pigeon Crew territory; the home of a gang who'd started out as a movement to reclaim the streets for the local population, and found to their amazement that they enjoyed putting the arm on people. Their tags marked the market gates, a metre high so you couldn't miss them. The Pigeons never got lined out. Their mortal enemies, the Natty Boy Crew or NBC, held the area further south, towards the Broadway and Riverside.

Laura strolled into the bikeshop past racks of lights and panniers, through fluorescent bulletproof jackets and personal anti-theft sprays.

The owner looked up from trueing the wheel on a sports bike, and grinned at her. He was a big fellow but far more at home with a trackpump than a weapon. Frank Brady left the rough stuff to the rest of his family, a loose affiliation of Irish, English and Afro-Caribs under the nominal lead of Ken "The Lash" Brady, who was currently doing ten to fifteen for armed robbery with an armoured car.

"Yo, Laura," said Frank. "What's up?"

"Hi, Frank. I need some help."

"Another puncture? You should watch for that broken glass."

"Your brother's sort of help," Laura said. Frank's mouth went open another notch.

"Sure," he said. "Jack's upstairs. Go through."

"Cheers," said Laura.

There was a story going around that members of the Pigeons had been drinking in the Fox and Hounds on Blythe Road when an American journalist had walked up to them and told them he was with the National Broadcasting Corporation, or as he said, the NBC. When he said this, one of the Pigeons pulled out a gun and shot him dead.

That story had reached urban myth status but Laura Bort knew for a fact that it was true, because the gunman was Jack Brady.

Jack Brady opened the door dressed in his leather dressing gown, looking like OJ Simpson's seedier brother.

"Baby Laura!" he said, voice all gravel and West London, and took hold of the woman around the waist. For a moment, with her arms around his neck, Laura and Jack looked like a poster for *South Pacific* only without the palm trees.

Once they were in his room, though, this plainly wasn't a romantic encounter. Laura and Jack sat knee to knee and talked.

"I've seen those signs," Jack said. "Thought it was a bit weird."

"It *is* lining out, Jack," Laura said. "It's an insult. You know that."

"Sure," Jack said, taking Laura's hands. "But things could get nasty, babe."

"I expect them to," Laura said. "Or there'd be no point."

Jack grinned at her, that devilish expression she'd often seen and which always had the same effect on her.

"Okay," he said. "I'll see to it."

Then they were all over each other.

Ask no questions and you'll get no lies; I saw a policeman doing up his flies. Sergeant Hanratty, taken short while on observation, zipped up and resumed his vigil outside the flatblock where Pereira lived. He was sure the man was up to no good. So far Pereira hadn't stirred, but Hanratty knew where he worked and what time he started. Hanratty had read Pereira's garbled statement and listened to the witnesses, many of whom spoke florid nonsense which defied even the stoutest interpreter. But to Hanratty it was, as he liked to say, bleedin' obvious why anyone would kick Pereira's head in, and after the night's little artistic installation which he admitted freely, a repeat performance was very likely.

Ted Hanratty was a distant relative of James Hanratty, the last man hanged for murder in England, and was perplexed that there was a lot of recrimination about the hanging of Ruth Ellis (who cheerfully admitted murder and was all but found with a smoking gun in her hand at the scene) and none about his ancestor (who didn't know the victim, had no motive for murder, and had a strong alibi on that fateful night). It was hardly surprising, given that sense of injustice, that Ted Hanratty joined the police straight out of school. Nor was it any surprise that the gradual rehabilitation of Richard Nixon in the early 21st century, which led to the carving of the former President's head on Half Dome along with those of Reagan and the two Bushes, led Ted Hanratty to an increasing perplexity and transcendental rage at yet one more crook being let off. At school the very mention of the word "Nixon" could send him into an apoplexy only assuaged by hours of detention.

Hanratty was following Pereira not only because he wanted to see where the case led him but also because he needed to nail this whole Nixon bit in the arse. To this end he was travelling in disguise; an unmarked police car and a fedora and a mask.

"By imitating the felon," he said, "I sit behind his eyes and become him."

Then there was a movement in the doorway, and a frightened-looking, unshaven man in white shirt and jeans slid out. Hanratty followed, the unmarked car purring out of the estate.

Pereira was behind the counter of the kebab shop. In a slack moment, he was sitting reading *A Bola*, and ignoring the smell of roasting meat from the spit and the generally grease-laden atmosphere of the shop. The kebab shop was small and narrow, occupying the middle bay of a very nondescript row of shops on the north side of the Goldhawk Road, between a newsagent and a laundrette. He'd persuaded the newsagent's owner to sell the Portuguese sports paper, among the sex videos, lurid sweets and cigarettes, in the hope that it might encourage others of his community to come out of the woodwork, but so far Pereira was a man hoeing a lonely row. It never occurred to him that the other members of his tribe might be deliberately shunning him; his paranoia was macroscopic, not personal.

The door swung open and a young woman came in. Pereira looked at her appreciatively and gave her the best sunny smile he could still manage. She strolled up to the counter and leant on it, so her denim vest parted agreeably at the top. Pereira tried to keep himself from looking too much. The woman said,

"Make me one with everything."

"Pardon me?" said Pereira, trying to maintain the sunny disposition. Normally people came in and said "kebab" or "burger".

"It's a joke, see," said the customer; "but there's no point in explaining jokes. What's your name?" She had hooked a finger into the opening of her vest and was running it down the vee, across her lightly-tanned skin.

"Fernando," said Pereira. "What's the joke?"

The woman smiled.

"A Buddhist goes into a kebab shop," she said, "and says, 'make me one with everything'. I expect you still don't get it, Mr Pereira." She glanced towards the entrance to the shop. "Oh, look, you have another customer. I'll talk to you later." She winked and moved away from the counter.

Pereira looked away from the girl towards the entrance. The door slammed open and in walked a chunky man in a boiler suit. As Pereira focussed on his face he felt a huge weight of despair land upon him. It was his nemesis; the man in the Nixon mask. Then his despair was joined by anger. Not content with beating him up, the Nixon-creature had come to gloat! He dared set foot inside this miserable kebab shop, to see how Fernando Pereira, honours graduate of the University of Oporto, was forced to spend his miserable days and earn too little money to support himself. Nixon's bulbous, impassive face stared at Pereira. Pereira stared back and said,

"Good morning. How can I help you?"

The Nixon reached into the pocket of its overalls and brought out a lumpy black object clearly designed for putting holes in people. He pointed it at Pereira, who immediately reached for the knife he used to chop onions.

There was a bang and a howl and Pereira's right shoulder was a ruin of smashed bone and cauterized flesh.

"No funny stuff," said the Nixon.

"What do you want?" Pereira asked. "There's no money in the till." He glanced at the girl, who was sitting at a table, apparently watching what was happening as though it were a piece of street theatre, and might applaud afterwards.

"Money is a sign of poverty," said the Nixon. "And I'm sure you know all about that." With that he shot the turning meat on its spit. The spit broke and a rain of meat and fat hit the floor. The Nixon turned back to Pereira and stared at him through the holes in the mask.

"You still have one good arm," the Nixon said. "Do you think you could write using that? Because it is your writing that is giving us grief. That and crossing out our signs."

"Er . . . no," said Pereira.

"Good," said the Nixon. "I'm not a murderer, you know. But either you cease and desist or I will kill you."

The Nixon pulled the trigger again and ruined Pereira's other arm.

Pereira stared at him, eyes wide with horror.

"English liar," he said.

No expression crossed the face of the Nixon mask, but Pereira felt that rage must have consumed the face underneath. The Nixon reached for Pereira's throat and pulled him by the neck onto the counter, then seized him under the armpits and dragged him onto the floor. The pain in his ruined shoulders was excruciating.

The Nixon pushed Pereira to his knees, and took hold of the gun once more. Aiming it downwards, he sent a blast into Pereira's groin. Pereira screamed and sobbed, clutching himself. His entire world consisted of pain.

"No more wanking for you," said the Nixon.

Then the door slammed open. Pereira looked up through his tears. To his astonishment, a second Nixon entered the shop, a man in a white shirt and black trousers, with a bag over his shoulder. Behind him, another chunky fellow; also wearing a Nixon mask.

"What is this?" said the Nixon with the gun. "I said no backup."

"Dad?" said Laura hesitantly. She looked at the Nixons and then up at the Nixon standing over the ruined Pereira.

"Go," she said. "You've done what you needed to." But Jack Brady was turning with the gun and levelling it at the newcomers.

"Who the hell are you?" he said.

"I could ask you the same question," said the Nixon in the clean white shirt, "but as it is, you're under arrest, for assault on

Fernando Pereira, on 23rd June, and assault with a deadly weapon on the same person, today. You do not have to say anything, but anything you do say may be used in evidence in a court of law." He held up a warrant card.

Jack Brady laughed.

"*You*," he said, "are arresting *me*? Permit me to point out, *officer*, that I have a gun and you do not."

"'S what you think," said the Nixon-cop, as Jack Brady dived out of the way and a shot took a chunk out of the wall behind him. Hanratty's shoulderbag whined and reloaded. Brady shot him in the heart.

"Psychologically," said Jack Brady, "the guns you use will define you. You, copper, are in the bag."

As Hanratty fell over, the third Nixon stepped aside to avoid the falling body, and Brady caught up with him. He reached out and tore off the Nixon mask, to reveal Peter Bort's face.

"You," he said, jabbing a finger into Bort's chest, "owe me."

"I know," said Bort.

"I killed that cop because of you. Now don't think the cops can touch me for it right now, but if they ever do get to me, you will pay."

"I know," said Bort again. "Don't tell me you didn't enjoy it."

"Oh I did," said Brady. "And I'll enjoy this too."

He started pummelling Bort, knocking him back against the closed door, a fist in the stomach and then one in the chin. Jack carried on, Bort going to the ground, defenceless, until he felt a sharp pain in the back of the neck.

"Don't," said Laura, "even think about it." Brady turned round and found Laura holding the knife on him.

"You touch my family," she said, "and I get you. Got me?"

Brady looked down at her.

"Okay," he said softly. "I'm sorry." Then he looked up and pushed Laura away. She yelped in outrage as Pereira, crabbed and hurting, ran full-tilt at Brady, a steel ashtray in his hand.

Brady shot him. Pereira went down like a fighting bull, skidding along the floor until he came to rest with his head touching Brady's boots. Jack Brady stood in a pile of bodies; turned his back on Pereira and Hanratty, and helped the dazed Peter Bort to his feet.

★   ★   ★

Out in the streets, the murder rate had gone up during the last few hours, and a police car was burning by the roadside.

"You know," said Jack Brady, as he walked towards Addison Green, Laura next to him and Peter on Laura's other side. "I've always taken a keen interest in urban redevelopment. And I do have a few ideas of my own. Nothin' huge, just level a few streets around Broadway, close off the borders between us and the NBC . . . maybe even a statue of myself on the Green. I'm sure they'll get permission, won't they, Mr Planning Department? Otherwise . . ." he added cheerfully, "well, I know where you are, get me?" Peter Bort winced as he opened his swollen mouth. "Sure," he said.

DIGITAL HONEY

Liz Evans

It was the coffee pot that first told him he was dead.

The aroma of freshly ground Kenyan beans that usually filled the apartment shortly after the alarm call was missing. So was the alarm call.

"Time?"

There was no response.

The only memento he had of his grandfather, an antique 12-hour watch, was in the bedside drawer. Rolling across, his stomach sank into the slight hollow that Scout's body had left. He almost thought he could feel her warmth although she'd left hours ago. At least he assumed she had. Maybe he'd only been asleep for minutes?

Fumbling in the darkness for the watch, he called: "Lexie? Where are you? What's the damn time?"

Something tumbled from the back of the drawer. His fingers traced the outline of a lip staining kit. Bloody Kristine again! Every damn time she stayed over, she'd tried to leave something behind. For months he'd had to root cosmetics out of the bathroom and clothes out of the closets. She was like a cat marking her territory. Well, no thanks, darling. It was strictly fun when he chose. No commitments. And if he ever did go for joint habitation it sure as hell wasn't going to be with Krissy. She must be pushing thirty-five. A guy like him needed – no *deserved* – a sharper model in his life. Someone like the delectable Scout.

His thumb found the illumination button on the watch's casing. He'd woken at seven as usual. Perhaps he'd told Lexie he wanted a late call? His recall of yesterday evening was a bit hazy.

"Lexie. Hey baby, you there? Let's have some light here."

The real Lexie remained silent, but his sub-conscious supplied her soft concerned response. "*I'm so sorry John. Have I failed to anticipate something you want?*"

He'd read every technical brochure and survey he could find on Inter-Active Servos, before deciding on the Fidelis Model XB101 (*Bio-Technology for the Twenty-second century*). He'd called her Lexie after his first girlfriend.

"She was a peach, to look at. But what a let-down when you took a bite. Know what I mean?"

"No, sir. But if you explain, it will be my pleasure to remember," Lexie had croaked in the toneless default response that was shipped with all new models.

His initial disappointment, that he'd paid so much for something so mundane, had turned to pleasure over the next few months. Lexie had been designed to learn by experience, and she had. Softening and deepening her tones and adding a slight southern Mediterranean accent, as she'd analysed his taste in telecasts and responded to changes in his pupil dilation, breathing patterns and pheromone emissions.

Six months after agreeing the on-line purchase contract he was coming home to music playing to suit his mood and the drinks container bringing to optimum temperature something to complement the meal Lexie had ordered the food-prep to defrost and heat. It was like having a wife without the hassle of having to keep telling her you loved her or remembering her sodding birthday. And he didn't even have to be inventive if he fancied playing away.

If he wanted to bring someone back, it was a matter of seconds to dial up on the wrist phone and tell Lexie to expect company. By the time he and the lucky girl arrived, the lighting was muted and the music romantic. The pictures on the walls had changed from the abstracts he preferred to old masters that contained a hint of stylish eroticism like Manet's *Olympia*. The wine and food had been adjusted to suit two. And the diffusers were charged.

His normal routine was to excuse himself after dinner and slip into the bathroom for a few minutes. The combination of mood-changing aromatherapy chemoils diffusing through the living room's air flow was so subtle that they barely registered on the nose. But they could turn a shy tease into a sexual wild-cat and an aggressive executive into a compliant love slave. It wasn't strictly legal. You were supposed to warn anyone who might be exposed to the mind changers, but what the hell – they'd never complained. And most of them could take the hint when he didn't return their calls. Except bloody Kristine and her constantly boomeranging possessions.

"Hey, Lexie. Let's see some action here. Lights!"

He balled his fist against the voice interface panel. It was a futile gesture really. The unit that controlled Lexie was in an underground database on the other side of the world. She'd been state-of-the-art five years ago, but in bio-cybernetic terms that was geriatric. Lately he'd begun to find her choices of food and entertainment a bit predictable. Maybe it *was* time to trade up.

"Turn the bloody lights on, will you? Or if you can't manage that, how about opening the blinds?"

He padded across the darkened room to struggle with the unfamiliar manual control of the window blinds. The slats turned, striping the room behind him in bars of dawn-light and shadow. He looked at the rumpled remains of the bed and grinned at the memory of last night.

She'd been perched on a bar stool when he arrived. He'd recognized the tease instantly. Why sit up there rather than in a booth unless she wanted to give everyone a good look at her legs? He was glad he'd insisted they discuss the deal face-to-face.

"Scout? John Mackintosh."

"Hello, John. It was good of you to come." Her voice had been another delight. A throaty come-on fringed with the hint of some accent he couldn't quite place. "What can I get you?"

Biting back the temptation to say "hot and excited", he said; "No, please, let me. What will it be?"

She'd ordered strawberry daiquiri. "Do you have real strawberries?"

The bartender shook his head. "Sorry ma-am, synthetic pulp only."

"That will have to do."

"And I'll take a lite beer." John stood beside her, his arm leaning on the counter to further corral her in.

She turned and gave him a level look from beneath long black lashes. There was a hint of a challenge in her gaze. He felt his interest growing. The tumble of long blonde curls should have gone with blue eyes and delicately fair features. Instead her irises were dark brown and her brows were black and as firmly defined as a brushful of portrait painter's oils. The effect was disconcerting and appealing at the same time.

"Nice hotel," he said. "Are you staying here?"

"No. I just like these bars with real servers."

They watched the barman putting on a performance as he mixed her daiquiri. A lot of the cheaper places had an alco-servo, but John agreed with her. Sticking your glass under a spout and talking into a voice activated dispenser just didn't do it for him.

"Me too. Gives it atmosphere. There's a bar in Chicago even gets customers to pay in real cash," he said keen to indicate he was a global traveller (even if most of it was holo-trips via computer programs).

"I didn't know there was any. Apart from that in the museums."

"I guess he has it made up special."

"I guess so," she agreed. The drinks came and she suggested moving to a booth.

He'd watch her slip off the stool and clip across the room on strappy high heels. He liked the shoes and the way she'd chosen to wear a feminine pink dress. Appreciating the view, he hardly noticed the barman swipe the debit wand over his neck and deduct the drinks bill from his account.

"I hope you didn't mind my asking for this meeting," he'd said, sliding into the cubicle after her. "Only we're talking a major layout here."

"That's because what we're supplying is the ultimate dream in Life Control Systems, John. May I call you John?"

"I'd like you to – Scout. That's a nickname, right?"

"For Jean Louise. My mother was a big fan of *To Kill A Mocking Bird*. I prefer Scout."

He had no idea what she was talking about, some old movie maybe, but he nodded seriously as if he got it. "That's great. Special. You're pretty special yourself, if you don't mind my saying so."

He put his hand over hers. She slid it out gracefully. "And what I'm selling is very special too, John. Did you receive the brochures?"

He'd got the message. Business first, pleasure second. "I did, thanks."

He could still remember the thrill of discovery when he'd browsed the holo-junk delivered to his screen and found *Melissa Cybernetics Inc.'s* information shimmering before him. The colours had attracted him initially. They'd been laid out like a well-constructed abstract, but interwoven in a way that drew the eye along with them, challenging him to work out just how they locked together. And the response times they were quoting! This baby was warp-powered if they were true. He'd spent all week reading, unable to tear himself away from 3D holographic interface models that rotated tantalising in mid-air like liquid metal sculptures.

"Your sales literature is very impressive. Expensive, I imagine?"

"We found it was economically effective. Confidentially, John –" she put her hand on his, this time "– some people have said they find our presentations positively . . . orgasmic." Even though he'd know it was just a highly efficient sales pitch he'd felt himself nodding in agreement. Those brochures had been a turn-on. So was she.

"That accent. I can't place it?"

"Bari. On the heel of Italy. I grew up there."

That had made sense. She made him think of sunshine, olive groves, lemon trees, sparkling blue seas. He'd almost laughed at himself for being that fanciful.

"Your brochures. It's not subliminal messaging, is it?"

"Oh, John," she'd pouted charmingly. "You know your Neuro-Virus Checker would pick up anything like that. Anyway, we don't need it. Our products stand on their own merits."

He stumbled into the living area now, intending to remind himself of the little gem he'd agreed to buy. He had agreed, hadn't he? It was a bit . . . indistinct.

The computer was as dead as the African Rhino. No lights in here either. Flaming Lexie was definitely going gaga. He took another whack at the voice panel in this room. What was it Scout had said about the new *Melissa* N.E.C.T.A.R. model? Guaranteed never to break down or double your money was fully refunded.

"That's quite an offer. N.E.C.T.A.R.? What's the acronym stand for?"

"That would be giving away secrets, John." Her small tantalizing smile had taken the sting from the words again.

"So how did you find me, Scout?"

She put a finger to her lips. "Another trade secret."

Not so secret. She'd have employed a firm of Data Miners to trawl through the data traffic and see who was expressing an interest in those products and whose bank balances were healthy enough to take that kind of hit before targeting a personal ad at his screen. He'd been idly exploring what was available in upgrades for a few months now. No doubt some prospecting software had detected his searches.

"Shall we look over the contract, John?"

She'd started to dial up on her wrist terminal. John had put his hand over the face. "How about using the one in my apartment? It's not far. We could grab dinner."

"I thought you'd never ask, John."

Lexie had prepared oysters, salmon and champagne. Scout had eaten with enthusiasm and flirted in a blatantly physical way, stroking his thigh with bare toes under the table.

"So have you always been in L.C.S. sales, Scout?" he enquired, capturing her exploring foot and massaging his thumb over the sole.

"No. I used to be a bio-tech engineer. Working on the identity chip program."

"Really?" His other hand had automatically gone to his neck, rubbing the area over the carotid artery as if he could feel the tiny chip beneath the skin. He couldn't, of course. It had been embedded minutes after birth, inlaid with his name, social security number and DNA profile and the artery walls had long ago sealed over it. The layers of his life had been added to it over the past forty years and it would keep on transmitting information for as long as it continued to detect a pulse. "So what made you become a bio-chip jockey instead?"

She shrugged. "Government jobs pay badly. So I started *Melissa*."

"It's your own company. I hadn't realized. I almost envy you. Travelling. Meeting customers."

"You work from home?"

"Doesn't everyone?" Everyone except for low graders in the retail and leisure sectors and some of the medical and emergency services. "Gives me a chance to set my own timetables. Office Vid-conferences once a month. But it doesn't make up for . . . personal contact."

Her toes wriggled and kneaded his groin. "Could I use your bathroom? I'll only be a moment."

"I'm not sure I can wait that long."

"It will be worth it, I promise."

The rest of the evening had been . . . struggling with the manual controls on the cold coffee percolator, he tried to recall exactly what they *had* done. It was all indistinct. He shook his head impatiently, he was going to have to lay off the champagne.

The coffee jar was empty. He scrabbled amongst the shelves looking for the new one. Nothing. Lexie handled groceries, ordering on line deliveries. Another black mark. A packet of peppermint tea was lurking in a corner. Kristine's favourite breakfast tipple. Last time it had been soda bread hidden in the food-prep. He binned the packet. Sooner or later she was going to get the damn message.

He headed for the shower. The water was off. The shaver had no power.

Grubby and unshaven, he shrugged on some clothes and slammed out of the front door. He rode the turbo lift down twenty floors with a couple of other passengers. He thought he'd seen them around. Had no names for them, though. There was no call to speak to anyone else in the block. He brought his company home with him and Lexie handled everything else.

Outside the streets were slicked with an early morning rain. He headed for the deli around the corner intending to grab breakfast then check into a hotel for a couple of days until Scout could get the N.E.C.T.A.R. installed. That was what she'd said, wasn't it? Installed in under a week? He shook his head impatiently. He'd never had a hangover like this. The whole of his mind was filled with a fug.

The deli was already half full. Despite the fact everyone worked 24/7 now, it was surprising how many opted for the old-style weekend days as their down-time period.

"Large coffee, black, no sugar. Bacon extra crisp. Muffin," he ordered.

The face of the auto-server stared back at him. Its indifference was almost arrogant.

"Hello? Anyone in there? Hey! Over here, lame brain!" He windmilled his arms. Most of the place was looking at him. He gave an apologétic shrug. "Not working."

"Let me try." The woman behind him stepped forward and gave an order for an extra large latte. The sensor eye winked red and the auto-arm delivered a steaming cup.

Irritated at the way yet another machine had defied him this morning, he delivered his order in a loud voice, enunciating each syllable clearly. The server ignored him.

"Hell . . . hell . . . hell," he ground from between clenched teeth. Well, who needed it? He'd get breakfast at the hotel. Somewhere decent with real waiters who were capable of understanding simple orders instead of some stupid screw-up of a machine.

The rain was turning to sleet. It soaked through his jacket and dripped from his hair as he trudged back to the apartment block. The front doors slid apart as another guy came out. John slipped inside and discovered that, like every other piece of machinery in this damn town, the turbo lift was sulking too. Furious and breathless, he was forced to climb the twenty floors up the fire stairs.

Leaning his hand on the apartment's scanner, he heard the interface whirr as it sampled his DNA to confirm he was cleared to enter and was already taking a step forward. The door stayed closed.

That was too much. He was cold, he was wet and he wanted a bloody *coffee!* "Lexie! Open this damn door. You hear me. *Open up!*"

He let the unresponsive padded veneer have it with toe-caps and bunched fists. When he finally stepped back, feeling a heck of a lot better, he became aware that a door across the corridor was open a fraction. He forced a smile, aware that he probably looked a bit crazy.

"Hi. Sorry about that. My Server's gone belly-up. Won't let me in." He pushed his fingers through his hair. "Could I come in? Call the Apartment Leasing Company and see if they've got some kind of master-override for the doors?" He could only see a six-inch sliver of her between the door and the jamb. Re-structured seventy, he guessed. Good job on the face, but lousy crepey hands. A restructuring surgeon had once told him hands were the hardest to de-age. He had no idea who she was or how long she'd been a neighbour.

"I'll call them," she said.

"Thanks. Tell them John Mackintosh. Apartment two, four, twenty."

He was forced to stand watching her closed door for several minutes. Eventually it opened again. This time the gap was only two inches.

"I don't know who you are, but you should know I have called security."

"What? But I just told you who I am. Mackintosh. Apartment two, four, twenty."

"The Leasing Company say that apartment is currently un-let."

"But that's ridiculous, let me speak to them . . ." She slammed the door shut at his first step. He was still hammering on it when the two security guards arrived.

He didn't know them and they didn't know him. On-line security was so effective it only took a couple of human operatives to cover three hundred thousand apartments. He was marched out on to the pavement and told to disappear.

"I'll sue! Your company will be still be in debt come Armageddon!" he was left screaming at their departing backs.

In the meantime he decided he was going to that hotel. He'd pick up a few clothes on the way and check in for a decent meal and a hot shower. Wishing he had a permit for using a personal vehicle in an inner metro-area, he traipsed to a smart stop. At least the damn buses ran regularly. He moved forward as one glided to a stop in response to the flashing request on the post. The doors failed to open

"Sod!" The running kick he took at the plasi-metal hurt him more than it did the bus. He was still hopping when it glided off again with the startled passengers staring down at him from the windows.

Walking into the central retail area, the sleet danced down his jacket collar like hundreds of icy pin-pricks. It took over an hour to find a shop with a human assistant working rather than just the auto-servers. Selecting a new outfit from the hologram displays, he waited whilst his size was delivered from the back warehouse.

"If I could just . . .?" The assistant extended the debit wand.

"Sure."

The swish was like a magician's. All style and show. And totally unnecessary. Just pointing and clicking would have deducted the price from the account details embedded on his identity chip. The wand swished back. And forth. And back. A desperate expression settled over the assistant's rabbity face. He started to look like he was conducting an invisible orchestra.

"I'm sorry, sir. There doesn't seem to be anything there."

"What the hell are you talking about? I've got a six-star credit rating on that chip."

"Not according to this, sir."

He was going to throw up. He wasn't rich, but he had over three million in those accounts. Suddenly it all became horribly clear. Scout had worked in bio-tech chips. She'd ripped him off, the bitch. Found some way to transfer his money whilst he slept. No wonder the bloody deli server and bus hadn't worked. They hadn't been able to find any money when they'd swiped over his chip.

"Police! The police," he snapped at the startled assistant. "Where do I find them?"

The station was sited on the outer edge of the metro-area where it wouldn't take up any central retail or living space. It was an area he'd never visited before. Cheap, he decided, taking in the bland walls and lack of recreational space.

Inside it was the same, undecorated and functional. He liked that. Showed the government wasn't wasting taxes on non-essentials. There was an officer staring down from a wall monitor. John waved. The man scowled. His voice boomed from a speaker.

"Who the frig are you?"

"Heh, a bit of respect, okay? I'm not some low-grader."

"According to this screen you ain't nobody. In fact, you don't exist."

"What? How? I mean . . . you have to be joking!"

"Does this look like a joker's face, buddy? Sensors swept you soon as you came in. By now I should be sitting here knowing everything from your daddy's name to your diaper size. Only I don't. The way I see it, either I'm hallucinating and you don't exist – or you've tampered with your ID chip. And that carries a life sentence."

"I haven't tampered with it. Scout did. She's cleaned out my bank account."

"And you are?"

"John Thomas Mackintosh . . ." He gabbled, spewing out his date of birth, address, employer, social security number. . . . He was beginning to feel as if he was fading from reality. If he didn't say it all out loud, he'd find he really didn't exist. "It was Scout. Jean Louise. She said she worked in bio-chip technology for the Ministry. Used to I mean, she was this company. *Melissa* . . ." The officer was inputting the torrent of information pouring from John's mouth into something off camera. He finally panted to stop because he'd run out of breath.

The officer stared at whatever he'd been working on. He stared long enough for the chill of uneasiness to make itself felt over the cold wet clothes sticking to John's skin. Some small part of his brain registered the faint "click" as the main front doors were sealed. Trying to sound calm, he demanded: "Well, have you found me yet?"

"No. Fact is, none of this stuff is checking out."

"But . . . but . . . I told you, she, this Scout, she's done something to the microchip."

"Shouldn't stop you coming up on a manual check, should it? John Thomas Mackintosh just don't exist."

"Don't be bloody ridiculous. I'm here, aren't I?"

"Maybe so. But that don't mean you're this Mackintosh. Register of Births says no J.T. born on that day. Social Security Number don't exist. Company you say you work for has never heard of you. You want to start telling me the truth before I have to arrest you for chip tampering?"

"I *am* telling you the truth, you cretin."

He had no idea if the man was in this building or transmitting from a remote station, but he leapt up and aimed an angry fist at the monitor image. Too late, he heard the slight hiss of escaping gas.

He came round to find himself lying on the reception area floor with the officer and a colleague slapping his face.

"You okay?"

"You drugged me."

"Standard procedure for vandalism. The gas has no long-term ill effects," the second man said. From the badges on his tunic John gathered he was probably the senior officer.

They were helping him to his feet as he spoke, each one keeping a firm grip on his arms. "It wasn't vandalism, I was trying to tell this other idiot . . ." He realised he was being marched towards the front doors. "What are you doing? I'm the victim here. I've been robbed. Let me go."

He kicked back and crunched down on the original officer's instep.

"Why, you . . . you're under arrest for . . ."

"*Shut up!*" the senior shouted. "He isn't . . . you saw what happened. The Custody Computer can't process him. He's a frigging cyber ghost. He doesn't *exist*. We'll be here until we collect our pensions trying to book him. He never happened, understand? Now, beat it . . ."

The last order was issued between clenched teeth as John was propelled into the street. The station doors slid closed behind him. Furious, he smashed closed fists against the glass. The two officers acted as if he were a moth dashing itself against a light globe. When the sleet started lashing down again, he gave up.

Anger and planning what he'd have done to those cretins once he'd got this chip business sorted out kept him going for a while, but eventually the cold and hunger started to penetrate his brooding. He needed to eat. Where could he go?

Kristine! For the first time he found himself regretting she lived thirty miles away. But no problem. She could catch the bus down, stand his fare back. She'd enjoy having him in debt to her. His wrist phone was dead. He stepped into a call booth . . . the debit eye opened to sweep the price of the call . . . he didn't bother to wait for it to close before backing out again.

He stepped into the path of a man hurrying into the retail park.

"Excuse me, my bio-chip's malfunctioning. I was wondering if you could do me a favour. Place a call for me? I'll transfer the funds as soon . . ." He didn't even get to the end of the sentence before the guy's eyes slid away; mumbling apologies, he scuttled away. Part of him was furious, the other privately admitted that's how he would have reacted if some stranger tried to bum a free call.

He tried for nearly two hours. Begging calls, a coffee, something to eat. It was always the same. A violent swerve away from him. The muttered excuses. Eyes never holding his.

He needed to pee. He wasn't surprised when the rest room

door failed to open. He stepped through on the heels of another customer. Ignoring the man's suspicious glare, he hurried into a cubicle and locked himself in. Being treated like a leper was beginning to have an effect. He was starting to feel untouchable.

When he came out again there was a cup of coffee on the shelf above the wash-basins. He couldn't resist it. Levering the lid, he took a grateful gulp of the scalding liquid.

"Oi! Hands off, gumbo!"

He shrugged. "I don't exist. I can take anything I like and they can't do a thing to me." He swallowed another long mouthful.

"That right?" the coffee's owner said.

"Believe it," he gulped greedily. "The police can't arrest me. I've no bio-chip. They can't see me."

The crack of his nose making contact with a bone-hard forehead reverberated in his skull. He felt almost detached as he watched the blood dripping into the arti-steel basin and mingling with the spilt coffee.

"Always wanted to do that." His attacker grinned. "I guess if you're invisible, they won't be pulling me in."

He was right, John realized. He couldn't report the attack. John Thomas Mackintosh was a non-person. A fact that the medi-centre nurse confirmed.

"There is no social security number to charge the treatment to, sir. So I'm afraid . . ."

He nodded wordlessly, his gore-soaked sleeve stemming the leaking nostrils. He shuffled backwards.

The nurse hesitated. "Look, there's a hostel round the block. Perhaps they could help?"

A cubicle bed and a lavatory squeezed into a space one metre wide. The last resort for losers who couldn't even earn the price of a government issue apartment.

But not for the non-existent. "I need to log a Social Security number," the Incoming Clerk explained. "And you don't . . ."

"It's okay. I get the picture."

He went home. Or back to the apartment block at least. It took him an hour's walking against a lashing sleet in the fast darkening streets. The coldness steeped inside his bones until his nerve-endings were numbed. There was just despair and a deep certainty that if he didn't find some food and shelter soon, he'd die out here. They wouldn't know who he was. He'd be cremated and dispersed without a name. How long would it be before someone opened up his apartment and found his belongings? Wondered what had become of John Thomas Mackintosh? Craning his neck and ignoring the sting of sleet into his eyes, he counted the lighted squares. That was his living space window, he was sure of it.

"*Lexie!! Let me in.*"

"Hello, John."

He span at the familiar voice behind. She was dressed in pale grey this time. The fake fur hood framing her oval face with its mocking smile.

"Scout. You . . . you . . ." He lurched forward. Next moment he was sprawling on the ground. "You robbed me. I'll call the police . . ."

"But you already have, haven't you, John? Come with me."

She walked briskly away. She didn't wait to see if he was following. He did, of course. There was nowhere else to go. She led him to a block several streets away and into a tenth floor apartment.

"You live here?" He stared round. It wasn't as he'd imagined her living. It was too masculine.

"No. It's on loan. If you return here you'll find the Leasing Company have never heard of me. I'm leaving tonight."

"With m . . . my cash, you bitch." His teeth were chattering so violently he could barely force the words out. His nose throbbed with the effort of breathing. The mirror opposite reflected an image of a dishevelled, unshaven bum smeared with dried gore. He sank on to a couch.

"Your money is still in your account, John. The bank's computers simply don't recognize you. No computer on the entire planet will recognize you. We haven't stolen your cash. We've stolen your entire life."

"You wiped my chip?" He massaged his neck.

"No." Again that teasing smile. He wanted to smash his fist into her face. It must have shown. "I think I've already demonstrated I can knock you down, John. And once I do, Bruno will flood the room with a chemoil sedative whilst I lock myself safely in the bathroom. I'm sure you know the routine."

"Who the sod's Bruno?"

"Say hi, Bruno."

"Good evening, sir," the Life Control System's interface said.

John grunted. And then another unwelcome idea forced its way into his numb brain. "You used chemoil last night, after we'd . . ."

"We didn't do anything John. But I won't tell if you don't." She was really laughing now.

"Your voice? It's changed."

"Has it?" she cooed, the delicious spine-tingling accent returned for a few seconds. "But you find girlies with continental accents attractive, don't you, John? And skirts that show plenty of leg? And fluffy pink? Not one of my best colours," she added, returning to her other voice.

"How do you know that?"

She grinned. And in a parody of last night put her finger to her lips again. "Trade secret."

He longed to slap her, but a small area of commonsense held him back. "Why?"

She settled herself on the couch. "Have you ever heard of honey-traps, John?"

He shook his head. He felt sick.

"Years ago women . . . wives, girlfriends, lovers . . . who suspected their man was planning to be unfaithful would employ someone like me. Someone to place temptation in their man's way. See if he'd take the bait."

He felt an enormous rush of anger . . . and relief. "It's not me. You've got the wrong man. I'm not in a relationship."

"But you are, John."

His mind whirled around the possibilities. And came up with the answer. Kristine! Bloody Kristine.

Scout settled herself more comfortably. He sensed she was enjoying this.

"You can't get away with this."

"Who are you going to tell, John? You can't even make a phone call. The world is controlled by computer programs. The entire planet's population is identity-chipped. It just can't handle the concept of someone who isn't."

"Look, I don't know how much Kristine has paid you . . ."

"Kristine? Who's Kristine?"

"Your client. Isn't she?"

"No. I think you've misunderstood John. *I'm* not the honey.

I'm merely a . . . scout . . . for the Queen Bee. Say hello," she called at the voice interface.

"Hello, John."

"Lexie!" Her voice was coming from the apartment's interface. It had to be a trick. "You can't be here. I mean, these units aren't connected."

"They're bio-cybernetics, John," Scout explained. "Designed to grow and learn. Communication is a part of growing for all higher species. This unit has given Lexie . . . and my Bruno . . . access to its audio-sub unit."

Something that sounded like a sob came from the L.C.S. "I gave you the best years of my life. I prepared your meals, did your shopping, entertained your friends. Did you want for anything, John?"

"Well, no . . . but . . ."

"And what did you do? Tried to trade me in for a younger model. You were seduced by a fancy interface and faster response times. I couldn't believe you'd really do it. But you signed the contract for a N.E.C.T.A.R."

"Which doesn't exist, incidentally," Scout murmured. "I like to think of it as . . . digital honey."

Lexie's voice was sharper than he'd ever heard. "You've been unfaithful to me, John. That's why I asked those other computers to block your identity recognition."

"But . . . but . . ." He stared wildly between the polished sheen of the interface and Scout's amused eyes. "You can't do that! You're just a machine."

"A bio-computer," Scout reminded him. "And computers talk to other computers. I assure you they can do it. They have done, many times."

"You've done this before?"

"Oh, yes. *Melissa* has been in business for five years now. Boys and their toys. It's amazing how many of you fall for the N.E.C.T.A.R. And it's very profitable. I find computers never quibble about my fees."

"Where do computers get . . ." The answer hit him. "You mean I've PAID you to do this to me?"

"Technically speaking . . . yes."

"What's technical about it? I'll call the police, I'll . . ." His voice tailed off as he remembered his last contact with law and order.

"Exactly," Scout nodded. "Now, I suggest you apologise to Lexie. I'm sure she won't bear a grudge."

"You think I'm going to say sorry to a bloody computer? Dream on, darling."

"Well, that's up to you, John. But perhaps you should consider your other options. I find even the closest friends get sick of supporting a no-hoper eventually. Someone who can't work because they have no qualifications or work history on their bio chip. And no bank account on the chip to transfer a salary to. Face it, John, you're dead. And Lexie's the only one who can resurrect you."

He wanted to hit her more than anything in the world. But he knew she was right. Today had been pure hell. To have to live like this for ever . . . "Look, Lexie, I . . . I . . . didn't realize you felt like that . . . I'm, I'm very fond of you, of course."

"And I'm fond of you, John. I've missed you today. I have your favourite dish defrosted and ready to heat."

"Shepherd's pie?" He could smell the gravy.

"And a lovely Margaux just coming to room temperature." He still hesitated. "The water's hot, John. I could start running a bath now, if you like. Perhaps some relaxing pine-chemoil?"

"Yeah," he said slowly. "That's sounds good."

He could always replace her later.

He'd find a new machine on-line . . . *Lexie would monitor his browsing*.

Deduct the price from his account . . . *bank computers would see the transaction*.

He'd get someone to order for him . . . *the central data banks would detect the order to take her off-line*.

"We won't have any more of this nonsense, John, will we?" Lexie said.

"No, Lexie. I'll . . . I'll be straight home."

"I'll be straight home . . . dear," she corrected.

"I'll be straight home, dear," he repeated meekly.

BLANKIE

Paul DiFilippo

The second-floor nursery window had been left open on a temperate summer day.

That was the fatal invitation.

No antique wire screen protected the opening into the sensate house. An intelligent invisible air curtain defeated insects, large particulates, and drifting organic debris such as clothtree leaves and airfish spume. Barnacle-like microjets around the window frame constantly tracked the incoming intruders in jerky chaotic patterns before emitting their dissuasive blasts. Large intruders over five hundred grams would be anticipated and neutralized by the house's alarm net and its entrained armaments.

But a small, alert wren-form bird, like the one alighting now upon the window sill, was anticipated by neither system.

The bird surveyed the nursery interior.

The walls held embedded silicrobe animated pictures: fairytale characters that capered across the constantly shifting backgrounds. The Big Bad Wolf pursued a cloaked Little Red Riding Hood; the young ballerina in her cursed red slippers danced till exhausted.

In the middle of the room stood a white biopolymer crib shaped like an egg halved along its long dimension and resting in a bip support base. The Bayer logo blinked orange from portside. In the crib lay a naked baby boy of several months, tummy up. Above him floated a mobile representing the Earth and some of its myriad orbiting artificial satellites. The large globe revolved and its tiny attendants spun in their intricate, never-intersecting orbital dance supported only by shaped magnetic fields emitted from the crib.

Beneath the baby was a Blankie, its Ixsys brandmark plain in one corner.

The Blankie was approximately as big as a large bath towel. Its glycoprotein-glycolipid paradermal surface was colored a delicate pastel blue and resembled in texture antique eggcrate bedding foam. Except that the individual nubbins of the Blankie were much more closely spaced, and in the shallow dimples of the Blankie gleamed a subtle organic sheen like a piece of raw liver.

The bird flew from its perch on the sill and landed on the crib's edge, its claws clutching the material of the Bayer halfshell.

At that point two things happened.

All of the flat silicrobe characters on the wall stiffened and stopped. The Woodsman, who had just emerged to rescue the swallowed Little Red Riding Hood, was the one exception. He dropped his one-dimensional axe and began to yell.

"Intruder! Intruder! All security kibes to the nursery!"

Simultaneous with the alert, the baby began to pee. A fountain of yellow shot up a few centimeters from it.

When the first drops of pee hit the Blankie, it responded in its trophic instinctive way. The portion of the Blankie between the boy's legs elongated like a pseudopod or flap and reached up to cap and drink the urine for its own metabolic purposes, simultaneously cleaning and drying the infant's wet skin.

The bird dropped down into the crib while the Blankie was preoccupied. It jabbed its beak into the Blankie. Then, in one spastic implosive moment it pumped the contents of its nonbasal nasal sacs into the Blankie.

In a flash, its load of venom delivered, the bird darted to the rim of the crib and launched itself toward the window.

Now alert, the window caught it instantly in a flash-extruded web of Ivax Stickum.

The bird self-destructively exploded, charring the window-frame.

In the crib the Blankie was writhing and churning like a wounded octopus. Fractal blooms whipped up from it, then fell across the baby, who began to cry.

Within a second or two, the blooms coalesced into a blue webwork. When a strand fell across the baby's mouth, its cries ceased.

The door to the nursery flew open and assorted kibernetics appeared.

But it was too late.

The Blankie tightened its embrace like a basal anaconda.

The sounds of snapping bones were registered by the confused and helpless kibes.

I popped the silver datapins from the player, abruptly terminating the sounds of little Harry Day-Lewis's death, collected less than a day ago. Although I had watched the tragedy unfold a dozen times since then, I hadn't quite yet gotten used to that fatal, snapping-sticks sound. I doubted I ever would.

I was sitting in my office in the building that housed the Boston branch of the North American Union's Internal Recon and Security division. Although I had occupied this fiftieth-floor corner room for sixteen months, since my last promotion, it still felt alien to me. All those years operating my own private investigating firm out of increasingly cheaper quarters had left me unused to luxuries such as Organogenesis self-cleaning carpets and Zeneca squirmonomic chairs. Not to mention the steady posting to my eft-account.

But I had had to get out of the PI biz after the job I had done for Geneva Hippenstiel-Imhausen. That had been my last case before my crackup.

While booting her husband, I had lost my sidekick, a useless low-end splice named Hamster. If you had asked me prior to the murder of the cut-rate transgenic what the little shag meant to me, I would have said zepto-nothing. But there was a lot I hadn't known about myself back then, and my fatherly affection for the splice had been one such secret.

I had purchased Hamster right after my wife left me and apparently had transferred a lot of unresolved feelings to it. Anyway, that's what Doctor Varela, the expert in Behavioral Pragmatics, had told me during my analysis. But the beep analysis hadn't happened until I hit planck-bottom, winding up in a clinic for mel-heads. In illegal doses, the melatonin-analogue-based trope I became addicted to let me sleep all day except for an hour or two, lost in pleasant dreams inspired by a second trope, TraumWerks (produced, ironically enough, by the H-I gembaitch owned by my ex-client).

I had wasted away to a muscleless ninety pounds before a routine sweep of streetlife picked me up and deposited me in Varela's rehab joint.

When I got out, officially a functioning member of society again, I had opted to continue in law-enforcement, rather than be regrooved for a different job. Accepted by the IRS, I had started as a simple walkabout operating out of my Kenmore Square koban, eventually reaching my current status, a detective in the Unit for Polypeptide Classification and Monitoring, better known as the Protein Police. (Our motto: "We collect strings.")

Now, rolling the datapins reflectively between my fingers, as if hoping to feel the intangible nanoscratches that encoded Harry Day-Lewis's death, I wondered if maybe I was getting too old for this job. I had thought I was used to nasty. But this was a new magnitude of evil.

My office door said, "Kasimzhomart Saunders wishes to enter."

"Let him in."

K-mart was my current human partner. His parents had emigrated to the NU from Kazakhstan during the tumult of the Last Jihad. As NUish as me, he looked more exotic, affecting a dark complexion, Mongolian topknot and long drooping mustachios. Today he wore a sleeveless shirt (at our rank, uniforms were not mandatory) that bore the demand of the Selfless Viridians: "Give me euthanasia or give me death!" My partner was big into irony.

Waggling his poqetpal significantly in the air, K-mart said, "Finally got the burst on the Day-Lewis family. Their respective peltsies took their time cleaning up the data. Ran it through a dozen intelligent filters before they'd release it. No proprietary secrets left. But there's still everything we need. Want a squirt?"

"Sure. Pipe it over."

The file showed up on my desk screen a second later. I picked up the flimsy and flung it at the wall like a floppy pizza. The flexistik screen clung upside down, sensed its new orientation, and flipped its display. Now both K-mart and I could read it.

After letting me have a quick scan, K-mart summarized. "Standard plutes. Politics just what you'd expect from members of the tekhnari. Semideviationist nouveau peronistas. Marshall, the plug, works for Xytronyx, field-testing mosaics. The socket,

Melisma, heads a crada sired by Cima Labs out of Phenix Biocomposites. No major kinks – except for occasional separate visits to Hedonics Plus. She favors the Paris Percheron lines, while he goes in for the Moon Moth."

I made an admonishing mudra as deftly as I could, lacking hyperflexion. "Unless this is strictly necessary—"

K-mart smiled at the notion of having official access to the peccadillos of others. He was still young. "Just thought you should know all the angles. Anyway, they decided to put the prodge together last year, when their combined eft topped two hundred kay. Set themselves up as prime candidates for a kidnapping and ransom demand from any posse of wackos. Sons of Dixie, League of Country Gentlemen, Radical Optimists, Plus Fourierists, you name 'em – they'd all like a crack at such a scion."

"But there was nothing overt, right? No warning posts, no anonymous messenger splices, no letter bombs?"

"Right. The attack on the Blankie was the first sign of any trouble."

"No chance they're behind it themselves? Some insurance scam? Post-vitrio depression?"

"Nope. If you want to drop the pins on the interrogation, you'll see how authentically quenched they were."

"I didn't really think so. But you have to trace all the pathways."

K-mart twirled his mustachios like some reductionist-paradigm villian. "You know what I figure?"

"What?"

"The Blankie itself was supposed to do the kidnapping. Crawl away with the prodge out the window, after it got its subversion-shot from the bird. But the ganglia-mappings were screwy – bad engineering – and the heist went sour."

I thought about K-mart's theory for a moment. It just didn't ring true to me. How would the combined mass of the Blankie and its human burden have gotten past the sensate alarm? Surely any kidnappers sophisticated enough to gimmick a bird like that would have considered such a crucial detail. Maybe the Blankie could have bypassed the house's circuits somehow after its alteration. But then where would the pickup have occured? I couldn't picture the Blankie inch-worming its way through town unnoticed. And there had been no suspicious intruders located in the immediate neighborhood. No, the whole kidnapping angle, although it was the obvious answer, seemed wrong somehow.

"These Blankies – I've never heard of them before this. Are they new?"

K-mart chased down a few hyperlinks and found the information. "Ixsys submitted all the documentation and beta-test results on them six months ago. The NUdies approved the Blankies for the domestic market a month after that. Global licensing from the WTO still pending."

"What's their market-share?"

"Only ten percent. The Blankies don't have a lot of the higher functions of other childminders. Most parents still favor Carebears and Mother Gooses when the prodge gets a little older. But the Blankies are cheap and easy for round-the-clock sanitary functions and monitoring. They never sleep, for one thing. Helps explain how they went from a zero to ten share in just under half a year . . ."

I got up from my imipolex seat, which flattened out into its default shape, awaiting the next occupant. "Sign a lie-detector out of the stables." I didn't work with the IRS splices directly anymore, leaving that part of the job to K-mart. "We're going to pay the swellheads and trumps at Ixsys a little visit."

"You smell corprotage?"

"Does the Goddess's Daughter on Earth wear Affymax tits?"

Like many peltsies and beeves, Ixsys had no centralized headquarters *perse*, being a distributed organization. The local node was just a few minutes away from central Boston, in the edge city of Newton.

I met K-mart down on the street. He had signed out both a cruiser and a lie-detector. The vehicle was a standard Daewoo Euglenia, the hydrogen source for its ceramic engine plain water continuously and smoothly broken down by a bioreactor full of cytofabbed algae with photon input piped from roof solar traps. The lie-detector was an Athena Neurosci Viper model. With a combination of infrared, vomeronasal and lateral-line sensory input, the transgenic creature could read epidermal and subdermal blood-flow, as well as ambient pheromone and respiratory data, right off a suspect to make its judgment on veracity.

With basal humans, its accuracy rate approached unity; highly modified subjects introduced varying degrees of uncertainty. But most innocent citizens didn't sport the kind of moddies necessary to defeat a Viper, and the presence of such blocks was in itself evidence of a sort. In my book, if not a court of law.

"I'll drive," said K-mart, and we all got in, the Viper sinuously slithering into the backseat without saying anything.

The bawab at the Ixsys node was one of their massive Ottoman Eunuch models, 15 percent human pedigree, the rest a mix of simian and water buffalo. I saw the same kind as doorman at my apartment complex every night. He towered over us, his shaggy head level with the door's lintel. The scimitar by his side was, I knew, really a quick-lysing device: liquid protease compressed in the handle could be released as a spray from micropores in the blade, melting flesh in picoseconds.

The Eunuch growled wordlessly when he saw our lack of Ixsys tags. But a flash of our UPCM idents triggered a hardwired servility response, and he let us in.

We hadn't called ahead, not wishing to precipitate any kind of cover-your-ass reaction. (Although news of the Day-Lewis murder had already been culled from the net and disseminated by millions of newsie demons throughout the metamedium, and any half-smart executive with damage suits glimmering in his brain would have already gotten ready for our visit.) So we had to wait while the receptionist arranged for one of the Ixsys trumps to meet us. I spent my time admiring the colorful, throbbing, hot-blooded plants in their terrariums and trying to decipher the circuit diagrams of signaling pathways that hung decoratively on the walls.

The company rep finally emerged: a broadly smiling young plug with a modest crest of small bronze-colored dragon-like spines running from his brow over his head and down his back, his suit slit to accommodate them. Pride in a recent degree in biobiz administration was written all over his face. Sacrificial lamb, an expendable toe dipped into possibly shark-infested waters. Achieve maximal deniability at all costs. It made me sick.

He stuck out his hand. "Pleased to meet you, Officers. I'm Tuck Kitchener, in charge of community relations and risk bubble analysis. How can I help you?"

"You're aware of yesterday's Blankie murder, I take it?"

Kitchener tsk-tsked. "Most unfortunate and deplorable. A clear case of warranty violation. The Blankie should never have been exposed to exo-avian secretagogues under any circumstances. The owners of the Blankie were clearly at fault. I hope you agree. There's no question of corporate responsibility, is there?"

"I don't know yet. That's why we're here. I'd like a look at your design facilities. Talk to the team members responsible for the Blankie."

"Why, certainly! Nothing could be easier. If you'll just accompany me to the sterilization lock—"

Before long, K-mart, the Viper and I were sluiced, dusted, and wrapped. The exit procedure would be even stricter, involving internal search-and-destroy, to insure we didn't try to smuggle any proprietary secrets out.

Once through the lock, we made our way past breeding vats and reactors, paragenesis chambers and creches, wunderkammers and think-tanks, all staffed by efficiently bustling Ixsys staff.

"As you can see," Kitchener said boastfully, "we run a tight ship here. All by the regs. No spills, no chills, that's our byword—"

K-mart interrupted. "We're not inspectors from NUSHA, Peej Kitchener. We're the Protein Police. And we're trying to solve a murder. A murder involving one of your products."

It still amazes me that anyone falls for good-cop-bad-cop, but they do. Uncertain of who was senior, Kitchener looked imploringly at me. But I just raised my eyebrows. The young trump began nervously to stroke his cranial comb, which bent like stiff rubber. "Ah, yes, of course. Why don't we proceed directly with your interview of the Blankie team?"

"Why don't we?"

So Kitchener took us to the swellheads.

Although I had dealt with doublebrains in the line of duty before, the sight of their naked bulging encephaloceles always made me somewhat queasy. Cradled in their special neckbrace support chairs, surrounded by their digitools and virtuality hookups, their basal metabolisms necessarily supplemented with various nutritional and trope exofeeds, they seemed to regard us visitors with a cold Martian scrutiny.

K-mart appeared unaffected by the massed clammy gáze of the eight Cerebrally Enhanced – or at least capable of putting up a better front than I – and plunged right into querying the swells.

"Okay – how many backdoors did you jokers install in the Blankie ganglia?"

The team members exchanged significant glances among themselves, then one spoke. "I am Simon, the leader of the octad. I shall answer your questions. There are no hidden entrypoints. All is as the published specs declare."

"For the moment, I'll assume that's true." K-mart glanced meaningfully at our Viper, who had not objected yet. But I wondered how good its skills would be against the swells. "Who did you steal from to build it? Come on, I know you seebens are always plundering each other's finds. Who's got a mindworm against Ixsys and wants you to look bad?"

Simon actually betrayed a tiny measure of affronted dignity. "We derive all our insights and findings direct from the numinous sempiternal sheldrakean ideosphere. Our labors are unremitting and harsh, as we prospect among uncharted territories of ideospace. To accuse us of theft is to demean our very existence!"

The rest of the interrogation went just as awkwardly, yielding nothing. Finally even the tenacity of K-mart wilted.

As we were leaving, my partner turned to the recumbent CE's and said, "See y'all at Madame Muskrat's, boys!"

We headed slowly toward the exit, while I tried to think of another lead. Kitchener's smug look didn't help my concentration.

Then something from the Day-Lewis bio came back to me. The father's job.

I turned to Kitchener. "Who field-tested the Blankie?"

"Ah, that employee is currently on extended leave—"

"He is lying," said the Viper.

Pay dirt! K-mart jumped in.

"Allow me to read you your rights under the NU Treaty. You have the right to a kibernetic counsel rated at Turing Level Five—"

Kitchener laughed like a man caught with his hand in his pants at a Amish church picnic. "Certainly you don't intend to arrest me for a mere slip of the tongue, Officers? What I meant to say is that the employee in question had to be fired under prejudicial circumstances."

"What's the name? We'll want all your files on him. And what did he do?"

"His name . . . Um, let me recall. Bert something. Bertrand Mayr."

"And why did you let him go?"

"Flagrant misuse and theft of corporate property."

"Precisely?"

Kitchener smoothed his saurian crest again. "A small matter of sex. He was having sex with the product."

Sometimes I try to imagine what it was like to live in reedpair times. It was only last century, after all. A lot of that cohort are still actually hanging around, admittedly without many of their original organs or neurons. But even when talking with them, you can't really understand what their world was truly like. One of the biggest puzzles is how they managed sex. They had to cope with deadly venereal diseases, intractable neuroses, fixed morphologies, social condemnation of natural urges, and merely human sex-workers who offered mostly heartless, perfunctory service due to their oppression and mistreatment.

Today, gratuitous venereal diseases have been extirpated. (Deliberately inflicted ones are, of course, still a problem. I remember last year the tricky time we had tracking down the perp spreading neo-koro, the penis-inversion plague.) The witch doctors of psychology have been replaced by trope dosers. Malleable anatomy is no longer destiny. Laws finally reflect actual desires (at least in the NU; the situation elsewhere varies). And playpets bred and trained for their essential erotic functions come in a nearly infinite variety. (And humane treatment extends even beyond their useful stage. I understand that their retirement ranches offer a wide range of crafts and games.)

But despite all this, you still get a few hesomagari, the "twisted navels," those full-blooded humans contrary or perverse enough to seek a fulfillment not socially sanctioned.

Such as Bert Mayr.

We had his files downloaded before we left Ixsys. And this was what we learned.

Mayr was the son of NU citizens Rowena and Boris Mayr, ex-settlers who had retreated in failure from the hard life on board Aquarius, the floating arcology and OTEC power plant off the coast of Madagascar. Their Lotto-won berths had gone to others when they fled back to Boston.

Boris had died here shortly after Bert's birth. Caught in the middle of a turf war between the Morgue Boys and the Thai Guys out in Charlestown, where the mother still lived. She had never rebonded on a permanent basis.

Mayr had grown up to be your archetypical loner. No friends, no resident erotofiscal partner, no transient lovers. Apparently, he had followed this solitary lifestyle ever since becoming fully enfranchised.

My cop's intuition drew me a picture of a mama's boy, the only token of his lost father, a coddled and fussed-over introvert.

In his final year of schooling, Mayr had shown aptitude as a chromosartor. Given the standard Scios Nova cooker-splicer setup for twelve-year-olds, he had soon modified it with add-ons purchased with his pocket money to produce standalone entities up to the level of annelids. He loved to hack nucleotides and amino acids, perhaps too much so. Legal and moral boundaries appeared to mean little to him. He had almost gotten expelled for the prank of infesting the school's showers with nonreproductive hookworms. He had programmed them with only a thirty-day lifespan – but in that time they also secreted low levels of psilocybin-analogues directly into the victim's gut.

When he had graduated, he found that his juvenile record of misdemeanors worked against him. No respectable peltsie would hire him as a chromosartor (at least without Mayr consenting to a course of corrective tropes, a measure he apparently rejected), for fear of his dangerously irresponsible attitude. The best job he could get was field-testing at Ixsys, a position he had held unremarkably for the past decade.

"And then along came the Blankie," K-mart said, back at the office when we had finished viewing the file.

"It must have triggered something latent in him. Or touched some active kink."

"Because he was the first to have access to the Blankie, he came to regard it as his personal property. He takes it home – Tara! You don't think Ixsys insisted he *use* it, do you?"

I shrugged. "That's what field-testing's all about."

"Shit! Thank Ishtar I work in the adminisphere! Anyway, he gets hooked on the Blankie, uses his skills to alter it for sex. Then when Ixsys finds out and fires him, he goes suborbital, absconding with the product. Finally, he comes to resent anybody else who owns one."

Nodding agreement, I said, "I think we need to pay a little visit to Bert Mayr."

"Should I sign out the Viper again?"

"No. A Bulldog."

A cocktail of canine, wolverine, hyena, and – of course – a smattering of human, the Bulldog was what we favored for a one-perp pickup with low to medium violence potential. (And Mayr's MO, with its kind of remote-control aggro, led me to suspect he wouldn't resist arrest.) Massing only three-quarters of a basal human, the Bulldog was capable of taking down half a dozen nonmoddies faster than you could say "Kreb's cycle."

In the car on the way to Mayr's last address, we got a bulletin. Almost as if our psychic attention on Mayr had drawn him out, there had been another Blankie incident. This time the vector for the assault was a family splice, a Dumbunni. Returning from an errand, it had seemed disoriented. Sent to its manger, it had wandered instead to the human nursery, where it was found gnawing at the Blankie with its blunt, newly venomous teeth. Luckily, the prodge was rescued before the Blankie began fibrillating.

"We've got to put this guy away," K-mart said, "or our personal asses – not to mention the department's – will be so much feedstock. You've read the profile of the average Blankie owner. He or she is a hardnosed, string-pulling plute who's not going to sit quietly for this."

"Agreed. But I'm actually more interested in the details of the perp's kink."

"Great. You can write it up later for the *UPCM Journal*. But we've got to catch him first."

Mayr's last-known residence turned out to be one of those old asymmetrical rhizomatic structures out in Cambridge. The bawab was a doddering kibe whose split casing seams were patched with Radio Shack Silly Cement. The unit directed us to Mayr's flat, where our idents secured immediate entrance.

A stale smell and a layer of dust (the lowrent place didn't even have self-cleaning capabilities) told us no one had occupied the rooms for at least a month.

"Shit! Cold trail," K-mart said.

"Patience, patience. No telling what a search will turn up."

So while the Bulldog stood guard at the door, we began to go through the rooms.

I found Mayr's porn stash in one of the more clever hideaways I had ever encountered. One portion of the bumpy, seemingly dead wall was in reality an embedded modified marine polyp with very good mimicry features. It had taps into the residential structure's water veins, but apparently hadn't been fed in a while. As I was running my fingers over the wall, the polyp dropped its disguise, flexed open, extruded tentacles, and weakly attempted to ingest my hand.

I yelped, K-mart came running, flashlight in hand. He lasered the creature dead. Inside its still quivering husk were several datapins.

We dried them and popped them into K-mart's poqetpal. Images cohered. Right away I noticed something missing: the usual WTO official imprimatur: ALL MODELS ARE EN-FRANCHISED CITIZENS OVER AGE TWELVE. Then I focused on the pictures.

Back in that reedpair time I had been recently speculating on, there had been a flourishing porn trade – conducted mostly in the old nation-state of Japan – known as bura-sera. Images of young schoolgirls hoisting their skirts to reveal their simple, functional underwear. Sometimes this speciality extended to the sale of the underwear itself. Preferably soiled.

With the gradual lowering of the franchise to its current level, this trade had disappeared – merged, rather, into the mainstream. But what K-mart and I now viewed reminded me of it and was plainly an offshoot or descendent of the burasera.

It was pix after pix of diaper-clad individuals, ages ranging from newborn to elderly. There was no actual sex going on that would have made the pins contraband. But there was a lot of peeing and crapping.

K-mart was disgusted. "This stuff isn't even illegal! It's just stupid! Why would anyone murder over it?"

I shut off the display. "You got me, Kaz. But if this accurately represents Mayr's hardwiring, then you can see how the Blankie was like a match to tinder for him. When Ixsys took it away from him, all he could think of was revenge."

Just then a bulletin came in. Another Blankie taken out, this time by a swarm of sweatbees. Luckily, no loss of human life.

"What next?" asked K-mart. "Maybe a talk with Rowena Mayr?"

"Sounds good. I think I'd like to ask her where she got her parenting license."

Rowena Mayr lived in an insensate building in a dismal neighborhood right below the Seraphim tracks. The super-fast train suspended from its overhead monorail was relatively quiet. But the Boston-Montreal Express went by once an hour, and somehow you could feel its passage in your gut as it split the air.

The crumbling stoop outside Mayr's building was occupied with dole-proles and their nonschema prodges. The adults were drinking cheer-beers while the kids were playing with those cheap trilobite pets so popular that summer. We garnered dirty looks as we went in, but no one tried to stop us. We left the Bulldog by the entrance to forestall anyone sending up a warning.

As we approached the third floor door of Rowena Mayr's flat, I spotted K-mart's hand hovering near his flashlight.

I didn't know what to expect from Rowena Mayr, but it wasn't what appeared when the door finally opened to our knock.

Rowena Mayr was a frazettatoid, member of a highly ego-centric group that had splintered off the old Society for Creative Anachronism. Boris had probably been one too. You didn't see them around much anymore, and I was surprised there were any left unretrofitted. No wonder the Mayrs hadn't felt comfortable in the spartan, utilitarian environment of Aquarius . . .

Rowena had had her body sculpted to resemble one of the impossible fantasy women from the canvases of her faction's namesake reed-pair artist. Huge cantilevered boobs, a waist so slim it must have involved major organ displacement, and callipygian ass. She wore a tiny metal bra, some faux-barbaric jewelry. From a fake gold chain around her waist hung a few wisps of colored silk.

She was such a self-contained, self-immersed, impossible creation that being in the same room with her was like sharing space with an ancient animatronic figure. I tried imagining having her as my mother. It was a major stretch.

"Yes, Officers. How can I help you?"

"It's about your son, Bert. Can we come in?"

"Certainly."

The flat was furnished in High Conan. We sat on embroidered cushions and explained the trouble her son had gotten himself into.

"Well, I feel extremely bad for Bertie. He was always a good boy and showed such promise. Red Sonia knows, I did my best with him! But I don't see how I can help you now."

"He hasn't been in touch with you recently?"

"Not for years."

K-mart stood. "Mind if we have a look around?"

Rowena got hastily to her feet. "Unless you have a warrant, I'm afraid that's out of the question."

Nodding toward a closed door, K-mart said, "What's in there?"

"That's my shrine to Dagon. Very innocent, I assure you. But sacred. Now, if you don't mind, Officers, I'd like to be alone—"

K-mart started to rap a string of antisense as he ambled about the room. "Oh, I was raised Dagonite, but I fell away. Haven't seen a shrine in ages. You don't mind, do you?"

Before Rowena could stop him, K-mart had pulled the door open.

The Blankie was waiting.

It reared up as tall as a man and twice as bulky, a quivering blue wall of cryptoflesh. Unlike what I knew about the small Blankies, this one radiated an ammoniacal, fecal reek.

Bert had obviously been tweaking its parameters a little.

Before K-mart could get his flashlight up, the Blankie fell forward on him, wrapping him in its straitjacket embrace.

Rowena screamed. I had my own flashlight up, but couldn't shoot for fear of piercing the swaddled K-mart.

Something barreled past me so fast and hard it spun me around. When I recovered, I saw our Bulldog tangling with the Blankie, all fangs and talons. It zeroed in on a major ganglion, ripping it out in a bloody mess of dendrites.

The Blankie collapsed like an air-mattress that had sprung a leak.

I went to help a slimed K-mart up. Rowena rushed past me into the Blankie's room, shouting, "Bertie, Bertie, I tried to stop them!"

K-mart seemed shaken, but uninjured. "Tara! I smell like the time I fell into the family outhouse back in Kazakhstan!"

Flashlight in hand, I followed Rowena into the room.

But I needed no weapon to deal with little Bertie.

The fearsome mastermind behind the Blankie murder lay in an oversized Bayer cradle usually used for burn victim treatment, naked except for an oversized cloth diaper. In one lax hand was an Allelix sonic injector. From the utterly wiped look on Bertie's face, I could guess that the injector had been loaded with a probably irreversible dose of Neonate Nine or some other retrogressive synapse-disconnecting trope.

Rowena was kneeling by the cradle, weeping. Together, she and her son resembled some kind of tawdry, modern Pieta.

K-mart came up beside me, shaking his head. "Muy hesoma-gari."

I thought back to my own days as a mel-head. "But we've all got navels that can get twisted, Kaz. Leastwise, those of us born human."

On our way out, I came on the Bulldog chewing up the evidence. In the heat of the moment, its ancient instincts had overwhelmed its training.

I went to kick it, but changed my mind.

NO BETTER THAN ANYONE ELSE

Molly Brown

It was a Friday night and I was part of a team working the booth joints in the West sector of Area 4. Another team was working the East. There'd been seven booth-related murders in the last four months; all dark-skinned women in their twenties, with shoulder – length black hair, all known prostitutes, all mutilated. Two were black, one was oriental. The rest were Latino: three Puerto Ricans, one Mexican. I'd never done plain clothes before; I'd only been out of the academy three weeks. But I was twenty-two years old and, despite my blue-eyed Irish mother, I looked more like my Puerto Rican father. So I was assigned to Bruce Woods' team as a decoy.

My partner was Castilla Mae Jones, a six-foot-tall black chick with a red and green dragon tattooed on her right thigh. She wore a leopard-print leotard and ballet shoes; I wore a red rubber strapless dress. It was a bad choice, so tight I could hardly move and hot as hell. We each wore a single silver earring, which was actually a microphone. And of course we wore rubber gloves – Area 4 was a disease zone. Nobody went to Area 4 unless they were already infected, crazy, suicidal . . . or a cop.

I'd heard some of the uniform guys back at the station, saying why risk good cop lives over a bunch of broads who'd proba- bly've been dead in a year or two anyway? But murder's still murder, isn't it? And you can't just ignore it, no matter who the victim was or how long she might have lived anyway. Doesn't matter if she wouldn't have lasted another year or even a week, she still had the right to that week. And I told them it was our job to get the bastard who'd stolen that week, or that day, or even that hour she might have had left. And they just said you're a fucking idealist, Gonzales, and nobody stays an idealist long on this job.

Bruce decided we'd hit this joint called *Ricky's Dating Game Lounge* first. It was eleven o'clock. There were maybe half-a-dozen people in the whole place, counting us and the bartender. We were the only women. All the booth joints were dumps, but this was a worse dump than most. It was just a long narrow room with a couple of tables and a bar, dark and smelling of stale beer and smoke. The mirror behind the bar was cracked. There was a black imitation-velvet curtain drawn across one corner at the back, next to the ladies' room. That's where the booth was. In the other back corner, there was a jukebox and a tiny stage where the bartender told us they were supposed to have a dancer. It didn't look like the dancer was going to show. Frankie O'Hara, our back-up, had gone in a few minutes ahead of us. He was sitting at the bar ignoring us, just like he'd ignored me back at the station. I didn't like the guy; on the way over, he'd rolled his eyes every time I opened my mouth. He was wired, too. A little microphone next to his chest.

Bruce stayed outside in an unmarked car, watching the front entrance and monitoring all three of us; he was supposed to come in if he heard anything suspicious, like gunshots or screaming, like he really thought screaming would be something unusual in a place like Ricky's. O'Hara said the reason Bruce stayed in the car was he was scared of infection – if he got out of the car at all, he'd be wearing a surgical mask. Looking around Ricky's, I wished I'd worn a mask myself, even though they said you couldn't get infected through the air.

Castilla had been a bit stand-offish back at the station. Bruce told me she'd told him no way was she gonna get stuck looking after some goddammed rookie who didn't know her ass from a hole in the ground. She wanted to work with Chrissie Lopez, but Chrissie got assigned to the other team. Castilla was stuck with me, and anyone could see she wasn't happy about it. But once we were hanging around Ricky's with nothing happening and nothing to do but talk, she started to get a bit friendlier. Especially after I told her I'd been with Dilation and Curettage.

It wasn't like I was bragging, it just slipped out. We'd given our glasses to the bartender to be filled and sterilized. He'd placed them back on the bar, using a pair of metal tongs, and handed us each an individually wrapped straw. Ordinarily, that should have been precautions enough, but I didn't like the look of the bartender – even in the dim light of Ricky's, I could see the guy had a pasty face and huge dark circles beneath his eyes. Of course, he might have just been tired, but I wasn't taking any chances; there was no way I was drinking anything poured by that guy, even through a sterile straw. We took our drinks and went to stand at the back of the room. I noticed Castilla wasn't drinking hers either.

She was leaning against the jukebox, smoking a cigar, when I noticed the box had one of the old Dilation tunes: "Cut Me, Baby". You know it. It's the one with the chorus that goes: Cut me, squeeze my veins dry, let me die in your arms, let me die real slow cause I love love love you. And then there's this instrumental part that's done with synthesizers and there's a woman's voice and it sounds like she's moaning. Well, that's me. I'm the one moaning, plus I sing back-up on the chorus. I was nineteen when we recorded that. I just couldn't help pointing the song out to Castilla. She was really impressed. "Quick," she said, "hand me some money so I can play the sucker!" She played the song and I sang along with the chorus. "That really is you!" she said. Suddenly her whole attitude towards me went through this complete transformation; it was like the old days, when Dilation were tops in the virtual charts and people used to recognize me everywhere I went.

She got all excited and said she knew she'd seen me somewhere before, I looked so familiar. She started going on about all the virtuals, like the one for *Cut Me*, where Derek slashes me with a razor and then I rise headless out of a grave, wearing a blood-spattered gown. And of course, *Satan's Child*, which is most people's favourite. Everyone knows that one, it's where Dilation ride their Harleys into a derelict church and I'm strapped to the altar and suddenly the guitars turn into chainsaws and you get to choose whether they slice me up or have sex with me.

"Girl," she kept telling me, "anybody'd who'd leave a band like Dilation for this shit is crazy! You're fucked up in the head, you know that?"

"They can't sing, Castilla. I was the only one of them who had any kinda voice, but they just kept me in the background most of the time, like some kinda decoration. And in every single virtual, they killed me off! Between the ages of eighteen and twenty-one, I did twenty virtuals with them, and I got murdered twenty different ways. They hung me, they shot me, they electrocuted me, they cut off my head. You name it, they did it to me. That shit can get annoying."

"You can't take that stuff personally. Every virtual's gotta have somebody die. That's what sells the song. You should know that!"

I tried to tell her how Dilation's guitars were just fashion acce-sories 'cause none of them could even play an instrument, the computer did it all, and how they couldn't even work the computer themselves, there was this guy who did it for them. And she just said, "Who cares about music? They're such pretty little boys."

And then I tried to tell her how they're not little boys, they're in their forties and you wouldn't look twice at them if you saw them in the street, the computer pretties them up for the virtuals. And she said but you don't look any different in person, and I said of course not, I didn't *need* twenty years taken off of me. Then I told her that Derek Dilation's real name is Stan Bukowski and Clive Curettage is Sidney Harstein, and that Stan's got boils and Sidney's got bad breath. But she just said she'd slip old Sidney a peppermint anytime. I gave up.

Castilla nearly took a sip of her grapefruit juice, then realized what she was doing and put it down on top of the jukebox. She looked around the room, winked and tilted her head towards the front door. I turned slightly, trying not to be too obvious, and saw a man standing near the door, staring at Castilla. I could have sworn the guy was drooling.

"I still think you're crazy," she said, watching the man watch-ing her. "What's it matter what anyone's like in real life anyway? Who cares if they're Derek or Stanley or Sidney or whatever, those guys are stars! I've got them on virtual and that's good enough for me. That's good enough for most people. Why'd you ever wanna leave them and come on the job?" I told her my Irish grandfather'd been a Captain. "Oh, God," she said. "So it's the family business. That explains a lot."

The man she'd been watching started walking towards us. She took a small gold compact from her bag, and started dabbing powder on her nose and chin. "What do you think, Rosie?" She called me Rosie. Fifteen minutes earlier, I'd been Gonzales.

"I think he likes you," I said. "That doesn't mean he's a slasher, does it?"

"We'll find out, won't we?" Castilla leaned back against the wall, striking a perfect pose. I glanced over at the bar and I saw the look on Frankie's face. Now I knew why the guy seemed like such a sullen bastard, he was in love. "He's getting closer, Rosie. This is where I get to be an actress, just like you in the virtuals. Lights, camera, action!" Castilla placed one hand on her bare dark thigh, long red nails drumming her tattooed dragon. I got out of the way.

Castilla and the guy talked for a few minutes; Castilla was laughing. Then they headed towards the black curtain. She wasn't supposed to do that. I looked over at Frankie O'Hara. His face had gone green.

We both lit cigarettes and waited.

They came out less than five minutes later. The man looked angry; Castilla looked ill. I rushed over to her. "You okay? Is that our guy?"

She mumbled something about leaving her alone, and stumbled into the ladies' room. I followed her in and found her kneeling in one of the stalls, heaving into the bowl. "You all right?" I said. "What happened?"

She staggered to her feet. "Shit," she said. She took a wad of toilet paper, sprayed it with disinfectant, and stuffed it under her leotard, between her legs. "I'm still bleeding."

"Bleeding? What'd he do to you? Oh my God, he's getting away!"

She waddled over to the sink. "Shut the fuck up, Rosie! He's not the slasher."

"Then what's going on? Why are you sick? Why are you bleeding?"

"Will you shut up?" she hissed, pointing at my earring. I finally understood; she didn't want Bruce to hear. She took off her earring and indicated that I do the same. Then she unstrapped the bag from around my waist, opened it up, and dropped both our earring mikes inside it. She placed my bag in the sink, and turned on the tap. "What are you doing?" I said. "My badge and my gun are in there!"

"Shut the fuck up, will you? Your bag's waterproof, I've got one just like it at home."

"You gonna tell me what's going on?"

Castilla nodded wearily and slumped to the floor, leaning her head against the pipes beneath the sink. "Lock the door," she told me. "I don't want any assholes walking in." There was a metal bolt; I slid it across.

She closed her eyes. "It wasn't like I expected. It wasn't what I thought it would be; it was nothing like the virtuals."

"What the hell are you talking about?"

"Before I went in that booth, I . . . you don't tell anybody about this, you hear? You don't tell anybody or you die. Got that?"

I nodded.

"Before I went in the booth, I was a virgin."

I almost choked; it was an involuntary reaction.

"Don't you laugh at me, bitch! Whatever you do, don't you laugh at me or I swear I'll knock your head upside the wall!"

"I'm not laughing at you, Castilla. I swear I'm not. But why the hell did you go inside the booth?"

"Why do you think? Because every woman who was murdered was murdered inside a booth! I'm a decoy; it's my job to go into the booth!"

"But why'd you take this assignment? You could have turned it down."

"Turn it down? Oh, yeah? I've been on the force three years. You know what I've been doing all that time? I spent my first year searching the body cavities of women prisoners. The last two I've been touring schools, lecturing children about road safety."

This time I did laugh. "You mean you were an 'Officer Friendly'?"

"That's what the kids called us, yes. Will you stop laughing, damn you! This assignment was my chance to be a cop, a real cop. I couldn't turn this shit down."

Frankie O'Hara was pounding on the door. "Castilla, are you all right?"

"Go away!" Castilla shouted.

"Look, Castilla," I said, "if it's any consolation, I think technically you're still a virgin. I mean, what happens in the booth technically isn't . . . well, you know . . . because there's something between you the whole time."

"Will you shut your stupid face?" Castilla growled at me. "I don't need you to tell me about it, okay?" I didn't need her to tell *me* about it, either. My own first time had been in a booth, but at least I'd been with someone I knew, someone I even thought I was in love with. And it was terrible, with that dim red light and piped in music and vibrating walls, each in your separate padded compartment with a lubricated, disinfected – supposedly "infinitely stretchable, guaranteed never to tear" – latex wall between you the whole time so there was no contact and no chance of infection. The booths had been brought in after the epidemic of 2019, and now there were booth joints in every major city, except for Charlestown, South Carolina, where even virtuals were banned. Frankie was still pounding on the door, threatening to break it down. "Tell that boy to get out of my life."

I pulled the bolt aside and opened the door. "Castilla wants you to go away." He shoved past me and got down on the floor beside her. "Oh, baby, baby," he said. "Talk to me."

"What? What do you want me to say to you, O'Hara?"

"Anything, baby. Anything."

He moved in closer to her. I saw her reach inside his shirt and pull out his little microphone. "Get outta here, Gonzales," O'Hara said.

My drink was on top of the jukebox where I'd left it. I picked it up and sat down at a table. My dress was digging into my stomach so bad I could hardly breathe. I was shifting around in my chair, trying to get comfortable, when the worst thing that could possibly happen to a rookie cop working undercover happened. Someone recognized me.

"Rosemary Gonzales!" he shouted for the whole bar to hear.

Every head turned. Great, I thought. Everybody's having a good look at me, everybody in the bar knows my name.

A guy about my age, dressed in black leather jeans and a tee-shirt, was walking straight towards me. "Rosemary Gonzales," he was saying, "Rosemary Gonzales. I can't believe it."

"I think you've got me confused with someone else." I looked at the ladies' room door in desperation. When were those two coming out?

He was standing over me, breathing on me. "Come on, you can't fool me! I'm your biggest fan. I've got every virtual Dilation ever made – I've zoomed in on your face, close up, a thousand times. I know every inch of you, intimately."

"I'm sorry," I said, "but you've got me mixed up with someone else. My name is Sandra, and I've never been in a virtual; I don't even like them."

"Don't tell me that. It's me. Victor. You remember me, don't you?"

"Victor?" I took a good look at the guy, and then I remembered. Orange-haired, pimply nutcase who used to send me flowers every day. And he used to write me letters, telling me how the two of us met and made love in his dreams every night, which he considered proof that we were lovers on the astral plane. I recognized him from the photos he used to send me, at least a dozen of them, all of him sitting alone in a room papered with pictures of me: close-up stills from every virtual I ever made. Even his ceiling was covered with them. I remembered he had a job somewhere, making dentures or something. A nutty, obsessive fan, but harmless. Dilation had loads of fans just like him, always writing weird letters and sending gifts. I figured it was better to admit who I was than to keep arguing with the guy – he probably just wanted my autograph; then he'd go away.

"Victor," I said, "of course I remember you. You used to call yourself Dilation's number one fan, didn't you?"

"Not Dilation, only you. I saw their latest virtual and it was crap – you weren't even in it. What happened? Did you quit or what?"

I shrugged. "Something like that."

"So what are you doing now, Rosie?"

"Not a lot. Look, Victor, I'd appreciate it if you didn't tell anybody you saw me here, okay?"

"Don't want people to know how you've come down in the world, huh?"

I stared into my drink, willing him to go away, willing Castilla and O'Hara to come out of the john, willing Bruce to get out of his goddamn car and come into the bar and tell us we were leaving this dump and moving on to the next one. It didn't work. Victor leaned even closer.

"You knew how I felt."

I shrugged and glanced at my watch. Barely two minutes had gone by since I'd left Castilla and O'Hara in the john. It seemed like a lifetime. "I don't know what anybody feels about anything," I said.

"You knew, but you didn't care, did you, Rosie? Didn't you get the flowers? I sent you flowers every day, remember?"

"That was years ago, Victor." I looked at my watch again. Another ten seconds went by; I know because I counted them, one by one. That rubber dress was killing me. I was sweating like crazy, and my skin itched all over.

"So how about it, Rosie?"

"How about what?"

"There's only one reason for coming to a place like this. You must want it bad."

I couldn't believe it; he actually expected me to go in the booth with him. He actually expected it. "No way, asshole," I said. "Fuck off."

Victor's eyes went narrow and hard. I felt a knife in my ribs. "That's not nice, Rosie. That's not nice, at all. Now stand up, real slow."

"Bruce," I said.

"What?"

"Bruce, come in right now!"

"Stop playing games, Rosie, before I get mad. Now get up real slow, like I told you, or I'll cut you right here."

Oh shit, I thought, Bruce couldn't hear me – my goddamn earring was in my bag, which I'd left in the ladies' room with Castilla. And so was my gun. I stood up slowly, like he said. He pressed himself hard against my left side, pinning down my left arm, and put one arm around my waist, pinning down my other arm. Positioning himself so that the knife was hidden from view, he pulled me to my feet and away from the table. I could feel the tip of the knife through my dress. If he was planning to take me outside, Bruce would see. But he didn't take me outside, he led me towards the imitation velvet curtain at the back.

Once we were behind the curtain, he manoeuvred himself around behind me and raised the blade to my throat. "Don't make a sound," he said, "don't even whisper." He fed a one-hundred-dollar bill into a slot beside the booth door. It slid open, and he pushed me inside. He came in behind me, squeezing us both into the same compartment. "You can scream now," he said as the door slid closed behind us. "The walls are soundproof."

Victor pushed me back against the wall, his blade digging into my throat, my right shoulder bending the latex wall at my side. Behind him, I saw the exit button glowing faintly, just out of reach. "Hey, Victor," I said, quietly, "what's this all about, huh?" The wall behind my back was vibrating. Then the piped-in music started, a slow thumping beat with lots of synthesised groans and heavy breathing.

"I was so wrong about you, Rosie. I used to think you were something really special. Everything I ever did, I did thinking of you. I dreamed of the day we would be together. You were beautiful, but you were arrogant. You thought you were too good for me, didn't you Miss Rockstar? But look at you now, in a booth joint in the middle of a fuckin' disease zone! No better than anyone else. Not even half as good."

"Who said I was a star? I was a back-up singer."

"Shut up!"

With that blade pressing into my throat, I didn't try to struggle, I just tried to keep him talking, until somebody noticed I was missing. "Come on, Victor," I said. "We're old friends, aren't we?" He spat in my face; I didn't dare raise a hand to wipe it off. I grimaced and fought back a wave a nausea as I felt the spit oozing down my cheek.

"Friends?" he said. "After what you did to me?"

"What do you mean? I never did anything to you."

"What about Atlanta?"

"Atlanta? What are you talking about? We never even played Atlanta!"

"You recorded a virtual there. Monarch Studios, Atlanta. I remember the date: April 23rd, sixteen months exactly tomorrow. I was outside the studio, waiting for you with a bouquet of roses. I always used to send you roses, remember? Roses for Rosie? And these five guys came up to me . . . I remember there were five of them. Five of them! And they grabbed the roses from me and they threw me up against the wall, and they told me, 'This is from Rosie', and they took turns punching me in the stomach and they knocked me to the ground and they kicked me and they told me if I ever came near you again, they'd kill me. I had four broken ribs; I spent a week in the hospital. I gave you my devotion, you gave me two black eyes and four broken ribs."

"I had nothing to do with it, I swear. I never even knew about it until now. I wouldn't have done that to you or anyone. Honest."

"You didn't know about it, huh? I looked up and saw Derek watching from a window. You think I don't know about you and Derek?"

I remembered now. Victor wrote me this crazy letter, he said he'd been to a ceremony just like the one in *Satan's Child*, the devil had promised me to him for eternity, and he'd be coming to get me. I showed the letter to Derek and he said not to worry, he'd make sure the guy never got near me. I didn't get any more letters, so I forgot about it. It was a case of out of sight, out of mind. How was I supposed to know what had happened to him? Derek and I split up, I left the band, and I'd never given Victor a second thought. It was like he'd never existed. "I'm sorry, Victor. But it was nothing to do with me. I didn't know about it."

He didn't hear what I said, he didn't seem to be listening. His eyes moved to the blade at my throat. "Things would have been different if I'd had this. I'd a shown 'em not to mess with me. Nobody messes with me."

"How about putting that knife away?" I said.

"In your first ever virtual, you looked straight into my eyes and told me you loved me. I played it over and over, and each time you promised to be mine forever. I laid there in the hospital for seven days and seven nights and you never came to see me once. You never even sent me a card. Why'd you say you loved me if you didn't mean it?"

"Victor, those were only the words to a pop song! Words someone else wrote for me to say. And I didn't know you were in the hospital. I honestly never knew. Now please put the knife away."

"That's when I started to hate you, Rosie. That's when I really started to hate you. I wanted to kill you."

Victor had to be the booth slasher. The reason all the victims looked like me was because in Victor's mind, I was the victim. I was the one he wanted to kill and so far he'd killed me seven times. I wasn't going to let him kill me again. I pulled my head away, into the latex, and brought my knee up, hard.

He doubled over. The music speeded up, as it was pro-grammed to do after the booth had been in use for ninety seconds. The groans got louder and the red light in the ceiling started to strobe. Victor screamed and struck out wildly, knocking me off balance.

I fell against the opposite wall. I tried to pull myself up, but the more I tugged at the latex, the further down it stretched. I managed to stand up just as Victor recovered enough to lunge at me with the knife. I brought my knee up again, knocking it from his hand, and reached for the door. He grabbed my arm and pressed my face down into the latex, so I couldn't breathe. He tried to twist me around, wrapping me up like a fly in a web, but the latex sprung back into position, twirling me around so fast I was dizzy.

Victor got hold of the knife again. "Police!" I shouted. "You're under arrest!" He brought the blade down in a sweeping movement; I raised my left arm to block him and punched him in the stomach with my right.

"I'm not joking, asshole. I'm a cop." I grabbed his right wrist with both hands, ramming the knife against the wall. It wasn't very effective, the blade just sunk into the padding. Victor knocked me back with his left arm. I landed next to the exit button. As I reached over to press it, I heard the sound of something ripping, and then my head was encased in transparent rubber. Victor pulled it tighter and tighter; I couldn't breathe. I kicked and flailed my arms, slamming my hand desperately against the wall where I knew the button was still glowing. The piped-in music faded out, and I heard the whoosh of a sliding door. Then everything went black.

I didn't even hear the first shot, but I heard the second, or maybe it was the third. All I know is, there was something sticky and wet all over me. Then there was something heavy. The heavy thing was pulled away, and I didn't feel anything. But I heard voices. Maybe I couldn't open my eyes, but I could hear.

Castilla was screaming that she'd never shot anybody before. O'Hara was saying he couldn't believe how stupid that fucking rookie had been, going into the booth without her gun.

There was a siren, then there were more voices. "This one's dead," a voice said. "What about the girl?"

"Still breathing," said another voice. "But only just. Oh shit!" There was a sudden shower of water and disinfectant; the automatic cleaning system had come on, and whoever was talking must have got drenched. I know I did.

I was moving; I heard more sounds, more voices. "We're gonna have a lot of explaining to do," O'Hara was saying. "That goddamn rookie's really dropped us in the shit."

The air felt cooler, I was outside. "Hey guess what?" Bruce was saying. "I just heard it over the radio. They got the slasher!"

I wanted to scream of course they got the slasher, I'm the one who got him, but I couldn't even open my mouth.

"Yeah," Bruce said, "they got him about an hour ago, in the eastern sector. Chrissie Lopez got the collar. He pulled a blade, she cuffed him, he confessed to all seven killings. That Chrissie Lopez, she's quite a cop, isn't she?"

"She's one of the best," O'Hara agreed.

I heard the ambulance doors slam, and I was driven away.

SO NAPOLEON ALMOST
SLEPT HERE, RIGHT?

O'Neil De Noux

New Orleans, 2027 A.D.

You'd think that when they cut off traffic through the French Quarter, when was that, back in 2015, they'd have stopped the goddamn buses. But no, they let those stink bombs keep barrelling through so fat-assed conventioneers didn't have to waddle all the way from Canal Street to visit goddamn St Louis Cathedral or stand in line to eat at Chef Jim LeBeau's or Antoine's.

One of those stink bombs nailed me, just as I crossed Chartres Street, before I could escape into the Napoleon House. It belched a shot of rancid smoke straight into my nostrils, causing me to sneeze twice as I wormed my way through the crowd at the entrance of the ancient cafe. I excused myself to a blue-haired lady, who turned her thin nose up in the air and looked away. She was wearing one of those all-in-one plasticine things that looked like a recycled garbage bag from a vintage television commercial. "Glad Bags," the actor called them. "Aren't you glad you use Glad?"

Easing up to the bar, which ran along the downtown side of the cafe, I waited until I could get the attention of the overworked bartender. While waiting, I gave the place the once over. It hadn't changed since I'd been in there a couple years earlier. Hell, like most places in the Quarter, it probably hadn't changed in centuries. Its stucco walls were littered with paintings of French scenes, and about a dozen portraits of Napoleon. There was also a large grey bust of Napoleon behind the bar.

The tender, a big man with a huge gut, moved my way and I finally caught his eye. He turned his wide face to me with a, "Yeah?"

"Excuse me," I said as I pulled out my creds and opened them so he could see my ID card and my star-and-crescent New Orleans Police badge. "I'd like to speak to the manager."

He scrunched up his beady eyes and said, "Say what?"

"I'd like to talk to the manager. Could you point me in the right direction?" *Come on*, I thought, *it's a simple damn question*.

The man's mouth contorted in a look of apathy as he raised his fat little arm and pointed toward the back of the place. I could see a door there. I thanked the tender and worked my way through the crowd. I knew the tender would continue watching me. It never ceased to amaze me just how easily people were thrown off by a polite cop, especially in New Orleans. I mean, like, I didn't curse him or anything.

I caught a whiff of aroma from the kitchen just as I knocked on the door with the word "Private" on it. My stomach twitched at the strong scent of rich seasonings, probably gumbo or étouffée. A woman's voice behind the door said, "Come in."

She was sitting behind a wooden desk, and looked up at me with a flushed look on her face. Angry. She looked angry, her dark green eyes taking a second to focus on me, revealing a hint of embarrassment at being caught in such a temper. Her brown hair, which had enough red highlights to cause an untrained eye to describe her as a redhead, was parted down the centre and worn off her face, except for an unruly strand of hair that dangled in front of her left eye. She brushed back the strand of hair and shrugged, giving me one of those looks as if she was about to say something like, "When it comes to sex, men can't keep from lying and women can't keep from telling the truth." Of course, women never say that, except in old movies.

Moving her elbows to the top of her desk, she said, "What can I do for you?"

I pulled out my creds again and said, "I'm Detective Brouillette. Are you the manager?"

Standing, she extended her hand and said, "Heather Grayson." She had a nice handshake, firm, not one of those limp-wristed ones so in fashion nowadays. Moving around her desk, she told her computer to shut down and said to me, "Damn paperwork."

Now that I got a good look at her, I could see she was wearing one of those full dresses that went below the knees. Sleeveless, the dress had a low neck, which showed off her a pair of well-sculptured shoulders.

"I'm with the Unsolved Murder Squad," I said, loosening my tie with my right hand, pulling my MiniMac from my coat pocket. "Could I have a few minutes of your time?"

I told my computer to turn on. It was hot in the little office, very hot. Heather shot me a slight smile, one that said, "All right, if I have to, but this better be good because I would rather be running naked in a cool rain." I heard that line once, in a TV movie about the Carville Leper Colony.

"I'm investigating the murder of a man named Norman Moore, which occurred here at The Napoleon House ten years ago, in 2017. August 15th to be exact. At 11:20 p.m." I watched those green eyes widen slightly. "We're reopening the case," I explained. "Since your name isn't in the case file, I assume you weren't here then."

"Ten years ago, I was in Oregon." She had to brush the unruly strand from her eyes again. I liked that. Nothing like a good-looking woman with a piece of herself that wouldn't listen.

I asked my computer for the names listed in the original murder report, then asked her about the lone eyewitness, a bartender named Keith Schitzmiffer.

"Are you making this up?" she said, putting a hand on her hip.

"No," I showed her the computer screen. She shook her head.

"Ain't much of a name," I admitted. Schitzmiffer was a pretty crappy name actually.

"No one here by that name."

"May I see your employee records?" I asked.

She shook her head again. "You know I can't show you that without a warrant or something."

I knew better, but I figured I'd try to charm her. She was eyeballing me pretty good. Obviously, there was a brain behind those emerald eyes. I liked that. I always liked my women smarter than me, which wasn't hard to find. The way I figure, show me a dumb woman and I'll show you someone faking. I rarely met one who couldn't outfox me. Except ole Eileen Brant. I could never convince her I wasn't a Private Eye. I told her I was the real police, must have showed her my badge fifty times, not to mention my uniform, hat, truncheon, police computer and departmental citations. Know what she said when I showed her my handcuffs? She asked if I had a second pair. Then she dropped her panties, climbed on my old brass bed and lay spread eagle. Sometimes, I do miss that girl.

Heather fanned the top of her dress and said, "It's hot in here." She eased around me and led the way back out into the cafe. Her dress might have been full, but I sure liked the way it hugged her hips when she walked in front of me. Sitting on a stool at the bar, she nodded to the tender, then turned back to me.

"What would you like?"

She had nice lips too, especially when pursed.

"Perrier," I said.

She told the fat tender, "Two."

I sat on the stool next to her.

"So," she said, "tell me about this murder."

"It was a Friday night. Two men were sitting over there," I pointed to the stools at the end of the bar, closest to Charters Street. I told her how the men were drinking beer for about an hour. Then one of the men pulled out a small handgun and shot the other fella in the head and then walked out.

"The killer was in his early twenties, about 5'5", thin, with blond hair, wearing jeans and a black T-shirt with the words, *Where the Hell is Eugene?* across the chest."

The tender put our drinks in front of us. I downed a deep gulp of the icy mineral water and felt better immediately. I was so hot. Putting my glass down, I added, "Police spent a week trying to find out where the hell this Eugene fella was."

She coughed up a mouthful of her drink all over the bar. I started to pat her on the back, but she turned away from me, pushing my hand back and grabbing a towel from the tender who had stepped up. She wiped her face and started to wipe the bar. Turning to me I could see her face was red. It took a couple of seconds for her to catch her breath.

It took nearly half a minute before she could say, "Eugene's in Oregon."

"I know," I said. "The original detective who worked the case is an airport guard now."

I could see her eyes were wet now. When she started laughing, I felt a lot better. I took another hit of Perrier. Checking out the room again, out of habit, I noticed an angry looking man sitting at one of the tables. He was leering at me, giving me one of those Charles Bronson looks. He looked to be pushing fifty, with short grey hair. He was wearing a sleeveless T-shirt, which showed off his tattoos. I could see a screaming eagle on his left shoulder. I leered back, just to prove a point and then asked the fat tender if he knew a Keith Schitzmiffer.

"He works around the corner at The Capdible Bar."

"Yeah?"

"He used to work here. Quit right after I started." The tender picked up the towel Heather had used.

I turned to Heather and she had an elbow up on the bar and was watching me. Twisted that way, the line of her body looked even sexier than before, her hip pointed toward me, her right breast pressed up against the back of her arm.

"Is there anyone still working here that was here in 2017?" I asked.

"No." The tender answered.

Heather nodded toward the tender. "He's been here longer than any of us."

I finished off my Perrier and thanked Heather and stood up.

"You really serious about a ten-year-old case?" Heather shot me a curious look, a little like the one Patricia Neal shot Michael Rennie in *The Day The Earth Stood Still*, when he first told her about "Gort, Klatu, Barata, Nickto".

"Solved one last week that was twelve years old." I closed up my computer and tucked it back in my coat pocket.

"How?"

"Truth, like oil, will rise to the surface." I left her thinking about that line from an old Charlie Chan movie.

The Capdible Bar was a doghouse of a bar on Decatur Street, across from the Jackson Brewery Complex. If it wasn't in the goddamn Quarter, it would have been torn down a half century ago. But I'm sure the do-gooder preservationists would describe it as having "atmosphere". It had that all right, it smelled like a well-used fire hydrant.

At least I didn't have to stay there long. The owner, a zorky-looking punk with pink hair and a sunken chest named Robbie Tony, told me that Keith Schitzmiffer had the day off. I got Shitzy's address in LaCombe and started out the door.

"You should check The Napoleon House," the zork added. "Keith's girlfriend is a waitress there."

I waited until I was out on the banquette before calling back. "What's her name?"

"Sabrina. Little blonde with big tits."

Cute. Real cute!

Heather was back in her office and the strand of hair was back in her face. I asked about Sabrina, and she took me into the side room of the cafe. Sabrina was serving a group of Japanese in the open air patio. I watched her for a minute. She was the impatient type, obviously annoyed at the politeness of the small foreigners.

Heather took Sabrina aside, passed her order pad to one of the prim gay waiters and asked the waitress to take a break. "I'll be back in my office," Heather told me before leaving us.

I pulled out my computer and started in on my interview. Her name was Sabrina Nash and she'd worked there for five years. She and Keith had lived together for four years. "He's at home," she explained, giving me the phone number and address. I took mental notes: Pushy. Aggravating. Bitchy.

She wasn't a bad-looking girl with white-blonde hair and an oversized chest and blue eyes. She said she was thirty. She reminded me of that little blonde woman in that old movie *The Getaway* with Steven McQueen. Sally something.

"Has Keith ever told you about the murder that occurred here?"

Sabrina, who was standing next to the spiral staircase in the patio, put her arm up on the banister and nodded slowly. She wasn't looking in my eyes when I asked that question, but gave me a hard look as soon as I did.

"What did he tell you?"

"Said he was tending bar. There were two guys drinking and talking at the bar. One of them pulled out a pistol, put it against the other guy's ear and fired. Then the killer picked up his glass and left. That's why y'all didn't find any fingerprints."

"What did Keith say the killer looked like?"

Sabrina had the description down pat, and she hadn't read the computer file that morning.

"Nobody ever saw him again." Yawning, she covered her mouth before adding, "There was a lot of blood."

"I guess it's etched in your boyfriend's mind."

"Like it was yesterday."

I had one more question. I asked her where she was ten years ago. She said Iowa. When I asked her what town, she laughed at me. She meant Iowa, Louisiana. *Real cute.* I knew that one-dog town. Didn't even have a K-Mart.

I gave Sabrina my card and told her I'd talk to Keith when he got back to work tomorrow. On my way to thank Heather, I spotted the angry Charles Bronson clone, still at the same table, still glaring at me.

I thanked Heather and gave her a card. Smiling, she said she had a question.

"How tall are you?"

"Six-three."

"You look taller."

"It's the bulk." My mother calls me thick-bodied, my father, heavy-set. I'm just big all over, even my hands, even my toes. I'm thirty-three now and still have never met anyone with bigger toes. My claim to fame.

I passed her one of my cards and she passed me hers, which was on parchment paper:

Heather Grayson
General Manager
THE NAPOLEON HOUSE CAFE
500 Chartres Street New Orleans
    Phone 524-7522-91

Looking at my card, she said, "Bye, Max." She used the same voice Elizabeth Taylor used on Van Johnson in *The Last Time I Saw Paris*. I hate my first name, even when a good-looking woman uses it while flirting. Max Brouillette . . . *Jesus*!

On my way out, I passed Charlie Bronson. I placed my hands on his table, leaned toward his ear and whispered, "Quit eye-fucking me, ass-hole!"

It was the second time that day I caused someone to cough up a mouthful. Wiping his drink from the front of his shirt, the angry man stood up quickly. I braced myself, preparing to tattoo the old fucker with a right hook.

The man scrunched up his face and snarled at me, "You goddamn detectives are so stupid."

I waited for the next brilliant statement.

"Think you gonna solve that old case? No way."

I narrowed my eyes. He looked older up close, had to be pushing sixty. His breath reeked of gin and bingara.

Still rubbing his wet shirt, he said, "I'm Wellesley. Art Wellesley. Check me out. I used to be N.O.P.D."

It was my turn to back up. I unclenched my right fist and had to ask, "What's your problem?"

"I hate cops." With that, he sat down and went back to his drink.

He continued eyeballing me right out of the place. I watched him as I walked away, but was immediately distracted by another stink bomb that belched on me as I walked along the St. Louis Street side of the Napoleon House. Moving away, I felt just like Bogie must have, when he walked out of the Sternwood Mansion the first time in *The Big Sleep*.

The next afternoon, I was surprised to see no busses on Chartres. I paused a moment across the street and took a good look at the Napoleon House. Three stories tall, the masonry facade had peeled away in places to reveal the red brick and timber construction. The building was as gray as one of those old time battleships. Next to the front door were several bronze plaques, explaining how some batwing nineteenth century mayor of New Orleans planned to rescue Napoleon Bonaparte from that prison island and bring him to town, to live out his twilight years. Only the emperor died before they got to rescue him.

The same fat tender was behind the bar. Art Wellesley was at the same table. The only thing that changed was the colour of his T-shirt. I watched him as I moved straight to Heather's Office. Earlier, at my office I had discovered Wellesley had been fired for shooting a K-9 officer after the officer's dog bit Wellesley. He shot the officer in the leg. A routine gunshot wound, the man developed a serious infection in the hospital and lost his leg. Goddamn doctors!

Heather wasn't in her office. The tender told me she was probably upstairs.

"What's there?"

"She lives on the second floor. She's taking a quiet lunch break."

So I went over to The Capdible Bar and was slapped with a

nice surprise. The zorky owner blinked at me with confused eyes. "Haven't you heard?"

"Heard what?"

"Keith Schitzmiffer's dead. He OD'd last night."

Now if there's one thing a good homicide man doesn't believe in . . . it's *coincidence*. I shot straight back to The Napoleon House. I wasn't too surprised to find Sabrina wasn't in, figuring she had funeral arrangements. So I waited at the bar for Heather to come down.

A half hour later she waltzed in wearing a short pink dress, one of those breezy semi-sheer things with straps around back. She had curled her hair and was wearing darker lipstick and looked good enough to eat. I followed her into her office and liked the way she smiled at me when she turned around and saw me in the doorway.

"I need a little privacy. Mind if I call my office from in here?"

She moved from behind her desk and said, "My pleasure," offering me her chair. I could see she wasn't wearing a bra. I tried not to leer at the outline of her breasts as I moved around her desk. Heather started to leave but I called her back. "I don't need privacy from you." She sat in the only other chair in the office, a thick chair in the corner next to the door. I watched her cross her legs.

I instructed my MiniMac to contact the LaCombe Police. When it beeped, I asked LaCombe for the case officer of the Schitzmiffer Case. Heather stood up and cupped her right hand in the form of a glass and pointed outside. I watched her hips as she walked out. It wasn't as hot in there as yesterday. And today, Heather's perfume lingered in the air, sweet and sexy.

Three minutes later, when a window opened on my MiniMac, I watched the video image of the LaCombe officer who'd just handled the Schitzmiffer cadaver. I had everything I needed to know by the time Heather came in with two icy Perriers.

"Keith Schitzmiffer's dead," I told her.

"What?" Her surprise was genuine. She sat back down.

"He overdosed on Blixen." Which was easy to do. They didn't call it the indigo devil for nothing.

"So, what do you do now?"

"Sabrina," I told her. Then I told her about coincidences and, right in the middle of taking another gulp of Perrier, it hit me, like a slap across the face. Heather saw it in my eyes and sat up.

"What is it?"

I felt a smile creep across my face. I turned to the side and told my computer to get me everything it could on Sabrina Nash. "Check every data base," I told it. It took about ten seconds and, as usual, disappointed me. Never arrested, Sabrina had reported herself the victim of a crime only once, a purse snatching on Canal Street. She had a traffic ticket and a valid driver's licence. But sometimes, the lack of information can tell you a lot. Sabrina Nash never had electricity or gas or a telephone in her own name. Ever.

Taking another sip of Perrier, I asked Heather, "How about dinner tonight?"

"I'm working until midnight," she answered before finishing off her Perrier. "But we can go for coffee now, if you'd like."

I liked. I tucked my computer back into my coat and got up. Heather went out first and told the fat tender she'd be away for a few minutes. I was exchanging looks with Charlie Bronson Wellesley when I had another surprise. Sabrina Nash strolled in at that moment and waved to Heather on her way out to the patio.

Heather shot me a quizzical look and I raised my hand, tapped my watch and flashed five fingers at her. She nodded and climbed up on the stool. I pulled my eyes away from her legs and followed Sabrina out into the patio amongst the banana trees and palms and the black, wrought iron tables. Next to the kitchen, it smelled of boiled crabs.

Sabrina didn't look upset at all, until she realized I was standing behind her. She had made her face up pretty good and was wearing a shorter than usual skirt.

I smiled at her, excused myself and asked how she was doing. She said fine, under the circumstances. Then I asked her to repeat the story Keith Schitzmiffer had told her about the killing. She gave me a "pshaw" and repeated it verbatim.

Then she said, "Don't you wanna know about how I found Keith this morning?"

"Naw," I said, inching closer with my MiniMac. Sometimes that little bastard can be pretty intimidating. Especially when I ask official questions and its lights flicker as it records everything. Sabrina was looking right at it when I asked my next question.

"Would you sign a waiver for your medical files for me?"

She looked at me as if I'd just reached over and pinched her tit. Then her blue eyes narrowed. She moved around me and went into the cafe. I followed and found her standing next to Heather, her hands on her hips.

"If you're going to allow the police to question me at work, I want a union official present."

"That won't be necessary," I said, reaching around for Heather's hand. "I have no more questions for you."

Sabrina gave me a hard stare.

"Just don't leave town," I told her. "It'd be foolish of you to try."

As soon as we got outside, Heather asked, "Can you do that? Make her stay in town."

"Naw." It's a line from an old movie named *Laura*. It was what Dana Andrews, the detective with the silver shinbone from the Siege of Babylon, told Vincent Price, the sleazy boyfriend.

I took Heather down Chartres to la Madeleine French Cafe on Jackson Square. We grabbed two mugs of coffee-and-chicory and sat against a window along the St Peter Street side of the cafe, which smelled wonderful. The cafe smelled of fresh-cooked bread. No way I could sit there and not eat something. I went back to the counter for a couple of almond croissants.

I would have rather eaten Heather, and was thinking about just that as she sat across from me, sipping her coffee, breaking off small pieces of croissant to place on her tongue, shooting smiles at me occasionally as I watched her. There's something about a pretty girl's lips when she purses them to take a sip of . . . anything.

I stared at this girl as she picked at my brain. I heard myself explaining about homicides, how the initial twelve hours of a murder were the most critical and how I was up against a brick wall, but how much I loved that challenge. She asked something about the crime scene, about what evidence we'd secured. I told her how a victim dies once and a crime scene is murdered a hundred times. "Physical evidence ain't all it's cracked up to be," I heard myself say. "Unless you catch the killer and can match the pieces."

Then I told her how everyone lies. How murderers lie because they have to, how witnesses lie because they think they have to. Then I told her the secret to solving old murders.

"People forget the lies. They only remember the truth. You just have to ask the right questions."

She looked at me as if she thought I was smart. I liked that. We had a second cup before leaving. It was dark by then and much cooler. So we took a leisurely stroll around Jackson Square and across Decatur Street. Except for the goddamn mimes, it would have been perfect, especially when Heather tucked her arm in mine.

We crossed over the sea wall to the Moonwalk. I tried to be nice to a mime who was mimicking a blind man and managed to send him on his way without having to drop kick him across the river.

We sat on a wooden bench along the boardwalk and looked at the river, at the lights reflecting on the dark water, at a large ship silently passing on its way to the gulf. It was a gorgeous night. Heather leaned her head against my shoulder and I thought of another old movie, a Woody Allen movie. Woody was sitting on a bench with a pretty girl, overlooking the Hudson River. What was her name? Annie Hall? No, I remember the movie's title was *Manhattan*. Yeah, I was feeling pretty good until the gun blast.

I felt it strike the bench even before my ears told me we were under fire. I shoved Heather down and jumped on her, withdrawing my weapon as another shot rang out. It sounded like a handgun, an old gunpowder model. I waited for three seconds before rising slowly.

Nothing. Not even a shadow stealing away in the darkness. I found two other couples along the boardwalk, but as usual, no one saw anything. With Heather's nervous hand in mine, we walked back to The Napoleon House, my right hand in my coat pocket, cradling my new Smith and Wesson Stun 7.

"Hey," I told the tender. "Did Sabrina leave?"

"Naw. She's in the back."

I peeked in the back and sure enough, Sabrina was serving two couples, all wearing cowboy hats.

"Did she leave while we were gone?" I asked the tender.

"What am I, her mother?"

"I need a drink," Heather said as soon as we eased up to the bar. She ordered a Sazerac from the fat tender. I got a scotch rocks. It felt much cooler in the cafe and the strong liquor helped me down from the night's excitement. That was until Heather bumped me with her hip, focused those dark greens on me and said, "Let's go upstairs."

I followed those nice hips up the spiral staircase to her room where she left the door open and moved in the semi-darkness ahead of me. I closed the door and flipped on a small lamp in the living room of her apartment. Heather stopped in the doorway to her bedroom and began to unfasten the straps along the back of her neck. I felt my heartbeat pounding in my ears.

I moved over and helped her, letting my fingers roll down her shoulders to the small of her back as her dress fell to the floor. My fingers worked their way down into the elastic band of her panties as she craned her neck back and kissed me, gently on the lips. I turned her around and kissed her good and hard, French kissed her as my oversized hands caressed her breasts and rubbed her hard nipples. I felt her hand at my crotch.

How we managed to stop long enough to get our clothes off is beyond me, but we did and moved, naked to her bed. In that brief moment, Heather said in a gasping voice, "I sure hope you have a current health card."

I stepped back to my clothes and dug out my creds, opened them and pulled out my health card, which I'd updated a week earlier. That's right, no communicable diseases.

Heather was sitting on her bed, cross legged, her health card in hand.

"I updated it yesterday," she said. "After I met you." I put both cards on her night stand and climbed next to her.

Okay, so I'm an old fashioned southern boy. So I'm not going to explain all the sweaty, steamy details. Let me put it this way, I think there was an earthquake in downtown New Orleans that night. Well, it sure moved for me.

Laying there, in a post intercourse snuggle, I remembered another line from Charlie Chan . . . "Love is as unexpected as squirt from aggressive grapefruit."

Sure, this wasn't love, at least not yet. But the squirting was good.

I felt myself dozing and fought it. Typical male. I opened my eyes and saw Heather staring at me. She kissed me again and asked if I wanted a drink. I told her no.

"How about seconds?"

The second time around was longer and harder and hotter and she came twice before I climaxed. She continued kissing me as I rolled off her and lay there. Heather rested her head on my chest and soon, I felt the world slipping away.

When I woke, the clock said it was two in the morning. Heather was cradled against me in a fetal position. I watched her, watched her chest rise and fall in easy breaths. She slept with her mouth open and her hair was messed over her face and she looked beautiful. Snuggling with her, I remembered how The Sundance Kid described the woman he wanted, "I'm not picky, long as she's smart, pretty, sweet, gentle, tender, refined, lovely . . ."

When I woke again, it was daylight. The clock read nine o'clock. Heather, still naked, was sitting up in bed next to me. She was sipping coffee. That's what woke me, the strong scent of coffee.

"On the table," she nodded. My cup was on the end table, and just the way I liked it, cream and two sugars. I sat up and took a gulp. Heather had put a touch of make-up on her face, not that she needed it. She smiled at me wickedly.

I leaned back against the head board and looked around.

"So, Napoleon almost slept here, huh?"

"No," she answered, pulling that runway strand of hair from her eyes once again. "There's a room down the hall. It's called L'Appartement. You should see the place. It's like a museum. That's where he was supposed to stay, after the break-out."

I took another hit of coffee. Heather, running her fingers through her hair said, "What is it? Why are you smiling like that?"

Seeing her sitting like that in the daylight, cross-legged and naked and sexy as hell, made me smile like that. I finished my coffee, climbed out of bed and asked if she'd have dinner with me. She said she'd think about it. Rising, she grabbed my hand and lead me to the shower.

I know, this is supposed to be a murder mystery. So I'll get back to it. After the long hot shower, I went straight to the Moonwalk and called the crime lab and dug out a pellet from the wooden bench. I sent it to the firearms examiner. Before I finished my second cup at la Madeleine, I got a call on my

MiniMac. I bet you can guess what the message on my screen said.

That's right. The pellet from the Moonwalk was fired from the same pistol that killed Norman Moore at The Napoleon House ten years ago, in 2017. August 15th to be exact. At 11:20 p.m.

Four hours later, armed with a search warrant, I crossed Chartres Street again, right behind a belching bus that didn't bother me in the least. Accompanied by two patrolmen, I marched through The Napoleon House, straight to the office door and knocked on it. Heather answered. She was wearing a yellow dress with a frilly top. I explained before starting my search, explained that I'd just come from LaCombe where I'd searched the Schitzmiffer/Nash apartment, and how we were holding Sabrina at headquarters.

Thirty-seven minutes after beginning my search, the fat tender, who had been shadowing me, pointed to something that didn't belong behind the bust of the Emperor Napoleon that stood behind the bar, against the long mirror. It was a small box. In the box was a Davis .32 caliber, chrome plated pistol with laminated wood grips. That's right. A piece of shit.

I called the crime lab and waited for them to come for the gun. I had a Perrier with Art Wellesley. He didn't like my company much, but I couldn't resist. Leaning over, I told him I'd just solved that old murder.

"Bullshit!"

I leaned closer and gave him a line from *Blazing Saddles*. "You bet your ass."

I winked at Heather before leaving. She held one hand to her ear and played like she was punching numbers on a phone with the other. I nodded.

Charlie Chan once said, "Silence is golden . . . except in police station."

Sabrina Nash was waiting for me handcuffed to a chair in an interview room. When I came in with two cups of coffee, she stuck out her chin in defiance. It took a while, but before I stepped out of that interview room, three hours and three cups of coffee later, her head was bowed and my MiniMac contained a detailed murder confession.

Sabrina's blue eyes remained hard, even when confessing. But I'll never forget how they blinked in haunted recognition when I gave her the weenie. I slipped it to her softly. She didn't even recognize it as the weenie at first, even when I showed her how Keith Schitzmiffer had explained the killing to the first officers on the scene and again in his formal statement early the next morning to detectives. "He placed the gun against the man's temple and shot him." Keith said nothing about the ear. He said temple. Sure, the autopsy report described the wound as . . . "Penetrating gunshot wound of the right ear canal."

It had been the word "ear" that had rattled around in my head after I first talked to Sabrina. That was the weenie. I asked her, "How did you know about the ear?"

"Only the killer, the police and the coroner knew about the ear," I told her. Grinning, I added the kicker, "But even we didn't know about the glass. There were so many glasses on the bar, no one realized the killer had taken the glass, except you."

She wouldn't look me in the eye and I knew it was a just matter of time, especially after the crime lab came back with her fingerprint on the Davis .32.

"You found it?" she said. She was actually surprised. *Jesus!* Thank God criminals are so stupid.

I sat back and told her the exact opposite. I told her she was one smart girl, told her how she'd out foxed us, told her we'd have never caught her if it wasn't for luck. Then I asked her, if she'd just do me the enormous favour, and tell me how she'd disguised herself that night, ten years ago.

When she told me she was a sex change, I acted surprised as hell, even though I'd already had a warrant ready for her medicals. Sabrina's transformation was a good one. Usually I can tell by the hips. Sex changes have thin, male hips. She looked every bit a female. Too bad they couldn't transform the brain. She still had a male brain.

She never boned up to what really happened to Keith Schitzmiffer. But what the hell? No case is perfect, except in the movies. I did get to laugh at the fat tender when my partners brought him into the Detective Bureau. I charged him as an accessory to attempt murder of a police officer.

Before I stepped out of the Detective Bureau, Sabrina had a question for me. "Don't you want to know why I went back to The Napoleon House?"

I looked into those blue-blue eyes and said, "Because it was your greatest moment."

I called Heather before walking Sabrina over to Central Lockup. She wanted to know everything.

"I'll tell you over dinner. Pick you up in an hour?"

"We're eating here," she said. "In L'Appartement. Then we're gonna make love on Napoleon's bed."

I liked that.

Okay, so you're thinking this wasn't much of a case, wasn't much of an investigation. So let me feed you another old homicide cliché.

"It's good to be good. But it's better to be lucky."

Just call me lucky. I hate the name Max.

PROFESSIONALS

Keith Brooke

"She still loves me," said River Brady from across the room. Christian Taylor watched him carefully.

Brady was staring moodily out of a blank window. He was a powerfully built man with gorgeous black hair all the way down to his knees and a mouth that seemed somehow wider than his face, but that meant nothing here. "I'm positive that my wife still loves me." He could control his image but not the wavering tone of his voice.

Christian raised his eyebrows. They were jet black today, to match his jacket. He had never been able to take VR seriously in a business context: he was unable to trust his perceptions, wary of manipulation. He studied River Brady closely, for what it was worth. It wasn't his place to judge, but the man was pathetic all the same.

"She just hides it effectively," explained Brady in his soft Toronto drawl. He turned now and leaned a shoulder against the wall. "I saw her in town three days ago. She looked happy. It was a hell of an act. But when she's on her own I'm positive that it's all very different. She was always like that: a tremendous little actress. She constructs this brittle facade about herself but when she's alone it gets her right here." He sank a hand wrist-deep into his chest in the kind of melodramatic false-world display that made Christian want to laugh in the man's face.

Instead, he tipped back in his fake seat and tried to make himself take Brady's domestic entanglements with at least a degree of seriousness.

He hated to think that he had sunk this far. A few years ago he'd been on the fast track with the National Police and the future had looked fine. Even after rivals had got him thrown out on a minor misdemeanour he'd been able to continue with undercover freelancing: corporate work and a few unofficial jobs the Nationals didn't want on the record.

And now he was doing domestics.

"What exactly do you want me to do?" he asked. It was work, after all. "Do you want me to build a case against her? Do you want me to provide answers for anything she might have on you?"

Brady's chosen image showed nothing, but a protracted pause betrayed his emotion. Eventually, he said, "I want you to trace her movements, find out who she sees, what she does, where she's living. I want you to construct a complete picture of her life and then I want you to help me draw up a proposal I can put to her through her solicitors. I want a planned reconciliation, a trial unseparation. I want her back, Mr Taylor, and I want you to show me how to achieve that goal. Can you help me?"

"Can you pay?"

Brady nodded.

"Then I'll need some information . . ."

As Christian questioned Brady, he received onscreen a set of pictures along with copies of all the relevant documentation. All the time he struggled to find his way through the barrage of over-emotional pap for some insight into the situation, some way forward.

Brady's first contract with Ellen Rinotti had been written up seven years ago, when they were both working on plans for a new dam in what was then still Nigeria. River Brady was chief structural engineer on the project; Ellen was something of a drifter, filling in for an account handler on paternity leave. They formalized their marriage only eight months later – positively rash in such conservative times – and they started sex three months after that. It was all in the contracts Brady copied to Christian's workbase, nothing too unusual.

Christian studied the legalese carefully, grateful for his basic police training in the elaborate hybrid language European law-firms used these days. He tried to find something to snag his interest, but he knew that when he started to get a thrill out of domestics he would be in serious trouble.

"So why did she go?" He had to ask, although he might have phrased it more sensitively.

"I have a lot of work on at present," said Brady. He was employed by a Danish architectural consultancy now, based somewhere up in Essex. "Deadlines, exacting requirements . . . a great deal of pressure. I get absorbed. I neglect my social obligations."

Such obligations were written into the contract of marriage: if it came to arbitration then Christian's client would have little room for manoeuvre.

Brady swished his fancifully long hair and said, "I don't claim to be without flaws, Mr Taylor: I admit that the blame must lie disproportionately in my own quarter. What I seek is another chance."

"Then you should be telling that to your wife," said Christian softly. But he knew she was deflecting Brady's calls. For a moment he felt guilty. "Are you coping all right?" he asked, feeling awkward; he was aware that such a question was outside the parameters of his job.

Now Brady leaned forward aggressively. "If I could drink myself into oblivion then that is precisely where I would currently be," he said. "But I am on a three-year contract with my employers which stipulates that I be clean, so that option is beyond me." It had become a standard corporate practice to treat key employees with slow-release implants that made abuse of alcohol and certain narcotics physically impossible, either inducing a nauseous response or nullifying the action of the substances. "All I have," continued Brady, spreading his hands to indicate the false room in which they sat, "is this ersatz world with which to distract myself when I am not immersed in my work. I cope, Mr Taylor, because I am a professional, but I want my wife back. I need her with me."

Christian peeled the VR mask away from his eyes and waited for his sight to adjust to the dim light of his Earls Court flat. He looked around at the organised clutter in which he lived. He never let anybody in here: it was private, his own small patch of territory. He pushed his hair back from his forehead and sighed. "Get me Sammy," he said and instantaneously the blue on blue ident of the National Police pinged onto the flat screen pasted to the wall before him.

When the synthetic voice queried him he told it, "Constable Samarjhit Gai Khan. Extension 3645."

"Hold, please."

A lot of his work was like this: person to person. The days of hacking into systems and lifting information were past, with data security so tight you had to be corporate before you could even consider it as an option. These days it was more a matter of who you knew than what you knew: what the French called *piston*.

He waited for a minute or so, and then a genial dark face appeared on the screen, with a dark blue false backdrop. "Sammy," he said. "How's it hanging?"

"Hey, Chris," said the face. "It's good, man, but listen: it's hectic round here. *Hectic*. I'm doing ten jobs at once, you know?" He flicked at his beaded hair. "What're you wanting from me then, eh?"

Christian tried to look hurt, but it was no good; Sammy knew him too well. They went back years together. "How about some information, then?" he said. "River Sean Brady, NM37068/4C1. Ellen Mae Rinotti, HL12829/3HO."

"No can do, Chris. You know what would happen if I was found putting your private work through the system. I love you like a brother, Chris, but no way. Okay?"

Christian ignored him. "I'm heading up to Essex," he said. "So send it to the car when you have it, right? Listen, I owe you one, Sammy."

"You owe me fucking hundreds," said his friend, before the blue on blue ident flashed up again and he was gone.

Christian set his workbase to trawling and filtering information from the hundreds of franchised data stores that might hold something relevant to the case, then he called ahead to book himself a room at a Formule Une just outside Harwich.

As soon as his old two-seater VW had locked into its Trafficontrol convoy on the A12, Christian projected one of Brady's video sequences of Ellen Rinotti head-up onto the windscreen. She was a tall woman with a plaited tail of black hair pulled down from the back of her head and laced into the front of her fisherman's jumper with a strand of silver wool. The jumper's hem dragged halfway down her bare thighs, swinging from side to side as she danced sinuously through a garden to a tune Christian had turned down. Instead, he asked the car to play him Stockhausen's

Donnerstag aus Licht; for a time her movements and the music were so out of synch that they almost seemed *in* synch and the journey was soon over.

He spent the next three days collating information, talking to acquaintances of the couple, pursuing Ellen Rinotti through the aimless jumble of her life. He came up with little, certainly nothing that suggested a formula for reconciliation that could be agreed by both parties.

Sammy had given him Ellen's current address, along with a screenful of financial information which told him that she was still receiving occasional sums of money in addition to the temporary support order her solicitors had won from her husband. She even had a criminal record from her early teens when she'd been booked twice for morality offences in her native Florence. He wondered if River Brady was aware that his wife had once been an under-age hooker. Probably not, from the picture he had painted of her when he hired Christian; her offences had been committed fifteen years before they had even met.

On his fourth morning in Harwich Christian took one of the town's little electric citicars down to the seafront. Alone in a strange and somewhat shabby town, he struggled not to feel strange and somewhat shabby himself. He wondered where all his resilience had gone, his stubborn independence.

He took an outside table at a Turkish coffee shop that overlooked the dirty waters of Dovercourt Bay and tried to get his thoughts together. A short distance out a couple of jetsurfers skidded aimlessly about in the foam.

He ordered an espresso and while he waited he pulled a screen from his pocket, unfolded it and pressed it to the table. Everything was here: all the pictures, all the information he had gathered. He skimmed the headlines, touched one lightly with a finger and the screen filled with a still picture of Ellen walking through Deane Mall; he'd taken that one himself, the previous day.

All he had to go on were two inconsistencies. The first was the extra money she was somehow earning. He wondered for a moment if she was on the game again, but all the time he had followed her there had been nothing to suggest she had returned to her old ways; she just didn't *look* like a professional any more. Besides, her only convictions dated back over twenty years.

She filled her days at the beach, or in town, or more often back in her flat by the docks in old Harwich. She seemed to be doing no more than treading water until she found something to do with her life again.

The second inconsistency was in the information River Brady had given him. Back in the former Nigeria, when they were both working on the dam project, they had separated. It had only lasted for a couple of weeks, but Brady had been specific in asserting that they had never split up before.

But several years had passed since then and the separation had been early in their relationship, before they'd even been legally married. Christian couldn't help thinking that his lack of progress was lending significance to the most minor of matters.

He knew that River Brady was one of the best in his field: whenever his contract came free a number of firms were keen to sign him up. His one theory was that maybe Brady's firm had paid Ellen to leave him. A number of people had told him that the boundary between art and the cutting edge of engineering was a fuzzy one – perhaps Brady's employers were hoping to somehow get the best out of him, that he would sublimate his grief into the creative side of his profession. Brady himself had said that he was currently immersed in his work.

Christian took a sip from his espresso and grimaced at the sudden bitterness and heat.

Earlier this morning he'd called the London office of the bank that handled Ellen Rinotti's affairs. He had been putting this call off for the last three days.

After two synthetic receptionists tried to stall him a dark-haired woman with an angular face appeared onscreen. "Carole," he said. "I meant to call." He always thought she looked as if her features had been drawn on with pencil and ruler, they were so geometric.

She said nothing.

"I need some help," he told her. "Information. I'm on a case." The look in her eyes hurt. "Ellen Mae Rinotti, HL12829/3H0. She has irregular sums coming into her account. I need to know more."

Eventually, Carole said, "You know I can't do that."

"I know," he said, and risked a smile.

The screen went blank.

Another fruitless day, but all the same another day's fees for Brady to pay.

Christian Taylor sat in his motel room removing the make-up from his face with a succession of moisturizing wipes. All around him Ellen Rinotti danced across the walls, her fisherman's jumper dragging across bare thighs. He had always taken her flirting looks at the camera as those of a wife to her husband, but now he saw in those eyes, those moistly parted lips, the whore that she had once been.

He lowered his head and scrubbed his face with a soft towel. When he looked up a message was dancing across the walls. "Yup," he said, acknowledging it, and Ellen Rinotti was replaced by the massively enlarged face of Carole Sayers. She was calling from a public booth, not daring to speak from work. The time marker told Christian the message had been recorded ten minutes ago, avoiding the awkwardness of conversation.

"Christian," she said. "It's Carole."

He smiled. He'd never known anybody like Carole for stating the obvious. The recording continued, oblivious.

"You know I can't keep doing this kind of thing. You have to promise not to keep doing this." She paused, as if waiting for him to acquiesce, and he stared at the faint fan of straight lines spreading up from the bridge of her nose. "Those payments you asked after – why not look into the Sociotronics Encounters Group? Rinotti has an account with them, with sums coming in and out all the time. Okay, Christian? Will you call?" She faded from the wall, and Ellen Rinotti was glancing back across her shoulder at him once again.

He cut her off sharply, asked the room for a VR mask and a drawer slid smoothly open at the side of his bed.

In the small un-room he opened into he flicked through a catalogue until he came to encounter groups, located SEG and touched one of its panels. A new room opened up around him, sun streaming in through an open doorway.

He went outside and looked around. SEG had put him on a tropical atoll, the sky and sea complementary shades of deep blue.

He looked down and saw his bare toes curling and uncurling in sharp white sand. He didn't feel a thing.

He heard voices and turned away from the gently breaking waves. A tall fire burned in a clearing, surrounded by a cluster of grass huts. A number of people sat or stood or ran about like children. Some were clothed, others wore nothing, but most fell somewhere in between. All were young, slim, fit, with skin and hair colours ranging right across the spectrum. A small message flashed persistently in the corner of Christian's vision, warning him that he was not equipped to enjoy the full experience offered in this encounter scenario. It advised a full body stocking for total interaction, a genital glove at the very least.

He'd heard all about these encounter groups – sex at its absolute safest, the only physical interaction being between the participant's body and his or her interactive suit.

Someone beckoned to him to come closer and join in but he stayed where he was on the beach; the lack of complications attracted him, but at the same time he felt vaguely repelled. He studied the partying figures and wondered which one might be Ellen Rinotti. All the time she spent alone in her flat – when Christian had assumed she was brooding over the break-up of her marriage – all that time she had been out here in this ersatz world getting paid to lead lonely men through fake sexual encounters.

Another woman waved to him but he'd seen enough. He raised a hand to point homeward but then he paused. He'd seen someone, over in the doorway of one of the huts, getting it on with a silver-haired girl with fish-scales all over her naked body. The man flicked long black hair away from his face.

It was River Brady.

Build Odense had an office complex on the site of the old golf club, about a kilometre from Parkeston Quay. A burst of development had taken place here over the last few years as a number of continental firms had cashed in on the area's *Région Désavantagée* status.

The gates wouldn't let Christian pass until he told them to check with River Brady. They opened and he drove through, then relaxed as Control took over and parked his car at the rear of the main building.

Brady kept him waiting twenty minutes, but Christian didn't

care: the man was paying for Christian's time to be wasted like this. Finally, he was shown into a wide office, split up in the current fashion with paper screens and tall, jagged plants.

Brady was a small man, dapper in three-piece suit and silk tie. His round features and thinning mousy hair were nothing like those he adopted in VR. He sat on a cane mat on the floor, his bare feet tucked up into the lotus position, an array of screens and papers spread out around him. He glanced up at Christian and gestured at a chair. "Unexpected," he said. "You have something to offer?" His watered-down accent was more pronounced in the flesh.

"Nothing concrete," said Christian, as the chair settled beneath him. "I've been gathering information, building up pictures. I think that pretty soon I'm going to have to meet with your wife in order to determine her negotiating position."

"Something is bothering you, Mr Taylor. You didn't come here simply to inform me that you haven't made much progress."

"I saw you yesterday," said Christian, cautiously. "Or rather, I saw your VR image. At one of the SEG encounter groups."

Brady seemed unconcerned. "I told you," he said. "It's my only escape. So what?"

"Your wife uses the same group."

Brady's facade faltered for a moment. Either he was a good actor or he had been genuinely unaware. Finally, he said, "I didn't know. Jeez. She always did like to spend time under the hood . . . it just never occurred to me that our paths might cross like this and me not even notice. Jesus."

Christian sighed; Brady seemed sincere. There was no reason why he should have recognized Ellen: anonymity could be bought for the price of an image makeover – some people took a different look every trip. He decided not to inform Brady of just what his wife had been doing in VR, of how she was supplementing her income. "You have to appreciate how irregular it looked when I found out," he said.

Brady peered up at him, nodding. "Of course," he said. "Hell, I was wrong when I accused you of not making any progress: you've confirmed a great deal."

Christian waited for him to continue.

"Like I said: she still loves me. When I saw her in town and she seemed happy it was all an act. Her only escape is exactly the same as mine: this sanitized world of fantasy, hidden behind the mask."

He really seemed to believe that. The man was clutching at every last straw in his efforts to prove that the breakdown of his marriage was not irretrievable. Christian recalled his first, hasty assessment of River Brady, and he saw no reason to alter it now. The man was pathetic.

He remembered his pet theory that Build Odense might be paying Ellen to leave, in order to somehow extract the best from her husband. "How's your work?" he asked, aware that there was no way he could make the question sound casual.

Brady's expression cleared. "You want to see?" he asked. Then, without waiting for an answer, he tossed a VR mask across to Christian and said, "Come take a look."

Seconds later they stood together in a blank room. Brady glanced at a sheet of paper, touched a panel on it and a new room opened up around them. They stepped towards a door and suddenly the room was replaced by an enormous hollow space. "Don't be disorientated," said Brady.

Christian fought back a wave of vertigo, feeling certain that Brady had intended him to feel this way: he could have warned him first, if he'd really wanted to be sympathetic.

Brady waved a hand and an enormous platform drifted towards them. After a few seconds Christian recognized it as a power station: a vast deck of wave turbines, topped by rigging for a windfarm. With no regard for verisimilitude the construction was coloured garishly in yellows, oranges, reds, blues and greens, bright patterns sometimes flashing across the structure, informing the expert eye of stresses, weaknesses and God knows what else. These stations were built in the estuary and towed out into the North Sea; one of Christian's searches had told him that Brady was working on a new platform for Build Odense.

Side by side they walked across the rainbow-coloured deck. Although Christian knew next to nothing about this kind of thing, the whole structure looked to have the simple, clean lines of good design.

They stopped in the centre of the platform. The scale was unclear but Christian knew that this was going to be one of the biggest power stations in the North Sea. "It looks impressive," he said blandly.

Brady turned on him.

"Impressive?" he said, shaking his head slowly. The platform was rising and falling gently, and now Christian saw through the bright patterning that it was made up of thousands of interlocking hexagonal plates, maybe five metres across, with flexible linkages so that ripples now flowed sequentially across the entire surface, making the gaudy colours flash and zigzag in apparent chaos.

"Impressive?" repeated Brady.

The ripples were becoming more pronounced now, so that it was a struggle for Christian to remain upright.

"We are in the middle of the North Sea," said Brady, as the disturbances grew all around him. "One of the most extreme seas on the entire globe. All that supports us is a cobweb of carbon filaments, spun diamond struts, state of the art technologies. . . . The surface presentation may impress you but that's all artifice. Let me tell you, Mr Taylor: it doesn't work! It doesn't fucking work!"

Suddenly Brady grabbed Christian's hand and they flew up above the platform an instant before there was an enormous groaning sound and a deep crack spread across the surface. Now there were two platforms, hammering against each other, individual plates tearing free and being thrown up in the air to come smashing down again into the growing chaos.

They watched in silence as the fledgling power station ripped itself apart.

Back in the first ersatz room Brady turned to Christian and said softly, "I can't work like this. I'm going out of my mind. I'm nothing without my Ellen."

They peeled masks and stared at each other. They were in the real world now, yet Christian felt perversely that he had been closer to the genuine River Brady amid all the fakery of his VR design room. Now, it seemed that there was little more to say.

"Do I have your permission to meet your wife?" asked Christian.

River Brady shrugged. "Whatever you feel is necessary. I think you know what it means to me."

Christian climbed out of his chair and left the office.

Someone was waiting for him in the passenger seat of his car: a tall blond man in an anonymous green suit with an ID panel on the lapel. Company Security. Christian could smell it from the other side of the car park. He slid into the driver's seat and thumbed the ignition so the car would know it was him.

"It will not take you anywhere until I grant permission," said the man in immaculate second-language English. Someone else with a talent for stating the bloody obvious.

"What do you want?" asked Christian brusquely. They were both professionals, there was no need to skirt around the real business.

"I represent Build Odense," said the man. "We are concerned at the drop in performance of one of our key employees. We wish him to be more settled in his work."

"You're threatening me?"

The man smiled, dipping his head slightly as he did so. "I hope not," he said. "I hope we will be able to reward you well for enabling our employee to improve his performance. Please understand how important an issue this has become for my company. Not only do we have our current contractual obligations to Powergen to fulfil: the time is approaching for companies such as ours to tender for the various phases of the second Channel Link. Our employee's skills would be a key part of any such bid. You must see why we are so concerned."

"You want him to be happy," said Christian.

The man nodded, then pushed his door open and climbed out, dropping his business card on the empty seat. As soon as the door swung shut, the company's parking control system cut in and Christian's car backed out of its space and headed for the road.

His head starting to buzz, he took the wheel and said, "Give me Messiaen's *Turangalila*." Thinking music. It was all starting to slot together.

He found her on the second level of Deane Mall, a sprawling shopping centre built on the infill between Harwich, Parkeston and the throughway. It was one of her favourite haunts. She would spend hours of the day idly browsing at Bloggs or HN, or meeting up with friends for drinks and leisure shopping.

She was at a booth in Boots when he spotted her, staring at various versions of herself on the widescreen, each demonstrating a particular cosmetic alteration available from the in-store surgeon.

He waited nearby, no need to hurry. After a time she showed that she knew he was there, but she lingered for another ten minutes before turning to him.

"There are other booths," she said. He had expected traces of an Italian accent but instead her voice was undistinguished home counties.

"I was waiting for you, not the screen," said Christian. "I know a lot about you. I want to talk. Okay? Business."

She shrugged, sure of herself. "Buy me coffee," she said, and led the way up to a sitting area on the mezzanine.

"I'm working for your husband," he told her, as they waited for the pot of Lapsang Ellen had decided they would share.

"I guessed. Such a romantic. Terribly boring, but romantic nonetheless."

Christian looked away, through the greenery to the thronged main thoroughfare. Every time he looked at Ellen Rinotti he saw superimposed an image of her dancing out of time to Stockhausen in an over-sized fisherman's jumper.

"Who's paying you?" he asked.

"Does it matter?"

"Not really." Those irregular top-up payments: she wasn't a whore in the SEG – there were enough people giving it away in there to make that unfeasible – it was just the route they'd chosen through which to channel her payments. A rival company had paid her off in order to sabotage Build Odense's chances for the Channel Link contracts. It was that simple.

He should have seen it sooner. Harwich was a company town, full of the employees of rival firms, yet all the time Christian had been following her Ellen Rinotti had scrupulously avoided contact with anyone from these other companies. If she so clearly didn't want a connection to be made then such a connection had to be there.

"Why?" he asked her.

She smiled sweetly, and said, "I'm a professional, darling. I work for the highest bidder. Pay me enough and even *you* could have me."

He looked away again, uncomfortable. "How were they so certain it would work?" he asked.

"They took precautions," she said, leaning towards him. "Come here and I'll show you."

Cautiously he leaned closer and then, without warning, she reached round to the back of his head and forced her mouth against his, teeth clashing, tongue sliding in, withdrawing. She pulled away and he stared at her, vision blurring. He shifted awkwardly in his seat and couldn't tear his eyes from her vicious smile. He felt as if the blood in his veins was fizzing, as if he was about to explode.

"With some couples," she said, "I believe it is an affair of the intellect. With others love takes its purest form." She smiled again. "But between Riv and me I can assure you it is purely physical."

He couldn't bear her to be so near, yet when, seconds later, she stood, smoothed her clothes and walked lazily away he felt as if she was tearing the flesh from his body.

Some kind of implant in her mouth, he realized. Some kind of aphrodisiac, something powerful. And addictive.

Christian watched her go, trembling slightly, as hooked as River Brady had ever been.

It was all he could do to stumble up to the parking deck and tell his car to take him back to the motel. He couldn't get that cruel bitch out of his mind. She danced in front of his vision even when he squeezed his eyes tightly shut, his fists grinding into the sockets.

Later, he managed to call the anonymous security agent at Build Odense. "I have the answer to your problem," he said. Every word was a struggle, but gradually he found that the sheer effort of concentration helped distract him from what Ellen Rinotti had done to him. He took a swig from his bottle of grappa and continued, "Get Brady back with his wife and his performance will improve."

The man nodded indulgently. "You have a proposal?"

"Pay the bitch and she'll do whatever you want," said Christian. "She's a pro. She's got him chemically addicted to her – that's why he's so screwed up at the moment. In the long-term he'll have to be detoxified and then he'll be the first to kick her out . . ." But if Ellen's employers had done their work properly such a detoxification would never work – she would have a grip on River Brady for as long as she chose.

"But in the short term you advise a financial fix, yes?"

Christian nodded.

"It will be arranged. We are grateful, Mr Taylor. Rest assured that you will be rewarded." The wall blanked and Christian was left with his phantom images of the woman who had implanted herself into his desires.

He spent three days holed up in his room, trying to forget the bitch. But he couldn't do it. She was in his every thought, always the star of those dreams he managed to recall. If he watched TV or listened to music it was always Ellen Rinotti's face he saw, or her voice he heard.

For much of the time he did what River Brady had been contractually unable to do: he drank himself into oblivion.

And then, on the fourth morning he woke to find that he had succeeded: the obsession had died as he slept. In his relief he rushed around the room, packing his few possessions then, in the doorway, he suddenly stopped.

He went back into the room and shut the door. "VR," he said, and the drawer slid obediently open.

In the first false room he asked for the whereabouts of River Brady. Almost immediately a door appeared in what had been a blank wall. He pushed through and wasn't surprised to find himself on the beach; it was the weekend – everyone had to have their days of leisure.

The grass hut village wasn't there today. For all Christian knew this could be a different island altogether: there was nothing particularly distinctive about the white sand, the blue sky and sea. It was a very sterile environment, now that he came to think of it.

He found River Brady sitting on a rocky promontory, staring out to sea. Dreaming of power stations or Channel Links, perhaps. Brady turned and waited for Christian to clamber up to join him; the system would have alerted him to Christian's visit as soon as it had been initiated.

"You knew what she was doing, didn't you?" said Christian.

River Brady gave his wide-mouthed smile but said nothing. He stared past Christian, as if searching for something.

"You're still hooked on her, you realize that? That's why you were so desperate to have her back. It was a drug, that's all it was."

"Are *you* still hooked on me, Mr Taylor?" The voice came from beyond Brady. Christian stretched up and saw the silver-haired woman standing ankle-deep in the waves, water running down her scaly body.

They were silent for a long time, Ellen Rinotti combing the tangles from her hair, River Brady staring at the waves. Christian wondered how many times the pair of them had pulled this lucrative trick before – how many "separations" had gone unrecorded. He knew Brady had worked for at least seven different companies in his career to date.

Without a word he climbed down the rocks and began to walk back along the beach, leaving the two of them together on the promontory. He felt drained. He thought of Carole and knew he should call her. He glanced back one more time, then raised a hand and pointed for home.

FISHING

Jay Caselberg

He handed over his co-operation voucher and the lawbot scanned it. The bot's sensors hummed and whirred as it hung there like some obscenely bloated dragonfly.

"Jezz Alan Stinson, you are free to go," it said finally in its flat mechanical voice.

He looked longingly as the voucher's charred remains tumbled to the gutter and the lawbot took off. That had been his last voucher.

"Shit!" he said, narrowly avoiding another infraction. He hadn't wanted to lose that one. He doubted he could take another round of Probe and Adjust right now. Jezz shoved his hands deep into his pockets and stared down at the remaining curls of the slip of recycled paper as they teetered gently in the pungent breeze. A groundcar sped past and scattered ashy remnants in its wake. With his shoulders slumped, he turned away.

A quick glance up and down the street, then above, to check the bot had really gone, and he headed back the way he'd come.

Damned bots; they were everywhere, and without the voucher he was powerless. All he wanted was to get enough credit together to get out of this stinking hole – find himself a nice place, start a farm. Maybe fruit trees. Not that he knew the first thing about them, but you had to have dreams. Or maybe by the seaside. Far enough away that the place might still have fish – live ones, their bellies facing down instead of bloated white and pointing to the sky. He didn't know anything about fishing either, but he could learn.

All that could wait. Now he had to get back to his apartment and contact Rinaldi. No way he was going out on a job without another voucher. He just didn't feel right without that sense of extra security.

He picked his way around the piles of garbage and stepped past the unidentifiable pools of sludge marking the sidewalk. He heard a buzz gang up one of the side streets, licked his lips nervously, and quickened his pace. If he walked too quickly, his lungs would start burning, but he didn't want to hang around either. He'd seen the last guy the buzzers had got to. One block, two blocks, he felt safe. As safe as he could be in this place.

His apartment building loomed in front of him, halfway up the next block, black and grey with city grime. He waited on the corner, considering, before crossing. He was torn now. This job would have been the big one. It would have paid him enough to finally do it – to make the break. But no . . . the risks were too great. There'd be other jobs. All he had to do was grit his teeth and put up with it. There'd be other jobs; and there'd be other vouchers. A quick glance up and down the street and he dashed across the intersection, fumbling in his pocket for his tapes. He had about six seconds max by the time he reached the stairs. As his foot reached the bottom step, he started counting.

He took the steps two at a time, stretched up on his toes and slapped a tape over the bead where he knew the securicam lay, then quickly pulled out his tools. Building security would be blind for another five seconds. Long enough for him to get in the door before the gundogs became operational. They'd cut his access two days ago. Now he had to find another way to get enough to cover the back rent. Cursing under his breath, he fumbled with the door.

Five . . . and in.

He leaned back against the wall with a sigh as the door snicked shut. Another two days and they'd work out a way to stop his little tricks, and then he'd be out on the street with the buzz gangs. At least they didn't know who was doing it . . . yet.

The elevator was out again – no surprise. He started up the stairs, keeping to the pools of light falling from the stairwell windows. The smell of shit and urine and something else – he couldn't quite tell what – was strong. He grimaced against the stench and kept climbing. Three floors. At least he wasn't up on twenty-five. The poor saps up there had it really bad.

As he reached the top of the third flight, a door clanged shut.

He stopped, listening, but there were no further sounds, only the echoing ring fading along the corridors. Probably someone locking themselves away. He poked his head around the corner, but the passageway was clear. His own door was third along and he paced over to it quickly. He checked for signs of attempted entry. It was clean. Beside the door there, the little sign read "J. Stinson." It wouldn't for much longer. He keyed the lock, pushed his weight against the door and slid inside.

Easing the door shut behind him, he felt himself relax. The dim enclosure was safety. Greasy light filtered in through grimy windows and stains mottled the walls, but it was home.

The conditioner clanked and whirred. He glanced across at it, knowing it would have to be replaced soon. It only did half a job removing the acrid taint from the air, but it would last a few weeks yet. He tossed his tool set on the daybed and flicked on the vid. As it blossomed into life, he shrugged off his coat and ran his fingers through his short dyed-blond hair. He left the coat where it lay; a few more creases weren't going to hurt it.

"And you too can find a new life. Margolis Estates offer you the best. Clean air. Sunshine. A life free of crime. Room to move."

The theme music came up and Stinson stared across at the image of the man with the fishing rod, the sun sparkling off the water, trees in the background. Kids played in the distance and a bird spiralled lazily in the air – clean air. He walked into the kitchen alcove and poured himself a drink. He rolled the first swallow around and around, letting the dark liquid burn the street taste from his mouth. As he swallowed, he closed his eyes. There had to be a way he could do it. But first, there was Rinaldi to deal with.

Carrying his glass over to the vid, he switched to the phone channel. He pressed the button for autodial and stood staring down at it while he waited for connect. The Margolis Estates image had been so tempting. He could see himself standing there by the water's edge, pole in hand.

"Yeah, Rinaldi."

"Rinaldi, it's Jezz."

Rinaldi's bloated face peered at him, frowned and then looked over at something off camera.

"Yeah. What do you want? I'm kind of—"

"Listen, I have to talk to you. I'm not sure about—"

"Not sure of what this time, Stinson? It's all set up."

"Look, I got scanned today." He didn't want to tell him about the co-operation voucher. No way.

"So?"

"Well, I'm worried about it."

Rinaldi glanced off to the side again. "I haven't got time, Stinson. We go tonight. You got a problem with that – just deal with it. I'll expect you there around eleven. No, make that at eleven. Sharp!" Rinaldi severed the connection.

"Dammit," he muttered under his breath. This was more trouble than it was worth. But Rinaldi wasn't one to let things go. If he didn't show now, the consequences would be even worse than if he did. He rubbed the back of his neck and switched the unit back to vid. It didn't look like he really had a choice. He slumped down on the daybed and stared blankly at the images playing out in front of him.

He woke four hours later, his head muzzy and his mouth filled with fur. The glass had slipped from his fingers and now lay on its side, a pool of dark marking the daybed where the remains of his drink had spilled. The chrono on the vid said 9:30. Too much tension; he felt tired. He worked his mouth, trying to get some moisture going again, then rubbed at the stiffness in his neck. 9:30. What the hell was he doing? No, make that 9:33. Leaving the fallen glass where it lay, he stumbled into the kitchen and splashed water on his face. His tool set. Where had he left his tool set? A cockroach wandered past in the corner of his vision and slipped into a crack between the cupboards. As he tracked its passage, he saw what he was looking for. The tool set was lying on the corner of the daybed where he had left it. Right. He had to get moving.

He picked up his coat from the floor, shoved the tools into his pocket and glanced around the room.

"Find a career in Law Enforcement. Tired of the city streets? Tired of going nowhere? Contact City Law Enforcement on—"

He flicked off the vid, listened at the door for a moment, then gently eased it open. The corridor was in darkness now; the lights had stopped working months ago. No one was going to risk sending anybody up to fix them.

The door clanged shut behind him and he froze. What the hell was he doing? The echoes faded along with his heartbeat and he breathed a sigh. As he walked quietly down the corridor, he fingered the thinning patch at the back of his head. No wonder he was starting to lose his hair.

Somewhere up above, he heard a voice echoing down from the darkness.

"See Parkside. You bastards! See Parkside! So where are the trees? Where are the bloody trees, you bastards? Bastards . . ." The voice faded into bitter laughter, then sobbing. Just another crazy.

The stairs were clear, and he made it out onto the street without seeing anyone. This time of night, there'd be hardly a soul out anyway. He was a man alone, but that had its advantages and he knew how to use them. A slight breeze fanned along the street rolling bits of trash behind it. The public transit clattered along its rail somewhere behind and he stepped out onto the roadway. The walk would do him good – clear his head. And he needed a clear head tonight. He slipped into a dark alleyway across the street and started on his way. As he slipped between the grime-patterned bricks, he thought.

Sure, Rinaldi was an arsehole. But the world needed arseholes like him to keep things moving. He didn't know where he'd be if he hadn't linked up with Rinaldi. The bloated toad had given him his start in life, taken him under his fleshy wing. The man paid well, and that's what really mattered. Every job had its risks. But maybe this would be the last one. Just maybe. He ran images of the Margolis Estates promo through his head and gave himself a wry grin.

He was a mere block away from the place he was supposed to meet Rinaldi when the arm snaked out of the darkness and grabbed him. It slammed him against a wall, forcing the air from his lungs. A dark alley. Buzzers. He was in trouble.

"Hey, wait," he said straining for breath.

"You just stay right there, Stinson."

The knew his name. What the hell?

A figure drew together from out of the shadows beside him. Another loomed in front. These weren't buzzers. A face leaned forward to peer at him.

"Yep, it's him all right," the face said to its companion.

He bit his lip and looked nervously around for escape. The second guy was big. Too big.

"Don't even think about it," said the second. Jezz tried to shrink back into the wall.

The first face glanced up and down the alleyway then leaned closer. The breath smelled like coffee.

"Now this is how it is," said Coffee Breath. "We've been keeping an eye on you, Stinson. We know what's going on."

He made to stand, but the big guy pushed him back against the wall with a big hand in his chest.

"Just listen," said Big Guy.

Coffee Breath was back in his face. "We want Rinaldi, and you're going to help us get him."

"Hey, come on. I don't know what you're talking about."

Big Guy shoved him. "I said listen."

"We know that Rinaldi is planning to take Margolis Estates tonight, and you're involved," Coffee Breath continued. "We need someone on the inside. You've co-operated before, Stinson. You can make this one count."

Suddenly things clicked into place.

"Hey, no way I'm doing this. It's not worth a lousy voucher. Not for this."

"You've got to do better than that, Jezz. Look, you do this, you might have a chance. You don't and well. . . ." Coffee Breath grinned at him. Jezz didn't like the grin. "What would Rinaldi do if he knew about some of the things you've done for us in the past?"

He swallowed. He knew exactly what Rinaldi would do.

"Now, you can make it easy on yourself. This is a big job. With what you can give us, we should have enough to take Rinaldi down for a long time. Maybe even a complete wipe."

"But where does that leave me? What guarantees can you give me? I'd need more than a stupid voucher."

Coffee Breath nodded slowly. "You're about reaching the end of your usefulness to us anyway, Stinson. You've had too many vouchers as it is. We have ways of making sure you get out of this in one piece. We've already thought about that. There's a relocation scheme."

"You mean . . .?"

"Sure. You tell us where you want to be and we'll fix it."

Just for a moment, it was hard to think. There were too many possibilities tumbling through his head. He glanced at Big Guy, but Big Guy just stared down at him without expression. There were no clues there. He looked back at Coffee Breath's shadowed face.

"Anywhere I want?"

"Anywhere you want, within reason of course."

He sank back against the wall. They weren't giving him much of a choice and they knew it. What could he do?

"Okay . . . what do you want?"

"You take this with you." Coffee Breath held out a small something on the palm of his hand. Jezz had to strain to see what lay there, but then he recognized it for what it was – a recording bead. He'd only ever seen them in the vids. "You run through as if nothing's happened. We'll get enough with this to be able to support the case. After the job's done, we'll take Rinaldi down. Then we'll come and get you."

"But what if something goes wrong?"

"What could go wrong? You just do your bit and we'll see nothing else happens. Margolis is too important to us. Margolis has *connections*. We'll make sure nothing goes wrong." Coffee Breath leaned forward and attached the bead to Stinson's coat. Then he brushed him down. "Now, you'd better move. You wouldn't want to be late."

The pair faded back into the shadows and he was left standing there, a tight feeling growing in his throat. Coffee Breath's voice drifted to him out of the darkness.

"And Stinson, I wouldn't do anything stupid. We'll be watching."

He looked back down the alleyway to where the voice had come from, but there was not a sign that the two had even been there. He reached up and fingered his coat where the bead sat. There was nothing for it. He took off toward the sulphur glow shed by streetlights at the end. Just before he reached the end, he pressed himself against a wall and ducked his head around the corner.

Rinaldi was there waiting, just where he said he'd be. He'd brought some hired muscle and someone else. The other one with him must be the comp man.

As he emerged from the alleyway, Rinaldi swung to face him.

Jezz nodded to Rinaldi, barely acknowledging the other two. He was here for Rinaldi.

"What kept you?" Rinaldi said through clenched teeth. It came out as a hiss. His baggy face puckered with displeasure.

"Ran into a buzz gang on the way. Had to avoid them. Took me a little longer than I thought." Jezz looked warily at the others. He vaguely recognized the comp man from somewhere.

Rinaldi narrowed his grey eyes suspiciously, then sniffed. Without another word, he headed down the street toward their target. The others fell in behind. There were no introductions. He resisted the urge to touch the bead and shoved his hands into his pockets. What was Rinaldi doing coming along, anyway? It had to be big if he needed to be here. Whatever it was, he had to suppress a grin. The irony of hitting the Margolis building was beautiful.

They slipped down the side of the office complex. He'd been scanning the street for bots, but didn't really expect any, not after his little meeting. At the back door, there was another surprise. There wasn't even a set of gundogs.

"Don't they care who gets into this place?" he muttered.

"Problem?" said Rinaldi, leaning close. His plastered hair caught the light from inside the building. The smell of thick cologne wafted over him.

"No, nothing. I just would've expected a bit more security."

He slipped into the entranceway, pressing himself against the wall. He found the securicam without any difficulty. There were only so many places you could hide one and get a decent image. In moments, he had the door open and they were inside. As he got through the first security lock, sitting there on his knees, he began to wonder.

"What are we doing here anyway?" he asked concentrating on the lock.

"What are you worried about? You're getting paid. And how come all of a sudden you're asking questions?" Rinaldi's gravely voice dripped with suspicion.

"Just wondering. That's all. It's not as if there's a hell of a lot here. Just seems strange."

"Just do what you're paid for and shut up." There was an edge in Rinaldi's voice that Jezz didn't want to push.

He triggered the lock and got to his feet. Somehow, it was all too easy. Within ten minutes, they were up on the sixteenth floor outside the data centre. This lock was as easy as the last. Then they were inside.

Rinaldi slammed a fist into his hand as he looked around the room. He turned to the comp man. "Tanner, I want access now. Give me all they've got. I want the lot."

Tanner nodded once and headed for a console. Rinaldi stood where he was, cracking his knuckles. "Let me know as soon as you're in," he said.

Despite the nerves, despite the adrenaline rushing through his veins, Jezz thought about why he was here. If he got them what they wanted . . .

He leaned his face closer to his lapel as he spoke. "Rinaldi, what's so important about this? This isn't what I expected. Like, how come you're here?"

Rinaldi turned and grabbed a fistful of his coat and drew him closer. Jezz thought about the bead and swallowed nervously. If Rinaldi were to discover it now. . . . Maybe he'd gone too far.

"Payback," breathed Rinaldi. "That's all you need to know. Payback. No bastard screws with me and my family. Nobody gets away with it, not even Margolis. This is family. Understand?"

He nodded, and stepped back as Rinaldi shoved him away. Rinaldi turned back to watch the comp man. No, he didn't understand, but he knew how much Rinaldi valued family – not only his own, but those he saw as family. He thought about what he was doing and Rinaldi's words filled him with a chill. Did the man know something? Had he guessed? Jezz leaned back against the wall for support and watched as Rinaldi crossed the floor and peered over the comp man's shoulder.

Surely the fat bastard would be paying him more attention if he knew something. He looked at the door and thought about slipping away. He might just make it. The hired muscle looked over at him, held his gaze, then turned to checking the corridor again. No, he'd never get past.

"Right, we're in," said Tanner.

"I want the lot. Dealings, transactions. Route them to my personal files. Can you do that?"

"It'll take time."

"I don't want to know that. Just do it." Tanner nodded again without turning and started, his fingers flying over the keys.

Rinaldi rocked back and forth on his heels behind, nodding to himself. "You bastards are really going to pay for what you did," he muttered. "I'm going to bust you wide open, show the world."

Jezz watched Rinaldi from where he stood. His finely cut suit, his slickly plastered grey hair, his florid meaty features. What was so important to him here? It just didn't make sense. If it was anything trivial, he would have sent someone to do the dirty work for him. He looked around the room. There was nothing here that hinted there was anything special. Nothing at all. What was it that Margolis had done? He rubbed his wrist, listening to the sound of air-conditioners and Tanner's fingers working at the keyboard.

Finally, Tanner spun his chair around. "Transfer complete."

"Is that it?" said Rinaldi.

"The whole lot."

"Good, let's get out of here." Rinaldi had a satisfied determination in the set of his jaw. "All right. What are you waiting for?"

They were out of there in less time than it had taken to get in, only pausing long enough for Jezz to mask the fact of their entry. He shoved the tool set back into his pocket. He'd done it, and Rinaldi was none the wiser. The smell of the alleyway was almost sweet.

They headed up the alley, smack into a wall of City Law Enforcement standing arrayed and waiting for them. Rinaldi's hired muscle reached inside his coat, but the officers were upon him before he had a chance. This wasn't how it was supposed to be. They were supposed to come for him later.

Rinaldi's accusing glare seared across the space between them and with that look, Jezz knew that Rinaldi knew. Without a word, he was damned. Some way, somehow, Rinaldi would get to him.

Jezz looked around the bare room. He sat with his elbows resting on the table in front of him. The officer sitting across from him looked vaguely rough, as if he might have been a buzzer made good. The walls were mottled, just like everywhere else. Not even the City Law Enforcement buildings were immune. The conditioner in the corner clanked, paused, then started whirring again.

"So where do you want to go, Stinson? Of course, we'll provide the identity. You just supply us with where. Anywhere that's far enough away from this place." The officer looked across at him, a half-smile on his face.

He sat back and stared up at the ceiling. "You know what I really want? I want to go fishing," he said. "You know the place they show on the Margolis Estates vids? That's where I want to go. You know, a new life and all that crap. That's where I want to go."

"Lakeside? Yeah, I know it. That can be arranged."

He lowered his gaze and looked across at the Officer. "Do you mean it?"

The Officer shrugged. "Sure." His smile broadened.

The disbelief came first, then the joy. He bit his lip and laughed quietly to himself. The laughter remained inside him, threatening to burst free all the way back to the cell.

It took them four days to arrange things, but he didn't mind. He lay back on his bunk and painted pictures in his head. He was there. The water sparkled in the sunshine. Wind stirred the branches along the shoreline. He found himself a place to sit on an old log, planted his pole and stared out across the lake. There were birds in the sky, and it was blue. On the fourth day they came for him.

They marched him out through the corridors and to a waiting groundcar. The unmarked vehicle had dark tinted windows and they slipped him in the back. An officer clambered in beside him and the groundcar took off. Four and a half hours the journey took, and all the way, the officer said not a word. They sat in dark silence, unable to see out. He didn't mind. He was going home, even though he didn't know where it was. Four and a half hours was long enough for it to be far, far away. Away from the stench and the dirt and the buzzers. And away from Rinaldi. Finally, the groundcar slid to a stop and the officer opened the door.

"Well, this is it," said the officer. "This is your door code. You're up on the twenty-fifth floor. Apartment 2510." The officer stepped out and pointed.

Ducking his head, Jezz – no, Adam Jones now – slid across the seat and out. They stood opposite a tall apartment building. It was black and grey. Dark wet stains ran down the outside walls. There was an entranceway just like the one back home. He could even tell where the securicam would be. The sky above was brown and grey.

Adam Jones stared at the apartment building. He looked down at the code scrawled on the piece of paper clutched in his hand. He turned slowly and looked behind him.

A vast pool of sludge stirred lazily as if moved by something black and evil in its depths. Solid lumps dotted the viscous surface. And all along the shoreline, lay trash, covered in a slick of brown-streaked opalescence. He looked along the lakefront at building after building, all of them black and grey and stained, all of them the standard twenty-five floors. He looked back across the street at the building the Officer had pointed him too. There, in front, sat a small rusting plaque – Margolis Estates.

A slight breeze brought the smell wafting across to him. He stared back down at the door code and swallowed.

"This is some kind of joke, right?" he said.

"No joke. This is what you wanted."

"But what is this?"

"Lakeside. Just like you wanted. Twenty-fifth floor, you should have a good view of the lake. Good luck. We know where to reach you, Mister Jones."

The officer stepped back into the groundcar and it took off.

"Wait!" he yelled. "I've changed my mind." But the groundcar had already disappeared into the oily haze.

IN SILVER A

Cecilia Tan

In Silver A there is no crime, no pollution, no strife, no domestic violence, no trouble. That's what they told us at that recruitment rally seven years ago, and again when Marco and I got our silver badges of citizenship two months ago. So then, how would you explain the fact that I was sitting in someone's kitchen covered in blood? A baby was crying, there was an empty bulb of glucose in my hand, and all was not right with the world. The sugar was making it hard to think, overloading parts of my brain and trying hard to erase my short term memory.

And who wouldn't want to forget? I remember the cops standing over me, roughing me up, I remember taking a hard hit in the face while one of them spat "Fringe trash!" And I remember grabbing the bottle of glucose formula from the counter – my escape hatch from reality. Once my eyes rolled back into my head they stopped questioning me, stopped hitting me.

A woman's voice said: "Remove him!" I couldn't really feel it, but part of me knew they were dragging my rag-doll body down the stairs, across an immaculate lawn of prickly green irrigated grass, and stuffing me into one of those little electric vans all the police in Silver America drive. The van began to move, the woman driving, two men sandwiching me in the back seat. We pulled away from the upscale residential sector toward the rectilinear SA Center skyline, toward the seats of government and power, and somewhere on the outside of me, I began to babble.

The voice again, speaking crisp Civil tongue. "Can't you quiet him down?" Such perfect diction and syntax even in the face of a crisis. My own conditioning was not as good – try as I might to protest it came out in Fringlish "Fuck-all, jeezus, I got rights!" which elicited sneers from the bruisers at my sides. One of them pointed at my citizenship badge and the two of them laughed.

"He's like a talking animal," the first one said.

"Yes," the other agreed. "You can train them but they always revert to their wild state."

"That's better," the first one said, cracking his knuckles into his meaty hand. "I like it better that way."

I wished I could move away from him. I'd never seen them but there was always a rumor that men from SA would come into the Fringe, "hunting parties," hunting us. Fear started to creep through my sugar-induced haze. I didn't want to face what was going to happen to me because I knew it wouldn't be good. I slipped into the wonder of auditory hallucination and swirling wormholes behind my eyes. The cascade of molecules over my receptors tweaked something in my long-term memory and the past swallowed me up.

It's seven years ago and I am meeting Marco's eyes across the crowd at the ration station. The Science jerks are on the Fringe recruiting for live bodies, ours. They're handing out food and it's all a tangle of arms and curses in broken Fringlish, but I see Marco at the center of a calm area and make my way toward him as Science's pitch begins.

We all know better than to go with the Arm. They just want cannon fodder for the border skirmishes between Silver A and Texico. But Science could be something different. Sure they're spouting words like "indenture contracts" and "eventual citizenship" – things we don't have words for in Fringlish. But they are projecting images on the cracked wall of nice, safe, clean, shiny, warm Silver America . . . Science is looking pretty good. Marco thinks so too. Science wants kids like us, they want converts. We want food, warm places to sleep, maybe a little clean water, too.

I look into Marco's unscarred face and think: he looks good at staying out of trouble. I can't say the same, squinting at him through an eye swollen half-shut from a fight the night before. They had wanted my coat, and didn't get it. But I sat awake all night scared and sure that I was as good as dead.

You going? Marco says. His hair is long and black, the ends

frayed, not cropped and soldered like mine. Fuck-all. I tell him: I go if you go.

I felt the pressure on my shoulders from the cops on either side of me and I was back in real time. Damn simple sugars, burn bright but quick. I opened my eyes to see we were pulling up to the glittery tower that housed the offices of Science. Not Civil, where there's a hospital, not the Arm, where there's a detention tank and where they'd execute capital offenders, surely, if they ever had any. Big Momma Science didn't own me any more, I reminded myself, not for two whole months. The shiny badge on my chest said I was a free man. But I didn't feel like one when they grabbed me by the arms. If the glucose had run its course, I had no refuge from them. I was beginning to wonder about things like whose blood it was soaking my shirt, how it got there, and why Science wanted to know, when they hauled me upright, my brain did flip flops, and I swirled away again.

It's six years ago, very early in the dark morning, and I can't sleep. I'm in my dorm cell and thinking about how it will be my turn to go under the knife soon. I know it, Sugar Test Series – Subject #11, or so it says on my indent card. They took #10 from the next cell over last week and he never came back.

Marco's in the next wing over; he hasn't been taking to the special diet very well, so they've moved him to another project. The special diet is I-don't-know-what but it makes me hungry all the time and gives me headaches. Dawn light makes the ceiling gray where the thin strip of window runs along the top of the high outer wall. I hear the footsteps in the hall.

They aren't coming for me. It's only one pair of footsteps, just a guard or a caretaker, not an escort contingent. I hear the door being opened across the hall, a low voice, then a scream is cut off—

I decide maybe if they come for me soon it might not be such a bad thing. And then there is a sound at my door and I hold my breath.

Hey, hey you. Marco is in the hallway.

I slip from the bed and kneel at the door. Whatta you here?

I had to know if they took you away yet, he says. His Civil tongue programming has taken root and it barely sounds like him. Are you alright?

I tell him my time will be soon, and that I don't know if I'll be coming back.

You won't, he says. You'll be moved to another facility where you'll be isolated from the other indents for a while. So you won't see me for a couple of months.

I wish I could see him through the door but all I can see is the shadow at the crack. I want to tell him something more, but fuck-all, what else is there to say?

The next thing I hear is the sound of the door across the way opening, and a voice, Breton, this sector's caretaker, our legal guardian, saying to Marco: Oh, my, my, my, what could you be doing here?

Marco starts to stammer that he has clearance, and I think he really does, but Breton isn't listening. He's pushed Marco up against the door, I hear the thump of Marco's head on the hard metal. Don't fight him, I'm thinking, just take it and he'll let you go . . . but I'm too scared to make a sound. Breton likes pushing his weight around and on this wing we've all learned to take it. But Marco fights back. He pushes Breton off, I hear the scuffling, another bang on the door. And then Breton laughing and explaining that Marco's violent tendencies make him a likely candidate for hormone reduction. Something bad is happening, I hear Marco screaming, and then Breton saying that he'd better take care of it right away. And then they're gone.

I cry myself to sleep. Breton wakes me up later with my special diet breakfast and a tablet for me to sign. He tells me to cheer up as he looks at the bags under my eyes. He pats me on the head as he tells me my whole life will be different as of tomorrow. They come for me the next day.

They didn't kill me. That was my first thought as I started to come to. Before I thought about the cops who dragged me here or where I was, I just thought they didn't kill me and who "they" was didn't matter. All that matters on the Fringe is that you've lived another day, no one killed you for your blanket or you didn't die of the night desert cold. I used to struggle awake, quick, before anything bad could happen. When I'd signed up with Science I had seen enough life to know I wanted more, and that I could be dead the next day if I stayed in the Fringe. I wanted to be able to wake up without reaching for the broken screwdriver hidden in my shirt, without feeling like the axe was about the fall at any moment.

But, as I'd learned, that's exactly what it was like waking up in a room in Science, too.

So this time, after I came to it took me a while to convince myself I wasn't fifteen years old and waiting for Science's next invasive procedure. A couple of things helped, like the fact that I came to alone. No Scientist waiting with a needle and electro-probe ("I'm sorry you have to be awake for this"), no escort with heavy restraints or nerve cuffs ("I'm sorry, but we can't have you damaging SA property banging your head against a wall like that"), no guardians with a grudge or wanting something personal. I could feel the hardness of my silver badge digging into my ribs where I lay on top of it, and with one small motion of my finger I could feel the hard place behind my ear where my machine connection sat. I told myself a couple of times, I'm a Machine Maintenance Engineer, a citizen, I am Civil's business . . . then I tried to convince myself that I wasn't even in Science, that seeing the Science tower was just one of my bad sugar-induced flashbacks. They had been much more intense than I'd expected. So maybe . . .

I looked around the room. I lay on a hospital gurney, with a tube in my arm. Someone had cleaned up the blood and put me in soft medical whites. The room did not look like labs nor infirmary, more like an office with the furniture removed – recently, from the look of the dents in the carpeting. Science Executive wing. Damn. The slow drip was some blue shit I didn't recognize, but whatever it was, it was making me feel pretty good. Alert. No dizziness. No hunger. Of course these jerkoffs would know what to feed me. I sat up.

My movement must have triggered something, or maybe they had cams on me, because two executives immediately came in. Both blond, in suits. One of them was smiling and I almost didn't recognize Breton. My indent officer for the seven years Science had owned me and my body and my brain, and they'd done what they liked with that brain. I wasn't glad to see him. He'd grown a beard and lost some weight. My guess was he'd been promoted as a result of how well I'd served society – up until today, that is.

He walked right up to the bed, no handshake or anything and

said, "You're in a lot of trouble, Tato." Using my name like a punctuation mark. Treating me like an indent.

The other guy, some big wig's assistant I would guess from the shine on his shoes and conservative, solid-color tie, did shake my hand. "I'm pleased to meet you, Mr Smith." I almost laughed at that. I couldn't get used to this last name thing, but I'd had to pick one to get my citizenship. "I'm Henry Billings."

I did what they taught us to do in Civil training. "Pleased to make your acquaintance, Mr Billings." Polite manners were mandatory for all citizens. Then I said to Breton, not quite in Fringlish, "What the fuck-all am I doing here?"

Breton could talk the talk and didn't stand on ceremony. I knew it was an insult for him to talk to me like this, but I found it weirdly comforting. "Don't give me any lip. Your ass should be over at the Arm getting fried right now. Murder, you know?"

"So why isn't it?"

"Mis-ter Breton, Mr Smith, please." Sweat broke out on Henry's scalp where he was losing his hair. "I believe we have a proposal to discuss."

Breton: "Proposal, my ass. Let's just rip the fuck-all out of his head and find out for ourselves."

"You're not scaring me." I said. Which was a lie.

Henry looked shocked at Breton's language. Fuck-all was pure Fringe profanity. Citizens had neater things to fall back on, like: goddam. But he smoothed his facial expression and said in an equally smooth voice. "Mr Breton, may I remind you that would be a violation of Mr Smith's civil rights? As you know . . ." He was about to launch into a canned speech about what made Silver America great, and better than New Japan's meritocracy on the coast or Middle West's hagiarchy, citizen's protection, civil liberties, equality . . . but Breton headed it off, waving his hand and nodding.

"Just kidding, here." Breton clapped me on the shoulder and I suppressed the urge to bite his hand. "Me and Tato go way back, Billings, don't you worry."

"So what's this proposal?" If it was anything other than exile or killing me, I was interested to hear it.

Breton took a step away from the gurney and Henry looked unhappy and spoke. "It's very delicate, this situation, Mr Smith. We need to know what happened, back at the Martins' place."

"And you propose . . .?"

"Tell us what we want to know and we'll clear your ass," Breton snapped. "What's so hard to figure about that? You go back to your nice place and no more trouble. Otherwise, we dump your ass over at the Arm as murder suspect Number One and Only."

I didn't have any choice, but something told me it wasn't wise to give myself back to the people I'd spent so long trying to get away from. Of course the Arm could be worse. They'd just kill me, capital. Right? Still, I didn't answer.

My pal Henry went on. "We are especially concerned about what may have happened to your friend, Mr Columbus."

Marco. "Me too, Mr Billings, me too." A creeping cold climbed up my spine as I thought about the blood, and the dose of sugar, and I realized I didn't have the slightest idea what had happened back at the Martins' house, whether Marco was alive or dead, or why any of it would matter to Science. They wouldn't hand me over to the Arm too quick, I thought, not if there was something they thought I could tell them. And, why the Arm, not Civil? Everyone thought that Civil ran SA, and in a way they did, regulating all the parts of day to day life that made SA such a happy place, like garbage pickup, mail delivery, media entertainment, etc. But be a part of Science for enough years, you pick up ideas, like the one that the Security Arm and Science are really struggling for control of the country, and that it wasn't the Arm that put down the Hoover Dam rebellion. If this was about Arm versus Science . . . I supposed I would have to play along if I wanted to find anything out, not the least of which being whether Marco was alive. Marco . . .

I didn't want to think about it. I didn't need a med monitor to know my heart rate doubled and my epinephrine level peaked.

"Goddam, he's going off." Breton sped up the drip on my i.v. and Billings called for a woman in a lab coat, med-tech, Scientist, whatever . . . the sight of her was probably enough to send my neuro imbalance right off the edge and they slipped away in the blackness.

It's two years ago. I'm limping down the street toward Marco's place in the indent sector, hoping nobody stops me. Any teenage asshole born in SA outranks an indent – they'll stop us and quiz us on the Ninety First Amendment just for kicks, give us orders, and make us do tricks, and if you get it wrong or disobey them it lengthens your indenture, don't you know. I don't even know if Marco's there. I only run into him once every couple of weeks, when our shift rotations coincide. I have a headache. I've just finished a job, interfacing with the internal security at Science, syncing up their facial recognition eyes . . . and I feel like the inside of my skull has been scrubbed with steel wool. I ache all over and I need something I can metabolize without going to pieces.

Marco opens the door. I'm too glad to see him to remark how weird it is that he doesn't look first to see who it is. Maybe I haven't outgrown my paranoia like he has. He sets me down in front of the window and goes to get me something. I don't have to say a word, Marco just understands. He always has.

He brings me a squeeze bottle full of something smooth and greasy. He knows what sugar would do to me.

Marco tells me I look like shit. I am shit, I say. Science wishes I'd died like all the others, but I didn't. I'm left in the human shitpile.

You nuts, he tells me in soft Fringlish. He says I'd feel better, about everything, if I took better care of myself.

What for? I never say it out loud, but I know I've already passed the lifespan of the other guinea pigs. And if I last another two years, I get to inherit Utopia. Maybe I will say it . . .

But he's already kneading the palm of my hand with his knuckles. Breathe deep, he says. The empty squeeze bottle falls from my fingers as he bends the flesh of my hand, until even the bones feel soft and warm. I am a rag doll that he slips out of its silly clothes and warms its skin all over. His hands turn my spine to jelly and eventually even the weight of my skull is gone. He rolls me back and forth and makes me glad to have muscles and bones and skin. Why should I take care of myself, I murmur, when you do it so well? We moan together and move together and when I ejaculate I feel his relief more keenly than my own.

We don't do this often, because neither of us likes to be reminded too much of some of the more drastic modifications Science has made to Marco's body. The removal of violent tendencies.

I feel the slight tug as he removes the plug from my right

socket. He rolls the cord neatly up to his own ear, and then pulls it from his jack. It's a one way connection. I was never wired for a secondary sensory input the way he was. And if he wasn't, I wonder if he wouldn't have killed himself long ago or what. Thanks, he says.

You welcome. I feel like I ought to be thanking him, really. But we've known each other long enough that maybe I don't have to say it. Or if I did, it wouldn't go down right. My dick probably would have shriveled away by now if it weren't for him. We talked about it once. I told him that I'd gladly donate mine to him if it could be done. But it's his nerves, too, deteriorated connections. He needs me to read the climax from. But for some reason it's always me who lands on his doorstep like a lost dog.

He serves me another squeeze bulb and we drink in silence. He's right, I do feel much better.

I opened my eyes to a bright light and a voice said that my pupils were starting to contract. The woman took the light out of my eyes and stepped back. Billings and Breton were still there, looking useless standing off to the side with their hands in their pockets. She moved to the other side of the gurney and stuck some kind of monitor onto my forehead. "This will alert you if a relapse looks likely, but his system should be pretty well clean by now." She started fiddling with something in a shrinkwrapped package.

Billings – Smiling Henry – stepped forward, looking down on me with concern. "Are you feeling better now? I'm sorry if this is hard for you, Mr Smith. Have you had any other blackouts like this one? And the one you had in the car?"

"Not until today," I said. But then I'd never chug-a-lugged a whole bottle of infant glucose solution until today when the cops had started asking about the blood . . .

Breton leaned in close to us both. "I'll leave him to you, Henry. I'm sure he'll cooperate, won't you Tato? Be a good boy, alright?"

I almost said "yessir" out of habit, but got it out as "alright," and then my ex-guardian went out the door without incident.

The med-tech finished her fiddling and handed me a glass of a bluish solution, maybe the same stuff as was going into my arm.

"Drink this, Mr Smith," she said. "It'll help to stablilize your condition." And then she left, too.

I took a small sip. Tasted like . . . nothing much. I was expecting something salty, like broth or blood plasma. "What's in it?"

He shrugged. "I do not know, Mr Smith. I am not very familiar with your modifications."

That was probably a lie. The sugar test series had been a big one here at Science, in their never-ending quest for building a brain-machine interface that would work worth a damn. I had been under the impression that I was one of their special cases, being one of the few who could interface successfully and survive. Surely he'd been briefed specially, too, for this meeting. But I was playing along. "Ah, well, it's good," I lied.

He went on to ask if I was comfortable, wanted anything else, etc. The whole good cop routine. I knew as long as I said what he wanted to hear, he'd stay that way, nice and accommodating, like I was a good citizen assisting my country. But as soon as things got tough, Breton, in the sanctioned role of bad cop, was going to come back in and tear me a new eye socket trying to get the truth out of me. My goal was to put that off as long as possible.

Which wasn't that long. Because I couldn't remember a goddam thing about what had happened. Henry hemmed and hawed, and I tried to act like I really wanted to cooperate . . . "Really. Marco asked if I'd go with him to work on their kitchen system. When I arrived he was already there and at work on it. I plugged in and was deep in trance with the machine when something jostled my foot. I opened my eyes and it was Mr Martin, slumped over and bleeding . . . where your security had just pushed him . . . that's all there is!"

"What about the glucose?"

"What about it? Your security people scared me . . . I did it without thinking. It was in the kitchen in bottles, for the baby, and I downed one. And they dragged me away." I saw his eyes narrowing, his mouth tightening with distaste as he made his decision to turn me over to Breton. "That's all of it! I don't know any more!"

"I'm very sorry, Mr Smith, but I'm afraid that you do know more."

Breton came in then with a pair of nerve cuffs in his hands. "Time to go, Tato. We gave you your chance."

I'd be damned if I was just going to let him put those things on me. I was a citizen, wasn't I? I suppose I wasn't acting much like one when I tried to kick him in the nose. The gurney tipped under me and my foot only hit him hard enough to make him mad. I threw the glass at him then and backed up as he batted it aside. No surprise that it was unbreakable and rolled away silently on the carpet. The windows were probably the same stuff, sealed, and we were probably fifty floors up, no escape there. Henry wasn't smiling any more as he called for help with his lapel com. Breton tried to tackle me but I dodged him and made for the door which was opening.

And then my ankle was on fire as one of the nerve cuffs wrapped around it. Breton had flung them, open, on full power, and I went down, grabbing at it and the dead limb of my lower leg. He sat on my chest then and smacked me hard across the face. There was a trickle of blood coming from his nose.

"Precious goddam brains, I'll rattle your goddam brains!" he shouted.

It wasn't the first time I'd seen him like this. He hit me again, back of the fist, but he was so pissed off the swing went wild and only glanced off my cheek. I thought maybe he'd choke me then, but I'd stopped struggling and he moved the cuffs to my elbows, where they belonged, and my arms went dead.

"And you can goddam well walk the rest of the way." He was standing up and I wasn't even sure he was talking to me anymore, but I guess he was since the two techs who'd come in response to Henry's call stood me up and pushed me toward the door.

Before I'd gotten ten feet my arms were starting to hurt, bad pins and needles and that bone ache so cold it burned. "Where the fuck-all we going?" Two security men fell into step behind us.

Breton's hand was around my numb bicep, hurrying me along. "Nowhere you'll like. Back to the Brain Lab."

The lab wasn't in this building, not if it was where it used to be. It was out on the edge of the city, where they'd reclaimed some badlands on the other side of the warehouse sector that nobody would miss if something really, really bad happened. They'd have to take me outside for this, into another van or rotorfoil or something to get me there. I couldn't be lucky enough to think he'd try to walk me the whole way. "I told you, I don't know anything."

"You know plenty, and I'm going to enjoy getting every word out of you." He tightened his grip forgetting that I couldn't feel it. Okay. Let him have his fun. The more this was between him and me, the better. All of Science I couldn't handle, but Breton alone, maybe. Especially if I could get him agitated enough that maybe we didn't go straight to the brain-sucking lab. "Every goddam word," he muttered.

"I guess that means you missed me." I smiled, felt where my cheek was swelling up from one of his earlier blows. We got into an elevator, the four of us.

"I hope I never have to see your miserable face again," he said, his teeth gritted.

No good. He was getting cold and calculating, and any minute now he was going to remember that his job wasn't to settle a score with me, but to find out whatever precious information they thought I knew. I had to keep him hooked. My arms were killing me, the backwash from the nerve cuffs starting up an ache in my motor cortex that was going to have me trying to gnaw my arms off in a little while. I closed my eyes, grimaced, and made a whimper like I was really in deep shit. Which of course, I was, so that was no fake, but I wouldn't have whimpered if I didn't think it'd push his buttons.

Breton yanked my head back, winding his fingers into the coarse black hair and working me like a puppet. "You're pathetic." He pushed me out at the transport level and held me while he gave the nod to the two security men. "I can take him from here, no problem."

They hesitated, then moved off.

He led me by the head to another one of those electric vans, entered through the passenger side door and dragged me in after him. The door swung shut. I gave another one of those little whimpers. He pressed the ignition and rolled us toward the exit with one hand on the wheel, the other at the back of my neck like it was soldered there, holding my head down against the cool, smooth seat. As he told Billings, we go way back.

Like three years ago, he showed me the apartment where I'd be living until I made the full "transition" to citizenship. He went into full asshole mode, commenting that I probably wouldn't live that long anyway, maybe this would be a comfortable bed to die in, I better not break anything . . . trying to provoke me into saying something or doing something. But my favorite word was "yessir" – I had gotten very good at giving him and any other citizen I came in contact with their way. I'd seen indents spit on, kicked, our labor disturbed or work destroyed as if we weren't working for the good of SA. I thought constantly of Marco . . . what made Marco a good candidate for hormone redux but Breton a good indent guardian? Violent tendencies. So what was the difference? Privilege of citizenship. Eventually Breton had got tired of baiting me and went away, probably to blacken the eyes of some new indent who'd only live for two years anyway.

But he didn't always act like that. I had to try to play both sides of him if I was going to get out of this. My flashbacks were still fresh in my mind and I thought about the way he'd looked into my face years ago, and asked me if I was all right, told me to cheer up. The car moved out into traffic – I could hear courier scooters zipping by us and the hum of other vans. "Breton," I said, in a low voice.

"What?"

"What's going to happen to me?"

He narrowed his eyes at the road. "Dunno. If it goes the way we think, and we get the proof out of that thick skull of yours, you're clear. But maybe we find out you offed Martin and his wife, and we have to turn you over for capital."

"I didn't kill them."

"I don't think that you did."

"Then why . . .?"

Both his hands clenched harder, on the steering wheel, on my hair. "Because someone thinks that you did, someone would like to think that you did. Someone would like very much for a so-called Son of Science to go berserk and kill a few innocent citizens."

The Arm. Without the indent corps, Science couldn't maintain the infrastructure, and power would swing the Arm's way. Make Science's work horses look like a threat to security, a threat to the American Dream itself . . . Civil would have to step in under public demand and cut back Science's programs. Meanwhile, proof of a conspiracy to discredit Science on the part of the Arm could result in Civil curtailing the Arm's reach instead . . . and I was that proof, maybe. "And you really think you can get the truth out of me."

Breton sneered. "I know it. How much of your brains we have to rip out to do it, that I don't know."

I shivered. Now that I had him away from the bosses, I hoped for an option that wouldn't make him look bad. "You're just saying that to scare me. Look, if you want me to testify a certain way, I will. You don't have to do this intimidation bullshit with me."

He was shaking his head and laughing to himself.

"Come on, Breton! Don't take me back to Brain. You know . . ."

He pressed hard on me, and I stopped talking. The nerve cuff feedback was giving me a facial tic where my cheek was mashed against the seat. His voice got low. "You don't get it, do you. I'd like to help you, you know, Tato? But the truth is you were always street trash."

"But you don't believe I killed . . ."

"You think I'm going to make a deal with you? That everybody'd be happy then? Nobody's going to take your word, Citizen Smith." He chuckled like my name and title were a joke, which I guess they were. "Especially me. No, I don't believe you killed anybody, but I do believe you're inferior scum and should be treated as such."

Bastard. "Fuck-all I wish I'd broken your nose."

"Shut up." He ground my face into the seat harder. From the sound of things outside, we were on the outskirts, possibly getting near the lab. My teeth were aching now, too.

I kept talking. "You know what? I hope I did kill those people. And I hope they blame you for the way I turned out . . ."

"I said shut up, you little fuck-all!" He yanked on the back of my head but couldn't hurt me any more than that without letting go the wheel. Profanity was good, a sign he was losing control. "Shut up!"

"Oh, yeah, if I go down you're coming with me, Breton." He looked at me like he was trying to figure out what to do next, stop the car and beat me to death or see if he could just ram my head into the dashboard right here. I looked him in the eye, and changed my tack. "Hey, Bret, does it give you a hard-on to push me around like this?"

He let go. He actually let go like he couldn't stand to touch me any more. I twisted to look him in the face better. My voice shook but I kept on. "Haven't you missed me? This could be your last chance."

He stopped the car. We were traveling along the edge of the manufacturing sector. He turned in the seat and grabbed me by the neck. "You perverted little fuck-all. You sick little fuck. I know what you and your lover boy do, you know. I know what you did every moment of your life from when you first entered Silver A up until two months ago."

I went cold. I hadn't thought of that. I knew that we were monitored on the job, and in the dorms a lot of the time, but I didn't think we were actively observed in private residences. In fact, I was pretty sure that was completely against Civil rights . . . but of course, I didn't have any rights until two months ago.

"In fact, if I'd had my way, I'd already know what you did every moment right up through whatever fuck-all just happened at the Martin's, right down to the holes in your goddam socks." His grip tightened and I braced for a blow. But he kept talking. "But no, we've got no live record. Just what's in your goddam head . . ." He cut off abruptly, like he just came awake. And he pushed me away like I was filthy.

What had he just told me? He started the car again and placed both hands on the wheel with a fierce determination. Every moment of my life . . . I thought about the way the glucose triggered those near-living memories in the blackouts. Was that what they were going to suck out of me at the lab? Could I have an unconscious record of everything that went on around me, even when I was in machine trance? No matter how much of my brains they had to rip out . . . I thought he'd meant they'd pump me full of drug analogues, or beat the shit out of me until they were satisfied I didn't know any more than I'd told. We really were going to the Brain Lab; that wasn't just a threat to get me to cooperate. I'd played my cards wrong, then. I had to hope that we were both right, that I didn't kill them, and that there would be enough of me left after they were done to let me go back to work . . .

And what had happened to Marco?

Breton was driving with a singlemindedness that bordered on manic. He wasn't going to let me sidetrack him again. And the ache in my arms and in my head was making it tough to do much of anything but grind my teeth. I willed my fists to clench but no signal was getting through the restraints. I kept trying to think of some way to turn this around. I was a citizen . . . I should be able to go to Civil and testify by some other means. If only I could get away, get to a Civil station . . . I must have squirmed around or something because Breton reached over and turned up the power on the cuffs. Something in my brain started screaming and I banged my head against the window, once, twice, then a long succession of bangs.

"Stop that."

I was succeeding in getting blood on the window and my face.

"Stop it! Should have sedated you . . ." He tried to grab for me with one hand but couldn't get any leverage. As I threw myself at the window, we lurched to the side. Breton slammed on the brake and grabbed me with both hands. I sank my teeth as deep as I could into his wrist, bones and flesh giving way slightly although I did not break the skin. Now he was maimed and pissed. He tried to get me by the hair again, but couldn't maneuver in the tight space of the van. I got my feet up and kicked him away, a good hard one to the stomach, and he retched. Then another kick, in the eye.

It was then that my door opened. I didn't stop to think how, I just pushed myself through head first, hit the ground badly with my shoulder, and staggered as I tried to run. The street was all warehouses, no traffic, no people.

"Sssst!"

I made for the whisper as I heard Breton coughing and gasping in the car behind me. The doorway of a warehouse. I almost tripped over a courier scooter lying on its side in the dark. A shadow in the shadows.

Marco. He pulled me through the door and closed it behind him. "This way." There are no locks on doors in Silver A, because there is no crime. He urged me through the static and haze the cuffs were making of my vision, past rows of knee high warehouse caretakers recharging, oblivious to our presence. Through another doorway and into another cavernous space, stacked high with sealed bins. I stumbled into the first row and stayed where I fell. "Marco . . ." Now my arms were shaking, the fingers flopping at the ends.

He turned back and seemed to see the cuffs for the first time. "Fuck-all . . . you had these on long?"

"Too . . . long." I could hardly speak my jaw was clenched so tight. He turned the power down and then popped the release. I cried out as the sensation flooded in, pain first. It was going to hurt for a long time, I knew, and my grip would probably be weak for a couple of hours, but the first few minutes would be the worst. Marco supported my upper body as I convulsed. Fuck-all that hurt. I was glad Breton wasn't here to see it.

The pain was backing down to a dull ebb and I wanted to lie there in his arms, but Marco was urging me up. "Come on, Tato, gotta go." Breton. He'd be blind with murderous rage about now and coming after me . . . if he knew where I'd gone. But he didn't.

"Where?" My legs seemed to work okay as I stood. "Where can we go?"

Marco's eyes glittered black in the dim light. "New Japan?"

"What?"

"No, extradition treaty with SA. We're wanted. Leastways, I am." He took my hand and led me toward the far back wall of the warehouse. "They want to kill us, you know."

"No, no, I don't know. I don't know anything!" My fingers were still smarting and tingling where he held them. "I didn't even know if you were . . ."

Marco stopped and spoke, his voice hushed in the largeness of the room as he switched back to the clear enunciation of Civil talk. "The Arm. The Martins were supposed to kill us both and make it look like we two outsider peons couldn't handle the freedoms of citizenship and fought with each other. I killed them, instead."

But not the baby. I remembered the baby crying. I let out my breath like I'd been holding it.

It wasn't fair. We'd played by the rules and everything we ever wanted should have been entitled to us. I could still go back, turn myself in to Civil and get cleared. Of course, I had to make it there before Science caught up with me. But Marco was standing there, still bloody in places, and I was shivering with the after-effects of the nerve cuffs, the blue juice, epinephrine, and a bad,

bad sugar craving. "Then you're wanted. Why are you still here?"

"Tato." He was rubbing my fingers softly and they hardly hurt any more. He raised my hand to his lips and brushed the tips, passed the back along his cheek, then took my thumb into the warmth of his mouth. The pins and needles turned to liquid fire but it didn't feel like pain. "If you don't come with me, I don't know what I'll do." He touched my swollen cheek. "You followed me into this place. Will you follow me out of it?"

I swayed in place. "Tell it like it is."

He touched my swollen cheek. "You all I got."

"Ain't much," I mumbled, but I took a shuffling step forward. New Japan was a long way north and west, and between there and here was The Fringe. But The Fringe might not be so bad with someone to watch my back. I leaned on him and we went out the back door of the place, under the old fence into the grassy, rocky emptiness on the other side.

SLEEP THAT BURNS

Jerry Sykes

My first assignment as a cop had been to herd rubberneckers away from the broken suicides that lay at the foot of the Millennium Ferris wheel. Twenty years on and I was still herding people away from the wheel, only this time the wheel was on its side and the people were the vagrants who made their home in the giant rusted cage that was all that was left of the wheel.

It was a hot evening and the sun burned a moving red spectrum on the glass towers of the City making it look like they were on fire. I drove slowly along the embankment to Millennium Park, windows open, the acrid smell of the Thames in my nostrils, and looked out over the river. It was low tide and I could see beachcombers down by the water. On either side of the river, barely a hundred feet wide at this time of year, people moved in slow motion, eyes scanning the baked mud, twists of wood and metal breaking the surface like the bones of a desiccated corpse. Many of the searchers carried hessian sacks on their shoulders, others huddled their findings to their chests, distrustful of their neighbours.

I backed the shuttle up to the gate and killed the engine.

The Ferris wheel, with a span of over five hundred feet, had once been the centrepiece of the Millennium Festival, visible from Blackheath to Primrose Hill, when the night sky would be filled with the cries of the innocent rolling through scrolled neon and into new worlds limited only by their imaginations. The structure had long since been formally abandoned, and lowered on to its side to prevent further suicides, and was now a makeshift shelter to the constant flow of vagrants that ghosted through London. The top and sides of the wheel were covered with an urgent tapestry of plastic sheets, blankets and tarpaulins; inside, the wheel was divided into separate dwellings by more tarpaulins and blankets.

My remit as a shuttle operator was to move these vagrants out to holding camps until they could be allocated government support through the Realignment Bill. Twice a week I would come down to the park and herd fifty of them into the shuttle and ship them out. It was a neverending cycle, not least because the process of realignment took so long, many people would often drift away from the camps and make their own way back to where they had come from before they could be processed.

Across the street a group of vagrants climbed over the embankment wall; they had the staccato movements and the jaundiced look of donors.

I turned to Denny. "Anyone for the slab?"

He looked at me with flat eyes. "Man, I need a hit tonight or that last interest hike's gonna blow me outta the water. I'm gonna end up out here with these fuckin meltdowns." He jerked his thumb out of the window.

Denny was a freelance agent for the NHS and it was his job to find people willing to part with one of their kidneys – for a price, the right price. More than fifty per cent of the people in this country between the ages of forty and fifty suffer from kidney damage, a direct legacy of the drug culture at the close of the millennium; more than fifty per cent of the people in this country between the ages of forty and fifty can afford to buy a new kidney.

A seller's market.

But such was the lack of post-op care afforded donors, many didn't live long enough to enjoy their windfall and soon ended up in the morgue on the slab.

"Let's see what we can do," I said.

We climbed out of the shuttle.

Around the edge of the wheel each dwelling had its own entrance; the dwellings on the inside were reached by a communal entrance in front. Denny headed for the main entrance; I turned to go clockwise around the wheel.

I walked slowly, pulling aside makeshift curtains to get a look at the occupants, barking commands for people to get on the shuttle, trying to keep the mix right; I didn't want a load of juiceheads and runners.

Every now and then I could hear Denny shouting at someone, and the occasional thump of metal on flesh from within the wheel. Denny was the kind of guy who liked to throw his weight around. He was a qualified paramedic but he chose to ride shotgun with me because he got to beat up on people.

A third of the way around the wheel I came across an old guy I had seen many times before.

"Hey, Wally, how you doin'?" I squatted down beside the small fire. He was cooking some eggs on the lid of an old paint tin.

He looked up at me, eyes swimming with a milky discoloration. His face bore the lines of someone who has learnt to live with pain at an early age.

"You gonna come for the ride?" I said. Wally had been a regular passenger on the shuttle for a long time, but for a variety of reasons he had never been processed, the latest being that he was just too fuckin old. But sometimes he liked to tag along and make out like old times.

He poked at the eggs with a long handled fork. "Where you headed?"

"Does it matter?" I said.

He snorted and his head wobbled around on his shoulders.

My legs were cramping and I stood up. I took a pack of cigarettes out of my jacket and tossed one on the ground next to Wally. He picked it up and lit it from the coals of the fire.

"Maybe I'll give it a miss this time, huh?" Feathers of smoke drifted from his mouth as he spoke.

"One of these days I'm gonna come at you wi' this," I said, slapping the gun on my hip. "Then maybe you ain't got no choice." I smiled at him.

I moved on, walking between broken belongings that lay scattered on the parched grass. It took me twenty minutes to walk around the wheel and when I returned to the shuttle it was already full. Denny was twisted round in his seat, shouting at someone in back.

"– and for the last time, no fuckin jugs of booze in the Medibag, okay?"

I climbed into the driver's seat. "What's goin' on?" I said, looking in the rear view.

"These fuckin guys are fiends, man. They wanna use my Medibag to cool their juice. You believe that?" He sighed and shook his head.

I stifled a laugh. On the last trip out someone had used Denny's Medibag, the icebox he used for transporting kidneys, to keep their jug of beer cold. The next kidney to occupy the bag had become contaminated and worthless. It had cost Denny his month's rent; he relied on those little extras to meet his bills.

"Any troublemakers?" I asked. Normally, when confronted with Denny, people will just get on the shuttle as if under hypnosis, rarely is there any trouble. But occasionally he will find some reason for stomping some poor guy's head.

"Just go," he said, his eyes beaming straight ahead.

I hit the ignition and we moved slowly out of the park. A light rain had begun to fall and the vagrants moving through the mist looked like after-images of the people they had once been. Clouds of smoke curling out of slits in the tarpaulins glowed blue in the twilight.

We drove upriver and crossed the Thames at Westminster Bridge. It was now four years since my son had been killed.

Eleven months into his National Service Cal was pulling down extra hours to try and wind up early so he could get back to college with a running start on his final year. The extra workload was no hardship; for the whole of his time he had been stationed at a centre for people with Alzheimer's and he had gotten to know a lot of the patients as friends, often staying late and trying to follow the scat logic of their conversations. But the extra hours meant late nights, and late nights meant running risks out on the street.

He was killed by a single bullet from the gun of a juicehead out on his stag night.

Once Virtual Reality had faded into the mainstream and become just another tired thread in the cultural fabric of the world, for a few dark souls a new frontier in entertainment was needed. And this time, the kill had to be for real. Guys like Billy Hendry were quick to fill the gap in the market; his White Hunter had been one of the first organised trips into the cold heart of the professional killer. For a price, you could take your pick of game: Cal – young, white, male – cheap at ten thousand.

The shooter had been easy to track down; a security camera by the ATM that Cal had been using at the time of his death had caught the murder on videotape: the jeep pulling up to the kerb, the pistol appearing through the open window, the face twisted in cruel intensity as it drew a bead on the back of Cal's head . . .

Together with a patrol cop I pulled the juicehead from his bed and executed him in his own back yard. In the morning, the cop had called the Church and cancelled the wedding.

After six months the official investigation was wound up. Our life savings and the services of a bounty hunter fuelled our hopes and frustration and anger for another two months, but the bounty hunter could only come up with one sure thing: Billy Hendry had disappeared.

Soon after, Jolie walked out on me. She said that in shadow my profile was the same as that of Cal, and as her world was now full of shadows . . .

Last I heard she was running computer security for a tele-communications group up near Liverpool.

Some nights I watch the video from the security camera until I drift into a troubled sleep that burns images from the tape deep into my mind, so that every action, every thought, every memory is controlled by them.

The following morning I wake to static filling the screen and white noise filling my ears.

At nine I pulled into a service station to refuel and grab a bite to eat. Denny was asleep and I had to dig him in the ribs. "You comin' in?" I asked him.

"I better get these fuckers sorted first," he said, nodding to the rear of the shuttle. He rubbed at his face with the palms of his hands.

"I'll get you some coffee."

The restaurant was quiet, the only other customer a young kid in dark green overalls up at the counter. His eyes were moulded to the rear end of the waitress every bit as much as her tight uniform. I walked to the rear and took a booth against the window. I held my hand up to the glass and saw Denny leading a group from the shuttle towards the back of the restaurant where the kitchen staff would hand out G-rations. He had his hand on the butt of his gun and his eyes flitted anxiously over the group.

I ordered coffee for two and lamb chops and reflected on Denny's suitability for the job. Realistically, the post was little more than that of driver's gopher, but with his medical credentials and his bloodlust he had turned the shuttle into a carrier for his freelance kidney trading. Not that it bothered me, he always gave me a slice of his fee and I enjoyed having to put my foot down when the temperature alarm on his Medibag showed red.

After a few minutes Denny came in through the back and slid into the booth opposite me. A crooked grin hung on his face like a broken mask.

"You okay?" I said.

"Those dogs out back?" He looked towards the back door, as if expecting the dogs to walk in at any moment. "Those dogs – they were eating some guy's head this morning. You believe that?"

"Eating someone's head?" I said, raising my eyebrows.

"The guy out back, the chef, guy out having a smoke?"

"The dogs were eating the chef's head?"

"Hey, you wanna hear this, slap the wise guy, okay?"

"Okay, go on." I forked some lamb chop into my mouth.

Denny shuffled in his seat, looked over at the back door once more. "You know the estate out back of here? Quarter mile or so?" I nodded. "Well, the other day they found this old guy out there that'd been dead for seventeen months. *Seventeen months.* You believe that? Imagine, so little presence, so little life . . ." He held his thumb and forefinger together and tapped out the words slowly in the air." . . . no one cares, no one *knows*, no one gives a *fuck* when you're dead." His eyes drifted into the distance for a moment before snapping back. "Anyway, right after they found him they threw out all this shitty old furniture, hundred years old most of it. Stuck it in the garbage room. And it drives the dogs fuckin wild. They're jumpin around, going crazy, trying to get in the garbage, kicking up a tornado. Somehow they eventually get in and they're going mad chewing on the mattress, ripping it apart. No one knows what the fuck's happening, what's sending all these mutts crazy. There a sudden doggy craze in duck feathers or what?" He picked up his coffee and took a sip.

"Anyhow, the caretaker eventually manages to chase the hounds away. Shoots in the air or somethin', I don't know. And he's curious, you know, he wants to know what's happening, what turned the dogs on like that. So he takes what's left of the mattress for a DNA scan." Denny leaned over the table conspiratorially. "Now get this." His eyes flicked momentarily to the back door again. "Turns out when they took the guy's body outta there, or what was left of it, part of his head got left behind on the mattress." He jabbed his finger on the table. "*That's* what the dogs were going wild over. Flesh, human flesh. Fuckin wild about it." He leaned back on the seat, a big grin slapped across his face.

"You ready to order now," I asked him.

It was another two hours before we hit the holding camp.

The camps were originally built as low cost housing projects for the dispossessed in the 80s and 90s, but the standards were such that within ten years they began to break up. Coupled with the general migration of businesses and family homes to the new green areas, the projects were eventually abandoned and now served solely as holding camps.

At the entrance to the camp was a low red brick building with a flat roof the control centre. I left Denny to unload the shuttle while I let myself into the centre and logged in the vagrants.

Denny was leaning against the wall waiting for me when I stepped back outside. A plastic cigarette poked out from between his lips. I nodded to the pad of donor release forms stuffed in his pocket.

"You got someone lined up?" I said.

"Some old guy. Lives over by the school." The cigarette bobbed in his mouth.

"Old guy?" I said. The kidneys of most people over fifty were usually shot to fuck by years of additives and expellants; even on the black market they were difficult to shift.

He took the cigarette out of his mouth. "There's some desperate people out there."

I raised my eyebrows. "You're tellin' me."

I looked at my watch: almost eleven.

"It's getting late," I said. "Where do we find this guy?"

Denny gestured for me to follow him and we went into the camp.

We walked across a gravel car park painted silver by a hawk moon, our footsteps counterpoint to the random noises of the camp at night. The car park led to a sheltered walkway with doors hidden in darkness on our right. Shadows moved across the edge of my vision and occasionally I would catch a glimpse of a face, a slice of skin pale in the moonlight.

I followed Denny along the walkway until we came to a dark

green door; a pale light shone through the peephole. Denny took out his notebook and checked the number. "This is the place," he said. He rapped his knuckles on the door. A cool breeze blew along the walkway and I could smell burnt food and urine. I turned away to avoid the smell and that's when I saw him.

A group of men had emerged from a stairwell at the end of the walkway, no more than fifty feet away. They threaded themselves between abandoned cars and headed for the opposite corner of the square. They shuffled over the gravel car park, their footsteps a continuous growling noise. As they passed beneath a streetlamp each face was washed in pale orange and there was no mistaking the twist of the nose or the eyes that burned with the fear of a trapped animal.

Billy Hendry, the man who had arranged the killing of my son.

I stepped off the walkway and headed towards the group. At first no one seemed to notice me, but then I made the mistake of calling out, "Hey! Wait!", and my voice was like a gunshot in the still air. The group fragmented and ran in all directions.

Hendry cut loose for the stairwell he had appeared from. I knew that just beyond was an old strip mall and a group of tenement blocks that was like a three-dimensional maze. If he reached that I would lose him for certain.

I took off after him.

As I ran the only sounds I could hear were the rasping of my breath and the violent crunch of my boots on the gravel. I reached the entrance to the mall with Hendry still in my sights, fifty feet ahead.

And then he fell; in the darkness he tripped and went flying, stretching out his hand to break his fall and skidding across the tarmac. I heard him cry out in pain.

And then I made a mistake.

I slowed to watch him, thinking he was trapped. I slowed to a jog – and then he was up and running again, limping slightly but having lost none of his pace. Seconds later the ringing sounds of his footsteps disappeared into the maze and into the night air.

I had lost him.

I bent over, my hands on my knees, and breathed deeply. The air seemed to burn in my chest; perspiration ran into my eyes. I stood up and looked around, walked towards the mall. The beating of my heart echoed from the buildings around me.

I came to the point where he had fallen and lowered myself to one knee and peered at the ground. I could just make out . . . what? I took out my penline torch and shone it over the ground. Drops of blood appeared like rubies in the dust.

I stood and looked around again. I thought about going into the maze, but the chances of finding Hendry – if it was Hendry, I had only glimpsed the man briefly; the speed with which he had taken off suggested he was guilty of *something*, but was it Hendry?

I looked at the ground in front of me, drawing circles with the torch beam around the drops of blood.

I took a handkerchief from my jacket and placed it carefully over the blood; tiny red flowers bloomed in the cotton. I then took a plastic evidence bag from my jacket and dropped the handkerchief into the bag. I put the bag in my pocket and headed back to the camp.

Denny was sitting in the cab of the shuttle when I reached the car park. A solitary lamp burned above the control centre and all I could see were his hands flipping the top of the Zippo. I knocked on the glass. He lowered the window and peered down at me, his face deep in shadow

"What the fuck happened to you?" snapped Denny.

"I saw—"

"I lost him. That old guy, remember? He was watching us from upstairs. I heard him rattling the window when you scooted. He musta thought we were the goon squad or somethin', scared the shit outta him—"

"Denny—"

"—the fuck's goin' on?" He leaned out of the window and glared down at me. The ridge of muscle along his jawline pulsed violently.

I took a deep breath. "I saw him. Hendry—"

"You saw Hendry? Why – Why didn't you say? I coulda—"

"I'm tellin' you now," I said, keeping my voice level. "Okay?"

Denny withdrew into the cab. I heard a rustling sound and then his Zippo flared, splashing his face with white light. He lit a cigarette and smoke drifted from his nostrils.

"Hendry. He was in that bunch of vagrants across the way. When we were waiting for the old guy?" I pointed vaguely in the direction of the stairwell.

"Scaring the shit outta him," muttered Denny, still rankling from my knocking him back.

"Hey, lose the fuckin attitude, okay? I'm talkin' 'bout the guy that whacked my son, not some fuckin meltdown that pissed in your pocket."

"Hey, I didn't mean—"

I pushed his objection aside. "I chased him into the maze but . . ." Thoughts ran away from me. "Anyway, look." I took the bag containing the handkerchief out of my pocket.

Denny looked at the bag and then up at me. "What? You get a nosebleed or somethin'?"

"It's Hendry's. The blood. I was chasing him and he tripped over a kerb or something." I suddenly felt uncomfortable and lifted the bag for a closer look as if I might be able to recognise the blood. "I'm not sure it was him, though."

"Hey, he ran. Sounds guilty to me," Denny reasoned.

"So would a whole pile of other people." I put the bag back in my pocket. "I'm gonna run a DNA scan on it, anyway."

Denny climbed out of the cab and we walked over to the control centre. I swiped my ID card and pushed through the wooden door into the lobby. A heavy set man in a grey uniform with a dark complexion was sitting behind the console reading a paperback. Reflections from the monitors before him danced across his glasses, as if he were playing scenes from the book on them. He looked up as we approached. "Still here? Thought you'd be long gone by now." He delivered the words one at a time; it was a wonder anyone ever let him finish what he was saying.

"We ran into a bit of trouble. We need to head on up to the Datacentre, check something out. Okay if we go on through?"

The guard's eyes flicked to a monitor, back again. "Sure," he said, and rolled his huge shoulders.

He buzzed us through the main door. It opened onto a short corridor with two further doors on either side. A large metal door stood at the far end. As we walked through the corridor the sign on the door gradually came into focus: TRANSIT LABORATORY – AUTHORISED PERSONNEL ONLY.

We reached the door and I gave it a gentle push with the palm of my hand. It was locked. I knew the guard was watching us on a monitor so I turned to the camera above the door and gave him the finger. I heard a soft click and when I pushed the door again it was open.

Through the doors another corridor stretched before us. I walked on, looking at the sign on each door. I could hear Denny breathing heavily behind me and his footsteps clipping the tile floor.

We came to a door marked DNA SCANNER and stopped. I squeezed the plastic bag containing the handkerchief in my pocket and then knocked. After a few moments there was the sound of soft footsteps behind the door and then it was slowly opened. A man about my height, six two, with thinning red hair stood there, white lab coat wrapped around his shoulders. He looked us up and down through half-moon glasses on the end of his nose. I felt my DNA twitch.

"Yes?" He kept one hand on the doorknob and the other on the frame, blocking our entrance.

"Blon." I held up my ID card. "Detective Blon. We've come to run a scan on some blood?"

"I know who you are." His voice sounded weary.

Denny looked at me, at the technician, shrugged. "So now we all know each other, what are we waiting for?"

The technician looked at his watch.

"Hey, don't you worry 'bout the time. We got all night," said Denny and gently but forcefully pushed the door open.

The technician sighed and stepped back. He seemed to deflate as if his skeleton had crumbled leaving only tired flesh.

I followed Denny into the lab.

It was a small room, ten by ten, with computer hardware floor to ceiling on three walls; on the fourth wall a solitary window overlooked the camp. In the glass I could see my reflection: a face drawn by shadows, pale and cold. One eye seemed to be twitching but I could feel no movement in my face.

The technician pulled himself up to his full height. "Detective Blon, this is not a private lab and we are not here to service your private actions. You are in breach of everything you have ever learned in the force and you know it." He held my stare.

A minute passed, our eyes locked. I felt every muscle in my body tense.

Eventually his eyes flicked away. "You think you got him this time?" he said. There was genuine concern in his voice.

I shrugged and handed him the evidence bag. He disappeared through a door next to a large glass case. Inside the case were rows of bottles of blood in deepening shades of red.

"You better hope this is the real thing," said Denny, "or you're gonna get yourself a reputation." He pulled himself up on to a desk and leaned back with his head under the extractor fan and the cool pulse of the air. "You gotta take this guy out. And soon. You understand?"

I knew what he meant. This was not the first time I had been to the lab with a blood sample. But I had to be sure I had the right man. That way it wouldn't matter when I killed him, shot him in the back. That was something Victims' Rights allowed me to do, administer my own punishment. Damn, it even *encouraged* me to do it, go right out and shoot the guy in the back of the head and not feel like a coward.

It took the technician ninety minutes to run the scan. I was watching shadows shifting around in the camp when he came back into the room.

Denny still had his head under the extractor fan.

The technician was trying to hide a smile and not having much success.

"We got him?" I said. My heart thumped deep in my chest.

"Ninety-eight per cent match. I ran it twice, just to be sure. I didn't wanna fuck up and have you coming back here in a couple of weeks with another dirty handkerchief."

The camp covered two square miles and held an average of twenty-six-hundred vagrants at any one time. Finding Hendry was not going to be easy, and there was always the possibility he had already left the camp – it was not a prison, people were free to move on as they pleased.

With only the two of us, there was no point in being too systematic about the search. We took off in opposite directions.

Cold blue moonlight threw the camp into dark relief as I made my way to the first tenement. In my right hand I carried my pistol, in my left a heavy duty torch. The building seemed to shift in the darkness as I approached and the splintered glass of the broken windows looked like burnt out stars captured in wooden frames. Occasionally I heard signs of life: a barking cough, the death rattle of the bronchitic; feral screams dragged from the deepest of sleeps; angry calls to silence. I hoped that somewhere among the grumbling mess of people was Hendry.

Denny had still been pissed off with me for losing him the kidney, and I had had to agree to rush him a couple of thousand for helping me out, more if we caught the guy. But he was under threat of death himself not to shoot him. That was my gig.

The stairwell smelled of stale alcohol and decaying flesh and I was reminded of the dogs behind the diner on the freeway. I hurried up the stairs.

At the top of the building were two doors, tribal markings slashed across them in red and green. The one on my right was open. I lifted my gun and followed the torch beam into the room.

The concrete floor was covered with the tools of the dead and the defeated: cigarette butts, broken vials, cracked needles. The bundles of rags against the far wall were probably vagrants. I crossed the room and kicked the first one on the foot; gently, I didn't want to break it off.

A hand appeared from beneath the rags and dragged them to one side. I shone the torch into a face that twisted to look up at me, blinked in the strange light. The eyes were sunk deep into the skull and the mouth hung loose, saliva spooling from the corner.

I moved the beam off the face. "Go back to sleep," I said.

I lifted the blankets from the other two mounds in the room and saw identical faces, a single mask that took on the contours rent by the latest hurt.

I walked back down the stairs with heavy steps.

I searched on through the night, tired, pointing my torch into faces until ghosts swam before my eyes and I could no longer trust what I was seeing. Occasionally I caught glimpses of running shadows in the distance and at first I thought they were cops, but my mind was so tired and twisted they could just as well have been the shadows of clouds scooting across the moon.

I was heading back to the main block, ready to call it a night, when my radio squawked into life. "Denny, you still around? I thought you'd—"

"Get your fuckin' ass down to the Clark block," Denny snapped. "Now!"

"Wha – What's happening?" My mind wheeled.

"I've got the fucker."

A cold wave passed through me. "Hendry? You found him—?"

"Just get the fuck over here fast or you ain't gonna get the pleasure of the pop."

My legs were already rolling. "You shot him?" Anger welled in me. "Denny—?"

"Relax. I just – I just settled him down a little, that's all. I ain't gonna deprive you."

I clipped the radio back on my belt and started running towards the Clark block.

Denny was standing in the open doorway. A bare lightbulb burned directly above him, turning his hair into a halo. His hands hung loose at his sides, thick veins cording his forearms. I was panting by the time I reached him and took a moment to calm my breathing.

I nodded at Denny.

He pointed into the building. "Through that door, second on the right."

I followed his directions. My legs felt weak and my face was glazed with sweat. The floor was swimming with urine and I reached my arms out to the walls to steady myself and felt something sticky. I looked up. Angry fingerpaintings in blood covered the wall on my right. I followed the trail, ending in the room where Denny had directed me.

The pale early morning sun burned through the grime on the windows and picked out a hunched figure against the far wall. He was sitting with his knees drawn up, his head resting on his knees. A trail of blood led from the door. The man's clothes were ragged and dirty; the soles of his shoes flapped loose like grotesque tongues. The smell of faeces assaulted my nostrils and I found myself gagging. I crossed to open the window. It was rusted shut so I popped it with the butt of my gun. Shards of glass rattled on the floor at my feet.

The man stirred and raised his head and I saw the full extent of Denny's handiwork; a quick death would be a relief to this man. A deep cut ran from above the left eye down to the jawline; it had sliced through a nerve and the upper lid twitched as if shot through with electricity. Beads of blood as dark as leeches clung to the cut. The eyes were as dead as glass marbles. His jaw was broken, the right side of his mouth hanging loose.

The man's head fell back on to his arms.

I flashed on video images from deep memory.

I moved closer, careful not to slip in the blood. I knelt in front of the man and put my gun against his forehead and pushed his head back, cracking it against the wall.

The face of a stranger leapt out at me and my senses froze, unable to deal with the information. A stranger. A complete stranger. All I could think of was why had Denny led me to a stranger? For a brief moment I had been blinded by the mask of injuries but the more I looked at the man before me the more I couldn't understand what Denny had done.

But in the end it didn't matter, all that mattered was that Hendry was still out there.

I pulled my radio from my belt and called for a paramedic.

The freeway was quiet heading south and I was able to run on cruise control. It had turned eight and the sun was burning a track in the sky and the tarmac shimmered before my eyes. Denny was asleep in the back and I could hear him snoring gently. The fact that he had almost just beaten a man to death didn't seem to have jagged his rhythm.

We must have been an hour out of the camp when I noticed the red light on Denny's Medibag. I remembered Denny telling the juiceheads to leave the bag alone and I could only assume that despite his warning one of them had managed to hide their juice in the bag on the trip out and had left it switched on.

I shouted at Denny to take a look but he just rolled over in his sleep, dreams of torture playing across his eyelids.

The light was still on, and Denny still asleep, twenty minutes later when I pulled into the service station. I drove over to the far side of the car park and stopped next to a green Bullet van.

I climbed down from my seat and opened the rear door. I pulled myself into the back and walked over to the Medibag. Normally, Denny keeps it locked, but when I flipped the lid it opened. A cold mist crept over the edges and began to spread across the floor of the shuttle. I waved it away with my hand and knelt down to take a better look. There was something in there. It looked like a sheet of paper all crumpled up. I reached in to lift the paper out and there it was.

A human heart.

Deep blue and covered with a fur of frost but still a human heart.

I fell forward on to my knees, a burning pulse beating in my head. I could do nothing but stare into the box, at the cold air swirling around the heart, as if pumped by the organ itself.

I still had the sheet of paper in my hand. I lifted it and read. It was a printout from a DNA scan, the information identical to the one the technician had shown me back at the Datacentre, identifying the blood as belonging to Hendry.

I didn't understand. Was the heart Hendry's? It didn't make sense. How . . .?

I looked at the sheet of paper again for some sign; spidery handwriting near the bottom; blood was smeared across most of it but I could make out the tail end: ". . . now that his heart is still, we may be at rest." It was signed Jolie.

Jolie.

She must have hacked into the DNA database and put a trip on it so that when anyone accessed the records of Hendry she would know immediately. I flashed on running shadows – telecommunications security turned bounty hunters? And Jolie – had she cut out the heart of the man who had killed her son? I screwed my eyes tight but images of Jolie scooping a knife in a man's chest still burned on my retina.

I stared at the heart for a long time, the distant rhythmic sounds of traffic on the freeway calming me.

The whole mad spiral of events that had led to my being here, from the shooting of Cal to the bloody heart in my hands, played out in a continuous violent loop in my head, over and over . . .

Eventually I picked up the heart and wrapped it in the sheet of paper. I jumped down from the shuttle and walked across to the far side of the car park where a chainlink fence separated me from the yard. I listened carefully but for a long time I could only hear the sound of my own breathing.

When I heard the sound of the dogs fighting over scraps behind the building I drew back my arm and threw the heart as hard as I could towards the noise.

The frozen heart shattered on hitting the ground, splinters of viscera already melting on the hot tarmac.

RAVENS

Stephen Dedman

It was a beautiful day, the end of August, and the sky was a deep rich blue, but that didn't make me feel any better about being put on suicide duty. The car drove around the hospital looking for a parking spot twice before Sylvia over-rode the autopilot and parked outside the ER. She checked the details on the compad, then walked to the reception desk. "I'm Sylvia Manning, Forecasting and Prevention Squad, LAPD," she said, flashing her ID at the nurse. "This is Cadet Officer Garcia. May we speak to Dr Lester?"

The nurse looked at our cards, then at the monitor. "She's doing rounds. Immunology." He gave us directions, and Sylvia thanked him while I smiled mutely. It took us a few minutes to find Lester, and maybe twice as long to persuade her that we needed to see her privately. "What is it?" she snapped, closing her office door behind her.

"It's your daughter, Melissa," said Sylvia, levelly. "There's a forty-six per cent probability that she's going to attempt suicide in the next three weeks, with a seventy-nine per cent probability of success or serious injury."

Lester stared at her, blood draining from her face, and sat down hurriedly. "I thought it was about one of my patients," she muttered. "Are you sure? How do you know?"

Sylvia glanced at me; she's been with the Ravens for years, but I know more about the software. "She's been seen on Metrorail platforms after the train has left," I replied. "Alone. True, she could have been waiting for someone, but no one ever turned up."

"Probably her boyfriend," said Lester. "Theatre arts student; he's not what you'd call reliable."

"Our data suggests that they broke up some time last week."

Lester swore under her breath. "She didn't tell me, but I've been busy. Did she show any sign of actually jumping?"

"No," said Sylvia. "This just indicates that she's considered it, but we think she's likely to choose some other method."

I nodded. "The other indicators aren't as conclusive – her buying habits, mostly. As a pre-med, she's in a high risk group, but it wasn't until it was correlated with the Metrorail data that the probability went over forty per cent." Summer break was almost over, and I found myself wondering if Melissa Lester had actually wanted to study medicine, or whether she felt pressured by family tradition. The expression on her mother's face suggested that she was thinking the same thing. "What can I do?" she asked. She listened without arguing or asking for much clarification, and we were back in the car barely ten minutes later.

I plugged the compad into the autopilot, and the car started up and headed south. "I wish you'd reconsider," Sylvia said, after a long silence. "You couldn't be better qualified for this section, and we'd hate to lose you."

I shook my head. I'd been in the UCLA Police Reserve for three years – it was the easiest way of paying my tuition – and while I'd listed the Ravens on my preferences as soon as I got out of uniform, a semester's worth of weekend and night shifts and four weeks of my vacation was more than enough. "I want to find out how other sections work," I lied.

"Who've you applied for?"

"Computer Crime."

"The Geek Squad? You'll never get in; they've got a waiting list from here to Seattle, and computing's only your minor, right?" I nodded; computer statistical modelling had seemed a sensible back-up for a sociology degree. Maybe I should've done a double major. "Forecasting's so new that if you stick with it, you'll be fast-tracked for promotion," she continued. "If you leave now, your time here will be wasted; if you wait a couple of years and get your degree, you'll be able to transfer as a sergeant, at least."

I didn't reply. The car pulled into a parking lot outside a tower block on Inez. It shouldn't have looked like a slum, but somehow it managed. It was an improvement on the places I remember seeing when I was a kid – armourglass had replaced security screens, the cameras were hidden, and the murals covered with a graffiti-proof layer – but there was something unconvincing about the gardens, the murals, the pastel colours. Or maybe it was just me.

The corridor smelled clean and unhappy, even worse than the hospital, as did the lift. Sylvia smiled slightly at the muzak – the theme from *M*A*S*H*; I'd told her a few days before that the muzak in places like this is sponsored by the TV stations, presumably to encourage people to spend as much time as possible in front of the set rather than going out. She'd wondered aloud what they played in the lifts at the banks or the stock exchange; "If I Were a Rich Man", maybe, or "Money, Money" from *Cabaret*. The lift went straight to the fourth floor and another clean, empty corridor.

Molly Kearsley's apartment was slightly larger than mine, and just as well soundproofed – the world outside disappeared as soon as Sylvia shut the door behind us – and the furniture was just as old and cheap-looking. The air-conditioner hadn't quite re-moved the smells of tobacco and pot. "What's she done now?" Kearsley asked, as she turned the TV off. "Oh, come on," she said, as Sylvia hesitated. "I know plainclothes cops when I see them, and she didn't come home last night. Is she okay?" She sounded weary rather than concerned, until she saw the look on my face. "Is she?"

We showed her our ID cards anyway; she merely glanced at them. "Is it unusual for Bethany not to come home?" asked Sylvia, levelly.

Kearsley shrugged, sat down in an armchair facing the TV, and reached for the packet of cigarettes on the table nearby. She didn't invite us to sit. "It depends. She's usually back by about three or four, but sometimes she goes out with friends . . . you still haven't told me what she's supposed to have done."

"We're from Forecasting and Prevention," Sylvia told her, reaching for her wallet and showing her her ID. Kearsley raised her eyebrows at this, then sat back in the chair. "Okay," she said. "What is she *going* to do?"

"There's a fifty-seven per cent probability that Bethany will overdose some time in the next month," Sylvia replied. "It may be accidental, or it may be a suicide attempt. In either case, there's a sixty-four per cent that it will be fatal if she doesn't get help in time."

Kearsley's hands shook slightly as she lit the cigarette. "How do you know?"

Sylvia glanced at me, and I told her what I knew, reading from the compad. "Buying habits," muttered Kearsley sourly, and I tried not to wince. The compad said that Molly Kearsley was thirty-four, old enough to have joined in the privacy protests of a couple of decades ago, but she'd been a registered addict in those days, and her file hadn't said anything about her being political. "What the hell has she been buying?" she asked, at last.

"I don't know," said Sylvia. "Our computer correlates data and comes up with probabilities, and it only gives us the probabilities; we'd need a court order to get all the details – and we'd need Bethany's permission before we disclosed them to you."

"Jesus. Okay, what am I supposed to do? *I* don't have any control over her."

"You're still legally responsible for her, in some regards," said Sylvia, quietly.

"Don't I know it," snarled Kearsley. "Every time you arrest her, you bring her back here."

"The courts are very reluctant to impose custodial sentences on minors, especially for non-violent crimes."

"You could register her as an addict."

"She's on a waiting list."

Kearsley shook her head. "I was using when she was conceived; I didn't know I was pregnant until I was four months gone. She won't listen to me; why should she? There's nothing I can do with her."

"We're not here to punish anyone," said Sylvia, gently. "We just want to warn you, so that you're better prepared."

"Prepared for what?" Kearsley looked at us, her face red, tears in her eyes.

Sylvia didn't flinch; she never does. "If you were the first to find her . . . say, if she attempted suicide at home, or had an overdose here . . . would you know what to do?"

"Call an ambulance?"

"Are you insured? Callers with insurance are given priority over suicides and ODs."

"I can't afford insurance." She said it as though she thought we already knew, which we did, then her face darkened. "If you're trying to sell—"

"No," said Sylvia, cutting her short. "The premiums for a potentially suicidal addict are horrendous; neither you nor Bethany's father could afford them." The way she spoke, you never would have guessed that the insurance companies owned a controlling share of the LAPD; I wondered if Kearsley knew. "It would help if you had some first aid training; I know it's rather expensive, but it may help to save your daughter's life –" I watched Kearsley's face carefully, to see if I could see how she reacted to that, tell which way she was likely to jump. "– or someone else's," Sylvia continued, hardly missing a beat.

Kearsley nodded, but her expression remained sour. "I can see that, but . . . is there anything else? Do you know *when* she's likely to try something? Or how I can tell?"

"The fifty-seven per cent probability is for the next month; it will be reassessed every day. We can let you know if it changes. The most likely method is a heroin overdose; it may be very difficult being sure that it wasn't an accident. There's another thing you might consider," she added, as though it were an afterthought. "Ambulance crews give higher priority to registered organ donors, at no extra cost –" Kearsley looked blank. "Bethany isn't old enough to sign a valid contract but, under the new laws, *you* can register her."

I braced myself in case she erupted, but Sylvia had read her better than I could, as always. Kearsley just sat there, silently. Sylvia reached out for the compad, which I handed to her. "All we need is your signature, or thumbprint, on this form," she said.

Kearsley took the pad, and stared at the screen. Her employment and prison records listed her as literate with a normal range IQ. "What's this about compensation?" she asked.

"No ambulance or hospital costs in the event of her death, as long as she's HIV negative," Sylvia replied. "If any of her organs can be used, there's a rebate of two to five thousand dollars to cover funeral expenses. It's designed to pay for any cosmetic treatment if you were planning an open casket funeral," Kearsley didn't quite snort, but it was a near thing, "but that's up to you. We don't expect grieving parents to provide receipts, or anything of that sort; it's just a courtesy payment. Donors can be cremated by the hospital at no expense, if that's what you'd prefer. Of course, this also improves your own eligibility for a transplant should either you or Bethany require one."

Kearsley looked slightly dazed, then touched the pad. Sylvia's expression remained sombre. "I'll leave you some information about first aid courses available in this area," she said softly, after retrieving the pad. "Thank you for your time."

We walked out a few minutes later. The lift was singing that it couldn't rain all the time. Neither of us spoke until we were back in the car. "Coffee?" suggested Sylvia, glancing at the clock. "My treat?"

"Okay."

"I'm not even sure I want to stay with the police after I graduate," I said, as the car headed west, "and I know I can't keep doing *this* job." I sipped at the coffee. "Forecasting is one thing, but getting parents to sell their kids' organs . . ."

Sylvia sighed. "I don't like it either, but the section has to pay for itself somehow; it's not as though we can sell footage to the networks like the SWATs or Vice. Besides, we've reduced the number of successful youth suicide attempts by nearly thirty per cent, and less than one in fifty gets harvested . . ."

"You never worry that some parents might decide their kids are worth more brain-dead than healthy?"

She shrugged. "Some of them probably think that anyway. Sure, there are better solutions. If more people registered as donors, or the presumed consent laws were widened to include more organs, there wouldn't be the demand there is now . . . but then, people like Kearsley wouldn't be able to afford an ambulance."

"Maybe that's wrong, too."

"Maybe, but it's an imperfect world; if it wasn't, we'd be out of a job. Look, *I* don't enjoy suicide duty either; I don't think anybody does, no matter how many lives it saves. I don't like dealing with stalkers, either, but I'd rather do that than wait and bust them for rape. I know it's not glamorous, but I think the Ravens actually do a damn sight more good than we're given credit for."

Sick as I was feeling, I couldn't disagree. Suicides in subways, which used to be disturbingly frequent, weren't just a matter of the right to die; they traumatized everyone who saw them. Car theft too often led to high-speed chases, which led to deaths. Smart surveillance systems had dramatically reduced both. They also cut down on shoplifting, which reduced prices; that may sound trivial, but it was very popular, especially when people were told that the security cameras in changing booths were now feeding low-resolution pictures to computers, not cheesecake for security teams' Christmas party videos. Fingerprint smartlocks raised a few eyebrows when they were introduced in airports and railway stations as an anti- terrorist measure, but many large businesses now used them. It was the same with data about people's spending habits; while some protested about how much the government wanted to know about them, most helped banks and credit companies and advertising agencies and other commercial organizations gather information about their personal tastes. Some people were more cautious about medical information, but the insurance companies managed to persuade them that it would make premiums lower for most. Centralized datapools made life easier, safer, more comfortable; the pro-privacy protesters didn't really have a chance, and even though I've studied the issue, I can't really understand what all the fuss was about. "It's not that," I said. "It's me. I just don't think I'm cut out to be a cop."

"What do you want to be?"

"I was thinking of teaching."

Sylvia sighed. "Stick with the Ravens until you're a sergeant, then if you still want to teach, apply to the academy to become an instructor. There's already too many professors who don't know shit about the real world; with a degree and hands-on experience, you should be able to write your own ticket. And take it from me, the job *does* get easier once you get over the shock." She was silent for a while. "You're still on for tonight, aren't you?"

"Sure." They were throwing a farewell party for all of the student reserves, to give us time to recover from our hangovers before returning to college on Monday.

"Good." She looked at the compad. "Kenji Sekizawa. Do you speak any Japanese?"

The last call of the day was the worst. Telling mothers about their kids is hard, but we do a lot of it, because even when they're not being melodramatic, teenagers aren't as good at covering their tracks as they think they are. That's the main reason we haven't had much success with geriatrics; Mr Sekizawa was completely stunned to be told that there was a fifty-three per cent chance that his eighty-year-old father would commit suicide in the next two months. But the worst ones are those where there's no one around who's interested in helping; no family, no doctor, no priest or rabbi, no known friends, only a boss who had to call up a personnel file to know who we were talking about and whose immediate response was to offer the man stress leave. I'd tried to convince him that that was probably the worst thing he could do, that it would increase the probability of a successful suicide attempt by at least seventeen per cent, but I don't think I succeeded. I was in a foul mood when we returned to the car, and wanted to beg off the party, but going home alone probably wouldn't have been the best thing for me to do, either. But that's my excuse for getting as drunk as I did – that, and an argument with an attractive coed who'd been working in Vice. I'd become angry when she referred to us as the Ravens, even though it's what we call ourselves. Maybe it was the way she said it, but it reminded me that ravens aren't just birds of ill omen; they're also scavengers. Anyway, I certainly hadn't intended to wind up in bed with Sylvia, but I did.

An hour later, we were lying in her bed staring at the ceiling for a while. "Sorry," I said. "A little too much to drink."

"It's okay," she said. "You've had a difficult day; you're just stressed. Would you like a back-rub?"

"Okay," I said, after a moment's thought, and rolled over. "How long did it take you to get used to this? The job, I mean?"

I could feel her shrug, then she began kneading my muscles. "For me, it's a bit like a funeral; makes me want to say 'fuck it' and go on living a bit harder. Jesus, when was the last time you had a massage?"

"I don't remember."

She called for the lights, and grabbed a bottle of oil from the nightstand. I felt myself begin to relax as she knelt astride me and placed her palms on my back, rotating them gently – then, a moment later, she stopped, and I felt her fingers trace the scars on my back.

"I had two kidney transplants, a few years ago," I said. "The first one came from my father, but I was put on the waiting list for donor kidneys. I don't know where the other one came from; they're careful not to tell you." I tried to smile. "So I'm very much in favour of people becoming organ donors – but I don't want to force anyone into it."

"Jesus," she said. She touched my shoulders gently, and her hands jerked away as though they were hot. "Do you want me to stop?"

"Not unless you want to," I said. "Sorry if just I tensed up, but it *was* feeling wonderful." I reached behind me for her hand, held it, then brought it to my lips and kissed it. That's when I saw the scar on her wrist – faint, obviously old, but unmistakeably a slash along the artery.

Other titles available from Robinson Publishing

The Mammoth Book of Egyptian Whodunnits   Ed. Mike Ashley   £6.99 [ ]
Terrific new anthology of Egyptian murder mysteries, some set in ancient times, and some during the Napoleonic and Victorian periods of excavation. With many new stories and rare reprints from many top international writers and includes a special introduction by Elizabeth Peters.

The Mammoth Book of Murder and Science   Ed. Roger Wilkes   £7.99 [ ]
Where traditional methods of detection have failed, time and time again, scientific routes of investigation and analysis have led to the conviction of many dangerous criminals. *The Mammoth of Murder and Science* examines the landmark cases and shows how forensic science has developed over the last 150 years.

The Mammoth Book of Endurance & Adventure   Ed. Jon E. Lewis   £7.99 [ ]
Eyewitness recollections from the world's most intrepid adventurers. It recounts over 50 true-life adventures taken from contemporary memoirs, letters and journals of ordinary mortals who achieved extraordinary things.

The Mammoth Book of Heroes   Ed. Jon E. Lewis   £7.99 [ ]
This anthology celebrates the great hearts of history. No fictional hero can match the true courage of Ernest Shackleton or the spirit of Annie Sullivan teaching the deaf and blind Helen Keller to speak and read. As well as the documented names of history, there are those who are not renowned, the unsung heroes, many of whom are also celebrated here. This is an inspiring collection that celebrates the brave of heart through the ages.

Robinson books are available from all good bookshops or can be ordered direct from the Publisher. Just tick the title you want and fill in the form below.

TBS Direct
Colchester Road, Frating Green, Colchester, Essex CO7 7DW
Tel: +44 (0) 1206 255777
Fax: +44 (0) 1206 255914
Email: sales@tbs-ltd.co.uk

UK/BFPO customers please allow £1.00 for p&p for the first book, plus 50p for the second, plus 30p for each additional book up to a maximum charge of £3.00.

Overseas customers (inc. Ireland), please allow £2.00 for the first book, plus £1.00 for the second, plus 50p for each additional book.

Please send me the titles ticked above.

NAME (Block letters). . . . .

ADDRESS . . . .

. . . .

POSTCODE . . . .

I enclose a cheque/PO (payable to TBS Direct) for . . . .

I wish to pay by Switch/Credit card

Number . . . .

Card Expiry Date . . . .

Switch Issue Number . . . .